THE *Secret* ADMIRER
ROMANCE COLLECTION

Can Concealed Love Be Revealed in 9 Historical Novellas?

THE *Secret* ADMIRER

ROMANCE COLLECTION

Molly Noble Bull, Kathleen Y'Barbo
Amanda Barratt, Lorraine Beatty,
Anita Mae Draper, CJ Dunham, Jennifer Uhlarik,
Becca Whitham, Penny Zeller

BARBOUR BOOKS
An Imprint of Barbour Publishing, Inc.

Print ISBN 978-1-68322-175-3

eBook Editions:
Adobe Digital Edition (.epub) 978-1-68322-177-7
Kindle and MobiPocket Edition (.prc) 978-1-68322-176-0

Published by Barbour Books, an imprint of Barbour Publishing, Inc., P.O. Box 719, Uhrichsville, Ohio 44683, www.barbourbooks.com

Our mission is to publish and distribute inspirational products offering exceptional value and biblical encouragement to the masses.

ecpa Member of the
Evangelical Christian
Publishers Association

Printed in Canada.

Contents

The Cost of a Heart

by Amanda Barratt

Dedication

To my dear grandmother, Elizabeth. Thank you for your continued love and support. I'm so blessed to have you in my life!

Soli Deo Gloria!

Chapter 1

July 1895

They'd quarreled that morning—she and Jackson. Argued about his latest scandal involving another woman and a hotel room at the Waldorf-Astoria. Or rather, she pleaded and he stared. Stone-faced. Except for that brief moment on the way out to the carriage when her husband grabbed her wrist in a noose-like grip and demanded in a low-cut whisper that she "keep smiling today."

Now at the Long Island racetracks, Lily Montgomery sat alongside fellow racegoers—mostly socialites like herself—smile wooden but firmly in place.

"My my, doesn't Jackson look dashing today, atop that fine black horse?" Kitty Carlisle waved a gloved hand at her own husband.

"He always looks dashing." Lily maintained her brittle smile. Never wavering. She'd performed this role often enough and, like a well-trained actress, remembered that the show must always go on.

The sham must always be firmly fixed.

The race began. Lily watched absently, having attended many of these events in years past. During their first year of marriage, she'd jumped and cheered, waving vigorously at Jackson as his horse rounded the track. Until he told her one evening in that granite-cold voice of his that she looked like an out-of-control poodle, with her "ridiculous hat" and "wild wriggling and waving."

She never cheered again, adopting instead, a pose of indifferent languor.

A gasp went up from the crowd. People rose to their feet, a wave of flowered bonnets and bowler hats, blocking her vision.

"What's going on?" Lily snagged Kitty's gaze. The petite blond stood on tiptoe, craning her neck. Whether the crowd muffled Lily's words or Kitty chose to ignore them, Lily couldn't be sure.

She turned instead toward a lanky youth, one of the tallest in her vicinity.

"Sir? What's happening?" She tugged on the sleeve of his jacket.

He swiveled around, a shock of black hair falling over his forehead. "There's been an accident. Didn't you see it, ma'am? The rider—thrown from his horse?"

She shook her head, feeling foolish. "I suppose I wasn't paying attention. Who was injured? Do you know?"

The youth stood even taller, as if proud to be the bearer of useful information. "Rider number twelve, it was. Yes, that's right. Number twelve."

The air leeched from her lungs. The waft of summer wind on her cheeks suddenly scorched her. Spots danced before her vision.

Number twelve.

Jackson.

"My land, ma'am! Are you all right?" The youth grabbed her around the waist and half-carried her to a vacant seat.

"Number twelve. . . My husband. . . Can you find out if he's all right? I don't think I can stand. . .just now." Blast her infernal weakness. Brought on, no doubt, by her constrictive lace collar and the lacing of her corset—meant to marshal her less-than-ideal waist to willow-slim.

"Of course, ma'am. Right away." The youth's eyes sparked with concern, before he took off, brushing past a gentleman with a drooping mustache and a corpulent lady carrying a fluttering parasol.

Lily waited, head bent, forcing breath in and out of her lungs.

In. Out. In. Out.

Keep breathing. Don't stop.

She hadn't seen the accident, lost in her own thoughts. Behaving as Jackson wanted—uninterested. Minutes passed, each dragging by like carriage wheels laced in lead.

Finally the young man returned, shoving through the crowd, despite angry protests from those he elbowed.

"And?" She found her feet. She must prepare to go to the hospital and be with Jackson, must be calm and strong. . .

"I'm sorry, ma'am." The youth's Adam's apple jerked. Her world swirled, a thousand memories flashing through her mind, as the boy said with his eyes what he did not with words.

Jackson Montgomery was dead.

Two Years Later
Newport, Rhode Island

Lily leaned toward the motorcar window, into the intoxicating fragrance of sea breeze and freshly trimmed grass. She balled her gloved hands into fists, willing the memories to return to the recesses of her mind with as much force as the rippling azure waves swept away from the shoreline and toward the vast expanse beyond.

Jackson wasn't waiting for her inside their marble mansion, that place of both paradise and prison. Not this time.

Not ever again.

Her gaze turned toward the front of the car, where Nathaniel Evans expertly manned the wheel. A navy chauffeur's uniform encased his wide shoulders, the matching cap partly concealing his walnut-hued hair. Sometimes she wished the man would turn around, offer a quick smile. But, no. Evans took every task most seriously, be it scouring the silver in his role as footman or chauffeuring her about in his job as driver.

At any rate, they were nearly there.

For a wild, insane instant, she nearly ordered him to stop the car. What a spectacle it would be if she gave into her longings. To divest herself of fussy hat, kid leather shoes, and silk stockings. Take them all off and race for the shoreline. Become one with the pounding waves and frothing surf.

What a story for the society columns *that* would make.

"Mrs. Jackson Montgomery, out of mourning at last, romped in the surf like a madwoman, just moments after arriving in our fair city."

The car stopped, halting her inane musings. Evans opened the door and held out his palm. She placed her gloved fingertips in it, his masculine strength swirling over her like an exotic fragrance as he handed her down.

Strong men. The most dangerous sort.

"Tired after your journey?" Evans's green eyes showed true concern.

"Do I look as wilted as last season's tea roses?" She laughed, though the boning in her corset scarcely allowed true mirth to escape.

"Some watering wouldn't go amiss." The slightest curvature of a dimple appeared on one side of his mouth. "But then, it's the beautiful flowers that need the most care."

He often spoke in such a way, her footman/chauffer. A compliment here, a gesture of concern there. Those compliments and gestures had been her buoy, helping to keep her afloat during her tenure as Jackson's wife.

But she wouldn't spoil the day with more thoughts of that nature.

"What about you? Don't you need watering after your journey?"

He shook his head, that country boy smile ready on his lips. "I'm more tumbleweed than hothouse bloom, Mrs. Montgomery. But I wouldn't say no to a glass of milk and piece of blueberry pie."

With the salt-laden breeze filling her lungs, laughter came easier. "What is it about men and simple cooking, anyway? I think every chef within twenty miles of here has it all wrong. They serve roast duck and crepes suzette, hoping to please. But a steaming bowl of beef stew and a slice of warm blueberry pie are what would really make the gentlemen happy."

"You may have just invented the newest fashion. Fancy-dress dinners served servants' hall style. Complete with the kitchen maid spilling the gravy and the butler boxing her on the ears." A warm chuckle rumbled from his chest.

"I may have to give it a try." She stepped away, sending a smile over her shoulder, and made her way toward the wide double doors leading to the foyer of what the papers dubbed "Newport's Grand Trianon." Otherwise known as Seacombe.

As if on cue for the most spectacularly staged show ever produced, Osbourne, her Newport butler, opened the door.

"Welcome again to Seacombe, Mrs. Montgomery. I trust your journey was without incident." The man's ponderous nose twitched ever so slightly whenever he spoke.

"Thank you, yes." She inclined her head and stepped into the foyer. The place had Jackson written all over it. He, along with Richard Morris Hunt, had designed every inch of the marble-columned, Palladian-arched vestibule. Lily hadn't been permitted so much as a suggestion. Not that she cared much. The house was perfect, embodying everything Jackson himself had revered. All splendor, with little substance. A metaphor for their marriage.

Even their lives.

Still, the artist within her appreciated the perfect symmetry of it all. At least

Jackson's tastes had not tended toward the outré.

She approached the small oak table and flipped through the cards and invitations atop the silver salver. Like a Metropolitan Opera performance, only the star names were present. Astor. Vanderbilt. Belmont. Kingsley. Wellington.

Hmm. . . A ball to be held at the Wellington mansion just a few houses down on Bellevue Avenue. A shiver skittered down her back. During the past two years, the customary period of mourning had been her safety net. Garbed in suffocating black silk, she'd nonetheless been left in peace. To mourn, society assumed. A grieving young widow of only twenty-three, recovering from the death of her beloved husband in a horseback-riding accident.

She'd mourned, yes. For Jackson's life, as explosive, colorful, and short as a burst of fireworks.

More importantly, she delved into the recesses of her shattered heart and began to pick up the pieces. Two years later, she was still gathering. But now, instead of her own clumsy efforts to bind together with schoolroom paste what needed to be fused with steel, she sought comfort in the refuge of a Father who would never leave, nor forsake.

It was time to test herself. To finish the business of healing and get on with that of living. She was no longer the girl who had donned Brussels lace and floated to the altar with stars in her eyes and true love's kiss on her lips. Nor was she the bruised and broken woman who sat alone in an opera box season upon season, while Jackson showered charm, jewels, and attention upon countless other women.

No, she, Lily Montgomery, had been rebirthed.

And it was past time the world knew it.

Newport. Like the circus of every child's fantasy, it put on a show worth viewing. A spectacle of brilliance. A display of pomp and circumstance, rivaling the unrivaled.

And he, Nathan Evans, was smack-dab in the middle of it.

Whistling softly, he drove down Bellevue Avenue, the lady of the house in the backseat. Bedecked in light purple, sparkling gems adorning her throat, wrists, and ears, she looked like a woman ready to conquer society.

Conquer it, she would, his lady employer. Only he rarely thought of her in such lofty terms. For the past two years, longer even, she'd been Mrs. Montgomery in his words, Lily in his thoughts.

"Are you nervous?" He didn't look behind him, concentrating intently on the road and the throng of other cars approaching the Wellington mansion.

"You've known me for how long, and you honestly have to ask that?" She was smiling now, he could hear it in the timbre of her voice, how when her lips tipped upward her tone became more melodious, slightly higher. "You're not known for being disingenuous, Evans. Why start now?"

He chuckled. "My apologies. Let me rephrase. Are you 'my hands are shaking' kind of nervous or are you 'I need to stop the car so you can deposit your dinner in the bushes' terrified?"

"Let's just say I'm a happy medium between the two." He'd made her laugh, and he reveled in the sound of it. When he'd first known her, she never laughed. Oh, she smiled all right, but he noticed right away those smiles never reached her eyes. Two years ago, that all changed. Slowly, her smile had turned genuine. And then, in the most glorious of moments—an instant he would never forget as long as he drew breath—she laughed. He didn't remember what he had said to prompt the occasion. All he remembered were those musical, light sounds and what they had signified to them both.

"Well, don't risk things by trying the duck croquettes. I heard from the Wellingtons' chauffeur himself just how awful they are. And to tell you the truth, I don't understand why anyone would want to eat duck anyway. They're cute little things, flapping their wings and quacking."

She laughed again, and he sneaked a glance—quickly. One gloved hand pressed over her dainty lips, a stray black curl tumbling down her cheek.

"Do me a favor, Evans. Promise me that you'll never attend one of Mrs. Astor's balls. You'll nauseate every guest in the house with your elaborations on how 'cute' their food was during its life."

"I think I can safely make that promise." Nathan parked the car and climbed out. Lanterns hung from branches, their glow illuminating the fountain in the middle of the manicured English-style garden. Music spilled onto the air, rich notes of violin and piano. If champagne could make melody it would sound exactly like whatever it was the orchestra played.

He opened her door, and she clasped her fingers around his. Every time he touched them, he marveled afresh at how delicate they were, so dainty and fragile, and yet how they twined with his and held with surprising strength.

The moment passed quickly, and she withdrew her fingers. She always did, never lingering. A pang of guilt speared him. Some nights, he lay awake staring at the ceiling, reliving those instants. . .wondering what it would be like to feel her hand without the protective sheath of her glove.

"So you're off?"

She nodded, the diamonds in her ears swaying.

"I know there will be a stir. You haven't seen many of these people for almost two years. Don't worry though. You'll still outshine them all. And when you need me, I'll be waiting. With the car, of course." He smiled.

"You're always so kind, Evans. Some days, I wonder what I'd do without your kindness." Her eyes gleamed brighter than any sapphire found in Tiffany's store window.

He swallowed, his tongue suddenly wooden. "Have a nice evening, Mrs. Montgomery."

She nodded, still smiling. He watched her go, her skirt brushing the gravel, head held high. Truly beautiful. The kind of woman who could make a man wonder why the single life held any pleasure whatsoever.

Make a man? Men who were Vanderbilts, Rockefellers, or Wellingtons. They could dream all they wanted, no risk attached.

Unlike men who were chauffeurs, footmen.

Such a world as his didn't permit such luxuries.

Chapter 2

Even the air seemed to glitter tonight. Or perhaps it was the mingling scents of hothouse roses and French perfume that made it appear so.

The notes of a Strauss waltz spun through the air, flitting and dancing, as couples swirled through the ballroom to the melody. Lily inhaled deeply, Evans's words filling her mind.

"You'll still outshine them all."

During the last ball she attended, Jackson had been at her side. As usual, he'd behaved as if unaware of her existence the entire evening, recovering from his amnesia only once to partner her in a single waltz. She'd always dreaded such occasions, breathed a weighty sigh of relief when they returned home.

But Jackson wasn't with her. And so help her, she would not end tonight in humiliation.

The Wellingtons—rotund mister reaching sixty and petite missus only a few years older than Lily—stood beneath their favorite showpiece, a van Dyck, receiving guests.

She glided across the parquet floor.

"Well, if it isn't Mrs. Montgomery. Lovely to see you after so long, my dear." Bram Wellington bowed.

"Thank you so much for inviting me." She smiled. "Your gown is exquisite, Alesia."

"As is yours, Lily. You look wonderful." Alesia Wellington returned the smile. "Why, if I didn't know better I'd say you were still a seventeen-year-old girl, learning the steps of the quadrille under the stern eye of our horrid dancing master."

"You flatter me. As we both well know, I'm no longer seventeen. And I haven't danced a quadrille in ages, so after tonight, society might decree I need another round at Mr. Beverly's School of Dance and Deportment." More guests crowded in and Lily moved on, so as not to hold up the line.

"Enjoy the evening. And be sure to save a spot on your card for me," Mr. Wellington called after her.

A wave of awkwardness assailed her as she stood near an enormous potted palm. How did one reintegrate into a world one had been absent from for two long years? She recognized a few familiar faces—Oliver Belmont dancing with Mr. Wellington's debutante daughter. . .Willie Vanderbilt in conversation with J. J. Astor.

But like an injured limb newly freed from a restrictive sling, the feeling of rightness was no longer there. And for a moment, she fought the urge to turn on her heel and run out the door, toward Evans and the car and the familiarity of home.

"Mrs. Montgomery?"

The voice made her lift her head, and she found herself looking into the eyes of Roland Kingsley.

"Why, Mr. Kingsley. What a surprise to see you here."

"A welcome one, I hope." Mr. Kingsley smiled. He'd aged some, since last she'd seen him. Probably his forty-fifth birthday had come and gone. A touch of silver around the temples that had not been there before, a few lines around the eyes. He was still tall though. And his smile still emanated genuine warmth.

"Very much so. It's been so long since we last had the pleasure of meeting."

"At. . .your husband's funeral, I believe it was." His brown eyes took on a pained expression.

She nodded. "You were so kind to come. And the gifts you sent. . .the basket of fruit was so thoughtful. I never had a chance to thank you afterward."

"No need for thanks. It was a kindness easily done. But if you wish to do me a favor, you could honor me with this dance."

Warmth spread through her at the thoughtful gesture. "I would be delighted. But I must warn you, I haven't danced in so long and am liable to tread on your feet." She gave a rueful grin.

"I consider myself duly warned." He took her hand and escorted her onto the dance floor.

"How are you enjoying Newport?" He led her through the steps with ease, turning her gently and expertly maneuvering among the other dancers.

"I've only been here two days. I took a walk along the shore this morning. Early. It's so much nicer when other people are not about." Slowly she found herself relaxing, even enjoying the rhythm and grace of the dance.

"I agree. Early morning is my favorite time for a walk. There's something serene about the stillness then. A sweetness to the air that it lacks at other times."

"My sentiments exactly. So tell me, Mr. Kingsley, how have you occupied yourself these past two years?"

"Work, mostly. I traveled to England last year. Stopped over at Blenheim Palace and saw the new duchess of Marlborough."

"How is Consuelo?" The dance ended and he offered her his arm. She placed her hand upon it, sensing none of the tension there that had always emanated from Jackson. Mr. Kingsley gave her a companionable smile and directed her out of the ballroom, toward the adjoining area reserved for refreshments.

"Unhappy. Their marriage was a sham right from the start. To be so miserable when one is so young and lovely. It makes the heart ache just to think of it." He handed her a flute of champagne, taking one for himself. Though, as they stood against one wall, she noticed he barely sipped from it. Jackson had always downed his drink in a single gulp.

"But there's more to life than happiness in marriage." She took the tiniest of sips from her own glass. The liquid fizzed going down and she resisted the urge to scrunch her nose. "A home. A place in society. Children." The latter she herself had never enjoyed, though she'd always longed for them. And once, she'd been so sure her hopes had become promise. . . .

"True. Though marriage is such a large part of one's life. Surrendering oneself to misery in any area is a bit like declaring that as long as one possesses the ability to see, they could rub along quite happily without the need to taste. And with so many sweet things on offer, life would be rather empty without the ability to experience them." He looked at her earnestly. As if he found her society enchanting. As if he was actually content ignoring the rest of the party and spending the evening with her and her alone.

Heat filled her cheeks. "And if one must accept? Wouldn't it be better to embrace the gifts the Lord chooses to give us, rather than be bitter over those we are denied?"

A weighty sigh lifted his chest, though he tempered it with another smile. "Very wise words, Mrs. Montgomery. I won't argue with them."

"I do enjoy a good debate. Though not a quarrel." She placed her almost full champagne flute on a tray offered by a passing waiter, watching as Mr. Kingsley did the same.

"Then I shall take care never to quarrel with you. The notion of doing so anyway sounds rather impossible. With your winning smile, I don't know how anyone could stay angry with you for long."

Jackson had always found anger at her easy. Even when she pleaded, cried. As if his heart were hewn of the same marble as the columns surrounding her now. Unbreached by any dart she might fling. Her father had been the same. Though not as outwardly violent as Jackson, he'd been unsusceptible to her little-girl coaxing, meriting her a scolding whenever she attempted to try.

"May I call on you? I would very much like to renew our acquaintance to a greater degree."

She started, was on the brink of saying no, but the look in his eyes disarmed her completely. This man sought her friendship. Nothing more. Didn't he? There was no danger in afternoon tea, a carriage ride to the seaside.

"As would I." She infused warmth into her smile.

"Good." The grin on his face made him look, all of a sudden, younger. "Now how about another dance?"

One would think that with only a single lady in residence, there wouldn't be much for the servants in Lily Montgomery's employ to do.

But there wasn't a chance of overmuch relaxation while Osbourne, the butler, remained within scolding distance.

Nathan brushed an invisible speck of lint off his jacket lapel, straightening his casual stance as Osbourne gave him a dour glance from his seat at the head of the servants' breakfast table.

Polly, the freckle-faced under housemaid hid a giggle behind her napkin, nudging him beneath the table.

"What's eating Oz?" she whispered, while Osbourne's attention was momentarily diverted by Mrs. Lakely, the housekeeper.

"He found a smudge of car oil on my nose earlier. Said I didn't wash well this morning."

"Aw, tell him to go jump in the drink. He knows just as well as any of us that your job as chauffeur is ten times more important than any piddling footman duties. He's just jealous that you get to drive Mrs. Montgomery around, while he's stuck here barking orders at this sorry lot." She took a generous bite of porridge. "How'd it go last night, anyway?"

"How it always does. I take her there, she goes to the party. I drink coffee and eat sandwiches with the other drivers until she's ready to come home." It took a heap of effort for him to shove aside the image of her—fresh from the party—a smile on her lips, cheeks flushed and eyes sparkling. She stifled yawns on the drive back, while regaling him with a rundown of the evening's events.

"It was awkward at first. But then Mr. Kingsley came to see me. It was nice after that. He took me around to talk to everyone. We danced together a few times."

Why did the thought of another man's hands clasping hers make Nathan want to ram his fist into something? She'd danced at parties before. . .though rarely with her husband.

Yet she hadn't been to a fete in two years.

Much had happened in the space of twenty-four months. A whole lot of it included Nathan feeling less like Lily Montgomery's servant and more like her friend.

Friend. Who was he fooling? She paid his salary, for mercy's sake. His job was simple: drive her where she needed to go and see she got there safely. He wasn't being paid to listen to her stories, tease laughter from those rose-hued lips.

He wasn't paid to. . .enjoy her company, long for it even.

But enjoy and long for it he did, like a mooncalf idiot.

"Did you hear the music, Nathan?" Polly's words pulled him to the present. The eighteen-year-old regarded him, blue eyes wide.

"I certainly did. You would've loved it, Polly. They played Strauss waltzes, a few polkas and quadrilles. Even from belowstairs, the music. . .well, it sort of swept over you. Like looking up at the stars at night and watching one streak across the sky. I wish you could've been there."

"Me, too. But the next best thing is listening to you tell of it. You have a way about you, when you say things. I wish you *could* be a teacher, Nathan. I'd like to have learned from you."

He swallowed. It had probably been a mistake, telling Polly of his ambition. But the confidence she had in him watered the thirsty roots of his dream, one born when he'd been a youth of fourteen, forced to quit school and go into service, because time spent book-learning didn't put bread onto his mother's table.

"Well, you won't have a chance to learn another thing from me, if I don't get a move on before I get tossed out on my ear." He stood, pushing his chair back from the table. Always, he did his best to be the first footman upstairs every morning, so he had a head start on laying the breakfast table. Gilbert tended to dawdle, but as Osbourne's nephew, never got much of a tongue lashing for it.

The hours passed. Laying the table, serving breakfast, polishing silver. Hanging the protective apron used for the latter task on its designated hook, Nathan's ears pricked as the bell rang. He strode to the call board. Front door. A quick check in the mirror assured his hair was neatly in place and his white bowtie had stayed straight.

Up the servants' stairs, through the foyer and to the large front door in less than a minute. Swiping a hand down his shirtfront, Nathan straightened his shoulders and opened the door.

A man stood outside. Nathan assessed him in a single glance. Medium height, stocky build. Brownish graying hair combed and parted to perfection. Gray suit, blue ascot. In one hand, the gentleman held his hat and walking stick.

In the other, he carried a bouquet of pink roses and white lilies.

Nathan's jaw hardened the moment he clapped eyes on those fancy flowers.

"Good afternoon, sir." He did his best to soften his features into a more footman-appropriate expression.

"And to you as well." The man gave a genial smile. "I'm here to see Mrs. Montgomery. Is she at home?" Without preamble, he handed his hat and walking stick to Nathan and produced a white vellum calling card. Nathan placed the items on the hall table, before glancing at the card.

Mr. Roland Kingsley scrolled the elegant black letters.

So it was him. The man who'd made certain Lily had an enjoyable evening. Nathan was grateful to him for that.

But something deep in his gut didn't like the look of those flowers. Not one bit.

"Give me a moment and I'll see. If you'll do me the honor of waiting inside, sir."

He left Mr. Kingsley craning his neck to better view a landscape painting.

Nathan turned the handle of the morning room door, stepping just inside. Lily sat at a rosewood desk, head bent over a sheet of writing paper. She wore her hair coiled high atop her head, a few stray ringlets curling around the creamy expanse at the nape of her neck. Attired in a lacy white blouse and maroon skirt, she looked like an advertisement for high fashion.

The room's decor only enhanced the scene. White and gold draperies sewn to match the upholstered furniture. A vase of fresh flowers topping a polished table. Twin gilded mirrors, one hanging above the marble fireplace, the other on the opposite wall.

He cleared his throat. "Mrs. Montgomery?"

She turned as if startled, a slight smile curving her lips upward. "Yes, Evans." She had a way of saying his name. Each syllable low and cultured, as sweetly polite as if he were the heir to the Vanderbilt millions, instead of her paid lackey.

"You have a visitor." He held out the silver salver bearing the calling card.

She took it in her hand, glanced down at it. Her smile deepened, a shade of rose enhancing her fair complexion.

"Show him in, please."

"Right away, ma'am." The notion he'd had of hoping she'd say no irritated him to no end. Society ladies received gentleman callers. It was a ritual that occurred in each one of the millionaire mansions dotting Bellevue Avenue. Since Mrs. Montgomery hadn't received more than a few close friends since her husband's death, it would have been highly unusual if she now turned her visitor away. Especially since they'd enjoyed each other's company the previous evening.

He found Mr. Kingsley just the way he'd left him. Getting a crick in his neck enjoying the Montgomery art gallery.

"She'll see you now, sir."

The man turned, flashing Nathan another amiable smile. "That's a very nice painting, by the way." He followed Nathan across the foyer and to the morning room.

Nathan opened the door and moved aside to let Mr. Kingsley pass. For the briefest of instants, he saw Lily Montgomery standing in the center of the room, smiling. Mr. Kingsley crossed the room and took her hand, bowing over it.

Nathan closed the door, quietly, as Osbourne and three previous butlers had taught him.

"The ideal footman is as unobtrusive as a well-oiled hinge. His job is not to be noticed but to make certain that those he serves have as smooth and effortless a passage through the waters of life as possible. That is the job of every servant. That is our honor and privilege."

He blew out a sigh.

Well-oiled hinge? Smooth and effortless passage?

His job exactly.

Chapter 3

Lily hadn't received flowers since her debut season. Not from Jackson. Not from any man. Single men didn't send such gifts to married women, and she'd been married so soon after her debutante ball.

As Mr. Kingsley handed her the bouquet, a smile in his eyes, her pulse did something it hadn't done in a long while. Sped up. Just a notch.

"Thank you." She tried to keep the tremor from her voice. "That was very thoughtful of you."

"I hope you don't think it too forward." True concern showed in his eyes.

"Oh my, no, of course not. They're very pretty." She moved to the bellpull, wishing she'd taken more time with her appearance that morning. Worn a different dress, perhaps. Laced her corset a bit tighter, a much-needed accompaniment, if she wanted to look even passable. "Please, won't you sit down?"

He took the chair across from her. "I trust you are well rested after last night's exertions?"

"Of course. I slept better than I have in quite a while." It had been one of the best evenings she'd had in some time. The enjoyment of dancing, the sight of familiar faces. The sheer fun of putting on a pretty dress. After the initial awkwardness, she'd felt almost seventeen again, especially with Mr. Kingsley as her escort.

The door opened. Evans stepped inside.

"You rang, ma'am?" His features were blank, his shoulders straight.

"Could you see that these get put in water?" She crossed the room and held out the bouquet.

"Of course." He accepted the flowers. "Do you require anything else?"

"Tea, perhaps."

"I'll inform Mr. Osbourne." Why was he behaving so formally? This wasn't the Evans she knew. Though he played the part of a proper footman, the remnant of a twinkle always lingered in his eyes, no matter the occasion. A special smile on his lips, reserved just for her. Was he feeling unwell?

But he left the room before she could make further inquiry.

She turned back to her guest, taking the seat across from Mr. Kingsley.

"Do you have a busy few months planned? You're probably eager to renew old acquaintances, seeing as you've been absent so long." Mr. Kingsley's gaze met hers, and comfort rushed over her. Few men looked at her as he did. Never her father. Jackson, only at first. As if she was a person of interest, worth bringing flowers to and conversing with.

It was an altogether foreign and completely pleasant sensation.

"I have rather courted solitude of late." She gave a small smile. "Not by choice, of course."

"Custom dictates choice." He ran a finger across the mustache obscuring his upper lip.

"How well you know the world in which we dwell." He wasn't a handsome man, by any means. Not like Jackson, dark and Byronic. Nor like Evans, with his farm-boy grin and wavy brown hair, grass-green eyes that—

Evans? Her chauffeur? Was she actually comparing Roland Kingsley's looks with that of her servant? Gracious. Maybe she hadn't slept as well as she thought.

But Mr. Kingsley did have a kind look about him, the sort she wished her father might've had. As if, in his gentleness, she could find safe harbor.

"Well, I do, as you say, dwell in it. But back to my question."

"I'm hoping to attend a few parties. Probably the Astors will hold their usual ball at Beachwood. I might even host one here. What would you say to that?" Opportunities to hostess as Mrs. Jackson Montgomery had been few and far between. To host such a party, one would expect the man of the house to be in residence. She had never been sure whether Jackson was coming or going, how long he intended to remain with her before heading off on another round of pleasure-seeking. But the thought of now opening her home, arranging such an event, held a certain lure.

"I'd say that any party hosted by Lily Montgomery is one worth clearing my calendar for. Such an event would take time to plan though."

She nodded. "I think I could still manage. Maybe right before everyone returns to New York."

"Sounds feasible. It's always amazing the wonders capital can do."

She bit her lip, hesitating before continuing. "I've been thinking about that. The capital part, I mean. I don't want to go through the rest of my life indulging in nothing but pleasure. While I was in mourning, I became acquainted with a certain Mrs. Dorothea Lincoln. She runs a home for immigrants who are left without family upon their arrival in the States. I visited the home and it seems such a worthy cause. But it's not very large. I think I might like to expand it." The words rushed out. She hadn't mentioned the idea to anyone before. Oh, wait. She *had* mentioned it to Evans. He'd been the one driving her there, and on the way back, she'd shared her thoughts. He'd listened so earnestly. . . .

"Lily Montgomery, lady patroness." Mr. Kingsley chuckled.

"You don't think it's a good plan?"

"I do indeed. I wager you could accomplish anything you set your mind to. But it's best not to be too hasty about these things. The reputability of such organizations can't always be trusted. I heard of an instance where a gentleman founded a charitable organization for the benefit of orphaned children, and it was only discovered after several wealthy patrons had given him financial backing that he was pocketing over half of the profits himself. I would hate for such a thing to happen to you."

"Perhaps the idea does merit more investigation," she said quietly.

"If you'll allow me, I'll check into Mrs. Lincoln once I'm in New York. You'll need someone to aid you in such matters."

She supposed his words should have brought her a measure of relief. After all, he, a highly respected man of mature years was offering her, a young woman with little experience of the world, his assistance. That was a good thing, a needed thing.

But it didn't quite match the new vision of herself as Lily Montgomery, capable woman. The sort of person who could stand on her own two feet and succeed at doing so.

Never mind high-minded new visions. He would only be helping. And she would hate to entangle herself and her finances in an ugly situation.

"Thank you." She smiled. "You're right. I do need help. I must admit I'm woefully inexperienced."

"No more so than any other woman." He offered a reassuring smile, and had they sat near enough, would probably have taken her hand. "And as for help, rest assured, you may always rely, in every circumstance, upon me."

⁂

By five in the morning, Nathan had memorized every crack and crevice in the ceiling above his bed. Whether the pain in his abdomen, growing worse by the minute, or the events of the past two weeks, was keeping him up, he couldn't say. At any rate, he hadn't slept worth a darn.

Since that first afternoon call, Lily and Mr. Kingsley had been inseparable. Every afternoon, at precisely one o'clock, the doorbell would ring and Kingsley would be waiting outside. He always brought gifts: flowers, a new book, a box of chocolates. And he always stayed closeted in the morning room with Lily, their laughter and chatter humming through the house like a hive of lively bees.

Then the evenings came. They dined at friends' homes. They dined together. They went to parties, balls. Took walks along the beach.

Nathan played driver at each one of these excursions. And every passing day, the knot in his chest burned like a smoldering firecracker.

Why was Lily throwing herself into this relationship? Kingsley was a nice enough fellow, genial and gentlemanly. He didn't talk down to Nathan or the other servants the way some rich stiffs did, treating them like a coatrack: useful but not worth the time of day. Kingsley generally made some pleasantry about the weather or Nathan's skill with motorcars.

It took the calm of a poker player and the control of a diplomat to answer Kingsley's remarks with proper respect.

Why? Why was his usually rational mind responding this way? It wasn't his business whether Lily consorted with Kingsley or the king of Prussia.

But it had become just that. His business. In the two years they'd shared together, he'd made it his business.

Worst of all?

He, Nathanial Evans, had allowed himself to care about Lily Montgomery—his employer. The woman who paid his salary, whose food he ate and pillow he lay his head on.

Not just a little schoolboy infatuation, no, sir. But the kind of caring that robbed his sleep, muddled his mind, confounded all manner of reason and sense. The kind that made him want to move heaven and earth in her defense, to give Kingsley a bloody lip and a black eye, even though the man had done nothing at all wrong.

It wasn't love though. Couldn't be.

Nathan sucked in a breath, the pain in his lower abdomen increasing, jabbing his insides like a pitchfork in the hands of an angry farmer. In the bed across from him, Gilbert snored loudly.

Now that he'd admitted all this to himself, one question remained: What was he going to do about it? Lily wasn't like those girls who worked in the kitchen or sold bread at the bakery downtown. No, she was special. Not your average jewelry store diamond, but the kind of gem Tiffany's kept under lock and key and only brought out to show their very favorite customers. Women like her weren't meant to be carelessly tossed into a box with all the other pearls and emeralds, but kept polished and cared for. Set apart.

In a fit of exasperation over some annoying antic, his mother had once declared that Nathan hadn't the sense the good Lord gave a pump handle. He tended to disagree, and deep down, he knew his mother did, too. The decisions he made were usually smart.

His feelings for Lily Montgomery?

Unimaginably stupid.

He couldn't act on them. Not now. Not ever. She'd sack him on the spot, and with good reason, too. But *not* experiencing them, locking them away and then burying the key? Well, one might as well have asked him to quit providing his lungs with air.

So there was his quandary, intricate and complicated.

He tightened his jaw. What in tarnation was wrong with his stomach? The pain had begun a few days ago, but he'd chalked it up to something the cook fed him. One never could be sure just what those French chefs put in their recipes. But it hadn't gone away, as digestive upsets tended to do. It had only gotten worse.

He glanced at the clock on the wall above Gilbert's bed. Almost six. He'd have to get up then. Would he manage?

His gut churned. A wave of nausea swooped over him like a black crow bent on vengeance. He managed to stumble to his feet and cross the room just in time to deposit what little remained of last night's dinner into the washbasin.

Gilbert sat up in bed, rubbing his eyes.

"What's going on?" His roommate's tone was as slurred as if he'd tossed back one too many.

"Not sure." Nathan collapsed back in bed. "But I'm feeling terrible. You'll probably have to manage without me today." If he was sick in bed, he wouldn't be able to drive Lily anywhere. That meant Kingsley would have to use his chauffeur. That also meant Nathan wouldn't be privy to their conversations.

"Don't worry about that. Gee whiz, Nathan. You don't look well. Your face is all pale and pasty looking. Do you want me to get my uncle to fetch the doctor?"

"No. It'll pass." The last thing he wanted was the butler peering down at him while he writhed in agony. The stress of dealing with Osbourne was probably what has caused the stomachache to begin with. Either that or the residual remains of those strange-tasting peppers.

"Well, all right." Gilbert lay back down. "If you're sure. I'm going to try and catch a few winks before that housemaid starts banging on our door." He pulled the covers over his head, sonorous nasal strains emerging two minutes later.

Would Lily be worried when Nathan didn't show up to serve breakfast? Would she even care? Probably not. Her plans for the day would consume all her thoughts. Especially now that she had such an attentive swain nipping at her heels.

He'd sort out his own thoughts later.

Just as soon as he got his blasted stomach under control.

Chapter 4

Y ou're leaving?"

Lily faced Mr. Kingsley across the morning room, his just-made announcement sending her heart into a downward spiral.

"I'm afraid so." He gave a weighty sigh, as if the news pained him. "But it will only be for two weeks. At the most. Just enough time for me to tend to my business in New York. Then I'll be back on the first available train."

"Still, why so sudden?" The past weeks had been a whirlwind. Not a day had passed without spending time in Mr. Kingsley's company. Their initial polite acquaintance had deepened into true friendship. Which in turn had deepened into. . .

"Necessary business. But don't worry. I'm sure every man in Newport would be thrilled to take my place and squire you wherever you need to go. Would you like me to arrange an escort?"

She shook her head. "No. I'll be fine. A rest will do me good. I haven't danced so much and so often in. . .well, ever." She laughed. "Go and have a good time."

"I won't enjoy a second of it on account of your presence being absent." He crossed the room and took both of her hands in his, gazing down at her with warmth in his eyes. "I'll miss you, Mrs. Montgomery. It would be a shame if I were to deny it."

Heat flamed her cheeks as she enjoyed the sensation of holding his hands. Though she had little experience of such matters, it seemed indelibly branded within her to want and long for the touch of a man. Jackson had rarely been physically affectionate, especially the gentler, sweeter things, like holding hands or putting his arm around her waist. It wouldn't have been proper for Mr. Kingsley to have done the latter, but he'd tried the former a couple of times.

"I won't deny it either," she murmured. "I'll miss you, too."

The door opened.

"Mrs. Montgomery?"

Lily turned. Her footman stood by the door. "Yes, Gilbert?"

"There's a matter needing your attention. It's urgent." She noted the anxiety in his eyes.

"One moment." She faced Mr. Kingsley again. "Good-bye then." He still hadn't released her hands, and she didn't attempt to pull away.

"Good-bye, my dear." He let go and crossed the room. At the door, he stopped and bowed, very seriously and politely. "Or should I say Mrs. Montgomery?"

She smiled at his antics, listening to his footfalls die away down the hall.

"Something awful has happened, Mrs. Montgomery. It's Nathan. . .er, Evans."

Her smile vanished, every muscle in her body tensing. "What? What's happened?"

Gilbert practically hopped from foot to foot. "He was sick this morning. I thought he'd just eaten a piece of bad beef. But it got worse. . . Dr. White told us the news. He's got acute appendicitis. They'll be operating within the hour."

Her heart slammed against her rib cage. The lacings of her corset seemed to leech every particle of air from her lungs.

Please, God, no. . .

"Take me to him. At once."

Gilbert started from the room. Lily fisted her voluminous skirt, holding it above her ankles to match his stride. Down the servants' stairs, through several long passageways. Finally, Gilbert stopped, puffing from exertion. "He's in there. Dr. White, too."

Once before, she'd been unprepared to see a man she'd seen as strong and invincible, prostrate and limp. The first time obviously hadn't taught her much, because it was happening all over again. Only much, much worse. Her throat tightened as she approached the narrow bed. Dr. White stood to one side, but Lily spared him only a glance.

Evans—no, Nathan—gave a weak smile as she approached. His tanned face was marble pale, the lines in his strong jaw tight.

"I'm sorry I won't be able to drive you around for a few days." He sucked in a gulp of air. Her heart ached for him, for the intense pain he was enduring.

"If you say one more word about that, I'll sack you on the spot. It's you I'm worried about, as a person, not as my driver." As if driven by something other than conscious thought, her fingers rested against his forehead. His skin, smooth and warm, was dampened by perspiration.

"As my lady commands." He reached up, covered his hand with hers.

"Mrs. Montgomery, we've arranged to have the surgery here rather than down at the hospital. We've taken the liberty of setting up the adjoining room as our theater. My nurse, Miss McGrath, will be assisting me." Dr. White's tone radiated the calm of over twenty-five years practicing medicine.

"Of course. Please, feel free to use anything you need that we might have."

"We'll be preparing the patient in just a few moments." His tone made it clear that it was time for her to leave.

"Yes. Just give me a minute more." She captured Nathan's gaze, wishing she could use every penny of Jackson's fortune to erase the pain in his eyes.

"You're going to be all right. Understand?" Traitorous tears burned her eyes. She blinked them back, unwilling to let him see her cry.

A calm smile edged his lips. "I trust God's providence. He decides my future. But I would very much like to continue driving that fine motorcar of yours."

"And so you shall." She stood, trailing her fingers across his cheek. "My prayers won't cease until I know you're all right."

Lily turned, brushing past the doctor. She crossed the hall and managed to make her way into the empty servants' dining hall. Sinking onto one of the backless wooden benches, she buried her face in her hands and let the tears trickle over her fingers. This was ridiculous. He was her servant. She shouldn't be collapsing into a blubbering heap.

Let him be all right, Lord. I know Dr. White is capable, but I'm still afraid. Guide his hands. Keep Nathan safe.

There. She lifted her face and drew in a steadying breath. The Lord would preserve Nathan, if it was His will. He loved and cared for both of them. And she needed him. Not just as a chauffeur but as a friend. She hadn't quite realized how much his friendship meant to her, but it hit her with full force now.

Nathan Evans was a true friend.

And the moments of waiting would be nothing less than agony, until she heard firsthand of his health and safety.

His mouth felt like cotton batting, his eyelids like weighted lead. His abdomen burned as if ringed in fire, and a woozy fog filled his mind.

Yet Nathan wasn't hallucinating when it came to the vision at his side. Lily's eyes were sapphire pools of concern. Her silk-smooth fingers caressed his forehead.

"Nathan. Wake up. Please." Her tone pleaded, drew him from the foggy shroud.

"I'm. . .awake." The words slurred from his lips.

"Oh, thank God!" She drew her fingers away and his head instantly started to ache. He nearly asked her to continue her ministrations but thought better of it. This was Mrs. Montgomery, an American countess. A common fellow like himself didn't ask her to stroke his forehead. No matter how blissful the sensation.

"Can I get you anything? Anything at all?"

"Draw the curtains a bit more, please. The light. . .hurts."

"Of course." It wasn't until she'd crossed the room and pulled the drapes that the irony of the situation struck him. She'd asked him to do the same once, when he'd found her in the parlor, eyes swollen from crying over an altercation with Jackson.

Another face, not half as appealing, loomed over him. Dr. White's bushy mustache twitched. "You're awake. Good. You survived quite an ordeal, young man. We almost didn't make it in time. But never fear. You won't have to worry about that offending organ ever again."

"That's nice." If he hadn't been so tired and his abdomen in such discomfort, he'd have laughed out loud. The good doctor talked about the bad appendix with the same matter-of-fact ease that a blacksmith would a faulty shoe.

Don't worry. The old brown stallion is newly shod and ready to go.

Yep, that was him all right. Nathaniel Evans, old brown stallion.

"I'll be back later this evening to change the dressing. Until then, Mrs. Montgomery has offered to care for you. Gilbert will assist you with. . .your more personal needs."

Mrs. Montgomery. What'd been in that sleeping stuff? Must've done some serious damage to his brain. He couldn't have heard right. Mrs. Lily Montgomery was to be his nurse? His fine lady employer who had never dirtied her hands to do more than pluck flowers?

"She's very capable. Nursed her mother for a year. You'll be in very good hands."

Being flat on his back and barely able to talk had its disadvantages. You had to take what you could get. Not that he didn't trust Lily. But he didn't much like the idea of her seeing him like this, feeble as an old woman.

Still, the thought of hours in her company was as attractive as a bowl of caramel apples to a boy denied sweets.

And he would relish every second of it.

Chapter 5

In her years as a socialite, Lily had rarely capitalized on her status as a woman of influence. But as she'd faced Dr. White and announced that she intended to oversee Nathan's care, she'd capitalized. Shamelessly. As a result, she'd achieved exactly what she wanted.

All of it had amounted to a rather heady feeling.

Nathan had slept for several hours after the operation, while she sat at his side, attempting to read a book. She only made it a paragraph or two before she set the volume aside and allowed herself to study him, memorizing every inch of his features. The way his hair curled slightly over his forehead. The tiny scar just below his right eye. How his lips parted slightly with each intake of breath. His slightly thicker lower lip, the narrower upper, the faintest growth of stubble. . .

A flaming blush whooshed over her cheeks. Perhaps her perusal was becoming a bit too intense. Best stick to assessing vital signs.

The gentle ticking of the wall clock and Nathan's even breathing proved a soothing symphony for her own emotions. Mother's sickroom had rarely been this calm. There had always been the sounds of tossing, moans, unrest. Lily had been compelled to sit there, hour after long hour. Compelled not by any financial woes preventing them from hiring a nurse, but from something deep within herself. A voice that said she'd never been a worthy daughter, a worthy person. Her mother's illness had been a chance to prove that voice to the contrary. Yet after long months of seclusion, she'd reneged. Her father hired a reputable caretaker, and Lily had entered her long-postponed debut season.

Her mother had died three months later, the agony wracking her body put to rest.

Lily wed Jackson as soon as it was proper, her own agony just beginning.

Nathan shifted on the bed. His eyes, green as the shrubs lining her avenue, opened.

"Hey." A small smile angled his lips upward.

"Oh. You're awake." She pushed a wisp of hair behind her ear. "I trust you slept well."

"All right, I guess. I feel a sight better than I did before the operation."

"I can imagine. Are you hungry?"

He gave a nod.

"Anything particular that you'd fancy eating? I think everyone else just had sandwiches. Everything has been rather topsy-turvy all day. But I can see to it you get whatever you want."

He reached up and rubbed a hand over his eyes. "Maybe a piece of toast. I don't feel up for anything adventurous."

"What about some broth?"

"That sounds good, too."

"Then I'll inform one of the kitchen maids." She stood. "I'll be right back." But before she could turn to go, he grabbed her hand, capturing it in a surprisingly strong grip.

"You didn't need to go to all this trouble to take care of me. I'm not that special." The warmth of his hands sent a jolt of electricity clear down to her toes, followed by a rush of longing. For what, she couldn't be sure.

She swallowed. "After all the kindness you've shown me, how could I not care for you in your hour of need? And you are very special. And very important. To me and to this house." She quickly disentangled her fingers, relieved when the unfamiliar sensation vanished. "I'll be right back."

Then she left the room, the remembrance of his hands within hers a hot coal in her already tumultuous mind.

<hr/>

There's no great loss without some small gain, had been one of his mother's favorite expressions. In this case, there'd been a small loss with great gain. Nathan had lost his appendix and gained hours of uninterrupted time with Lily. At first, he'd been in too much pain to fully appreciate the experience. But four days later, able to walk and tend to his own personal needs, he had to admit every ounce of pain he'd endured was well worth it.

Though he didn't actually need a nurse, she continued to stay, spending several hours a day with him. And with Kingsley gone, the demands on her time had decreased considerably.

They talked. About everything and nothing. Childhood stories. Current events. She made him laugh with her rendition of Mamie Fish's ill-fated attempts to drive a motorcar. He coaxed her into a fit of giggles sharing the tale of the time when the cook at his first job dropped into a faint during an important dinner party, and Nathan had been marshaled into preparing the soufflé.

She sat beside him now, after he'd finished the story, a thoughtful expression on her face, one hand toying with the diamond teardrop on her earring.

"You've had quite the exciting life. You've met a lot of people, traveled to places you never thought you'd go." She dropped her hand and met his gaze. "If you'd stayed on the farm in Pennsylvania, you wouldn't have had all those experiences."

"Uh-huh." He nodded, folding his hands atop the quilt covering his legs. Sunlight flittered through the room's one window, warming the room and adding a golden hue to her creamy skin. "There's just one thing. . ."

"Yes?" Lily leaned forward.

He hesitated. Though the boundaries of propriety had continued to slip between them like a little girl's hair ribbon tilting to one side, the threads separating his class and hers had never truly fallen. They held fast, less constraining perhaps, but still secure and intact. Sharing with her—not as a listening ear for her thoughts and plans, but revealing a piece of himself—one rubbed raw by life's hard blows and usually kept shoved in the back of his mind, would mean a sight more to him than it would to her. Still, she waited, the look in her eyes confirming her interest.

"I wanted to become a teacher."

Her eyes widened. Not with shock or annoyance but plain, simple interest. "Go on." She must have realized the words sounded a bit imperious, because she added: "Please, tell me more. . .Nathan."

He needed no second invitation. Just the sound of his name on her lips was enough to make him willing to pledge the world to her. She had such a way of saying it, quiet and breathy and sweet enough to make him want to pull her into a closet, lock the door, and find out for himself if her hair was as soft as it looked, if the top of her head would rest just below his chin, if he would ever tire of inhaling the scent of roses. He already knew the answer to the latter. He never would. The more he held her, the more he'd ache for it.

"The whole idea of me being a teacher is a big joke though. I don't even have a high school diploma. When I was fourteen, my father got sick and was unable to work. As the oldest, with four young ones under me, school was no longer possible. I do my best to study, even now. I visit the library on my days off and read every chance I can. But there's no piece of paper proving I have any greater intelligence than one of those ducks your rich friends are always devouring."

"You don't enjoy being a chauffeur?"

Was he imagining things, or did a flicker of pain flash across her fathomless eyes, even if for only an instant?

"I consider it a privilege to work under your employ." He chose his words carefully. The last thing he wanted to do was give her the impression he didn't care. When in reality, he cared far more than he'd ever admit. "But I guess I've always wanted more. Kind of like how you want to open that halfway house for immigrants. Which, by the way, is an amazing plan."

An adorable blush took up residence on her cheeks.

"That's your dream. And I've no doubt you'll succeed. Teaching is mine. There are so many young people, just like I was, who have the ability to make something more of themselves, become something great, if only to rise above the lot circumstance has dealt them. But it's sort of like the safe upstairs. To get your hands on the treasure, you first need to find the key. I believe education is that key." He must've gotten some crazy look on his face, because, as he spoke, she regarded him with an expression of rapt interest.

"Why, that's brilliant." She seemed to exhale, rather than verbalize the words. "I can't remember the last time I heard something so. . .so inspiring. You have such passion, Nathan. I want to help you in any way I can."

"Just hearing those words is help enough." He swallowed. "Besides"—he added a grin to his words—"you do help me. You pay my salary. And living in New York gives me access to a lot of things I wouldn't have had on the farm. I wouldn't change the life I've lived. I just want to, someday, open another chapter."

A rap sounded on the door. Mavis, Lily's maid, stuck her head inside.

31

"If you please, ma'am, Mrs. Worthington-Chamblee has arrived and is waiting in the drawing room."

Lily smiled at the maid with the same courtesy she showed to all her servants. His chest tightened at the sweetness of it, at the special woman whom he had the privilege of knowing.

"I'll be down momentarily."

Mavis shut the door.

Lily stood, sending the scent of roses wafting over him. He found himself wondering, after he was recovered and she no longer sat with him, how long that smell would linger in his room before dissipating forever.

Her shoulders straightened. "This conversation may be over, but I'm not finished with it. I'm going to help you. I don't know how yet. But I will. Just you wait and see."

Chapter 6

I want to do something special for you. Is that all right?"

A ridiculous smile unfurled on her lips as Lily stood in her bedroom. Birthdays had never been much of an occasion during her marriage to Jackson. A diamond bracelet or a pair of opera glasses would be presented to her at breakfast, and there would be the end of it.

But on this, her twenty-fifth birthday, Nathan wanted to do something special for her. And though it probably violated every rule in the servant-employer code of conduct, she wasn't about to say no. Since Mr. Kingsley wasn't in town, there wasn't a single person who actually *cared* to celebrate with her. Nathan, apparently, did.

And for heaven's sake, was it so wrong to revel in the caring?

He'd instructed her to meet him outside, as if they were going for a drive. She was to wear attire suitable for outdoors. That was all he'd told her.

She stepped down the stairs, feeling pretty and girlish in a dress of pale blue and cream lace. A practical straw hat adorned her upswept hair.

Pretty? Girlish? All she had to do was look in the mirror to see the truth. She wasn't petite. Nor girlish. Hardly pretty. As Jackson once said, she reminded him of a beer barrel, ugly and round. Even now, the words stung.

She shoved them aside. She wouldn't think about that today.

The motorcar stood outside. A grin tipped one corner of Nathan's mouth. Despite his recent ordeal, he looked hale and hearty, wearing his usual chauffeur uniform.

"Ready?" He held the door for her. Not, however, the door to the backseat where she usually sat. But up front. With him.

She chanced a furtive glance, making certain none of the servants, or anyone else for that matter, was watching. No one was. So she grasped his hand and let him help her in. He closed the door, started the engine, and jumped into his own seat.

"You look. . .very nice." His gaze found hers for a brief instant before he maneuvered the car out of the driveway. Sitting so close to him made her even more aware of his scent. . .something spicy and masculine. Was he wearing cologne?

Whatever it was—it smelled altogether tantalizing.

You do not mean that, Lilian Grace Montgomery. Your chauffeur does NOT smell tanta-lizing. No ifs, ands, or buts about it.

"Where are we going?" She fiddled with the ribbon securing her bonnet, trying to block out persistent thoughts of that cologne.

"Secret. Not telling, Birthday Girl." He winked.

"Is this the moment when I discover you're not actually my chauffeur but an abductor in disguise?" She grinned, liking the way he smiled when she teased him. As if he was the brother she never had, she, his impish sister, giving him what for.

The glint in his eyes mesmerized her.

Perhaps she didn't feel quite as sisterly as she ought.

They continued their drive. As he drove, Nathan whistled. Jaunty tunes she'd never heard, which reeled her in, made her tap her foot, and long to join in.

But proper ladies didn't whistle. Because finishing school hadn't included that in their standard curriculum.

At last, Nathan stopped the car. He climbed out and assisted her down.

The seaside stretched before them. Not the one Newport society frequented, proper and well kept. But the real seaside, sparkling cobalt water stretching as far as the eye could see. Pearly white sand that begged one to forsake shoes and stockings, ladylike rules and propriety. The wind rushed over her face, warmed by the sun. The sort of seaside where one could forgo bathing hats and sun parasols. The sort of seaside where one could simply. . .be.

Nathan busied himself with carrying items and setting them on the sand. He proceeded to spread out a blanket, and she rushed to assist him. The quilt tangled in the wind like a child's kite, and laughter bubbled from her lips as they worked to secure it to the ground.

He set the picnic basket on top, dusted off his hands.

"Now I've got just one question for you. Do you know how to swim?"

Lily gasped. "What? Here? Now?" For a society lady to swim required a concealing bathing costume, along with a specially made cart that drove one several feet out into the water, stopped, and allowed one to bathe shielded by a protective awning.

He nodded, his hair teased by the wind. It had grown longer during his recovery, the golden-brown strands curling slightly over his forehead.

"No. We're going to swim in the Mediterranean a year from now. Of course, now."

"I. . .I don't know."

He closed the distance between them, coming toward her and taking both her hands in his. "Adventure is like salt, Lily. Without it, both porridge and life are tasteless. Bland. Though I won't go as far as to say fun makes the world go round, it does help it spin a bit more merrily."

He did have a point. During her years as a stifled socialite, her life had been bland. Now that her fetters to Jackson had been severed, she didn't want to go on like that anymore.

"I'm not sure, Nathan. . . I don't have my bathing costume. And even if I did, I can't. . .get into it without help from Mavis."

He reddened first then chuckled. "All right. I have another plan though." He disappeared behind a clump of trees, returning a couple of minutes later, dragging what looked like a miniature raft attached to a length of rope.

"You okay with a little ride?" Amusement glinted in his eyes. As if he were enjoying, truly relishing, every moment spent with her. As if thinking up this day gave him as much pleasure as doing something for his own benefit.

So she tossed propriety to the wind and nodded, matching his smile. "I suppose so."

"Come here." He held out his hand and led her toward the water's edge. "Pardon me." He bent and unlaced his shoes, rolled up his pant legs. Most young ladies of her acquaintance would have looked discreetly away. At first, Lily averted her eyes.

But then she caught a glimpse of his tanned, muscular legs.

Gracious me, he's. . .

Handsome? Well built? Not afraid of hard work?

All of those things and more.

He shucked his chauffeur's jacket and vest, until he was down to a simple shirt and trousers. Then he waded into the water, the raft following along. He dropped the rope, gave her a teasing grin, and scooped her into his arms as if she weighed no more than a feather pillow.

She shrieked as he lowered her atop the raft, a spray of water splattering her skirt.

"You all right?" He steadied the raft with one hand, the other holding on to the rope. Showing the same care as when he drove the car over bumpy terrain, as if to reassure her that her safety mattered.

She nodded, settling herself more comfortably on her seat of logs.

He pulled on the rope, wading deeper into the water. Waves splashed the sides of the raft, the craft bobbing along. Water misted onto her face and clothes, but at this moment, she could not have cared less. The sun shone high and bright overhead, the sparkle of the water like a thousand rapidly shifting panes of glass.

"Having fun?" Nathan glanced at her. He'd gotten himself soaked through, his shirt plastered to his chest. He didn't seem a bit winded though, surprisingly, considering all that exertion.

"Completely."

He continued to tow her around, never straying too far from the shore. She gazed up at the sky, closed her eyes—

The raft tipped. Dangerously. Lily scrambled for balance, slipped.

Water closed around her in a sudden rush of cold. The skirt of her dress weighed her down. She fought for air. Her feet sought solid ground and found it against the sandy bottom.

Nathan grabbed her around the waist as if to steady her. She coughed and sputtered.

"I'm so sorry." His eyes, so perfectly green, radiated absolute distress. "I did *not* mean for that to happen. Not at all."

She must've startled him by bursting into giggles, for his gaze turned from distress to astonishment.

"I'm all right, Nathan." She managed to stop laughing long enough to speak quietly. Gracious, the man seemed truly upset.

"But you're all wet."

She laughed again. "Since when did a little water harm a person? I'm fine. Actually, the water feels quite pleasant."

Nathan looked her up and down as if to assure himself that, yes, she was unharmed.

"You're sure?" He took a step closer, so close that the heat from his body radiated over her. She drew in a breath of salt and water and him. That uniqueness of fragrance that was Nathan Evans to the core. She inhaled again, savoring.

"I've never felt better in my life," she whispered.

If he took half a step closer, he'd be pressed right against her. Close enough for her to twine her arms around his waist, bury her nose into the side of his neck. So incredibly, painfully close.

His gaze bored into hers for a second longer.

Then he stepped away and steadied the raft.

"We'd better get back to shore if we want to have our picnic." He held the raft steady as she climbed aboard, her skirt sloshing around her.

She wiped a hand across her face, clearing the water. Then focused on the shoreline, coming ever closer. Not on Nathan, taking even, careful strides, all to keep her safe.

The shoreline. Focus on the shoreline.

Not on him.

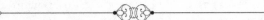

As long as Nathan drew breath, he doubted he'd be able to erase from his mind the sight of Lily Montgomery, lady of fashion, with her bodice plastered to her skin, her wet hair straggling from beneath that hat, attention fixated on him.

She wasn't like most of those deathly thin socialites who looked as if they'd never eaten a day in their lives. She had curves. Blast it all!

He gave the silver coffeepot an extra hard rub. If only he could scour away his thoughts as easily.

She'd looked so completely beautiful, even with her unruly hair and ruined dress. And as they stood together, close, too close, he'd breathed in that rose fragrance that could turn his mind to useless mush in half an instant.

The rest of the afternoon had been pure, unadulterated sweetness. She'd dried off with his jacket, and lay in the sun, staring up at the sky while he assembled their picnic lunch. They'd dined on cold chicken and potato salad, followed by a frosted birthday cake. Nathan had ordered the whole thing prepared at a local café and picked it up earlier in the day. The cake had sure been pretty, all that white frosting and fondant pink roses. He'd lit a single candle and announced she must make a wish. His heart had hammered in his chest as she closed her eyes and gave a blissful smile then blew out the candle. He hadn't asked what her wish had been. He wasn't sure he wanted to know.

Now, a day later, Nathan occupied himself in a way that would please Osbourne—polishing the silver with just the right amount of shine. It always drove Nathan crazy with irritation when Osbourne performed his usual inspection of the task, holding up a piece and craning his neck to see if his reflection was visible.

As if on cue, Osbourne entered the room.

"All finished, Evans?"

Nathan nodded, watching as Osbourne picked up one piece then another. He trained his gaze on the butler's pantry window, waiting until the man finished.

"Very good." As usual, he bit out the compliment as if the giving of it physically pained him. He turned but stopped at the door and swiveled back around.

"You're a good lad, Evans. A hard worker and a respectful young man." The almost congenial tone issuing from Osbourne's lips sounded nothing like the usually cantankerous butler. Nor the way he rested his meaty hand on Nathan's shoulder.

Nathan stiffened under the man's touch. What was this all about?

"Thank you, sir," he answered. "I appreciate the opportunity to continue my employment."

"I know you do. But there are certain circumstances, occasions, where a man tends to doubt another man's loyalty. May I be quite frank with you?"

Nathan resisted the urge to squirm under the man's hand. "Please do."

"I know Mrs. Montgomery's behavior toward you has been a bit. . .shall we say, unorthodox. Caring for you as she did after your operation. You see, Evans, in a position such as mine, one tends to see everything. Note things that a casual observer might miss. After over forty years in service, I notice more than most. Just keep in mind, lad, I'm always watching. And if. . .certain behaviors continue to occur. . .well, I need a man I can trust. Implicitly, with everything and everyone in this house. Don't fail me." He gave Nathan's shoulder a weighty clap.

Nathan stood, unflinching.

"Now, you'd better get back to work." He moved toward the door. Then turned once again, a smile on his lips. The type of gleeful smile Nathan imagined villains in his favorite adventure stories would don right before abducting the beautiful princess. "Oh, by the way, I thought you'd like to know Mr. Kingsley has returned. No doubt, he'll continue his attentions toward Mrs. Montgomery." And with that, Osbourne left.

Both palms flat against the table, Nathan lowered his head. So Osbourne suspected. The wily codger had probably put two and two together when both he and Lily returned looking less presentable than when they'd left. Of course, the man would stick like a barnacle to his promise. If anything suspicious occurred between Nathan and Lily, he'd be sacked on the spot. Probably some excuse would be made up to tell Lily about her disreputable chauffeur. Would she believe whatever crime story the butler concocted? Would she care, or would she just forge a friendship with her new chauffeur, as she had with Nathan?

A weighty sigh heaved his chest. No doubt she'd marry Kingsley within the year, move to his house, be driven around by whatever lackey he employed.

Lord, help me to make sense of the mess I'm in. I don't know why You've allowed me to care about Lily, when she'll never be more to me than the lady who authorizes my paycheck. I don't understand. Give me clarity. Give me peace. And thank You in advance for Your help.

He stood to his full height, some of the heaviness easing from his chest. He'd given the matter to the Lord. The One who promised peace and wisdom.

The One who always knew best.

Chapter 7

Contrasting this picnic with the one she'd been on with Nathan was like comparing black against white. Or a Worth gown versus a linen smock.

Lily couldn't be sure which she preferred. Worth gowns were pretty, as was this picnic. Liveried footmen ferried crystal serving dishes from table to table, and a three-piece orchestra strummed out a Haydn sonata. Every lady wore an elaborate hat and pastel dress, men light summer suits and bowler hats.

But linen smocks were more comfortable—like her picnic with Nathan. There she hadn't felt a bit self-conscious, even when her dress hung on her like a waterlogged burlap bag. There she'd let herself eat her fill of that amazingly delicious cake, without worrying what anyone might think. There. . .well, what did it matter? She wasn't there anymore, but here.

Mr. Kingsley had returned, profusions of "I've missed you" on his lips and a volume of Shakespeare in his hand. A belated birthday gift, he said.

How sweet he was—to think of her amid his busyness.

"Enjoying yourself?" He accepted another helping of foie gras from a waiter. The hostess of the picnic, Mrs. Livingston-Hockley, had an obsession for all things French and planned her menu accordingly. She had a passion for all things Versailles and Marie Antoinette, too, though after what had happened to that sorry royal, Lily couldn't understand why.

"Immensely." She nibbled on a baguette slice.

"How are your party plans coming?"

"Pretty well." A footman held out a tray of pear and peach tartlets. My, those did look tempting. All golden brown and sprinkled with crystalized sugar. Though what would Mr. Kingsley think if she gave in to her urge to take two? Best not test it. She daintily accepted one—the tiniest pear piece she could find—and plated it. "It's to be a costume ball, you know."

"And who are you posing as?"

She watched as he also took one small pear tart.

"I'm not telling." An impish smile lifted her lips. She'd decided to dress as an English shepherdess, but she certainly wasn't letting him know that. It would be a surprise, one she hoped he'd be pleased with.

"What color is your dress then? That way I'll know what sort of flowers to bring."

"Blue. But you won't hear another word about it." Her attention was diverted by Mrs. Livingston-Hockley's young daughter, Amy. Though children were generally neither seen nor heard at gatherings such as these, a few mothers had decked their young ones in enormous hair bows and sailor suits and brought them along. Amy's hair bow had gone crooked, and fat tears dripped down the seven-year-old's cheeks.

Mrs. Livingston-Hockley stood on the opposite side of the lawn, giving directions to the orchestra and not paying a whit of attention to her daughter.

With a quick word to Mr. Kingsley, Lily pushed back her chair, hurried across the lawn, and knelt down beside the little girl. Of course, the grass would probably stain her pale lilac skirt, but the sadness in the child's eyes was far more important than any mere item of clothing.

"What's the matter, sweetheart?" She brushed her fingertips across Amy's cheeks, wishing she'd brought her reticule so she could offer a handkerchief.

Amy's lower lip trembled, her pudgy face red and flushed. "Mary Sue said I'm as. . . as fat as her mama's pug dog. She says I'd better not eat anything for the next ten years, else I won't be able to get a handsome prince like Cinderella did. I. . .really, really want a prince like Cinderella." She burst into another round of blubbers.

Lily drew in a breath and smiled at the girl. "First of all, Amy, you are a beautiful young lady. No matter what Mary Sue or anyone says to you, it doesn't change the truth. And handsome princes, if they are truly good men, will look past our outward appearance and see the people we are inside." She pointed to her heart. "And I know you are very beautiful there, too."

"You mean a handsome prince will love me even if I do look like a pug dog?" Amy had ceased crying and regarded Lily with wide, interested eyes.

"A true prince will love you always. He won't care whether you're as rich as the Vanderbilts, or poor like Cinderella. It won't matter to him if your nose gets all red when you cry or if your teeth are a little crooked." She opened her mouth to show Amy her slightly crooked bottom teeth. "A true prince will always care for you, no matter what. But it's your job to recognize the true princes from the villains who might look like princes. And never, ever give your heart away until you're absolutely sure."

Amy sniffed, wiping her nose on the back of her sleeve. "Mary Sue isn't as smart as you. She doesn't know about true princes. Thank you for telling me, Mrs. Montgomery."

Lily smiled, pulling the girl into a gentle hug. Amy nestled into her embrace, wrapping both arms around Lily's waist. She inhaled the scent of soap and chocolate, reveling in the sensation of holding this sweet child. What a wonder it would be to experience this joy every day. Imparting wisdom to, loving, a little girl of her own.

An ache swelled in her chest.

"Now, you go find Mary Sue and tell her what I just told you." She released the girl and reached to straighten her pink hair ribbon.

"I will!" Giving her one last happy smile, Amy scampered across the lawn.

Lily turned. Mr. Kingsley stood a few feet away, leaning against a tree, watching her. She got to her feet, smoothed the front of her dress, and crossed to where he stood.

"What was that all about?" He offered her his arm and led her back to their table.

"Just giving some womanly advice." She smiled up at him, liking the way her hand rested on his arm. As if it had been there for years and would continue to remain so.

"You left that little girl smiling. You do that, Lily Montgomery. Make people smile. Bring joy into their lives." He pulled out her chair and pushed it in once she sat down.

"You really think so?" The compliment warmed her heart the way the sun warmed her skin. She could easily grow used to hearing such words every day, a balm to the scars left by her marriage to Jackson.

"I know so. And what's more, I want to. . .hope very much to. . ." He looked down at his plate. Despite the chatter and laughter of the nearby guests, a sense of intimacy lingered between them.

What was he going to say? Did he care for her? Did she, for him? What was love, anyway? Was this it? Her only prior experience had been with Jackson, and she realized now that her feelings for him had been no more than girlish dreams and fantasies, as light and void of substance as the cream puffs that sat in the center of the table. Did a true prince lie in her future, as she'd promised Amy? Was he to be found in the man before her?

Mr. Kingsley seemed to hesitate. "Never mind. There'll be time enough to say what I wish later." He lifted his glass of lemonade, as if to make a toast.

"Indeed." But the smile he gave her made her believe he wished later came sooner instead.

There was a time when one had to quit holding on to hope. Admit defeat, let the best man win.

Nathan had come to that point in his feelings toward Lily Montgomery.

Since Kingsley's return, he and Lily had been as inseparable as before. And as they grew closer, Nathan sensed his own distance with Lily lengthening. Like a rope, stretched tighter and tighter, tested further and further, until it reached the breaking point. They had only two weeks left in the Newport season. And if Nathan didn't miss his guess, Lily and Kingsley would announce their engagement before the end of it.

Never mind her care of him after his operation. Never mind their conversation, the smiles passed between them. Never mind their picnic—standing next to her in the water, two seconds away from kissing her senseless.

In Lily's eyes, it meant nothing.

What did matter, though, was ascertaining one thing. He'd prayed about it and felt the Lord's peace about pursuing the truth.

He had to make sure Kingsley would treat Lily as she deserved. There was no way his own life could hold any remaining speck of joy if he heard of Lily's later unhappiness.

So he'd investigate Kingsley. Ascertain that the man's motives were as honorable as first impressions would have one believe. All it would take was a telephone call to New York, to the office of a lawyer, a man Nathan had met while serving as footman during a house party on the Hudson River. The man would help him; Nathan had little doubt of that.

One telephone call.

Then he could give her up and hope and pray for his heart to follow.

———————————◦◦◦———————————

Nathan got the answer to his telephone inquiries a week later.

He opened and read the hastily penned note.

A howling anxiety whirred through his mind.

Chapter 8

With the ball only hours away, a heady rush of excitement swirled through Lily, making it difficult to concentrate on much of anything. The house hustled and bustled as a crew of decorators transformed the immense ballroom into a veritable feast for the eyes. Flowers in abundance. Potted ferns. Every chandelier had been polished until it glittered and gleamed, the floor waxed and scrubbed.

The evening promised to be a success.

And maybe, just maybe, Mr. Kingsley would finally tell her what he'd been hinting at all week. She wasn't quite sure what it was, but a lady could hope, couldn't she?

Hope that he might confess his feelings. Hope that they might. . .well, get married and begin a life together. She didn't truly love him, that much she could be sure of. But love was for schoolgirl romances and fanciful novels. A genuine liking could—would—be more than enough. For her, at least. Why couldn't it be?

Because she sensed the. . .*more* in all of it. The more of teasing and laughing, passion-filled kisses and wanting to belong to one heart and one alone. But *more* wasn't always realistic.

It was time for her to become a realist.

She fiddled with her fountain pen, propping one elbow atop her writing desk. Morning sunlight floated through the parlor window.

A knock sounded on the closed door.

"Come in." She put aside her pen and turned.

Nathan stepped inside. He wore his footman uniform and a dark expression in his eyes.

"Good morning, again." She'd seen him an hour ago at breakfast, when he served. Was he announcing callers at this early hour?

He didn't return her smile. In one hand, he grasped a folded piece of paper.

Curiouser and curiouser. . .

"Do you have something for me?"

"Yes." He made a move to pass her the paper, but at the last second, drew his hand back. "There's something I need to talk to you about."

"Of course." He seemed so grave. Was something wrong? Was he ill again? Did he need leave to visit a family member? She'd give it to him, of course. He could depart straightaway, before the ball even.

"It's about Roland Kingsley." He gritted out the name as if it were a bad taste he wanted to spit out.

Her nerves tensed. What accusation did he have against Mr. Kingsley? For Nathan obviously wasn't in here to tell her the man had come to call.

"I did some checking. . .into Mr. Kingsley. His family, finances, and so forth."

A hot, heavy rage doused her. Her servant had investigated the man she planned to marry. How could he. . .? Why would he. . .? How dare he!

As if oblivious to the swirl of anger inside her, Nathan continued. "I'd spare you, if I could, but I must tell you the truth. He's almost bankrupt. It's a secret. Nobody really knows it. But my friend, a lawyer, ferreted out the information."

Bankrupt? Her brain caught onto that single word and turned it over and over and over. *Dear Lord. . .*

"Why? Why would you do this?" The words rasped from her lips.

In two strides, he crossed the room. The expression in his eyes was one of intensity and raw earnestness. Grasping her by both shoulders, he pulled her from the chair. His arms wrapped around her waist, shocking her with their strength.

"I love you, Lily. That's why. You have become so much to me, and I had to find out if Kingsley was as good as he appeared. I couldn't stand the thought of you marrying someone who wasn't the person you deserve to be with." For a long moment, his gaze seared through her, intense, unwavering.

Then before she could think, react, even take another breath, he kissed her. His arms melded her against him, his lips sought hers with the urgency of a man long denied. Her knees turned liquid, her senses swimming—

She jerked away. And then did something she had never, not once, no matter how much he'd deserved it, done to Jackson.

Raised her palm and slapped him. Hard. The impact reverberated through her hand, sharp and stinging.

Nathan stumbled, eyes wide with shock and pain.

Her body trembled, as if caught in an intense bout of chills. "What are you thinking? You have no right, no right at all to meddle in my private affairs. And you have far less of one to do what you. . .what you just did. As for you saying such things to me. . . You are nothing more than a servant in this house. I know we have been friends, good friends, but you have overstepped your bounds in this." She raised her chin, standing tall, proud, and every inch in control. "And you will leave this very day. Pack your things and go belowstairs to collect what salary is owed you."

He stared at her, his skin pale, gaze unblinking.

Silence hung between them, heavier than New York fog.

"At least I can say I tried. You were warned that the man you are entering into an understanding with is only after you for your money. He doesn't love you, Lily. He doesn't deserve you. And now you know."

It wasn't true. He did. He did love her. How could he look at her and not mean the things he said? Roland Kingsley cared about her. She was sure of it. They would have a safe and happy future, complete with children to love and dote upon.

Yet as she met Nathan's gaze and read the terrible truth written there, that future and those hopes faded away, like breath gasping from dying lips.

"Go. Just go." She turned her back toward the window. Listened to his footfalls move away from her. The door closed with a click that echoed of complete and total finality.

She was going to be sick. If what Nathan said was true, then she'd been an inch away from repeating her very worst mistake. Signing away her life, and very probably her devotion, to another undeserving wretch.

"A true prince will always care for you, no matter what. But it's your job to recognize the true princes from the villains who might look like princes. And never, ever give your heart away until you're absolutely sure."

Her stomach roiled, anxiety making her heart pound. Tears blurred her vision.

Where are You? Lord, help. . .

No answering rush of peace. No verse popped into her memory. No. . .anything. Just emptiness and tension and more emptiness.

She lowered herself onto the sofa, curling her body into itself. Squeezing her eyes shut, she fought to remember how to breathe.

Help me, she cried inwardly. *Somehow, someone help me.*

Nathan left without taking a cent of his earnings. He briefly told Osbourne of his dismissal, turned away without waiting to watch the man crow, tossed his few belongings in a knapsack, said good-bye to Polly.

Then he left. Out the back entrance, down Bellevue Avenue.

What a joke. The chauffeur leaving on foot.

He walked, face to the wind, passing fancy motorcars and coachmen-driven carriages. As he neared the empty shoreline, his feet scuffing up sand, the crash of waves and screech of gulls increased in volume. Where exactly he was heading was anyone's guess. It wasn't like he had ten other prospective employers lined up to take his pick from.

He chucked the knapsack on the sand, crossed both arms over his chest and stared, gaze on the frothing water. Salt spray burned his eyes.

Or was it. . .?

Tears.

Nathan Evans, chauffeur and all-around errand boy, crying tears of loss over Lily Montgomery, society princess.

A woman he could never have.

A woman he loved with fierce and total devotion.

His throat tightened, aching. He'd kissed her. Known for the briefest of minutes the rightness of her lips against his, the sensation of his arms around her waist. It had been perfect. Undeniable. Indescribable. Perfect.

The sting of her slap still reverberated through him. The look of outrage in her eyes. As if he were some kind of criminal, worse than dirt.

All he'd done was tell her the truth. Tell her he loved her.

His secret admiration was no longer secret. He'd spilled it. And like clean water, sloshed from a bucket, it lay on the ground to be stepped on and muddied.

Tears ran down his face, hot and angry. He swiped them away and picked up clods of dirt, throwing them as hard as he could into the water. His breath came in short pants.

He didn't quit. Kept throwing, kicking, venting until his heart thundered and he collapsed on the sand, spent.

He let his face fall into his clasped hands.

"Why, Lord? Why did I tell her? It would have been better to keep it secret. Then she would never know. Then I wouldn't be left with this. . .this rejection. I don't understand. Why are we taken down paths that lead nowhere? Is it to test us? Well, I'm passing this one about as well as I passed second-grade reading. Lousily."

Life was a cruel ringmaster. It drew one in, reeling and wooing. Then when you got to the point of no return, it dropped a cloud of pain and misery so thick and stifling it left you unable to breathe.

"Why do bad things happen, Mama?" He'd been eight, sitting beside his mother on the front porch. The sky had been a perfect color blue, the wind whispering in the trees.

His mother had looked at him with one of her beautiful smiles. Even now he could see that smile. Turned it over in his mind, remembering.

"If Jesus is so good, why does He let the badness in?"

And her answer. . .what had it been?

Oh. Yes.

"I don't know, Nate. I don't expect anybody, even the Reverend Jones, does. Some things, I don't think we're supposed to know. Because if we knew everything, there would be no need for faith. And I think God wants us to have faith. It's all about trust. Knowing for sure and certain that no matter how hard the road gets, we're not on it alone. He's always walking right there with us, holding our hands through the ruts and helping us over the hills. During the clear stretches, He's there, too. Always there, Nate. That's what you need to remember."

"I remember, Mama," Nathan whispered. "I remember."

No matter what happened in life, Mama lived by those words.

"Always there, Nate."

Always there. A reason for everything. The reason for this, Nathan didn't know. Maybe he never would. Maybe his relationship with Lily hadn't been for him. Maybe he'd been there, through the broken moments of her marriage and the healing afterward, for her. Put there by a sovereign God who always had a purpose.

He drew in a deep breath. Let the air fill him while peace cleansed his soul.

"All right, Lord. What now? I don't have a job. I have about ten dollars to my name. I don't even have a place to sleep tonight. But I guess You already know that. So show me what to do. I've got faith, Lord. I figure I don't have much else going for me, but I've got that."

He looked up at the sky. The blue of afternoon darkened into the gray of evening. There'd be a party at the Montgomery mansion tonight. Kingsley would be there, his charming facade hiding the secrets within. Lily would smile at him, probably forgetting that only hours ago she'd stood in the parlor and been kissed by a man who loved her with everything inside him.

Forget about the party? That he could do.

Forget about Lily?

Never. He had little of his own, but he had those memories to cherish.

Faith. He had that, too.

Two things to hold on to.

Chapter 9

The evening had perfection written all over it. From the elegant decorations to the scrumptious food to the carefully tuned musicians. There wasn't a thing that could go wrong. Not with Jackson's money behind it all.

Tonight would be a night for the memory books. For the society columns.

So why did darkness cloak Lily? Why did the smile on her face feel as false and stiff as those she had donned during her marriage to Jackson? She was supposed to be happy tonight. After all, isn't that why people threw parties? To celebrate? To have fun?

Neither felt appropriate for her current mood.

Nathan's accusations toward Mr. Kingsley filled her mind. As did the nagging sensation that they might possibly be true.

If they were, where did that leave her?

A duped woman yet again. Duped by her longing to be cherished, despite her appearance. Duped by her desire to be loved.

Well, she was through. She wouldn't repeat earlier mistakes, no matter her other faults.

And tonight's maneuvers would be a test of Mr. Kingsley's true motives.

She looped her arm through his, smiling up at him. He'd dressed in a male counterpart of her female shepherdess costume. Had it been mere coincidence? Or was something deeper going on there?

"I'm tired of dancing." She'd only danced three, one with Kingsley, two with other guests. But she was weary. Of dancing. And secrets.

"Me, too." He looked down at her fondly. What a consummate actor he was. If he was as poor as Nathan let on, maybe Mr. Kingsley's next career should be the stage. "Besides, I've been hoping for a chance to talk."

They made their way into the gardens, the strains of "The Skater's Waltz" drifting on the warm, summer air. Light shone from neighboring mansions, all of which would be shut up in a matter of days. These monuments to wealth and beauty would soon become as quiet and dark as tombs for the next ten months, until those who owned them decided to return again, filling them with the powder-thin veneer they called social intercourse.

She was heartily sick of the whole stupid ritual.

"Shall we sit here?" Mr. Kingsley motioned to a secluded stone bench.

Lily took the proffered seat, folding her hands in her lap. She looked up at him, forcing adoration into her gaze.

"Mr. Kingsley. . .Roland. Will you allow me to be bold? Permit me to say what you may think too forward?"

His eyes took on an ardent look. "You know you can tell me anything, my dear. There is nothing that you could say that would make me think any less of the beautiful woman you are."

"Good." She reached across the space between them and took his hand in hers. The music inside had switched to a jaunty march. The rhythm matched that of her heart.

To use a cliché, this was a moment of truth, if ever one existed.

"Over the past weeks we have spent together, I have grown to. . .feel something for you. Something I wondered if I could ever feel again. But I have a secret. And I can't continue to nurture these feelings, until I can be sure that you are made fully aware."

No change in his expression. In fact, he actually scooted closer.

"I'm listening."

"To put it bluntly, I feel the terms of my husband's will are not quite as they should be. In fact, if I were ever to remarry, I would receive nothing from him. This house, the one in New York, and all of his assets would revert to his younger brother, Jeremy. Jeremy currently lives in Chicago."

As she spoke, Mr. Kingsley's expression shifted. Not drastically in a gape-mouthed astonishment kind of way, but there was a tension in his posture that had not been there before. If she'd thought any of this mattered, she'd have told him long ago. That though she was an heiress in society's eyes, she was an heiress only as long as she remained a widow. But she hadn't dreamed, hadn't even imagined. . .

She hurried to continue. "I know this probably doesn't matter a bit to you. But I consider myself an honest woman, and I want to be quite frank about anything that concerns myself. Especially since you seem to wish to. . .to. . ." Here she dipped her head and peered up at him through lowered lashes. Her outward expression was everything a well-brought-up woman's should be. Inwardly, her heart pounded and anxiety coursed through every vein. ". . .enter into an understanding with me."

There. She'd laid it all out.

And in the space of a second, the sickening blow of reality backhanded her full in the face. Before he even said a word, he revealed the truth. In the way he drew back, not much, but enough. In the way his breath came in quick bursts.

In the utter shock in his eyes.

She fought against the battle of her own emotions and continued to look as trusting and demure as ever.

Now, sitting perfectly erect on the opposite edge of the bench, Mr. Kingsley cleared his throat. "Mrs. Montgomery." He said her name with unapologetic formality. The time for "Lily" and "my dear" had evidently come and gone. "You have misunderstood me if you were under the impression I intended to become—"

She couldn't endure such blank platitudes. Not after the day she'd had.

With great control, she lifted her hand, regally halting him. "You needn't trouble yourself to explain. You're no longer a wealthy man. Don't bother to deny it. I know.

You can no longer marry me because I haven't enough cash to pull you away from the poorhouse's brink."

His statuesque pose softened. Slightly. "I won't deny it."

"Then your courtship of me was not in the least a pursuit of myself?" She despised herself for the tinge of desperation worming itself into her words.

"I can, at least, give the honesty I denied you before. I think very highly of you, but you are right, I do not. . . My feelings toward you are not romantically inclined. My first wife, God rest her, was a beautiful woman whom I loved deeply. I could never hope to find her equal again. What I did to you was wrong, and for that I am sorry. I do not dare hope that you could find it within yourself to forgive me. . .or to say nothing of what you have learned."

The boning in her corset jabbed her ribs with every exhale. "I won't say anything. You have my word. But you have wronged me, Roland Kingsley. Courting me for weeks under false pretenses, about to propose marriage. . ." She swallowed, the roof of her mouth dry and cloying. "Make no mistake about the long and bitter wrong you have done." She got to her feet, the sounds of a polka providing a backdrop for their final moments together. Like a tragic heroine in an opera, she lifted her chin and looked down at him. This man who had almost coerced her into repeating the mistake that cost her so dearly before.

"Good-bye, Mr. Kingsley," she said simply and turned and walked away, clinging to the final, tattered threads in her cloak of polite behavior.

The climb up the stairs to her room seemed to take an eternity. When at last she closed the door, she crossed the room and stood in front of the full-length mirror, fingers of firelight the only illumination.

For a long, quiet moment, she stared at herself. More plain than pretty, little willowy slenderness evidenced in her curvaceous form. Roland Kingsley's first wife had been beautiful. So stunning that no woman could ever hope to equal her. Lily, of course, possessed nothing more than her supposed cash to recommend her.

How had Mr. Kingsley done it? Had it reduced him to inner gagging to gaze at her as he had? Had calling her "my dear" made him inwardly recoil?

What would he have done if they had married? He could not have kept up his lover-like facade forever. What would it have done to her? To realize that once again, she'd married someone who did not love her? Would the pain have been as deep, scalding her heart and burning her with blistering intensity, as it had the last time?

Tears pricked her eyes as truth whispered within her heart. She hadn't loved Roland. She hadn't even truly loved Jackson. What she'd been looking for in the affections of both men was a realization of her own worth. That, through the eyes of another, she could, just maybe, see herself as beautiful. Beloved. Cherished. Despite her outward flaws and inner insecurities, she wanted this. Wanted it with a deep, driving ache.

"You've been doing it all wrong, precious daughter. No one sees you in greater beauty than I."

The words seemed to come out of nowhere, gently spoken to the inner places of her heart. Her throat clogged with emotion.

"See yourself not as man sees you but as I do. I love you. I died for you. And if there had not been a single human being on earth besides yourself, I would have done no less."

"Truly, Lord?" Oh, how she wanted this. Wanted to let the healing oil of Jesus' truth salve the scars etched into her heart by the world's careless hands. To reject the lies she had been told—that because of her outward appearance, her inner held no worth.

"Always."

She wept. Cried out to the Lord in those tears, crying for forgiveness for believing the lies all those years. And slowly, sweetly, she began to heal. Felt the hands of the Lord mending, redeeming those hidden, wounded places. It wasn't painful, nor did it make her hang her head in shame, the way the words of her father and Jackson had. As if the Lord truly understood what it was to feel rejected.

Of course He did. He understood because it was what His people did to Him time after time, day after day. They ignored His outstretched arms, pursued meaningless pleasures rather than His embrace. Spent time in attaining wealth, friends, fame, while all the while He looked down, knowing that such things would never bring true peace.

She was guilty. Hadn't she run after the world's acceptance rather than His? Even this party tonight had been a plea to reenter the society that seemed to spurn her.

Oh, she was guilty.

Lord, forgive me.

She continued to sit in the presence of the Lord, freedom replacing bondage.

And then she thought of Nathan. The one man who didn't care whether she was an heiress or a kitchen maid. Who'd called her beautiful. Who'd kissed her and declared his love. Who'd held her hand as if he wanted to hold her heart.

A true prince will love you always.

She'd let him go. In her foolish pride, she'd lost him—her true prince.

But she could try to find him. Beg his forgiveness. At the very least, she owed him an apology.

Let me find him, Lord. Even if I cannot repair the damage I have done, let me find him. Just let me try.

Today he was leaving Newport, leaving Lily. And once he'd gone, there'd be no coming back.

In the course of his new life, there wouldn't be any cause to see her again. He'd already decided, last night, not to find another job in service. God had a different call in his life—bringing education to those who needed it most, bringing with that education, hope. It was what he'd always dreamed of, wanted, and planned for.

Still, no burst of excitement filled his heart. Or if it did, it dimmed and flickered like one of those newfangled electric lightbulbs. His plans had a hollowness to them, now that she would never share them.

Help me to trust You, Lord. I know You've got a good plan.

He'd spent the night in a cheap rooming house and now made his way for the last time, down Bellevue Avenue. How often he'd driven this same stretch. Every turn, every passing mansion, was as familiar to him as his own face. He knew when to slow a car to avoid a bump, when to keep to the side of the road to avoid horse droppings.

Amazing. What had been so familiar would soon become as distant as a far-off galaxy.

Wind swept over his face, ruffling his hair and sending cleansing air into his lungs. His steps slowed. This was foolish. He should've taken another street. He knew the town well enough to do so. Any path, even one that took him down a dark alleyway, would be less dangerous than this route. The one that would take him past Seacombe.

But like a compass to the north, he was drawn there. No matter the ruination it might wreak upon his already tumultuous heart.

There. Her house. Stately and grand and familiar as ever. Though Jackson had been the one to design the place, every brick seemed to breathe her name.

A rush of longing, sharp and insistent, gusted over him with more force than the wind.

He let his gaze linger a moment more then resolutely turned away. He'd made his pilgrimage. Time to leave the shrine behind.

The rumble of a motorcar registered in his mind, though only barely.

"Nathan."

Blast it, was he now going crazy? Would the sound of her voice fill his brain at every turn, the way the hero in Edgar Allen Poe's story couldn't escape the beating of a heart?

"Nathan!"

That voice again. He couldn't take it, couldn't—

His breath hitched.

For there she was. Running toward him. Not from the direction of her house but from a parked motorcar a block away. And not just any motorcar. The one he'd practically lived behind, driving her around during those long, blissful days.

Her hair swirled around her face, her dress held high above her shoe tops.

And she raced toward him as if her very life depended upon reaching his side.

For the space of a second, she seemed ready to fling herself into his arms. But she stopped a couple of inches short, her bodice heaving with quick breaths.

He regarded her, this woman he'd braced himself into never laying eyes on again. This woman that he loved, despite all manner of rational sense.

"You can't drive a car." The words slipped from his mouth.

The slightest of smiles bloomed on her lips. "I'm not an idiot, Nathan Evans. What do you think I've been doing while you've been driving me around? Powdering my nose? I've been watching you. And I've learned a great many things."

"Really?" He wanted to close his eyes. Why was she here? He didn't want this picture of her, so real and beautiful, invading his dreams for years to come. Call him a coward, but it pained him with an almost physical ache to look at her.

"Yes. You taught me how to smile when my world was falling around me. To laugh just for the joy of it. To dream because we have only one chance to live life well. I want to live life well. But not alone, Nathan."

The tears shimmering in her eyes nearly undid him. She shouldn't be crying. She'd done enough of that in years past to last several lifetimes.

But he said nothing. Didn't take a single step toward her. Perhaps the memory of yesterday still burned too sharply. Or perhaps he knew, deep down, that she had more to say.

In a single motion, she captured both of his hands in hers, her gaze never leaving his.

"Do me a favor. See me. Not the lady of society or the woman who paid your salary. But me. Lily Grace Montgomery. I'm not perfect. I'm not even rich. To be honest, I have very little to offer you. But what I have, I offer. Me. Myself. All of me. I offer it to you, knowing you have every right to reject it. But I don't want to get to the end of my life with the regret of never trying."

This was real. Happening. The woman he'd adored from a distance was standing in front of him, laying out her heart. For him. Him!

Thank You, Lord. . . .

Worry flecked her gaze, as if she feared his rejection. So he smiled and drew her against his chest.

"I don't have much either, Lily. Like you, I'm not perfect. And you already know I'm not rich. But one thing I do have in abundance. A heart full of love for you. And a longing to make you my wife so fierce I can scarcely stand it."

She looked up at him, her eyes brimming with love and wonderment. A tear trailed down her cheek.

"You want to marry me?" Her words came out in a whisper.

"Oh, Lily." He pressed his lips to hers, kissing her softly, reverently. He drew back, her forehead brushing his. "I have wanted, still do, and will always want to marry you."

"Me, too. Marry you, I mean." She kissed him, letting her lips trail across his, teasing, tempting. "You were a fine chauffeur, Nathaniel Evans. But I have a feeling you're going to be an even better husband."

"I'll still be your chauffeur." He fingered a strand of her silky hair. "Part of the time. I'd miss driving that fine car."

She laughed.

There were plenty of good moments in life. Moments of pleasure and joy. But few perfect ones. This moment, holding her in his arms, heartbeat to heartbeat, sunlight shining down on them?

A perfect moment.

Made even more so as she smiled, cuddling against him. "I don't care whatever you are, or wherever we are. Just as long as you're mine."

ECPA bestselling author **Amanda Barratt,** fell in love with writing in grade school when she wrote her first story—a spinoff of Jane Eyre. Now, Amanda writes inspirational historical romance, penning stories that transport readers to a variety of locales. These days, Amanda can be found reading way too many books, watching an eclectic mix of BBC dramas and romantic chick flicks, and trying to figure out a way to get on the first possible flight to England. She loves hearing from readers on Facebook and through her website amandabarratt.net

The Advocate

by Lorraine Beatty

Dedication

To Diane for all her help on this story. I appreciate you so much.

Chapter 1

He rode into town astride a black stallion, a recalcitrant cloud of dust swirling around his shoulders. He sat tall and straight in the saddle, one hand resting on his thigh, the other expertly holding the reins. His black hat was pulled low over his steely blue eyes, his full lips a tight line above his angular chin. Behind him a body dangled across the horse. Mitch Kincaid had found his man and brought him in dead or alive. No one escaped Sheriff Kincaid's brand of justice.

"Oomph."

Jolted from her thoughts, Hannah Davis glared at the young boy who had bumped into her before directing her attention once again to the man riding into town. The famed sheriff of Riverton, Mitch Kincaid, the perfect man. She frowned as he rode past. He wasn't astride a stallion but an ordinary sturdy bay mare. His black hat was pushed back on his head as he held the reins with both hands. Plodding along behind him came a second horse with a rider, hands tied in front of him clutching the saddle horn.

Hannah sighed. Apparently her imagination had gotten the better of her. But one fact was clear. Sheriff Kincaid was the most handsome, most heroic man she'd ever seen. As he moved on up the street, she realized she was still staring. What would the people here think? Whirling around, she entered the office of the *Riverton Chronicle*, the newspaper her aunt Polly owned and operated in the east Texas town.

She'd arrived in town two days ago only to learn the sheriff was out hunting down a horse thief. But now he was back, and she would finally meet the man who had haunted her dreams for nearly a year. Unable to keep from smiling, she hurried inside. If her aunt was amenable, she could soon have a real job as a reporter. Her father had tried hard to discourage her interest in publishing, but it was no use. And thanks to the era in which she was born, she was living on the cusp of great change for women—and she was determined to be part of it and become a reporter. Coming west was the best decision of her life.

Now she needed to find a moment to slip away and introduce herself to Mitch Kincaid. Her opportunity came later in the morning when her aunt left to check with one of her advertisers.

Hannah quickly covered the distance between the paper at the end of the street to the jail located near the middle of town. Taking a deep breath, Hannah smoothed her skirts down, patted her hair up, and assumed her sweetest smile. The one that never failed to mellow her father. With a copy of the *Chronicle* in one hand, she gathered her courage and pushed open the door to the sheriff's office. Her nerves quivered and her throat constricted. Finally she was going to meet her hero. Mitch Kincaid, the man who tamed a town, the man she'd dreamed about, and the reason she'd come to Riverton in the first place.

She stepped into the dim room, letting her eyes adjust. The sheriff was nowhere to be seen. A large wooden desk—*his* desk—sat in the middle of the room, the top cluttered with papers. On the wall behind it a row of rifles, propped up and securely locked in the cabinet with a narrow chain, caught her attention. Slowly she turned, taking in the rest of the space. A few chairs, a table with coffeepot, a barrel of sand, and a large collection of WANTED posters on the wall, several of which had black lines drawn through their faces. Were those the ones he'd captured?

Cautiously she peered through the open door at the back of the room, catching sight of the jail cells. Her heart skipped a beat. Were there any criminals in them now? Was she all alone with some dangerous outlaw? Maybe this wasn't such a good idea after all. Suddenly feeling alone and isolated, she shivered.

"Can I help you?"

Hannah gasped and spun around. It was him. Mitch Kincaid. He was taller than she'd expected and leaner. Up close the shoulders were even broader than they'd appeared on horseback. And those eyes. Not steely at all but bright, clear sky blue.

"What do you want, miss? I'm busy."

Hannah scrambled to collect herself. "I'm uh. . ." She cleared her throat. "I'm Hannah Davis, Polly Wilson's niece. I just came by to give you a complimentary copy of her newspaper." She smiled and held out the newly printed pages.

He turned away and went to his desk and sat down. "I know who you are, and I don't need a copy of the *Chronicle*."

She hadn't expected her hero to be rude. "It will keep you informed of all the events taking place in town. I would think that would be a valuable tool in your line of work."

His blue eyes, now more gray and steely, met hers. "I know everything that goes on in this town."

The door opened and a short scruffy man tromped in. "Here's the mail, Mitch. Got a big bundle today. Howdy, miss. You're that niece of Miss Polly's, aren't ya?"

"Yes, I am. Hannah Davis." She shot a sharp glance in the sheriff's direction. At least someone here was polite.

"I'm Leroy, one of Mitch's deputies. Glad to make your acquaintance. You plan on staying long?"

A deep voice spoke before she could respond.

"Two weeks."

Hannah looked at Mitch, still focused on the mail. "No. I'm here for an extended stay. I might even settle down here permanently." How dare he suggest otherwise. Her image of the perfect hero was crumbling fast.

Leroy chuckled and headed back toward the door. "I'm going to mosey through town. I'll be back later. Nice to meet you, miss." Still chuckling, he left closing the wooden door with a loud bang.

Hannah faced Mitch again. He was ignoring her, sorting through papers on his desk. She would not be ignored. She'd come too far to meet this man, though now she was beginning to wonder why. "I see you're running for reelection. Why aren't there any posters of you around town? Your opponent has banners and signs everywhere."

The sheriff squared his shoulders, pushed back from the desk, and came toward her. Up close he was an imposing figure. The leather gun belt squeaked as he moved, and his black boots thudded firmly on the planked floor. She took a step back, but he took her arm and turned her toward the door.

"I have work to do, and I'm sure you can find something more interesting to entertain yourself."

Hannah locked her knees, refusing to be pushed out the door. The man was insufferable. She jerked her arm free and faced him, looking up a long way before connecting with those blue eyes. Her heart skipped a beat, but she ignored it. "What did you mean by two weeks?"

A shadow passed over his eyes like a cloud on a summer day. His posture shifted forward, and she found herself enveloped in his presence. "I know your type. You Eastern girls come out west to see the cowboys, live the adventure, but when you get here and see how hard life is, you hoist up your skirts and take the first train headed back. Two weeks from now you'll be ready to brush the dust of Riverton off your fancy skirts and get back to your tea parties."

The arrogance of the man. "You don't know anything about me, Mr. Kincaid. I'm not some hothouse flower that sits around in drawing rooms gossiping all day."

Mitch raised an eyebrow and quickly scanned her attire with his gaze. She knew what he was thinking. Her dress was one she wore frequently back home in Cincinnati, but it was far too ornate for the rustic little town.

"I'll be back here in two weeks just to prove you wrong."

Mitch shook his head. "Good day, Miss Davis." He showed her his back and returned to the desk leaving her fuming at the door. "Good day to you, too, Sheriff. Though how much longer you'll have that designation is doubtful. No one even knows you're running for office."

Hannah squared her shoulders, lifted her chin, and marched out, leaving the door wide open. Let the man get up and shut it himself. The gesture gave her a deep sense of satisfaction as she made her way down the wooden walk to the newspaper.

So much for her romantic notions. From now on she'd focus on her next objective. Becoming a reporter.

Mitch stared at the open door. Miss Hannah Davis had gumption. He hadn't expected that. Finding her standing in his office had hit him like an ax to his chest, yanking him backward in time to a year ago and the moment he'd met Lydia. The only difference was Hannah was a blond. Otherwise from her intricately styled hair to her fussy ruffled and bowed dress, she was an Eastern girl through and through. He'd been generous in giving her two weeks. Pushing back from his desk, he stood and walked to the door glancing outside and down the sidewalk. He caught sight of the woman, flouncing along obviously still upset with his remark. He watched her a moment longer then stepped back inside and closed the door.

There was something different about this Eastern girl. He suspected she had a spine—something the other women lacked. Maybe she'd last longer than the others. There'd been a look in her green eyes that had been missing from Lydia's. Determination. No. Come to think of it she'd been determined to use him as a toy and leave him humiliated and wounded.

He wouldn't make that mistake again. Ever. No matter how pretty the green eyes. He eased back into his chair. Hannah possessed a different kind of determination, the kind born of being used to getting her own way. Still, there was something soft and appealing about her, and he'd found battling with her stimulating. She flared up easily and stood her ground. Not once had she used the typical feminine wiles to lure him—no coy smiles, no fluttering lashes, no dropping of handkerchiefs to get his attention.

Leroy traipsed back in a short while later, and Mitch glanced up to get his report.

"All's quiet for the moment."

"Good to hear."

The older man slouched in the wooden chair opposite the desk. "Well, unless you count the hullabaloo over at the hotel with Willard Greenly yapping about what a great sheriff he's going to be. The man wouldn't know a six-shooter from a Winchester."

"I think the people know that."

Leroy rubbed his chin. "I wouldn't be too sure. I heard some folks saying it's time for a gentleman sheriff."

Mitch took a moment to temper his response. "A gentleman can't handle a bunch of drunken cowboys on a Saturday night."

"He could if there was no Blue Bull Saloon to worry about. Greenly is claiming he'll close down the saloon and Miss Beulah's, too."

"Talk is cheap, Leroy. I'm not putting much store in what Willard Greenly is saying."

"What did that pretty little filly want? She sure did brighten this place up." He clicked his tongue. "She looked like a splash of sunshine standing there when I walked in."

The description fit her perfectly, which sent a barb of irritation along Mitch's nerves. "Not sure. She said she came to give me a newspaper. I think she just wanted to meet a real Western sheriff. You know how those Eastern girls are."

Leroy chuckled. "Not as well as you do."

Mitch aimed a glare in the man's direction, causing him to raise his hands in surrender and stand. "I'm going. But I wouldn't mind seeing her again. I might have to drop by the newspaper office and pick up my copy in person."

"Do it quick. She'll be gone before you know it."

"I don't know. There's something different about that one. Mark my words."

Mitch sincerely hoped not. His ego had already been trampled by one self-centered female. He sure as shooting wasn't going to give the time of day to this one.

So why couldn't he get her out of his mind?

Chapter 2

H annah pushed through the door to the newspaper office, exhaling a deep breath. Her rapid departure from the jail had drained much of her irritation toward the sheriff. Aunt Polly looked up from the press when she entered.

"What happened to you? You look like you just lost your best friend."

Hannah joined her, inhaling the familiar scents of ink and oil and metal and newsprint. Any chance she had she would go to the printing room of her father's paper just to smell the scent of news being made. She pulled the crumpled copy of the *Chronicle* she'd shoved into her pocket. "I went by the sheriff's office to take him a copy of the paper."

"And why would you do that?"

"I thought it might keep him apprised of the goings-on around here."

Polly sighed and crossed her arms over her chest. "Why don't you speak it plain, Hannah? You've been itching to meet that man since you arrived in town. I just don't know why, except for the fact that he's too devilishly handsome for his own good."

"I was just trying to be friendly. I want to meet everyone in town." The look of skepticism on her aunt's face remained. Might as well confess. "I wanted to meet the man who tamed this town and captured the Rankin gang."

Polly shook her head. "You're too much like your father. Is that why you begged to come here to stay with me, so you could write an article about him?"

"No. I just wanted to meet him. He captured my attention, that's all."

Polly raised her eyebrows. "Land's sake girl, you have a fascination with that man. I'm shocked."

Hannah hastened to explain. "Daddy printed an article about him last year, and I was intrigued. He seemed like a man worthy of the label hero. Now I'm not so sure."

"Be careful who you label as hero. Mitch Kincaid is a decent, honorable, courageous man, but he's no hero. No man is, Hannah, and as soon as you put a man up on that pedestal, you'll be disappointed every time."

"Are you saying he didn't clean up Riverton and capture the outlaw gang?"

"He did as far as I know. I didn't live here then. Your uncle Charles and I didn't buy the paper and settle here until years later. After he died I took over and I always assumed that the tales about Mitch were more legend than actual truth."

"Can you tell me why he isn't campaigning? I see banners and handbills and bunting all over town for Willard Greenly but not a one for the sheriff. Did he get elected last time without any effort?"

"This is our first election. Mayor Danvers and his buddy Horace Cosgrove, who owns the bank, have convinced folks they need a more respectable image for their sheriff. Since the railroad came through last year, the town fathers have taken on some highfalutin ideas about how things should be done."

"So Mitch, I mean the sheriff, could lose the election?"

"It's likely. Cosgrove usually gets what he goes after. More's the pity."

"Then why won't he campaign? He should be talking to people and giving speeches."

Polly shrugged. "You've met him. Can you see him skipping around town kissing babies?"

Polly had a point. The sheriff wasn't the type to try to charm people into voting for him. And most certainly not the type to sing his own praises. He was a no-nonsense, straight shooter. A fact that added to her admiration and appeal. She'd seen enough of the smooth, polished gentlemen back east, the kind who dressed to the latest fashion, dropped names, and made sure they were seen at all the right places with all the right people. A man who knew who he was and his place in the world was very attractive.

"What happens if the sheriff loses? What happens to the town then?"

"We're not threatened by the outlaws on horseback anymore, or the rustlers or even the rowdy cattlemen coming into town. Our danger now is from the businessmen, the manipulators, and the ones bent on controlling the town's future."

"And you think the other candidate is in league with those kinds of men?"

"All I know is that there are a few men who became rich when the railroad came through. The banker holds a lot of mortgages. More than a town this size should have."

"Maybe you should investigate. Surely there were laws broken. Can't you have your reporter, what's his name, Emmitt Jones, look into it?"

"The only thing Emmitt looks into is his whiskey glass at the Blue Bull Saloon."

"Maybe I should look into it."

Polly straightened and planted her fists on her hips. "I knew it. I knew you'd get around to asking me to let you be a reporter. No. It's out of the question. I know it's different back in Cincinnati."

"Yes, it is. Women are working in offices and newspapers, and soon they'll be able to work in any job a man can hold."

"Good for them. But not here. Riverton is still very traditional. There is a clear place for women, and reporting the news isn't one of them."

Never one to take no for an answer, she pressed on. "What if I was discreet and used a nom de plume?"

"What makes you think you can find out things that a man can't? This new breed of settlers are merchants; the town council has all but pushed out the original members. Its' a very select group now and they rule the roost."

"They may not talk to me, but I know who holds the secrets and knows the truth about everything that goes on."

"Who?"

"The wives. What do you say? I'm new, asking questions won't seem unusual for me. Maybe I can find out about how that banker got all his money. And if he did so legally or not."

Polly held up her hand. "I'll admit I'd like to get the scoop on Cosgrove. He's a crook to his core. And the mayor isn't much better. This slick lawman he's brought in is cut from the same piece of cloth. They all have the smooth attitudes of con men if you ask me."

"So I can look into this? See what I can find?"

"I'm going to regret this. Fine. But if you discover anything, I'll hold you to our promise to use a pen name. No one will read it, let alone believe it, if it's written by a woman."

Hannah hid her gleeful smile. She intended to change that notion forever.

Two days later, Hannah gathered up the handbills she'd designed and waved at her aunt, eager to set her new plan in motion. "I'll be back soon."

"Hannah, I'm telling you this is a bad idea. The sheriff is not going to take kindly to your interference."

"I'm not interfering; I'm helping. If he doesn't put up some kind of notices, he could lose the election."

"Don't say I didn't warn you."

Hannah tried but couldn't keep the smile from her face. A man like Mitch Kincaid was proud and fiercely independent. Not to mention stiff-necked. All he needed was someone to step up and do what he wouldn't. Posters were the perfect solution for his campaign. He would be grateful for her initiative. And concern.

The sheriff's office was empty when she walked in, dimming her enthusiasm. So much for her grand entrance. "Hello. Is anyone here?"

"Who's that?"

Hannah gasped. She hadn't expected anyone to answer. Cautiously she walked toward the door leading to the cells and peered around. A man sat on a cot staring back at her from behind the bars. She took a tentative step closer. Who was he? A hardened criminal? A killer? "I'm Hannah. I was looking for the sheriff."

"He's gone to get grub from Miss Mona's place."

"Oh. Well, I'll wait then."

"What ya got there?" The man rose on unsteady legs.

"Oh. Posters to help with his campaign for sheriff."

"Good." He nodded his approval. "He needs to remind people what he's done for this town. He's not good at tootin' his own horn."

"So I noticed." She studied him a moment. "You have a high opinion of the man who put you in jail."

"Oh, I'm not in jail. I'm just recuperatin'. Sometimes I get a little too inebriated, and then I forget to take care of myself. Every now and then Mitch will arrest me and bring me here where I can get a warm bed and a couple good meals."

"I see. That's very generous of him."

" 'Tis, it 'tis. But don't go telling anyone. It's our little secret. Most folks don't want nothing to do with me since I lost everything. Mitch, he understands."

"So how long are you here for?"

The man chuckled. "I can leave anytime I want." He pushed against the bars and the door swung open slightly. I ain't really locked up. But I ain't leaving till I get my food."

"Chester, Miss Mona sent you a real hearty breakfast this morning."

Hannah spun around as Mitch came through the door carrying a large tray of deliciously smelling food coming from beneath the napkin-draped plate.

He glared then stepped past her, opening the cell and handing the tray to Chester. "What are you doing here?"

Chester chuckled. "She's come to help you, Sheriff."

Mitch held her gaze a moment then walked back into the office. "I don't need any help."

"Not with your job. With your run for office." She laid the stack of posters on his desk. "I made these up for you to put around town."

Mitch didn't even glance at the papers. With one swipe he shoved them into the trash bin beside his desk. "Good day, Miss Davis."

Hannah sucked in a breath and let it out in a huff. "You had no call to do that. I came here to help in your campaign, and you won't even look at the flyers."

"I didn't ask for your help." He leaned over to retrieve the papers at the same moment she reached down, and their hands touched. Hannah was keenly aware of his nearness, the scent of leather and soap and the muscled forearm below his rolled-up shirtsleeve. She yanked her hand away and stepped back. Mitch pulled the papers from the bin and looked at them. His mouth settled into a thin line, his jaw twitched, and she could see the pulse in his neck throbbing rapidly. She held her breath. Was he going to shout at her? Arrest her?

Slowly he handed the small stack of flyers back to her. "I'm only going to say this once. I don't need your help. I'm not campaigning, and I don't have time to waste on women who think they know how I should run my life." He turned his attention to his desk dismissing her.

"Do you not understand that you could lose this election if you don't do something?"

"The folks of Riverton know who I am and what I've done. If they want me as their sheriff, they'll vote me in."

"Not if Willard Greenly has anything to say about it. He's out there charming everyone, making promises and kissing babies while you're in here doing nothing. I don't understand."

"You don't have to. If you don't like things here, you know where the ticket office is. There's a train leaving tomorrow morning."

Furious, Hannah huffed out a breath and whirled around. Of all the insufferable, hard, unfeeling men she'd ever met. And to think she came all this way to meet her hero. Ha. Nothing heroic about him, just a dull-witted country sheriff who couldn't see beyond his dreary office.

She grasped the door handle, stopping when the sheriff called her name.

"Shut the door this time."

She tossed a glare and an insincere smile over her shoulder then stepped out and slammed the door behind her. So much for her romantic fantasies about the great Mitch Kincaid. She was a fool to come all this way on a whim. But she wasn't about to go back to Cincinnati. Aunt Polly had given her permission to investigate some of the goings-on around town. This was her chance to be a reporter and show everyone what a woman could do.

Chester's words surfaced. Would a hard, unfeeling man look out for one of the town's less fortunate? Sheriff Kincaid was a contradiction, and she wasn't sure she liked that.

Mitch leaned back in his chair rubbing his chin. The woman was becoming a burr under his saddle, and he had no idea how to chase her off. He doubted he'd done anything just now to discourage her. He'd seen the determination bloom in her green eyes. Eyes the color of spring grass shaded with long thick lashes. Her silky hair was hanging down her back today, and he'd found himself wondering if it felt as soft as it looked.

The woman was churning up feelings he hadn't felt in a long time, and he didn't like it one bit.

"Sheriff, thanks for the meal and the bed." Chester set the dinner tray on the edge of the desk. "I'm feeling better now."

"Good to hear. You still helping out at the livery stable?"

He shrugged. "When I'm able."

Mitch knew he meant when he was sober. "Miss Edna is looking for someone to whitewash the fence around her place. If you're interested."

"Sure. I can do that."

Mitch stood and retrieved the man's hat from the rack. "Try and keep some of the money this time, okay?"

Chester nodded. "I will. I appreciate your kindness."

Mitch waved off the gratitude, watching with affection as the older man sauntered toward the door. He'd been a stand-up citizen once, until he'd lost his farm and his family. Now he worked odd jobs and spent the money on drink, sleeping in the alleys and empty sheds. The least Mitch could do was see he got a hot meal and a clean bed every now and then.

Chester turned back at the door. "You know, you shouldn't be so hard on that a little gal. She's got a good heart. She wants to help people. My Mary was like that. She just couldn't help herself when she saw people in need. She had to jump in and lend a hand. That's a special thing. Not to be brushed aside."

"You may be right, Chester, but I doubt Miss Davis will be in town long enough to help anyone."

Chester grinned and pointed a bony finger. "I think you're in for a surprise. That filly is a champion. You mark my words."

As much as Mitch hated to admit it, the man might be right. Most women would have stayed away after the initial meeting. Miss Davis had returned. In her overly frilly gown and her hair curled and arranged to perfection. Typical Eastern female.

He stood and moved to the window, staring out at his town. But she wasn't like Lydia. Nothing like her, with her soft voice and her liquid eyes, and her mouth that could speak so sweetly every lie that flowed from her lips.

He'd learned his lesson the hard way. She'd ripped his heart open and left him exposed for everyone to see and laugh at. No. No more Eastern girls for him. Pivoting, he went back to work, but the image of fiery green eyes lingered in his mind.

Hannah laid the flyers on the worktable at the newspaper before going to the small office in the back. Aunt Polly was working on her editorial. She looked up and frowned.

"What is it? Oh, let me guess. This is where I say I told you so."

"Yes." Hannah shook off the last of her irritation. The reality of the sheriff had shattered much of her fascination with the cranky but oh, so handsome man. "I'm fine. I thought I'd start looking into things around town."

"Playing reporter you mean." She held out an envelope. "This came for you."

Hannah took the pale blue paper and scanned her name written in flowing calligraphy. "Who's it from? Who's Florence Cosgrove?"

"The banker's wife. I introduced you to them at church last Sunday."

"Yes. I remember." Slipping the card from the envelope, she read the invitation then glanced at her aunt. "I've been invited to her home this Friday for afternoon tea and to meet some of the ladies of the town."

"I'm not surprised. I've been hounded with questions about you since you got here. Now you can answer them yourself."

Hannah tapped the card against her fingertips. "More importantly, this is my opening to do some investigating."

Polly sighed. "Don't get carried away. If you ask too many questions, these ladies will shut you out."

"I know. But I have a plan for that, too." Hannah gathered her determination. Just because one plan hadn't worked out didn't mean the next one wouldn't. She knew exactly how to win over the ladies of Riverton.

Chapter 3

Mitch strolled the boardwalk Friday afternoon, keeping his attention tuned to anything unusual or out of place. He was a firm believer in making his presence known. His twice daily strolls through town let people know he was on the job and made them feel safe and secure. The town was growing though, and the walks were taking longer than they used to. In the year since the railroad had come through, new businesses had popped up like gopher holes. Attitudes were shifting as well. The new arrivals weren't as easygoing, and they demanded he keep a close eye on their stores. Many of them were starting to complain about the saloon and Miss Beulah's.

Applause drew his attention to a small crowd in front of the Hallmark Hotel across the street. Greenly was giving another speech. The man had a smooth tongue and an easy manner that many took at face value as sincerity. Mitch had another name for it. Snake oil.

"It's time we made the name Riverton synonymous with respectability. The railroad has opened the way for great prosperity, and we want to be seen as a town where families can settle without fear of renegades and saddle bums shooting up the streets." His gaze landed on Mitch, and a slow smile shifted his features. "There was a time when the town needed a common gunfighter as sheriff, when appointing a fast gun and a hard fist was the only way to maintain peace. Those days are gone. We need someone who can deal with problems in a civilized manner, a man who knows the written law and will enforce it. Not a glorified bounty hunter who chases rewards and leaves the town unprotected."

Mitch fumed. Greenly was making it sound like all he did was track down the faces on the WANTED posters.

Greenly raised a hand in the air. "We'll send a clear message that their kind isn't welcome in Riverton anymore."

Mitch pushed away from the post and headed back to his office. If only it were that simple. Tell the outlaws to stay away. Post a sign that says we're respectable and all will be well.

Greenly knew nothing about upholding the law or how to deal with outlaws. But he did. And he made sure he kept one step ahead of them. But it was getting harder. The truth was, the sudden growth of the town was stretching his two deputies pretty thin. He needed to hire another man, but the town fathers hadn't seen fit to increase the budget to make that happen.

Hannah's taunts echoed through his mind. Were his days as sheriff numbered? He had no plans for his future. He liked Riverton and figured he'd be here till they plowed him under. Maybe he should take out an ad in the *Chronicle*. No. He'd stand on his record and on his work.

Hannah set her fine china cup lightly into the saucer, smiling at the women gathered for tea at Mrs. Cosgrove's home. "Yes, it's true. The bustle is making a comeback. However, it's smaller and lighter and narrower, which will make it more ladylike."

"Oh, my. I can't say I'm pleased." Maude Danvers sighed loudly. "I sometimes envy the farmers' wives. They don't have time to worry about fashion. They wear practical clothes, which are undoubtedly more comfortable."

Florence Cosgrove tilted her nose upward. "But not as fashionable. Fashion is a reflection of a civilized society."

Hannah listened as the women debated the merits of high style. She'd spent much of her time regaling the women with the latest news from back east. The fashions, the trends, the scandals, the newest plays and music, and the growing trend of women in the workplace. A subject that had stirred a little controversy.

Florence stirred her tea and looked at Hannah. "Tell me, Miss Davis, do you actually work for your aunt at the paper?"

The stunned look on the woman's face spoke volumes, causing Hannah to choose her words carefully. She'd made huge inroads into the women's circle today, and she didn't want to jeopardize it. "Oh, no. I do help some, sweeping, and sometimes I'll help her write an article. My father owned a large paper back in Cincinnati so I understand how things work."

"So you approve of women working in offices and doing a man's job?" Naomi Bower peered over the rim of her cup.

"It doesn't matter if I approve. It's happening. The world is changing and we have to accept that."

"Things are certainly changing here in Riverton. Which is why we need a new sheriff. Someone more worldly and respectable."

Hannah dabbed her napkin against her mouth to still her defensive response. "I understand he's been sheriff a long time. Five years or so."

"Yes, and he's competent, I suppose, but our former mayor was the undertaker." She huffed. "Hardly the image we want to send back to potential settlers. They want to come to a town that is safe and filled with honest, hardworking people like themselves."

Hannah nodded. "The sheriff certainly has a chip on his shoulder toward women from the East."

"Oh, that's because of Lydia."

Florence nodded. "Yes, I did feel sorry for him in that matter. It really was a distasteful series of events."

"What happened?"

Maude leaned forward. "She set her cap for him from the moment she came to town. She was here with her father for the opening of the new rail line. She lured him into her web right off. The sheriff was quite smitten with her, but when he asked her to stay here and marry him, she brushed him aside and climbed on the train and went back east."

"It was quite humiliating for the man."

Hannah lowered her gaze. No wonder he'd been so harsh.

"I suppose, but really a man like him thinking he could marry up. Arrogant attitude if you ask me."

"Rosemond, don't be a snob. You're no better than she was looking down on people."

"I didn't mean it like that. But he's a small-town sheriff. She was a New York social-ite." She arched her neck as if to say that explained everything.

"Love can close any gap." Hannah pressed her lips together. She hadn't meant to say that out loud. "Ladies, I have enjoyed this afternoon immensely. Thank you so much for including me. I hope you'll invite me again."

"Of course. You're a breath of fresh air. You'll have to tell us more about those new gowns the women are wearing. Perhaps show our local seamstress."

"That's a wonderful idea."

"Before you go, we'd like to invite you to join our historical society."

"I didn't know you had one."

"It's newly organized. We felt that in the light of the railroad and the sudden growth in Riverton it was important to record our history. You would be a welcome addition."

"I would very much like to be part of that worthwhile cause. In fact, I could mention to my aunt about publishing an article about your society. Provided, of course, you are looking for more members."

"We are. An article in the paper could call attention to our mission. A thorough history will require input from everyone, in particular the families who originally settled this area." Hannah pulled on her gloves and looped the handle of her reticule over her wrist. "Mrs. Cosgrove. Has my aunt ever printed a report on your get-togethers?"

"No, why?"

"I was thinking it might be time to start a society section in the *Chronicle*, a place where you could share your events, report on what happened and who was there."

Mrs. Cosgrove inhaled a deep breath. "That would be wonderful. Do you think she'd be agreeable?"

"She is overworked presently, but if I offered to write the piece she might. Of course, unless you ladies would be offended by a woman writing for the paper. . ."

"As long as you were the one doing the reporting. We can be assured that you'll do an honest job. Like you said, times are changing."

"Thank you. Your faith in me is humbling. I'll speak with her the moment I get to the office."

Hannah felt light as a feather as she hurried to the paper. Her first step into the small world of Riverton society had been a success. She'd made friends, gained trust, and created a position for herself. She'd also learned more about Mitch. The only sour note in her afternoon. No wonder he was so distant and prickly. She'd like to snatch the hair right out of the head of that Lydia woman. She was familiar with the type. Selfish and uppity, they enjoyed using people as entertainment with no thought to their feelings.

Her heart ached for Mitch. He was a proud man, and he deserved better than the likes of a woman like that.

Chapter 4

Mitch rested his hands on his gun belt Monday afternoon as he listened to the shopkeeper's complaint. Someone had been stealing his crates of nails from behind the store. "Do you always keep the extras out here?"

"I have been. They take up too much room in the store. But they're in great demand."

Mitch glanced around the area behind the shop. Tucked between two other buildings it should have been safe unless someone knew the extra supplies were kept there.

"What are you going to do about it, Sheriff?"

"I'll keep watch tonight, see if anyone shows up. You say it always happens on a Tuesday?"

"So far. That's the day the wagon drops off the order. I want this scoundrel caught."

"In the meantime, I suggest you either keep these inside or build you a sturdy container and lock them up."

"Sad day when a man can't keep his belongings on his own property."

Mitch couldn't disagree. "The town is growing. More people means more opportunities for things to go missing."

"Well, I hope the new sheriff can keep things under control." The merchant winced and lowered his eyes. "Sorry. I just meant we need more oversight."

"Right." Mitch bid good-bye then strolled out of the alleyway onto the boardwalk. He couldn't be everywhere at once. The rise in crime was inevitable. But putting on an air of respectability wouldn't deter thieves. Willard Greenly had no idea what he was facing when he got elected.

When? Was he starting to have doubts about keeping his job?

"Hey, Sheriff." Claude Dixon, the druggist, nodded and smiled as he passed. "I see you're checking on things more often these days. Makes me feel good to look out and see you're on the job."

"That's what you pay me for."

"True enough. But I'm glad to see you've started to campaign a little. Greenly is shouting his case all over town. Those posters of yours will make people stop and think twice before they vote in a weasel like Greenly."

"What posters?"

"The ones that say 'Vote for Kincaid.' They're popping up all over town." He pointed to one tacked on a post farther down the sidewalk.

Even at this distance, it had a strangely familiar look about it. The closer he got, the more his anger burned. The post had his name in big letters, and below it read: THE

BEST MAN FOR THE JOB. Why couldn't the woman take no for an answer?

"Nice poster, Sheriff."

Mitch ignored the comment and glanced around the street. He could see at least half a dozen more flyers attached to posts and walls. He started to take down the nearest one when he spied the object of his irritation coming toward him. She wore a pale blue dress with few frills, and her determined pace made the skirt swirl around her feet pleasingly. Her hair was tied with a ribbon on top of her head. The look of excitement on her face almost made him change his mind about approaching her. She had a smile that could melt any heart. But she had a will that needed corralled.

She hadn't noticed him yet, so he stepped forward, grabbed her arm, and steered her toward the post. "Is this your doing?"

She blinked and tried to pull her arm from his grasp. "No. I have no idea who put this up."

"They're all over town. I thought I made myself clear about no campaigning." Her green eyes widened and he felt her tremble under his hand. His conscience flared. He hadn't meant to frighten her. He released her, exhaling a tense breath.

"You did. I'm sorry. I don't know what happened. But I'll take care of it immediately." She reached up and pulled the paper from the post, crying out, "Ouch!" She grabbed her finger.

He was horrified to see blood trickling down her fingers and into her palm. Speechless, he took her hand, pulled a handkerchief from his pocket, and covered the cut. "Don't you know any better than to pull something from a wooden post?" His protective instincts flared. He shouldn't have let his irritation get the better of him.

"I was trying to rectify the mistake."

"You wouldn't have to if you'd listened to me in the first place." He marched her down the walk and into his office keeping her wrist in his hand as he pulled ointment from the drawer. Pouring water from the pitcher into the bowl, he plunged her hand in.

"That stings."

"I know." With the cut cleaned, he applied ointment and wrapped a clean bandage around her finger. He looked into her eyes, relieved to see the pain and fear were gone. Her green eyes were clear and staring directly into his. He realized with a jolt that he was still holding her wrist, the skin warm and soft under his fingers, and so delicate he could feel her pulse beating under the surface.

He wanted to look away but found it impossible. She was so close he could smell the lavender scent of her hair. He tore his gaze away, struggling to tame the wild rushing of his heart. "I'm sorry. I didn't mean for you to hurt yourself." She made no move to pull free of his grasp.

"I should have been more careful. I didn't think about splinters. I will on the next poster I take down."

"Don't bother."

Her eyes brightened. "You mean you'll leave them up?"

"No." He released her. "I meant I'll take them down myself."

"Oh."

Her mouth drooped into an adorable pout, and he felt like he'd just kicked a puppy. "I appreciate your enthusiasm and your support, but I don't need any woman directing my life. Is that clear?"

"But if you don't stand up for your job, you could lose it to that slick—"

"That's my concern. Not yours."

"Fine. If you're content to let five years of dedication go to waste, far be it from me to try and stop you. Good day, Sheriff."

Green eyes snapping, she pushed past and started for the door then abruptly stopped and whirled around to face him. "Don't worry, Sheriff. I won't be bothering you again. I know a lost cause when I see one."

Mitch ran a hand through his hair, wishing he had a gang of outlaws to go after. A hard ride through the open range was just what he needed to clear his head. He'd been spending too much time in his office, too much time doing paperwork and not enough keeping the peace and bringing bad guys to justice. Too much time thinking about the appealing Miss Davis. He'd formed a bad habit of looking for her whenever he made his rounds. He'd even considered looking in on the newspaper office. Thankfully he'd avoided that mistake.

Leroy tromped in, bringing with him the smell of tobacco and horse. "I just saw Miss Davis storming away. You two have another set-to?"

"I want you to go around town and take down all those posters. Then see if you can find out who put them up. I'm going to ride out to the Echols' place. He found a dead heifer this morning and he thinks there might be rustlers moving in."

"We haven't had rustlers around here for two years."

"And I want to make sure we don't have any now."

Mitch grabbed up his gun belt, took a rifle from the shelf, and set his hat on his head, ignoring the voice inside that called him a coward and a weakling for running away from his feelings. "I'll be back later."

Chapter 5

Hannah coddled her anger toward Mitch the rest of the day. Why wouldn't he listen? She'd watched him as he made his daily strolls around town. His keen eyes took in every detail, his politeness extended to everyone. Yet he carried about him an authoritative air that silently warned there would be a price to pay for misconduct on his watch.

She couldn't imagine Riverton under the care of Willard Greenly. He would alienate the townspeople within a week. He would ignore the needs of the simple citizens and only concern himself with those with influence. A death knell for a town like Riverton. There had to be a way to encourage the townspeople to vote for Mitch, to remind them of what he'd done for them, how important his contributions and how sterling his character. Virtues not to be dismissed because a polished Eastern man was flooding the town with empty promises.

A poster displayed on the side of the millinery store caught her attention as she started to cross the street. Somehow this one had been missed. Carefully she tugged it away, remembering how gentle Mitch had been earlier as he'd tended to her cut. She couldn't deny her feelings any longer. Her heart had raced as he'd held her wrist. His touch had been gentle despite his sharp tone. He'd felt badly that he'd caused her injury. She'd seen the regret in his eyes. Mitch was the protective type who stood guard over all those under his care—men, women, children, and females who irritated him. But for a moment, she thought she'd seen something more in his eyes. Admiration. Was he attracted to her? Or was she so desperate that she was starting to imagine things because her own heart was already involved?

Maybe she really was a silly Eastern female. Folding the paper, she slipped it into the pocket of her skirt, aware of voices coming from the alley beside her.

"I don't know about this. It don't seem right somehow."

"He's already lost. You know that. Greenly has the vote in his pocket. I'm just looking to seal the deal. One dollar. One vote."

"A dollar. Just for voting for Greenly?"

"I know you can use the money, Zeke. That will go a long way to feeding those five kids of yours."

"True, but I don't think my wife would like this."

Hannah held her breath, frozen in place, not wanting to reveal her presence. Her stomach knotted at what she was hearing. Vote buying. It was distasteful and appalling. There had to be a law against it.

The voices lowered and she lost the conversation. Turning, she took a step away as the two men emerged from the alley. The taller man strode past her as if she were invisible, the other, a farmer from the looks of him, shoved his hand in his pocket and shuffled down the boardwalk as if ashamed at what he'd done. As he should be. She had to tell Mitch.

She glanced at the sheriff's office. She'd just told him she wouldn't interfere, but she couldn't let this go. It was wrong, and he was the sheriff after all.

Gathering her courage, she retraced her steps. As she started forward she saw Mr. Cosgrove step from the bank. The tall man sidled up to him. Eager to hear what was being said she quickened her steps, trying to look preoccupied with the paper in her hand.

"I'll add his name to the list."

"I hope you have it in a safe place. It'll come in handy after the election."

"The safest." Cosgrove chuckled and slapped the tall man on the back. "Keep up the good work, Jenkins."

By the time she reached the sheriff's office her indignation was boiling over. Mitch was seated at his desk when she entered. For a moment his blue eyes lit up then darkened. Obviously not pleased to see her again.

"Whatever it is, the answer is no."

"I just overheard something I think you should know about."

He raised an eyebrow. "Greenly kiss another baby, did he?"

Obnoxious man. "No. This is important. I heard a man selling his vote for a dollar." He didn't flinch or look surprised or even interested.

"And?"

"*And?* Don't you understand someone is going around buying votes for your opponent? You need to do something."

"What do you suggest?"

"Arrest him. Put the guilty ones in jail. I heard Mr. Cosgrove say he kept a list of them."

He stood and moved to the front of his desk perching on the edge. "I admire your indignation and your sense of civic responsibility, but there's no law against selling your vote."

"Then pass one. Today."

"I'm the sheriff, Miss Davis. Not the town council. They decide what's lawful in Riverton."

"Then tell them what's going on. Tell them to make it a crime. Find out who's behind it and bring them to justice like you did the Rankin gang. That's what you're good at." The pleasant look on his face darkened suddenly. The thought skittered through her mind that this must be what he looked like to the criminals he captured. She hoped she was never on the wrong side of him.

"Oh, I see now. You read the article that no-count writer did last year." Bracing his hands on his gun belt, he stared her down. "Let me set you straight. There was no Rankin gang. There was no single-handed capture and no shoot-out in the middle of town."

"But the Nolan boys that were trying to tear up the town. That part was true, right?"

"No. They were drunk and starting to bust up the saloon. I went in and arrested them. End of story. As for the other," he rubbed his forehead. "The gang was me and my brothers. Three cattle rustlers killed our father in cold blood. My brothers and I set out to track them down. Hank found them holed up near Rankin, Texas. By the time Clay and I showed up, only the oldest boy was still alive. Their wild living had caught up with them. I brought him in to the marshal at Holcomb. Hank and Clay went back to their families. I stayed on in Holcomb as a deputy. When Riverton was looking for a new sheriff, the marshal suggested I look into it. I did. End of story."

"So you're not a hero? You didn't kill a dozen men and capture a ruthless gang single-handedly?"

"Is that what you think makes a hero? Do you think killing a man is exciting? Watching a man twitch and draw his last breath gives a man any kind of satisfaction? I saw my father die. There was nothing heroic about it."

Hot, scalding humiliation burned through every nerve in Hannah's body. She'd never thought about the reality of killing, of bringing men to justice. How could she have been so ignorant? Thoughtless. She looked at Mitch, who had taken a seat behind his desk again. She wanted to cry, to beg his forgiveness, but she knew he wouldn't welcome the gesture. He was a proud man and more heroic than she'd ever imagined, far exceeding her childish ideas of what it meant to be a hero.

She searched for words, but none surfaced so she quietly turned and left. There was nothing she could say that would repair the damage she'd done.

Chapter 6

Mitch's revelation about his father and his brothers nagged at Hannah for the next couple of days and interfered with her rest at night. If the news article about him had been embellished, then what else had been twisted to make a better story? And if the real truth about Mitch wasn't accurate, then what about Willard Greenly? Was he what he seemed?

There was only one way to find out. Her spirits lifted at the thought of doing research and the expectation of what she might discover. She'd been relieved when she'd learned the sheriff had been called out of town for a few days to testify in a case. It gave her time to sort through things in her mind.

She'd written her first report of the historical society, and the grateful ladies had arranged for all the women in Riverton to meet at the church to share their stories about the beginning of Riverton. Hannah had become a special friend to the women, most of whom were wives of prominent businessmen in town. She hadn't had a chance to bring up the question of vote buying, but she'd learned Cosgrove had become wealthy overnight. Some of the talk around town was that he'd called in loans and undervalued mortgages because he knew about the railroad coming through town long before it was announced. One of those properties had belonged to Chester Goodman. Looking into the banker's practices was next up on her list of things to investigate right after the election. What fueled her excitement today, however, was her new project. She'd decided to write a series of articles in support of the sheriff. Anonymously. If Mitch wouldn't advocate for himself, she'd do it for him.

Dressing quickly in a simple skirt and jacket, she hurried from her aunt's house and walked quickly toward the paper. Halfway there she saw Mitch. Her heart beat triple time. He was back and strolling along in that laconic way of his, making his presence known and letting people know he was on the job.

She fought off the urge to stop and watch him and quickened her steps more. Watching him could become a habit she might not want to break. After a stop at the telegraph office, she continued on. Donald, the young apprentice who worked for her aunt, looked up and smiled as she entered. "Morning, Donald."

"Miss Hannah, I want to apologize again for putting up those posters for the sheriff. I thought I was helping."

Hannah waved him off. "That's all right. Where's my aunt?" He gestured toward the office. The older woman was hunched over her desk and glanced up when she entered. "Hannah, come look at this. It was shoved under the door this morning."

Hannah assumed her most bland expression. She'd slipped the article under the door of the newspaper office early this morning so Polly would find it first thing when she opened up. Crafting the articles about Mitch to disguise her writing style from her aunt had been difficult. Pretending to be ignorant of the posts would be even more so. Hannah perused the post. "Who wrote it?"

"At first I thought you might have, but the style is all wrong."

"What are you going to do with it?"

"It's good, and the people of this town need to be reminded of what Mitch has done. I'm going to print it. Someone has to campaign for the sheriff. Might as well be the *Chronicle*. After all, that's what we do."

Hannah managed a sweet smile, but her insides were all jittery with excitement. Now she could proceed with the other articles. The *Chronicle* was a twice-weekly paper, and there were two weeks until the election. That would allow her to write four pieces about Mitch. Hopefully she could make the townsfolk see what she saw—a man of honor and integrity who truly cared for the town and its security. A man who would dedicate his life and even sacrifice it for them if necessary. She prayed the people would see the light and cast their vote for him.

Now she had to start her investigation.

"Aunt Polly, do you keep back issues of the paper?"

"Yes. Why?"

"I need to do some research. How far back and what about the papers from before you took over?"

"The past issues of the *Chronicle* are in the storeroom. The old copies of the *Post* should be there, too, though I have no idea where to start looking. Those go back seven or eight years. What are you looking for?"

"The truth." Pulling off her jacket, she laid it and her reticule on the side table before pushing through to the storeroom. The air was thick with dust and the smell of old paper and dry rot. She hoped her aunt had taken precautions to preserve the back issues. Her father always stored his in metal boxes and paid a special storage service to keep them in a cool location.

It took nearly an hour, but she finally located the box with the papers from five years ago. Spreading the issues out on the table she started to scan the contents. The truth was here someplace, and once she found it she knew exactly what she was going to do to make sure Mitch was elected sheriff again.

Hannah awoke on Wednesday morning filled with bubbling excitement. Her first article on Mitch had come out today, and her stomach fluttered at the thought of how he would react. Not well if she had to guess. She managed to keep her secret even though she felt badly about deceiving her aunt, but it was the only way to ensure it got published. She'd encouraged her aunt to put it on the front page. Time was running out, and Greenly gained ground every day. There was no guarantee her plan would work, but she had to try. Mitch deserved to remain as sheriff.

A quick glance at her lavalier watch showed she would have to hurry to meet with the women today. They were organizing an ice cream social on the church grounds for this weekend, and Hannah had volunteered to help. Having all the townsfolk in one location for an afternoon would give her an opportunity to ask questions under the guise of being new and curious.

But first she had to pick up a copy of the newspaper.

Riverton Chronicle
September 14, 1881

Election for Sheriff

Riverton's first election for sheriff is under way. Speeches are being given, promises made, and qualifications presented. Change is the theme of the day. A more qualified man is required for the office. We need a sheriff who sees into the future, who will polish our image and attract more settlers so Riverton will become a beacon of decency.

What is the most important requirement for sheriff? Experience.

Candidate Greenly made his qualifications known. But what about the other candidate? He's remained silent during this election, choosing to devote his time and energy toward doing his job—protecting Riverton and its citizens. Sheriff Kincaid has served our town faithfully for five-and-a-half years. He held the position of deputy in another county before coming to Riverton. In that time he has maintained the peace, protected the citizens and their property, and fostered goodwill among the people. He has conducted himself with honesty and dedication, and a deep sense of appreciation for the laws he's sworn to uphold and the people he's chosen to protect. I believe that experience should be rewarded.

The Advocate

Chapter 7

Leroy shuffled into the office, pulling Mitch's attention from the telegram he'd been reading. The bank over in Stanleyville had been robbed, and the sheriff there thought they might be heading in the direction of Riverton. Mitch had mentally filed away their description just in case.

"Morning, Mitch. I brought you a newspaper. Thought you might be in the mood to do some reading."

Mitch leaned back in his chair, the wood and old spring mechanism protesting at the pressure. "I have plenty to read right here."

"Well, the kind of reading I'm talking about is more personal in nature."

He laid the paper down, bottom of the front page facing up so Mitch couldn't miss what he was referring to. Mitch leaned forward, scooping up the paper and quickly reading the text. The headline read simply Election for Sheriff. His gaze zoomed to the byline. The Advocate. "Who wrote this?"

Leroy shrugged and tugged at his beard. "Makes you sound real honorable-like, don't it?"

"It's putting my private life out there for everyone to see." Mitch clenched his jaw.

Leroy tapped the paper. "Any of that untrue?"

"No, but I didn't approve this, and the paper has no right to print things about me unless I do."

"That so? Well, then, I guess you'd better go see Miss Polly."

That's exactly what he intended to do. Fisting the paper, he grabbed his hat and stormed out. If he wanted the whole world to know his business, he would have stood on the street corners like Greenly and blurted it out for them to hear.

"Sheriff Kincaid."

He slowed and touched the brim of his hat as Mrs. Cosgrove approached. He hoped she wasn't in a talkative mood. It was all he could do to appear calm and pleasant. "How are you today?"

"Fine. I just wanted to let you know that I, for one, appreciate all you've done for the town over the years. You've conducted yourself with dignity and kindness. And a firm hand."

Stunned, he nodded before he could find his voice. "Thank you, ma'am."

Mrs. Cosgrove's smile broadened. "I was hoping I could prevail upon you to help us set up for the ice cream social after church this Sunday. We can always use an extra pair of strong shoulders."

"I'd be happy to help."

"Wonderful. Good day."

With some of his indignation siphoned away by the woman's surprise attack, Mitch resumed his steps toward the *Chronicle*. Mrs. Cosgrove rarely gave him the time of day unless it was to complain about how he wasn't doing his job. What had changed her mind? He glanced down at the paper in his fist. Had she read the article by The Advocate?

A rush of heat flooded his body and he tilted his hat a little lower, feeling as if he was exposed to the entire town. This had to end. Today.

Inside the paper office, he looked for Hannah first. Had she seen it? Was she involved somehow?

Donald came toward him, wiping his hands on a rag. "Hello, Sheriff. Can I help you?"

He glared at the boy, ignoring the sting of remorse that pricked him. The boy had nothing to do with this. "Where's Polly?"

"In her office."

Mitch lunged forward, entering the small room unannounced and waving the paper when she looked up. "What is this? Since when does the *Chronicle* start revealing private information?"

She glanced up, pen in hand. "You read the article, I see."

"Everyone has. I want a retraction."

"We only do that when an error is made or the information has been revealed as false. What part did you object to?"

"All of it."

"Are you saying it's all a lie?" She took the paper and looked at the article. "It says you have been sheriff here for five-and-a-half years. Is that true?"

"Yes."

"And it says you were a deputy up in Holcomb, Texas, for a short while before taking the job here in Riverton."

"True. It's the other things."

"The part where you're called honest and dedicated, or is it the line about maintaining the peace in our town that angers you?"

"I don't want an article published about me without my say-so. Who's behind this?"

"I don't know. The article was shoved under my door one morning when I came in."

"And you printed it without knowing who wrote it?"

"Sheriff, I know you think it's somehow demeaning for you to go about town asking folks to vote for you. But you can't win an election by burying your head in the sand. This is a reminder of what you've contributed to the town during your time here. I can't see any harm in publishing something that casts you in a very favorable light."

"So you're not going to remove it?"

"No. Willard Greenly takes out space in the *Chronicle* every day singing his own praises. You're getting the same exposure for free. Consider it a blessing."

Mitch never felt so out of control. "I don't like this one bit."

"That's unfortunate, but my job is to inform the public and keep them apprised of what's going on in town. There's an election and, like it or not, you're involved. Unless you would like to acknowledge that Greenly will win and withdraw from the race?"

It was clear he was getting nowhere. A new thought surfaced. "Is Hannah behind this?"

"My niece? Hardly. I had the impression you two weren't even speaking these days."

"Where is she?"

"I believe she had a meeting with the ladies historical society. They're at the church if you'd like to speak with her."

Defeated, Mitch settled his hat on his head, spun on his boot heel, and stomped out. He wasn't used to losing battles.

Chapter 8

Riverton Chronicle
September 17, 1881

The Value of Words

*Being informed about a candidate's qualifications for office is crucial if we're to cast
our vote wisely. Each man will try to convince you he is the right man for the job.
We must weigh carefully the words that are put forth. Promises are easy to make
and easily forgotten once the voting is over. A man can claim to be many things, but
how do we know the claims are true? Look to the actions of the man and his past
behavior.*

*Sheriff Kincaid goes quietly about his business, with humility and kindness,
keeping a watchful eye on the town and its citizens. His experience was earned here
in Riverton under your observation. Contrast that with the claims of his opponent,
who cites several years with the Pinkerton Detectives and intense study of the law.
How do we know? We must trust that the stranger is honest and that he sincerely
wants to be our sheriff. This reporter intends to find the truth about the credentials
of both men.*

The Advocate

Hannah bit the bottom of her lip. The second article had been published yesterday. Had Mitch read it? She'd seen him around town but managed to avoid getting
too close. Her main motivation for keeping her distance was her irrational fear that
if he looked into her eyes he'd know right away she was the one writing the articles
about him. The other reason, one she kept trying to deny, was that he might also see
how much she cared for him. She wasn't sure when she'd realized she was in love with
Mitch. Maybe she had been since she'd first read the article about him. All she knew
for sure was that winning his heart was her dream. Accomplishing that, however, was
impossible. Secretly she'd hoped the articles would be like anonymous love letters and
would show him how she felt, but after the first one had been printed, his reaction and
his anger had told her that he would always see her as that girl from back east who
refused to mind her own business.

She'd considered ending the articles, but ensuring he won the election was more
important than winning his heart. It was her own foolishness that had trapped her
affections for him. He was not at fault in that regard.

Shaking off her melancholy, she slipped her arms into her white lace blouse and buttoned it up. It was the coolest thing she owned, and today's social on the church lawn would be warm. Next she gathered her lavender skirt and lifted it over her head, letting it drop over her petticoats then fastening the clasp in the back. She'd volunteered to help and she wanted to be comfortable. Today was no place for one of her fussy gowns. After tying a matching lavender ribbon around her hair she stared into the mirror, frowning at the direction of her thoughts. What would Mitch think of her attire?

She huffed out a breath and hurried downstairs. Aunt Polly was packing up cookies and sweet bread in baskets that would be served along with the ice cream. "I can take those with me. I'm ready."

"Thank you, dear. I want to change out of my church clothes. I'll see you there."

The church was only a short distance from the house, and Hannah could hear the activity on the grounds as she drew near. Tables were being set up in the shade of the oak tree, and the women were fussing over the food table placed nearby. Several men were turning the cranks of the ice-cream churns that had become so popular. She spied Florence Cosgrove and started to wave when she realized the woman was talking to Mitch. She stopped. Her heart pounding. She hadn't expected him to be here. Looking around she searched for another place to take her baked goods. As she looked back, Mitch's gaze snagged hers and she froze. Her breath caught in her throat. He looked so handsome. The light blue shirt he wore matched his eyes, and the crooked smile on his face wrapped around her heart like a morning glory vine. He came toward her, his gaze never leaving hers.

"I'll take those." He held out his hand for the baskets.

She handed them to him unable to find her voice. She forced her feet to move, searching frantically for something to say that would ease the horrible tension between them.

"I think we're going to have a big turnout."

"Everyone likes ice cream." Inwardly she rolled her eyes. That was an intelligent response.

"I know I do."

When the baskets had been delivered to the table, Mitch tipped his hat and walked off, leaving her confused and rattled. Then she realized he was simply being polite, the way he would to any woman.

With effort, she shook off the disappointment surrounding her heart. She needed to think beyond her own feelings. Today's social provided her the perfect opportunity to ask questions, poke around about the unusual number of foreclosures and that vote-buying scheme. If she could find that list of names, maybe she could use it to prove to the voters that Greenly wasn't the right man for their sheriff.

She was still waiting for a reply to the telegram she'd sent last week. Her father had influential friends back east, and she'd requested information on Greenly from one of them. Mitch's opponent claimed to have worked for years with Pinkerton. She had the resources to find out if that was true or not. She'd also asked her contact to see what else he could find on Mr. Willard Greenly. She had a pretty good idea what they'd discover, but she wasn't sure what she would do with that information when it arrived.

A group of men were gathering near the small barn on the grounds. Greenly's voice could be heard rising above the rest. Chester shuffled up to the group only to halt when Greenly pointed at him.

"Right here is a prime example of the kind of people we will no longer tolerate in Riverton. When I'm elected, I won't stand for the riffraff and layabouts sullying our streets, threatening the decency of our town."

Hannah fumed. "Are you saying that only the well-off are allowed to live in Riverton?"

"Certainly not. But we want industrious folks, people who contribute to the welfare of the town. Not slackers and drunkards."

Chester raised his hand. "I have a job at the livery."

"The wages of which you spend on drink."

Hannah was fuming. "So you'd force people like Chester to leave? What about those who are sick or injured? Would you forbid them to live in Riverton, too? What if someone suffers a reversal of fortunes, like losing their land or their family through no fault of their own? Would you chase them away, too?"

"If a citizen of Riverton cannot support himself and be a productive member of society, then he must look elsewhere for his food and shelter. We're not going to condone beggars and wastrels."

The crowd was eerily silent. Greenly's voice had risen considerably as he'd warmed to his topic. The stunned expressions on the faces showed their shock. Greenly suddenly realized he might have gone too far and cleared his throat. "Well, uh, of course, things happen, and when a neighbor is in need we would, of course, step in to help—only until they could get back on their feet, of course. Riverton isn't a charity town."

Hannah crossed her arms over her chest exhaling a pent-up breath. "That man is despicable."

Mitch moved up behind her, leaning forward and speaking softly into her ear. His nearness sent a warm rush through her veins. "I'd be careful how far you push Candidate Greenly. I suspect the man has a short fuse when he's challenged."

"Someone needs to challenge him. He's going to destroy this town if he gets elected." She made a quick decision. "I've been in touch with a friend of my father who works for the Pinkerton Detective Agency."

"You doubt that he worked for them?"

"Don't you?"

"I've made some inquiries of my own. Nothing back yet. Let me know what you hear." He moved off.

Hannah watched him go, wishing they could have talked awhile longer and compared notes. She consoled herself by sitting with Chester awhile longer before moving off to see what else she could discover. The ice cream social was a success. Everyone was having a good time despite the stumping by Greenly.

She wasn't going to let this golden opportunity pass her by. She might even push Greenly a little more. Even he wouldn't strike back at a woman, especially a close friend of Cosgrove's wife.

Chapter 9

Mitch mingled with townsfolk, greeting farmers and ranchers from outlying areas who only made it to town every few months or so. Glad-handing wasn't his strong suit, but he did carry a deep affection for the people of Riverton. They'd welcomed him in five years ago, a young man with little experience and a strong determination to turn the rowdy town around. He'd hoped that would be enough to keep his job, but lately he was beginning to wonder.

He had mixed emotions about the two articles The Advocate had written so far. Mostly touting his qualifications and his experience. The parts that made him uncomfortable spoke about his character. His humility and kindness. He didn't know what that had to do with being a lawman. Still it had spurred folks in town to come up to him and express their appreciation and their support in the upcoming election.

What he wanted to know was who was writing them. Leroy kept teasing him that they were written by someone with a fancy for him. A notion he refused to even consider.

After a short break to stroll through the town to make sure no one was taking advantage of the nearly empty streets, Mitch returned to the church grounds. Most of the ice cream and pastries had been consumed. A small group had gathered around Greenly again as he sang his praises to all willing ears.

As he approached he heard the voices rise and the tone turn angry. A fist went up in the air. He focused on the man he recognized as Will Caddy, a man always spoiling for a fight, only to realize that Hannah was right beside him. He'd seen enough gatherings like these turn ugly in a flash, and he had a sense this was going to be one of them. He quickened his steps as the crowd grew louder and started to move around. Greenly held up his hands and the shouting increased. Shoving began and quickly escalated.

"Hannah."

He ran toward her only to lose her in the scuffle. He stepped into the fray shoving aside bodies as he searched for her. He saw her pushed against the barn wall and his blood boiled. He plunged forward, pulling her against him and fought his way to a safe place. He settled her against the side of the barn and looked her over for injuries. "Are you all right? Did they hurt you?"

She shook her head and looked into his eyes. Fear dulled the green eyes. He rested his hand on her cheek. "Are you sure you're not hurt?" He wanted nothing more in that moment than to pull her into his arms and protect her forever. But he had a more pressing matter. If he didn't do something about this fight, more people could be hurt. "Stay here."

He spun and strode back to the fracas. So far only fists had been thrown, but soon the guns would come out. He saw Greenly in the middle making a feeble attempt to stop the ruckus. Neither his words nor his actions had any effect.

Mitch pulled his gun from his holster, aimed at the sky, and fired two shots. The report stopped the men in their tracks. Once he had all their attention, he lowered his gun but didn't holster it. "I don't know what you men are fighting about, but it's over. Now."

"But, Sheriff—"

Mitch set his jaw. "It's done. These nice ladies have gone to a lot of trouble to put this shindig together, and I don't want to see it ruined. You can either stop the fighting or we can all go down to the jail and discuss things there. Your choice."

The men reluctantly moved away, several of them tugged off by their wives. Thankfully, the ruckus settled. Greenly came toward him, loaded for a fight.

"I had things under control."

"If you say so." Mitch holstered his gun.

"That's exactly what I've been saying. You pull your gun when a reasonable approach would suffice."

"Your fancy words weren't getting anywhere."

His concern now was for Hannah. He looked for her. She was still standing against the barn, her hands at her side, her green eyes wide. He went to her, gently guiding her through the barn door and pulling it shut behind him.

"You're sure you're all right?"

She nodded, but her eyes were moist.

"What happened? How did it get started?"

She wiped her eyes. "I'm not sure. Greenly was talking about the town growing and new businesses coming in. Someone said those new businesses were going to be built on land that had been stolen from them. Someone asked if Greenly was going to look into the foreclosures over the last year. Greenly tried to divert their attention to something else, but more men spoke up. I was going to ask about it, too, but then the shouting started and the shoving and then you were there. Thank you, for saving me."

"You shouldn't have been there in the first place. Men can get riled pretty quick. You could have been seriously hurt." He tilted her chin upward with his fingers. "I don't want anything to happen to you."

"You don't?"

His thumb caressed her soft cheek. "It's my job to protect you."

"Why? Because you're the sheriff?"

"Yes, but that's not all." He leaned down. It would be so easy to steal a kiss. They were all alone, and she was so beautiful. He gripped her shoulders, looking into her eyes. "You need to be careful. Don't put yourself in dangerous positions. I may not be around to pull you out next time."

"I can pull myself out. I would have this time, but I was caught off guard."

Mitch set his jaw. Stubborn woman. "You're going to do what you want anyway."

"Yes, I am."

He turned and left. His last image of her was standing defiantly in the barn with dust particles floating around her head from the sun streaming through the window. It was hard to maintain his anger and concern when all he wanted to do was pull her into his arms and kiss her sweet obstinate lips.

He was a fool.

Chapter 10

Riverton Chronicle
September 21, 1881

Our Sentinel

Our sheriff took immediate steps to quell a possible brawl on the church grounds. He is a man of action. A man who aggressively maintains peace, not one who waits for disruption then attempts to stop it. What kind of sheriff do you want watching over our town? A man who confronts the threat with authority or a man who knows the law written in books but not its practical application? The merchants have a right to expect protection. But filing charges and waiting for the court system to administer justice is a lengthy process. Riverton is growing, but in our haste to be respectable let us not toss aside the very real need of a man who can take charge and settle disputes with fairness and respect.

The Advocate

Hannah read over her third article, printed in the latest *Chronicle* one more time and now held her fourth and final in her hand, ready to secretly submit it. This was the last one. The election was tomorrow. She wasn't sure her advocating on Mitch's behalf had guaranteed him the election. She was aware of the stir they caused if the many overheard conversations were any indication. But she wouldn't know for certain until tomorrow when the votes were cast. She'd prayed daily over every word she wrote, asking for His blessing on her endeavors. Surely God wanted a good man like Mitch for the town's sheriff.

She refused to think about what would happen if Greenly was elected. Picking up an envelope, she folded the article and slipped it inside, sealing it and printing THE ADVOCATE in block letters on the front. A glance at the clock told her she was running late. Normally she would slip out of the house early and shove the envelope under the door of the newspaper office for her aunt to find when she came in. She might not make it today.

Quietly she stepped from her room reminding herself to avoid the third step from the bottom on the stairs that creaked.

"I'll take that in for you."

Hannah whirled, coming face-to-face with her aunt. Her hand was extended and a knowing smirk softened her features.

She wiggled her fingers. "Hand it over. I'll save you a trip and you can enjoy the muffins I have waiting in the kitchen."

"How did you find out? I was so careful."

"You were. At first. I really didn't know it was you writing those articles until the third one." She grinned, slipping the envelope into her skirt pocket. "You got careless and let your emotions show through."

"No. I was very cautious about that. I rewrote each one several times to make sure it sounded completely professional and objective."

"And you did a good job. Most people wouldn't have noticed. But I know you, and I know that somewhere along the way you've fallen in love with our sheriff."

Hannah raised her hand to deny it. "No, I haven't. He's the best man for the job, and since he wouldn't lift a finger to help himself win, the least I could do was remind everyone what he had contributed and how well qualified he was for the position."

"It's all right, dear. I understand. I just hope the man appreciates what you're doing for him." She patted her hand. "How does he feel about you?"

"He doesn't. I'm not his type. He wants a nice, docile, complacent woman. I'm certainly not that."

"That might be what he thinks he wants but not what he needs. Give it time. Maybe after the election, things will change."

"You won't tell him, will you? You won't tell anyone, promise me."

"Of course, I won't. But I think it was a fine thing you did for Mitch. You're right. He is the best man for the job, and if the voters have any sense at all they'll vote him back in office."

Hannah spent the rest of the day helping the ladies at the historical society and did her usual stealthy surveillance of the activities in the town. Since she'd started her investigating, she'd managed to find several interesting goings-on and called attention to oversights that she'd printed in the paper under the name J. D. Wright. The initials for her father—Joseph Davis—and the Wright as a play on words.

She saw Mitch ride out of town midmorning causing her spirits to sag. They rarely spoke since the moment in the barn at the social, but at least she could comfort herself with glimpses of him around town. She knew to the minute when he would make his strolls along the streets and made sure she was out and about at the same time. Silly, but it was better than not seeing him at all.

Would he understand what she was trying to do with her articles? He'd quit complaining about them to Polly after the second one was printed. She wasn't sure if he'd just given up or if he'd come to appreciate them. Worse yet, what if he hadn't even read them? Perish the thought.

Late in the afternoon Hannah offered to make the deposit at the bank for her aunt. The small lobby was bustling with activity. As she left the teller window, she noticed Mr. Cosgrove and his man Jenkins huddled in the doorway of the banker's office. A paper passed between them surreptitiously. Casually she moved closer, straining to hear their conversation.

"Are these the latest names? Greenly has to win for our plans to work. I've got the list, don't worry."

Jenkins nodded. "You know Chester has been spouting off about you stealing his land. He says you changed the dates on his mortgage so you could foreclose."

"No one is going to listen to that old drunk. You just make sure Greenly has all the votes he needs."

Hannah kept her face averted until she heard the voices dying off. The men had left the bank and the door to Cosgrove's office was wide open. If she could find the list of those who'd sold their votes or, better yet, the mortgage papers from Chester's land, she could prove his land had been stolen from him and maybe Mitch could get it back.

Slipping into the office, she slowly closed the door. Quickly she scanned the papers on the large desk. Next she opened several drawers but didn't find any list. The large file cabinets weren't locked, so she selected the one with the letter *G* and searched for one labeled GOODMAN.

"I knew you were a troublemaker, but I never suspected you were a thief."

Hannah whirled around, her body hot with humiliation. "I was just looking for—" What could she say? *Something to prove you are a crook.*

"Whatever you were looking for is unimportant. I think it's time you were taught a lesson." He took her arm and steered her to the chair and shoved her down into it. "Jenkins."

The man appeared and started to ask a question, but Cosgrove halted him. "Get the sheriff. Tell him I found a thief in my bank that he needs to arrest."

Hannah's heart raced. "No. I didn't mean any harm. I was just curious."

"Hold your explanation for the law."

Hannah bowed her head. How was she going to explain this to Mitch? He already disliked her. Now he'd have more reasons to keep his distance.

Chapter 11

Mitch took hold of Hannah's upper arm and marched her out of the bank. She'd tried to explain, but he refused to let her speak. He didn't want Cosgrove twisting anything she had to say. And he would. No doubt. But Mitch also knew Hannah, and he knew whatever was behind her snooping she'd only been trying to help someone.

Inside the jail he walked her to the back and opened a cell door. His heart tightened. He didn't want to lock her up, but if he didn't Cosgrove would raise a ruckus, and no matter the outcome of the vote tomorrow Mitch would be out of a job. Not until the door was closed did he dare a look into her eyes. She was scared and angry and oh, so vulnerable that he wanted to wrap his arms around her and comfort her, but he couldn't.

"You want to tell me what you were doing in that office?"

"I heard Cosgrove and Jenkins talking about the new names of the people who sold their votes. He said he had the list. Then he mentioned Chester and I thought if I could find either the list or maybe Chester's mortgage I could prove Cosgrove had stolen it and you could get it back."

Mitch rubbed his forehead. "Even if you had, that's not up to me. That would be a matter for the judge to decide."

"But if I could find that list, then we could expose those people and make them vote their heart and not their money."

"Hannah, it doesn't work that way. Right now the only one who broke the law is you." His voice had risen as he spoke. He hadn't meant to shout, but he was worried what might happen to her. "Breaking into someone's office is a criminal act. If you don't understand that, then you should catch the next train back to Cincinnati before you find yourself in trouble I can't get you out of."

As if suddenly deflated, she sank onto the cot. He couldn't help notice how out of place she looked. Her rose-colored dress, the cameo at her throat, and her soft honey-toned hair didn't belong in his rough and dirty jail cell.

"How long do I have to stay here?"

"I don't know. It'll depend on when Cosgrove comes to press charges."

He couldn't look at her any longer. It hurt too much. He turned to go. He had a lot of thinking to do.

"Mitch, I'm sorry. I didn't mean to make trouble."

"I know. You never do."

Mitch tried to block out the image of the lovely Hannah locked in his jail. He came up with as many reasons within the law to release her as he could. Though he doubted the banker would agree to any of them. Cosgrove would want to press charges to the hilt. An unfamiliar sound reached his ears and he strained to make it out. When he realized it was Hannah crying, his heart ached. There was nothing he could do for her. Well, there was one thing. He could pray that Cosgrove would grow a heart before he got here. He wasn't a religious man, but he believed and he read his Bible when he could.

Mitch stared at the door to the jail then at the clock on the wall. It had been nearly forty-five minutes, and Cosgrove had yet to show up. Maybe his prayers had been answered. A commotion outside on the sidewalk brought him to his feet as the door opened and Mrs. Cosgrove entered. What was she doing here? "Good day, ma'am?" Slowly Horace Cosgrove entered the office and stood a few feet behind his wife, his expression grim.

"Hardly a good day, Sheriff, when you arrest a fine young woman like Hannah. I'm here to see that she's released immediately."

"Does this mean your husband is not pressing charges?"

"He most certainly is not." She glanced over her shoulder at her spouse. "In fact, I'm here to verify her accusations." Opening her reticule she pulled out a piece of paper. "I believe she was looking for this. It's a list of the people who foolishly sold their votes for a few pieces of silver."

Mitch took the list. There were names here that surprised him. "You know that vote buying isn't illegal. I can't arrest either these people or your husband."

"More's the pity. I know that, but Horace is going to make an announcement that those who took money for their votes are released from their commitment and are free to vote as they please. Isn't that right, dear?"

Cosgrove swallowed, his face pale. "That's correct. I made a big mistake."

"All right." Relief washed through Mitch as he picked up the keys and went to the back to set Hannah free.

She was gripping the bars, her face angled between the rough iron rods. "Did I hear Mrs. Cosgrove correctly? She found the list?"

"She did, and apparently she influenced her husband not to press charges."

She stepped out of the cell and into his arms." I'm so sorry, Mitch. Really."

She stepped back, leaving a cold aching sensation in his chest. He followed her out into the office, struggling to sort out the strange feeling in his chest.

Mrs. Cosgrove hurried forward and gave Hannah a hug. "I'm so sorry for all this."

"It's not your fault. I was wrong to look through your husband's office."

"Well, you should have come to me. I know where he hides things he wants to deny. I found the list in his safe at home. And I think he understands the consequences if he tries to win an election underhandedly."

"Thank you. I can never repay you for this."

"You already have. You have been a delightful addition to our town, and we look forward to more of your inspiring ideas. Don't you agree, Sheriff?"

Mitch looked into Hannah's green eyes and saw hope. Did she want him to agree? "I'm sure the folks here would like that." He watched as that light of hope faded from her eyes. He wasn't sure what he'd done, but the rift between them was as wide as ever.

He would never understand women.

Chapter 12

Mitch angled his hat on his head before turning to face his deputy. "Keep a sharp eye, Leroy. I'm turning in. Voting starts early tomorrow, and I want to make sure nothing disrupts the process."

Leroy nodded and took a seat at the desk. "Like an eagle. You gonna vote for yourself?"

"A man's vote is private. You know that."

"Well, you can count on mine, Sheriff."

"Thanks." Mitch strode out of the office and down the boardwalk toward Mrs. Foster's Boardinghouse. He normally took his evening meal with the other boarders, but he wasn't in the mood to listen to the chatter around the table. He wasn't hungry anyway. Every time he thought about how he had to drag Hannah to the jail, his gut knotted. He couldn't imagine what she'd been thinking when she decided to snoop around Cosgrove's office. His prayers for her had been answered in a way he never could have imagined. Apparently Mrs. Cosgrove ruled the roost in their household. She'd cut her husband off at the knees and exposed his scheme. He'd always heard that the money in the Cosgrove home belonged to the wife. Apparently that was true.

Mitch stepped through the door hoping to make a quick dash to his room, but Alice Lincoln stopped him with a smile and gentle hand on his arm.

"I'm so glad to see you. I just want you to know that you can count on my vote."

"Thank you. I appreciate that." He took the steps two at a time then closed and locked the door behind him. His room was generous. Mrs. Foster had given him the best one in the house facing the street with a shady tree outside the window. He had a desk, a comfortable chair, and a soft bed. Everything a man would need.

But lately he'd been feeling cramped in the space, edgy to move. He kept thinking about a house of his own, some land and a woman to share it with. A woman like Hannah. After pulling off his boots, he slipped his suspenders from his shoulders then dropped back on the bed, staring at the ceiling.

Any chance he'd had with Hannah was gone. He'd rebuffed her friendship from the first time he'd met her, shoving her into the same cubbyhole as Lydia. The arrest today had only sealed the deal. His big mistake was scolding her. But he'd been terrified of what might happen. He wanted to shake her and kiss her at the same time. Part of him admired her courage and determination, but the other wanted to wrap her in cotton wool and keep her safe away from even the smallest dangers.

He'd seen the look of hurt in her green eyes as he'd reprimanded her for her foolishness. Then he compounded it by telling her it was time for her to go home. He didn't want her to go home. Ever. He rubbed his eyes. No use crying over spilled milk. Tomorrow would be a long day. He needed to rest. At this time tomorrow he'd either be employed or looking for a new job. At the moment neither option stirred any emotions. The only feeling he had running through his heart was for Hannah and his deep regret for chasing her away because he was afraid of risking his heart again. Maybe a man like him didn't deserve to be sheriff.

Riverton Chronicle
September 24, 1881

Vote Today

Today you will cast your votes for one of two men running for the office of sheriff of Riverton. One man claims he's the answer to the coming boom in commerce and expansion of our town, that under his leadership Riverton will be a beacon of respectability. Settlers will look to us as the place to raise their families in safety.

The other has had little to say about what he will do if he stays in office. But we all know exactly what that will be. He will be honest, he will walk the streets of our town, keeping a watchful eye on everyone and everything. He will settle disputes with simple strength. He will take the less fortunate under his wing and make sure they are cared for. He will stay up all night to catch a thief that is robbing an honest merchant.

His clear blue eyes see the way things really are. Not how he'd like them to be or how they might become. He is our anchor. Our steady compass in the storm. Dependable, honorable, good-hearted, loyal, honest, brave, and humble. The very definition of a sheriff.

I know who I'm voting for tomorrow. Search your heart, and I hope you'll realize that the man in office today is the man we want for tomorrow and into the future.

The Advocate

Hannah stared at the latest edition of the *Chronicle*, her gaze focused on her final article as The Advocate. It was printed on the front page, but she realized now that she should have written it for the Wednesday edition instead. Today was the election. A Saturday, so everyone could come to town to cast their vote. All those who lived outside of town probably wouldn't think about picking up a paper. They'd come to Riverton to get supplies and vote then head back home.

Not that it mattered. It was out of her hands now. She'd done all she could to help Mitch get elected sheriff. It had proven to be a pointless gesture. He probably hadn't even read them after the first one had been printed.

She shoved the paper aside and stood, walking to the window and staring out at the town she'd grown so fond of. She had friends here, a purpose, a home with her aunt, and the potential to be a reporter—of sorts. Yesterday's events had revealed the dangers of getting overly involved. Maybe exposing criminals wasn't as exciting as she'd imagined.

She certainly hadn't enjoyed being hauled off to the jail like an outlaw. But that's what she was. She'd crossed over into criminal activity. A shiver chased up her spine as she thought about the hard, unforgiving look on Mitch's face as he'd marched her to the sheriff's office. Her heart squeezed knowing she'd lost any chance with him. He would never forgive her, and he would never care for a woman so brazen as to rifle through the bank's files.

But it was his scolding that had ripped her heart to shreds. He wanted her gone. He practically ordered her to pack up and get out of town. Which is what she'd decided to do.

"Hannah, what are you staring at? Something going on outside?" Polly came and stood beside her, glancing from her to the view out to the street.

"No. Nothing unusual."

"Oh, I see. Still stinging from your big adventure yesterday? You know, when I agreed to let you do a little reporting around town, I never imagined you'd get so involved. There's a point at which you need to turn over what you discover and let the law handle things."

"I told him, but he wouldn't do anything about it."

"So you thought you could do what an experienced, knowledgeable professional couldn't?"

"But I was right."

"And was it worth what it cost you?"

She shook her head. She'd lost respect, created an enemy, and lost the man she loved.

Polly wrapped an arm around her shoulders. "You're young and enthusiastic and I daresay spoiled and indulged. You are a crusader at heart, and when you see something that needs changed you charge ahead. But you have to learn restraint, patience, and when to stand up and when to fight another day."

"The fighting will be over today."

"Yes, either Mitch will be elected or not. I'm praying he will. Let's leave it in the Lord's hands, shall we? Have you voted yet?"

Hannah shook her head. "I can't imagine how Mrs. Cosgrove got the town fathers to agree to let us vote in this election."

"After his vote-buying plan was exposed, I guess it was the least he could do. Let's go cast our votes, then we can come back here and work on a special edition to announce the winner."

Tears stung Hannah's eyes as she thought about Mitch losing the election. She'd only meant to help with her articles, but her behavior yesterday may have erased all her good intentions. "He has to win, Aunt Polly."

Gentle arms wrapped her in a warm hug. "You love him, don't you? Maybe things will work out once this election is over."

"No. I've thought it over and I'm going back home. I've already bought my ticket. I'm sorry it's so sudden, but there's nothing for me here now."

"I wish you wouldn't leave. I like having you here, and I enjoy having you help around the paper. Please, don't make another rash decision."

"It's not rash. I came out here chasing a silly infatuation and I got what I deserved. I tried to make my fantasy come true."

"Don't give up hope. Sometimes dreams do come true when we least expect them. Let's go vote for Mitch. Our two votes could sway the election."

The rest of the day dragged on. Hannah wandered down past the Hallmark Hotel, which was serving as the polling location. People came and went. Often a small line would form of those waiting their turn, but Hannah could read nothing into the faces of those who had voted.

Finally the clock on the wall ticked down to seven. Hannah's palms were moist and her heart thudded in her chest. The counting would begin. Part of her wanted to dash to the hotel and wait with the others for the final tally to be announced. Another part of her wanted to hide here at the *Chronicle* in case the news wasn't good. Then she could grieve in private.

The shouting from outside pulled her from her contemplation. It was over. But who had won? Polly hurried to the door and opened it. Stopping the first person that passed by. "Who won?"

"The sheriff. By two hundred and fifty votes."

Hannah sagged in the chair. Her eyes filling with tears. Her prayers had been answered.

"Did you hear? Mitch won. Good job, Hannah. Let's go congratulate him."

The thought of facing Mitch sent a wave of apprehension along her nerves. How could she face him after yesterday? "No, I don't think I should."

"Hannah, you need to face up to your mistakes. It's the right thing to do. Come along."

Reluctantly, she followed, trying to tamp down her emotions. All she had to do was say congratulations, smile, and then leave. She just had to remember to not look into his eyes or she'd dissolve into a puddle of female histrionics, which would only drive him further away.

She squared her shoulders as they neared the sheriff's office. She could do this. After all, the only thing that mattered here was that Mitch retained his job. He would be happy and go on to serve the town with honor. Her feelings shouldn't enter into the picture at all.

She forced a smile and followed her aunt into the office.

Chapter 13

Mitch shook the hand of the local butcher, accepting his congratulations, and then did the same with the blacksmith. His office had seen a steady stream of well-wishers since the vote had been announced. The attention made him uncomfortable, but he couldn't deny he'd breathed a huge sigh of relief when the outcome had gone in his favor. His faith in the folks of Riverton hadn't been misplaced.

He glanced up as Polly and Hannah entered. The office suddenly became stuffy and small. There was so much he wanted to say to her, but this was not the time. She looked like a spring day in a flowered dress that brought out her beautiful eyes. She'd taken to wearing less fussy clothing the last few weeks, which only enhanced her beauty.

Polly came and gave him a hug and a soft pat on the shoulder. "I'm so glad you're staying on as sheriff. We need a man like you around here."

"Thank you. I'll do my best to earn the people's trust."

"You already have that, Mitch. They showed that with their votes."

Hannah caught his gaze. "I'm glad you won."

Mitch's throat constricted, and he wasn't sure what to say, so he said the first thing that came to mind. "I told you I didn't need any help."

She went pale and for a moment he thought she might faint. Polly gave him a scathing glance then tugged Hannah away and out the door.

What had he said? He never knew how she would take things. It was exasperating. When he finally left the jail and returned to his room, thoughts of Hannah haunted his dreams all night, leaving him eager to get to the jail and keep his mind occupied with work and not the lovely Eastern girl with the stubborn chin and the challenging green eyes.

He arrived at the office earlier than normal the next morning, finding Leroy slumped in the desk chair sound asleep. He didn't begrudge the man some shut-eye. He worked hard and Mitch would be unable to do his job as efficiently without him. He nudged his friend awake and motioned him to go home.

"You're here early."

"Have to justify the faith the town's placed in me."

"If you ask me, you need to thank that Advocate person, too. He made the folks here take a hard look at the campaigns and see through Greenly's empty promises."

Mitch doubted that. After the first article he'd barely glanced at the others. Mainly to make sure the man wasn't printing anything that was untrue. He avoided them because they always made him sound better than he was. He doubted anyone thought that highly of him.

Moving to his desk, he sat down, enjoying the sensation of being in charge. He belonged here. In this job. He tugged on his shirt and removed the badge pinned there. The small silver star was battered, bent, and worth little money. But to him it represented who he was and what the Lord had called him to do. His role was to protect the town of Riverton and serve the folks who lived there.

He pinned the badge back in place as his door opened and Polly Wilson strolled in, laying a paper on his desk. It was a one-page edition of the *Chronicle* announcing his election as sheriff.

"I thought you might like to have a copy. Purely for sentimental reasons."

"Mighty nice of you, Miss Polly, thank you." She stood at his desk, clearly having more to say.

"I hope you know that you didn't win this election by yourself."

"Ma'am?"

"You owe a huge debt to The Advocate. Without those articles reminding folks what a good job you've done, Willard Greenly would be sitting in that chair and you'd be looking for work."

"I doubt that."

Polly arched her eyebrows and leaned toward him. "Did you read those articles?"

"I glanced at them."

"And do you know how many folks changed their minds once they had time to think about them? You refused to lift a finger to prove to the town that you wanted to remain in office. Many folks thought you didn't want to be sheriff any longer. Those articles showed them that you did and that you were the right man for the job."

She had a point. He'd never thought about it that way before. He considered his lack of campaigning to be a sign that he was confident and secure. He hadn't considered the people might think he didn't care. "Then I'll have to thank The Advocate. If I knew who he was."

"I know. And if you had a thimbleful of sense, you'd have figured it out already. There's only one person in this town who was willing to fight for you and make sure you got reelected."

Mitch frowned. The only person who had nagged him about that was—

No, she couldn't be The Advocate.

Polly pressed her lips together and exhaled softly. "I can see the wheels finally turning in that thick male head of yours. I suggest you read those articles again with your full attention and look between the lines at what isn't said. If you don't have a change of heart, then maybe you're not the right man after all." She walked to the door and then abruptly turned back again. "Oh, and I wouldn't take too long making up your mind because she's leaving on the morning train."

"Hannah is leaving?"

"Isn't that what you told her to do? Besides, there's nothing for her here. Is there?"

Mitch set his elbows on the desk and raked his fingers through his hair. Hannah was leaving. Hannah wrote the articles. Why? His gaze fell to the *Chronicle*, and he noticed that there were other papers beneath the first page. The four articles by The Advocate. He picked up the first one and started to read, this time with visions of Hannah scratching out the words at her desk.

It wasn't until he got to the last article that his heart sped up. This one was different in tone and subject. He hadn't read it. He'd been too busy on Election Day. Now he took his time, and what he saw opened his eyes. This could only have been written by a woman in love. Was this how Hannah saw him?

How had he been so blind for so long?

Fear. That's how.

He'd felt the attraction, he'd suspected she had feelings for him as well, but the thought of risking his heart again was too painful to even contemplate, so he'd pushed her away time and time again. And he could lose her. He glanced at the clock. The train left in fifteen minutes. She was probably already on board.

Grabbing his hat, he charged out the door, praying that he wasn't too late and that he could change her mind. He had no idea how he'd do that, but he could be stubborn, too, and he'd find a way.

Chapter 14

It was hard to see her last glimpse of Riverton through tears. Hannah ducked her head and dabbed at her eyes with her lace handkerchief. It was for the best. Her big adventure out west had been a failure. Mitch was right. She didn't belong here. She couldn't be a frontier woman no matter how much she wanted to be.

Things had always worked out for her in Cincinnati, but she could see now that much of that had been due to her father stepping in, smoothing over her errors. In Riverton she had to finally face the consequences of her impulsive decisions, and it had left her with a broken and shattered heart.

The irony was that her desire to help Mitch and show him how she felt had been lost on him. Not only did he not read the articles; he didn't understand the emotion behind them.

"Miss Davis, I need you to come with me."

Hannah's heart froze at the sound of the familiar deep voice. She looked up at Mitch who stood beside her seat, blocking the aisle. His face was shadowed by the brim of his hat. She swallowed to clear the tightness in her throat. "Why?"

"For attempting to bribe an officer of the law."

What was he saying? "No. I did no such thing. You're mistaken."

He reached down and picked up her valise with one hand then took her arm with the other, urging her to her feet. "We'll discuss this at the jail."

"But the train is leaving soon."

He ignored her and steered her out of the train car and to the platform. Leroy stood on the ground, and he took her baggage. Mitch jumped down then helped her down the steps. He took her arm again and strode toward the jail. By the time they arrived, her legs were tired from trying to keep pace with his long stride.

She couldn't imagine what she'd done. Her surprise was giving way to anger. He'd better have a good reason for his actions.

He removed his hat, smoothed his dark hair back, and gestured for her to be seated.

She clasped her hands tightly in her lap, trying to control her rising anger. "I hope you'll make this quick. I don't want to miss my train."

"I only have a couple of questions."

She looked at him more closely. His whole demeanor had changed. His blue eyes were filled with concern; his shoulders were bent toward her. He reached for a stack of papers and handed them to her. She gasped softly when she recognized the articles she'd written as The Advocate. How had he found out?

"Did you write those articles?"

Her first impulse was to deny it, but there was no point now. Mitch was probably going to scold her again. Well, she wouldn't listen. "Yes, I did. Now may I leave?"

"Why did you write them?"

"Because you were too bullheaded to do anything to win the election. You just expected it to happen without any effort."

"Is that all?"

"No. You were the better candidate. After I learned about the vote buying I wanted to give you some help. The election was unfair. I just wanted to even the odds."

"What about this last article? What was your reason for writing that one?"

Her cheeks flamed. She'd hoped he'd never see it, but he had. "I'm not sure. I guess I got carried away." Moisture pooled in her eyes and she dug frantically into her reticule for her handkerchief. A strong hand held out a clean one for her. She took it, avoiding looking at Mitch. He came to her side, stooping down and resting his large hand on hers.

"Hannah, I'm sorry. I've been a blind fool. I didn't want to see what was right in front of me. You. I don't want you to leave. I want you to stay in Riverton."

She looked at him, searching his chiseled features for the truth and afraid to believe what she saw in his blue eyes. "What are you saying?"

"I'm saying I love you. And I think after reading these that you love me, too."

"You do? But you told me to leave."

He pulled her to her feet, slipping his hands around her waist. "I was afraid. But I know now that you're what I need. Times are changing, the town is changing, and I need a woman with imagination and courage to help me face the challenges. A woman who likes adventure."

She laid her hand against his face, thrilling at the whisker-roughened skin. "Are you sure?"

"I knew from the moment you walked into my jail. Will you marry me?"

"Yes. But on one condition: I still want to be a reporter."

"I have a condition, too. You can report all you want, but when it crosses the line into my job, you have to step aside and let me take over." He pulled her close. "I couldn't bear to lose you. I want to keep you safe."

"I think we have a deal, Sheriff." She laid her hand on his chest, the rapid beating of his heart mirroring her own. He drew her against him and she slipped her arms around his neck. "My hero."

He grinned then captured her mouth, kissing her with all the promise of their future and fulfilling all the dreams and fantasies she'd ever had about her heroic Western sheriff.

Lorraine Beatty is a multi-published, bestselling author. Born and raised in Columbus, Ohio, she currently lives in Brandon, Mississippi, with her husband of forty-four years. Lorraine has written for trade books, newspapers, and company newsletters. Lorraine has lived in various regions of the country as well as in Germany. She is a member of RWA, PAN, and ACFW and is a charter member and former president of Magnolia State Romance Writers.

Too Many Secrets

by Molly Noble Bull

Dedication

*To Bret, Burt, Bren, Bethanny, Hailey, Dillard, Bryson, Grant,
Grace, Jana, Linda, Angela, Carmen, and Noe.*

But to God give the glory. I can do nothing without Him.

But my God shall supply all your need according to his riches in glory by Christ Jesus.
PHILIPPIANS 4:19

Chapter 1

L ooks like the stage from San Antonio pulled in across the street."

Luke followed the hotel employee's gaze and peered through the front window. "Yep, it's here all right." He glanced at his pocket watch. "Twelve noon. Right on time, too." Then he looked back at the man behind the main desk. "Doc Carter asked me to pick up a package for Mr. Franklin and drop it by the Franklin farm on my way home. It's medicine. Is it ready, sir?"

"Mr. Ambrose Franklin." The desk clerk paused. "Yes, here it is." One eyebrow lifted. "I'm new in town, and you look familiar. But I can't recall your name."

"I'm Luke Conquest. Mr. Franklin's neighbor."

"Oh." He handed Luke a small wooden box. "I understand Mr. Franklin's been sick off and on for a long time now."

"Yes, sir."

"Well, tell him I send my regards."

"I'll do that, Mr.—"

"Pearson."

Luke glanced around the dark, expensive-looking hotel lobby with its crystal chandeliers and polished floors. The word *Frio* meant "cold" in Spanish, and the Frio Corners Hotel was named for the Frio River. The hotel was new, and this was the first time Luke had come inside since it opened. The furniture gleamed like store-bought polish. Slick and smooth. And it smelled like beeswax. It could be a long while before he stopped by the hotel again, and he wanted to take it all in before moving on.

He opened his mouth to tell Mr. Pearson how much he liked the hotel when the entry door opened. The most beautiful girl Luke had ever seen stepped inside. His heart pounded so hard that he did a double take. She looked tall, too.

Why, she was near as tall as he was.

Young women that fine didn't arrive in the Texas hill country every day. He wanted to savor every moment of that experience.

Her gold-colored hair reminded him of mountain honey and wheat while still in the field, and it looked as soft as a feather pillow in fresh-smelling ticking. It was wrong. But he couldn't stop staring. Her blue eyes sparkled with excitement like she had a zest for life. He couldn't look away.

Like a swan on a quiet lake, she floated toward the center of the room. Four young children followed after her.

A warning light went off inside his brain.

The young woman was married and probably somebody's mama. As a church elder, Luke should walk out of here right now and never look back. He hesitated. Maybe he was wrong. As if he'd been hog-tied by an invisible rope, he stayed put. Besides, she looked too young to be the mother of that bunch.

Slim and straight, she glided across the polished floor with confidence and grace. He'd never seen royalty, but he pictured them looking like her. She walked up to the main desk and rang the bell. *Ping.* Her shiny yellow hair looked as alive as she did, brushing her shoulders below her brown homemade-looking bonnet, and she held her head high as she stood in front of the counter, waiting to talk to a hotel employee.

Mr. Pearson continued sorting papers. Apparently he hadn't noticed her yet.

She coughed, and when he turned around, she smiled as if she talked to strangers behind desks every day. But even in the darkened lobby, Luke noticed that her brown skirt and white blouse looked old and shabby. So did the children's clothes. What a contradiction. A princess dressed in rags.

"I'm Miss Abigail Willoughby from Atlanta, Georgia." She had a heavy southern accent. "And these here are my brothers and sisters."

Brothers and sisters. Luke breathed a sigh of relief. *She isn't married.*

The young woman rested her hand on the shoulder of the taller of the two boys. "This is Tommy. Next comes Margaret. Then Louise, and finally Albert."

Luke moved a little closer to the girl and the children.

"I'm lookin' for Pastor and Mrs. Andrew Johnson," she went on. "They asked me to meet them here."

"I haven't seen them. Are they expecting to meet you here today, ma'am?"

"Well, yes and no." She shrugged. "They didn't exactly know when I'd arrive. And I don't rightly know where they live—this being my first visit to Texas and all. Would you mind lookin' to see if they left me a note or something?"

"Why, I'd be glad to. Just a minute. I'll check." Mr. Pearson turned around and looked through a stack of notes and letters. "Miss Abigail Willoughby." He pivoted, handing her a white envelope. "Here, ma'am."

"Thank you kindly, sir."

She paused to read her letter. Tommy, standing behind Miss Willoughby, pushed his younger sister. Margaret whimpered when her head hit the wooden counter. The little girl stuck out her tongue, pointing it at Tommy. The boy pulled a lock of her red hair. Margaret cried louder.

Luke reached out—prepared to pull the two apart if it came to that. He considered a fight between two children in a nice hotel like this unacceptable. Yet the battle had started right there behind their big sister's back, and Miss Abigail Willoughby appeared to be unaware of it. Or didn't care.

In her white blouse with buttons all the way to her chin, Miss Willoughby looked as calm and stress free as a white-tailed dove.

"Stop that, Tommy." Miss Willoughby didn't bother to turn around but just kept reading her letter. "If you want the candy I promised, that is."

"Yes, Abby."

"That's better." She returned her gaze to the man behind the counter. "The letter says that Pastor Johnson and his wife went to San Antonio and won't be back for several days. They said if I arrived while they were away to stay here at the hotel until they returned. They also promised to pay my fee. And would you happen to know where a Mr. Ambrose Franklin lives? I need to talk to him as soon as possible."

Luke stepped forward. "My name is Luke Conquest, and I know where Ambrose Franklin lives. In fact, I'm on my way there now. And I would be happy to drive you and the children if you would permit it, ma'am."

The man behind the desk frowned. "Are you kin to Deputy Conquest, the one that got shot dead in a shoot-out?"

"He was my pa."

"Well, I heard of him, but I don't know you from Adam. So I can't let you take this young woman anywhere. Wouldn't be proper." He looked back at Abby. "I'd take you myself, ma'am, but I just have too much work to do here at the hotel. Book work and all. You know how it is this time of the year—and with the Christmas season coming up before you know it. I'm sure you understand."

"I'm an elder over at the church on the hill, sir," Luke explained. "That should count for something."

A woman was mopping the floor off to the side. She turned and smiled up at Luke. He recognized her and smiled back.

"Why, Mrs. Eastland. I didn't know you worked here now."

"Started last week." She sent Mr. Pearson a stern look. "I know Luke there, sir, and I can vouch for him. He goes to our church just like he said. I think you should let him take the woman and the children wherever they need to go."

"Would you like for this man to drive you, ma'am?" Mr. Pearson asked Abby.

"Yes, I would."

Luke nodded. "Then we better get started. It's a long drive getting there, and we have to go through the hills."

"All right."

Abby's smile reminded him of a sudden sunburst breaking through a dark sky. He couldn't resist grinning back at her.

"Oh." She touched her forehead with the palm of one hand. "I almost forgot. Our trunk and suitcases are still on the stage." Abby glanced toward the entry door. "Would you mind having someone carry them into the hotel for us so they will be here when we get back?"

Get back? Luke thought.

"I figured you'd be staying at Mr. Franklin's place until morning, ma'am."

"Oh, my, no. I never intended to do that."

"It could be rather late if we drive back here tonight."

"I don't mind getting back late." She sent him a pleading look. "But I don't have much money left. The little I have has to last me. So I can't pay you much for the trip."

She looked desperate.

"Don't worry," he said. "There will be no charge."

"You are very kind."

He hadn't planned to drive all the way back to Frio Corners tonight and then drive back to his ranch in the middle of the night. But he would gladly do it just for the privilege of being with Miss Willoughby for a while.

Luke gazed at the entry door again. "Guess I'll go out and carry in your luggage, ma'am."

"I'd be much obliged."

The stagecoach was parked across the street in front of the café and right next to his wagon. Luke hauled the heavy trunk just inside the door of the lobby and went back for the suitcases.

"Put them in room five," Mr. Pearson said, "and here's the key." He put a key on the counter, motioning toward a hallway at the far end of the lobby. "I would help you. But as you can see, I'm entirely too busy."

Busy doing what? The desk clerk had hardly moved since they came in.

Luke loaded the luggage into room five, locked the door, and handed Miss Willoughby the key. "Here you are. So, I guess we can go now." He pulled out his pocket watch again and checked the time. "It's after twelve. Have you and the children eaten?"

"No, but we don't need anything."

"Yes, we do," the oldest of the two little boys said. "I'm hungry."

"Me, too," the others echoed.

"They fix picnic lunches over at the café across the street. Why don't I buy us all something for lunch? We can stop and eat it along the way."

Abby blushed. "I hate to put you out like that. And as I said, we have no money to pay you, sir. You've done way too much for us already."

"Please, let me do this. I would consider it an honor."

Her blue eyes widened. "Helping us is an honor? How?"

"I'm a member of God's family, ma'am. Christians help one another."

Abby smiled when Luke put the wooden box under one arm and took her arm with the other, escorting her and the children across the street to his wagon. Mr. Conquest was a thoughtful person, and she would call him Luke—at least in her dreams. He had on the kind of boots that cowboys wore. Abby tried not to notice that he was also handsome.

A pretty young woman with dark hair stood in the shadow of the café, peering at her. Abby considered asking Luke who the woman was but decided against it. He'd done enough for her and the children. It wouldn't be polite to bother him with more questions and demands.

Chapter 2

Abby held an empty wicker picnic basket on her lap, gazing at Luke in the wagon seat beside her. The children had enjoyed their lunches and especially the candy, and she was glad she bought a few more sticks for later. To be truthful, she wasn't thinking about candy at the moment and couldn't stop looking at Luke Conquest.

He'd looked tall and lean, standing in the lobby of the hotel in his black cowboy boots and tan trousers. A hat covered his dark hair now, but earlier she'd noticed how the honey-colored lights in his chocolate-brown eyes set off the deeper brown of his thick, curly hair. He held the leather reins with confidence, and his hands looked as rough and untamed as the state of Texas.

Hills surrounded them on all sides. Birds chirped overhead.

"Just look at all the birds," she said.

He grinned. "Some of them already flew south for the winter."

Abby kept looking at Luke, but with her eyes lowered so he wouldn't notice. A crisp breeze chilled the air, and it appeared to get cooler the higher in the hills they went. She'd put on her old brown cape and covered the children with an extra blanket. Clearly autumn was here, and winter was banging at the door.

Yellow, gold, rusty-red, and brown leaves clothed trees higher on the hills. Yet the valleys looked green enough to tempt hand-fed cattle and horses, not to mention the wild animals that probably roamed the countryside.

Abby wondered what kind of trees they were seeing—maples, maybe. The woman on the train said that maple trees grew in this part of Texas.

They had left Frio Corners hours ago, and the wagon broke down before they had driven three miles. Luke fixed the loose wheel and got the wagon moving again, and they had been going up and down rock-filled roads ever since.

In fact, Abby had bumped up and down on the wooden bench so many times that she wondered how she kept from falling off and tumbling headfirst to the hard ground. But according to Luke, they had almost reached the Franklin farm.

Anything would be better than her life as a child and young adult in Georgia. But all that was in the past. She had always dreamed of marrying a churchgoin' man. Now that dream was about to come true, and if Ambrose Franklin looked half as good as Luke Conquest, she was going to love living in Texas.

Abby glanced in the back of the wagon to check on her brothers and sisters. All four children slept on a patchwork quilt.

"Are they asleep?" Luke asked.

She released a big sigh. "Yes, thank goodness."

He chuckled. "They are fine-looking youngsters. Lots of energy, too."

"Oh, I reckon they are full of energy, all right."

Luke looked at her for a moment without saying anything. She wondered what he might be thinking.

"You mentioned Pastor and Mrs. Johnson," he said. "Guess this is none of my business. But how do you know them?"

"After the children and I decided to come to Texas, Ambrose suggested in one of his letters that I write to his pastor. So I did. Ambrose said he lived a long way from town, and I should stay with them until he could have someone pick me up."

Luke nodded. "Then are you and the children related to Mr. Franklin?"

"Not yet."

"What does that mean? You're either related to him or you're not."

"Well, Ambrose and I are..."

She hated trying to explain why she and Ambrose planned to marry in just a few days. The circumstances might seem strange to an outsider like Luke Conquest.

"I'm Ambrose Franklin's intended," she said softly, half hoping he wouldn't question her further.

"His what?"

"We have never actually met, but we have corresponded. And I am to be his bride."

His mail-order bride, she thought.

"Are you *sure* this is what you want to do, miss?"

"Of course, I'm sure. I've waited all my life to marry a God-fearing man and have a home of my own."

He frowned. "But am I correct in saying that you have never actually seen him?"

"Why would I need to? I reckon I know everything worth knowing. We have exchanged letters, but I will be meeting him face-to-face for the first time today."

"I see. Well, what has he told you about himself, if you don't mind me asking?"

"Not that it is any of your concern, but he said that he worked in mines in California and around here for a while. Now he lives alone on a farm he owns free and clear. Our parents are dead, and he doesn't mind that I'm bringing my sisters and brothers to live with us. Now I would call that a good man, wouldn't you?"

"I never said he wasn't a good man. He is. But there are a few things about Mr. Franklin you might want to know."

"No." She shook her head. "As I said, I know all about Ambrose Franklin that I need to know."

She saw his facial muscles tighten like he was looking down his nose at her. He probably guessed how poor they were and how unworthy she was. Yes, she felt guilty accepting a marriage proposal from a God-fearing man like Ambrose when her own father was...

Abby bit her lower lip, and her heart attempted to break out of the prison she'd tried to keep it in. She hated men like her father, and her late stepfather never worked a day in his life. Abby's poor mother supported the family until the day she died.

She glared at Luke. "I don't need a perfect stranger like you to try to turn me against the most decent, most honorable man I ever knew." Abby lifted her chin. "I'll judge Ambrose, if you please."

"Suit yourself." Luke peered down the road ahead.

He's angry with me now.

But why should she care? Luke Conquest meant nothing to her.

Nobody spoke again for a long time. Luke pretended an interest in surroundings he'd seen a million times—the hills—the streams—the trees just putting on their fall clothes.

The path they were taking edged the river. Luke blinked against the water's blinding sparkle, against water that was always cold. As a child, he'd seen muddy rivers and creeks when the family left the hill country and drove east to Grandma's, but the swirling Frio River was always clean and clear. He could see all the way to its rock bottom, and he loved to hear the rush of hasty waves as they twisted and swished on the long journey to the Gulf of Mexico.

Still, he couldn't stop wondering if the lovely Miss Willoughby was nothing more than a gold digger out to marry a rich and ailing man. In any case, she was in for a big surprise.

A small rock cabin stood on a rise just ahead.

"Well, ma'am. We're here."

Abby smiled, gazing at the house.

"The roof needs a little repair," Luke said, "and the brown shutters could use a coat of paint. Otherwise, the house looks pretty good."

Luke pulled the horses to a stop and tied up the reins. Then he jumped down from the wagon. "May I help you down?" he asked.

She hesitated.

Maybe she was still peeved with him for saying what he did. Good thing she didn't know what he'd been thinking.

At last she said, "Yes. Please, help me down from the wagon."

"What about the children?"

"I think I'll just leave 'em here sleeping in the wagon while we go inside. They should be all right, I think. I don't plan to stay long."

"Very well."

He reached out and grabbed her around the waist in order to lift her down. She felt lighter than a newborn calf.

As soon as her feet touched the ground, she wiggled out of his grasp and hurried toward the front steps of the cabin. Luke snatched the wooden box with the medicine in it from the back of the wagon and followed her up the steps to the front porch.

At the door she knocked, waited, and knocked again.

"Don't knock," Luke said. "Just go on in. Mr. Franklin will be resting anyway."

Abby hesitated. Then she went inside.

A big rock fireplace dominated the interior of the main room, and he saw her looking at it as soon as they went inside. Abby continued to survey the darkened room, and he noticed when she took a special interest in the bed in one corner. Mr. Franklin lay on it, snoring loudly.

"Hello," she said.

Nobody answered.

"I think he must be sleeping," Luke said.

Abby nodded and moved closer to the bed. One quick look, and she whirled around, staring at Luke.

"This man can't be my Ambrose," she exclaimed. "He looks old enough to be my grandfather. Why, he has a long white beard that hangs over the edge of the quilt like he was Saint Nicholas or something. Who is he anyway?"

"That's Ambrose Franklin, ma'am, your future husband."

Chapter 3

Abby wanted to scream. "There must be some mistake," she whispered to Luke. "This man is ancient."

Luke nodded. "He turned ninety on his last birthday."

"Ninety! Then there must be a younger Ambrose Franklin around here somewhere. We came to the wrong farm."

"There's no mistake, ma'am. This is the only Ambrose Franklin that I ever heard of, and I have lived in the Texas hill country all my life." Luke turned to Ambrose. "Isn't that right, Mr. Franklin?"

The old man's eyes were closed, but when Luke said the words *Mr. Franklin*, he opened them and looked around. "Who goes there?"

"It's me, Mr. Franklin, Luke Conquest. I came to bring your medicine and a few other things." Luke laid the wooden box on the table by Ambrose's bed.

"Well, speak up, son, and say them words again." Ambrose cupped his hand behind his ear. "These old ears of mine ain't working right just now."

"I said that you are the only Ambrose Franklin in these parts."

"I reckon I am—least I ain't never heard of nobody else by that name. And all my kinfolk? Well, they live out in Cal-e-forn-e." He peered at Abby. "And who is this here young lady?"

"Forgive me," Luke said. "I should have introduced you sooner. This is Miss Willoughby—your bride-to-be—arrived on the stage today all the way from Georgia."

"Land sakes, girl. Get yourself over here so I can take a look at ya."

Abby inched toward the bed. She was sick to her stomach. As they say, she could lose her peaches all over the hardwood floor at any moment.

Ambrose glanced at Luke. "Would you mind handing me my specs, son, so I can see Miss Willoughby here? These days my eyes ain't working no better than them ears of mine."

Luke did as the old man requested.

Ambrose squinted at Abby through his glasses. "Well, my word. She's a beauty, ain't she? I 'spect she's about the prettiest young lady I ever seen. Ain't that so, Luke?"

"You said it, sir."

Abby noted the flash of mockery in Luke's eyes when he said those words. She smiled at Ambrose as if she hadn't noticed.

"Are you ready for us to get hitched up, girl?" Ambrose asked.

The word *no* shouted from Abby's brain.

The look in Luke's eyes said *sarcasm* in big letters. It was accompanied by a one-sided grin. Her face felt hot like it always did when she was upset or embarrassed.

Abby lifted her chin a notch. "Yes, I am ready. When will our wedding take place?"

She couldn't believe she'd agreed to go through with the marriage. She never would have if Luke hadn't set her off like he did. Now it was too late to back out gracefully. She swallowed.

Ambrose motioned to his frail body under the blue patchwork quilt. "I'm pretty laid up, as you can see. And the preacher—well, he and the missus ain't here. They are out of town; won't be back for another week. So I reckon we can have the weddin' the day after the preacher and the wife get home."

"Will the ceremony be held here or at the church in Frio Corners?" Abby asked.

"I reckon I'm thinking the church—that is, if Luke here would be willing to drive me there and be my best man."

Luke nodded.

"Then I guess it's settled."

Abby was still too stunned by everything that had happened to speak. The men might have settled things between themselves, but her stomach was anything but settled. A case of nausea had invaded her body shortly after she heard Ambrose snore for the first time and grew stronger when she saw that long white beard. The churning inside still bothered her. Nevertheless, she forced the edges of her mouth upward in a fake smile.

"You're mighty pretty, all right." Ambrose raised his head from the pillow, and bracing himself on one arm, he gazed at Abby. "I just wish we was already hitched. That way you could stay here in the cabin and help me get over this sick-spell of mine." He shook his head. "But it wouldn't be right—you being an unmarried girl and all—unless some older woman came with you. And that ain't likely. Why, I can't think of any but Luke's late mama willing to come out here and nurse me the way she did.

"Nellie Conquest was her name," he went on, "and Nellie and Luke and Luke's pa lived just across the fence line from me. Luke still does. Anyways, Mrs. Conquest would come over here every day to cook and clean. Now that she's gone to her reward, I ain't found no replacement—none but you, Miss Willoughby. It pains me to say it, but I reckon I won't be seeing you again 'til the wedding."

A sense of relief swept over her.

Abby had noticed a rundown barn out back when they first drove up. She should probably offer to stay in the barn until after the wedding so she could care for Ambrose and her sisters and brothers could get to know him before the wedding, but the children were looking forward to staying in that hotel and eating store-bought food. Was it wrong to give in to worldly pleasures once in a while?

The children would have plenty of time to get to know Ambrose after the wedding. Maybe Luke knew of a single boy willing to run and fetch for Ambrose until after the ceremony.

Abby looked down at Ambrose. "Mr. Conquest brought your medicine, and I'm going to fix you something good to eat." She patted the old man on the shoulder. "Do you like chicken soup, Mr. Franklin?"

"I reckon I do. And call me Ambrose, Abby, like you done in all them letters."

"All right. Do you have any chickens?"

"I got plenty in the coop out back."

Abby cringed. She'd never liked killing animals, and it probably showed in her face.

"I'll kill a hen and get it ready to cook," Luke put in. "You can give Mr. Franklin his medicine, Miss Willoughby, and straighten up the place a little. How does that sound?"

"Good. Thank you."

Luke left by the back door.

Before reaching for the medicine, Abby glanced out the window just as the children climbed down from the wagon. "Ambrose, it looks like my sisters and brothers are awake and heading this way. I'll introduce you to them and give you your medicine, and then I'll get them involved in something outside that will keep them occupied. It wouldn't do for them to bother you when you're trying to rest."

"Thank you, Abby."

"And while the children are playing the quiet game," she went on, "I'll fix supper and get the house in order."

It was late afternoon by the time the chores were done and the soup was warmed. They all had a supper of fresh milk, biscuits, and chicken soup, and then Abby, the children, and Luke rode back to town.

Abby still felt guilty for not offering to stay in the barn and serve as Ambrose's nurse, and from the smirk on Luke's face, maybe he also thought she should have agreed to do it. Something caused him to step back from her, and if there was another reason, she couldn't think what it might be.

She'd hoped that she and Luke would become friends. But he seemed cold to her now. As a result, she had nothing to say to him that Luke would care to hear during the long drive back to Frio Corners. He had nothing to say to her either. If Abby's siblings hadn't asked Luke one question after the other, the silence in his wagon might have been overwhelming.

Yet Luke glanced in her direction several times. The mocking tone in his smile filled her with embarrassment.

At last it was too dark to see anything but the full moon, peeking out between clouds so dark she wondered if they existed at all.

Luke probably expected her to run out on Ambrose now that she'd actually seen him. He likely expected Abby and the children to take the next stage out of town.

Well, she wouldn't—even if she had the money for their tickets—which she didn't. She had faults. Some said she was too bold and always jumping to conclusions, but she wasn't a quitter. Abby would marry Ambrose—just like she said she would.

So what if Ambrose wasn't what she expected? Abby shook her head. At ninety years of age, Ambrose was *nothing* like she expected.

Still, even Luke admitted that Ambrose was a good man, and according to his letters, Ambrose attended church services every time he could.

But Ambrose deceived her—no question about it—just like her stepfather did. He failed to mention in his letters some important facts about his life. Wouldn't that make him guilty of the sin of omission?

Her late mother warned her never to trust men. She should have listened. Abby should have asked questions, and she should have demanded that Ambrose tell her more about himself. His date of birth would have been a good place to start.

The Bible said that Christians must forgive others if they hoped to be forgiven. Jesus said, "Father, forgive them; for they know not what they do." Abby needed to forgive Ambrose and also Luke. But how could she ever forgive Gary?

Gary. She wouldn't think about him now.

And Luke didn't like her as he seemed to at first. Perhaps he doubted her integrity, and Abby could see no way to change that.

When they finally arrived at the hotel, Luke got out of the wagon and helped her down from it. He still hadn't said more than two words to her since they left the cabin, but at least he cared enough to act like a true gentleman.

Lanterns hung from the eaves of the hotel, creating enough light to make it possible for her to actually see people and objects. The children jumped down with an air of excitement, as if they couldn't wait to go inside. Abby didn't move an inch after Luke set her feet on the ground.

"Thank you for your kindness, Mr. Conquest. I really appreciate you taking us all the way out to the farm to meet Ambrose. And someday I hope to return the favor."

"How?"

Abby frowned. "How what?"

"How do you plan to return the favor?"

"Oh, that." Abby casually tossed her head back and wiped a curl from her forehead. "I'll bake you a cake or a pan of cookies after Ambrose and I are married. You do like cookies, don't you?"

He nodded. "So you're really going to marry him?"

"Of course. Why else would I have traveled all this way?"

He shook his head. "Well if that doesn't beat all." He glared at her. "Good night, Miss Willoughby. Guess I won't be seeing you again until the day of the wedding, but it wouldn't be right not to wish you good luck. You're going to need it." He turned and started to walk off.

"Wait," she said.

He stopped and turned.

"Can you suggest a young man willing to go out and stay with Ambrose until the wedding? You know the people around here. I don't."

"He needs help all right, and I've been trying to find someone. A rich old man like Mr. Franklin could die on you—before you ever say, 'I do.'" Without another word, he climbed up into his wagon and drove off.

Luke waved the leather quirt over the horses' heads. The animals moved forward at a fast pace.

He sensed that Abby was watching him, and he wanted to turn around and look at her—see her lovely face and form one more time. But he wouldn't.

Luke guided the team through the main street of town and onto a set of bumpy ruts.

Miss Willoughby wasn't the princess he thought her to be—not by a long shot. And why did she smile all the time—as if she didn't have a care in the world? If she wasn't already an actress who performed on a stage, she should become one. Abby would outshine them all.

Luke yawned. He should have spent the night at the hotel in town. He was so sleepy, he couldn't keep his eyes from closing on their own, and the horses looked exhausted. If that wasn't bad enough, the moon had dropped behind the clouds again. He could barely see his hand in front of his face.

He slowed, turning the wagon around.

Sure, he might see Miss Willoughby at breakfast in the morning at the hotel. But what was she to him? Abby was an engaged woman and an opportunist—if not an actress and a gold digger.

Still, she had to be the prettiest gold digger in the state of Texas.

Chapter 4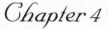

S ue Ann Reynolds went to the hotel early the next morning to see if she could learn the identity of the young woman with Luke on the previous day. The hotel was also new, and she'd heard the interior was worth seeing.

The hotel clerk was busy reading a letter of some kind and didn't look up when she came in. As she stood waiting to talk to him, thoughts of what happened on the previous day flooded her mind.

She'd just left the general store and was strolling in front of the café when Luke Conquest escorted a tall golden-haired girl and several children toward his wagon, parked across the street from the hotel. Sue hid in the shadows because she didn't want Luke to catch her spying on them.

Sue Ann had been in love with Luke Conquest all her life. Now that he was finally talking to her after church on Sundays, this stranger came to town. She wondered who the young woman was and what she was doing in Frio Corners.

Maybe she was Luke's cousin from out of town. She'd never heard that Luke had a sweetheart. But what if he did and the golden-haired girl was the one? These questions needed to be answered in order for Sue Ann's dream to come true—the dream that said she would become Mrs. Luke Conquest one day.

She'd also dreamed that someday Luke would take her arm as he took the arm of the young woman. Luke and the woman had gone inside the café as if she were special to him, leaving the children behind in the wagon.

Sue Ann had considered walking over and questioning the children to discover the woman's identity. Who would know?

"May I help you, miss?" the hotel's desk clerk asked.

Sue Ann was so lost in her own thoughts that his question startled her for a moment. But it also forced her back to the present.

She had to say something but had no idea what to say. She'd hoped to come up with a reason to ask him about Luke and the young woman without being obvious. But so far, that hadn't happened.

Then someone said, "Sue Ann? I mean, Miss Reynolds."

She turned. "Luke. What are you doing here?"

"I might ask you the same question."

Sue Ann had to think fast—come up with a reason for being there that made sense. "I've—I've wanted to see the inside of this hotel since it opened," she said. "This morning I decided to come inside and finally see it for myself."

Luke grinned. "I came here yesterday, and one of the reasons was to see the inside of this hotel."

She returned his smile as a thought burst forth. *Was the other reason to meet the golden-haired girl?* But she said, "It's really nice in here, isn't it?"

"Yes, it is."

The golden-haired girl came out of the same door from which Luke had just emerged. Did this mean that—? No, it was wrong to think such thoughts. Still. . .

"Miss Willoughby." Luke had smiled as he and Sue Ann had their brief conversation, but his smile disappeared as he gazed at the golden-haired girl. "Meet Miss Sue Ann Reynolds. She is our church organist and an old friend from school."

If Sue Ann could have fallen through the floor of the hotel and disappeared forever, she would have gladly done it. A Christian shouldn't have the kind of thoughts she was having, and she knew it. Miss Willoughby still stood in the doorway, smiling as if she really meant it. The word *Restaurant* was written in big letters over the door.

So the two had breakfast together. But what went on before that? And where were the children? Perhaps they were rented out to Mrs. Zack, the owner of the café, or some other unsuspecting person.

"I'm glad to make your acquaintance, I'm sure," Sue Ann finally said in a monotone.

"I'm glad to meet you, too, and I hope we can become friends."

Friends? Sue Ann doubted that would ever happen, but it was nice of Miss Willoughby to suggest it.

Without looking at either of them, Luke stepped up to the hotel desk. "I would like to check out, Mr. Pearson."

The desk clerk was looking down. But all at once he looked up. "Right away, Mr. Conquest. Anything else?"

"Yes. Put Miss Willoughby's breakfast on my tab, please."

"Very well. And what about the children? Did they eat, too?"

"No, they are still sleeping—as far as I know."

Sue Ann knew she was blushing because she felt heat bursting from both cheeks. Yet Miss Willoughby continued to smile as if nothing unusual had happened. If Miss Willoughby wasn't a fallen woman, she was close to it.

Luke was still paying his bill, and this might be a good time for Sue Ann to leave.

"I guess I better go now, Miss—Miss Willoughby. I'm glad I met you and all, and please, tell Luke it was nice to see him, too."

Miss Willoughby's perpetual smile increased sevenfold. "I will do just as you asked me to. And I hope you have a nice day."

For Sue Ann, a nice day was not a possibility. But at least she was leaving the hotel before something even more embarrassing took place.

As Sue Ann crossed the street to the café, she kept thinking about all she'd seen and heard. Luke Conquest was not the Christian man she'd always thought him to be. Yet she still wanted to marry him.

She'd planned to have breakfast at the café. Now she would go to the church and practice her songs for Sunday. She didn't feel like eating, and playing the organ always cheered her up.

Luke noticed when Sue Ann headed for the church. He didn't want to talk to her. At the same time, he felt guilty for having such thoughts. Sue Ann was a nice Christian girl and a pretty one at that.

But he had no romantic feelings for her. Clearly Sue Ann had feelings for him, and if he ever had a secret admirer, it would be her.

Secret admirer. Luke barely knew Abby. Yet he admired her more than he was willing to admit. Was it possible for a man to love a woman at first sight?

When he could no longer see Sue Ann's green dress and matching bonnet, he stepped out of the hotel lobby and onto the stoop outside. He planned to stop by Jim's blacksmith shop, and he would need to pick up the mare he'd bought from Pastor Johnson before he left town.

Nobody could break that wild and spirited animal. But Luke intended not only to train her but tame her—no matter how long it took.

He crossed the rocky street and stepped up onto the covered walkway. He needed to get his town business over and done with and get on out to the ranch. Ordinarily, he would have completed half a day's work by now.

Jim Turner was Luke's best friend, and he'd been helping Luke find a single young man willing to nurse Mr. Franklin back to health. If he'd found someone, Luke could drop him off at the Franklin farm on his way home.

He thought of Miss Willoughby again. Memories of her seldom left him now. Luke liked her. At the same time, he didn't trust her. Nevertheless, he'd wanted to invite her to sit at his table at breakfast that morning. She probably expected it. Yet her friendly smile told that she wasn't offended one bit when his invitation never came.

Well, it wouldn't look right—them sitting at the same table and Miss Willoughby being a betrothed woman and all. Mrs. Eastland was clearing some of the other tables as they ate eggs and bacon, and at least *she* knew they sat at separate tables. Still, people in small towns like Frio Corners talked, and gossip at a time like this was something none of them wanted.

The entry to the blacksmith shop was propped open. Jim Turner had his broad back to the door, hammering a piece of metal against an anvil. At six feet, four inches, Jim Turner was a giant of a man, and some, back in their schooldays, called him names like Washtub and Fat Boy. Jim was the biggest man in Frio Corners, and in Luke's opinion, he also had the kindest heart. "Mornin', Jim." Luke paused in the doorway before going in. "How's business?"

"Slow." Jim turned around and smiled. "What brings you into town so early in the day?"

"I wanted to talk to you. Have you found anybody willing to stay out at Mr. Franklin's farm and help him out? I brought him some new medicine yesterday, and he's still looking poorly. What he needs is somebody willing to stay day and night. I stay some, but not all the time."

"I know." Jim laid down his hammer and moved forward, lessening the space separating them. "And I think I might have found someone."

"Who?"

"Robert Benton. You remember him, Sue Ann's cousin. The boy's going to school back east come January—says he wants to be a doctor. But he needs a job now."

"He sounds fine," Luke replied, "but Mr. Franklin never pays folks much. You know what a tightwad he is, and him with all that money tucked away somewhere."

"Robert knows how Mr. Franklin is with money. He's mostly lookin' for experience helping sick people."

"So when can he start?"

"Today, I reckon." Jim's gaze moved from Luke to the tub by the anvil.

Luke thought he looked nervous.

"I guess I'll go on over to his house then and tell him to pack his things."

"Yeah, that's what you should do all right." Then Jim didn't say anything for a long moment. "Seen Sue Ann lately?" Jim finally asked.

"I saw her awhile ago over at the hotel. Looked to me like she was headed over to the church."

"Probably went to practice her songs for Sunday."

"That's what I figured, too."

Luke had known Jim long enough to know when there was something he was itching to say. Getting Jim to actually say it was another matter. Luke just wished Jim would spit it out and get it over with. He'd wasted enough of the day already.

Jim shrugged, putting both his hands in the pockets of his overalls. "Are you planning to take Sue Ann to the shindig here in town on Sunday?"

"The barbecue over at the church?"

"Yeah." Jim looked down as if he were embarrassed to say more. "So are ya taking her?"

"Hadn't planned to, no." Luke held in a grin. "So why don't you take her, Jim?"

"Me?" Jim shook his head. "A pretty girl like that wouldn't want to go out with someone like me."

"How do you know 'til you ask her?"

"Naw. I can't do nothing like that. I wouldn't know what to say."

"Just say, 'Sue Ann, I would like to take you to the shindig at the church on Sunday. How about it?'"

"What if she says no?"

"Say, 'Thank you kindly for considering my invitation, and I hope you'll go out with me some other time.' Then you walk off."

"No, Luke. I couldn't do that. She'd laugh at me."

"Has Sue Ann ever laughed at you in her entire life?"

"No, I can't say that she ever has."

"Then she wouldn't laugh at you this time either. Now, I'm going to walk out of here and go over to Robert Benton's house—see if he will come work for Mr. Franklin. As soon as I leave, I want you to close your shop, put a BE BACK IN AN HOUR sign on your door, and head on over to the church. Do you promise to do that?"

"I'll think about it."

"Think fast, Jim. Neither of us is getting any younger. My papa and mama were halfway to the altar by the time they were my age, and I don't even have a steady girl."

Luke hung around outside after he left the blacksmith shop to see if Jim would do as Luke suggested. He'd almost given up when Jim suddenly left the shop and headed out.

He was about to go on over to Robert's when he happened to glance toward his wagon. Someone was seated where Abby sat on the previous day, and it sure wasn't Robert. What was Abby doing there? He hurried over to find out.

"Miss Willoughby. What are you doing here?"

"Waiting for you."

"What do you mean, 'Waiting for me'?"

"The children and I are going out to that farm Ambrose owns to help him out a bit," she explained. "And we will need a ride in order to get there. But this time you won't have to bring us back to the hotel. We'll spend the night in Ambrose's barn."

"You'll do no such thing."

Her blue eyes widened. "I beg your pardon."

"I said, 'You'll do no such thing.' People talk in a small town like this. It wouldn't be proper for a young unmarried woman and young children to stay out at the farm without a chaperone. Besides, I think I've found a young man willing to do the job—just as you suggested. In fact, I am on my way to see him now."

"And if he refuses to take the job, what will you do then, Mr. Conquest?"

"I'll find someone else. Robert Benton isn't the only out-of-work young man in Frio Corners."

"Is that his name?" Abby slanted her head to one side, causing a cascade of blond curls to fall on her shoulder. "Robert Benton."

"Yes, and he's a fine boy, too—plans to become a doctor. We'll be lucky if we—if I can hire him for Ambrose."

She started to climb out of the wagon.

"Where are you going?" he asked.

"Back to the hotel." She climbed down from the wagon without his help. "The children will be waking up soon. I'll need to be there so we can all—so we can all do nothing together." She started to walk off.

"What do you mean, ma'am?"

"The excitement of living in a hotel will soon wear off," she explained, "and then the children will want to go out and play. Where do children play who live in one room of a very nice hotel? There would be places to play on Ambrose's farm. But here?" She shrugged.

"Maybe I could help," Luke said. Then he wished he'd kept his mouth shut. He was already in too deep with this young woman and didn't need to get in any deeper.

She stopped and turned. "Help? How could you possibly do that? You live miles from here on that ranch of yours."

"That's true, but. . .I'll be driving in to church on Sunday. I feed my animals before daylight. I can spend the whole day in town if I want to. So I could pick you and the children up before church and. . ."

"And what?" she asked.

He thought of the church barbecue. He hadn't intended to go. He'd planned to leave as soon as the service ended and grab something from the café. But now? Maybe he would attend the church social after all—for the sake of the children, of course. Poor little kids—penned up in that hotel like that. He owed it to Mr. Franklin to see that his future family was cared for until he could do it himself.

"There's a barbecue on the grounds after church on Sunday," Luke said. "We could all have our noon meal there. Later, I could drive you and the children out to visit Mr. Franklin, and after supper, I could drive you back to the hotel."

"But what about your ranch, Mr. Conquest? You need to be there early on Monday morning, and if you take us all the way out to Ambrose's farm, you might not feel like getting up early the next morning."

"I have a ranch hand helping me some now. So I have more free time than I once did. I should be able to take you and the children out to visit Mr. Franklin and still get home in time to do my chores the next morning."

"Well, if you're sure it wouldn't cause you any trouble, I guess the children and I will accept your kind offer. Otherwise, I doubt we would see Ambrose again until the day of the wedding."

"Oh, yes, the wedding," Luke said without interest. "When is it?"

"We will be married as soon as possible after Pastor and Mrs. Johnson return."

"That's what I thought."

He glanced across the street. Tommy, the older of Abby's two brothers, stood on the stoop in front of the hotel.

"Abby!" Tommy shouted, "come take us to breakfast. I'm hungry."

"I'm coming," Abby called back, hands on her hips.

Her face flushed, and Luke thought she looked plenty disgusted. She probably hadn't liked it when Tommy shouted at her from across the street. But then she smiled like someone had pushed a button or something.

"I'll stop by before nine on Sunday morning and drive you and the children to church," Luke said. "Is a little before nine all right with you, ma'am?"

"A little before nine will be fine."

Miss Willoughby was beautiful, all right, but she sure was a hard woman to figure out. But mostly, she belonged to someone else. He would need to remember that.

He stood there watching until Abby and Tommy went inside the hotel. Then he set out for Robert Benton's house.

All at once he saw a flash of green. Sue Ann and Mrs. Peabody were standing in front of the café talking. Were they just chatting—or gossiping? Everybody knew that Mrs. Peabody was the biggest gossip in Frio Corners.

Chapter 5

Luke waited while Robert Benton packed and told his parents good-bye. Then Luke bought supplies at the general store and loaded them in the wagon. He had two more stops before returning to the ranch.

He parked his wagon in front of Pastor Johnson's home. There were several houses on that street, each with big yards. The minister had a stable behind his house with pastureland behind it. After talking to the young man who was taking care of the pastor's animals until he returned, Luke tied the spirited young mare he now owned to the back of his wagon. He would drop Robert off at the Franklin farm, and then he would head on home.

Luke smiled internally. On Sunday he would drive Abby and the children to church, and they would attend the church social afterward—to help out Mr. Franklin, of course.

The next day after a noon meal in the hotel dining room, Abby and the children were about to go to their room when she noticed an elderly couple talking to the desk clerk. Somehow she guessed they were Pastor and Mrs. Johnson, and when they hurried toward her, she knew for sure.

The old woman moved ahead of the man, and the nimbleness of her movements and the warmth in her eyes when she smiled reminded Abby of someone much younger.

"Well, hello." The older woman offered her hand in what Abby hoped was friendship. "We are the Johnsons. Are you Miss Willoughby?"

"Yes." Abby shook the woman's hand.

"That's what the desk clerk told us. We had to cut our trip short, and I'm so glad we did since you are here."

Deep wrinkles creased the faces of both the pastor and Mrs. Johnson, and only a thin layer of gray hair remained on the pastor's head. His wife's face was almost as pasty white as her hair. Yet there was something charming about Mrs. Johnson—beautiful in the true sense. The pastor seemed nice, too, but more reserved with worry lines on his forehead. Was something bothering this man?

Abby introduced them to the children by name, and Mrs. Johnson gave each of them a hug.

What kind and loving people, Abby thought.

"You can't know how happy Andrew and I are to see you and the children," Mrs. Johnson said. "The desk clerk told us that you visited with Mr. Franklin."

Abby nodded. "Mr. Luke Conquest drove us there."

"But you are so young," the pastor said, almost in a whisper, and then he shook his head. "Then you've thought this through and plan to marry Mr. Franklin, regardless of his age?"

Abby's jaw tightened, and she looked down at her shoes. "Yes, sir."

"I see."

He will think less of me now. Yet she glanced up and smiled.

Then the pastor did. "So when is the wedding?" he asked.

"Andrew," Mrs. Johnson interrupted, "I don't have time to prepare for a wedding right now. I'll need to concentrate on the doings on the church grounds after the service on Sunday. Had you forgotten about the barbecue?" She turned to Abby. "Something came up, and they had to change the original date. So that's why we came back early."

The pastor gazed at his wife. "So when should the wedding be, my dear?"

"I don't know." Mrs. Johnson paused. "I'll let you know when I do." She turned to Abby and smiled. "Until then, I want all five of you to move over to our house. We have a big backyard for the children to play in, and I can use an extra hand to help with the preparations for Sunday."

Tommy smiled. "Big backyard, did you say? Is there a tree we can climb?"

"Yes, young man, and one of the trees has a rope swing dangling from it. The children in the neighborhood love that swing. I think y'all will like it, too. But there is only one swing, so you will have to take turns."

"Oh, we will." Tommy looked over at his brother and sisters. "Won't we?"

The other children nodded. The old couple laughed.

"We are so glad you are finally here," Pastor Johnson said. "Strangers are always exciting in a small community like ours. Why, we had barely stepped out of the stagecoach when Mrs. Peabody rushed right over and told us you were here. She's a member of our church."

"We haven't eaten," Mrs. Johnson interrupted. "Have you, Miss Willoughby?"

"Yes, we have."

"We will need to grab something to eat at the hotel before we go home, and Mrs. Eastland bakes delicious pies. Why don't you and the children eat pie while the pastor and I have lunch?"

Tommy nodded his approval, and when he clapped his hands, the other children did, too.

After the meal, they set out for the Johnson home, leaving the trunks and suitcases to be picked up later.

Abby squinted against the afternoon sun, taking in the trees and other plants as they walked along. The morning was cool but not cold, and the air was flavored with pleasant scents Abby was not familiar with. The woman on the train had said that perfume was made from some of the local trees in the area. Abby wondered if the fragrances she smelled came from some of them.

The children moved ahead of the adults and were practically running by the time they reached the white picket fence that surrounded the Johnsons' two-story home. No sooner had they entered the yard gate than the children scattered, heading for the backyard. Abby assumed they were looking for the swing Mrs. Johnson mentioned.

"You ladies go on in the house," the pastor said. "I need to drive my wagon back to the hotel and pick up that trunk Miss Willoughby mentioned and all the suitcases, including ours."

"You go right ahead, Andrew," Mrs. Johnson said. "I'll show Miss Willoughby around the house, and then I have to clean this place. The house has to be plenty dirty by now."

"I'll help you with the cleaning," Abby volunteered.

"No, dear. You're our guest."

"That's even more of a reason I should help. What all do you have to do?"

"I need to start a wash for one thing. We dirtied up a mess of clothes while we were gone on our trip."

"Then I'll do the sweeping. Where do you keep the broom?"

Mrs. Johnson laughed. "In the broom closet. I'll show you where that closet is after I show you your room and where the children will sleep."

Abby followed Mrs. Johnson up the stairs.

The older woman indicated a door to their right. "Your room is here." She opened the door. "We call it the Sunshine Room. The windows are on the south and on the east, facing the morning sun, and the curtains and the patchwork quilt are both yellow." She pointed to a small chest of drawers. "You can keep your things in there and use the desk if you have letters to write. I always leave writing paper, pen, and ink in the desk. Feel free to use them."

"The room is lovely," Abby said. "And the material in the curtains is so thin and delicate; I can see right through it. How did you know that yellow is my favorite color?"

"It's my favorite, too." Mrs. Johnson smiled, pushing her spectacles closer to the bridge of her nose. "And I'm glad you like your room."

Abby brushed her hand across the top of the quilt, and then she picked up the edge of it to inspect the stitching. "Did you make this beautiful quilt?"

Mrs. Johnson blushed. "Such as it is."

"You are too modest, ma'am. The handwork is excellent."

"Speaking of handwork, I need to get that wash started. So come on now and let me show you the girls' bedroom. It's one door down from this room. The boys will be across the hall from the girls."

Mrs. Johnson showed Abby the children's bedrooms and the location of the broom closet. Then Abby went outside to check on her brothers and sisters.

They appeared to be taking turns swinging. Since nobody was pushing or fighting as far as Abby could see, she went back inside and grabbed the broom. Later, she drifted into the parlor and stood at a window, looking out at the street in front of the house. She wanted to get acquainted with her new surroundings.

All at once, Sue Ann and a middle-aged woman in a purple bonnet walked by, studying the Johnson home as if they were searching for something or someone. They walked to the end of the block, but instead of going inside one of the houses, they turned around and strolled slowly in front of the house where Abby was staying for the second time. Then they stopped in front of the house as if the Johnson home was a good place to have a conversation.

The strong scent of Mrs. Johnson's flowery perfume announced that she had entered the parlor. "Oh, here you are, Miss Willoughby." Mrs. Johnson joined her at the window. "Why, look who is walking by—Miss Sue Ann Reynolds and Mrs. Peabody. Miss Reynolds is about your age, and Mrs. Peabody's husband owns the general store here in Frio Corners."

"I've already met Miss Reynolds, but I haven't met Mrs. Peabody yet."

"You'll meet her at church on Sunday. But how do you know Miss Reynolds?"

"She paid a visit to the hotel while I was staying there."

Mrs. Johnson's forehead wrinkled. "Was Mrs. Peabody with her?"

"No. At least I didn't see her."

"Well, then." Mrs. Johnson smiled. "Let's go over to the divan and sit awhile. I think a little chat before I go in and cook supper would be nice."

The two women in front of the house took one long look at the Johnson home and continued on down the street toward the main part of town. Abby and Mrs. Johnson moved over to the divan and sat down.

"There are so many questions I want to ask you, Abby, and some of them are downright silly, I guess."

Abby tensed, wondering what questions she wanted to talk about, and then she forced a smile. "Ask anything you wish."

Mrs. Johnson cleared her throat. "You said your real name was Abigail, and that's such a pretty name. So is Abby. But I've never known anyone named Abigail—except the Abigail mentioned in the Bible, of course. So I just wondered how you got that name."

Abby released a deep breath. "My mama is dead now, but I'm named for her mama—my grandmother, Abigail Grant."

The woman looked at Abby with warmth and compassion shining in her gray eyes. "I'm sorry for your loss. Do you have any people left in Georgia?"

Abby shook her head, trying not to let the pain in her heart show on her face. "Besides my brothers and sisters, there was only my mother, my grandmother, and my—my father, and they are all gone. It's only the children and me now."

"I see."

Nobody spoke for a long time. Mrs. Johnson rubbed the edge of one eye as if a tear might be hiding there. Evidently, Mrs. Johnson was tenderhearted, and somehow Abby had touched her heart.

At last she said, "Did I mention, Miss Willoughby, that we're serving barbecue and pinto beans at the meal on the grounds after church on Sunday? I was hoping you'd serve the beans?"

"Of course, I'll be glad to serve the beans or whatever else you might want me to do."

"There will be lots of chores," Mrs. Johnson went on, "and we'll need to be at the church as soon after daylight on Sunday morning as we can. Is this all right with you, dear?"

Sunday. Her heart pulled into a hard knot. Luke was picking up Abby and the children at the hotel on Sunday and driving them to church. How could she have forgotten?

Mrs. Johnson frowned. "Abby, are you all right, dear? You seemed so far away for a moment."

Abby blinked. "Forgive me. I daydream from time to time. But Mr. Conquest was kind enough to drive the children and me out to the Franklin place the day we arrived on the stagecoach and also promised to drive us to church on Sunday. It would be awful if he drove up to the hotel to get us on Sunday morning and discovered we left the hotel without telling him."

"Throw that worry in the garbage can and set fire to it." Mrs. Johnson nodded as if to confirm her last statement. "My husband is a very trustworthy person. If I tell Andrew to leave a message for Luke at the main desk of the hotel, he will. So go up and write that message. Andrew could be home at any moment, and as I said, there is writing paper, pen, and ink in the top drawer of the desk in the Sunshine Room."

Abby went upstairs, wrote her letter, and read it over to see how it sounded. Then she folded it in half and went downstairs.

In the entry hall, she heard voices that seemed to be coming from the kitchen, and she went in that direction. As she grew closer, it became clear that Pastor Johnson had returned with her trunk and suitcases and that he and Mrs. Johnson were talking in the kitchen.

Abby froze. To listen in on their conversation was not something Abby was willing to do. Should she let it be known that she was about to go into the kitchen? Maybe she should call out, cough real loud, fake a bout with sneezing, or simply turn around and go back to her room.

As she stood there deciding, she heard Mrs. Johnson say, "Andrew, did you hear what else Mrs. Peabody said right after we stepped down from that stage today?"

"No, what else?"

"I don't know where this garbage came from. But Mrs. Peabody said that Miss Willoughby came here to marry old Mr. Franklin because he is rich and that Abby must have known he had part interest in that silver mine."

"The one near Silver Mine Pass?"

"Yes, and that's not all. Mrs. Peabody implied that Luke and Miss Willoughby committed adultery right there in the Frio Corners Hotel on the night she arrived."

Committed adultery? Every muscle in Abby's body stiffened against this outright lie.

"I don't believe a word of it," the pastor said.

"Neither do I, and I feel so sorry for Luke and Miss Willoughby. Should we tell them what people are saying?"

"Absolutely not. We must love and protect them instead."

Abby raced up the stairs to her room, falling on her bed and sobbing until there were no tears left. Had all the wicked gossipmongers that had plagued her in Georgia followed her to Texas?

She would need to give Mrs. Johnson Luke's letter as she promised to do. And she and Luke could never be friends now. She must stay away from him—for her good and for his.

Chapter 6

An hour later Abby went down to help Mrs. Johnson with supper, and she took Luke's letter with her.

"Oh, there you are." Mrs. Johnson had been washing dishes, but she turned around, wiping her hands on her apron. "Is that the letter?"

"Yes, ma'am." Abby reached out and handed her Luke's letter.

Mrs. Johnson nodded, putting the letter in the pocket of her white apron. She was smiling, but it slowly faded. "Are you all right, dear? Your eyes are a little—"

"Red? That's because I've been crying. But I will be fine." Abby manufactured the best replica of a smile ever. "It's not easy moving all the way across the country and knowing that I will never go back to Georgia—even for a visit. But I will get over it, in time."

In her mind, Abby hadn't lied. One of the reasons she was crying was because she'd moved far from the land of her childhood. It just wasn't the main reason.

Mrs. Johnson put her arms around Abby in a grandmotherly hug. "Just so you know, Andrew and I already love you and the children, and that love will only grow in the days and weeks and years ahead."

Abby wanted to hug the woman back, and someday soon she would—just not today. If all her other problems weren't enough, she would soon marry a ninety-year-old man.

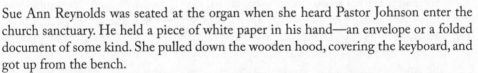

Sue Ann Reynolds was seated at the organ when she heard Pastor Johnson enter the church sanctuary. He held a piece of white paper in his hand—an envelope or a folded document of some kind. She pulled down the wooden hood, covering the keyboard, and got up from the bench.

The pastor hadn't noticed her yet, but even half hidden behind the organ, she could see that he looked refreshed and well since his vacation and more joyful than she had seen him in a long time. The visit to San Antonio must have been good for his spirit as well as his health.

"Welcome home, Pastor. How was your vacation?"

He looked up and smiled. "Miss Reynolds, what a nice surprise. The trip was wonderful, but it's good to be home."

"How about the pain in your back?" she asked.

"All gone, thank you. In fact, I felt so good that I walked all the way to the church instead of riding my horse like I normally do. The late afternoon air was so cool and

127

refreshing, and I love to listen to the crunch of autumn leaves under my feet. The fall season inspires me with all these colors, and I love to hike down roads this time of the year. It recharges my creative side and makes sermon writing easier." He took a deep breath, a contented smile on his lips. Then he seemed to remember his purpose. "I need to drop a letter off at the hotel," he said. "But I stopped by the church first to pick up any mail that came in while I was away."

"You shouldn't overdo, Pastor. We need you here at the church. Let me drop that letter off for you. It's on my way home."

"You make me sound like an old man."

"It's just that your congregation cares about you, sir."

"I know. But I enjoy walking now. It makes me feel better."

She nodded. "Walking is very good for your health, but if you don't mind me saying so, it is a new hobby for you. You need to take it slow at first. Let me drop that letter off for you. I insist." She reached out as if she expected him to hand her the letter.

After a moment, he did.

On the way to the hotel, Sue Ann unfolded the message and read it to pass the time. She'd expected the message to have something to do with church business. She never expected it to be a message from Abby to Luke Conquest.

She thought again about the possibility that Luke and Abby spent a night together. She couldn't stop thinking about it, and she should never have shared her assumptions with Mrs. Peabody. But it was too late to take back her words. Mrs. Peabody had probably told a lot of other people by now—perhaps destroying any chance Sue Ann might have had of marrying Luke.

Instead of going to the hotel, she went straight to the garbage can in the alley behind the café. She stood there a moment, clutching the letter as if it were glued to her hand. Then she let it drop.

Guilt scorched Sue Ann's brain as well as her heart as she walked away. She knew she'd done wrong. Was it too late to make amends?

She raced back to the alley. Some distance away, she smelled smoke. Mrs. Zack, the café owner, stood by the garbage can, watching as it burned. Sue Ann turned around and hurried away. She could only hope that Mrs. Zack hadn't seen her.

The sin of bearing what might have been a false witness against a neighbor was wicked enough. Now Sue Ann must add more sins to the list. Was it possible to stop a trail of evil deeds once they were started?

If only she could sit and visit with Jim for a minute. He said he knew the Lord personally, and just talking to the kindhearted blacksmith always made her feel better. But Jim could turn away from her if he ever learned what she had done.

Early on Sunday morning, Luke parked his wagon in front of the hotel and went inside—right up to the main desk. Mr. Pearson had his back to him, so Luke rang the bell.

The desk clerk turned around, and Luke said, "Miss Willoughby and the children are expecting me. Will you let them know I am here?"

"I'm sorry. They checked out of the hotel the day Pastor and Mrs. Johnson got back to town. Miss Willoughby and the children are living with them now."

Luke paused. "I see. Did she leave me a note?"

"Not that I know of."

The muscles in Luke's jaw tightened. "If you see Miss Willoughby again, please tell her that I got her message. She will know what I mean."

Then he turned and headed for the door.

Mrs. Peabody was standing in front of the hotel when he came out, and she was the last person he wanted to see at that moment.

"Oh, Mr. Conquest," she said. "I was hoping to see you this morning."

He nodded politely. "Mrs. Peabody."

"Have you heard the news?" she asked.

What news? Luke thought, but he didn't say anything.

"No, you couldn't have heard because I just heard it myself. Anyway, Miss Willoughby and old Mr. Franklin are getting married this morning over at the church after the Sunday service. Robert Benton drove him into town a while ago, and Mr. Franklin insisted on being married today come hell or high water. I guess everybody is invited. Are you going?"

"No. I won't be going to church this morning. I need to get back to the ranch. So if you will excuse me." He tried to go around her. "I'm kind of in a hurry."

The woman frowned. "Well, of course. Don't let me stop you."

"I don't plan to," he said under his breath.

<hr />

Abby climbed out of bed on Sunday morning, thinking she would attend a service at the church and then serve pinto beans at a church gathering. How could she have known that Robert Benton would drive Ambrose in from the farm before the service began or that later she would stand beside a chair with wheels on it, waiting for Pastor Johnson to say the words that would make Ambrose Franklin her lawfully wedded husband?

The church barbecue became a wedding reception. A big man named Jim served the pinto beans; she didn't know his last name. Sue Ann Reynolds stood right beside him, serving the avocado salad.

Ambrose and Abby were seated in chairs at the reception, side by side at a long table. Only his chair had wheels. She looked around for Luke but didn't see him. He hadn't attended church that morning either. If Luke had kept his promise to Ambrose and stood up with him during the wedding ceremony, maybe she wouldn't feel so lost right now. Luke's mere presence always lifted her spirits.

How long must she keep her deepest secret—that she was in love with Luke Conquest? Her throat tightened. Forever, she supposed.

Even before the scandal broke, she'd planned to stay as far from Luke as possible. But why did that have to mean marriage to Ambrose Franklin? Would the torture ever end? Maybe she should never have left Georgia.

Abby knew the Bible said the Lord knows a person's true thoughts and feelings, and she was ashamed of hers. Abby loved Luke Conquest and always would. But nobody else would ever know.

She saw a flash of movement. Ambrose fell forward. Horror choked her, and her mouth opened as if it had a brain of its own. *His face is in the pinto beans.*

Abby screamed.

Luke was trying to read his Bible and forget that he didn't attend the wedding. He'd told Mrs. Peabody at the hotel that he wasn't going to the wedding, and he didn't. Still, he felt guilty for not standing up for Ambrose during the ceremony as he had promised.

He heard a knock at the door. Luke put down the Bible and opened the door. Robert stood in the doorway; his face was as white as a baby sheep after a good washing.

"I drove Mr. Franklin to church this morning just like he told me to, sir, and. . . and. . ."

"What happened, Robert? Is Mr. Franklin all right?"

"No, sir." Tears gathered in the young man's eyes, and one or two slipped down his cheeks.

"Come on in, Robert, and sit yourself down."

Robert nodded and did as he was told. "I knew Mr. Franklin was sick, sir—sicker than normal. I wanted to take him to see Dr. Carter. But he made me drive him to church instead, and he and Miss Willoughby got hitched."

"Married?"

"Yes, and then Mr. Franklin fell into a bowl of pinto bean soup."

"He what?"

"He's dead, sir."

Luke stiffened. "Oh, no!"

"The doctor said that Mr. Franklin's heart wasn't working right."

A deep sadness started in Luke's heart, spreading throughout his body. "How is Mrs. Franklin doing?" he finally asked.

"She's all right, but it happened so fast. Like I said, I knew Mr. Franklin wasn't feeling well, and I wanted to take him straight to see the doctor. But I never expected something like this. I sure don't think Mrs. Franklin expected it. It was like she was taken aback and having a hard time believing that her new husband was dead."

"How about the children?" Luke asked. "How are they doing?"

"Fine." Robert cleared his throat. "They really didn't know Mr. Franklin yet, and you know kids. Bad things just run right off their backs like stock dip off cattle after they walk through a dipping vat."

Despite the bad news, Robert's comment made Luke smile. "Are you planning to drive back to town tonight?"

"Yes, sir, but I came horseback."

"I'll need to saddle my horse. We can ride along together."

Luke spent the night at the hotel in town. The next morning, he barged into the pastor's office without knocking.

"I came as soon as I could," Luke said breathlessly. "When's the funeral?"

"This afternoon." The pastor hesitated for a moment. "I reckon you knew Brother Franklin better than anyone. I was hoping you would say a few words at the service. Are you willing?"

"I'd be glad to."

"I kind of figured you would." The pastor indicated the wooden armchair in front of his desk. "Please, sit down. I have things I need to tell you."

Luke sat down, waiting to hear what else the pastor would say.

"Maybe you don't know about all the gossip that's gone on around here since Miss Willoughby, I mean Mrs. Franklin, came to town. But now that Ambrose is gone, I'm obliged to tell you because you are being gossiped about, too."

"Me?"

"You."

Luke knew what people must be thinking without being told. Some folks tended to get the wrong impression about situations even when their assumptions were wrong, and he had seen Abby a lot when she first arrived.

"Does Mrs. Franklin know about the gossip?" Luke asked.

The pastor nodded. "I think so. But at least she and the children own the house and the farm. At least, I *hope* they do."

"Hope?"

"There could be a problem with Brother Franklin's will, and it has also come to my attention that he was never rich like we all thought."

"What about the silver mine?"

"Rubbish. He owned one share in a silver mine that never paid off."

Luke left the pastor's office with some of his questions answered, but not all.

He kept remembering the tender way Abby treated Mr. Franklin and everybody else she knew, and he loved her brothers and sisters—almost as much as he loved Abby. He intended to watch them from afar in order to keep them safe and help them in any way he could. He would do the things a husband would do in the hope that one day he would become the head of that family.

At first he couldn't think of a single thing he could do to help, but after he thought about it for a while, he made a list. He could chop wood for their woodstove and put it in the woodpile at the back of the house whether Abby wanted his help or not. He also planned to doctor her cattle when any of them looked sick and fix any broken fences he came across in his daily visits to the farm.

He wanted to drive Abby and the children to town and to church on Sunday, but he knew it would only start another gossip storm. And Abby had already been through enough.

Pastor and Mrs. Johnson urged Abby and the children to continue living with them. "There is no reason for y'all to live way out in the country on that farm when we have plenty of room right here in town."

But Abby insisted; she and the children would live on the farm. She'd always dreamed of a home of her own. Besides, the one visit to the church in Frio Corners was enough to convince her to move away. She was shunned by some in the congregation, especially Mrs. Peabody, and on her wedding day, too. Only Mrs. Eastland and a few others talked to her after the service. But for the barbecue, would anyone have attended the wedding reception?

Three weeks after Ambrose died, the pastor called Luke into his office again.

"Mrs. Franklin and the children are having a hard time since Ambrose died," the pastor explained. "I'm thinking it's going to get worse. Mr. Franklin never had time to change his will after he married Mrs. Franklin, and a niece from California inherited his home and land. Mrs. Franklin and the children weren't left with so much as one penny. They're living in the house now, but I got a telegram from California. The niece is ready to leave for Texas. Mrs. Franklin and the children could soon be out in the street with no money and no place to go."

"Does Abby know?"

The pastor nodded. "I went out and told her as soon as I got the news."

"How did she take it?"

"She smiled as you would have guessed, but I've learned to see through those smiles of hers. So, please, keep checking on her like you've been doing." The pastor paused and shook his head again. "My wife and I have plenty of room in our big old house, and as you know, they stayed with us before. If need be, they can stay with us forever." He paused. "Do you have any ideas as to what else can be done to help them?"

Luke shrugged. He knew what he wanted to do—marry Abby. But he doubted she would have him.

The pastor looked Luke in the eyes. "What Mrs. Franklin needs is a husband." The pastor didn't say anything more for what seemed to Luke like a long time. At last he said, "You have a lot to think about, Brother Conquest. Let's talk again in a few days."

Chapter 7

L uke sat in a pew on the aisle at church on Sunday morning, thinking about what his pastor said the last time he talked to him and waiting for the service to begin. *"What Mrs. Franklin needs is a husband."*

Imagine. Was he urging Luke to marry Abby? Of course, that was exactly what he wanted to do, but that was impossible with Abby feeling the way she did about him.

Sue Ann was at the organ, playing soulful hymns barely above a whisper. Jim, seated on a pew a couple seats ahead of Luke, couldn't keep his eyes off her. Luke's thoughts centered on Abby. He kept wishing she were so close he could reach out and touch her hand—comfort her in her time of need.

———————◈———————

Abby stood by the kitchen table, spooning boiled mush into Albert's bowl. She couldn't stop thinking about something the pastor said shortly before they moved to the farm.

"As Mr. Franklin's widow, you own the house and the land it sits on," he'd said. *"Let's hope nothing changes that."*

She hadn't paid much attention to those words the first time she heard them. Now they came back to haunt her like a prophecy that came true. All she could do now was try to put all her worries out of her mind. So far, at least the children didn't know they would soon be homeless.

Abby sidled up beside Margaret and scooped another spoonful, dropping the white pottage onto Margaret's plate. Tommy stared at his empty bowl, waiting for it to be filled.

"Abby," he said. "I thought today was Sunday."

"It is."

"Then why didn't we go to church this morning, and why are we having mush again? We had it for breakfast."

How should she answer? Abby couldn't share with the children most of what was going on, but she could share some things.

Abby dropped the last of the mush in Tommy's bowl. Then she went around and took her seat at the head of the table. She hadn't had anything to eat all day, and that was all right with Abby. She wasn't hungry—not much anyway.

"Well," Tommy went on, "why didn't we?"

"Some folks in town and at that church don't like me very much." Abby noticed the worried looks on the faces of the children. What would they think when they learned everything?

"Why don't they like you?" Tommy dipped his spoon in the pottage and lifted it to his mouth.

Abby shrugged. "Who can say?"

"Do they like us?"

"I'm sure they do."

"So why can't we at least go to town? You said we were out of flour and things, and I'm getting tired of mush. We've been having it for almost every meal."

Abby gazed down at her bowl. Thank goodness the children didn't know her bowl was empty.

"I can't answer that, Tommy," she finally said. "But I am sure Pastor and Mrs. Johnson will visit us again soon, and they always bring food when they come."

She wouldn't tell them that Miss Betty Franklin, Ambrose's niece from California, could arrive at any time or that she wouldn't be bringing food but an eviction notice. The telegram said she was ready to leave for Texas, meaning that Miss Franklin could kick them out of their home at any time. Were all the bad things that happened in Georgia after their mother died happening again?

After the noon meal, she went out back to the henhouse to see if any new eggs had arrived since last she looked. She once said she would never kill an animal, but hunger changed things. Fried chicken sounded better by the minute.

She found two eggs in the henhouse and put them in the wicker basket. She supposed the wicker basket belonged to Miss Betty Franklin now.

As Abby was leaving the henhouse, she saw a flash of black out of the corner of her eye. She looked again.

A nice buggy pulled by a single bay horse was driving up to the front of the house. Folks with buggies didn't often drive all the way out here.

Miss Franklin. Had the woman from California arrived earlier than expected? If so, the eggs in the wicker basket also belonged to her. Abby dashed inside, through the house, and all the way to the front door.

Abby hadn't prayed in a long time, but her mother always said that Christians prayed in the name of Jesus for needs like food and shelter. She prayed, and then she opened the door before hearing a single knock.

Pastor and Mrs. Johnson stepped inside.

Relief filled every part of her, and Abby was already smiling. "Oh, it is so good to see you. Please, sit down." She hesitated, waiting for them to take their seats on the divan. "I didn't recognize that fancy rig y'all drove up in today," Abby said, taking a chair across from the divan.

"The buggy is new," Mrs. Johnson explained. "Our banker gave it to us, and he got a new one. But the horse is ours."

A white cloth was draped over the wicker basket Mrs. Johnson held. She removed the cover and handed the basket to Abby. "This is for you and the children."

Abby saw food inside, and a quick gush of tender feelings covered her like a warm blanket. Her lips trembled slightly, and she felt like crying. Was it normal to cry when a miracle had just happened? Pastor and Mrs. Johnson had brought her gifts before but never only moments after she prayed.

It was as if the tears now moistening her eyes had been hiding there all her life and suddenly poured out like a flood. Abby wiped them away with the back of her hand.

Mrs. Johnson got up and hastened to her side. Pastor Johnson got up, too, but not as quickly, and trudged over to join the women.

"What's wrong, dear?" Mrs. Johnson asked.

Abby wiped her eyes again. "Nothing, *now*. But just before y'all got here, I prayed. God answered, and here you are with a basket of food."

"And there's more in the buggy," the pastor pointed out, "and money, too."

"Oh, no." Abby wept audibly. "I don't deserve this. Why, I hadn't really prayed in ages and ages—not since I was little."

"God loves you and the children." Mrs. Johnson handed her a white handkerchief.

Abby buried her head in the older woman's shoulder, holding the handkerchief and trying to stop crying before the children came in and saw her. What was wrong with her today? She almost never cried, especially like this, and here she was weeping into the sleeve of Mrs. Johnson's blue dress. She sat up and wiped her eyes with the handkerchief.

"Thank you." She sniffed. "Thank you for coming today. Thank you for the basket of food. Thank you for everything."

"Better thank God first, young lady." The pastor gave her shoulder a soft pat. "He's the One behind the giving. He loves His people more than we can imagine."

"We love you, too," Mrs. Johnson said. "Why, you and the children are the family we never had."

The pastor nodded in agreement. "I reckon you and those little ones are a part of our lives now."

"Should we pray?" Mrs. Johnson asked.

"Yes." The pastor bowed his head, and then Abby and Mrs. Johnson did.

Abby was so filled with emotions from all that had happened since they arrived that she didn't hear much of the pastor's prayer. But she knew he was talking straight to God on their behalf and that he asked the Lord to bless all five of them.

Did God hear when she prayed? She'd never thought so. But now she wondered. Maybe He did.

Pleasing scents floated out from the wicker basket. Abby leaned over and took a whiff. "Oh, this looks so good. Is that chicken I smell?"

"Fried chicken and roasted potatoes. And if you'll have us, we'd like to stay for supper."

"I'd love for you to stay for supper." If they only knew how starved Abby truly was. "Let's make it an early supper, if it is all the same to you."

Later when the children had eaten the last of the fried chicken and only chicken bones remained on their plates, they went outside to play. Then Mrs. Johnson leaned forward in her chair.

"Did you know that your name, Abby, has a meaning?"

"No." Abby shook her head. "I didn't. What does it mean?"

"I read somewhere that it means 'her father's delight.'"

Abby glanced down at her plate. Her stepfather delighted in her, all right, but not in a good way. After a moment, she forced a smile and looked up again.

Pastor and Mrs. Johnson were looking out the west window as the sun dipped lower in the sky. She knew she should make some sort of comment, but she just couldn't.

The pastor and his wife turned back to Abby. "It's getting late," he said, "and we have another stop to make. So I guess we best go."

"Please, stay," Abby said almost in a whisper.

"You looked a little sad just then when you said that, dear," Mrs. Johnson put in. "Is something wrong?"

Abby looked away again, spreading out a wrinkle in the skirt of her gold print dress. "No, nothing's wrong. If I looked sad, it's because you are leaving."

But it was a lie. Plenty was wrong. Her whole life was wrong.

An old saying she'd heard from her grandmother came into her mind. *"Good people don't air their dirty linen in public."*

Maybe Pastor and Mrs. Johnson didn't know that she knew what the people at the church were saying about her, and she refused to tell them. She preferred to bear her pain in secret as she always had.

"Please, tell us what is wrong." Mrs. Johnson reached out and hugged her again. "Whatever you tell us will be in confidence."

Abby felt the muscles around her mouth tighten, a clear indication that more tears battled to get out. She wanted to tell all her secrets to these good people—shout so loud the windows shook. But she wouldn't. Her grandmother said she shouldn't, and her grandmother was always right.

At last she said, "There's a scripture verse I knew as a child. I can't remember it now, but it begins with 'If any man is in Christ.'"

"That's in 2 Corinthians," the pastor said. "If any man be in Christ, he is a new creature: old things are passed away; behold, all things are become new." He paused but only for an instant. "According to the Bible, Abby, God would like to be your friend. But the Lord expects you to move toward Him first. He moved toward you by giving His only begotten Son to die on a cross in your place."

Abby had always thought of God as judgmental, like some of the people in Georgia she knew as a child. She'd never considered that the King of the Universe would like to be her friend. It seemed too good to be true. Still, she tucked the thought inside her brain, promising to think on it again in the days and weeks to come.

Luke sat on the front porch of his ranch house, gazing at the western sky at sunset. Since Mr. Franklin's death, he'd thought about a certain scripture—the one about caring for widows and orphans. Abby was a widow now, and her brothers and sisters were orphans. Should he marry Abby to keep her from starving and keep her brothers and sisters from being placed in an orphanage?

Oh, he loved Abby, all right—had since the moment she floated inside the Frio Corners Hotel. But how could he trust her?

Did she come to Texas to marry an old and rich man that was on his deathbed, and was she only pretending to be surprised when she learned he was ninety years old? He wanted to believe that she was innocent of all charges.

He saw a buggy in the distance. The pastor and his wife had said they might stop by for a visit, and they would be driving the new rig the banker gave them. At last, the buggy stopped in front of the house.

"Brother Conquest," the pastor said as he helped his wife up the front steps, "it's great to see you again."

"Thanks for coming." Luke indicated his front door. "Shall we go inside?"

When his guests had settled onto the faded brown divan and Luke was seated across from them, he leaned forward and tilted his head at an angle. "I've been reading scripture verses in the Bible about caring for widows and orphans," Luke said, "and Mrs. Franklin is a widow now. The children are orphans, and they will all be out in the cold when that lady from California gets here. Somebody has to help them. Like you said in your sermon this morning, we should treat others like we would like to be treated. If I were in a fix like she is, I'd want somebody to step forward and help me. As a pastor you know that sometimes we have to make sacrifices for the better good."

The pastor grinned. "Would marrying a beautiful woman like Mrs. Franklin be considered a sacrifice, Brother Conquest?"

Chapter 8

Luke froze for a moment. "Well, now." He hadn't expected the minister to ask a question like that, and he certainly couldn't tell Pastor Johnson how he really felt. Or did he already know?

Luke scratched the back of his neck when it didn't itch. "Maybe I should up and marry her then—Mrs. Franklin, that is. Not that I actually want to marry her. True, she is a fine-looking woman and all, but as I see it, it's my Christian duty."

Pastor Johnson chuckled. "As you say, sometimes Christians have to make sacrifices to prove their faith," the pastor said. "They must become brave. Look at Daniel. He faced lions because he thought it was the right thing to do. And what about David? He didn't put on armor before facing that giant, Goliath. Did he?"

Was Pastor Johnson joking with him? It sure sounded like it.

"So when do you plan to marry her, Brother Conquest? My thoughts are, the sooner the better. As you said, that lady from California could be here at any time. I don't have anything planned for tomorrow."

"Tomorrow?" Luke swallowed. "That's mighty soon, don't you think? I haven't had time to ask Mrs. Franklin for her hand in marriage yet. Besides, that young mare I bought from you is as wild as a hurricane one day and as gentle as a spring breeze the next. I never know what to expect from that filly, and I need to break her before she gets so out of control I can't ever rein her in."

The pastor leaned back in his chair, putting his feet on the footstool in front of him. "I know what I would do if I were a young man like you."

"And what is that, sir?"

"After breakfast tomorrow morning, I'd clean up real nice and go knocking at Mrs. Franklin's door. I'd asked her to marry me, and that would be it."

"And then what?" Luke asked.

"Well, I'd clean up my house real nice. Women like clean houses. And then I'd prepare to meet my bride up at the church."

"And what time tomorrow will this wedding take place?" Luke asked.

"I think four o'clock tomorrow afternoon sounds good. Is that all right with you, Brother Conquest?"

"I guess so."

"Then I'll see you and Mrs. Franklin at the church tomorrow at four. And bring the children. We love those little ones."

Luke nodded. He would marry Abby. It was what he'd wanted all along. But he still didn't know why she left the hotel without telling him.

———————————◦❊❊◦———————————

Luke and Abby were married the very next day just like the pastor said they should be. Abby insisted on a marriage of convenience—no love involved. Under the current circumstances, what choice did Luke have but to agree?

Pastor and Mrs. Johnson insisted on keeping the children at their house for the first few days after the wedding. Abby didn't seem to like the idea but finally agreed to it. At last Luke and Abby got in his wagon and headed for the ranch.

"I'm hoping you'll like my ranch as much as I do," he said. "And I want to show you around the place. But it could be too dark to see by the time we get there."

Abby smiled, but her eyes didn't.

His ranch was in a big valley with hills all around as if protecting the land from intruders, and there were a lot of trees. Most of the trees in the valley stayed green even in winter, but the leaves on some of the trees wore fall clothing. Trees in rusty red and gold, brownish orange, and shades of warm brown dotted the hills with color.

"Are the beautiful trees I see up in the hills maples?" she asked. "A woman I met on the train from Georgia said that maple trees grow around here."

"They do, but I don't have any on my place. We call the fall-looking trees in all those pretty colors Spanish oaks."

She smiled. "Spanish oaks. I like that."

He wanted to show her his barn and especially the round pen where he was training his mare. But it was almost dark by the time they arrived at the ranch. He would have to show her around on another day.

———————————◦❊❊◦———————————

On the first morning after they married, Abby prepared a wonderful-tasting breakfast for the two of them—eggs, bacon, biscuits, and hot coffee.

"This is the best meal I ever ate," he said.

She smiled when he said that. But again, her eyes showed a kind of fear he was unable to define.

Abby's skills in the kitchen continued after her brothers and sisters arrived, and Luke was impressed with the way she cared for the house. She was also a good mother to her brothers and sisters and would make an excellent mother to their children, if they ever had any.

He tried to work his young mare in the round pen every day, eager to get that wild and half-crazy animal broke so he could ride her, and sometimes when he worked his filly, she pitched him. He remembered the tender way Abby ministered to Mr. Franklin the one time she visited him at his farm before he died, and Luke pictured her nursing him back to health if he ever got really hurt during the taming process.

Luke had thought what just about everybody in Frio Corners thought—that Mr. Franklin was hiding a lot of money he'd made from a silver mine. But now he knew the truth. Mr. Franklin never got any money from that one share he owned. All he had when he died was his house and the little farm it sat on.

He'd misjudged Abby, too, with regard to Mr. Franklin. She didn't know he was old or rich when she came to Texas to marry him. She'd expected a nice man about Luke's age or maybe a little older. Still, the more he got to know her, the more Luke thought Abby was hiding something. Nobody smiled *all* the time.

He tried to gentle Abby as a man gentles an unbroken horse—a friendly grin here, a pat on the shoulder there, and hugs as often as possible. But Abby kept pulling away. The warm smiles she was so capable of looked forced and unreal. He made other mistakes in his quest to tame Abby—like when he said something funny, meant to make her laugh, and his jokes turned sour. He knew because she never laughed at any of his jokes. In fact, she never laughed at all.

Why didn't he ever learn? It was said that a smart person never made the same mistake twice. Now they had been married going on three weeks, and he was still making some of the same mistakes he'd made the day after their wedding.

One day Abby was ironing one of Luke's shirts, and he was watching her. It was a warm day for December, and the woodstove was all fired up in order to warm the iron she used to remove the wrinkles from the batch of clothes she was ironing. The kitchen was hotter than a cook oven on the hottest day in summer.

Abby looked cute all bent over with a hot iron in her hand and a stray curl falling across her forehead. He just had to say something.

"I like the way you look right now, even with sweat rolling down your face like that."

Abby frowned—like she thought his friendly remark was insulting.

In hindsight, it probably was, and Luke wanted to make things right. So he tried to ignore the strong clue she was sending. He got up from his chair at the kitchen table and moved toward her. He grinned; she didn't.

She was pressing out the wrinkles from one of his blue work shirts, and he wanted to remember the way she looked forever. He moved around behind her, and putting his hands on her tiny waist, he gave her a big hug.

"Stop that!" she shouted.

Sharp fingernails cut into his fingers and hands.

"Hey, that hurts."

"Then leave me be."

He'd hoped for a different outcome, and when he removed his hands, part of his heart went with it. He stepped back then, holding his hands above his head like he was under arrest.

She turned around, glaring at him and holding the hot iron in front of her like a shield. In that instant, he knew she hated a man's touch, even a loving one, and he wondered what could possibly have happened in her past to cause such a reaction.

He should have demanded to know what was going on inside of her head. But he didn't want to make matters worse.

So he said, "Sorry, Abby. I didn't mean to scare you, and I appreciate the good job you are doing ironing my shirt."

She smiled then and went back to her ironing as if nothing had happened. But something *had* happened, and Luke intended to discover what it was.

Three days later, they were in the kitchen again. She was slicing tomatoes and lettuce for a salad. He sat at the other end of the table drinking hot coffee.

She looked up from her slicing and said, "If tomatoes could talk, would they call themselves to-may-toes or to-mah-toes?"

He laughed because her question was clever and downright funny. However, she must have been offended because the sweet expression on her face disappeared.

Luke wanted to make amends. He got up from the kitchen table and started toward her. Maybe she knew he wanted to kiss her. If she didn't, he knew.

"Stay away from me!" She grabbed a tomato and threw it at him.

He ducked. "Stop that!"

"No," she shouted, "because you are exactly like Gary."

"Who's Gary?"

"My stepfather, Gary Willoughby. He laughed in my face, too, just like you do."

Luke had thought Mr. Willoughby was her *real* father. He hadn't known she had a stepfather. In that moment, Abby's happy, cheerful demeanor totally crumbled. He was able to see more of the inner torment behind that covering she always wore.

"What's bothering you, Abby? Please, tell me. Maybe I can help."

Her smile returned—as if somehow she'd managed to paste it on her face by sheer effort. "It's me that should be helping you," she said in her sweetest of voices. "What would you like for supper?"

He would not allow it to end this way—not this time. If they hoped to have any kind of marriage, they must be completely honest with each other, and there could be no secrets between them. Abby's secret was like a boil he'd had on his arm once. The longer he waited to lance it, the bigger and more painful it became. He was determined to lance the boil that was deep in her heart. He just didn't know how to go about doing it.

"Something must have happened in your childhood, Abby, something I don't know about. It's time you told me what it is you've been hiding. And why do you smile all the time?"

"My grandmother told me to smile no matter how people treated me. Satisfied?"

"No, I'm not. What's really bothering you?"

The anger he saw in her eyes previously, returned. "Nothing! I'm not hiding anything."

"Yes, you are. I can see it in your eyes!"

She threw down the bowl of salad. Bits of lettuce and red tomatoes spilled on the floor. "I have nothing more to say. Leave me alone."

"Abby, I want to help you. So tell me what's bothering you, right now. Hear?"

"How's this?" She pointed her finger at Luke, trembling with rage, and her voice grew louder and shriller with every word. "I didn't have a last name because my father ravished my mother. How's that for truth?"

Luke swallowed. He knew she had problems but never dreamed they were that bad. He wanted to hold her, comfort her. Yet he just stood there—unable to say a word.

"We never knew who my real father was. Mama and I lived with my grandmother until Mama married Gary Willoughby. But Gary wasn't willing to just have my mother and the four kids they had together; he wanted me, too, and not in a good way. If I hadn't managed to get away from him each time like I did, I would have ended up just like Mama." She glared at him. "Now you know."

"Oh, Abby, I'm so sorry. If only I'd known sooner." His voice cracked with emotion. "Let me help you, please."

"I don't need any help!" she shouted. "I never have. Get out of this house. I never want to see you again."

"This is *my* house—in case you forgot," he said in a loud voice. "But I'm leaving, all right. I'm going out to break that mare of mine. She's almost as stubborn as you are. But before I go, I want to know why you didn't leave me a note at the hotel, telling me you were leaving and where you would be living."

"I left a note," she countered. "Why didn't you keep looking until you found it? Maybe it's because you are a horrible person—just like Gary."

Luke walked out the kitchen door then. It slammed shut behind him.

He'd always worked his wild two-year-old mare in the round pen so if he got pitched off, somebody would find him. Abby probably assumed that was where he was going, but today he wanted something different. He would work the mare in the brush some distance from the house and try to forget what she just said.

There was a knock at the front door. Abby paused, hoping it wasn't that woman from California. She pulled her shoulders back, opened the door, and stiffened.

Sue Ann Reynolds stood on her front porch, the one who had started all the gossip as well as the girl who was standing in the shadows near the café on the day Abby arrived from Georgia. Abby was convinced that the church organist had strong feelings for Luke because her interest in him shone in her eyes whenever he was nearby.

Was Sue Ann here for a catfight or for some other reason? If she came because she still wanted Luke, she could have him as far as Abby was concerned.

"Come on in and sit down," Abby said at last.

"Thank you." Sue Ann's mouth turned up at the edges, but her eyes weren't smiling. She ducked her head and sat down on the divan. "I came to apologize."

"Apologize?"

"I'm sorry, Abby, for the trouble I've caused." She looked down at her hands folded on her lap. "I—I started all the gossip and destroyed the letter you sent to Luke."

Abby couldn't believe what she'd just heard. She'd always known the gossip started the day Sue Ann saw Luke and Abby at the hotel at breakfast time. But she hadn't known that Luke never got her letter or that Sue Ann was responsible for it.

"Then Luke never got my letter?"

"No, I dropped it in a trash can. But I am a different person now. I made Jesus the Lord of my life."

"You what?"

"I'm saved," Sue Ann said with an awed smile. Her face glowed with a new humble contentment. "I'd gone to church all my life. But Jim Turner, the blacksmith, introduced me to the one true God for the first time. Then Jim and I fell in love and are getting married in a few weeks. I've done some terrible things, but, please, forgive me, Abby. I hope we can be friends now."

Friends? Abby had offered Sue Ann friendship when she first arrived in town, and Sue Ann stabbed her in the back.

"By the way," Sue Ann said, "that Miss Franklin arrived on the stage today all the way from California, and she didn't know that you and the children would be thrown out of your home. She seemed sorry and wants to meet you."

"She wants to meet *me?*" Abby put the palm of one hand against her chest as if she were somehow pushing Sue Ann's words into her heart. "Really?"

"Yes."

Abby was speechless. Two people actually said they were sorry for hurting her. Nobody but her mother, her grandmother, and of course Luke had ever done that, and she wanted to remember the moment forever.

Though in some ways Sue Ann sounded like a fire-and-brimstone preacher, there was a warmth about her now and a kind of joy. Abby had only pretended to be happy. Apparently, Sue Ann *was* happy.

"Jim said that his father died when he was small," Sue Ann said. "But now that he invited the Lord into his heart, he has a heavenly Father."

Abby had never had a real father—and needed one, even if it meant forgiving someone like Gary. But this "being saved" business was new and seemed a little strange.

"Would you like to go to heaven when you die?" Sue Ann asked.

"Of course." Abby shrugged. "Who wouldn't? What do people have to do to get there?"

"Repent of all their sins and follow the Lord."

"Follow the Lord." Abby leaned forward in her chair. "How would I do that—unless I had wings?"

"If you want to follow the Lord, Abby, you do what Jesus did and what He said to do. First, you repent. Then you study God's Word, the Bible, and believe it is true." She paused. "Would you like for me to teach you the sinner's prayer?"

Abby froze, and a dash of resentment slowly blended with the uneasy feelings in the middle of her stomach. "Are you calling me a sinner?"

"I'm calling everybody sinners, especially me. Nobody is perfect, and that's why we need a Savior. Jesus paid for our sins on the cross so that we wouldn't have to go to hell. He lived in heaven before He came to earth as a baby, you know, and Jesus knows how to get there."

Sue Ann gazed at her for a moment. Abby thought she might be praying. "Luke's a good Christian man, Abby, and you are lucky to have him."

Abby nodded, glancing at the clock on the wall above Sue Ann's head. It was almost four, and he'd been gone for what seemed like a long time. Did something happen? She started to get up.

"I've kept you too long, haven't I?" Sue Ann got up and stood by her chair. "Well, I have to go anyway. But I hope you will think about all I've said."

Abby looked away and nodded, gazing through the doorway to the back kitchen door—hoping—praying that she would see Luke standing there.

She must also have walked Sue Ann to the front door and told her good-bye, but as Abby hurried out the back and headed for the round pen, she couldn't remember doing it. All she could think about was Luke. She'd treated him badly with her counterfeit smiles. Yet she loved him with a passion.

But when she got to the round pen, she discovered that Luke wasn't working his mare. Surely he wasn't riding an unbroken horse out in the brush somewhere. She prayed for his safety and was determined to find him.

The wind had whipped up. The air was icy cold. Snow was rare in the Texas hill country. Yet a light snow carpeted the ground under her feet. She put her hands in the pockets of her brown coat, wishing she'd brought a coat for Luke. His light jacket wouldn't be enough to keep him warm on this unusually frosty day in mid-December.

Luke lay under a tree. She ran to him, and then she just stood there, afraid he might be dead. Her breath caught. She wanted to scream, and if she still had a heart, it was breaking.

He *was* dead. She knew it. If only she hadn't chased him away. Now it was too late to tell him how she really felt.

"Oh, Luke, I love you so. Please, don't die," she said out loud. "I should have told you sooner, and I'm going to say the sinner's prayer and follow Jesus. But I need you here with me."

He reached out and touched her hand.

"You're alive!" Tears moistened her eyes as she knelt down beside him.

"Yes, Abby," he said slowly, "and—and I love you, too. I have since the day we met." He squeezed her hand.

Then she smiled. Only this time, it came from her heart.

"I got bucked off my mare." His voice sounded stronger. "The breath was knocked plum out of me, but I'm gonna be fine." He squeezed her hand again.

She squeezed back. "I need to apologize for—"

"No, Abby, you don't. But it's mighty cold out here. Your hands are like ice. Will you please lean over and kiss me before my mouth freezes shut?"

Abby laughed, and she knew it came from her heart—just like her smile. Then she kissed him. It was a long kiss and full of love—a love that would last forever—and then some.

Molly Noble Bull has a Texas cattle ranch background and once lived in the Texas hill country where her historical novella "Too Many Secrets" is set. She has published with Zondervan, Love Inspired, and others. *Sanctuary,* her long historical, won the 2008 Gayle Wilson Award in the inspirational category and tied for first place in a second national contest for published authors that year. *Gatehaven,* Molly's gothic historical, won the grand prize in the 2013 Creation House Fiction Writing contest. *When the Cowboy Rides Away* won the 2016 Texas Association of Authors contest in the Christian Western category and was a finalist in the 2016 Will Rogers Awards for western writers in the Inspirational category. Please visit Molly's website at www.mollynoblebull .com, her page at Amazon, http://bit.ly/mollynoblebull, and her page on Facebook, Facebook.com/molly.n.bull.

Love in Store

by Anita Mae Draper

Dedication

To my husband and kids who willingly took on household chores so that I could pursue my dream. I am humbled by your faith and support, and blessed that we're a family.

If we confess our sins, he is faithful and just to forgive us our sins, and to cleanse us from all unrighteousness.
1 JOHN 1:9

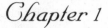

Chapter 1

Two long whistles warned Janet of the train's departure, effectively stopping her from discussing the transportation schedule of her family's freight delivery business. As she backed away from the mail car, the clerk raised his hand in her direction before sliding the large door closed. If only she could jump aboard and head down the rails to a distant destination.

"Hey, Janet! What are you waiting for?" Neil yelled across the platform without caring who heard him.

After a final look at the disappearing train, she hurried over to where Neil waited in their freight wagon.

He released the brake as she neared. "If you weren't my only sister, I'd leave you in the dust."

"Fine by me." She raised her face to the sky, nose high, as she always did when he spoke nonsense. "I'm twenty-two and old enough. I'll just catch the next train to Billings."

Clicking his tongue he got the team headed toward home. "You would, too, wouldn't you?" His sidelong glance held a hint of concern. "It would kill Pa if you left."

"Which is why I'm still here." Despite her dreams of leaving Miles City, she wouldn't go while Pa was alive, and he wouldn't leave with her as long as he had a business to run and sons to guide.

Neil didn't stop until he reached Hazelton's store on the last block of Main Street near the bridge. He fished a crate out of the wagon and then carried it inside.

Up in the seat, Janet held her back straight and her hands in her lap like a lady, in case Adam happened to notice she was there. A minute later, he accompanied Neil out onto the wide sidewalk in front of his store.

Her heart fluttered. She didn't need to see his face to know his eyes were gunmetal gray.

"Two more and that's it for this load," Neil said.

Janet shifted, her gaze catching Adam's long-legged movements beneath the brim of her slouch hat. Wide shouldered and muscular, he carried a crate into his store with ease.

She peered through the large window for a final sight of him, but the reflection of a large tree across the road distorted her view. On several occasions she'd spotted Adam lounging against that tree with a book or magazine in hand. One of these days she would stop and start a discussion on whatever topic had caught his attention. If only she had the nerve to do it.

"I'll stop by in the morning and pick that up," Neil said, his voice breaking into her musings.

"Good enough," Adam replied.

Janet turned her head to smile at him in greeting—but he'd already gone back inside.

With her spine straight and her chin up, she reminded herself that there was always the train, and no matter which direction, it was on its way somewhere.

The following morning after she'd cleared breakfast away, Janet walked across the yard from their large, two-story house to the building where the family worked their freight business. She found Pa and Ben standing in front of the wide sliding doors of the wagon room.

A burly man who said what was on his mind, Ebenezer Smith laid his hand on his eldest son's shoulder. "Be on your guard, Ben, and don't let your brother talk you into any side trips to see that girl he's mooning over."

Ben pulled on his leather gloves. He nodded. "I hear you, Pa. We won't be dallying on the way home."

As Neil approached with the team, Janet handed the meal sack to Ben. "There's enough for three days if you're careful. God be with you."

"Thanks, sis." He kissed her cheek as he always did before leaving. As the oldest son, Ben had spent the most time with Ma before she'd gone to heaven, and her passing had left him with a deep commitment to the family. A few years ago, his own wife had joined Ma. Ben accepted each day as a gift, showing his love in small ways that gave hope to Janet's quest for a loving husband who did the same.

Neil, on the other hand, was like a stubborn splinter she couldn't dislodge. Hands on his hips, he scrutinized her face. "How'd you get ink on your face already? You haven't been in the office yet."

Janet stood her ground, knowing her face was as clean as it had been after she'd washed it earlier that morning. She would have liked to stick her tongue out, except Pa was hitching up the team behind Neil and could look up at any moment. "Enjoy your trip."

"Where's Jack?" Pa asked.

"Coming." Jack carried in a small barrel, which he proceeded to tie down in the back of the wagon. "You're all loaded except for whatever Hazelton has going out. Don't forget to stop by his store."

Janet's heart lurched at the sound of Adam's name. No matter how many times she told herself that the man wasn't interested, she couldn't get her heart to listen.

She headed into her office as soon as the team pulled away. She didn't want to change the ribbon on her typewriter machine because of the mess it made of her, but it had reached the end of the spool and she had paperwork waiting to be processed. If she did get covered in ink, at least she'd have three days to scrub it off before Neil came back to bug her about it.

Except when she opened her supply drawer, she couldn't find any typewriter ribbon tins, never mind one with a new ribbon inside. After spending several minutes searching the desk drawers and shelves of her eight-by-eight-foot office, she knelt down on the new planked floor to see if it had rolled under her desk.

From that position, she saw Jack's boot step up from the hard-packed ground of the freight shop onto her new floor. "You praying?"

"No, but I ought to because I can't find what I'm looking for." She started to rise and he held out his hand, which she accepted. She didn't know why Jack, being the third son, had an ingrained sense of courtesy lacking in his brothers, but she was grateful God had made him that way.

He handed her a slip of paper. "Can you run uptown for us? We'll need those after dinner, if it's possible. Add whatever you need to the list."

"Sure enough." She tucked the list with Jack's hen scratch into her pocket. "Pa doesn't want to go today?"

"He's helping me with that broken wheel."

Which left her to run the errands. And since she needed a typewriter ribbon, she would have to visit Adam's store at some point. First or last? Last, she decided, as it would prolong the heady sense of anticipation of their meeting, with nothing to stop her from running home in misery afterward when he failed to acknowledge that she was alive.

But there was always hope.

Adam unpacked the fragile porcelain bonbon dishes from the first crate. Since the catalog hadn't given full descriptions, he hadn't known what he would receive after telling the dealer to send an assortment of special items not usually found in a general store.

He smiled when he pushed away a handful of straw and saw the pink fluted vase dressed in floral accents and covered in a shiny glaze. His mother had one just like it. Memories rushed in and he closed his eyes. His chest tightened as if a band squeezed the air out of his lungs. Leaving his past lying in the crate alongside the delicate vase, he rushed outside.

She'd had one like it.

He sucked in the morning air with its whiff of wet vegetation from the banks of the nearby Tongue River. Across the road, the pastoral scene of the park drew him forward until he stood beneath his favorite tree. He would clear his head and shore up his emotions while keeping an eye on the store.

Why had he ordered pretty, delicate things to attract women when they only reminded him of what he had lost? Why—because he'd thought it was the better solution to avoid answering all the friendly questions men asked when making purchases. They wanted to discuss the weather and his background, the railway and his past. No matter what was going on in the world, they wanted to know about him.

And that was his business alone.

Women, on the other hand, tended to talk among themselves as if he weren't even there. Several times he'd been privy to personal conversations better said in someone's kitchen than a general store where anyone could hear and then retell with embellishment, yet he'd seemed to be as visible as a pickle keg.

That suited him fine. He liked running a store. It was talking with the customers that clammed him up tighter than an oyster.

A woman strode down the opposite side of the street with a familiar purposeful gait. Normally he didn't notice such things, but he'd once overheard someone say it was a pity Janet Smith had been raised by a family of men without a woman to influence her behavior.

Adam was sorry she had lost her mother, and thought she'd turned out just fine. Not that he had an opinion one way or the other.

She clutched a sack in one of her swinging arms, which meant the men had probably sent her on another round of errands. And she was headed to his store.

Back inside, Adam guarded himself against unwanted memories. He lifted the ten-inch vase out of its straw nest and set it on the glass-topped display case.

Footsteps announced Miss Smith's arrival. "Oh, that's pretty."

Without answering, he set the vase inside the case on the center of the top shelf where customers could see it from the front as well as down through the glass countertop.

"What else did you get?" She peered over the side of the crate.

He lifted it off the counter and set it on the stool behind him. Answering her question would invite a response. A response would lead to a discussion. A discussion today meant more talk the next time, which could allow room for personal questions. It would be better if he concentrated on business.

"What can I do for you?" His practiced tone was steady and businesslike. He swiped the chaff from his counter to avoid looking at her.

"I need a typewriter ribbon." She plunked her sack on the counter without care for its contents.

He cringed at the sound of metal clunking on his glass counter. While she leaned forward to see better, he raised the sack and slid his hand across the smooth surface to check for cracks.

"Did I break it?" Her voice held enough remorse to soothe his irritation.

"Not yet." Needing a cushion of some kind, he reached for a magazine he'd been reading earlier and set the offending sack on top of it with care.

"Yes, well." She brushed something away from the side of her face. "About that ribbon?"

By far, Janet Smith used more ribbons than anyone else in Miles City. She must be writing a book to go through ribbons like she did. Or was she replacing them before they were worn out?

He set the box holding the tins of typewriter ribbons between them. It wasn't any of his business how many ribbons she used as long as she had the money to pay for them. Yet, while he waited for her to choose one, the price he'd have to charge niggled at him. The Smiths worked hard and didn't have a wallop of money to throw away.

She looked over each tin as if choosing a jewel, and then picked one that was identical to the rest. "I'll take this one."

Her satisfied tone was like a punch to his gut. No matter how much he wanted to keep quiet, he couldn't stop his words from spilling out. "At seventy-five cents apiece, it's a good thing they can be flipped over and used until the ink dries out."

He closed the lid at the same time her mouth opened.

She stared at the tin in alarm.

So, she hadn't known. He turned away to tuck the box back in its place, moving slow to give her time to recover.

As the impact of his words rolled through her thoughts, Janet tapped the new tin with her index finger. Three ribbons at seventy-five cents apiece was the same price as two gallons of ink. Pa wouldn't like to hear that at all. For that money, she could write the invoices the old-fashioned way for the rest of her life.

"You're right, Mr. Hazelton. It's good they made them so a person could flip them over. Here you go." She set her money on the magazine, lest it clink against the glass, and then picked up her sack. Hoping for a smile, she peeked up at him from under the brim of her hat.

He slid the magazine to the counter's edge. After rolling it into a U shape, he poured her money into his other palm. "Thank you for your business." Without a look in her direction, he continued to empty the crate he'd been working on when she'd entered his store.

She pocketed the tin with the new typewriter ribbon and walked away with the sound of straw rustling in her ears.

One smile from him would have brightened her day. She would even have forgiven him for laughing at her silly mistake of not using the typewriter ribbons until they were worn out, if only he had looked at her so she could see his face alight with humor.

But as usual, he'd barely acknowledged her.

As she passed one of the city's several saloons, someone bellowed out. Chairs scraped across the wooden floor. Not wishing to get bowled over when someone came flying out, she rushed past the open door.

She was thankful to have a houseful of God-fearing men who shared the workload and didn't waste their evenings in a saloon. With Sam at business school, she didn't know how he spent his time away from the family, but prayed he kept Pa's teachings in mind no matter what he did.

Later that evening, Janet looked out the kitchen window while washing up the supper dishes. The sight of black typewriter ribbons bordering the pumpkin patch showed off her foolishness for anyone to see. She had thought the used cotton ribbons useless for her office but strong enough to train pumpkin tendrils to stay in their space. At the end of the season, she had planned to salvage the rain-washed ribbons and store them for the next year.

But if there was a chance she could save the family money, as well as her pride, she needed to get the typewriter ribbons out of the garden before Adam spotted them and said something to Pa or her brothers.

"You're good with that, Janet?" Pa asked.

"Pardon me?"

Pa stood at the door with his hand on the latch and Jack by his side. "We'll be at the Thompsons' if you need us." He gave her a measured look beneath his thick eyebrows. "You all right?"

His regard warmed her right through. It also gave her an idea. "Yes, Pa, and don't worry if I'm not here when you get back. I might be in the office."

"I don't like you working out there alone when it's dark."

Jack raised an open hand toward her. "If it's your poetry you're working on, I could bring your typewriter to your room."

Pa scowled. "You'll do no such thing. You think I want to hear that clacking through the night?" His features softened as his gaze fell on her. "Do what you have to, girl. We'll check on you when we get back—wherever you are."

The glow of his love enveloped her as she finished the dishes. Once in the garden, however, the sight of her own foolishness pushed every feeling away. Whether she could get the ribbons back on the spools wasn't her worry. It was that Adam would discover what she'd done and think less of her when she wanted him to look at her with admiration instead.

Her hands blackened with sticky ink as she worked at knots weathered by the sun. In the fading light, she saw where an extra stubborn tendril had wound itself around the ribbon and tightened the final knot. She needed the scissors to cut it loose.

She carried the loose mass of the first two ribbons to the freight room in her outstretched hands, for the first time wondering where she would put them. The workshop table seemed like the perfect choice except it was littered with wood chips and axle grease.

Stepping into the office, she surveyed her domain. Along with the new floor, Pa and the boys had built a desk with counter space along one wall. She let the ribbons fall onto the clean wood surface. It was her mistake. She would sand the stains out, if that's what it needed.

She left her office to search the work area where Pa and her brothers kept their tools and treasures, careful not to touch anything that mattered. The scissors were half hidden between some tins at the back of a shelf and she yanked them out, eager to get the third ribbon cut and put away before Pa and Jack got home.

In her haste, the end of the scissors knocked one of the tins off the shelf. It hit the hard-packed ground with enough force to spring the lid open. Janet's heart plummeted to the bottom of her ribs as the familiar letters written by Ma's own hand spewed onto the dirt.

Instead of smearing them with her inky hands, she left them where they lay and ran to the garden to finish her task. Later, when her hands were clean, she'd pick them up and put them back in Pa's hiding place. Perhaps she'd read one or two to bring back the memory of sitting on Ma's knee while she read poetry in a soft voice to her young children. Janet had fallen in love with the cadence of the words, which inspired her to create her own poems. Someday she'd hold her own child on her lap and pass on Ma's legacy.

Janet lay awake for most of the night. She'd scrubbed her fingers raw with a small brush, and the cracks in her skin stung.

Dreams came and went. Hazy visions of coffee tins with Ma's letters spilling out. Unreadable words with inky smears. White notepaper with red hearts. And sometime during the night, Adam's face appeared with a smile just for her.

She awoke with her heart pounding in her chest and the agony of knowing she cared for a man who wouldn't even look her way.

Her morning prayer was for release from whatever hold Adam held on her heart. A vision returned—a letter with red hearts. She squeezed her eyes closed and prayed again, longer this time, with as much faith as she could pull together.

The simple explanation was that she'd picked up Ma's letters and replaced them in the tin before going to bed. Thoughts of Ma in the evening always led to dreams of her.

But it didn't explain why Janet spent the day composing poetry with Adam in mind, much to her own annoyance.

By evening, however, Janet had come up with a plan to win Adam's smile. If she couldn't get him out of her mind, she'd find a way to keep him there.

All she needed was the nerve to carry out her daring deed.

Chapter 2

Word of the new fancy items must have spread through Miles City because Adam had more people coming through his door than ever before. Most of them, both men and women, came to look at items they had only read about. The ones with more money and experience, congratulated him on ensuring the progress of the new state.

Several days after uncrating his new purchases, a gaggle of women entered his store.

"There it is." The mayor's wife pointed at the pink vase. "Do you think it's from Italy?"

Adam backtracked out of there. If they asked him a direct question he'd answer; otherwise, he wasn't about to stand around discussing pottery. He busied himself with tidying up the items on display, while keeping an ear open for the ladies across the room.

While straightening a pile of assorted magazines, a folded paper dropped out. He set it aside until the magazines were all aligned. Since he couldn't take action without knowing what he was dealing with, he unfolded the paper with its floral design and read the neat, but unfamiliar, script:

I saw you brooding beneath the tree, if only your thoughts were just of me.

It wasn't addressed to anyone, nor was it signed. The outside was blank.

Deciding it must have come in with the magazines, he flipped through them looking for more. And then he searched the floor and around the area. When he didn't find another one, he aimed it at the wood box and was about to let it go when he had a thought.

What if someone dropped it before it was finished and came looking for it? Perhaps someone lost it on the way to being delivered. Or what if it was unrequited love, and the person who received it threw it out?

He was still mulling over the possibilities when the ladies took their leave. Although they didn't buy anything, the admiration in their voices told him he was headed in the right direction with his store.

Adam decided to hold on to the note for a while. He pulled open the drawer where he kept his cash and other valuables and tucked it inside so it would be handy if someone asked for it. Of course, if *he* had lost it, he would never inquire if someone had found it, but there was no harm in keeping it safe.

A few days later he came in from the back storeroom and found the mayor bent over the counter looking in the display case. "Hello, Mr. Eider. Is there something you're interested in?"

The mayor straightened. "Afternoon, Adam. I see you've been changing your stock around."

"Yes, sir. With the new hardware store opening on top of the other stores, I thought I'd try selling something other than coffee and pickles."

"Yes, the air is quite different in here." He cocked his head. "Is that perfume I smell?"

Adam gave him his best sheepish look. "A crate of soaps and toiletry items came in yesterday. The ladies seem to like them."

"I don't know if I should laugh or offer congratulations. You never struck me as a ladies' man, but you're bringing in quite the arsenal to attract their attention."

"Don't say that." Adam held his hands up as if the mayor had pulled a gun on him. "Why, I brought in a good supply of toiletries for men as well. They're over here if you'd like to look."

"Some other time, Adam." He looked down at the pink vase. "The wife and I are celebrating thirty years next week. She has her heart set on that vase."

Adam took the vase out of the display case and set it on the counter. "Congratulations, sir. Mrs. Eider has a good eye for the beauty of fine workmanship."

"There's just one thing, Adam. I believe one of the reasons she wants it is because it is unique. No one around here has seen another like it. But—" He shrugged.

"No worries, Mr. Eider. I believe the pottery manufacturer only makes one-of-a-kind items. The shape might be the same, but not the colors. It truly is a unique piece."

"Fair enough. What do I owe you?"

Adam told him the price, adding, "If you'd like me to keep it here until you're ready for it, that won't be a problem. I have a spot in the back so no one's the wiser."

"That's fine, Adam, just fine." The mayor was almost to the door when he snapped his fingers and turned around. "You could think of changing the name of your store. Call it something special to show what you're carrying."

Adam nodded. The thought had visited him a few days earlier.

He walked outside and looked up. *Hazelton's Store* was a good name, but the mayor was right. He needed something with flair. A title that would appeal to both genders and still convey the uniqueness of his shop.

***

After a personal picnic in the park, Janet found Adam in the street staring up at the top of his building. He didn't pay her any mind as she took a stance beside him. Shielding her eyes from the noon sun, she looked up, too. "What are you looking at?"

He snapped his head over and glared at her. "You snuck up on me."

"I did not. As usual, you weren't paying attention." With another glance up to ensure nothing was about to fall on her head, she entered the building. Unlike the businesses that were all joined together on the congested blocks of Main Street, Adam's store was filled with light from windows on three sides that allowed customers to have a good look at what was on offer.

She slid the hand she'd used to shield her eyes into her pocket and caressed the smooth folded notepaper filled with sweetness for Adam's eyes alone. Yet hiding it in such a lighted area without him discovering her in the act would be anything but simple.

Adam trailed after her. "What can I get you?"

"Oh, I'm just looking. It seems the whole city is talking about the different things you're bringing in, and I wanted to see for myself before you sold it all."

Pride gleamed in his eyes as he swung his arm out in an arc to encompass the interior. "Take as long as you like. I'll be over here if you need help."

She studied the contents of a display case showing decorated egg cups, porcelain bonbon dishes, and the like, while he wrote in a notebook. Her plan was to drop the note into something, but that was proving difficult since most items with open tops were inside the cases. And then she spied the two valises standing beside the rounded lid of a steamer trunk. What if she merely dropped her note behind it? Surely he'd find it when he swept the floor. But how to distract him from the room so she could do what she needed to do?

The sound of stomping feet on the sidewalk rattled the glass in the front window.

Adam glanced at his pocket watch and then walked around the counter and headed to the door. Half a dozen young lads blazed in and stopped short as Adam raised his hands. "Welcome, boys. You have two choices. Settle down and act like a paying customer out for a stroll, or stand outside and look through the window."

Behind Adam, Janet saw her chance. She backed up to the trunk.

One of the boys angled his head to look up. "Is it true you're selling toys, Mr. Hazelton?"

While Adam nodded at the boy, Janet reached over and dropped her love note near the back of the domed lid, except instead of sliding down the back, it balanced on the edge.

"Yes, I am," Adam said. "Now, mind your manners or I'll chase you out myself. They're over there." He jerked his thumb over his shoulder in her direction.

One puff of air would topple the note over the side, but Janet had run out of time. She eased over to the counter.

"Yes, sir," the boys chorused, already on the run to get to the back corner toy display.

"If you break anything, I'll be calling on your folks," Adam called after them.

"Well done," Janet said.

He turned to face her. "Ah, you're still here." His gray eyes glinted as they looked at her—not through her, but at her.

Her pulse pounded in her ears. How long could she stand there under the force of his gaze without babbling about how he made her feel? Dragging her eyes away from his, she turned to the door. "Not for long. Since you have your hands full, I'll be off. Your store is always changing. I'll be back soon."

"Hey, Mr. Hazelton?" one of the boys called out. "Are these wagon wheels supposed to fall right off?"

Janet smiled as she walked away. That is, until she remembered her parting shot about being back soon. How soon could she return to find out if he located her note?

Not long if it didn't go over the edge. How long could she stay away without knowing? Already, her knees grew weak at the thought of him reading her heartfelt words.

At the end of the day, while locking up the storeroom, Adam's gaze fell on Mrs. Eider's pink vase. As the black cloud of devastating pain enveloped him, he dropped to the floor with his head between his knees. Waves of self-loathing poured over him as he immersed himself in memories he refused to forget. Why had he lived when he'd been the cause of others dying?

For several minutes he sat there before struggling to his feet. With the weight of his sin pushing down on his shoulders, he trudged to a house so devoid of life even spiders didn't bother spinning their webs in the corners.

Adam lay in bed the next morning and stared at the ceiling. He'd flipped and flopped during one of his worst sleepless nights ever, probably caused when the pink vase triggered memories of his family home.

But today was another day to get through, and he wouldn't allow his despondency to drag down the spirits of others.

Dressed in his finest, the mayor was waiting at Adam's store when he turned the corner onto Main Street. "Happy anniversary, sir."

"Thank you, Adam. I snuck out while the missus was making my breakfast."

Adam unlocked his door and led the way inside. "I have the vase back here."

"I thought it prudent to give it to her now instead of having her wait all day. She's a very impatient woman."

"A good plan, sir. She'll have a day to remember, for sure." Adam wrapped the vase in a piece of soft flannel, and then covered it with brown paper. However, instead of tying it with a string as he usually did, he cut a length of pink ribbon to secure the package. "There you go. I wish you both all the best."

"Thank you, Adam. I'll tell her you said so. Good day." He rushed out the door with his present cradled close to his heart.

Adam stared at the doorway for a long time. He'd ordered the vase, among other things, to resell as a way to make a living. Yet, that one item was a permanent memory for a special event in two people's lives.

He took out a new journal and then reached for a pencil. On the first page, he wrote down the date and that it was the thirtieth anniversary for Mr. and Mrs. Eider. If nothing else, he'd be able to wish them a happy day when the next year rolled around. He tucked the journal into the drawer he kept his valuables in, but paused before he pushed it closed. For the first time in years, he had thought about the future outside the realm of business.

He surveyed the showroom. Shelves and display cases filled with tins, toiletries, and fragile items. Stacks of luggage, crates, and linens across the center aisle. A back corner of items for youngsters. Where had the vision come from to have something special for everyone?

The Emporium. The name entered his mind like a locomotive on full steam.

Something for everyone, and the opportunity for anything. He liked it very much.

With the eagerness of someone with his life ahead of him, he strode down the center aisle. As he passed the trunk, a white paper fluttered and dropped down the back. Reaching down, he fished out a folded piece of floral notepaper, similar to the one he'd found days ago near the magazines. He opened it and read:

My heart beats faster when you are near, lean close to me so you can hear.

No one was in the store, and the mayor had been his only customer so far. Considering that it was the Eiders' anniversary, there was a good chance the mayor had dropped it in his rush to get back home.

Adam took out the first note he'd found and compared the script. A perfect match. The mystery was solved. If the mayor didn't come looking for his love note, Adam would take a run out to his place later and discreetly return them both.

Chapter 3

After three hours of typing, Janet shook the tension out of her wrists. Her speed increased by the week, but she still had a long way to go before she'd call herself proficient.

Neil leaned into her office, his hands on either side of the doorway stopping him from pitching forward. "You got a minute? I need your help."

He'd been moody for weeks. She'd first noticed it when he hadn't made fun of her for covering herself in ink from the typewriter ribbons after she'd cleared them out of the garden. Instead, he'd spent the rest of the evening in the barn with the stock.

Rising, she stretched. "Sure, what can I do?"

"Come with me to deliver the Emporium sign."

"I've been working all afternoon, Neil. I need to get supper started."

"Let Jack do it. I could use some advice."

"You're asking me for advice?"

His faced turned ruddy. "You're a girl, aren't you? Who else am I supposed to ask?"

She realized that the older brother who worked so hard at making her feel young and foolish was asking her for mature, womanly advice. The tension of bending over her machine eased considerably.

Pa appeared behind Neil. "It's all ready to go. Stay and help Hazelton hang it, too."

Janet perked up. "Hazelton? The Emporium sign is for him?"

"That's what Adam's calling his store now," Neil said. "Are you coming?"

She looked at Pa. "I sure would like to see some of the fancy things everyone's talking about."

Pa chucked her under the chin. "You go on, then. Supper will be ready when you two get back."

They had barely left the yard when Neil shook his head. "He never chucks me under the chin like that."

"If he tried it, you'd probably jerk back in alarm." She bumped his elbow. "I remember when he was washing your mouth out with soap every time you came home from school."

He laughed. "That's true enough."

"What did you want to ask me?"

"I'm sweet on Molly Saunders and want to show her my intentions."

"Your intentions? That's serious. Does Pa know?"

"Pa knows I'm sweet on her, but won't let me stop in when we're out delivering that way. I see her when I can. There's always a herd of ranch hands surrounding her, and I'm hoping to give her something special so she knows I'm serious."

"How serious?"

"To marry her, if she likes my gift."

He pulled the team to a halt outside Adam's store.

Janet placed her hand on his arm before he could jump down. "And if she doesn't like it?"

"Then she's not the girl for me, silly." He jumped down as if it made the most sense in the world.

Janet went over the conversation in her head. Somehow she had missed Neil's question, for it seemed like he told her what he wanted to do without asking her advice. Considering his attitude, that was probably for the best.

With a ladder on each side of the facade, Adam and Neil took down the old sign and then carried it around to lean against the side of the store.

While they were doing that, Janet went inside and searched behind the trunk for her second note. When she didn't see it, she decided it was time for number three.

A crystal lemonade set stood on a lace doily on top of one of the display cases. Once the men were back up the ladder hanging the new sign, Janet sauntered over and dropped the third note down into the pitcher.

By the time Neil and Adam walked in, she was surveying the toiletries across the main aisle with her hands folded behind her back.

Adam turned as he entered. "Thanks, Neil. Tell Jack I appreciate his workmanship."

"I'll do that. Mind if we have a look around a bit?"

"No, of course not." Adam nodded to her as he passed.

Neil approached her side. "Well, what do you think?"

"What do you mean?"

He leaned close with his back to Adam. "I mean for Molly. Come on, sis, we just talked about this."

"You said you were getting her a gift."

"Well, yeah, but you don't think I'm going to pick it out. That's what you're here for."

Janet stepped back, not caring who heard her. "Oh, no. I am not picking out something that will be the catalyst to decide your future."

"What?"

"You heard me. I'll help all I can, but I refuse to make the decision of what she gets."

"Well, fine then. I'll pick one myself."

Janet crossed her arms to hide her quaking hands. If he wasn't her brother, she'd—

Adam threw her a curious glance before moving toward Neil.

Realizing he must have heard the whole thing, she sagged against the counter. She'd only agreed to help because he'd asked her to, but if she'd known he was going to stake his future on it, she would never have come. Even if it meant not seeing Adam this week.

Adam tried to concentrate on Neil's problem, but he kept looking over in Janet's direction. He hadn't followed the complete conversation between the siblings, but when he saw the angry color darkening her cheeks, he felt he had to step in and do something.

Neil clasped his hands together on top of his head. "How am I supposed to know what a woman wants?"

"Who is she? Does she live around here?" Adam turned so that Janet was behind him where he couldn't be distracted by her.

"Molly Saunders. A rancher's daughter."

"How well do you know her?"

"Well enough to marry her."

Adam spun around at the sound of metal striking metal.

With a grimace, Janet raised the silver-latched lid of a tea chest off the rim of a nearby tin. "Sorry, it fell. I think I'll wait in the wagon."

Adam took a deep breath and then released it slowly as she left. He turned back to Neil. "Your gift must come from your heart if you expect it to reach hers."

Neil shook his head. "I don't even know what that means."

"Look around and see if something attracts you. Then close your eyes and imagine yourself giving it to her. How do you think she'll receive it? For example, look here at the trinket boxes. There's a crystal one, a silver one with embossed roses, and a wooden one with inlaid doves. Of the three, which one appeals to you?"

"I know that she prefers lilacs to roses, and she likes birds, too, but I can tell you right now, all of these cost too much."

"If you can't afford these, Neil, how can you keep a wife? You'll need to provide her with clothes, shoes, linens, and all sorts of little things."

Neil stared at the trinket boxes, deep in thought.

"Where will you live? Will she expect you to live on their ranch? Or at your place with your family? If it were me, I'd be asking what she expected before asking her to share my life. Otherwise, you might end up sharing hers."

Adam knew he'd talked himself out of a sale, but he couldn't allow Neil to do something rash without speaking his mind.

Sure enough, Neil left without a gift, although he said he would probably be back.

As they pulled away, Adam looked up at his sign with the realization that the new store was having an effect on the old Adam. First, he'd started making notes about his customers' private lives, and now he was offering advice without being asked. Heartfelt words had poured out of him like those from a preacher, or a father—or a friend.

He reached for his duster and started cleaning. If he wasn't careful, he'd be spilling his past to whomever would listen. Then once word got out, the good people of Miles City would be traipsing to his store—not to buy his goods—but to throw rocks through his windows.

He continued down the counter, picking things up and moving them farther down, while melancholy caught him in its grips.

When he picked up the lemonade pitcher, however, a flash of white drew his attention. He peered through the crystal and then tipped it over. Out poured another folded floral note.

Setting the pitcher down carefully on the doily, he stared at it as memories of the mayor's anniversary filled his mind. Eider hadn't returned that day, so after supper, Adam had carried the two love notes to the Eider place where the mayor had said he'd never seen them before.

Perplexed, Adam had put them back in the drawer when he returned to work the next morning.

And now there was another one.

The problem was that there were so many strangers coming to look at the items in his store, he couldn't hazard a guess who was leaving the notes, or for what purpose. Carrying the duster and the note, he went behind the counter to his stool. He couldn't say why he hesitated opening the note, yet apprehension set his pulse beating in his ears.

When he couldn't take it any longer, he unfolded the floral notepaper and read:

I've loved you longer than you can guess. Love me, trust me, and I'll confess.

Love? Someone was professing their love? He tapped the note on the glass counter. Was Neil using his store to leave love notes to Molly? He compared the script with the others. They all matched, but it didn't mean it was or wasn't Neil's since Janet took care of all the paperwork for the family.

He paced the length of the store for several rounds before taking up his duster and continuing his work. When he reached the end of the counter, he'd made a decision.

Janet returned to Adam's store three days later to thank him for whatever he'd said to Neil. Her brother had gone from brooding to pensive, without any more talk of Molly. It didn't matter to her who he married, except she had prayed it would be God's will, and if so, there wasn't a rush. She was curious to discover if that's what Adam had told him.

Adam looked up and nodded to her before giving his attention back to the seventy-year-old Lowell twins who were trying to decide between a trunk and two valises for their journey home to Canada.

She moseyed around the store with her hands behind her back. Only a few weeks ago she'd been lamenting the fact that Adam never looked at her, never mind smiled. Now, he threw her a look whenever she entered his fancy emporium. One of these days, he might even smile.

Her heart jumped when she saw her love note peeking out from under the pile of magazines. Strange. She'd been sure he'd found it.

As she continued her stroll, she caught sight of the second note on the back edge of the trunk, which happened to be surrounded by the men.

She carried another note in her pocket, but it didn't look like she'd have the chance to leave it behind.

"I want my own suitcase," George, the younger twin, announced.

"Me, too. We'll take them both," his brother said.

After they paid, Adam grabbed a suitcase in each hand. "Allow me to carry them to your buggy."

Janet didn't waste the opportunity. She'd seen Adam's coat hanging along the back wall in the storeroom and before she thought twice, she raced in, shoved the fourth note into the pocket, and ran back out to stand in the corner amid the toys and games.

By the time Adam returned, her breathing was back to normal.

He stood beside her. "I have a rocking horse on order."

Her pulse galloped. He was conversing with her of his own accord. "Any child would love that. I see lots of toys for boys, but I don't see a tea set."

"It's in the display case behind you."

She turned to admire it. "Oh, yes. It's very pretty."

"Pretty things for girls of all ages."

Was he flirting with her? She angled her head to gauge his expression while basking under his attention. "I can imagine Santa Claus sitting here entertaining the children with tales of his reindeer. Or even you, reading that poem, 'A Visit from St. Nicholas.'"

"Me? Why me?"

"It's your store," she bantered.

Two young women crossed the threshold, their eyes alight with merriment. Janet's enjoyment fled as she recognized Diana Webb and Doris Orson.

"Janet! Isn't this grand?" Diana held her arms out like a pastor reaching out to his flock.

Doris zipped from one display case to the other. "I want to see the hair combs. Where are they?"

Adam dipped his head to Janet. "If you'll excuse me, Miss Smith."

For several moments she stood there, going over their conversation, wishing he hadn't left. When Diana and Doris started throwing glances full of questions her way, she pretended interest in the merchandise without losing sight of Adam. Then Diana said something too low for Janet to hear and he bantered back. Diana giggled. Doris blushed.

Janet's heart ached. This was a new Adam, charming and attentive to everyone who walked through his door. Perhaps, like the Lowell brothers, he was a twin and had changed places with the Adam she'd pined after. It only proved that she knew less than nothing about him.

Was she foolish to pursue a man in such a way? To declare her love when he hadn't given a reason to show he cared for her any more than an item in his store?

Adam removed a silver floral hair comb from his display case and handed it to Doris.

Janet eyed the distance from Adam to the storeroom, wishing she could take back the fourth note.

The thought dissolved as Adam led Diana to a mirror on the wall beside the storeroom door, opposite the toy corner. With her hat off, and holding a hand mirror, Diana turned this way and that, preening, while Adam waited by her side.

Janet ran from the stifling room. Outside, with her hand on her bodice, she forced herself to breathe deep. Had the change from general store to emporium changed the man she'd fallen in love with into one she couldn't look at without seeing heartache?

Chapter 4

Adam drew on an extra reserve of patience as he assisted the two young ladies who seemed to know Janet and yet hadn't acknowledged her other than the initial greeting.

"Do you think the comb complements my hair, Mr. Hazelton?"

With Janet waiting on the side, Adam tried to hurry his customers along. "Yes, it looks lovely."

"Aren't you the gallant one."

Her attempt to bat her eyes was so ludicrous, he grinned. He felt a warm hand on his arm and turned to find the second young lady, also hatless, standing very close.

"I want to try on the sapphire pendant." She stared into his eyes.

Sweat poured into Adam's hands. The lady stood too close for propriety. He backed away slowly as if any sudden movement would spark them into action. "I'll just go get it."

He turned to plead with Janet for help, but she was gone. How could she leave him like this? He sighed and headed to the jewelry case. Footsteps echoed his from the other side of the counter, pausing when he stopped to retrieve the piece and continuing as he walked back to the wall mirror. He held out the red velvet–lined tray with the pendant, hoping the young lady, or her friend, would take it.

Instead, she faced the mirror and rested her fingertips on the hollow of her throat. "I want it right here."

Her friend lounged against the trunk wearing a mischievous, telling smile.

Adam didn't like being the brunt of their wiles, but in his position, the best thing was for him to bear it and try to avoid them in the future.

He fitted the pendant around her neck. "It's not fair that you know my name and I don't know yours."

She peered up at him in the mirror. "I'm Diana Webb, and she's Doris Orson. We're not married, but we're old enough."

He coughed into his hand. "I see." He gestured to the mirror. "Well, what do you think, Miss Webb?"

After they left with their purchases, Adam escaped to the water closet to wash the sweat off his face and hands. He hadn't planned on catering to little vixens—they hadn't even entered his mind when he'd changed the direction of the store. What would he do if they came back?

Still shuddering, he pulled his drawer open and retrieved his journal. He had started writing notations about what his customers liked, or didn't like, and somewhere along the way he'd started listening to everything they had to say. Instead of blocking out their chatter like before, he strained to hear their small talk. Nothing had changed. They still spoke of the weather, their neighbors, and politics, and these observances filled the pages of his journal, but they also included who was sick, or visiting from the east, or who was sweet on whom.

On a fresh page, he added the names of Miss Diana Webb, Miss Doris Orson, and their purchases. He didn't need to write anything further because he was sure he'd remember them for the rest of his life.

The idea crossed his mind that he could hire an assistant to take care of any customers he didn't wish to deal with, but he tossed the thought away. It was the nature of his business to handle all sorts of people, and he wouldn't shirk that duty, regardless of his past, or their nature.

After church on Sunday morning, Emily Dundas blocked Janet from leaving her pew. "I know you don't have the patience for ladies groups and tea parties, but the Ladies Social Club needs your help."

"No, Emily." Janet lowered her voice, mindful of lingering parishioners. "I always feel like they're judging me."

"Nonsense. They know you lack certain"—she twirled her hand elegantly—"social graces on account of being raised without the benefit of a mother. If anything, they look on you with pity, not judgment."

Janet dipped her head at Emily's brutal honesty.

Emily drew her into the aisle, her arm around Janet's shoulders. "Besides, you're mixing us up with the Ladies Home Society. The Ladies Social Club has one purpose only, and it has nothing to do with society."

"Emily, I refuse to take any more lessons on deportment. It's time wasted when I have so many other things to do."

"No, it's nothing like that. We need your advice on men."

Janet jerked back. "What on earth?" Was everyone mad? First Neil wanted her advice on women, now Emily on men.

"You live with four brothers, all of marriageable age. The ladies would like to know more about them before putting them on the list."

"What list?"

"The list for eligible bachelors, silly. There are far too many men compared to women out here, and sometimes it's hard to tell the good ones from the not so nice. So, we're making a list."

Janet shook her head. "I can't be part of this. You're making judgment calls."

"No, we're not. We're trying to save women from being ruined by men of questionable character by introducing them to upstanding men in our community. Churchgoing men with good morals."

"I don't know..."

"Well, I do. I'm getting older by the minute and want a husband and babies, and so do the others. We'll all have a better choice if we know who's available, and whether you help us or not, your brothers are going on the list."

With that, Emily marched toward a group of women and said something out of Janet's range.

Janet headed home, confused by their furtive peeks in her direction.

"You took your time getting home," Jack said as she walked in the door. He handed her a plate of the previous night's stew.

She sat at the table, around which Pa, Ben, and Neil were already eating.

Jack sat down beside her. "What were you and Emily talking about?"

"That's none of your business."

"Maybe not, but with the gaggle of girls watching you two, it was entertaining."

"She has a dumb idea and wanted my help."

Jack dipped his day-old biscuit into his stew. "Oh?"

The inflection he put on that one word caught her attention.

He dipped his biscuit again. "Emily's a smart girl. Are you sure her idea doesn't have merit?"

"Well, yes and no." Since she didn't see any harm, she explained what Emily had said about the Ladies Social Club. "What I can't agree with is that men will be judged on what we know of them, in other words, hearsay."

Pa cleared his throat. "A man's reputation is generally who he is."

"Not always."

"I said, generally. Seems to me that the ladies are trying to protect themselves, especially the ones who are alone."

Jack dipped his biscuit again. "So Emily's looking for a husband?"

Janet glared at him, but the effect was lost as he continued to eat.

"I wouldn't mind being on the list," Ben said.

Humbled, Janet bent her head. Ben's wife had been such a sweet girl. When she'd died from the fever after only eighteen months of marriage, Ben had lost his exuberance for life.

Neil leaned forward in his chair. "Count me in."

"What about Molly?" Janet and Pa chimed in together.

"I'm a teamster, not a ranch hand. Anyways, it's hard to get to know someone you never see."

"Son, if you want to take a job there, I'll understand."

"No, Pa. I've been doing some praying, and if Molly and I are meant to be, we'll find each other."

Neil's nod at Janet told her she'd had a part to play in his decision. Thinking back, however, she wondered if it hadn't been more of Adam's influence than hers.

"Janet, I think you should join this Ladies Social thing." Pa looked at his sons for signs of dissention before continuing. "Just to get things rolling, the boys will fill you in on whatever the ladies want to know."

Janet looked at her brothers with new eyes. They shared a home and she thought she knew them, but did she really? This was a very interesting turn of events. "Well, then. If I was looking for a husband, I'd want to know what he liked, and what he couldn't stand. What he considers his skills, strengths, and even his shortcomings. Also, his relationship with God."

While cleaning the dishes, she considered how Adam might answer her questions. What was his relationship with God? He didn't attend her church, but he could be a member of one of the others in the city. Or he may not go to church at all.

She almost dropped a dish at the thought of how little she knew of the man she professed to love.

Adam paused his dusting at the sound of boots clumping on his sidewalk.

"Howdy, Hazelton." Neil entered with a small crate in his arms.

Adam used his duster to point to his stool behind the counter. "You can set it right there, Neil. I suspect it's that shipment of watches I ordered."

"Uh-huh." Neil set it down gingerly before coming back around to stand in front of a display case. Bracing himself against the glass counter, he looked down at the assortment of egg cups.

Adam hid his duster on a low shelf. "Anything I can help you with?"

"Yeah. Remember the last time I was here, a week ago? When we hung the sign?"

"Sure I do."

He offered his right hand. "I appreciate what you told me even though I wasn't too happy at the time."

Adam hoped his surprise didn't show as he shook Neil's hand. "You're welcome."

Neil drummed his fingers on the glass.

It was plain he had something to say but didn't know how to say it. Since Neil had opened up to him about his personal life once before, Adam felt it wasn't untoward to cross the bridge once more. "What's on your mind?"

Had Neil come to claim his love notes? Adam had set them out as a trap for a few days and then changed his mind. He reached into the drawer for them.

"The Ladies Social Club wants to know if they can add your name to their list."

Adam dropped the notes back into the drawer. "You have me at a disadvantage, Neil. What's this all about?"

"It's a list of bachelors for the ladies. So they'll know who's in the running."

Sweat broke out in Adam's hands. "Not me." He backed away as if Neil was going to lunge at him and drag him out of there.

"Yeah, that's what my sister said, but she said the other ladies insisted I ask you."

"Janet said not to put my name on a bachelor's list?" Adam's mind raced. Why? Not that he wanted to be on the list, but why didn't she think he should be on it? "Did she give a reason why I shouldn't be on it?"

Neil threw him a curious look. "The ladies want God-fearing men of good morals and temperament." He shrugged. "Maybe she doesn't think you qualify."

Adam didn't know what to say. Whether he attended church or not wasn't anyone's business. If he allowed them to question that, then what would they want to know next?

"She's right," he snapped. "I don't want to be on the list."

"Why not?"

Adam crossed his arms in defiance. "Because this is a matchmaking scheme, and I want no part of it."

Neil straightened. "That's interesting."

"It's also democratic. What's the use of having a democracy if there are no dissenting votes?"

"Look, Hazelton, I don't know what got your spurs sharpened, but I'll tell the ladies you're not interested."

"You can't tell me you're on it."

"I am, and believe me, with all the men out there looking for women, there are plenty who are fighting to get on this list. The problem is that some of them aren't the type innocent church ladies should be matched up with, if you get my meaning."

Clouds moved across the sun as he spoke, dimming the showroom. By the time he stomped out the door, a wall of rain obliterated the view of the park across the street.

Adam's mood darkened along with the light level at the thought that he'd been the object of the women's discussion, never mind that they had decided whether he was suitable to marry one of them. It wasn't anyone's business if he married or why he didn't, because his personal life wasn't open for discussion.

He paced the showroom floor. Who decided whether the ladies were suitable for decent men? Why, those two vixens who had cornered him awhile back were probably members of this social club, although calling them ladies was stretching it. If there were so many men looking for women, why hadn't they been picked?

And why didn't Janet think he should be on the list? Everything she knew about him was based on what she saw of him in the store, and that wasn't enough to judge his character.

Just because he didn't go to church didn't mean he wasn't a God-fearing man. His fear of God's retaliation is what kept him away from church.

He stopped at the door and faced the street, now a slimy sheet of mud. Had she heard something about his past from her brothers? In their transport business, they were always on the road, talking to someone somewhere. But why would his name come up?

His new wall clock bonged five times. After ensuring the back door was locked, he reached for his coat, which he hadn't worn in two weeks due to the dog days of summer. But with the rain pounding down, he took it off its peg.

His gaze fell on the parlor safe tucked under a small worktable. He'd been so preoccupied with the thought of being talked about, he'd forgotten to lock up the cash. Still wearing his coat, he locked the day's intake in the safe.

As he reached the front door, the room lit up from a flash of lightning. A moment later, thunder rumbled above his head. He didn't mind walking in the rain, but a thunderstorm was something else.

He secured the door and then walked back to his stool where he shoved his hands into his pockets. His left knuckles scraped across a paper fold. Without thought, he pulled out another sheet of floral notepaper.

The white dazzled him with brilliance as lightning flashed through the windows, followed in an instant by a thunderous boom. He tossed the note in the drawer and slammed it shut. Why read words of gentle love when he needed the feel of heaven's wrath pounding on his soul?

Chapter 5

J anet squeezed the crumbly dough together in her hands. Her thoughts wandered to Neil, who should've been back already with Adam's answer, but he was probably riding out the storm somewhere. If Adam joined the Ladies Social Club, she could lose him to the girls who were trained to be ladies. She slammed the dough on the table.

"I thought we were having biscuits," Jack said from the doorway.

"We are." She picked up the dough and then slammed it down again.

Jack put aside the towel he'd used to dry his hands. "How about I take over before you turn them into rocks."

"What?" She stared at the fragile biscuit dough. "Oh, dear."

Leaving him to salvage what he could, she poured hot water into the basin and washed her hands. Little clumps of dough floated in the water like the thoughts hovering in her mind.

What if Adam didn't want to be on the list? Did that mean he already had someone in mind, or did it mean he didn't want to get married at all?

She'd left him four notes expressing her love, and other than putting them back where he found them, he hadn't given her a single indication that he had read them. Had he even mentioned them to anyone? Had he tried to deduce who they were from? A bit of investigative work would have pointed to her before too long, especially when her brothers admitted her penchant for poetry.

Her plan wasn't working. She had wanted to break through his haze and make him aware of her. She'd done the job too well.

The door swung open. Neil swept inside with water streaming from his hat and clothes. "I was gonna wait until it let up, but that might not happen for several hours and I didn't want to spend my evening in the Silver Star Saloon."

Janet took his wet coat to hang behind the stove. "Did you talk to Adam?"

He cast a critical eye on her. "I did. You seem anxious for his answer."

She tucked a wayward strand of hair behind her ear. "The ladies want to know, and I'm meeting them tonight."

"I don't think so," he said, shaking his head. He lifted a muddy boot. "You'll ruin your pretty dresses if you don't wait until it dries."

She bristled at his tone, until the image of washing yards of muddy hemlines came to mind. "At least there's nothing wrong with your eyes."

He studied her. "No, there isn't. And I'm beginning to see more than you want, I think."

Janet's heart thumped against her ribs. "What do you mean?"

Jack let the oven door bang closed. "Someone tell Pa and Ben to wash up."

"I'll go, since I still have my boots on." Neil's last look before he went back into the storm told her he wasn't done talking yet.

On Sunday, in preparation for an upcoming wedding, the preacher talked about the bond between a husband, wife, and God. He stressed the importance of harmony between marriage partners and the need to seek God for His direction. Such a bond would strengthen them in times of adversity. An excellent reminder of the importance of choosing a Godly man to share her own life.

At the completion of the service, Emily waited in the aisle, smiling in her direction.

"Morning, Emily," Jack said, blocking Janet's view.

Janet raised her hands to push him forward but paused with her hands inches from his back at something in his voice.

Emily peered around him as if he hadn't spoken. With her eyes on Janet she said, "Hello, Jack." She beckoned to Janet. "I have to talk to you."

In front of her, Jack's shoulders dropped. Glancing back, he stepped into the aisle. "I'll see you at home."

As if she hadn't heard a word he said, Emily took Janet's arm and pulled her through the groups of parishioners on the church grounds.

Janet's gaze followed Jack. Instead of socializing with the men, he headed homeward. Like a veil lifting from her eyes, she saw Jack as someone ready to start his own family. She thought back to the supper table when they'd first discussed the Ladies Social Club. Jack's interest had peaked when she had mentioned that Emily was one of the ladies organizing the club. Did Jack feel toward Emily the same way she felt for Adam? A sobering thought.

Emily tugged her arm. "Well, will he?"

"Will who what?"

"Silly. Will Adam Hazelton let his name stand on the bachelor's list?"

"I don't know. Neil hasn't said."

Emily stepped back in mock alarm. "Why did Neil ask him? You should have done it."

"No, I won't. I asked my brothers, and that was enough. Asking Mr. Hazelton would be too forward."

"Wait, there's Neil over there." Before Janet could stop her, Emily raised an elegant hand. "Mr. Smith? A moment of your time."

Neil, Ben, and Pa looked over from the circle of men conversing.

"Neil?" Emily persisted.

Janet turned away from Neil's knowing look.

He ambled toward them.

She'd avoided him since the storm, not wishing to divulge her secret, lest he say something to Adam that she wasn't ready to reveal.

"Miss Dundas. Janet. I'm at your service."

His gallant response might have hidden the amusement in his voice from Emily but not from Janet who knew better.

Emily stepped forward. "Mr. Smith, thank you for allowing your name to be added to the list of available bachelors in our community. On behalf of the Ladies Social Club, I ask that you convey our appreciation to your brothers, as well."

The eloquent words weren't lost on Neil, whose chest seemed to expand before Janet's eyes.

"I will, Miss Dundas. Was there anything else?" His eyes flickered to Janet, daring her to ask.

"Janet?" Emily nudged her.

Forced to question him in public, she attempted to follow Emily's gracious example. "The Ladies Social Club would like to know if you've asked any other gentlemen if they would be interested in putting their names forth, and in particular, Mr. Hazelton of The Emporium."

She held her breath, waiting for the words that would decide. . .what? It wouldn't decide anything unless she knew the reasoning behind it. She let her breath out with the realization that the answer didn't matter one whit. "If you two will excuse me, I've just remembered something important I have to do."

"Janet?"

She didn't turn at Emily's call. In the corner of her eye, her father and brothers turned as one in her direction. She kept walking, increasing her stride until she was far enough away to break into a very unladylike run.

Neil labored with the heavy crate. "You selling rocks now, Adam?"

"I suspect it's the books I ordered. It'll be awhile before I get to them, so you might as well bring it back here." Adam led the way into the back room. "Thank you, Neil."

The crate landed with a thud. Neil straightened. "Books, huh. Schoolbooks, or reading books?"

"Reading books. Science books. Bibles," he added beneath his breath.

"Did you say Bibles? I thought a drummer usually sold those."

Adam shrugged. "I have someone who wants a Bible, and the Bible drummer isn't here. I might as well stock them since I seem to carry a bit of everything else."

"Want me to spread the word?"

"That will be fine." He locked the door after Neil with a satisfying click.

If someone had told him when he first opened his store that he could triple his customers by ordering things no one wanted, he would have laughed at them. But that's what had happened. Instead of having his customers order what they wanted, sight unseen from a catalog, he took the risk by ordering what he thought they might like. He was grateful to people like the Smiths who helped spread the word.

And speaking of the Word, it was time to see what all the fuss was about. He pried open the crate to the familiar sight of fluffy golden straw. As if in reverence to the content, whoever had packed the crate had set the Bibles on top so that a mere sweep of his hand revealed several Bibles of varying sizes, some heavy and decorated, others compact with tiny printing.

The last layer contained a black leather-bound volume with a gilded cross and the words *Holy Bible* on the cover. It matched the one he'd owned years ago—the one that had burned with the rest of his possessions—except the leather wasn't worn smooth in places, and the pages showed no sign of being turned.

He set the Bibles on a back shelf instead of bringing them into the showroom like the other books in the crate. He'd sell the Bibles if someone asked for one, but he wouldn't put them on display like someone who believed in the stories of Jesus' miracles and God's love.

And yet love was the reason he'd ordered them, because the note he'd found in his coat pocket had mentioned Solomon's Song. Something about it had nagged his memory, but he hadn't been able to latch on to it other than to remember his siblings' whispers in the dark after the evening scripture reading.

Curiosity compelled him to reach for the simple black Bible. He balanced it in one hand. With his other hand, he drew the fourth note out of his pocket and read:

Solomon's Song shows love so fine, so hold me close and say you're mine.

He turned to Solomon's Song and skimmed over the words until the meaning caught his attention. He started the chapter again from the beginning. When he finished, he pondered on the words. Love in all its forms had been revealed on the pages.

Someone had left notes in his store, with each expressing love in a deeper sense. First in thought, then physical, then emotional, and back to physical of a deeper nature. More attachment every time.

If the notes continued, what was next? How many notes before he discovered the author? So far, he had sat and waited for the answer. Tomorrow he'd start investigating, even if it meant the author was on the run. Time to see who was playing the game of love and keeps.

With the love note back in his pocket, he set the Bible on top of the others.

For the first time in a long time, he was looking forward to a new day.

Chapter 6

An older man meandered around the showroom without any apparent wish to buy. Adam didn't recognize the lone man at first but then remembered something from a few weeks previous.

"Mr. Lowell?"

The man turned, showing sad, red-rimmed eyes.

Adam made his way over. "I was sorry to hear about your brother. How are you keeping?"

The inane words bounced off Mr. Lowell's melancholy. "Not well, I'm afraid. I think he's behind me, but when I turn, he's not there."

Adam surprised himself by reaching out and patting the older man's shoulder. "You shared something special that most of us will never experience. I don't expect it will ever feel right again. Is there anything I can get you, sir?" He dropped his arm as a thought occurred. "Did you ever use those suitcases I sold you? If you have no use for them, you can return them for your money."

Mr. Lowell shook his head. "Thank you, no. To see them sitting by the door is a memory of the past, and a dream for the future. At this stage, Mr. Hazelton, it's the only thing I have left." He extended his hand. "I appreciate your concern. You're a good man, Hazelton."

Shoulders sagging with the weight of his pain, he shuffled out the door.

Adam stared down the street after him. The exchange hadn't been pleasant, yet he felt as if he'd accomplished something decent. For a few minutes, he'd shared Mr. Lowell's pain.

Later that week, Adam's day brightened when Janet entered the store. She headed right to him, wearing a smile that warmed his heart.

"Hello, Janet." Her name slipped past his lips without thought.

For a brief moment, her eyes looked into his with an emotion that made his fingers tingle as if long-frozen blood thawed in his veins.

She turned to the man by her side. "Pastor Keyes, meet Adam Hazelton."

A sudden punch to Adam's stomach couldn't have surprised him more.

The preacher extended his hand.

After a brief hesitation, Adam shook it. "Good afternoon, sir. Welcome to my store."

"Thank you, Mr. Hazelton. Janet mentioned you have some Bibles for sale."

"She did?" He didn't recall her being in the store in the days since the shipment had arrived.

"Neil told me." She looked around the showroom. "Where are they?"

Adam wished he'd taken his own advice and hired an assistant. "They're back here."

In the storeroom, the preacher picked up the compact Bible. "Interesting."

Janet's gaze scanned the room. "What are they doing back here? Neil said they arrived several days ago."

Adam shrugged. "I haven't decided where to display them."

Her direct look searched his eyes, moving across the bridge of his nose as if each of his pupils revealed a different soul.

Janet caught her breath at the pain reflected in his eyes.

He glanced at his pocket watch. "If you'll excuse me." With his long apron flapping around his knees, he marched straight through the showroom and kept going across the street.

Instinct told her he was headed to his tree. She'd often seen him there, but as far as she knew, he didn't leave while customers were inside.

The pastor picked up the largest Bible with the leather-embossed board cover. He allowed his fingers to trail across the gilded geometric design. After putting it down, he lifted the simple black leather-covered Bible showing the gilded words and cross. "How long have you known him, Janet?"

"Adam? I mean Mr. Hazelton? Since he moved here a few years ago. Mostly through transporting his goods from the station to the store, but we also make deliveries for him. Why?"

With the black leather Bible in his hands, Pastor Keyes nodded toward the front door. "His past is catching up to him. He'll need someone strong to help him through it."

Leaving him to look at the other Bibles, she walked back into the showroom and stood at the end of the counter. She had watched Adam often enough to know that he kept his personal things in a drawer. What would he do if he discovered someone had been in it?

She took the fifth note out of her pocket as her pulse thrummed in her ears. Pastor Keyes could walk up behind her at any moment. Or Adam could walk through the door and catch her in the act. He would know she was the one leaving the notes. What would he say?

Without rethinking it, she reached over and pulled open the drawer. She paused at the sight of the other love notes tucked into each other like spoons. "Here's another one, Adam," she whispered. She dropped the note on the rest and closed the drawer.

Adam hadn't returned.

She went back to check on Pastor Keyes.

He held the compact Bible in his right hand, and the black leather one in his left. "I'll take these two."

In the showroom, he laid the two Bibles on the counter before bending to peer inside the display case. "I think I'll look around while you see if your Mr. Hazelton is ready to come back inside."

"Oh, but he's not *my* Mr. Hazelton."

Pastor Keyes laid a knowing look on her that would have matched King Solomon's. Since she refused to lie, she pivoted toward the door and left him to explore Adam's treasures.

They met at the door.

"Are you all right?" She reached out to touch his arm but stopped with her hand in the air as if it encountered an invisible barrier. His stern bearing warned her that whatever vulnerability he had shown in the storeroom had been displaced by a side of him that brooked no room for weakness.

"Has the preacher found something to his liking?" He strode past her, his voice loud enough to carry to the storeroom and back although the pastor stood right there. All business, Adam rounded his counter where he braced himself on the glass top. He flinched as his gaze fell on the two Bibles lying side by side before him. "Which one did you choose?"

"I'd like them both."

"Both of them?"

Something akin to panic flared on his face before he doused it as he had at the door. "You want both of them," he repeated.

"Yes, I have someone in mind for each of them."

"They are for sale, aren't they?" the preacher asked.

His challenge brushed Adam's nerve endings the wrong way. "Yes, they are. Like everything else, they come in and they go out. Nothing lasts."

"Do you need cash, Mr. Hazelton, or may I put it on account? Providing the Community Church at the end of Main Street has an account?"

"Your church doesn't have an account here. I'll start one for you today if you think your flock will agree."

"That will be fine. We don't shut the doors before the guests arrive, Mr. Hazelton. In fact, I'd like to think we don't shut them at all."

Adam didn't care if the preacher locked the church doors and tossed the key in the Tongue River. However, the sight of the preacher tucking the black leather Bible in the crook of his arm shot an arc of pain across his chest. He had discovered the Psalms one morning and now began each day by skimming bits of David's trials. Something in the young shepherd's fearful journey had reached out to Adam's pain.

But there were other Bibles in the back. Different cover, same story.

"I'll write that up and send it over today." With the sale complete, he nodded to send them on their way.

"Mr. Hazelton, we're having an outdoor service followed by a picnic this Sunday on the church grounds. You're welcome to join us for both, or just the picnic if that makes you feel better. We won't judge you either way. I believe you already know a lot of the good folks who'll be there, so you won't be a stranger to anyone but yourself." He smiled to emphasize his words.

It sounded to Adam as if the preacher had thrown down another challenge.

The preacher smiled at Janet. "Janet and her family will be there, won't you, Janet?" Yup, definitely a challenge.

Janet lowered her eyes in a feminine move he'd never seen on her before. "Yes, I'll be there."

Whether it was the preacher's challenge, or Janet's confirmation, something propelled him to say, "I'll see you on Sunday, then."

He should have said he'd changed his mind as they were walking away. He could have said it before they got to the door. He would have yelled it down the street if it hadn't occurred to him that if he went, he might discover the author of the poetic love notes.

Sunday morning found him dressed, polished, and brushed better than he'd ever been for the store, although he'd changed his mind a million times over the past few days. He planned to arrive after the service ended and before the meal started, which would give him time to investigate without having to sit through a sermon.

Halfway through the morning, after his small rented house had started to close in on him, he decided to get the love notes from the store and bring them along. Perhaps he would even show one of the first ones to Neil, who was used to seeing signatures in his line of work.

As he collected them from his drawer, he counted them to ensure he hadn't dropped one and accidentally kicked it under the display case. He expected four, yet counted five.

With confusion mounting, he unfolded them and laid them out on the counter. There were five. The most recent one said:

Your smile brings sunshine to my life. Oh, that I could become your wife.

He slumped on the stool, his gaze glued to the notes. Over the course of their delivery, the author spoke of love, trust, and marriage. Yet she had gone into his private drawer in secret. Where was the trust in that? Or, was that the confession she had warned about when the third note had read:

I've loved you longer than you can guess. Love me, trust me, and I'll confess.

If the author had no respect for privacy, what else would she do? Was she a raving lunatic? He had to find out who it was before the farce went any further and destruction of property or worse happened.

He numbered the notes in order and then swept them together. Not all of Miles City would be at the church picnic, but there would be enough to start him on his quest.

Chapter 7

J anet chose to sit beneath the old apple tree that grew close to the church instead of on a blanket like most of the congregation was doing. She had an ulterior motive in that she wanted to keep an eye on the street in case Adam came along. From the way he acted with Pastor Keyes in the store, however, she didn't expect him to show.

She wished she had the courage to ask him how he stood on the important things of life. If that lesson had been offered with the other social graces, she would have attended for sure. Could her feelings really be love if she didn't know who he was inside?

She withdrew the note she'd spent most of the night composing—the boldest she'd written yet, where the dullest of men would have no cause to misunderstand. With his sharp business acuity, Adam was anything but dull, yet after weeks of dropping visual hints she was no closer to him than any other customer in his store. Would God place such a man on her heart if there was no hope of a future together?

As the service began, she tucked the note into the folds of her skirt where her pocket was located, while turning her ear to the pastor's voice before it dissipated in the breeze. His message was a familiar one on remorse and redemption, meant to heal wounded hearts and replace despair with hope. Pastor Keyes often used the outdoor service for this message as he could reach people who would normally never step into a church without being pushed or pulled through the doorway.

It wasn't a surprise then, to see nonparishioners listening on the fringe of the gathering, but no matter how often Janet looked, Adam wasn't one of them.

Neil joined her at the conclusion of the service. "Hey, Janet, I thought I caught sight of Hazelton over this way."

She had prayed for guidance, hoped Adam would appear to give her an indication of what she should do next. What she didn't want was Neil telling her what she ought to do. "As you can see, he's not here."

He gave her a sharp look. "What's all this about? I know you're sweet on him—"

"Shhh." She swatted his arm. "What does it matter if I am? I know nothing about him, and he doesn't even see me."

"Of course he sees you—"

"Not in the way I see him, Neil. Not in the way Em—oh, never mind." Horrified, she stared at his boots. In her misery, she'd almost told Neil that Emily had her eye on him, while knowing that Jack had his eye on Emily. She'd never been inclined to play matchmaker and wasn't about to start now. They could sort out their own love interests like she was doing.

The crowd wavered before her. "Just leave me alone." Her shoes crunched on the twigs and stones under the tree's canopy as she ran toward the outhouse—the only private place around where she could wallow in her misery.

Adam heard the voices and laughter of the picnic before he reached the church grounds. Within seconds, his stomach growled in response to the tantalizing smells emerging from the laden tables where the women worked. His gaze scanned the crowd for a familiar face. If no one stepped forward to welcome him, he'd walk on past as if that had been his intention all along.

The flash of a blue dress in the corner of his eye caught his attention. Janet had worn a similar one to his store, once. Instead of finding Janet, however, he spotted Neil standing alone beneath the apple tree.

As Adam headed toward him, Neil bent down and retrieved something off the ground. Adam caught sight of a folded sheet of floral notepaper similar to the ones in his pocket. Perhaps the day would prove fruitful after all. "What you got there, Neil? Someone sending you love notes?" he asked.

Neil turned slowly. He stared at Adam for what seemed like minutes. "It was here, on the ground. It's pretty plain it's meant for you, not me. Here, read it."

Adam took the note and read:

You run your store with your own hand while my finger aches for your wedding band.

"Why do you think it's for me? I'm not the only storekeeper around. I've never even been here before."

"Uh-huh. Well, the girl who wrote it was just here."

"You mean you know who wrote them?"

"Them?" Neil looked around. "There's more of them?"

"Yes, here." In his hurry to present them, one floral paper escaped from Adam's hand. Neil snatched it in midair before it hit the ground. Adam handed him the rest in silence.

Neil took his time reading them. "What's this mean?" He pointed to Adam's scrawl in the top right of each corner.

"It's the order I found them."

Neil read them again in order. "Where were they?"

"Here and there among the shelves and things in the store. One in my coat pocket. Oh, except for the final one, which was actually in my private drawer. I'm not too pleased about that one."

"And you haven't guessed who it is?" Neil's tone held amusement, as if Adam was a dunce for not figuring it out.

"Not yet. It's why I came today. I want to know who's been playing games with me."

Neil handed the pile of notes back. "She's not playing games, Hazelton. Even I guessed it weeks ago." He grinned. "I am enjoying this, however. Might even keep you guessing."

Adam shoved all the notes back into his pocket. "You're not going to tell me?"

"Calm down." Neil's expression sobered. "That's my sister's handwriting. She's the poet."

"Your sister?" Adam held his breath as his heart skipped a beat. "You mean Janet, right? You don't have another sister off at school somewhere like your brother, Sam?"

"Nope. Just Janet." He gestured to the people lining up for the food. "I'll leave you alone to chew on that, while I get a plate of the real stuff. I'll be here if you need support."

Support? Why would he need support? Again, he sought out Janet. His heart jumped as he found her sitting on a blanket with some other women. He was about to go to her when he spied the two vixens who'd cornered him in the store sitting on a blanket nearby. They looked his way.

He hurried after Neil. "Wait up. I can't think when my stomach's growling." It wasn't the support Neil meant, but it was what Adam needed at the moment.

The frenzied tapping on Janet's forearm knocked the ice cream off her spoon. "Hey, watch it." She fumbled to scoop the creamy lump off her blue dress.

"There he is, Janet, with your brothers." Emily's nudge dumped the melting blob back in Janet's lap.

Her attempt to sponge up the sticky mess spread it in a wider circle. Giving up, she followed Emily's sight line to where Adam relaxed beside Neil and the rest of her family. Had she seen him there earlier, her elation would've shot to the moon.

Emily leaned into her shoulder as she always did to impart confidential information. "Neil said that Adam wouldn't let his name go on the eligible bachelor's list. I wonder why."

"I don't know, Emily. Could be that he doesn't want to marry." A sudden, horrific thought exploded in her mind. "Perhaps he's already married."

"He can't be as no one has ever heard of a Mrs. Hazelton." She peered at Janet with narrowed eyes. "Have you?"

"No, I can honestly say I don't know anything about him other than that he owns the most interesting store around."

"Look, Janet, he's coming this way." Emily rose to her feet. "I'll ask him myself."

"No, Em." Janet tugged at her hand, trying to pull her back down.

Emily ignored her other than to whisper, "Mind your manners, Janet." She stepped away from the blanket to stand in front of Adam. "Mr. Hazelton. Such a pleasant surprise to see you here today. Would you care to join us?"

Adam tapped the brim of his hat. "Another time, perhaps." He stepped around her, his eyes on Janet. "Miss Smith, would you walk with me?"

Janet felt light-headed and wobbly, unsure if she could stand. Emily's gape was reason enough to try it though. She accepted his hand and he pulled her up in a warm, firm grip without making her wince. A hand strengthened by years of honest work like Pa's and her brothers'. But why was he here?

"I didn't think you'd come today."

He made a sound that could have been a grumble, or a chuckle if he'd allowed it to hit the open air. "Would you believe my stomach told my feet to march when my nose smelled the food?"

Between his teasing voice and laughing eyes, her own stomach did funny flips. "Mr. Ha–zel–ton."

Janet dipped her lashes as she recognized the singsong voice of Diana Webb.

Adam tucked her arm in his and began walking as if he hadn't heard his name.

"There you are." Diana rushed in front of them with Doris by her side.

Adam tapped his brim. "Ladies." His gentle pressure on Janet's arm directed her to circle them on the right.

The ladies sidled over to block that way, too. Doris stepped forward, almost toe to toe with Adam. "We're members of the Ladies Social Club and we want to know when you'll put your name on the bachelor list."

"It won't be on it. If you'll excuse us." His arm pressure signaled Janet to try again.

Diana moved faster. "Why not? Are you taken?" Her eyes flickered to Janet and back.

His hand tightened. Not enough to hurt, but enough that Janet felt his sweat soaking into her sleeve. She addressed the interlopers. "You've interrupted a private conversation. Mr. Hazelton was kind enough to give you an answer, and you are now on the verge of overstaying your welcome."

Janet took the lead to move around the two gaping women.

"Well done," he murmured. "But you didn't have to stand up for me."

"I stood up for me. Those two were wasting my time as well as yours."

"I see. Am I holding you up from a scheduled engagement?"

"No. I'd just rather spend time with—" She coughed into her cupped hand. Saying she hadn't expected him to attend was one thing. Spilling out refrains of love was something better left for a time when they weren't surrounded by curious onlookers.

They reached the corner of the church property as the loud ring of metal striking metal announced that horseshoes were being pitched. She turned back to see her brothers waiting their turn. Neil glanced her way.

Across the street, the railroad tracks glistened in the hot sun, the perfect place to maintain her good reputation where she would be seen without being heard. Before she could suggest it, however, she became aware of Adam's stiffness. More so than usual, even as he looked down Main Street toward his store.

To ease his tension, she placed her hand on his arm, since he had already given silent approval to do so by linking her arm in his earlier. "Shall we walk the perimeter, or cross over to the tracks?"

His eyes flicked to her hand. "I'm not the marrying kind."

She snatched her hand back and tucked it in her other one. "Why are you telling me this? We've never even had a personal conversation."

His gray eyes glinted. "Because you proposed to me." He held up the handful of floral notepapers. "Let's see. . .*'hold me close and say you're mine. . . Oh, that I could become your wife. . .'*"

Heat spread upward from her chest, tightening her throat and setting her face aflame. The papers wavered in front of her. "Stop."

"And here's the most recent one. . .'*my finger aches for your wedding band.*'"

"Put them away." She pushed them to his chest. "Please."

"What was it—a game?" He cocked his head. "You don't know anything about me. Not once did you ask about my family, if I'm widowed, or even married."

"That's not fair! You put up a wall between yourself and everyone else. You never asked how I was doing. You never even smiled at me." Memories of how he used to be coursed through her veins like a runaway locomotive. She stamped her foot. "It's a wonder you have any customers at all."

"Pipe down, you two." Neil appeared by her side. "You're making more noise than the horseshoes."

Behind him, a sea of faces in varying degrees of amusement watched their every move.

Adam pocketed the notes. "I'm done here. Thanks for the invitation, but I don't think I'll be back."

Chapter 8

By the Saturday after the church picnic, Adam was tempted to put up a sign that only buyers would be permitted in the store. Gawkers could look through the window. Of course, he wouldn't do it, but thinking of work took his mind off Janet and the way he'd treated her in front of the whole church.

Their personal conversation had gotten out of hand when he'd buried his true feelings under a stern veneer. He'd callously read her poems aloud, and the painful emotions that played on her face had pulled his heart in all directions. Yet he hadn't stopped because she needed to understand that he wasn't a man she could love forever. If she did, sooner or later he'd let his guard down and confess his past. And she'd never look at him the same again.

For his sanity's sake, he couldn't risk it.

A wagon pulled up outside and Neil jumped down. Adam noted the empty seat where Janet sometimes sat. He'd been relieved when she hadn't accompanied her brother on the other two deliveries this week, but had hoped he'd see her on the Saturday run.

There were two crates in the wagon. Neil carried the smaller one inside. "I'll need a hand with the other one, Adam, if you have a minute. What did you order this time that's so big, if you don't mind me asking?"

"I got a deal on toys for the Christmas season, so I ordered enough to fill my back corner. There might be a rocking horse in here, or a dollhouse. Dolls, trains, could be anything."

They set down the crate between the potbelly stove and the toy display.

Neil wiped his forehead with his sleeve. "I've never seen so many toys in one place. Pa says toys are for idle boys who grow up to be fools." He eyed a train set with longing.

"Does he say the same for girls?"

"No, he let Janet have a doll so she could practice being a ma."

Adam's heart constricted as an image of Janet cradling a baby in a rocking chair by the stove came to mind. He cleared his throat. "Some parents don't have the money to buy toys when they have a houseful of little ones."

Neil spread his arms to encompass the corner. "You don't feel bad that little kids come in here and see all these, and their parents don't have the money to buy them?"

"I never thought of it that way, but, no, I don't. It gives them something to dream about. Something to strive for when they're wondering why they have to work so hard. Besides, you walk into any shop in this city and you'll find things priced so high only a few can afford them, but they're still on display. At least I let the kids play with these

184

when their folks come to shop."

"And speaking of shopping." Neil pointed to a porcelain creamer on display. "I'll take that one. I was rushing to get through kitchen duty last night and broke ours."

Adam told him the price while wrapping the creamer in a soft cloth and then in brown paper with a string around it. He cleared Neil's change from the counter and then opened his drawer.

"That the famous drawer my sister got into?"

"Yes, it is." Adam stared at the bottom of the drawer, remembering how much of a deal he'd made when no harm had been done.

"I see you still have the notes. You want me to bring them to her?"

Adam's breathing quickened. If he kept the notes, there was a chance she'd stop by for them herself. He closed the drawer. "How is she?"

"What are you asking, Adam? She's alive, and she's hurting. I can't tell you more than that." He headed toward the door but stopped halfway there to add, "Like I said before, let me know if you need my support."

Adam awoke the next morning with an urge to read how the shepherd David was faring. He reached for the black leather Bible before he remembered that he'd sold it to the preacher a couple of weeks back and hadn't gotten around to ordering a new one yet.

He read a bit from a couple of books he had on a shelf, but neither one satisfied him.

After breakfast, he walked down Main Street as he usually did, but when he reached the corner, instead of heading west to go to the store, he turned the other way. Before long, a song from his childhood beckoned him toward the open doors of the church by the tracks. He silently sang along as words he hadn't thought of in years flowed over him, their truth touching his soul.

When the song ended, he strained to hear the preacher's voice.

It wouldn't hurt to go in and listen to the service. Maybe sing a few songs. And then at the end, he would ask the preacher if he could buy the Bible back.

He ignored the turned heads as he slid into the back pew. Raised in church, he knew the routine, so when they started singing the final hymn he slipped outside and around the corner until everyone had left.

The preacher looked up as he entered. "Hello, Adam. It was nice to see you in church today."

"I hadn't planned on it, but. . .well. . .here I am." He shifted his weight from one leg to the other, and fiddled with his hat. "I was wondering if you still have that black leather Bible I sold you. I'd like to buy it back. Or you can pick another one from my stock regardless of the price."

"That's generous of you, Adam. However, I've written on the dedication page, so you probably won't be able to sell it again."

Adam's heart dropped a notch. "Well, if it's a gift for someone, then that's that." He turned away.

"Adam." The preacher held the Bible open to the front page. "Read the name."

Adam ran his fingers over the edge of his hat brim. What did the preacher have in mind?

The preacher waited with a patient smile.

Adam looked down. He swiped at his eyes and read the name again. "What's this?"

"I bought it for you, Adam. But I needed you to come looking for it." He gestured to a pew. "Sit with me awhile."

As soon as church was over, Janet hurried home. She'd seen the looks cast her way, then to the back of the room, and back at her. After their public discourse at the picnic, the only reason the parishioners would have acted that way was if Adam was in the building.

She'd braced herself for their meeting and then been disappointed when she hadn't seen him after all.

Footsteps hit the hard street behind her. "Wait up, sis."

Recognizing Neil's voice, she slowed her pace.

"Did you see Adam in church today? That was a nice surprise."

In response, she made a noncommittal sound.

"Do you remember those notes you wrote him?"

She groaned and picked up her speed.

"He still has them. He keeps them in that drawer."

"Neil, why would you tell me that?" She swung her arms to go faster. "Do you want me to go steal them back? Huh?"

"No, I just thought you'd like to know."

"Well, I don't," she snapped. As a thought occurred to her, she turned around and headed back to church.

"Wait! Now where you going?"

"I have to talk to Emily. Go get dinner for Pa. I'll see you soon."

Since she didn't hear him following her, she assumed he did as she asked. For the past week she'd pined for Adam, even though there was no hope for them. Heartsick, is what Pa called it. But no more. He had been at church and hadn't even stayed to nod at her, never mind say a greeting. He couldn't have been plainer in his actions.

She found Emily waiting with her family while her brother brought their surrey around.

"Emily, a word, please." No sooner had she dragged Emily out of earshot than she whispered, "Sign me up."

Emily leaned back to take a good look at her. "Sign you up for what? We only have one list, and that's for bachelors."

"Well, there should be one for spinsters, too. Just do whatever you're doing to let the men know I'm available."

Emily frowned. "Are you sure, Janet? Adam—"

"Don't even say it, Emily Dundas. He's not interested in me, and I need to take my mind off him."

"But you can't let a man court you when you have another one on your heart." Emily placed her hand on her bodice as if shocked by such an idea.

"It was one-sided, Emily, so it doesn't count. Let me see the bachelor's list, then."

"Oh, Janet." Emily hugged her, right there on the street. "Come with us for dinner. The Ladies Social Club is meeting this afternoon at our place."

Janet bit her bottom lip a moment. "They're expecting me at home."

"We'll stop by your place first, then. Don't worry. Come on."

Later that afternoon after the meeting, Emily drove Janet back home. "Are you going to tell me the names you wrote down?"

Janet sighed. "I didn't write any."

"Oh, but you must have. I saw you scribbling something."

"You really want to see?"

"Yes."

Janet handed her a piece of paper and then took the reins so Emily could read it.

"Oh, dear. Are you sure?"

"Yes." She handed the reins back to Emily and pocketed her paper. A minute later, she took the paper back out and stared at the five names. Each time she'd picked a bachelor from the list, she'd mentally sized him up against Adam. And then she'd written down the better man's name. She'd chosen Adam five times.

"How was your afternoon?" Pa asked as she entered the house.

"Good. I haven't been to a tea party in a long time."

"You missed our visitor. He left about thirty minutes before you walked in the door."

"He?"

Neil came in the door behind her. "Janet, you missed Adam."

Shock sent her wits flying. "Why was Adam here?"

"He didn't say. Perhaps you should ask him yourself the next time you see him."

They went back to what they were doing as if nothing absurdly important had happened while she was gone. What had Adam wanted? Surely nothing to do with their situation, because according to him, there was nothing between them.

The only thing to do was hitch a ride with Neil the next time he had a delivery. Unless she chickened out. Or came up with an excuse to stop by in the morning.

The next morning, however, they needed her to stay behind while all four men went on a delivery with the two wagons.

As she washed up the breakfast dishes, she told herself it was for the best because the last thing she should do was rush into Adam's store with high expectations that he'd changed his mind, only to find that his visit was nothing of the sort.

Anxious and confused, she headed to work intending to take her mind off all matters of the heart.

She saw the note as soon as she stepped into her office. A folded sheet of notepaper, similar to the ones she'd left for Adam, lay beside her typewriter. Her pounding heart kept time with the cadence of her footsteps as she crossed to it.

Ever so slowly, she picked it up and unfolded it. Her tears fell in rivulets down her cheeks and under her chin at his poetic words:

> *Meet me under the apple tree,*
> *We'll speak of our past and things to be,*
> *And then if you still want me,*
> *I'll offer my ring on bended knee.*
>
> > *Adam.*

She clasped the note to her bodice, held it there as she prayed. She read it again, slower, taking in each phrase to ensure she understood the meaning correctly. The thought crossed her mind that Neil was playing a joke on her, except she recognized the script as Adam's.

She was almost out the door before she realized that he probably wouldn't be there now; after all, he'd left the note the day before and wouldn't know when she stepped into her office.

Inspecting the note, she saw where he had written, *Monday, 5:30 p.m.* in a corner. How was she ever going to wait?

Chapter 9

At 5:00 p.m. Adam tucked Janet's love notes into his pocket. In front of him on the counter lay the black leather Bible. Beside it, a thin gold band. He was ready to present himself to Janet and then accept her answer, no matter how she responded.

Except he still had a customer in the store.

"Pardon me, but it's closing time," he said.

The elderly woman raised her cane and set it down half a foot to the right. Then she turned in line with it. "What's that you say?"

"The store is closed now. It's five o'clock."

She lifted her cane and moved it back where it was originally then followed it around. She did the same thing twice more until she faced the door.

Thinking she was leaving, Adam opened the door for her.

She didn't move. "Joe isn't here yet."

He closed the door, lest another customer think he was open. "Who's Joe?"

"Joe Nash. My son." She shuffled back around to look at the painted lamp shades.

Adam stepped outside to look up and down the street but didn't see anyone who could be Joe.

The woman shuffled to the next display case.

"Mrs. Nash, what time will Joe be here?"

Shuffle, shuffle, shuffle. "When he's done."

Adam prayed for patience. He couldn't leave the woman outside alone, and he wasn't about to leave her in the store. Although he'd already locked the back door, he checked it again while ensuring Joe wasn't waiting out that way.

The clock clicked on the quarter hour.

Adam's hands began to sweat. The most important day of his life and he was stuck in his own store.

"Mrs. Nash, is there something you'd like to buy?" He didn't want to have Joe arrive and then have to wait for them to pay for an item. That would take time that he wasn't willing to share with them.

"Not yet."

Adam heard an outfit coming down the street. He ran to the door. "Joe?"

The young bearded man tied off the lines. "That's me. Ma ready?"

"Joe's here," Adam called out as he led Joe through the door. "Thank you, Mrs. Nash. I hope you'll stop by again." He held the door open.

"I want that one," Mrs. Nash said.

Adam groaned. He closed the door and then walked down behind the display cases to see what Mrs. Nash was pointing at. "This one?" He held up a silver trinket box.

"No, the porcelain one beside it."

Adam glanced over his shoulder. 5:25 p.m. He handed the box to the woman. "It's on me. Good-bye."

"How much?" she asked, passing it over to Joe.

"It's a gift. Thank you, again." Adam turned away.

"We always pay our way. How much is it?"

He told her the price.

Excruciating seconds passed as she counted out the exact amount.

"Thank you, again."

"Aren't you going to wrap it?"

He stared at her. "Yes, of course."

She harrumphed.

By the time Mrs. Nash and Joe were out the door, it was 5:31 p.m. and Adam was beside himself. With the Bible tucked under his arm, and the ring in his pocket, he sprinted down Main Street. He couldn't even be sure that he'd locked the door properly, but he didn't care. Hopefully, Janet was still there.

Puffing, he arrived at the churchyard.

The area under the apple tree was empty.

Chest heaving, Adam sucked in gulps of air. He couldn't believe she wasn't here. Had she been and gone? Or hadn't she come at all? Holding on to his sides where painful stitches ached, he walked toward the apple tree. As he neared, he caught sight of a brown skirt on the ground on either side of the tree.

He strode forward and around to find her sitting at the base of the tree hugging her bent knees, her head resting on them.

"Janet?"

She raised her head. "Adam? Are you really here?"

"I sure am, sweetheart. Sorry I took so long. I had this customer, and—"

"It's all right. You're here now." Her smile dazzled him.

Adam dropped to her side under the apple tree. "I have something to tell you. I won't lighten or embellish it because you need the facts. What I'm about to say may change how you feel about me, and that's all right if you decide to take back what you said in these notes."

He withdrew them from his pocket and laid them on the ground between them. A light breeze fanned the papers. He imagined them blowing away as soon as he confessed, and reached for a stone to place on top of the stack.

"When I'm done, if you still want me, hand the notes back as confirmation that you still believe the words to be true. If you decide you can't live with seeing my face every morning for the rest of your days on earth, take the notes home and burn them. I won't try to change your mind."

She picked at the ground until a pebble dislodged in her fingers. Her knuckles turned white from the grip. Her actions said she was strong enough to face the truth. Was she strong enough to forgive it?

He held up his Bible. "I had a Bible like this once. It was a gift from my mother before I could even read." Closing his eyes, he used both hands to rest the top edge of the Bible against his chin. "I lost it in a fire."

He forced himself to look back at the house as it had been that night. To remember the breeze fluttering the curtains as he sat on the windowsill. "I lit a smoke up in my room, close to the window so that the breeze would take the scent away. I was on the threshold of manhood, old enough to drink and smoke but respectful of my folks who couldn't abide either habit." He picked up a twig and spun it around with his fingers as if turning time back to that moment. "It was almost bedtime when Ma called me down-stairs for something. I squeezed the burning tip off the smoke, tossed it out, and shoved the rest of it into my pocket for later.

"I should have guessed the breeze would blow the burning ashes back into the curtain, but all I could think was to get rid of it before they found out." A lump grew in his throat as he heard Ma's voice calling up the stairs. He cleared his throat before continuing.

"It didn't matter. One sniff and Pa knew what I'd been doing up there. He said he was tired of arguing and I was to stop or move out. I stomped out and rode to the nearest saloon." He paused, unable to admit the depths he'd allowed himself to fall into—no, not fall, he'd done it deliberately with full knowledge—willingly under his own steam. "Witnesses said the barkeep sent me sprawling into the street. Too drunk to get up, I crawled into an alley and passed out."

At Janet's gasp, shame from the depths of his soul seeped out of his pores, soaking him in sweat. He couldn't look at her innocence and see himself reflected in her eyes.

Rising, he walked a few yards away. "I saw the black smoke as I rode back the next morning. I rode hard, but it was too late. Everyone was gone. Ma. Pa. My brother and kid sister. My Bible." He stared at his Bible and saw the charred remains of the original one lying beside what was left of his sister's doll. His eyes stung as if still feeling the effects of the acrid smoke. It filled his airway and clung to each breath until he pushed the tenacious memories behind him.

Minutes later, he faced her squarely. "I haven't had a smoke or touched alcohol since that night, and I can never forget what I did to them. It was ruled an accident, so there was no punishment." His harsh laugh escaped before he could pull it back. "I committed the most despicable crime and got away with it. Even God tried to forgive me, but I wouldn't let Him because I didn't deserve to go unpunished.

"And then I started finding notes from someone who was thinking of me, wanting to be with me, of loving me."

Tears ran unchecked down her blotchy face. That she felt his pain, took some of his away. He crouched beside her. "And because of her love, and with the preacher's help, I've opened my heart to God and accepted His forgiveness."

A sob escaped her lips before she could smother it with her balled-up handkerchief. He turned toward the tracks to give her a moment of privacy. He was tired of hiding. His heart cried out for her to accept him, but if she didn't. . .if she didn't, he would stay and be a testament of God's love.

At the sound of rustling paper, he clutched the Bible to his chest and turned.

———————————◆※◆———————————

Janet picked up the pile of notes as Adam's pain engulfed her heart. Although he spoke with maturity, his remorseful words resonated with the cry of youth, when he'd felt challenged to assert himself as an adult and had failed. He'd carried his pain in silence, believing he wasn't worthy of love.

The notes had broken through a barrier she hadn't known existed. Only God could have filled her heart with love for a man she barely knew, extending that love with hidden poems to catch his attention.

She held them up. "My heart was full of unrequited love as I wrote these, and now, I want to keep them."

He flinched and closed his eyes, but not before she saw the bleak emptiness.

Rising, she rested her hand on his arm, near his Bible. "Adam, I want to keep them forever close to my side, as a reminder of our courtship."

"What?" His voice trembled. "Are you sure?"

"Yes, I've always been sure. You're the one who balked."

His eyes simmered with emotion. "Only because I tried to protect you. Each time you came to the store, I followed you with my eyes, while my arms ached to hold you—like this." He reached for her.

She leaned forward in anticipation, eager to seal the promise she saw in his eyes. Their lips met and warmth flooded through her, melting the last of her doubts away. When he lifted his head, she rested hers on his chest, not ready to lose the comfort of his arms now that he'd welcomed her home.

He kissed the top of her head and then pulled away. "You caught my eye long before I found the first note, but I wouldn't allow myself to think about tomorrow. Now, I'm eager for it." He reached for her notes. "Let me see those."

She handed them over without question.

He flipped through them until he found the one he was looking for and placed it on top of the rest. "I have to get this right." He sank down to one knee.

Giddiness welled up as she realized his intention.

He pulled a thin gold band from his pocket and held it up to her. "In my note, I promised to offer my ring on bended knee—even though you proposed first."

She rolled her eyes with exaggeration, knowing he would tease her with it for the rest of their lives.

His face grew serious. "I have fallen in love with you. Will you marry me?"

Brimming with happiness, she nodded. "I will, my love, I will."

Epilogue

A few months later in early December, Janet followed Emily down the aisle. Beside her, Pa patted her arm, his way of saying everything would be all right. Friends and neighbors smiled as she passed them, wearing her mother's silk ecru wedding dress, updated to 1890 fashion with Emily's help.

At the front of the church, Adam waited in his best outfit, his eyes shining with the love he'd saved for her alone.

She basked in its glow, knowing he saw the same reflected on her face. She'd stepped away from convention to show her love to the man God had placed on her heart, and she'd been rewarded with more happiness than she'd ever imagined.

From his spot of honor beside Adam, Neil caught her eye. But instead of his usual teasing look, he nodded with approval.

Janet stopped a few feet away from Adam. She turned to Pa and kissed his cheek. "I love you, Pa."

With great ceremony, he placed her hand in Adam's. "Your mother would be proud of you."

With a slight squeeze and nod, Adam let her know he also felt their mothers watching from above as they took the holy step together.

At the close of the ceremony, they sealed their vows with the traditional kiss. Flushed from the contact, a moment passed before she realized Adam had slipped a folded piece of paper into her palm before turning to thank the pastor.

She almost laughed out loud. The courtship was over, but the love notes would continue to provide a source of mystery and entertainment for some time to come.

Her heart sang with joy.

Anita Mae Draper's historical romances are woven under the western skies of the Saskatchewan prairie where her love of research and genealogy yield fascinating truths that layer her writing with rich historical details. Her Christian faith is reflected in her stories of forgiveness and redemption as her characters struggle to find their way to that place in our heart we call home. Anita loves to correspond with her readers through any of the social media links found on her website at www.anitamaedraper.com. Readers can enrich their reading experience by checking out Anita's storyboards on Pinterest at www.pinterest.com/anitamaedraper.

The Last Letter

by CJ Dunham

Dedication

For Red Pen, a.k.a. Nancy Dunham. Thank you, Mom, for editing every copy I've ever written, and rewritten, and rewritten. You not only made me, you've made me the writer I am today. And for Ferron, who is my support, and my "Cyrus," the love of my life.

Chapter 1

I
t was a day of stark contrasts, almost more than she could bear.

The heavy winter sky had thrown off its gray shroud. A luminous spring day, the most brilliant Emilia had seen since before the war, beamed above her. Its lapis blue mirrored the distant lake, and the water sparkled as if competing with the brightness of the sky. All around her the world was flooded with color, yet here she was, still wearing black.

With somber steps she continued down the cobbled main street of Canandaigua, New York, with another letter in hand. As she passed the fabric shop, she gazed with longing through the window at the rows of calico fabrics: they came from her father's warehouse. "Papa," she whispered, the ache choking her voice. For the first time in over a year she had the desire to take up needle and thread, but who would she quilt for now? She had sent Papa and her only sibling, Johnny, off with handmade quilts, but they had been killed in the battle of Melvern Hill three years ago. She had made quilts for her fiancé, Asa, and his comrades, who were freezing under threadbare blankets, but it wasn't the cold that had reduced the company from one hundred to twenty men. A quilt is a comfort not a shield, and last year Asa also fell; for him it had been at the Battle of Cold Harbor.

Asa! As she thought of him all the fondness came back. He was a good man. He would have been a good husband. They would have had a good life. But now all she had left was a weekly ritual of mailing letters to him. They had made a vow before he left that they would write faithfully to each other until the last day of the war, and so she continued to send letters. It seemed a morbid thing to write one's dead fiancé, but it wasn't really. More than once, Emilia had caught her father talking to her mother's picture after she died. He confessed it eased his grief. Well, this ritual gave relief to both Emilia's grief and integrity.

On she walked, past the milliner, barber, and bread shops, as she did every Monday. But today was different: the bells of the Methodist Church began to ring, followed by a succession of bells of three other churches. Among the clamor came the incompressible cry, "Lee has surrendered! Lee has surrendered!" The town went wild. Hats flew up in the air. Like the breaking of a dam, people began to flood the streets as word spread.

The letter fluttered in her hand with a rising breeze. Dated April 10, 1865, it now marked the last letter she would send to her deceased fiancé. The war was over.

At this moment it seemed easier to be brave in the face of danger than in the face of this emotion, but she managed to lift a foot, then another, and make what would be the last offering to Asa's memory. As she walked, the jubilation seemed to nip at the heels of her grief. Hand bells began ringing like a swelling tide, flowing down the street behind her while she maintained a slow, methodical gait.

When she got to the post office, Mr. Andrews, the postal clerk, wore an uncharacteristically grim expression, a stark contrast against the flags and ribbons blurring past the window. He didn't reach out to take her letter either, just stared with what appeared to be watery eyes. He was an older man but didn't have the dewy eyes of the aged. Tears of joy would have been understandable considering the victory celebration erupting on the other side of the wall, but his was the countenance of a pallbearer. The wrinkles around his mouth and eyes trembled slightly, as if cracks in a stone that was about to crumble.

Emilia parted her lips to ask if he was all right, but a lump lodged in her throat, and she saw that her hand was likewise trembling. Until now she hadn't realized how much this ritual had sustained her, given her a purpose.

A man entered the post office. With a vague glance over her shoulder, she saw that he was tall, broad shouldered, and filled the doorway. He wore the blue uniform of a Union officer, yet he was so young, only in his twenties. His face was shadowed under the brim of his stained hat, but she could see his dark brown eyes looking back at her.

She extended the letter to Mr. Andrews. He accepted it while looking at her with that intense expression in his eyes. "Miss Davis," he said as she turned to leave. His words caught her like a snag on her shoulder, and how she dreaded snags! She was not a perfectionist, except with quilts, and of late with the penmanship of her letters. She had surrendered her last letter, so what could he want?

"Miss Davis," the postman hesitated. "You have a letter."

"I just handed it to you, sir."

"No, you have *received* a letter."

"I believe there must be a mistake." Emilia had distant relatives, but they were just that, *distant*. She knew them by name only, and that because they were recorded in the family Bible, but she couldn't tell where they lived, and they certainly wouldn't know Emilia's address. Yet Mr. Andrews held up a letter.

"Miss Davis." His voice cracked. "It's from Asa Wilson."

A long moment of silence passed between them. Her mind couldn't fully attach to the words he spoke, as if he'd uttered them in a foreign language. Again she parted her lips to reply, but nothing came out; verily her mind couldn't even form the astonishment into a single word. In a timid gesture he extended the envelope.

She looked at the crinkled envelope and saw her name: Emilia Davis, 221 Downy Lane, Canandaigua, New York. She forced her eyes to look at the return address. 1st SGT Asa Wilson, XVIII Corps, Washington City.

"It can't be!" Emilia gasped. A shadow moved behind her. It was the officer as he took a step toward her then hesitated. "How can it be?" she asked Mr. Andrews, who could only offer a shrug. This had to be a cruel joke, and crueler still in this setting of unbridled reverie. "Asa Wilson died June second last year. You know that." Blood drained from her lips. "Who would do—"Then it struck her, what this could mean, and she snatched the letter from his hand. Her breath shook with a rising tremor as she ripped open the envelope.

"It can't be," she mumbled as she shot the postman a pleading look. "Could it be that he's still...that there's been a terrible mistake and he's still..." *It's a joke, it's a mistake, this is wrong, wrong*, she told herself, but hope is a sudden flame when ignited.

She slid the letter out of the envelope and looked at the signature. It was signed Asa Wilson! Written in pencil, the handwriting was similar, but the down strokes heavier. Irrational as it was, the first thought that came to her mind was, *What has this war done to him?*

Mr. Andrews came around the counter to steady her hand, but it was too little too late, for next she saw the date at the top of the letter: June 2, 1864: the day Asa died. This had been his last letter to her.

Now it felt as if all the blood drained out of her head. Fainting, all she was aware of was something warm pressing against her back, and realized that it was the soldier's chest as he caught her.

Chapter 2

I'll fetch water," a deep voice spoke in her ear as she was lowered to the bench outside the post office. The officer left as the clerk began patting Emilia's hand.

"You just rest here a bit," he said.

"No."

"Excuse me?"

Emilia lifted her chin, drew a breath, composed herself, and slid the letter in the envelope that had appeared on her lap, presumably placed there by the postman. "I wish to return home."

"You need to rest!"

"I need to think. I need to go home. I'm going home. Now!"

Mr. Andrews called after her about seeing a doctor, but her mind had gone as numb as her ears, and her frame stiff as a dressmaker's mannequin as she moved back down the street.

❦

The letter clutched to her breast, Emilia walked beneath the lane of cottonwoods to the low white gate of Downy Lane. Papa always had a sense of humor, and as he was in the textile business, he deemed it the perfect name for their small but cozy property.

The cottage was five rooms short of a manor, Mama once said. But as Emilia approached the porch, she thought that, though it was not impressive or large, it was the most beautiful dwelling she'd ever seen. How she loved the Grecian-style porch with its small but proud pillars! The family had done well in textiles. Since girlhood she'd fallen in love with the sight of rolls and rolls of cloth the way a sailor falls in love with the sea. Cloth had become her life, and her skill as a seamstress was unmatched, even by the tailor.

No longer able to maintain servants, Emilia entered the empty house and collapsed in her favorite button-upholstered chair. It was situated next to the parlor bay windows. More than for the view, she adored this spot because of the potted tree beside the chair. It was an orange tree, and even she had laughed at Papa's foolishness for trying to grow oranges in New York. It never did produce fruit, but, oh, the fragrance of its blossoms filled the entire room! This was where she was wont to sit to read the Bible, to pray, and, once upon a time, to sew. Today, it was where she sat to read Asa's last letter.

Just then she noticed the figure of a man at the gate. It was that scruffy-looking officer from the post office. He was indeed tall, his shoulders almost too wide for the blue coat. The double row of gold buttons down the front added to his impression of height. He could have been the face of war with that misshapen hat, the miserably untrimmed dark beard and mustache, and the brooding yet intense brown eyes shining from under the brim. Perhaps he had come to ensure she had arrived safely home? But there seemed to be another agenda as he stood there with a saddlebag slung over his shoulder. Then as suddenly as he had appeared, he turned away and disappeared under the dappled shadows of the cottonwoods.

This near encounter made Emilia more acutely aware of her aloneness as she slumped in the chair, the letter burning as if a hole in her chest. Distant cheers and horns and clanging bells pealed out like the rolls of unwelcome thunder. It was unlike Emilia to tremble, as she did now, praying for strength as she read the letter:

Dear Emilia, [Emilia winced: Asa had always written Dearest]
I must be brief as I haven't much time. [Oh, the irony of that line! It was unbear-
able.] I wish for you to know that despite all the sacrifices I've made for this war,
I am grateful I was here to help preserve the Union and to do my all to end the
blight of slavery in this land. But I do not wish for you to think of my hardships.
Rather, think of me resting on these cool nights, gazing up at the stars as they bloom
in the ever-deepening blue of night. I have missed you more than you know. I have
thought of you daily, especially at night, wishing I could share these views of heaven
with you. I have cherished each of your letters and have slept with them as I dream
of better times.

Emilia turned the page over, angling it into the sun in an effort to read the pencil marks.

Kansas has just become a state in the Union, and I find myself aching for a new
life out west. This may sound strange, but I want to own a store and live free, out
on the wide-open plains away from all this turmoil and strife. If anything should
happen to me, I want you to know that I have come to admire you above all other
women. When this war ends, after the mourning has past, I wish for you to think of
starting a new life, of living under brighter skies and embracing a beautiful hope of
your future.
I have been cheered by your goodness even in these harsh times. Whatever you
do, don't stop sewing, for your quilts and your grace are a gift to all who know you.
Emilia, carry on to that brighter place, and know that you are loved.

Emilia dropped the letter in her lap. Why, why did Asa have to write like this now? Why did his last letter have to be the first time he wrote with such a sympathy of expression? Now she felt something more than fondness for him, she felt the stirrings of love—unrequited love!

A wagonload of people flew down the road, shaking cowbells, of all things, and shouting, "The war is over!"

I know, I know! she wanted to shout back. *That's all I know. The war is over, the war is over! Everything is all over!* As if in a voiceless reply, the verses Papa had taught her from Psalm 139 shot through her mind: *"If I ascend up into heaven, thou art there: if I make my bed in hell, behold, thou art there. If I take the wings of the morning, and dwell in the uttermost parts of the sea; even there shall thy hand lead me, and thy right hand shall hold me. If I say, Surely the darkness shall cover me; even the night shall be light about me."*

Picking one of the last blossoms left on the tree and placing it inside the letter, she vowed, "Yes, Asa, I will find that brighter place."

The screen door banged like a gunshot. Emilia jumped at the sound. Only now did she see a horse and carriage parked near the porch. Lost inside the last letter, she had not noticed the arrival of a man—who was now standing in the entryway, staring at her.

Chapter 3

Miss Davis?"

Emilia sprang to her feet, alarmed, until she realized that it was only Mr. Langley, the family banker and financial adviser. Emilia's shoulders dropped in relief.

"Miss Davis, good morning," he said with a nod.

"Mr. Langley," she returned. "What brings you here?" Though she hardly needed to ask.

"One could barely make you out, dressed in black, sitting in shadow." He had been urging her for months to discard the mourning dress and join him on outings, both of which she'd refused. "Have you heard the news?" he spouted, an actual note of enthusiasm in his otherwise monotone voice.

"How could I not?" she retorted, walking toward him while yet another rider whooped and shouted as he rode down the lane toward Main Street. "It is good news." It was her turn to be monotone, feeling as if a dam had burst and the full effects of the war were just now tumbling down upon her. "Shall we?" she asked, stepping out onto the porch.

"Why, yes, yes, of course," he replied, following. "I meant no impropriety. I'd forgotten you had to let Opal go as well."

"I find it difficult to believe that you could forget anything, Mr. Langley," she threw back over her shoulder as she found a seat on one of the wicker chairs on the porch. Although he was only in his late thirties, his eyes drooped and gave him the appearance of a man ten years his senior. His goatee was not only trimmed to perfection, it came to such a point as to appear to tuck into the V of his starched high-necked collar. It was hypocritical, she knew, to judge him for the dishwater gray of his eyes, but if only poor Mr. Langley had some color in them; something to give them the appearance of depth.

"The end of the war will bring about remarkable changes, not only in the financial climate of the country," he said, drawing a chair up next to her, "but in other respects as well, I hope."

Emilia was not blind to his intentions, nor was she receptive. "But that is not why you've come, Mr. Langley."

"No," he leaned back, "it is not. Unfortunately. This is a business call. I'm hard pressed to tell you that there is no other recourse. Downy Lane must be sold. Without your father's income, well, the estate funds are running out."

Emilia looked out over the estate. There was not an inch of lawn that did not hold a family memory, and the whole of it seemed infused with the footfalls of every Davis who had lived here since the days of the Revolutionary War. How was it that war marked the beginning and the end of this place?

"Miss Davis." He leaned forward, and she noted that the fragrance of his hair tonic was stronger today. "I understand that your female sympathies run deep and that this is a most distressing time for you; however, it's time to move forward. You cannot stay here alone, not a young and lovely woman as yourself. It's not safe. It's not done."

"Are you ordering me to give up my home?"

"I'm only the harbinger of bad news, not the instigator of it. The proceeds from this property will support you in a boardinghouse." She bristled. He saw it and smiled. "I found a charming one with a lakeside view."

"I need time to consider it." Oh, how could she bear it, to lose Downy Lane, to live in a boardinghouse!

"My dear Miss Davis, I don't see that you have a choice."

Emilia was sure Papa was rolling in his grave this very instant, and as he had been buried with his Colt Paterson revolver, she imagined he was pointing it at Preston Langley this very instant. She shut her eyes in a censoring gesture for allowing such an unchristian thought.

"I already have"—he hesitated—"several offers for the estate. I took the liberty of drawing up the papers—"

"What?" Her head swung around, her eyes targeting his, and it was probably a good thing the Colt Paterson had been buried with her father.

Mr. Langley threw his hands up. "I don't want to see you deposed from your home but feel duty-bound to ensure your future, Emilia."

It was not only the fact that he used her Christian name but how he used it that incensed her. "Mr. Langley—"

"Preston, please."

"Mr. Langley," she continued, "I will consider your advice. Good day." She marched toward the screen door until he said:

"Perhaps you would join me at a lecture tonight? It's being given at the Methodist Church by a Mr. Isaac Goodnow from Kansas."

"Kansas?" She turned. "Did you say Kansas?" The words from Asa's last letter jumped before her eyes.

Encouraged, Mr. Langley continued: "Yes, he founded the town of Manhattan to help create a Free State." He had placed his words well, knowing how Emilia detested slavery. "He will be giving updates on the settlement, and because he is a former Rhode Island teacher, it promises to be a very stimulating oration." Who but Preston Langley would propose a speech for a first date? Yet it worked, because of Asa.

"Indeed," Emilia said, "I would be greatly interested in attending this lecture."

Chapter 4

Mr. Goodnow's lecture was more powerful than most sermons Emilia had heard. He was the leader of a group who'd left in 1855 under the auspices of the New England Emigrant Aid Company to populate the antislavery vote in Kansas.

Isaac Goodnow's purpose for traveling back to the eastern states was to raise money for the improvement of their Blue Mont College, the second in the country that would admit women. So they weren't just lobbying for equal rights for the blacks but also for women?

The more Emilia heard, the more her heart burned. Her face also burned when she saw that same officer sitting in the congregation. She almost didn't recognize him out of uniform, in a simple cotton shirt and brown wool pants and a nearly clean-shaven face. He now donned a close-trimmed chin-strap beard and a mustache. He listened to the lecture with that same sober, intense expression in his eyes.

To every soul there comes a defining moment, an instant when one decision can change the rest of one's life. For Emilia, such a moment was imminent, and she could feel its approach as Mr. Goodnow continued: "Kansas is a place where the elements can beat against you like the devil himself. But it is also a place where the stars shine out in their golden splendor. It has become a promised land for those of us who have left our homes here to establish a new life out on the frontier. We have not only built a town but a college that admits students regardless of race or gender. Any who would like to support our school, your donations will be consecrated to a magnificent cause. To any present who feel the call to join us, you will find that a promised land awaits you, too.

"I would like to take this moment to announce that one of our citizens built our general store ten years ago."

Now Emilia's ears began to burn, straining on every syllable as he continued. "However, family matters are calling him back to Rhode Island. He will be selling his mercantile to—" Before he could utter another word that fire shot down Emilia's legs, and she bolted up onto her feet with her palm flashing high in the air.

"I'll buy it!" Her voice boomed louder than it ever had in her nineteen years.

"Excuse me?" Mr. Goodnow politely inquired, unruffled at the interruption.

"I said, I'll buy it," Emilia replied as her hand sank down to her side. What was she doing? This was madness, but it wasn't hers. It was Asa's. This was what he wanted, and what did she have to lose? A future in a boardinghouse?

She raised her hand back up, acutely aware of the officer's stricken expression, as if this was a personal affront to his male ego. That put her hand up even higher. "Mr. Goodnow, I want to buy that mercantile. I've lost my father, my brother, my mother, and my fiancé to this war." This fact was painfully emphasized by the black dress that still donned her small frame. "If anyone needs a promised land, it's me. I helped my father run his textile business, so I am qualified to run that store. If your college admits women, why not your town? If Manhattan has a female shop owner, then it will stand as an example, a testament, of a truly Free State. And it would serve as a boon to your school. I pledge to donate five percent of the store's profits to Blue Mont College, making me both a donor and a settler."

"What are you doing?" Preston gasped under his breath, grabbing Emilia's elbow. He stood up, and she knew it was to make a public excuse for her wild behavior, but before he was fully erect she saw Mr. Goodnow look down from the pulpit at the officer, as if to get his opinion. They knew each other? Emilia jerked her arm away from Preston's grip and looked directly at the officer, saw him discreetly put up his hands and shake his head no.

How dare he? But Mr. Goodnow shocked the forming protest right out of her mouth when he looked over at her and said, "I see no reason why you can't purchase the mercantile, Miss—?"

"Davis, sir, Emilia Davis."

"If you have the means and the gumption, if you also pledge to be a Free-Stater, we welcome you to Manhattan!"

Emilia gulped then said, "I do, to both," and with her hand up in the air, it felt as if she had just been sworn in—but to what? She was both surprised and relieved at the power in her otherwise quivering voice. She promptly sat back down, stunned by her actions, ignoring Mr. Langley's censoring whispers. The closing song was "Rock of Ages." Every time those words were sung, she could have sworn the congregation sang, "shock of ages." What had she done?

At the close of the meeting, Emilia's tension doubled when that officer approached. Unlike most men, the closer he got, the more handsome he became. Now she *was* being foolish, and she shook her head as if to reset her wits.

"Miss Davis," he said in a deep voice. She was glad he spoke softly; with a voice like that he could easily sound formidable. "My name is Cyrus Holden. We met briefly at the post office this morning."

Her face flushed. "A pleasure to meet you properly this time. I hope I caused you no inconvenience."

"I was glad to help and am encouraged to see you looking so well. I hope I'm not being intrusive if I offer some advice?"

"That what? Women have no right owning property? That we are incapable of taking the reins of our own lives? May I lay your need to advise to rest, Mr. Holden. My acquaintance, Mr. Langley," she gestured to him by way of introduction, "has been informing me on the horrors of such for the past ten minutes."

"Begging your pardon," Mr. Cyrus Holden tipped his head as if in an unconscious gesture to show deference, "but a single woman of legal age *can* own property. However, the law states that once a woman marries she must relinquish all wages and property to her husband."

"Well, then, I will be sure not to marry the first prairie dog that comes along." What was meant as sarcasm was taken with humor as his slight grin proved that he was enjoying her wit.

"I've heard it said that a dog is a man's best friend," he retorted, "but I haven't heard that said of a woman. Yet. Perhaps you enjoy breaking all conventions?"

His ease unsettled her. "Am I to understand that you are encouraging me to purchase the store?"

"The law is on your side in that respect, but not in another."

"And what, pray tell, is that?"

"Even in Kansas, the law allows a woman to purchase property but not own a trade license. In effect, you can own the store, but you cannot do business out of it."

"That's absurd!"

"I didn't write the laws. If I did, many of them would read differently, including this one."

"Why would the law allow me to own a store but not sell from it? How preposterous!"

"Yes, it is!" Mr. Langley broke in. "All of this is preposterous, Miss Davis! Tell me you are seeing reason at last?" But Emilia ignored him, keeping her eyes leveled on Mr. Holden.

"To ensure your new endeavor," Mr. Holden continued, "may I suggest you find a man you trust to take out that business license for you?"

"Ah," she said, "and you propose to be that man? I own the store and you bank the profits?"

"No, Miss Davis, I was merely," he shot a look at Langley, "suggesting you find a man you can *trust*." With that he mimed tipping a hat and walked out of the church.

Oddly, Mr. Langley was silent on the matter of the store as he drove her home. Not a censoring word passed his lips, only a farewell kiss, which he presumptuously placed on the back of her hand.

Chapter 5

The irony of life redoubled: on the day that the world turned black, Emilia wore color.

One week after the church meeting, Preston Langley had sold Downy Lane and the textile mill and on Monday had the documents for the purchase of the Kansas store ready for signing. The first thing Emilia did upon rising on this, her final Canandaigua morning, was to fold her mourning dress in tissue paper and lay it to rest in the trunk. Next, over corset and petticoat, Emilia slipped on a flowery chemise dress. It felt like a baptism from depression and loss. Even as the fabric flowed over her shoulders, hips, and legs, like cool spring water, it also felt like a smug insult to the memory of President Lincoln.

Only days after Lee had surrendered, the president had been assassinated. Now the entire Union had come under a mourning pall. Fireworks were doused while victory speeches were burned. Buildings were covered in black crepe, and grown men openly wept in the streets. Once again church bells rang out, but now they tolled with the ominous tones of a dirge.

And this was the day Emilia cast aside black for a cheery floral dress! But she couldn't bear another hour, another second, of that mourning dress; not now that she had the hope of a new life. It was as if she had regained her youth, and upon arriving at the bank, her hand couldn't sign the purchase documents to her new store fast enough. The instant her foot left the shadow of the bank, she was on a carriage to New York City.

But once at the train station platform, life wove an unexpected thread around her ankle. It stopped her dead in her tracks when she nearly ran into a boy clinging to a pole. No more than seven years old, his eyes were pitiful, filled with the same desperation she felt pounding in her chest. His hair was almost blond—was it the natural color, or was it coated with dirt? His clothes were ragged; frayed twine held his shoes together.

"Pardon me! I didn't see you there," she said. No response, just a doleful stare from his large eyes. "Are you lost?" Emilia knelt beside him and brushed a finger down his cheek. "Shall we find your parents?" When she reached out to take his hand, he jumped up and grabbed her in a neck lock. The unexpected force of his body threw her backward. It was then she felt his small body trembling: he was terrified.

She stood, holding him, and he clung to her with a fervor she had never known. Scanning for potential parents, when she turned full around, she saw a train being loaded with children of every age. The only adults were the few who stood at the loading steps, ticking off names on a piece of paper as each child boarded.

"What is this train?" she asked one of the women in charge.

"Hello," the woman smiled, and it was a welcome relief for Emilia hadn't seen one of those in days. "My name is Margaret DeHaven. Is this one of our boys?"

Now the boy wrapped his legs around her, as if holding on for dear life. Never had she seen, much less felt, a child in such a state, and she found her own arms wind as tightly around his waist, as if she, too, were clinging to him for dear life.

"Why are only children boarding?" Emilia asked.

"My dear," the middle-aged woman replied, her salt-and-pepper hair thin but comely, and the early lines on her face indicating a woman worn with work. "This is one of many orphan trains. We are the Children's Aid Society, dedicated to finding homes for the tens of thousands of abandoned children in New York City. This train will travel to the Missouri border. Flyers will announce its arrival at stops along the way, and farmers and homesteaders can come to the stations to adopt a child. They need help, and the children need homes." Peering around to the boy's face, she said, "Oh, yes, this is one of ours."

"He's frightened," Emilia said.

"Madam, I assure you, the children are given much care, and it is a far better place they go to than these filthy streets of hunger."

Another one of those defining moments came, and again Emilia seized it. "What if someone wants to adopt a child right now? Save you the expense and time? Save him the trauma?"

"We are eager to place them in a Christian home wherever it can be found. The children must be loved and well cared for, and we follow up to ensure both giver and receiver are happy with their situation. Is your husband in agreement with this?"

The last of the children were being boarded. Emilia knew she was out of time, that the boy would soon be pulled out of her arms, and how he clung to her! Never in her life had she felt needed, and certainly not with such ardor.

"Miss DeHaven, I am not married, but I am the owner of the mercantile in Manhattan, Kansas. If anyone needs another pair of hands, it is me, and he will grow to be a great help and strength, I am sure. I promise I will care and provide for him, and take him to church every week."

Though Miss DeHaven's eyes were sympathetic, she shook her head. "I'm afraid a single woman doesn't constitute a family, Miss Davis."

Why did tears sting along her lashes? What had come over her? All she knew was she couldn't bear to be parted from this boy. "This war has taken my family. I am alone in this world, but I have ample inheritance, and I'm joining the New England Emigrant Company, leaving upon the hour to Kansas to support their noble cause. There can't be a finer place to raise a boy."

"And if I were to tell you that this boy is deaf?" Miss DeHaven arched a brow. "That he hasn't spoken a word since we found him on the Lower East Side?"

That only caused Emilia to hold him even tighter. "I wouldn't say anything. I would ask a question."

"And what is that?"

"What farmer or settler will adopt a deaf boy?"

Miss DeHaven drew a breath, the same concern evident in the tightening expression crossing her face. "It isn't my decision, Miss Davis. This is wholly unorthodox."

The boy must have understood the look on the agent's face for he burrowed his face into Emilia's neck. "I've learned that when God opens a door, sometimes we have to act swiftly before it closes again. What if I am this boy's open door, Miss DeHaven?"

The woman paused, and it was strategic, her eyes conveying an unspoken message. "It will have to come up before the committee, and as you can see, there is no time for that. He is slotted to board *a* train today."

Emilia thought the agent would pull the boy from her arms, but instead she withdrew to the orphan train, where she boarded with the last child. Emilia wondered if this was her chance to run or if she should wait and hope the agent returned with permission? But the train doors closed, and she realized that Miss DeHaven was turning a "deaf ear."

Seizing the chance, Emilia darted through the station as fast as she could while carrying a boy, purchased another ticket, boarded her train, and dropped into the seat with the boy still clinging to her. For the second time in less than two weeks, she sat stunned in the aftermath of a rash decision. What had she done? But instead of being awash in regret as realization and sagacity set in, she was overwhelmed with relief as she held him even tighter.

Chapter 6

After two days of mindless rain, the train at last stopped in Chicago. Emilia purchased clothes and shoes for the nameless boy. Dipping a handkerchief in the clear water of a rain barrel, she washed his face to reveal adorable features and starred eyelashes. He looked at her then, really looked, as if studying his choice, and she wondered if perhaps he would have a fit of regret and run off. To the contrary, he raised a cleaned finger and traced her face, as if learning the features of this newfound friend. She smiled, and he smiled back. The fear seemed to wash from his eyes like sheets of rain down a train window, and in its place were clear, fresh eyes filled with wonder.

"My name is Emilia," she said, pointing to herself. He didn't respond, just watched the movement of her lips. "What is your name?" He made no effort to speak or make a sound. "Well," she concluded, "how about Josiah? He was a boy king of Israel who did great things. What do you think? Josiah? Jo-si-ah," she pronounced as she pointed at his chest, repeating it several times. He smiled, whether in agreement or amusement she couldn't tell.

At the Missouri-Kansas border, they took a Wells Fargo stagecoach to Fort Riley then a wagon to Manhattan. The more the coach jostled and bumped over the unfamiliar terrain, the more Emilia felt afraid, and the more Josiah seemed to come alive with excitement. She may have been a stranger in a strange land, but he appeared to be born to this environment.

Manhattan proper was nothing more than a wide dirt street that dipped into the Old Blue River at one end and disappeared into a copse of trees at the other. The short stretch in between was all that constituted the town, comprised of clapboard or white rock buildings.

The driver reined the horses to a stop halfway down the street, in front of a filthy, dust-covered building. She was about to ask where the store was situated, when to her sheer horror she looked up and saw the word MERCANTILE on the wind-blasted sign over the porch roof. There were signs of a nice coat of white paint under a layer of dirt, and the structure was sound—at least the walls stood confidently upright. It wasn't a full two-story, but the vaulted roof appeared to hold the promised upstairs apartment.

Her trunk and bag were tossed onto the ground beside her, and the wagon pulled away. *Wait*, she wanted to call after it, terrified at being left in this dismal place, but where else was there to go?

When she went to unlock the door, the door swung open at touch. "Hello?" she called, but only the echo of a barren room answered. Emilia was not given to female hysterics as so many of her sex were wont to display. But when she looked inside the store, she could have miraculously fainted and screamed at the same time. Every shelf, hook, and counter was barren—the store had been robbed! But it was far from empty: a windstorm had deposited half of the state of Kansas inside. Dirt was piled up against the walls and counter as deep as a New York snowbank. But instead of white water crystals, her store had been socked in with dry brown filth.

Josiah ran up and down the mounds—this was a haven for a boy. But for Emilia, a young woman of refinement, it was the exact opposite. Oh, the regret, the humiliation! This was no promised land; it was desolation. She was ruined before she began. Exhausted beyond reasonable limits, weary from the hot train ride, and sunbaked and bruised from the wagon, she collapsed against the doorway and sobbed out loud.

"The cottonwood seeds are about to fly," she grieved, "and Papa and I would have danced in them like snow at Christmastime." Clinging to the doorjamb like a sailor in a storm, she shut her eyes against the stinging regret. "The plum tree flowers are turning into fruit, and Opal and I would have made jelly, with extra sugar because they're always tart." Pressed against the side of the doorway, the hoop skirt bowed up against the other side, a lopsided bell, the base of the whalebone frame cracking. "Johnny and I would have run down the bank in the heat of the sun and splashed water until one of us fell into the lake."

How could she have willfully left Canandaigua for this inhospitable wilderness? Was this how Jeremiah felt in the bottom of the pit? How dare she compare herself to suffering prophets, but even Paul's prison was a clean house. "I could be sitting in the parlor under the orange tree right now. What have I done?"

Just then she looked down and would have sworn Life itself was laughing, for she spied one item the thieves had left behind: a shovel!

Chapter 7

Night was falling when Emilia forced herself to take the first step into her ruination. Beleaguered, she dragged the boy up the stairs in the hope of finding a clean spot to eat the last of the crackers and cheese she had purchased at the fort.

Only days ago she had stood inside Preston Langley's posh bank and signed where he pointed. The one document she had read was the inventory sheet. On the list were stores of canned food, which Emilia had counted on to sustain them until a personal order was placed. Now what would they eat for the next two weeks? Or would a shipment take even longer? Where was she to buy food in the meantime? The only store in Manhattan was this mercantile.

The one reprieve in all the mess was that the small apartment over the store had been safeguarded from the storm by a secure door. Unlocking it, Emilia found a tidy room. Nerves eased as she scoped out quaint living quarters. It held a side table with a washbowl and pitcher, and a decent bed with a cheery quilt. A braided run on the floor, and a kerosene lamp mounted to the wall, finished off a plain yet tasteful room.

The boy refused the bed, hiding under it instead. "Josiah?" she said to herself. "Darling, what kind of a life did you have on those streets?" Terrified of the dark, he refused to come out. Emilia scooted the rug under the mattress so at least he would be up off the cold floor, and he appeared thrilled, rolling himself inside it.

Laying down on the bed, she prayed but one thing in the aching darkness, "Forgive me for not putting him on that train."

Emilia spent the bulk of the morning shoveling dirt until her arms gave out. "I swear, half the street is inside my store!" she exclaimed. "Perhaps I should sell the dirt back to the town," she joked, knowing Josiah couldn't hear but treating him like a hearing child nonetheless.

Bless the boy's heart, he was as helpful as he was energetic, and he rallied to Emilia's side as soon as he saw the shovel drop. It appeared he thought himself quite a man the way he attacked the dirt with the blade.

The blacksmith saw their plight and came with his beefy arms to help. He informed her that the townsfolk were having a day of respect as the body of the fallen president was being conveyed on a train to its final resting place in Springfield, Illinois. "I only came to the forge today to fetch a tool. I can take over here, ma'am. You and the boy head on down to the river to cool off."

Emilia was more than obliged to do so. At the riverbank, like an answer to prayer, she was greeted by cottonwood trees! Their seeds were swollen with tuft, like pillows about to burst at the seams. Soon they would fall like a summer snow shower, and when they did, she promised herself she would dance in it with Josiah.

The water was clear and cold, soothing sore muscles as she bathed her arms and face. Josiah, on the other hand, stomped through the water, as if a river was the greatest invention he had ever seen. As he did, he caught sight of someone upriver and waved. Emilia leaned over the bank to get a glimpse, saw a man about her age, his face shaded by a hat. His stance and build looked familiar, but before she could get a good look, he disappeared into the trees.

Back at the mercantile, she found that the blacksmith had removed all of the dirt and swept the floor clean. Well, at least now it no longer looked like a dump heap—just an empty store. On the counter she found a cloth napkin cradling fresh jerky and three carrots. Next to it was a note written with blunt strokes:

Well tell women to come tamarow to hep you clean. They well be rit happy ta met you.

Exhaustion would have been a kinder state than the one that claimed Emilia. After eating their meager but delicious dinner, she dropped into a deep stupor on the stair-case that led up to the apartment. When she woke, it was dark—and the boy was gone! Frantic, she searched the town and the river, to no avail.

Had he run off? But then she remembered the prominent hill that stood a few hundred paces behind the store. Josiah had been eyeing it throughout the day. Frantically, she ran toward it, her skirt flapping around her heels. Panting, she charged up the hill. Once at the top, she spotted the boy's small dark form as he sat staring up in wonder at a sky bursting with stars.

Her first impulse was to scold him for running off. But the sight of the adorable boy brought a wave of relief, and his wonderment was contagious. She found herself gazing up at the great expanse. Out in the raw and wild and open air, standing above the dark and endless prairie below, it was as if she stood halfway between heaven and earth. Never before had she seen so many stars. Mr. Goodnow was right: they did shine out in golden splendor! The Milky Way was more vibrant, more brilliant, more resplendent than anything she had ever witnessed in her life. Here, the seeds of eternity floated in this immensity. She gasped then laughed when stars began to fly around them as a meteor shower streaked through the glittering heavens. The sight brought her down to her knees behind Josiah, and she wrapped her arms around his small shoulders. He wasn't surprised; he must have sensed her presence. She laid her cheek on his hair and whispered, "Wish, Josiah, make a wish!"

Suddenly, a shadow moved in the nearby brush and then stood up to the full height of a man! Emilia seized the boy and bolted upright to flee.

"It's only me," the dark form exclaimed, "Cyrus Holden!"

Instinct drove her to the bottom of the mound before the words sank in. Whirling around, she looked back up the hill and saw his black silhouette standing against the glittering Milky Way. It would have been a marvelous sight to see any human form set off by such a backdrop, even his, but that stance. . .that form. . .it was the same as the man she had seen at the river that afternoon. This Cyrus Holden had followed her all the way to Kansas, and was spying on her! What kind of man—with what intentions—would do such a thing?

She fled into the darkness in the direction she hoped was the mercantile, pulling little Josiah along so fast his feet hardly touched the ground. Not until she got to the store and locked the back door behind them did she pause to breathe. Chest heaving, she slid down the door into a heap on the floor, Josiah locked protectively in her arms. Stiff Emilia, the walking mannequin, began to shake.

Just when she thought she had gathered her wits, there came a knock at the door. Emilia pressed her back against the wood, as if her petite frame could stop an intruder.

"Miss Davis? It's Cyrus Holden, from the church meeting in New York," he said through the door, followed by another knock. Should she yell back, threaten him? Or remain silent and hoped he left? "I'm sorry I frightened you. Please accept my apology."

"I have a gun!" she shouted back through the door. Her blasted temper! But the words had already shot out of her mouth. "Did you hear me? I have a gun—and—I can use it! I will shoot you through the door if you don't go away!"

There was a pause before he replied, "Well, yes, you could shoot the door, but the bullet would fail to pass through the wood with sufficient velocity to stop an intruder. Such an action could be a waste of your bullet. And if you did manage to shoot me, it would be a greater waste, as I am the one person sworn to protect you."

Now fear took a deep curtsy to temper as she jumped to her feet and yelled, "I don't know why you're here, why you're following me, Mr. Holden, but rest assured I will file a complaint against you with the peace officer of this town!" There was a pause as she rocked nervously on her heels, wondering if there even was a sheriff in this want-to-be town.

"I would be happy to oblige you," he answered. "I can take your complaint now, or you can come to the telegraph office in the morning where I've set up my desk."

Joints stiffened with the realization, and she stood frozen to the spot with the word *what* stuck on her lips. "What"—it finally shot out—"what are you talking about?"

"Ma'am," and by the soft hum of his voice she could tell he was leaning against the door. Oh, if only Papa hadn't taken his revolver with him! If only she could test his little bullet-piercing-wood theory! "Mr. Goodnow hired *me* to be the peace officer of Manhattan."

Half words and chopped syllables stumbled over her tongue, and it was just as well they didn't find a voice as they would have been unintelligible. She fell back on the only word her brain could form tonight: "*What?*"

"Miss Davis, I am the peace officer. I'm sorry I frightened you. I came to tell you that it was only me on the hill."

"So who's going to keep me safe from *you?*" she yelled back. "And what kind of peace officer has a jail in a telegraph office? What kind of a simpleton do you think I am?"

"Ma'am, I don't think there is *anything* simple about you."

"Well, I'm not a fool. A peace officer in a telegraph office? What would you do with your criminals? Wire their mothers to come spank them?"

There was another pause, and she was sure he was smirking. "Uh, no, ma'am. I intend to keep the peace, not criminals. This isn't Carson City."

"Well, I don't believe you, Mr. Holden. I demand you tell me why you are following me."

"I didn't mean to upset you, Miss Davis. I only meant to allay your fears. I'll leave now. I expect I'll see you in the morning for that complaint against me."

He was laughing at her! When she heard him walk away, she threw open the door. It was difficult to be enraged when he turned back, his body relaxed, a sheepish expression on his face. "I demand you answer me. Why are you following me?" In that moment she realized she had just thrown open the door to her would-be stalker. Yet irrational pride kept her from slamming it on him.

"Begging your pardon, ma'am," he said with that tight-lipped smile. Fear would have reasserted itself as he towered a head above her, but when he took off his hat, it signaled a gentleman in her presence. That was, until he said, "But one could say that it was you who followed me to the church meeting. I had arrived there first, after all." How dare he? And then he dared even more. "I met Mr. Goodnow before the war, and the plans were in motion for me to come settle that very claim whereon you just trespassed. Could it not be concluded that *you* are following *me*?"

With that she did slam the door on him.

"Good night, Miss Davis," he said through the door. She was sure he was tipping his hat as he said it. "If you need anything, I'll be just down the street...with a real gun."

After locking the door, Emilia held the key in a trembling fist—trembling not from fear.

Chapter 8

Apeace offering from the peace officer," Mr. Holden said as he stood at the front door to the mercantile, presenting a tin plate of freshly cooked eggs, a loaf of bread, and two apples. Emilia was speechless.

"This was wholly unnecessary," Emilia exclaimed, more irritably dismayed than pleasantly surprised, for now she would have to be polite to him.

"I was too forceful last night, Miss Davis," he said as he handed her the offering. "I've spent the past two years giving orders to men, not conversing with ladies. I was a brute and wish to apologize and explain. I was originally stationed here at Fort Riley. When the war broke out, my troop was sent to Virginia."

"Virginia?" Emilia whispered, the name heavy on her lips.

"Yes, ma'am."

"My fiancé fought there. His name was Asa Wilson. He fell at the battle of Cold Harbor."

Cyrus Holden's throat constricted. He turned his hat in his hands as if trying to keep his balance. "We lost over six thousand there." He as quickly redirected. "As I said last night, I had staked out a claim here before my reassignment, in the hope I would return."

That gave Emilia pause, realizing what he meant. He continued, his head slightly bowed as if he struggled, in vain, to not tower over her. His speech was low and careful, reflecting an apologetic tone. "When we first met in Canandaigua I had already been relieved of duty. I was required to report back here at Fort Riley and was mustered out yesterday. I wasn't following you, Miss Davis, but I can see how it might have appeared that way."

"I'm afraid I've let my losses get the better of me," she said. "I apologize for my untoward behavior. Thank you for the food." How thankful she assumed he didn't know, for this would be the only meal for the day.

"I am deeply sorry for your losses," he said. "As for your store, I hope you will feel comfortable filing a report of the robbery, giving me a list of what was stolen."

The town had come to life today, apparently the "day of respect" for President Lincoln over, and wagons, men, dogs, a runaway cow, and a pig had occupied the street this morning. Now she saw a gaggle of women heading toward the mercantile.

"Uh, yes," Emilia said, stunned by the sight of the entourage. "I have a copy of my inventory." After setting the plate of food down in front of the boy, who charged at the eggs with the speed of a hawk, she retrieved the inventory sheet and handed it to him.

"I'll make a copy," he said. "Could you come sign the complaint in an hour?"

"Yes, thank you," Emilia responded just as the older woman leading the brigade marched up onto the porch, holding an ear trumpet. It was made from an animal horn with an ivory earpiece at the point. The other women were holding buckets, mops, and rags. Mr. Holden nodded to them and departed.

"The sewing circle meets today at the church," the older woman announced. "But we've canceled it as we've been informed of your arrival and demise. I'm Mrs. Vandemark." She spoke loudly, her tongue and lips hitting every consonant with precision. She carried herself as if she were the town matriarch and made the introduction for the seven other ladies.

The women were efficient if they were nothing else, and they had mopped and scrubbed and washed down the store, including the porch and exterior walls, before noon. As the service project came to a close, Emilia took off her work gloves and said with a flourish, "When my first shipment arrives, I will make a cake to celebrate our new life here in Manhattan, and you are all invited to join us!" But as she looked out over the gathered churchwomen, their expressions fell—none more so than Mrs. Vandemark's.

"Ladies," Mrs. Vandemark announced, "we are finished here." With that, she turned and marched out of the store. The rest of the women offered their good-byes, but their countenances were altered, and they quickly retreated to the church.

"My," Emilia commented to Josiah, "but they close up shop quickly, don't they?" So what if the townswomen were a little backward in their manners? She had friends! Scooping up the boy, she whirled him in a circle on the now gleaming wooden floor.

Chapter 9

Had she, or Manhattan, been altered? An hour later, as Emilia walked hand in hand with the boy to the telegraph office, this place seemed to have transformed from a dingy backwater settlement to a lovely little town. The stained-glass church windows glowed in jewel tones, the open shops and offices seemed to smile, and the cheerful songs of unfamiliar birds sang out from the rooftops.

At the telegraph office, she found a wiry little man in a printer's apron sitting behind a desk, the telegraph machine on a table behind him. Mr. Holden was in the back of the office, seated at a battered little desk beside a cot and a wood-burning stove. When he saw her, his face brightened. He returned the inventory sheet and had her sign the complaint, written in ink.

She then dictated a wire to Mr. Langley, in whom she'd entrusted the trade license, stating that the store had been robbed during its vacancy, that it was urgent he restock with all the merchandise on the duplicate inventory sheet in his possession, and to include an additional month's supply of food for two, and a pair of boy's trousers and white shirt suitable for church.

"How long will it take for the message to be received?" Emilia asked.

The man spoke with the speed of a dying clock. "That depends on the gauge of the copper wire, the distance between repeater stations, and if there is a thunder storm, in which case lightning can speed the signal. All things considered," he finally summed up, "within the hour."

There was, at least, relief in that. And Mr. Langley being a timely man, the order would ship in a day. With the advent of the railroad connecting all the way to Kansas City, she could conceivably have food in two weeks. But what to do in the meantime?

The women were polite yet always in too much a hurry to chat. Except for Mrs. Vandemark, who shunned Emilia altogether. When Emilia went to the schoolhouse, the teacher stammered about not being trained to teach a deaf child, and Josiah's enrollment was rejected. This was the worst blow of all, and Emilia clenched her teeth every time she thought of it. She had been blasted with a cold front long before winter had set in, and she didn't know why.

Over the ensuing week, Emilia made several attempts to speak to Mrs. Vandemark, but the woman wouldn't deign to even raise the ear horn. It came to a head when Emilia made a more forceful attempt to confront the woman after the next church service, but the matriarch turned away.

"What have I done to breed your contempt?" Emilia erupted, in the sanctuary no less. But she was determined to leave this partially deaf woman no excuse for ignoring her. She failed to ascertain the acoustics, however, and her voice rang out clear as a bell *inside* the church. The mingling congregation fell silent and turned to look at them, including Cyrus Holden.

Mrs. Vandemark spun around like a spring ready to snap. "Indeed," she said, matching Emilia's tone. "It is not I whom you've offended, but God!"

"What did I do to incur your displeasure?" Emilia begged.

"You know very well what you did!" The woman shook her ear horn. "Feigning innocence in the face of such a sin *should* breed contempt."

"What sin? What did I do? Say it," Emilia challenged. "Say it for everyone to hear!"

The spring did snap as Mrs. Vandemark stabbed the point of the horn at Emilia and declared, "I'll do more than that!" Whirling, she marched out of the building.

After this, the townswomen looked on Emilia with pity, but none did more than smile. Dispiriting as this was, at least she and the boy didn't face hunger. The Lord did provide, and it came in the form of an anonymous person. Each night fresh meat was left hanging in a burlap bag outside the door. Did she have a secret admirer? But what kind of an amour leaves *dead birds*? Yet when she and Josiah blessed their dinner each night, she thanked the Lord for the bounteous gifts and asked that He bless the giver threefold.

She believed it was Cyrus Holden's doing until she learned that he doubled as a carpenter for the college and was spending most of his time finishing an extension before the upcoming semester. The blacksmith, perhaps?

Throughout all of the struggles, Emilia had kept Asa's last letter tucked up inside her sleeve as a reminder of why she had come out here. Though only paper, she had hoped it would feel warm, like a hand on her wrist. Instead, it felt cool, like a shackle.

Fortunately, the shipment arrived in only ten days. It had taken two wagons to transport such a comprehensive inventory from Kansas City, and to her surprise, Cyrus Holden was one of the drivers. "I was already there picking up lumber for the college," he explained.

The unloaded crates created a towering maze throughout the store, and Josiah raced around and climbed up them for hours. But the wooden crates posed a problem for Emilia: the lids were nailed shut, and the crowbar she needed was packed inside one of them. Mr. Holden retrieved a tool from his wagon to assist. She gritted her teeth: once again she was beholden to Mr. Holden! While he pried off lids, Emilia unpacked, and to her astonishment there were additional supplies she had not ordered. "What are these?" she asked, taking out stacks of metal pans and screens, and an entire crate of small picks.

"It looks like mining supplies," he offered.

"What on earth would anyone here do with mining tools?"

"There's a gold rush in Colorado. I've heard that prospectors are going through Fort Riley for supplies, but the shortest route to Denver is here, through Manhattan. Once they learn that your store has reopened, I bet they will stream through here and buy up half your inventory."

Emilia was stunned. "How very insightful of Mr. Langley to include such items." When she dropped the pick back into the box, Asa's last letter slipped out of her sleeve and fell into the packing straw. Before she could reach for it, Mr. Holden had already retrieved it. When his eyes met the name on the envelope, a painful expression darkened his face. Had the sight of a war correspondence triggered unpleasant memories for him?

Vividly, she recalled that day at the Canandaigua post. The embarrassment of fainting into this man's arms, compounded by his male arrogance at the church when he tried to dissuade Mr. Goodnow from offering her the store, had prejudiced her heart against him.

But he had changed out here, or at least her perception of him had. And never more so than in this fleeting moment, as she became inexplicably aware of every nuance of his person. Of his scent: he smelled of sawdust and lye soap. Of his height: even bent over his half-stance made her feel small but safe. Of his hair: it was thick and wavy, and the sunlight filtering through the storefront window glinted across the highlights.

When she reached out for the proffered letter, her arm brushed his, and her skin tingled with the sensation of his muscled arm through his shirtsleeve. She became acutely aware that he hadn't shaved this morning and actually found the ruggedness attractive. Still stunned by the unexpected sight of the letter, his lips had parted and revealed not only a scar on the upper lip but also an adjacent chipped tooth. She imagined the butt of a rifle striking him dead in the face, breaking that tooth, and found herself wondering what emotion lay behind his often brooding expression.

What had awakened her senses to him? It wasn't just his physique or attraction. It was pain. That expression that crossed his face was one of suffering, and empathy had opened her heart, and then her eyes, as she looked directly into his. All this had transpired in a matter of seconds, but routine and random thoughts had stilled, and time with it. It was as if she had suddenly stepped out of sync with the harried dance of everyday life and found herself exposed to the pull of a strange and new—what? Emotion? Perception? Recognition? Contrition? Perhaps there was another word for it, one her mind refused to form.

In that moment, something beyond will had brought her eyes up. It was as if an external pull drew them to his eyes—and her heart closer to her chest as it began to pound harder. He not only met her gaze, he held it. But it wasn't with curiosity or any form of earnestness. Those brown eyes revealed. . .an apology and the longing to speak.

He drew himself upright and handed her the letter with an obvious, "You dropped this."

"Oh, yes, thank you." She never knew the throat could flush until she felt heat shoot up her neck. "This is *that* letter."

"Yes, I recognize it."

"Asa wrote about his new vision to come out west. I have clung to it in the hope it would buoy my resolve."

"Has it?"

Even her lashes felt heavy as she dropped her eyes from the weight of what had become her life. "No."

He put on his hat, the cue that he was about to leave, and her heart dropped back into place. If he didn't bow out soon, she knew this awkwardness between them would become glaringly apparent, and she sensed he did, as well. "I've been working at the college," he explained. "I plan to finish the window casings tomorrow, leave around three o'clock. There are some extra boards I would like to bring over, to build shelves so you can stock more inventory."

"Thank you, but you must let me pay you."

"That's not necessary, Miss Davis."

"Well, then, supper it is." What else could she do? She refused to be indebted to him. "I'm not a very good cook, so dining at this establishment might prove a trial of your manhood."

"Better your trial by cooking than some of the other rites of passage I've heard about." He grinned. "Tomorrow, then, and I'll come with my best courage." With a nod, he left.

As if with his own little show of manliness, Josiah labored to stack the crates and then climb his self-made summits. All the while, Emilia's thoughts kept returning to that night she saw Cyrus Holden's silhouette against the Milky Way. He could not have struck a more impressionable scene if he had staged it. Despite her best efforts, she couldn't shake that image of him standing among the stars.

Shopkeeper duties kept her busy the whole of the day, emptying crates and stocking shelves. Colorful boxes, tins, and shiny bottles, polished metal utensils and a large candy jar, transformed a barren room into a mercantile in a matter of hours. A surge of enthusiasm lifted her spirits and was soon accompanied by curiosity when she discovered another unusual item. Coiled neatly inside the pair of boy trousers was a silver whistle on a cord. She cocked her jaw as she wondered why Preston would include a whistle, of all things. Could it be he had someone here in Manhattan reporting to him? Telling him that she had taken in a deaf boy? A whistle! How perfect! If Josiah ever became lost, he could "call" to her! It was the gift of peace of mind. How intuitive of him. She put it around Josiah's neck at once, showed him how to blow it, and indicated that he was to wear it at all times. One would have thought it was pure silver the way he admired it.

Had Preston also been responsible for the nightly gifts of food? Well, she concluded, prairie hens and whistles showed the workings of a practical mind, not overtures from a secret lover. But when she looked into the last crate, she had to revisit her assessment of the family advisor. Carefully, if not lovingly, placed on top in a nest of straw, was a velvet box the size of a folded letter. Opening it, inside she found—a bottle of perfume! It was made of orange frosted glass with an embossed label that read "Orange Blossom" and "New York Perfume Company."

Emilia cradled the bottle in her hands, gasping, "I don't believe it!" Pulling off the stopper, she smelled the fragrance. "Orange blossoms!" she exclaimed in a weeping laugh. Dabbing several drops into her palms, she rubbed them together, cupped them to her face and inhaled the scent.

"Josiah!" she called out, and she looked up to see that he was standing on a crate at the top of his highest summit yet. "Josiah, do you know what this is?" She rushed over to him, careful not to spill a drop, and let him smell it. He scrunched his nose as if to say, "Girly."

"Oh, Josiah, my papa had a potted orange blossom tree. Its scent brought a part of him back to me. Of all the things of home, I miss that tree the most. And here it is! I can't believe it! Who would send this to me? Who could have possibly known?" And the only plausible answer was Preston Langley.

Suddenly, she was aware of someone watching her. Looking over, she saw Cyrus Holden standing just outside the opened front door, not wanting to intrude. Was he early, or was it that late? Emilia straightened her skirt. "Please, come in." Quickly, she inhaled another waft of the aroma before replacing the bottle in its box and safe-housing it in a drawer.

Mr. Holden rolled up his sleeves and went to work, hanging shelves on the bare wall. As he finished, she quickly filled them with more of her wares. "Yes," she exclaimed with hands on her hips, surveying her mercantile, "it looks like a store, indeed!"

Emilia served canned ham, a jar of applesauce, crackers, and cheese, and it proved a better meal than she had expected as they dined on a blanket behind the store. It was odd that he brought his saddlebag with him to the meal. Daily bumping and rubbing had created a crease in the leather around the square contents.

"Well," she said at the conclusion of the meal, "it appears you have bravely survived this trial of manhood."

"I would find it a most pleasing ritual any day of the week," he replied. He cleared his throat, put his hand on the saddlebag. "There is something I need to give you, Miss Davis."

The tone in his voice, the serious expression on his face, sent her heart racing, and she became scared—of what? No, she didn't like the way he made her feel. Routine, order, the control of a needle creating designs of her making, these made her feel secure. The flushing, surging emotions he triggered were unacceptable. A tide may be powerful, but one doesn't have to stand in its pull.

"You don't owe me anything," she waved off. "I wish I could do more to thank you, Mr. Holden." She led Josiah back into the store, leaving Cyrus Holden to follow. Her intention was to finalize the evening with idle conversation. This was cut short, as if with a knife, when she laid eyes on a peculiar object tacked to the wide-opened front door.

"Is something wrong, Miss Davis?" His eyes followed her gaze until he saw it, too.

Posted on the mercantile door, for all to see, was a piece of cloth twelve inches square. On it was embroidered a symbol, done with a fine and artistic hand. Wrenchingly gorgeous scarlet thread formed a bold and elegant letter *A*. Had it been left on the counter, she might have thought it another secreted gift from someone who assumed her name began with an *A* for the familiar spelling of *Amelia*.

But the accompanying book propped up in the storefront window, for all to see, left no doubt its meaning—*The Scarlet Letter*, by Nathaniel Hawthorne. Who? Why? But the meaning was abundantly clear. This book was about a character named Hester

Prynne, a young woman found with child in 1642 Puritan Boston, who was forced to wear this defaming emblem.

This was the scarlet letter *A* for *adulteress*.

Her face burned until it surely matched the color of the threads. Her mouth fell slack, her hands dropped. So that was why the women had shunned her. When Emilia had taken off her work gloves, they had seen her barren ring finger and judged her for being an unwed mother.

Furious, Cyrus ripped the fabric off the door. "Emilia," he said, his voice charged with emotion, "I'm sorry. I'll burn it. No one's seen it yet, I'm sure."

A wave of shock threw her back against the counter. Opposite that sensation of stepping outside the whirling circle of life, she felt as if it was crushing in, sucking the breath out of her.

"He's not even my son!" she choked.

"I know, I know." He approached her, the fabric wadded inside his fist. "He doesn't look a thing like you or Asa." He took her by the shoulders and lowered her onto one of crates. "It wouldn't matter if he were." Cyrus's voice was distant, even though he was kneeling right beside her. "You would still be the same to me," he said, his words garbled in her head.

"No, no," she stammered, then shouted toward the door, "He *is* my boy. Josiah *is* my boy!" Her face was wet, and only then did she realize she was crying. When Cyrus tried to dab at her cheek with a handkerchief, all she could see was that swatch of fabric with the scarlet letter before her eyes. "Go!" she cried. "Go away. Please, go away. And tell them, tell them all, that Josiah *is* my boy!"

Her vision cleared enough to see Cyrus walking through the doorway with the condemning piece of cloth in his hand. "No, leave it, Cyrus. Leave it. It's mine." Deliberately now, he crossed to the cash register, opened the drawer, and placed the scarlet letter inside. Was this his way of saying someone would pay for this?

The sun seemed to set the next instant. How long had it been since Cyrus had left? Emilia was in the same spot, only now Josiah was in her arms. He didn't understand this dark change that had come over his proxy mother and had climbed into her lap, seeking reassurance. As darkness filled the store, she began singing to him, as a mother would sing to her child,

"Sleep my child and peace attend thee, all through the night.
Guardian angels God will send thee,
all through the night. . . .
I my loved ones' watch am keeping,
all through the night. . . ."

Chapter 10

"Word is you be open and sell'n min'n supplies." The man lisped through the gaps in his teeth. He was the first of the prospectors to come into the store. How the word of her mercantile had spread, she didn't know, but a steady stream of settlers and miners began passing through Manhattan.

Now that the war was over, the Homestead Act had become the siren call to more than just Asa. Former soldiers and settlers from throughout the Union and Confederacy turned a trickle into a flood of travelers over the ensuing weeks. It was as if someone had raised a sluice, and a river of people, oxen, horses, and donkeys streamed through eastern Kansas and converged down this street. The soldiers from the fort were now assigned postwar to protect not only the railroad workers but these visionaries as well, and added gallantry to the town as they rode abreast the wagon companies in their blue uniforms.

With this flood came sales. Emilia sold out her inventory three times over. It was exhausting to run the store, keep the books, and supervise Josiah. The restocking went smoothly thanks to Cyrus, whom she was on first-name basis with, though that was the extent of their familiarity. Her temper was at a constant simmer over the scarlet letter, and his brooding demeanor had returned, except with Josiah, whom he taught how to plant a garden behind the telegraph office, whittle sticks into fishing poles, dig for arrowheads, and shoot a slingshot.

The college also brought in business, and she kept well stocked with school supplies. She paid Blue Mont College the promised five percent of her profits and was respected in at least that circle.

Emilia had written several letters to Preston, who feigned ignorance at the hinted gifts, but more surprises continued to arrive with the shipments. After the perfume, she received a quilting hoop with an attachable stand. She hadn't sewn since Asa's death, and now with the townswomen's condemnation, her heart wasn't in it, even if she had the time. Even so, she kept it propped up behind the counter, brushing fingertips over the polished walnut frame as a child might a candy jar. It boasted unique blade marks that proved it handcrafted, and it spoke to her heart that Preston would send something so endearing.

Cyrus had picked up the first four store shipments, and he had signed the invoices in pen and ink. But the fifth he had signed with pencil. Why should that matter? Yet something about this gave her pause.

The next shipment likewise held a secreted gift. Nestled in the packing straw was a blue porcelain teacup and saucer, hand painted with translucent white roses, and a tin of orange spice tea. In payment for the delivery, she had made Cyrus the first cup of tea and then teased him for the way he cradled the diminutive cup and saucer in his large hands.

"It's not a bluebird egg," she ribbed, "and stop staring at it like it's going to hatch. Just take a sip!"

He'd pinched the small handle in his fingers and drank the tea in one gulp.

"Dear, sir!" she had exclaimed. "It's not a bottle of whiskey!"

"Some men can't be reformed, Miss Davis," he teased back.

"We'll see what the reverend has to say about that," she said and offered him a coy smile.

During these weeks, he proffered none but that tight smile. She knew he wanted to make inquiries about the scarlet letter, but leaving a piece of cloth on a door wasn't a crime.

After a month and a half, Emilia's temper got the best of her. As if taking up the gauntlet, she pulled the scarlet letter out of the cash register drawer and marched over to the church. Throwing open the door, she strutted up to the circle of women bent over a quilting frame. Startled, they looked up, needles suspended in the air. Emilia tossed the fabric square out over the taut fabric. The red threads caught the light as the scarlet letter came to rest in the center of the quilt.

Eyeing the women carefully, Emilia was shocked to see that only one woman appeared to recognize it: Mrs. Vandemark. For the others who were still clueless, Emilia tossed the book, *The Scarlet Letter*, out onto the fabric, where it bounced once before coming to rest beside its condemning counterpart. Now that the connection was made, several gasped, others covered their mouths.

"I have come," Emilia announced, "to return these items to their rightful owner."

The silence was nearly choking, most of the women mortified by the sight of the letter and book.

"The embroidery is lovely," Emilia continued, cooling her tone, channeling her temper into quiet dignity. "It shows great skill with the needle." Mrs. Vandemark wriggled uncomfortably. Could it be this bull of a woman had regrets? "Perhaps a scarlet letter is befitting me, befitting us all. Did not the Lord say, 'Though your sins be as scarlet, they shall be white as snow'?" Emilia shot Mrs. Vandemark a look. "In this situation, I wonder if the Lord might'n say, 'Let she who is without sin cast the first scarlet letter.'" Emilia planned to turn on her heel and leave then, but Mrs. Vandemark shot up to her feet.

"We left our homes in Rhode Island," she spat, "to come out to this barbaric country and establish a *Christian* colony, a town of *upright* women." The woman's voice gained force even as her hands trembled. "May God forgive you," she continued, "as you repent. But Manhattan is no place for—for—"

"An adulteress?" Emilia blurted, shocking all the women. "You didn't even take the time to learn one iota about me. Am I a widow who lost her wedding ring? You don't know. Was I abused by an enemy soldier and thus in need of help and understanding? You don't know. Or did I claim a scared little boy who was bound for an orphan train? You don't know, Mrs. Vandemark."

"Irrelevant!" Mrs. Vandemark punched the air with a fist. "The boy deserves a father!"

"As I deserve a husband!" Emilia stepped into the words. "But some of us are destined to be alone. It would be nice if those of you who have fathers and husbands wouldn't judge those of us who don't. Doesn't the Lord call upon us to lift up the hands that are weary? Not slap them down for their emptiness?"

Emilia's lip belied her tone when it began to quiver. "When I had nothing left, God gave me a new home and a son, if Josiah chooses so to be. It is not enough for God to give us gifts; we must likewise claim them. And I claim mine. But these items," she stabbed a finger at the emblem and the book, "do *not* belong to me, nor any woman for that matter. And now that I have returned them, I bid you ladies adieu."

With that Emilia walked with lighter steps back across the street. But when she returned to her mercantile, it felt as if she still possessed the scarlet letter—*A* for *Alone*. Her own words boomeranged back: "*Some of us are destined to be alone.*"

Chapter 11

In the aftermath of her confrontation with Mrs. Vandemark, many of the ladies had warmed up to her. Soon thereafter Emilia received a letter from Preston. It was a Friday, one she would never forget. She had expected an accounting sheet in yet another attempt to discourage her from this venture. Instead, she received what he proclaimed to be his last letter, insisting she return home—and marry him!

Months passed with cooler weather moving in, signaling an early and hard winter. Emilia had made several attempts to write Preston but couldn't bring herself to accept his hand. Was she in love with him or just drawn to the lifestyle he offered? It was clear he admired her from afar, but that wasn't love, was it?

With growing clarity, Emilia recalled the suitors at the New York dances. Many of the young men were handsome from a distance, but up close on the dance floor, all she could see were their crooked teeth or bitten nails or pockmarks or wiry sideburns, and she as quickly lost her feelings of attraction toward them. Preston was no different, but was *she* the one being judgmental now? Was it vanity to reject a suitor based on physical appearance?

Yet Cyrus Holden *was* different. Even up close he was handsome. In truth, she saw his flaws—the broken tooth and scarred lip, the crook in his nose, the early creases of hardship around the eyes—but the sight of him still turned her stomach to jelly.

As she thought about all these men, she began to realize that all were attractive, each in his own appearance and style. But Cyrus, he was her kind of handsome. And it wasn't just the incredibly pleasant assemblage of his features. It was his countenance that drew her to him. She didn't love *how* he looked so much as who he *was*. It was then that it struck her: even if it had come from the silent and unseen reaches of her mind, she had thought the word *love*.

In the end, it didn't matter if she was in love with or just attracted to Cyrus; he hadn't asked her to marry him and made no signs that he ever would. She had to be sensible. It was a Tuesday when she was working up the courage to accept Preston's hand. It was apparent that he already knew about Josiah, so that was a nonissue, she was sure—and what a life Josiah would have; he'd want for nothing.

Josiah was occupied playing with a ball on the stairs when Emilia stood at the counter and forced herself to take up pen and paper. But no sooner had she written the salutation than the bell Cyrus had installed above the door jingled.

Looking up, Emilia saw a young family enter the store. The woman was maybe a few years older than herself. It was half past eleven, and she already looked worn to the bone. They had but one child, a boy Josiah's age, who watched the ball with longing eyes, and Emilia could tell at once that he was worked hard.

The young woman took off her bonnet, and sunflower yellow hair fell around her face. Her eyes were light blue, but her complexion was worn and blotched, her lips sunburned. She had been robbed of her debutante face, but her expression was worn down from something more than the elements: bitterness seemed to set the wrinkles around her mouth.

With a jutted chin, she eyed a bolt of calico cloth on the shelf. She pointed to her worn dress and, in a matter-of-fact tone, said to her husband, "*Ich brauche ein neues Kleid!*"

The husband pointed to a knife in the case and shook his head. "*Nein! Wir brauchen eine gute Jagd Messer. Ich werde für ein bevor ich diesen Preis bezahlen.*"

Emilia couldn't understand a word they said. Several Bulgarians had come through last week, and their accents sounded similar.

As the young couple conversed, Josiah's eyes grew large, and he slowly rose to his feet, staring at them. Gooseflesh shot down Emilia's arm. Did he sense danger?

The husband paid for a can of kerosene and a fish hook, shook his head again at the knife case, then bade the wife and son to follow, which they did, returning to their covered wagon outside. All the while Josiah gaped at them. Emilia could sense his small heart beating faster as they pulled away, but before she could come around the counter, he bolted out the door.

"Josiah!" Emilia raced after him. Outside, she found Josiah on the porch, rigid as the sticks he whittled. He stared after the rattling wagon. "Josiah?" But he wouldn't acknowledge her. Looking down the street she saw that his gaze was fixed on the boy, who was now peering out through the split in the canvas at the back of the wagon.

Gripping the edge of the wagon, the boy suddenly called out to Josiah: "*Komm! Bringe deinen ball und spielen in den wagen!*"

Like a pup released from a cage, Josiah sprang into the street and raced after the wagon. This shocked Emilia, but nothing could have prepared her for what he did next. Josiah opened his mouth, and with a crackling voice, called out loud and long: "*Warten! Warten! Nicht verlassen!*"

Emilia froze in place as Josiah ran faster. She grabbed her ears, wondering if she had heard right. Was that the wagon boy's voice she'd heard? Was this some trick of the prairie wind?

The boy slapped the side of the wagon, urging Josiah on, and called out again in his language. A second time Josiah shouted: "*Komm zurück! Komm zurück! Ich will mit dir reden!*"

He could speak? He could speak! Josiah could *speak*! Dazed, Emilia stared hard after Josiah, as if that would clarify the confusion and doubt colliding in her brain.

As if elated at the sound of his own voice, Josiah continued to shout out, and it was the most beautiful voice Emilia had ever heard: Josiah could talk! He wasn't deaf! He wasn't mute! All this time, he hadn't spoken because he couldn't understand anyone. Had the shock and trauma of losing his family here in a foreign country sent him into his silent world? And then he found a woman who cared, so he clung to her. Only he was no longer clinging to Emilia. He was running away! She felt the tether that had bound them stretch thinner and thinner the farther he ran, until it snapped when Josiah jumped into the wagon with the boy, disappearing inside the cover.

"Josiah!" Emilia's lungs burst. She grabbed up her skirt and flew after him. "Josiah! Josiah!" With all the force in her lungs, she screamed, "Josiah!" The wagon stopped, the husband and wife jumped down to see what was wrong. "My boy, my boy Josiah is in your wagon!" Emilia shouted.

Cyrus, who had been watching from the telegraph office, ran to the back of the wagon to retrieve Josiah. But the husband, thinking Cyrus was grabbing his son, seized Cyrus by the belt and threw him back. Cyrus blocked the ensuing blows before pinning the man on the ground, yelling, "Stop! I don't want your son!"

The German woman began tearing at Cyrus's shirt in an effort to pull him off her husband. Cyrus sprang back and whipped a badge out of his pocket. The husband's hands went up in the air, and the wife stepped back.

"Two boys," Cyrus said, holding up two fingers and pointing to the wagon.

The husband threw back the canvas and saw his boy laughing with Josiah, both oblivious to the skirmish on the other side of the tarp as they wrestled for the ball. The husband pulled Josiah out.

"Josiah!" Emilia ran toward him, but the German woman acted as if she recognized Josiah, and blocked Emilia from him as she grabbed Josiah by the arms, crying out, "*Diederich? Bist du das?*"

Emilia lunged at the woman, grabbing her arms in an effort to pull her away from Josiah. "No! That's Josiah! That's my boy. Give him to me!"

The young wife responded with unintelligible words, sweeping the boy up into a powerful armlock, all the while stroking his hair.

"Stop!" Mrs. Vandemark appeared in the middle of the foray, ear horn in hand, and this time she held it like a weapon. "I'll speak to them. My grandmother was German."

"German?" Emilia gasped. Josiah was German? She began to realize how little she knew about him.

As Mrs. Vandemark communicated with them, the wife turned her back on Emilia and tightened her grip on Josiah, a clear sign of ownership. Emilia would have lunged at her had Cyrus not grabbed her from behind and said in her ear, "Emilia, we're going to work this out. No one is taking Josiah." Was it the sound of his voice or the reassurance of the town peace officer that calmed her?

After several excruciating minutes, Mrs. Vandemark turned and said, "She claims they came over last year with a large group from Germany. There was something about Josiah's family coming late or being held back at the island. I assume she meant Ellis Island. I construe that they wintered over in New York City, getting jobs to pay for the journey to Kansas. In the spring, they agreed to assemble at some place I didn't understand. She said Josiah's family did not show up. They heard that they had all died of a fever. Now this woman claims to be overjoyed to find the boy alive. Says he is German and belongs with his own people. They will take him out to the German settlement in central Kansas and give him a good home."

"No," Emilia's voice cracked. "He's my boy!" Cyrus held her even tighter, which meant her case for the boy was getting weaker. "How do I know you're not lying?" she said to Mrs. Vandemark.

"I'm sorry," the elderly woman said. Were her eyes misting? Was she having pity on Emilia? "I keep that scarlet letter beside my bed as a reminder. God as my witness, I am sorry." She looked from the wagon to Emilia, and said in a softer tone, "I am sorry."

"We don't know these people are even telling the truth!" Emilia cried as she twisted against Cyrus's grip. He turned her around, facing him.

"Would you force him to stay?" he whispered, his voice breaking, too.

"You're the lawman. Stop this!"

"Emilia, there's no basis in law here. He's not a relation, and you have no adoption papers."

She grabbed his shirt, her breath on his chin as she looked up into his eyes. "You know he's my boy."

"We will give him a choice," he whispered back, arching a knowing eyebrow. "Law or no law, if he chooses to stay, I will defend that with whatever means necessary. Understood?"

The underlying meaning was clear: Josiah did love her, and he loved this place. There was no way he would choose to be carted off by strangers. "All right," she said. Her throat constricting when she turned around and saw that the woman had already put Josiah back into the wagon.

"Wait," Cyrus said, his deep voice booming. It stopped the man and woman in their tracks. "Josiah," he pointed in the wagon, "Diederich." Cyrus pointed to the store. "He choose."

Everyone was stiff, but no one more so than Emilia, every fiber of her being locking up. The German woman eyed Emilia, challenge flaring in her eyes, yet she submitted with a nod. As if acquiescing, she walked to the front of the wagon and climbed up on the seat board. "Hunfrid!" she called, and the husband put up his palms to pacify Cyrus and took his place at the reins.

Emilia's chest began to cave as the wagon pulled away. "Cyrus!" Only then did she realize he was standing behind her, now squeezing her arms with reassurance. He had no doubt of the outcome, why should she?

"Go," he said in her ear, "call to him."

Emilia walked out into the center of the street, now lined on either side with a crowd of people. A storm wind was rising, shaking her skirt. Not since the day she had arrived with Josiah had this street been so quiet. Dread constricted her chest, and it took a moment for her to draw in sufficient air and call out: "Josiah!" The wagon rolled on, the oxen plodding as if to give her and the boy ample time. As the distance increased between them, she took several steps and cried out again, "Josiah! Josiah!" No response. Now Emilia panicked, and she began to run after the wagon, calling over and over for the boy, but he never answered. He didn't even peer out. "Josiah!" she cried with all the force in her body, shaking her fists as if to give the sound more thrust. "Deiderich!" she tried in the vain hope he would respond to that name.

She never stopped calling for him, stumbling to the end of the town, even after the wagon disappeared in the trees. "No, no, no!" she rasped from a failing voice.

The town collective had pressed into the street, as if they would call with her. She felt them before she turned back around, but her eyes sought one man, and when she saw him, she ran to him and began beating him on the chest, shouting, "It's your fault! It's your fault!" Breaking into a sob, she said, "I trusted you. I trusted you!"

Cyrus didn't raise a hand to stop her. Instead, he stared off down the road as if too stunned to believe it himself. He reached up at last to touch her arms, but she flailed, stepping back, glaring up at him.

"He didn't come back, Cyrus." Turning to look into the copse of trees, all she could think was how Josiah had run to the boy, how he had shouted out in his native tongue—how happy, how excited he was to at last understand and be understood. He had never tried to communicate with Emilia. How isolated he must have felt!

Fourfold pain was the catalyst that brought Emilia to her knees. "He didn't want me. He didn't want to come back." And she cried, for that was all she could do. Just like her father, just like Johnny, just like Asa, Josiah was gone.

Chapter 12

Snow filled the air as angry clouds piled overhead. The storm swallowed up the sky in one massive gulp. All the while, Emilia sat in a stupor on the porch in front of her now truly empty store, buried in grief. The townspeople had dispersed hours ago, all except for Cyrus. He kept his distance but sat close enough that if she spoke he would hear it.

At last he broke down and said, "Say the word, and I'll go after him. I'll bring him back." Not until she heard the desperation in his voice did she realize how deeply he had bonded with Josiah.

"He didn't want to come back." The wind began whipping hair across her face, and she did nothing to restrain it. Let it come, let it sting. "He didn't want me." Snow began to pour as if all the cottonwoods of Downy Lane shook overhead; shook in anger, shook in pain.

"He can speak, Emilia!" Cyrus said. "I'll bring him back. We'll learn to communicate with him. Hear him say it for himself that he wants to go off with those people."

The wind created maddening designs in the blustering snow. The cold; it was cruel, but the crystalline patterns forming within it were beautiful. In contrast, this aloneness she felt was cold, it was cruel, but she could see nothing in it that was beautiful. Her life was starker now than it had ever been.

"You didn't see the look on his face," she mumbled, staring at the white air. "When he saw a boy his age, a boy he could understand, a boy he could befriend. You saw how fast he jumped into that wagon." Her voice gained momentum with the wind. "You heard him speak for the first time! You heard him shouting in German! I don't speak German, Cyrus. He might as well have been deaf all these months. He couldn't understand a word I said."

And then it came down to it. "He didn't even try to speak to me. Not one syllable. But he laughed and chattered on with that boy like, like, like I don't know what, but it wasn't like me! He never ate well, and now I know it's because I didn't know how to cook his kind of food." Snowflakes hit her in the eyes; the cold burned, but not more than the tears. "But the way he clung to me, the feeling of my arms around him, it made him feel like, like. . ." Her voice trailed off, and she dropped her head onto her knees.

"Like a son."

"I was a fool. Poor Josiah. He clung to me because I was the first person to speak kindly to him." She laughed over yet another irony, "Mrs. Vandemark was right. He deserves a father, and that was something I could never give him." She looked down the street but could only see white, as if nature was erasing him from her life. "I should have realized it months ago when you said he didn't look a thing like me or Asa."

And that was the moment it hit, hit with a blast in the face that did not come from the storm. Snowflakes melted on her lashes and she blinked fast, but not against the cold. As realization sank in, she stood, and she turned and stared at Cyrus. Her lips parted, but only hot breath passed over them for a full minute before comprehension broke the shock into words. "Asa. That night, the night of the scarlet letter. . .you said— you said he didn't look a thing like *Asa*."

Slowly, Cyrus rose to his feet. Clouds of breath formed in front of his mouth as his chest began to heave. As he stepped toward her, she stumbled back, gasping, "How—how could you know?" She gulped frozen air. "How could you know what Asa looked like?"

"Emilia, I can explain. I came to Canandaigua that day to find you. . .to tell you. . . to give you something."

"The saddlebag. It was Asa's, wasn't it!" she blurted. His silence was the confirmation. She stumbled back across the porch. "How could you have his saddlebag unless— Unless you—you were the one who shot him!"

"What?" He looked as if *he* had just been shot. "No!"

"You not only saw him at Cold Harbor, you shot him!" Like a mindless dance, every step she took back, he took toward her.

"The cold is affecting you. I'll tell you everything, but please go inside, Emilia."

"Don't call me that! I'm Miss Davis to you!"

Snow melted on her cheeks. He must have thought she was crying for he reached inside his pocket and pulled out a handkerchief, a stub of a pencil falling out with it. The pencil rolled toward Emilia before stopping on a miniature snowdrift between two boards. She stared at it. There was something significant about that pencil. He'd had it when she'd arrived here months ago. She frequently saw him writing at his desk, but he always used a fountain pen. He never used this pencil, yet he carried it with him.

Fingers pressed against pounding temples as the truth fell into place. "That pencil," she gasped. "You had to sign an invoice with it." He didn't answer, just studied her face, trying to read it through the wind and white. "The lead marks—heavier on the down strokes!" she blurted, yelling on the wind even though he was only a few feet away. He started to reply, and then he understood: she had pieced together the truth.

"Asa's last letter," she charged, "written in pencil. The handwriting was different. Heavier on the down strokes! It wasn't his handwriting. It was yours! You *did* know him. You shot him and wrote that last letter!"

"Yes!" Cyrus shouted, his voice fierce, but not from anger. "No! Emilia, I didn't shoot Asa! He was my friend. He was shot by a Confederate—not me! I fought off two soldiers trying to *save* Asa!"

"So you were there? You knew him?"

Cyrus heaved a long breath. "Yes. I was with him when he died."

Involuntary pants chilled her lungs, her chest, her heart. A coldness poured through her veins as she paced, her hands suspended beside her head as if trying to physically grasp the thought.

"Emilia, go inside, get out of the cold."

"Miss Davis!"

"Emilia!" he shouted back, all his pain breaking loose. "All I ever knew you as was Emilia."

"You never knew me, Mr. Holden! We never met before that day at the post office."

"I did know you. Asa. . ." His voice trailed off as he winced against the pain. "You were all Asa talked about." His voice dropped into his chest, and she could barely make out the words. "He told me all about you, read all your letters to me, until I felt I—I knew you. And I came to"—he chewed on that scar on his lip before finishing—"to respect you above any woman I have ever known. My mother was a hard woman, my father harder. I was on my own by the time I was twelve. All I wanted was. . .a home. I worked on farms, on the canal, at a general store. I met a lot of people. But it wasn't until I went to war that I found the one person I admired above all others."

He looked back over his shoulder—at what? Was he ashamed? Afraid she'd see the deception on his face? But when he looked back he matched her gaze. "Asa told me about his promise to write you every week until the last day of the war." This took her aback. How could he know that unless he was telling the truth? He continued: "At Cold Harbor he was shot in the abdomen. He was bleeding out, and we both knew he only had minutes to live. That's when he made me swear to write you his last letter. I had to honor his dying wish." He threw his head to shake off the wet tendrils falling into his eyes. Once more, in a sudden jerk, Cyrus looked back.

"You knew Asa. All this time you didn't even tell me! His letter—*you* wrote it, *you* signed his name. It was a lie, all of it!"

"What was I supposed to do? Lie to you or lie to a dying man? But I didn't lie, Emilia, not in what I wrote. It was all true. But to keep my promise, I signed Asa's name. What would you have had me do?" Were those tracks of melting snow or tears running down his face? "Lie to Asa or pretend to you?" His chest heaved. "What, Emilia? Tell me, what should I have written?"

They stared at each other, Emilia incredulous, Cyrus unnerved. He wiped his wet face with his wet hand. "I came to Canandaigua that day to tell you how your fiancé died—valiant—and to confess that I had written that last letter."

Emilia was stunned beyond words. Cyrus looked back a third time, straining against the wind.

"I can't—I can't do this anymore," Emilia stuttered. "I can't take this anymore. Any of it! Everything's gone," she shouted on the wind. "Now even Josiah's gone! Asa's dream to come out here, to buy a store, it was all a lie. I never wanted to buy a store, Cyrus! I did it for Asa, and now you tell me that he didn't even want it!"

He put his hand up to her face. "Emilia, stop!"

"Don't tell me to stop! You're the one who's lied to me."

He shook her arms and shouted, "Listen!"

"No! I've heard enough. Preston Langley has proposed, and I'm going to accept. I'm leaving—!"

"Emilia!" He shook her again. "Listen! Stop talking and listen!"

"So you can lie to me again?"

To her complete surprise, he whirled her around, pinned her against his chest, and said in her ear, "Emilia, just listen."

How dare he grab her! She should be furious; she should stomp on his feet, but she couldn't move. The way he held her. . .the feeling of his hands, warm around her wrists. . . What did he want her to listen to? He didn't say anything. All she could hear was the blood and wind rushing through her ears. . . And then something else. . .in the distance. . .

"Did you hear that?" he half shouted. "A whistle?"

Whistle? Now she clung to his arms as she held her breath until it hurt. There, three times in a row and then nothing. "A whistle. I heard a whistle!"

Cyrus whirled her back around, hope and fear burning through his face. "Josiah's whistle!"

"It can't be!" She trembled, first with anticipation, then denial, and then terror. How long could a boy last in this blizzard? How soon until his limbs and mouth went numb, and then they'd never find him in time?

Cyrus bolted and ran for the stable, Emilia close on his heels. Once inside the livery, Cyrus shouted, "Stay here! I'll find him!"

"No! He's *my* boy! I'm going, too!"

Cyrus looked helpless in the face of maternal ferocity, as if he'd rather face the entire Southern armies alone than go against this one woman. He reached down and pulled her up onto the horse behind him. He snatched his officer's coat off a hook and threw it around her shoulders. She hardly had time to shove her arms into the sleeves before the horse galloped out of the stable.

"Josiah!" they both shouted as they came upon the thicket at the end of the street. The horse stamped against the cold. Emilia held on to Cyrus's waist as they alternately cried out and listened for the boy. She burrowed her face into Cyrus's back as she sobbed out a prayer. Soon thereafter, they heard it: one long, dying whistle.

Cyrus charged the horse in the direction of the sound. "Josiah!" his deep voice boomed as he reined the horse to a stop. Nothing. "Josiah!"

Emilia drew her deepest breath with her deepest prayer, and she cried out as only a mother can cry to heaven, "Josiah!"

"Come on, come on," Cyrus urged under his breath, "one more whistle."

But instead there came a faint cry, "Mama! Mama!"

Emilia flung herself off the horse and into the snow, Cyrus a mere breath behind her. They ran through the trees in the direction of the small voice, where they found Josiah curled up between a rock and a tree.

"Josiah!" Emilia cried with both voice and tears. She threw off the coat and wrapped it around the boy as Cyrus lifted him up. "He's shivering, violently!" she exclaimed, shouting against the wind just to be heard two feet away.

"It's a good sign," Cyrus called back. "It means his body is still fighting the cold!" But no amount of reassurance would give Emilia the strength she needed as her own limbs were becoming stiff and numb. Every cloud of breath she panted was a plea for divine help, and to her amazement her legs plowed through the wind with greater speed than she alone possessed. Cyrus put the boy in her arms and lifted them both up onto the horse. Springing up, he mounted behind them, trying to shelter them with his body as he spurred the horse into a charge.

Back at the mercantile, Cyrus helped Josiah into dry clothes. He wrapped the shivering boy in the one blanket from the bed, started a fire in the stove, and laid the exhausted boy down beside it. Frozen to the bone herself, Emilia sat behind Josiah, allowing him the full measure of the fire's warmth, and placed his head on her lap. She stroked his wet blond hair in the hope of reassuring him after his harrowing ordeal.

But instead of closing his eyes, he opened his mouth. Chattering, he tried to talk. "So–ree," he said.

Emilia leaned down. Had she heard right? It was one thing to shout for help in a storm, another to try for the first time to converse. "Josiah?"

"So–ree," he chattered again.

"Sorry?" Cyrus prompted.

"*Ja*," he mumbled through a quivering jaw. "Yees."

Now Emilia's lip quivered. "Josiah, why would *you* be sorry? I'm the one who let you go. I'm the one who's sorry. I'm so sorry!"

"Me," he pointed to himself with the one finger visible above the quilt. "Me run to vagon." His accent was thick, but she could understand him. "I no vant go away. I vant play, talk to boy."

"He can speak, he can speak!" she mouthed to Cyrus, struck by the realization as if for the first time. Josiah was speaking to her! After all these months of believing he couldn't speak, yet talking to him anyway, she had been teaching him English and hadn't even known it.

Cyrus's lips trembled, and his hand slid into Emilia's hair as he fought back rising emotion. Their eyes met before he withdrew his hand.

"Woman hold me." The boy crossed his arms over his chest as if unsure his words were clear. "Woman hold mooth." He tugged at the blanket to loosen his arm enough to reach up and put his hand up over his mouth. Emilia's blood ran cold as she realized that not only had Josiah not wanted to leave her, but she had allowed another woman to haul him away.

"Far over"—his brows knit as he searched for the right word—"away. Boy push, make me free. Me jump. Run. Run. They look. I hide. Scar–red." Scared!

Reeling from this realization, Emilia began rocking Josiah in her arms. As she held him tighter, she noticed that he had stopped shivering. "Josiah, I swear I will never let anyone take you from me ever again. Understand? You're my boy, you're my boy. I love you," she whispered. He craned his head around to smile up at her, blinking through still-wet lashes. But the effect of the extremities of the day sapped what strength he had left, and he closed his eyes and fell into a peaceful sleep.

"He's going to be all right," Cyrus said, leaning in toward Emilia, "but you've got to get out of those wet clothes."

Only then did she realize that she was shivering uncontrollably from the cold that sailed through every crack in every board, but she didn't care. Truth had numbed her mind—the truth of her own failing. Why had she not insisted Josiah be taken out of the wagon, to see his face when he was asked to choose? Why had she not acted? Never again, she vowed. With a new sense of daring to face the truth full-on, Emilia looked over at Cyrus. The firelight flickered in his eyes as he looked back, matching her gaze. The truth had been revealed about Josiah, the mystery of his silence solved. But what was the truth about this man sitting next to her? "Just tell me," she said at last. "Cyrus, tell me what is in the saddlebag?"

A white wind beat against the storefront window as he leaned away, as if ashamed. "Your letters to Asa," he said at last. He took a deep breath. "Emilia—Miss Davis—there are no words to express my condolences for the loss of your fiancé. I'm sorry—"

She put up a tired hand. "It's too late for that. Asa is far behind me now. That schoolgirl I was when he left is long gone." She looked out through the window at the raging darkness beyond, shivering painfully despite the warming stove. "I don't know what's real anymore. I don't know what to do. I don't know what to feel. I don't know what to believe."

After a long moment of silence, Cyrus got up and left the store, the little bell over the door chiming good-bye. Well, his job was done; the lawman had saved the boy and seen them safely home, and the soldier had confessed to writing the last letter. There was apparently nothing left for him to do or say.

As she sat alone in the mercantile with Josiah, another puzzle piece fell into place. That night in the church in New York, Cyrus had shaken his head no to Mr. Goodnow. For the first time it occurred to her that he wasn't telling the founder to refuse her the store. It was Cyrus who had written the last letter, and so it was and always had been Cyrus's dream to buy this store. He said it himself, that he had made a claim here before he even left for the war. No, Cyrus had been shaking his head to indicate he *wouldn't* buy the store after all, giving it up for Emilia.

There was no question. She would have to relinquish the store to Cyrus. The next question was where would she and Josiah live? Perhaps that boardinghouse overlooking Canandaigua Lake would look better with Josiah in it?

It was true that Preston represented the life she had lost, with the comforts and finery she loved, and that from the moment she stepped into this store and saw piles of dirt and empty shelves, she had longed for home. When she saw the beleaguered and sunbaked faces of the passing homesteaders, she hated this harsh land. But now as she sat alone in the mercantile, Cyrus's withdrawal stung more than she'd have anticipated. Now she couldn't bear the thought of leaving Kansas, and it was because she didn't want to leave Cyrus.

But perhaps more painful than leaving him was living so near him but never being *with* him. Of the many things she had learned, the most profound was that there were several, if not many ways to love a man. And when that love wasn't returned, there were as many ways to feel pain.

After kissing Josiah's forehead, Emilia dropped back against the end of the counter as the cold penetrated to the bone. Shocked, she looked up when she heard the bell over the door jingle. It was Cyrus! He was returning with a blanket, and leaning into the wind to close the door. Why had he come back? Without a word, he crossed the store and sat beside her, whereupon he wrapped her in the blanket and pulled her into his arms.

Emilia was equally as astonished by the gesture as she was at the sight of the blanket. Though frayed and stained, she recognized the design. "This is one of my quilts!"

"Asa gave it to me" he confessed. "It was one of the quilts you sent for his comrades. You can't imagine the effect when I opened the brown paper and saw this. In all my life I had never seen, much less been given, a thing of beauty. Until then, I had felt hopeless and couldn't close my eyes without reliving the battles or hearing rifle and canon fire in my head. But when I wrapped myself in this quilt, I imagined instead the kind hands making every stitch—while sitting beneath an orange blossom tree. It saved me, Emilia."

Emilia arched up. "How did you know?" Of course, Asa had told him. "The orange blossom perfume—that was from you?" He only shrugged. "The quilt frame? The teacup?"

"I wanted to give something back to you. I never meant to lie to you, Emilia. I should have explained myself that first day. I had assumed that months before you'd already received that last letter. When I saw you through your window, sitting beside that little tree, you looked distraught. I knew I couldn't tell you then.

"Once I knew you were coming to Manhattan, I thought I'd tell you here. I tried several times, but it seemed it was too late to broach the subject. Just when I thought to leave the past where it belongs, you put it all together."

Warmed by the blanket, warm in his embrace, she finally stopped shivering and began to relax. . .until he handed her a stack of envelopes tied with a string. They were her letters to Asa. Accepting them, she found they were heavier than she expected.

"You carried these all the way from Virginia?" she murmured.

"I thought they would bring you comfort."

"No. They won't," she shook her head. "They will remind me of my shame."

"What shame?"

"That I didn't really love him. I was fond of Asa, but losing everything has made me realize how much I was in love with an idea and a way of life. That sounds horrid, doesn't it?"

He smiled, fully, sincerely. "No. A way of life can be an important thing."

She sighed and said the inevitable: "This store was supposed to be yours."

"Ah, you put that together as well," and he gave a wistful glance around the store.

"You never wanted to be a peace officer, did you?" The dashing snow sounded as soothing as rain now that she was sitting beside a warm stove—with Cyrus.

"I had hoped to trade my gun in for a plowshare. Mr. Goodnow is helping me until I can build my home on my claim."

"A dugout?" she asked. He shook his head. "A sod house?"

"I've spent my life looking for a home. It will be built of solid rock, a two-story with a shingled roof. It'll have two bedrooms upstairs, one for Josiah. Downstairs will have a parlor with wide windows to let in the sun so a woman can sew to her heart's content."

"What did you say about Josiah and sewing?"

"You're not going to marry Preston Langley." It wasn't a question.

"My dear Mr. Holden, I am not a soldier."

"You can't marry that man." His tone was flat.

"He's a sensible choice," she said, even though she knew now she could never marry

Mr. Langley, or any man, except. . .except the one she had fallen in love with. She could hardly admit this fact to herself, much less Cyrus.

"For three reasons," he said.

"Is that right? Pray tell, what are those reasons?"

"First, because he deceived you. Mr. Goodnow informed me that Preston Langley is the owner of this store."

"What?" Emilia jerked upright.

"It appears you trusted your family banker too much, Emilia. You signed it without reading the document."

"No! He wouldn't do such a thing!"

"It's my guess that if you married him, he would sell the property, pocket the equity, and you would not be the wiser because a woman surrenders all her possessions at the altar. If you refused him, he would sell the store, leaving you homeless, and thus force your hand."

"And if I rejected him altogether?"

"Then he'd get his revenge for being refused."

"That's criminal!"

"True, you are not a soldier, certainly not one under my command, but as a gentleman and a friend, I must tell you not to marry Mr. Langley."

"What's the second reason?" she probed.

"You belong out here now. Josiah belongs out here. This town needs you."

"What is the third?"

"I need you. I—" If they hadn't just faced a blizzard together, and if Josiah hadn't nearly died out in the elements, the expression on his face might have been comical: a soldier intimidated by a woman. "During the war my regard for you was very high. It wasn't until the war ended, until I met you, that my regard became something more. I have come to. . .to love you, Emilia. What I'm saying—what I'm asking— I mean, Josiah is like a son to me as well, and it seems only sensible that. . .well, that—"

She took his face in her hands. "You already told me in the letter. I just didn't see it until now. Thank you for honoring Asa's last wish. Thank you for being his friend. Thank you for giving up this store for me and for leaving food for us when we were hungry, for the anonymous gifts, and for, for—" She faltered, but the unspoken words *loving me* must have shone through her eyes. He took her face in his warm hands and said, "I do." His eyes queried hers, searching for the confirmation of her love.

"I do, too," she whispered, their faces so close, their lips almost touching. "Does this mean we're married now?"

"Mrs. Vandemark would love to chew on that one." He grinned.

"Yes, I suppose she would. We would get matching letters!"

They chuckled. He took her hands in his, kissed her fingers, and asked, "Will you say those two words to me at the altar?"

She took his hand, brought it up to her face, and spoke into his fingers. "I will."

Chapter 13

When the first day of spring arrived in Manhattan, Kansas, the gray of winter fell away like a woman casting aside a mourning dress.

A rising wind blew back the cloud cover as an artist pulls back a sheet to reveal a masterpiece. All at once the sun beamed down on the endless sweep of shoulder-high prairie grass. As Emilia stood on Holden Hill in her wedding dress, she felt as if she were surrounded by a great sea of green. Last summer, all this had appeared harsh and bleak, but now, as she looked out over their patch of Kansas, the scene of living colors took her breath away. In the breeze, waves and waves of green flowed through this vast stretch of grassland and "splashed" glittering seed heads against the rocks at the base of the hill. One could run through this sea all day without sinking, lie at its depths without drowning. Even the sound, *swoosh, swoosh, swoosh*, reminded her of the sea, and she knew now she had not abandoned the Davis legacy; she had merely relocated it.

It was as if a lifetime had passed since that day at the post office and the last letter had marked the beginning of the first day of her life. How she missed Papa and Johnny and held fond feelings for Asa! She hugged the breeze as she imagined that they were watching her now, at peace and rejoicing in the peace she had found. Mr. Langley did repossess the mercantile, but little did he realize that when he sold it to the highest bidder, a Mr. Cyrus Holden, he had inadvertently returned it to Emilia. Now she and Cyrus would run the mercantile together. He would stock half for the needs of the miners and farmers, and she would stock the other side with all the bright bolts of cloth and other necessities a prairie woman could wish for.

Mrs. Vandemark ceased using that ear horn, and to everyone's astonishment she heard every tidbit of gossip just fine. Not only was she more receptive to the newcomers in town; she took a special interest in Josiah, using her German to help him master English.

And as for Josiah, he thrived at school and made friends, wrestling and fishing with the other boys. But he did have considerable trouble speaking when around a certain doe-eyed girl.

As Emilia stood on the hill, trying to take in the view and the new life she had found so far from Canandaigua, she felt as if she were surrounded by so much more than a living painting of gorgeous scenery, more than new friends and a soon-to-be family. She was, and always had been, surrounded by grace.

As she turned to hurry back down the hill, to return to her waiting groom and his best boy, she was taken aback when she saw that Cyrus was already at the base of the hill, apparently too anxious to wait for his bride. He was wearing his Sunday suit with what looked, from this height, to be an orange blossom in his coat pocket! He put a fatherly arm around Josiah, who stood at his side. Emilia sighed: her boy looked like a little man! Cyrus had gotten a suitcoat and matching trousers for him. He had the same blossom in his coat pocket and the two were the handsomest men in all of Kansas!

Both appeared to be awestruck as they gazed up at her, and it was then that she realized what a scene she struck, backlit by a massive glowing cloud. Her dress fluttered about her ankles with the same excitement that fluttered in her heart, and she ran down into their waiting arms.

CJ Dunham is an author, presenter, and storyteller. She has performed across the country, given creative writing presentations, and published a fully illustrated children's book, and her work has appeared in national magazines. A mother of five and grandmother of thirteen, Dunham enjoys cycling and pretending she can paint. Learn more: authorcjdunham.com and @CJDunham1 or @AKALM.net.

The Outcast's Redemption

by Jennifer Uhlarik

Dedication

To Michele, who endured a thousand late-night text messages as I worked on this story.
Thank you for the many wonderful ideas, helpful brainstorming sessions,
and unwavering friendship you offered through this process.
I couldn't have done it without you! (It's your turn next. . . .)

Chapter 1

Ma, my diary's missing. Again." Maisie Blanton stormed into the kitchen, hands fisted. "How many times do I have to tell Charlotte to leave my things alone?"

"When did you last have it, dear?" Ma remained focused on the noon meal preparation, rather than turning to face her.

"I wrote in it after breakfast then hid it under my pillow. Now it's nowhere to be found."

Ma glanced over her shoulder. "Since breakfast?" She shook her head. "Your sister couldn't have taken it, honey. She went to see Patricia right after her morning chores. Perhaps you left it somewhere else?"

"I've checked my whole room."

"I thought you were supposed to be at the café by now." For some reason, Ma's voice sounded just like Charlotte's.

"What? Ma, you're not making sense. Why would I need to be at the café?"

"Maisie, wake up!" Someone jostled her from her dream. "You're late for work!"

Maisie snapped her eyes open and glanced to the window across the room.

Sunlight. Very bright sunlight.

She bolted from the desk where she'd fallen asleep reading the previous night, the chair tipping over in her haste. Her neck and shoulders protested the sudden movements, particularly given the strange sleeping position. "Charlotte! Why didn't you wake me sooner?"

Before the girl could answer, Maisie flew into action. She brushed and arranged her hair then splashed water on her face. Thankfully, she'd slept in her clothes, so she wouldn't lose time donning umpteen layers of underpinnings.

Charlotte helped change to a clean dress then gave her a shove toward the door. "Go."

"Tell Ma and Simeon I love 'em."

Maisie darted out the front door but stopped at the sight of a beautiful blue, hand-painted vase, filled to overflowing with Texas bluebonnets, which sat in the center of their porch. She stared a moment then glanced up and down the street. Surely someone was playing a prank. Sighting a rolled paper protruding from the vase, she unfurled the message: *"For the prettiest gal in town, Maisie Blanton."*

She stared at the writing, noting the little flourishes on the *M* and the *B* of her name. Heart pounding, she gingerly lifted the vase. It was breathtaking.

"Maisie, go!" Charlotte hissed from behind her. "You're gonna get fired."

Oh, no! Vase in hand, she sprinted the block to the Blackwater Café, paused an instant to catch her breath, and, trying to seem collected, stepped through the back door.

Heat greeted her as she barged through the kitchen and plucked an apron from atop a nearby crate. Whether from the already-cranking woodstove or the glare from the café owner's wife as she cooked, Maisie wasn't quite sure.

"So glad you decided to grace us with your presence," the other woman sneered.

Mute, Maisie swept into the dining area, vase still in hand, and slinked toward the café owner.

"I'm so sorry I'm late." She set the heavy vase on the counter then wound the apron around her waist. "It won't happen again."

The man glared. "I'd believe you, but this is the fourth time you've said those very words to me."

Heat warmed Maisie's cheeks as if the truth slapped her. "Yes, sir. I'm very sorry." She couldn't afford to lose her job. It was hard enough to get her position, given the circumstances. "I beg you, sir. Please. . .one more chance."

The tendon near his jaw popped repeatedly. "I haven't gotten the orders yet. Get to it. But this conversation isn't over."

"Yes, sir. Thank you."

She retrieved a pad and a stubby pencil, her heart still pounding.

"And what is this?" He waved at the vase.

Her cheeks warmed. She dared not say she'd found them on her doorstep with a cryptic, yet flattering note. "I thought they might brighten the place up."

He shook his head and stalked toward the kitchen. "Get to work."

At the sight of her father's old friend, Rocking D Ranch owner Robert Dempsey, seated near the window, her heart rate slowed. At least there was one friendly face in the bunch.

"I'll be right with you, Mr. Dempsey." She shot the balding gentleman a lopsided grin and hurried toward the only other occupied table. As she neared, her steps faltered.

"Thomas?" The name dribbled from her lips in a breathy whisper.

Sporting his most charming grin—the one that used to turn her belly to mush—Thomas Eddings stared back at her. Suit-clad, hair slicked neatly. Looking like a fine Eastern gentleman. "Howdy, Maisie. It's been a while."

Her belly knotted. A while? Almost two years to be exact. "What are you doing here? I thought you were studying in New York." He'd nearly crushed her when he'd left to pursue medical training.

The bell on the front door jingled, and Lucky Tolliver entered. The mere sight of the roguishly handsome cowhand set her stomach to quivering, though why was a mystery. He rarely said more than hello before giving her his order. Not much different than most other townsfolk, though at least he was polite.

"Perhaps you've heard about my pa?" Thomas's words jarred her from her thoughts.

"Your pa?" On occasion, she'd overhear conversations in the café, but she was hardly included in the latest town gossip. More often, she and her family *were* the gossip.

"It's his heart. Ma called me back to run the ranch until he improves."

After the way Mr. and Mrs. Eddings had turned against her family, perhaps this was God's judg—

She cut off the uncharitable thought. The Eddings family had been like an extension of her own for many years. "I'm sorry, Thomas. I hadn't heard."

His expression turned grim. "Maisie, I came today to say I'm sorry. For the way I left so suddenly without a word, for not writing. My folks still haven't come around, but I've done a lot of thinking while I was gone, and I needed to apologize to you. I never intended to hurt you."

She cleared her throat to rid herself of the knot threatening to choke her.

When the door to the kitchen jostled, Maisie shot a panicked glance toward it then back to him. "I'm sorry, Thomas. I need to get to work. Can I get you something? Coffee? Some eggs?"

He shook his head and rose. "No. I only stopped by to see you for a moment. I don't want to get you in any trouble."

Tears threatened to overrun her lower lashes.

"I'll see you soon." He hesitated, pecked her on the cheek, and headed toward the door.

Thoughts and emotions swirling, Maisie stared after him.

On his way out the door, he glanced at the flowers. "That's a real pretty arrangement, by the way." He grinned at her. "Suits a pretty girl like you."

Lucky Tolliver's gut clenched. Had that blasted dandy just kissed Maisie? By golly, he had, and the way her mouth was hanging open, she might just have liked it.

His boss, Robert Dempsey, looked mildly amused from where he sat across the table. Confound it. Wasn't nothing amusing about this situation. Not to him.

"You all right over there, darlin'?" Mr. Dempsey called, drawing Maisie's attention.

In a flurry of motion, she grabbed the coffeepot and mugs before heading their way. "I assume you'll want coffee, gentlemen?"

Mr. Dempsey nodded. "Yes, please."

She shifted toward him. "How're you, Lucky?"

Warmth threaded through him at the way his name sounded on her tongue. A smile tugged at the corners of his mouth. *As long as I'm around you, I'm right happy, Maisie. Did you like the flowers I picked you?*

He opened his mouth to speak the words, though at the sight of the perfect oval face that flitted through his dreams every night, his mind went blank. "I'm, uh. . .good."

Simpleton. He broke their gaze.

She sighed and filled two cups.

Mr. Dempsey reached for his. "Was that Cyrus Eddings' son you were talking to?"

Maisie nodded. "Thomas. He's returned from New York to help with his family's ranch."

"Cyrus's been bad sick for a few weeks."

"I certainly hope the people of Blackwater will be kinder to his family than they were to mine."

Her vibrant green eyes filled with unshed tears that set Lucky's chest to aching. She was much too young to know that kind of pain.

"Darlin', I know you're hurt, and I'm sorry things went the way they did, but please don't let this fester into bitterness. That won't harm anyone but you."

She stood a little straighter. "I'm not. I'm still working my way through Pa's journals, and once I find the truth, everyone will know why he turned the way he did." Maisie set the coffeepot down and retrieved her pad and pencil. "Now what can I get either of you besides coffee?" Her full lips curved into an unconvincing smile.

Goodness, but she was beautiful.

"How about a thick stack of flapjacks?" Mr. Dempsey grinned. "With lots of butter and syrup."

"Of course." She scribbled something on a pad then turned to him, blond wisps working loose from her bun and brushing her fair cheeks. "Lucky?"

I'm powerful hungry this morning, ma'am. How's about a whole mess of scrambled eggs, bacon, some potatoes. And would you grant me the favor of your company whilst I eat, Miss Maisie? At her expectant look, his tongue rooted in place. "Uh, flapjacks. Please."

He was an idiot. Probably for the best that he could never loosen his tongue to invite her to sit with him. What interest would she have in a big, stammering oaf? Especially one with his past.

"Two plates of flapjacks." She jotted the order then glanced again at him. "It's unusual to see you on a Tuesday morning, Lucky. It's real nice."

He twisted to face her, his heart beating like a thousand stampeding horses. Nice— to see him? He nodded, tried to smile. *It's always real nice to see you, too, Miss Maisie. I think you're about the sweetest gal God ever created.* Mr. Dempsey's boot landed hard against his shin, and the table shook, coffee sloshing over the sides of both their cups.

"Yes, ma'am." A knot formed in the pit of his stomach. *Speak, fool.* But he could tell any further attempt at words would only jumble on his tongue.

Maisie's brows furrowed in disappointment. "I'll, um, have those orders out shortly." She turned toward the kitchen.

He clamped his eyes shut and rubbed the heel of his palm against his forehead.

"Son, what's wrong with you?" Mr. Dempsey shook his head. "You can talk the ears off a cornfield, but you walk in here and forget how to string more than two words together."

Lucky reached for his coffee. He wasn't experienced with women like some men, nor did he care to be if it meant bedding a different woman every payday. He didn't have the polish—nor the money—that the Eddings fella obviously had. Lucky was a simple hired hand, simple enough that any time he came near her, even a smile got twisted and came out all wrong.

"You gotta pursue her. Let her know how you feel." Dempsey prodded. "Make an offhand remark about the flowers."

Those thunderous hooves beat a stampede through his chest again. He loved her, had from the first time he'd laid eyes on her. But the idea of speaking those things aloud set his innards to quivering. He shrugged. "I don't know how."

"Son, she don't bite. Just speak up, get to know her. You won't find any gal as good-hearted, and you both could use a friend. You'd be good for each other."

He had no doubt she was good-hearted, given who her father was and what he'd done for Lucky before his death.

Lord, I can only hope we might be good for each other one day, but what do I have to offer her?

Lucky shook his head. "A gal like her deserves friends who are honorable and decent." Everything he wasn't.

Dempsey leaned in. "I don't hire dishonorable men, Tolliver. You may have done some questionable things, but you've paid your debt. Sheriff Blanton saw the good in you. I've lived by the motto that every man deserves a second chance. This is yours. Quit thinking of yourself as the scoundrel you once were and start living like the man you want to be."

Lucky sipped his coffee. What was it that Dempsey saw in him—or that Maisie's dearly departed pa, Sheriff Jonathan Blanton, had seen in him six years earlier? He was a good-for-nothing cattle rustler, or rather, the kid stupid enough to stand guard while the rustlers scoped out a herd. And lest he forget, an attempted murderer. Like he could forget. Had Sheriff Blanton not convinced him to testify against the other gang members, he'd have been the guest of honor at his own necktie party.

"Sorry, Mr. Dempsey, but I don't know who that man is."

Chapter 2

"Margaret Ann Blanton!" Ma's voice boomed through the house, nearly shaking the shingles from the roof. Despite her frail condition, she could still muster a convincing sternness when needed.

"I'm coming!" Maisie sighed. The answers she sought would have to wait until after Sunday services. She marked her place in Pa's journal and trudged from the bedroom.

Ma stopped her at the front door with a firm stare. "I know you're not thrilled about going to church, young lady," she whispered, likely so neither Charlotte nor her brother, Simeon, might hear, "but I could've used the help preparing."

Ma's pointed words stung like a hoard of angry bees, particularly at the sight of the heavy-laden picnic basket she held. "Sorry, Ma." She ducked past, relieving her mother of the burden.

Charlotte had harnessed the team and readied the old farm wagon for the drive to church. But for Ma's feeble health, they could've easily walked there before the service, but in her present condition, such a trek would so tire Ma, she'd be unable to participate in the worship or picnic afterward.

They loaded into the wagon and, with a cluck of her tongue, Maisie started the team toward the little church. Moments later, they drew up in the busy churchyard. Ma smiled and nodded to the other families, unaware or unaffected by their cool responses. They weren't lost on Maisie. Perhaps because she was older, she'd seen the changing reception of the townsfolk as Pa had begun his slow fall from grace. At first they'd asked after his health. When he insisted things were fine, their concern grew to irritation and eventually to anger. As hard as Ma and Pa had tried to keep things from her, she'd been painfully aware of the rumblings within the town of removing Pa from his position as sheriff. That had finally happened after Ma's accident.

"Come, children." Ma shepherded them inside. Maisie headed for the back row, though Ma cleared her throat and nodded to a spot farther forward.

Maisie shot her a pleading glance. When Ma didn't back down, she chose a pew in the middle of the church and, standing beside it, allowed her family to file in before she took the aisle seat. Once settled, Maisie scanned the faces in the room. All familiar, all unwelcoming—except for Thomas, who stood across the church smiling unabashedly at her when she glanced his way. Irritation niggled at her.

Mr. and Mrs. Dempsey seated themselves next to Simeon, Mr. Dempsey clapping the boy on the shoulder. "How're you, young man?"

"Real good, sir."

The rancher grinned. "Stand up there, son." When Simeon complied, Mr. Dempsey eyed him closely. "I reckon you've grown about three inches since I last saw you. Another couple, and you'll be man-sized."

Simeon beamed. "Yes, sir. Ma says I'm outgrowing my pants faster'n she can sew new ones."

Robert Dempsey laughed.

His wife, Agatha, turned a knowing glance in Ma's direction. "Oh, Georgette, I recall those days. Just ask if you need help sewing."

As Ma nodded, the rancher turned to Charlotte. "And look at you, little lady. You get prettier every time we see you." He gave one of her blond braids a playful tug.

Charlotte's cheeks flushed. "Thank you, sir."

Just as Mr. Dempsey turned Maisie's way, someone stepped up beside her in the aisle.

"Good morning, Maisie."

At Thomas Eddings's courtly bow, her stomach clenched. She longed for the days when she and her family were acknowledged in church, but somehow, Thomas's attention felt more like she was being made a spectacle. Perhaps two years ago, she'd have welcomed it, but so much had changed now.

"You look lovely this morning."

She forced a smile to her lips. "Good morning, Thomas."

"I see there's still a bit of space in the pew." He nodded toward the far end of the row. "May I join you?"

She cast a quick glance around the room, noting the various reactions of the parishioners, everything from glowering stares to hushed conversations carried out behind people's hands. Did he not notice the chilly reception, or did he not care? Either way, she really didn't want to attract any more adverse attention, but what reason could she give him without seeming rude?

"I suppose—"

A flash of motion at the far end of the row caught her attention. Maisie's heart quickened as Lucky slid into the empty space next to Mrs. Dempsey. As he sat, the ranch hand's warm brown eyes flashed her way, and he nodded almost imperceptibly to her. A knot filled her throat at the silent greeting, slight though it was.

She turned back to Thomas. "I suppose the space has been filled. I'm sorry."

Disappointment flitted across his features, though he smiled. "Then I will look for you at the picnic afterward."

He excused himself and took a seat directly across the aisle from her.

The idea of sitting with Thomas Eddings at the picnic grated. She'd much prefer Lucky Tolliver's quiet company, but that would never happen.

Lucky waited his turn to exit the small building, glad when the citified dandy, Eddings, stepped outside. He'd been shameless in his attempts to garner Maisie's attention before and during the service. Church was hardly the place for such trifling behaviors.

He fixed his eyes on Maisie's golden hair. Beyond her stood her ma, younger sister, and brother. Mrs. Blanton was far more fragile than during his stint in the town jail. In those days, she'd swept into the building each day with her son on her hip, a basket of food in hand, and a smile on her face. She'd practically run the place, even though it was her husband's office. Now, her face was gaunt, eyes rimmed with dark circles, body withered and frail. The smile that once brightened his dreary days was replaced with a look bordering on pain—whether in body or heart, he could only guess.

The line moved, and the Blanton family filed out, Mrs. Blanton greeting the pastor while Maisie slipped outside and disappeared. His gaze darted to the window as she scurried past, arms wrapped about her waist. His gut knotted. Was she sick? Without thought, he slipped out of line and weaved around to the side door. Stepping into the sunshine, he hurried to the corner and perused the churchgoers as they prepared for the picnic. Maisie wasn't among them. She couldn't have gone far. He scanned the faces a second time then looked toward the street. There she and the fancified dolt stood, deep in conversation.

Disappointment threaded through him. Mr. Dempsey had encouraged him to ask Maisie to sit with him after church, try to have a conversation with her, but she'd run off before he could ask.

Uncertainty nibbled at his thoughts. He could attempt to interrupt them with the excuse that he wanted to be sure she wasn't ill. But what if he got tongue-tied again? It was embarrassing enough in front of her. He'd only make a bigger fool of himself if he turned into the stammering idiot in front of that polished blowhard. The thought set his heart to pounding.

He closed his eyes. "Lord? What do I do?"

"Follow your first instinct." Mrs. Dempsey sidled up next to him. "She's had a hard time coming to church since her pa died. I promise you, checking on her will do you both some good."

"She's talking with that Eddings fella."

Agatha Dempsey's brows arched. "Look again."

Eddings stalked back to the churchyard, hands shoved in his pockets, as Maisie rounded a corner out of sight.

"Go after her."

His throat knotted. "Maybe you should, ma'am." He shrugged. "She don't really know me."

"You've got a good heart, Lucky. Let her catch a glimpse of it." She gave him a gentle push toward his horse.

Lucky's feet stalled. At Agatha Dempsey's encouraging nod, he drew a deep breath and shuffled toward the hitching rail, thoughts churning. He'd be a fool to let the gal who visited his dreams slip off by herself iffen she were in a bad way. A mighty big fool. Surely he could utter a few words to her. *You under the weather, ma'am?* Simple enough.

Hardly.

He mounted the big bay, and followed Maisie's path. At the corner where she'd turned, he paused to peruse the empty street but found no sign of her. He headed down the road, checking each alley and cross street until he saw her duck around a corner near the café. She must be heading home. Lucky's heart rate quickened. He hadn't hoped to watch her find the second vase of flowers he'd left on her porch. Dare he spy on her?

Lucky tied his horse at the café's hitching rail and followed on foot. From the cross street nearest her house, he huddled behind the corner of a building and watched as she stalked up the path toward her door. She slowed, stopped. For an instant, she stared. When she glanced up and down the street, Lucky ducked out of sight but peeked again a moment later. He waited for the pretty smile to bloom when she unrolled his note, but instead, she crumpled the paper and threw it on the porch. Maisie picked up the vase and stalked inside, slamming the door after her.

He ducked around the corner and pressed his shoulders to the building, gulping air as if he'd taken a mule kick to the gut. What had he done? What woman didn't like flowers? Thoughts reeling, he turned toward his horse.

Before he reached the café, hoofbeats echoed down the street beyond. In no mood to see anyone, he waited for the rider to pass, and only a moment later, a bald-faced paint with ghostly blue eyes dipped into view.

The sight of the hauntingly memorable horse knotted his belly even further.

Chapter 3

As Maisie poured a fresh cup of coffee for a customer, the bell on the front door jingled. Lucky Tolliver ducked inside, book in hand, and took off his hat. His eyes settled on her, and excitement fluttered her belly. She must stop such schoolgirl foolishness. The man came every payday and sat for hours to sip coffee, read a book, and have a meal, but he never spoke other than to place his order. Even if the handsome young ranch hand were to show some interest—which he obviously didn't have—he didn't need to become involved with her. In this town, she was no better than poison.

"Afternoon, Lucky. Sit wherever you like."

He chose his usual table near the window.

Maisie faced the customer again. "Can I get anything more for you, sir?"

The man declined, and Maisie shuffled off to take the order from the couple at the neighboring table. Two slices of pie. Once she'd run the order to the kitchen, she approached Lucky's table.

"Do you know what you'd like this evening?" She poised her pencil over the notepad.

"Were you feeling poorly?"

She jerked to meet his deep brown eyes. "Pardon?" Had he truly spoken a whole sentence to her?

"At church." He held her gaze for an instant before shifting his attention away.

Maisie blinked, mute.

He shrugged. "You, um. . ." He fidgeted with the cover of his book. "Never mind. Ain't important."

Her eyes stung with the threat of tears. How long since anyone in this town had asked after her health? Outside of the Dempseys, no one seemed to notice—or care. Why he'd have noticed, she couldn't fathom. "Truth is, I wasn't feeling particularly well on Sunday. Thank you for inquiring."

He gave her a halting nod but said nothing more.

The stinging of her lower lids intensified, and a knot gripped her throat.

From the kitchen, the cook called that the latest order was ready.

"Excuse me, please."

Just inside the kitchen, she pressed her back to the wall and gulped several deep breaths.

The owner's wife glared. "What's wrong with you?"

A very good question. Lucky Tolliver's unexpected question had nearly reduced her to tears.

"Well?" the woman prodded from her station at the stove. "If you ain't dying, get this pie out to the customers, or I'll tell my husband you're shirking your duties again."

Biddy. Maisie squared her shoulders and met the woman's eyes. "I'm not shirking my duties. I needed a moment, if you don't mind." She wiped her eyes on her apron, retrieved the plates, and swept out of the kitchen.

"Here you are." She served the young couple and returned to Lucky's table. "Sorry for the interruption. What can I get you today?"

"Uh. . ." As usual, he avoided her eyes. "Fried chicken. Mashed potatoes."

She sighed inwardly. Four words. Of course, it was too good to last. "Anything more?"

He glanced toward the young couple. "Apple pie?"

"Fried chicken, mashed potatoes, and apple pie." She scribbled down the order.

"And coffee."

Maisie noted it on her pad. "I'll bring it directly."

By the time she delivered the order to the kitchen and returned with a mug, he was engrossed in his book.

It was for the best.

Within a short time, her other customers departed, leaving only Lucky. Rare for a Saturday, though it was still early. Maisie collected the dirty dishes and ran them back to the sink, taking a moment to rinse them since business was slow. No sooner had she begun than the bell on the front door jingled. She dropped the plates into the hot water to soak, dried her hands, and hurried into the dining room.

Two dark-haired men seated themselves at a table near the back wall. As she approached them, Lucky tugged his hat on, settling it low over his eyes as he rose. He placed something under his coffee cup on the table and, book in hand, slipped out with only a tiny nod in her direction.

What on earth. Was he coming back?

She watched through the window as he rode off then looked back at the remaining two horses at the rail. A magnificent black horse, its coat shining in the sun, stood next to a smaller paint. Its body was mainly a chestnut color, its neck and underbelly splashed liberally with white, though its bald face and light blue eyes gave it an eerie appearance.

Reeling in her attention, she retrieved the item Lucky'd left under his coffee cup. A two-dollar bill—far too much money for his uneaten meal—and a scrap of paper with something scribbled on it.

She turned to the two men, who both watched her. "Can I help you gentlemen?"

The first shoved his hat back to reveal angular features and cold gray-blue eyes, similar to the horse at the hitching post outside. "Gimme a steak. Rare. And coffee."

"Make that two steaks." Having already removed his hat, the second man pushed a mop of dark hair back from his eyes, which mirrored the peculiar blue of the other fella's. Brothers, perhaps, or some family relation.

"Rare as well?" Maisie gripped the scribbled note Lucky had left her.

He cocked his head, the waning afternoon light playing against his prominent cheekbones. "Ain't no other way to eat a steak."

"Yes, sir. I'll have those out to you directly."

She turned toward the kitchen, but the second man grabbed her wrist.

Heart pounding, Maisie spun. "Please unhand me."

"Anyone ever told you you're real pretty?" The man's grin chilled her.

Maisie squared her shoulders. "Yes. My father, *the sheriff*. Now, please, unhand me."

The first man glared across the table. "Let her go."

His grip eventually loosened. "My apologies, ma'am."

Knees like butter, she slipped into the kitchen, bee-lined for the back door, and turned Lucky's note toward the sun: *Be careful. Bad men.*

Stomach churning, Lucky rode down the street. Coward. He didn't deserve a gal like Maisie. Not when he'd leave her alone with two dangerous outlaws just to protect his own skin. And for what? Would Percy or Kane Freeman have recognized him? Perhaps not. He'd been a rowdy orphan, just barely seventeen, when he'd last seen them more than six years ago. He'd done a heap of changing since then.

But maybe they would have. They *were* cousins of Dale Freeman, the leader of the rustling gang he'd testified against, and it was his testimony that got the gang lynched. That'd make him memorable.

He couldn't say for sure, but he'd always wondered just how connected Percy and Kane were to the rustling operation. The first time they'd come by the hideout after Dale brought Lucky into the fold, there'd been an all-out war between the cousins. Dale had been willing, at first, to let Lucky in as a full-fledged member of the gang. After Percy and Kane's visit, he'd been left to tend the horses and do other mundane tasks. They'd obviously held a lot of sway over Dale for that to happen, even though they were rarely ever around.

For all he knew, they'd shown up in town now because they were looking for him, to settle the score.

He shouldn't have left Maisie in the café alone with 'em, not when he knew what they were capable of. "Lord, I should be making sure she's safe, not protecting my own sorry hide." He shook his head. "I had more of a spine at seventeen than I do now at twenty-three."

Go back and watch.

The thought came so suddenly, he drew to a sudden halt. Go back. . .to the café? The idea knotted his stomach. Not the café. He could keep an eye on the restaurant from the mercantile across the street.

Lucky turned the corner and secured his mount in front of the newspaper office then headed down the nearest alley and wound his way to the mercantile.

At the store owner's greeting, he nodded. "Mind iffen I look at your books?"

"Up front." The man motioned to the shelf.

Perfectly positioned to pretend he was looking while keeping an eye on the horses across the street, he grabbed a book and opened the cover, thumbing absently through the pages. A weight lifted from his shoulders when other diners arrived and filtered through the café's door across the next half hour. The more customers, the less likely the Freeman brothers would hassle Maisie.

The setting sun's rays reflected off the café's large window, making it impossible to see inside, so he prayed and watched for the pair to exit the building.

"It's nearly closing time," the shopkeeper called. "Are you finding what you need?"

He jerked at the unexpected question. "Yes, sir." He snapped the book he was holding closed and paced to the counter.

The man looked at the book's spine. "You sure this is the one you wanted?"

"It's a gift." He pushed the book of Elizabeth Barrett Browning's sonnets toward the man.

Recognition flared in the fella's eyes. "Like those pretty vases you ordered?"

With a sheepish grin, Lucky paid for the slim volume and turned. Outside the café, the Freeman brothers prepared to mount up.

"Pardon." He turned back to the counter, desperate for some reason to stay a moment longer. His gaze fell on the ledger book where the man kept track of the credit he'd extended to store patrons, and an idea struck.

"Yes?" The man stepped back to the counter again.

"I, uh. . ." His tongue threatened to freeze. "Iffen I was of a mind to do a favor for a friend, would you be willing to tell me how much they owe you?"

"What friend would you be asking after?"

He dropped his voice to a confidential level. "Sheriff Blanton's widow?"

The gentleman flipped to the appropriate ledger page. "Thirty-five dollars and twenty-eight cents."

More than a month's pay for him. He could only imagine how much that would translate to on Maisie's meager earnings. A year's worth? He dug in his pocket, produced twenty dollars, and slid it across the counter. "Put that toward her account, and I'll bring you the rest later. And I'll ask you to keep this between us. I don't want the family knowing."

After the man wrote a receipt, Lucky headed toward the door again. The café's hitching rail stood empty as he exited the mercantile and slipped back to the alley.

Thank You, Lord.

He should check in on Maisie, make sure they hadn't acted inappropriately toward her. But what would she think of him leaving her there alone, especially after his pointed note stating they were bad men? She'd think him a coward. His heart pounded. It'd be best to disappear for now, wait to see her another time. Perhaps she'd forget his spinelessness by then.

He tucked the book under one arm, pulled his hat brim lower on his forehead, and crammed his hands in his pockets. Long strides carried him down the narrow alley toward the newspaper office where he'd left his horse, though when he rounded the corner, he stopped at the sight of Percy Freeman.

"Pardon." His nerves crackling, Lucky dipped his head so his hat brim shielded more of his face and turned the other direction. Kane Freeman blocked that path.

"Lucky Tolliver." Percy stepped up behind him.

He swung around to see both men. His only options were to stand and face them, or backtrack. He took a shuffling step back.

"Thought that was you in the café," the elder brother, Percy, continued.

He swallowed, took another step back.

"Wasn't you feeling neighborly? You didn't stay and say hello." A humorless grin stained Kane's lips.

Lucky backed up a couple of more steps. "Don't want no trouble, fellas."

Percy smirked as they both closed in. "Neither do we."

Both men's gazes darted past him to the alley entrance. He dared not look.

"Well, there you are, Lucky!" Maisie Blanton called. "When a gentleman invites a lady on an evening stroll, it's customary to wait for her out in the open. Not in a dark alley surrounded by all this trash."

Jaw slack, he turned so he could see Maisie without losing sight of the Freemans.

"Are you ready?" She settled a hand on her hip and smiled, green eyes glinting.

"Yes, ma'am." He looked at the brothers. "'Scuse me." He gave a curt nod and settled a hand against the small of Maisie's back, high-tailing it onto the street.

"Are you all right?" Maisie asked after they'd walked a good half block.

He kept his pace until he reached the street where he'd left his horse. There, he searched for the Freemans before he drew her to a halt. Heart hammering, he turned on her.

"What in the name of Pete do you think you're doing?"

Chapter 4

Maisie drew back at Lucky's sharp tone. "If you must know, saving you. I saw those men had you cornered, so I—"

"I didn't warn you so's you could save me. I warned you so's you'd steer clear of 'em. You shoulda left well enough alone."

Ungrateful man. And she'd been intrigued to the point of nearly throwing herself at this fella? "Pardon me for caring." She drew back out of his reach then turned back toward the café.

Lucky caught her arm and, after a glance up and down the street, nodded toward his horse. "Come with me. We need to get out of sight. They're still around here somewheres."

"I have to get back to work. My boss allowed me a short break, but I still have to close up."

As if he hadn't heard, he stowed something in his saddlebags then jerked the reins free and swung into the saddle. Only then did he stretch out his hand to her as if expecting her to abandon her job and ride away with him.

"Did you hear me? If I don't get back, I'll lose my job."

Lucky nudged the horse nearer and leaned down. "I ain't trying to scare you, but your job's the least of your worries with these men." He spoke in a confidential tone. "They're killers, among other things. Now, please, come with me?" He held out his hand again. That time, something in his expression compelled her to take it. In one quick motion, he helped her up behind him.

Maisie's hands instinctively settled at his waist, a little thrill winding through her. At almost nineteen, she'd never ridden double with a man other than Pa and never figured she would, given the things folks in this town thought of her family.

Lucky urged his horse into motion. "You know someplace in town where we can get out of sight?"

"I'm quite serious. I must get back to the café, but there's a small barn out back if you feel compelled to hide. The owner uses it to store some broken chairs and such."

"Any chance I can talk you into not going back to work tonight?"

Not going back to that blasted café was her dream. She'd rather work the family ranch, but all hope of that died with Pa. They owed too much on the property, and she was barely making enough at the café to keep food on the table, but. . . "I had a hard enough time finding that job. The owner's all but promised he'll fire me if I do anything more wrong."

He loosed a long breath but turned the horse toward the café. They rode in silence,

Lucky searching the streets constantly as he took them on a circuitous route back to the Blackwater Café.

Whoever those men were, they'd certainly gotten Lucky talking. It was as if someone had knocked the rust from his jaw and oiled his tongue up good and proper. Now if she could just keep those words flowing. But when she drew back, prepared to ask how he knew them, Lucky tugged her arms tighter about his waist. Her thoughts turned to sludge and her insides wobbled at his nearness.

Blast it all. How easily she could go weak kneed and addle brained.

She jerked her thoughts back. "Who are those men, and how do you know them?"

His face clouded. "Nobody important."

"Is that so?"

He glanced back. "Trust me when I tell you they're bad fellas. You should cut 'em a wide path."

A decidedly guarded answer, not unlike the ones Pa used to give her when she'd ask him specifics about his job—and particularly about why he wasn't doing it there at the end of his tenure as sheriff.

"What aren't you telling me, Lucky?"

He stiffened as he turned down the little alley leading to the barn behind the café. "Some questions are better left unasked." He swung his leg over the big bay's neck and slid from the saddle then turned to help Maisie down.

Feet on the ground, she pinned him with a glare. "I don't like secrets. There's been too many of those in my life, and I'm tired of it."

The old Lucky returned then. He looked away and shrugged. "Just. . .trying to protect you."

Despite the reemergence of his timorous side, she shook her head. "I don't need protecting. I'm the daughter of a lawman. Pa taught me to ride, rope, track, and shoot, so I wouldn't need a man. I'm more than capable of protecting myself, thank you very much. Now will you please tell me who they are?"

After a moment, he shook his head. "Better you don't know."

Sighing, she brushed past him into the café.

Lucky sat beside the small watering hole and shook his head. What on earth had he been thinking? *He'd left.* The moment that doorway swallowed her up, he'd ridden to her house, tucked the book of poems against her door, and ridden back to the Rocking D. And that was three days ago. At the least, he shoulda made sure she got home unharmed, but she'd rattled him, asking what he was hiding. Despite being the sheriff's daughter, she was somehow blissfully unaware he'd spent time in prison, and the thought of spilling those details scared him senseless.

"There ain't much hope anyhow. The only way you can talk to a pretty gal without getting tongue-tied is when you're scared for her safety or upset at her recklessness." He attacked the weeds that threatened to choke the edge of the watering hole.

She didn't help matters. The minute she spouted off about her abilities to rope, ride, and shoot, he'd gotten so blasted discombobulated, there'd been no chance. Had her pa truly taught her those things so's she wouldn't need a man in her life? He tossed the weeds to the side. It didn't leave him much to be optimistic about. Not that he had any to begin with.

The bigger issue was Percy and Kane Freeman's sudden appearance. In hindsight, he should've mentioned their appearance to the new sheriff. But the lawman—formerly Sheriff Blanton's deputy. . .and the man Lucky'd shot while attempting to escape capture—had plenty of reason to hate him. The man had lingered between life and death for a week before he'd finally pulled through. All the more reason Lucky avoided the law as much as he could.

He moved down and attacked another handful of weeds near the water's edge, as well as pulled a few stones from the shallows. "Lord, I shoulda expected to see Percy and Kane Freeman, but I didn't. Guess I figured since I'm trying so hard to right my wrongs that You'd keep that part of my life from returning to haunt me. Now that I know they're here, I got a real bad feeling that they're up to no good, and I fear Maisie's in some danger. Because of me."

In the distance, a horse and rider cantered his way. Lucky continued working at the weeds and rocks until the man finally neared.

"Howdy, Joe." Lucky stood to face his fellow ranch hand.

Joe Coppen leaned on the saddle horn, his expression grim. "Boss wants you back in the ranch yard directly."

Concern knotted his shoulders. "Is everything all right?"

"Don't appear so. The sheriff wants a word with you. You best come along."

The sheriff. That didn't bode well. Lucky wiped sweat from his hatband then tugged his hat back in place. "You know what he wants?"

"Can't say for sure, but I can surmise." The latter part leaked out like a breath, almost too soft for Lucky to hear.

Lucky swung into his saddle and clucked his tongue. Within minutes, he rode into the ranch yard, his neck and shoulders aching with tension. Joe trailed up beside him. At their approach, Sheriff Ed Warburn and Thomas Eddings, of all people, stepped off Mr. Dempsey's wide front porch and strode out into the sunshine. Lucky's muscles knotted even tighter. Thankfully, Mr. Dempsey was close on their heels.

"Tolliver, git off that horse," the sheriff barked. "I need a word with you."

His tongue turning to cotton, he obliged the lawman. "What can I help you with, Sheriff?"

The lawman stopped a foot in front of him, glowering. "Where were you two days ago?"

He resisted the urge to step back to distance himself from Warburn. "I was here. Doing my work. Why?"

"Because some of my family's cattle are missing." Eddings barged toward him. "I remember you from years ago. If you'd throw in with rustlers then, what would stop you from stealing cattle again?"

He fisted his hands, his heart pounding. It would feel good to punch that dandified troublemaker in the nose. Somehow, though, he kept himself under control. "I didn't. I swear it. I was here, and Mr. Dempsey knows it."

"Was he, Dempsey?" The sheriff turned, finally putting some space between them. Lucky breathed a little easier.

"Thinking back, Lucky helped me deliver a calf that morning, then me and several of the boys—including Lucky and Joe, there—moved part of the herd for a couple hours after that. That afternoon, they went off to do other chores separately."

Sheriff Warburn squinted at him. "Can anyone vouch for your whereabouts that night?"

Lucky shrugged. "I was in my bunk. Ask Joe." He turned to the other cowhand, still sitting in his saddle.

"Lucky was in his bunk when I went to sleep. Can't promise nothing after I drifted off, though."

He glared at Joe, while the sheriff and Eddings pinned Lucky with their own fiery gazes.

Lucky shook his head vehemently. "I was here. All night. I ain't lying."

"You got some way to prove that?" Warburn prodded.

Mr. Dempsey swiveled toward the lawman. "You got some way to prove he wasn't, Ed?"

The lawman clenched his teeth. "Not yet."

The dandy stomped off a few feet. "Find some proof, Sheriff, or every rancher in this county will wake to find their herds missing."

Lucky glared at Eddings a moment then turned to the lawman. "Sheriff, I promise you, I had nothing to do with it. But I might know who does."

"Oh?"

"A week ago Sunday, I was leaving town after church and saw a bald-faced paint walking through town. Then this past Saturday, the same horse showed up at Blackwater Café, along with a big black. Those horses belong to the Freeman brothers. Percy and Kane."

"Ain't never heard of 'em," Warburn growled.

"They're cousins of Dale Freeman, and I reckon they might've had something to do with his rustling gang back then. Start looking with them, sir. Not with me."

"I'll look wherever the evidence points, and right now, it's pointing straight at you."

Chapter 5

Nothing. Absolutely nothing. Maisie flipped the page of her father's journal and read about a scuffle in the saloon. Would she ever find the truth of why he quit on his job? She skimmed the remainder of the entry and turned the page:

February 9, 1866

Monty Stebbens reported that thirty head of his cattle have gone missing. Ed and I rode out to his place to take a look and found there weren't any tracks to follow. It's troublesome. How do thirty head of cattle up and vanish without a trace? We spent several hours hunting but didn't find much before dusk. We'll resume the search tomorrow.

Her brows furrowed. Thirty missing cattle and no tracks to follow. Very odd. She flipped the page but realized it was time to return to the café. Maisie marked the page, snapped the journal shut, and hurried back to work. Once she slipped inside and wound her apron around her waist, the restaurant owner departed for his office.

Maisie made the rounds of the four occupied tables, checking to be sure the customers had all they needed. Two tables paid her and departed.

"Of course, you know who Warburn suspects," one of the men at the remaining tables whispered.

The other man nodded. "He needs to do more than *suspect*. That kid was trouble years back, and he's trouble now. Dempsey was a fool for hiring him."

Maisie's attention piqued at the mention of Robert Dempsey. Straining to hear, she turned to the recently vacated table nearest the two men and, back to the pair, stacked the dishes.

"I hear Warburn's brought him in for questioning."

Questioning one of Mr. Dempsey's men? That wasn't good.

"Perhaps Tolliver's *luck* has run out."

Maisie jerked as if struck.

———◆◆◆◆———

Lucky met Sheriff Warburn's gaze from across the lawman's desk. "Maisie Blanton waited on 'em in the café. There were other customers that came in after I left. She'd be able to tell you their names. Maybe they could vouch that the Freemans were there."

Warburn leaned across the desk, his eyes hard. "I'll say it again. I don't really care if two blue-eyed men were in that café. What I'm trying to figure out is where Cyrus Eddings' cattle have gotten off to."

His hackles rose. "And I'm telling you, it wasn't me who took 'em. I swore to myself I wasn't going back to prison once I got out, and I been doing my best to stay outta trouble. I stay around the Rocking D, work hard, keep to myself. I go to church on Sundays and have a meal in the café on paydays. That's it."

"So iffen you keep to yourself, then there's plenty of time you coulda slipped away and taken a few head of cattle."

"No!" Lucky slapped the surface of the desk. "You're twisting my words."

"Warburn." Robert Dempsey stepped toward the desk. "That's not what he said, and you know it."

"I know nothing of the kind. And I said you could stay as long as you let me do my job. Butt out."

"Ed, as a friend, I'm asking you to hold off in your questioning for a couple minutes. Do you mind?"

"You can ask. Ain't gonna do much good, though. I got a job to do here."

"I'm real sorry to hear that." Mr. Dempsey turned and settled a hand on Lucky's shoulder. "Son, I'll be back in just a few minutes."

He swiveled toward his boss. "You're leaving?"

"Don't say a word, you understand?"

Lucky nodded. *Lord, I'm being railroaded here, and Mr. Dempsey's leaving. I could really use a friend about now.*

As soon as Dempsey slipped out the door, Warburn resumed peppering him with questions, though Lucky focused on the front of Warburn's desk and tried not to listen. The constant accusations only served to anger him. He'd done *nothing* to deserve such treatment.

Within ten minutes, Mr. Dempsey barged into the office again, Maisie Blanton in tow.

His head began to pound. He never should've told Warburn she could attest to the Freemans being in town. Her involvement could put her in danger, not to mention cause her to question more about his past. He was a fool.

"Sheriff?"

At Maisie's firm call, Lucky cast a sidelong glance her way. Her expressive green eyes fixed on him for an instant before she focused on the lawman.

"I understand there's a matter I can help with?"

Warburn faced Mr. Dempsey. "What'd you bring her for?"

Maisie strode up to the corner of the desk. "Mr. Dempsey says you're curious about two men who dined in the Blackwater Café the other night?"

"Seems Mr. Dempsey's out of line. I didn't ask for you."

"I see." Maisie glanced around the room, paced to the corner where she collected another chair, and settled it particularly close to Lucky. As she sat, her hand brushed his arm, lingering, it seemed. The tiny gesture infused him with a little strength, and perhaps a mustard seed's worth of faith that this could somehow work out.

"What do you think you're doing?" Warburn eyed her.

She folded her hands primly in her lap and lifted her chin. "I know my father taught you to track down all the leads, so I'll wait until you're ready to speak to me." Maisie smiled politely.

Warburn's expression grew severe.

Maisie nodded. "Please, don't let me interrupt."

"You already have, and iffen you were anyone other than Jonathan's daughter, I'd escort you outta here right now. But because of the respect I *used to* hold for your pa, I won't do that." He folded his arms. "Tell me what you got to say, then see yourself out."

The confidence in her green eyes faltered at Warburn's pointed comments about her father, though she recovered and, standing, fished something from her pocket.

"As is his routine on paydays, Lucky came into the Blackwater Café last Saturday. I was just returning from the kitchen when two men entered and sat down across the room from him. Lucky didn't even get his food, just got up and walked out. But he left this note on the table." She handed a scrap of paper to Sheriff Warburn.

The lawman snatched the paper, read it, then shifted to Lucky. "Iffen you really wrote this, you'll know what it says."

He nodded. "It was a warning. Said 'Be careful. Bad men.'"

Mr. Dempsey glanced over Warburn's shoulder at the paper and laughed. Warburn's jaw clenched.

"After the men departed the café," Maisie continued, "I saw them corner Lucky in an alley across the street, so I approached and helped him excuse himself. It was obvious to me that he was trying to avoid them. I never got their names, but Lucky said they were killers."

"What'd these fellas look like?" Warburn's words were short.

"About your age—early thirties. Both had dark hair, one cut short, the other one shoulder-length. Neither had shaved in a few days. And both had cold blue eyes." She looked as if she were about to sit then thought better of it. "Oh. One of them rode a paint horse with a bald face and eyes just as blue as the men's. The other rode a big black horse."

Lucky held his breath. For several long moments, Warburn stared at the note Maisie had produced. Why she'd kept it, he couldn't imagine. Finally he met Lucky's eyes.

"None of this absolves you of any wrongdoing, Tolliver. So there was a couple odd-looking fellas in the café, and you had a scuffle with 'em in the street afterward. That doesn't explain where Eddings' cattle have gotten off to."

"The evidence doesn't point to him either, Ed," Mr. Dempsey chimed in. "Until you can prove he took those cattle—or was even near Eddings' ranch, you got no case. You're just letting past circumstances color your judgment."

The sheriff glared, first at Dempsey then Lucky. "You're free to go for now, but I'll be watching you, Tolliver. Any more cattle go missing, and you'll be back here."

Warburn stalked toward the door, opening it so they could file out.

Lucky rose, though Maisie blocked his path. Her warm green eyes twinkled as she looked up at him. Without a word, she hugged him, arms circling his ribs for the briefest of moments before she pulled away again. A shy smile curved her lips as she headed toward the door.

His mind reeling, whether from the brush with the law or her unexpected gesture, he wasn't sure. The one thing he was sure of was that he liked the way she looked at him just then, and he liked the feel of her even more.

But Percy and Kane Freeman could ruin everything—his future and any life he'd dreamed he could have with pretty Maisie Blanton.

Chapter 6

"Are you ever going to turn out that light so I can sleep?" Charlotte's voice dripped fatigue.

Maisie rubbed her knotted neck muscles then stared back at the rickety desk. "Soon." Not until she'd finished searching through Pa's old WANTED posters.

The younger girl sighed. "Fine, but don't blame me when you wind up late for work tomorrow."

Maisie glanced back and rolled her eyes.

The bed creaked as her sister propped her head on her hand. "Who do you reckon paid so much on our account at the mercantile?"

She could easily guess. Thomas Eddings had been to town a few times and stopped by to see her at the café. He'd shown up across the street at the mercantile to buy supplies just a day or two before they'd discovered the generous gift. He certainly could have paid some on their bill then.

"You think it's the same person as left you the flowers and the poems?"

Maisie faced the desk again, staring at the thick stack of papers before her. "Go to sleep, Charlotte."

"I'm trying, but you won't turn out the light."

Ignoring her, Maisie flipped through each paper, studying the names and likenesses, noting Pa's scribbled notes of arrest dates, convictions, or hangings. Those with hanging dates, she shuffled into one pile. Any drawings that looked similar to the men from the café, she placed in a separate stack.

"I bet Thomas is leaving you the flowers. He's always been so romantic."

"Charlotte, hush. I'm trying to concentrate." This task would've been so much easier if Lucky had just told her who the men were. Then she wouldn't feel compelled to ferret out the truth. But something told her to follow this rabbit trail just a little further—for Lucky's sake, if not her own curiosity.

"Well, isn't he? You used to think Thomas was quite charming."

"Thomas Eddings is an incorrigible flirt, nothing more."

Lucky, on the other hand. . . Mr. Dempsey's hired hand seemed to understand the pain and hardships she'd endured in a way Thomas Eddings never would. Perhaps she was allowing his good looks and mysterious nature to charm her just like Thomas's gregarious nature had years earlier, but she doubted it. When Warburn had badgered Lucky with questions and accusations, his responses were that of a man accustomed to trouble, and they'd stirred something deep in her heart. At the sight of the frustration, fear, and anger in his deep brown eyes, she'd wanted him to know he wasn't alone. She, of all people, understood how it felt to be vilified for things completely out of her control. It's why she'd instinctively hugged him.

But she hadn't expected her belly to flutter so fiercely, nor her cheeks to heat as they had.

"*You're* incorrigible. A secret admirer leaves you two bunches of flowers in a matched set of expensive vases, and you're not even interested in finding out who he is."

Maisie twisted again to face her sister. "Yes, I think Thomas paid the bill, and, yes, I'm certain he left the flowers and the book as well. But right now, I'm trying to find the names of two men Lucky Tolliver and I saw in the café as well as solve the mystery of what happened to Pa. What do I care about flowers? Now, please. . .hush."

She turned back to the posters. An instant later, a wadded paper *thunked* the top of her shoulder and skittered across the desk. With a huff, she smoothed it to find the note from the second vase of flowers: "*Maisie, in all my born days, I ain't met a gal as sweet as you.*"

She faced her sister. "Where did you get this?"

Charlotte giggled. "You left it on the porch, so I saved it for you."

"Girls," Ma called from down the hall. "Get to sleep."

"Yes, ma'am." They answered in unison.

Maisie dimmed the lamp a little and twisted to look at Charlotte one last time. "I'll be done soon. I promise." She held her finger to her lips, cautioning her sister to be quiet.

Once the girl closed her eyes, Maisie laid the note aside and whittled through the posters. As she neared the bottom of the stack, she lingered over one. The likeness was a good resemblance to the elder of the two men. Same angular features, strong jawline, and dark, close-cropped hair. The next poster showed an unmistakable likeness of the longer-haired man with prominent cheekbones. The list of aliases revealed one common name between them—Freeman. Percy and Kane. As Lucky suggested, murder was among a litany of crimes.

As Maisie set the two posters to the side and reached to extinguish the lamp, she once more picked up the crumpled note, tracing the little flourishes that marked the first letter of her name. In all his born days, Thomas hadn't met anyone as sweet as her. She shook her head. Was he playing coy, using such colloquial terms? He'd never speak in such a manner. It didn't matter. She wouldn't be drawn in by his frivolous games.

She set the note aside, gathered the various stacks of posters, and shuffled them back into one. As she laid it in the center of the desk, a name on the top poster caught her attention. Dale Freeman, leader of a cattle rustling gang. Her father had scribbled a hanging date in the corner, but at the bottom, she focused on the name among the "known associates" section.

Luke "Lucky" Tolliver.

A circle highlighted his name, and beside it, Pa's familiar scrawl filled the bubble:

Arrested April 4, 1866.
Sentenced May 7, 1866.
Six years.

Her jaw went slack.

Her Lucky—a convicted cattle rustler?

───────────────◈───────────────

From where Lucky saddled his horse, he had a perfect view of the road leading onto the Rocking D. So when Maisie Blanton bobbed into view atop a handsome sorrel, he grinned. Oh, that she might have come to see him. A laughable thought. Surely, she'd come to see her friends, the Dempseys. At least he'd be able to thank her proper for helping at the sheriff's office a few days earlier. He finished his task and met her at the center of the yard.

"Afternoon, Maisie." He took hold of her horse's bridle.

"Afternoon, Lucky."

"I, uh, don't think I thanked you." He willed his tongue not to stall. "For talking to the sheriff."

"That's actually why I came."

"It is?" Then she *was* there to see him. His stomach knotted.

She motioned to his horse. "Were you going somewhere?"

"Yes, ma'am. Gotta finish checking out a watering hole."

"May I ride with you?"

He'd imagined riding with her often but never hoped for such a pleasure. Mute, he nodded.

"Where to?" she asked as he swung into the saddle.

"This way." He reined his horse around, and she fell in beside him, seemingly deep in her own thoughts for several long minutes.

Lord, You made me a happy man by bringing her here today, but. . . He risked a peek at her. "You. . .wanted to talk to me?"

She startled. "I'm sorry. Feeling nostalgic, I guess. The ranch bordering the Rocking D was my family's old homestead. I miss it something fierce."

He'd known the land next door was the Blanton's place. Upon his release from prison, he'd headed there first, only to find the place abandoned. The sight of it had caused an ache in his chest, particularly when he found the grave marker where Jonathan Blanton took his final rest.

"I'm real sorry." At her whispered thanks, he pressed on. "You said you came out to talk. . .something about the sheriff?"

"No. Not directly. I just, well, I—" She stopped short. "I'm stammering like a ninny."

He knew that feeling all too well.

"You were so cryptic about those men, so I pulled out Pa's old WANTED posters."

A sick feeling washed over him.

"I found Kane and Percy Freeman's posters among them. I see now why you were concerned."

Had she come only to confirm his feelings, or was there more?

"I also found this one." She held out a rolled paper, her gaze full of questions.

Dread's cold tentacles wormed through him. With a silent prayer, he reached for the poster and unrolled it. At the briefest glimpse of the old Freeman Gang notice, Lucky drew the bay to a sudden halt and stared at his horse's neck. *God, help me.*

Silence lingered for a long moment.

"Well?"

"What do you want me to say, Maisie?" She must hate him. His secret was out, and she would turn and run at any moment.

But she didn't. Instead, she reined her sorrel around to face him. "I want you to talk to me, Luke Tolliver!"

He found her green eyes full of compassion.

"I've been serving you meals in the café for nigh on half a year now, but we've never really talked. You and Mr. Dempsey asked me to vouch for you, and I did. Without question. Now I'd like to know a bit about the man I spoke for. Where'd you grow up? What was your family like? How'd you get involved with cattle rustlers?"

Once she knew his past sins, it'd end any dreams he might have for them. Nothing for it now, but to plunge ahead. He urged his horse forward again, and she fell in beside him.

"I was an angry kid looking for a family. Dale Freeman and his gang took me in."

"What about your real family?"

He shook his head. "Ma died birthing me, and Pa died in the War between the States. I was their only child. When Pa left for the war, I got shuffled around between a bunch of aunts and uncles who didn't want me. That's when I fell in with the Freemans. I was a stupid kid hungry to belong, and they were like the older brothers I never had. Teased me and pushed me around, but all good-natured-like."

"So you like getting pushed around?"

"No, I...I didn't mean—" Lucky jerked to look at her but found mischief in her eyes. He quit stammering and chuckled.

"There! You *can* laugh. I was wondering."

He shook his head. "Don't hear you laugh much either."

She sobered. "Suppose I haven't in a while."

"Why?"

Her face clouded. "I'm asking the questions. How'd you get caught?"

Lucky rolled his eyes. "I'm surprised you don't know. I was standing watch whilst the gang scouted a herd to rustle. Your pa and Deputy Warburn crept up on me. Woulda gotten the drop, but Warburn jostled a rock loose at the last instant."

"What happened?"

"I, uh...I shot Warburn. In the chest."

Maisie's eyes rounded. "You were the one?"

His belly knotted. Surely now she'd ride away without a backward glance.

But she didn't.

"I always wondered. Pa never talked much about his job to us kids. Only with Ma."

"It was me, sure enough." Not a day went by that he didn't beg for God—and War-burn—to forgive him.

"So what happened? How'd you go from an outlaw to this fella?"

A grin curved his lips as he drew up near the watering hole. "Your pa happened."

"Pardon?"

He dismounted and helped her down. "Like I told you, my kin took little interest in me. Guess I was used to that. But from the minute your pa locked me in his jail, he told me I could amount to more than a useless thief. He was real firm, but kind, too. In the beginning, I pushed him away, but him and your ma were real persistent. She'd bring me meals every day and spend an hour talking. They convinced me to testify against the other gang members, said I could save my own neck iffen I did. I'd get prison. They'd get hung. Guess I started believing 'em, that I could do better for myself. So I testified, and I went off to prison for six years."

Maisie's brow furrowed in confusion. "So you went into prison a hardened criminal and came out a good, upstanding man, just like that?"

He pulled at his earlobe. Iffen he wasn't mistaken, she'd just called him *good*. "Wasn't just like that. Your pa wrote me letters whilst I was in. Talked about startin' over. He'd write me scriptures or tell me what the Lord had done in his life. He showed an uncommon concern, something no one else had done before. He was like the pa I wished I had."

She stiffened, her features hardening. "And how long did he write to you?"

Lucky shook his head. "I. . .I don't know. The first three years that I was in prison. Thereabouts."

She laughed, though the sound lacked mirth. "I shouldn't be surprised."

" 'Bout what?"

"I mean no offense, Lucky. I'm very happy Pa's attention helped you when you needed it. But it also upsets me. While he was becoming like a father to you, he became a stranger to his own family. He grew more distant every day. He started shirking his duty as sheriff. He'd disappear for days with no explanation. Things got so bad, I had to quit my schooling to help at home. And the town was left wondering where their lawman went." Her eyes clouded, fat tears welling against her long lashes.

"In that same time, things grew strange at home. We'd wake to find items moved around in the barn or the kitchen. Things started disappearing from the house—my diary, my sister's favorite doll, a blanket my baby brother was partial to. Ma and I thought we were going crazy, and Pa just dismissed it. When I pressed him for help, he grew angry and withdrew more. Then one night, he returned after being gone for several days, and a corner of Simeon's blanket was hanging from his saddlebags. When I asked about it, he denied he had it. Lucky, I know what I saw. It was my brother's blanket, all right."

Lucky shook his head in confusion. "What happened?"

"Nothing. I searched the house and barn. I never did find it, but I tell you, it was there. In his possession. And he acted like I was loco when I brought it up."

"That doesn't make sense. Why would he hide your brother's blanket?"

"You're right. It doesn't make sense. His behavior turned odder every day, almost like *he* was going mad. Then Ma had her accident."

"Accident?" A shiver snaked down his spine.

Her tears flowed then. "The windmill wasn't working, and Pa wasn't home to fix it, so Ma climbed up to see about it. Only the ladder rung broke." Maisie closed her eyes, as if to block the memory. "The fall nearly killed her. She was unconscious for two weeks. Broke a bunch of bones, cracked her skull. When she woke up, a lot of her memory was gone." She opened her eyes again, her expression a mixture of pain and rage. "And Pa's response was to crawl into a bottle and drink himself to death."

Chapter 7

At the jingling of bells, Maisie turned in time to see Mr. Dempsey enter the café. Disappointment wound through her when Lucky didn't trail in behind him. A few feet inside the door, the rancher beckoned to her with an urgency that caused her to hurry to his side.

"Is something wrong?"

"Is your boss here, Maisie?" He spoke in a confidential tone.

"Yes, sir. In his office. Would you like to speak to him?"

"Fetch him, please. But first, put in an order for Lucky's favorite meal."

She swallowed. "You're worrying me, Mr. Dempsey. Is he all right?"

"I'm sorry, darlin'." He shook his head. "Sheriff Warburn just arrested him for rustling."

The breath leaked from her lungs slowly. *God, You have to help him. Please.* Thoughts swirling, she scribbled Lucky's customary order, delivered it to the cook, and asked her boss to come to the dining room.

Grumbling about the interruption, the café owner approached Mr. Dempsey. The men spoke in hushed tones. She held her breath when their eyes darted her way more than once, her boss shaking his head vigorously. Finally, Mr. Dempsey handed him something—money for the meal, certainly—and shook his hand. Rather grudgingly, her boss nodded and stepped behind the counter.

"Pack up Mr. Dempsey's order and go with him."

"Yes, sir. When should I be back?"

The man glowered at Dempsey. "Tomorrow."

Her eyes widened. "I can't afford a day without pay."

"You'll get paid. Now collect the food and git." He nodded toward the kitchen.

Maisie scrambled into the kitchen, wrapped each plate with a cloth, and settled the dishes in a crate before hurrying outside to Mr. Dempsey.

"What happened?" She settled herself in the wagon.

"Two more ranchers are missing cattle." Mr. Dempsey turned the team toward the jail. "Warburn swears he's looked for the men Lucky described, but nobody's seen them or their horses. Sheriff's threatening a hanging iffen Lucky doesn't produce the missing livestock."

"A hanging! He can't do that! Not without a trial."

"I'm afeared Warburn's more interested in getting even with Lucky for his past than finding the truth."

Her stomach knotted. "So what're you hoping I'll be able to do?" She couldn't force the sheriff to abide by the law.

"Just keep Lucky's spirits up whilst I work at this another way."

When they pulled up outside the sheriff's office, Maisie hoisted the crate from the wagon and burst through the door. Inside the lone cell, Lucky sat on a bunk, head cradled in his hands, seemingly unaware of anything happening outside the bars.

"What'd you want?" Warburn eyed her.

"I'm here to see Lucky."

Lucky looked up.

"He ain't receiving visitors."

Shoulders slumping even more, Lucky returned to his former posture.

"Leave off, Warburn," Mr. Dempsey called as he entered. "Iffen it were anyone else, you'd allow 'em a visitor or two." Taking the crate from her, he deposited it on Warburn's cluttered desk. "I purchased this food from the café for Tolliver." He unwrapped the plates for Warburn's inspection.

The lawman poked at the food with a fork then eyed Mr. Dempsey. "Looks clean." He carried the food to the cell and opened the slot. "Come get your dinner, Tolliver."

Lucky rose, but just as he reached for the plates, Warburn released both. Fried chicken, gravy, potatoes, and pie slopped to the floor, dishes clattering after them.

"Clumsy fool!" Warburn huffed. "You'll be cleaning that up."

"You did that on purpose, Sheriff!" Maisie stormed toward the cell. "You should be the one to—"

"That's enough outta you." The lawman whirled on her. "You hope to stay in my office, you'll keep a civil tongue."

She gritted her teeth. "My father would be ashamed of you."

"Maisie." Mr. Dempsey looped an arm around her shoulders and pulled her away. "It's not worth it."

"Reckon I couldn't eat much anyway. Ain't hungry." Lucky used the plates to scoop as much of the ruined food as he could then held it out to Warburn. "You want to take this and bring me something to clean the rest of this mess with?"

The sheriff dropped the dishes in the crate beside the door then turned to the three of them. "I'll be back directly. You two"—he pointed to Mr. Dempsey and her—"don't get within five feet of that cell. Understood?"

Maisie folded her arms and glared, though Mr. Dempsey nodded compliantly. Once Warburn stepped outside, she spun to face Lucky again. "Are you all right?"

He gripped the bars. "I'd be lying if I said yes."

Maisie's chest ached. If only she could offer him some comfort. "Blast that sheriff. He's being downright ornery."

"Unprofessional, more like." Mr. Dempsey settled a chair in the middle of the room and guided her to it. "Maisie, stay with him. I'm going to contact the U.S. Marshals and see iffen we can't get some help searching for those men."

The U.S. Marshals? *If* he could get them, and *if* they'd arrive quickly, it would be a big help. Unfortunately, those were some mighty big *if*s.

"Tolliver?"

Lucky looked at Mr. Dempsey. "Yes, sir?"

"The prophet Isaiah wrote that 'no weapon that is formed against thee shall prosper; and every tongue that shall rise against thee in judgment thou shalt condemn.'"

"Yes, sir. Sheriff Blanton wrote that scripture in his letters to me."

Dempsey nodded. "The next part says that's a heritage from the Lord to God-fearing men. Trust in Him to help you out of this."

Lucky chewed on Mr. Dempsey's words. Were those things truly his heritage? He'd pondered the verse many times through hardships in prison and since. But in this present circumstance, it was hard to hold on to faith when he *knew* he was being wrongly accused.

He'd come to a meeting of the minds with God in the Texas State Penitentiary, thanks in large part to Maisie's father. While awaiting trial in Blackwater, the lawman had given him a Bible and encouraged him to read the scriptures. He'd carried too much turmoil and anger then, but the Good Book had somehow ended up among his things at prison. In his letters, Sheriff Blanton had spoken about God as if He were a personal friend, someone whom he could confide in and trust. It hadn't taken long before Lucky cracked the book open and, much to his surprise, found an unexplainable peace in the words he read.

Lord, I could use some peace now. And I surely wouldn't mind iffen You'd confirm to me what Mr. Dempsey said. Is it truly my heritage? No weapon formed against me can prosper?

He glanced Maisie's way. Concern creased her brow as she attempted to smile. The tiny gesture wobbled, then faltered completely. Lucky paced back to the bunk, collapsing with a sigh.

"Is there anything I can do?" Her voice was so small, it squeaked.

"Don't rightly know what it would be iffen there was."

Confound it. This was *not* how he wanted her to see him—caged like some animal. It'd be too easy for her to believe he was the old, rabble-rousing Lucky rather than a man trying to change his life.

"Lucky?"

He peeked her way.

"What'd my pa say to you in his letters?" Her voice held a hint of longing and sadness.

She was thinking about the letters at a time like this? He shook his head. "No disrespect, but what does that matter?"

"Please, tell me."

"I don't know, Maisie." He scrubbed a hand over his face. "He told me to believe God could change me and give me a new life. Wrote me scriptures to commit to memory. Sometimes he wrote about you and your family." That was the reason he'd come back—to be near the people he'd come to know and love through Jonathan Blanton's glowing words, the family he'd come to think of as his own. "As things went on, he asked questions about the Freeman gang. Never understood why, given they'd all been hung. And there toward the end, the letters grew. . .darker, somehow. Ain't real sure how to describe it. Then they stopped." He missed them, missed 'em fierce.

The door swung open and smashed against the wall. Startled, Lucky shot to his feet, his heart pounding. Maisie also jerked from her chair to face the door. Warburn, silhouetted against the opening, chuckled hollowly.

"Well, dad-burn it. I figured I'd catch you too close to that cell door, missy."

Maisie lifted her chin. "Then you must think me stupid, Sheriff. Think what you like, but I'll ask you to treat me with some respect. I've done nothing to cross you."

Lucky grinned at the irritation that lit Warburn's eyes.

The lawman brushed past her and unlocked the door. He set the bucket and old scrub brush inside. "Clean up your mess, Tolliver. Now." He clanged the door closed again, locking it before he stalked to his desk.

Lucky pushed his shirtsleeves to his elbows and scrubbed the floor.

Lord, it surely feels like there's weapons forming all around me, and I'm helpless as a newborn calf. Could use some of that heritage about now.

"By chance, did you save any of those letters, Lucky?"

He glanced up. "Yes, ma'am. Every last one."

Her brow furrowed. "Where are they now?"

"Under my bunk at the Rocking D."

"Would you mind if I read them?"

Lucky sat up. "Reckon not, but why?"

She shrugged. "It may be nothing."

Surely it was, but iffen those letters got her out of here so's she'd quit staring at him so helpless. . . "I don't mind. One of the other ranch hands can get 'em from under my bunk. They're all there."

"Thank you. I'll be back later tonight."

Chapter 8

Just the sight of Pa's chicken scratch on the first envelope had left Maisie breathless and wanting some place private to read the words he'd penned to Lucky. So she'd ridden to their former homestead. Once she'd turned her sorrel into the dilapidated corral, she let herself into the house.

Dust particles danced in the slanting sunlight that penetrated the grimy kitchen windows. The big farm table stood in its usual place, though thick dirt covered the surface, rather than the dishes and food that she was used to. The kitchen was empty, everything removed long ago.

Familiar, yet not.

She shut the door, found an old rag in a drawer, and cleaned a corner of the table. Her hands trembled as she opened the flap of the first envelope and unfolded the letter within:

July 20, 1866

Dear Lucky,

Perhaps you don't want to hear from me, but I felt compelled to write. If you don't care to read on, I'll understand. If you do, I'm obliged.

In my nearly ten years as sheriff, there's never been a man in my jail who has stuck in my mind like you. Even Mrs. Blanton agrees. We've lain awake nights praying you'll fare well in prison. More than that, we're praying you'll search your heart and begin to make changes to become the man God intends you to be. The real Luke Tolliver is buried in there somewhere. You just have to find him.

A lump grew in her throat. Pa and Ma had prayed for Lucky? She had no recollection of that. Her eyes strayed to the date of the letter again. It was written a month after her twelfth birthday, the one at which Ma and Pa had given her her first—only—diary. Perhaps, if it hadn't disappeared, her writings might have jogged her memory of Luke Tolliver. Though, perhaps not. Pa was always careful not to share sensitive details about his job, and he'd only become more tight-lipped the older Maisie got.

Probably because while Pa was encouraging Lucky to become a better man, he was becoming a lazy drunk who got fired from his post.

She fought down the ire that came with that thought. Her anger toward Pa wouldn't help Lucky. Far better to stay focused—but for *what* she had no idea. Hopefully it would stand out once she read it. She turned again to the short letter, which ended with her father's reminder that in Joshua 1, God instructed His people to be strong and courageous and that He would be with them wherever they went, and how in Hebrews 13,

God promised He would never leave nor forsake His people.

"If those things are true, God, then why have I felt so alone these last several years? You have abandoned me and my family, just like Pa did."

She crammed the letter back into its envelope and produced the next. As Lucky had said, her father wrote many scriptures, encouraging him not to let the difficulty of prison sway him from changing his life. Yet the verses only produced ugliness in her chest. How could Pa have been so unreserved with Lucky while withdrawing from his own family?

Maisie read the second letter, then the third. By the time she opened the fourth, Pa's hypocritical words had knotted her belly. As she read yet another scripture, she shoved back from the table. She'd get to the bottom of this. Tucked away under her parents' bed, she pulled out Pa's journals and rifled through the contents until she found the books that corresponded in date to the letters he'd written Lucky.

Back at the table, she matched Lucky's letters to the dates of Pa's journal entries. She found one journal entry from five days before the first letter, and one a week after:

July 15, 1866

Today was a somber day in Blackwater. After their convictions, the Freeman Gang took their places on the gallows. The judge ruled that Lucky Tolliver should watch, and I had the unfortunate task of making sure he was present. By the time the last man hung, Tolliver was shaken to his core.

I can't explain why he's any different than most of the men I've arrested, but there's something that's drawn both me and the missus to him. He's rough, for certain. But if my gut is right, he's redeemable. It pained me to see him so traumatized by the hangings and not be able to offer him some comfort.

July 27, 1866

I have a strange sense that Blackwater hasn't seen the last of the trouble that has so recently plagued us. I can't express what I'm feeling—just a sense that I've missed something important. Maybe I'm jumping at shadows, but I haven't been able to shake the feeling for days now. It bears watching.

The second letter, dated in early August, corresponded to a journal entry of the same date:

August 3, 1866

A young man stopped Maisie and Charlotte outside my office today as they were walking home from school. It's not often people make my skin crawl, but this fella did. After I shooed the girls on home, he said he was passing through but was short on money, so he was looking for work. Wondered if anyone was hiring cowhands.

He had a mop of dark hair and cheekbones that seemed to protrude from his face in too obvious a way. He smiled a lot, talked decent enough, but there was something chilling in his blue eyes. Nothing I could put a finger on. Just a sense of evil. The fella stuck around town for a couple hours then rode on. I'm hoping he's drifted on without further trouble.

Maisie's heart thudded. Cold blue eyes, dark hair, and cheekbones too obvious for his face. She rubbed her arm where Kane Freeman had grabbed her in the café. Sure sounded like the same man.

As darkness fell outside, Maisie rubbed her eyes to clear her bleary vision.

Pa's letters to Lucky had spoken so glowingly of her and her family, showing the deep love she remembered him showering over them. And she could see the care, concern, and respect he held for Lucky.

Yet the journals showed a different side—a man who, over the months after Lucky's conviction, became driven in his work. He'd written journals about several private encounters he'd had with both Kane and Percy Freeman. Unnerving encounters where the pair had promised vengeance for his part in their kin's hangings. When some isolated instances of rustling began to crop up again, Pa became obsessed in his determination to catch the pair, though his own writings said they were like ghosts.

The further into his journals and letters she read, the clearer the picture became. He'd disappear for days to search for the brothers but always came up empty. The local ranchers and townsfolk grew frustrated that he never seemed to be around to look into matters:

March 23, 1867

A mystery was solved today, but in the most unsettling way. Some weeks ago, Simeon's favorite blanket went missing. The boy's been distraught without it. It reappeared today, a good ten miles from our home as I followed the Freeman brothers. Found the blanket draped over a low-hanging tree branch. When I pulled it down, there was a message written on it—in blood. "You took our kin. Now we'll take yours."

I suspect they must've taken the blanket from the clothesline after Georgette washed it. They're toying with me. Makes me angry but all the more determined. I will get them. My family's safety depends on it.

A chill raced down her spine. She'd *seen* Pa ride into the ranch yard with the blanket spilling from his saddlebag, seen him carry it into the barn. What had become of it? She skimmed the next few pages to see if perhaps he'd written more.

April 6, 1867

I am worried. I was on the back side of the ranch tonight and found Charlotte's missing doll. Just like Simeon's blanket, it went missing, though not at the same time. Today, it turned up hanging from a tree limb by a perfectly tied noose. I hid it in the barn with Sim's blanket, held for the day when I finally catch these evil scoundrels and use the stolen items as evidence to put them away. Their threats will not sway me.

So the blanket *had been* in the barn—and Charlotte's doll, too. Might they still be? Maisie bolted up, scattering letters across the floor as she did, and hurried outside.

Chapter 9

Lucky woke as the outer office door opened, allowing him a brief view of the street. Perhaps an hour past dawn. He blinked heavily, only slightly aware that the sheriff entered before sleep pulled at him again.

"I'm telling you, Sheriff." A girl's plaintive voice broke into his solitude. "Ma's beside herself. It's not like Maisie to stay out all night."

Maisie? Lucky threw off the scratchy wool blanket, sat up, and rubbed his eyes.

Sheriff Warburn lit a lamp on his desk before he turned to Charlotte Blanton. "I'm sure she's fine. Just go on home, and she'll show up. Might already be there."

Fear gripped him. "Sheriff." He went to the bars of his cell. "This young lady's got a sincere concern. Ain't right, you dismissing her without looking into things."

Warburn's heated gaze bored into him. "You mind your own business, Tolliver. No rustler's gonna tell me how to do my job."

"You at least need to look for her!" His thoughts flashed to the night in the alley. "Iffen Percy and Kane Freeman are still about, they might've. . ." His words trailed off as his gaze shifted to Charlotte. Wouldn't do to put ideas in her head.

"Thought I told you to shut up."

He looked again at the lawman, heart thudding heavily against his ribs. "Please. Go look for her."

"I'm warning you, boy."

Lucky pressed his eyes closed. *Lord, help. You gave me Sheriff Blanton and his family to think of as my own all them years ago. Now, when I might be able to repay 'em some little part of what I owe, I'm stuck in here—and by no fault of my own.*

A thought struck like lightning.

"Charlotte?" Lucky pinned the girl with a look. "You got any friends around town that could ride somewheres with you?"

Her face puckered in confusion.

"Men. . .or older boys?"

Warburn took a step toward the cell. "Just what're you getting at, Tolliver?"

"Thomas Eddings was outside the café. Would he do?"

He rolled a glance heavenward. *Are You really going to make me rely on that flirtatious tenderfoot for help, Lord?* "Anyone else?"

She shook her head. "There's Simeon, but he's younger than me."

He gripped the bars until his knuckles blanched. "Maisie was planning to head to the Rocking D yesterday afternoon but said she'd be back to town afterward. Go find

Eddings and ask him iffen he'll ride out to the ranch with you. Ask Mr. Dempsey iffen he's seen her recent-like."

Eyes brimming with tears, Charlotte nodded. "I will."

"Good girl."

Warburn swung to face Lucky. "You best hope that girl doesn't run into trouble, Tolliver! Any harm comes to her, and it'll be on your head."

"No, Sheriff, it'll be on yours."

He paced to the cot and sat as a fervent prayer began to bubble from his lips.

"Mr. Dempsey?" Maisie knocked on the Rocking D ranch house door. "Mrs. Dempsey?" *Please answer.* She scanned the yard then glanced toward the early morning horizon. Were they already gone? She knocked again, louder.

This time, the door jerked open. Mr. Dempsey's brows shot up as his gaze settled on her. "Maisie? Is everything all right?"

"May I come in?"

"Of course." He waved her inside. Maisie hefted the gunnysack she carried and headed to the kitchen.

"You're here awfully early, Maisie," Mrs. Dempsey called as she poured coffee at the stove.

"Yes, ma'am." Her eyes stung with unshed tears as she looked between the pair. "But I finally understand, and I need your help."

Deep lines creased Mr. Dempsey's brow. "Understand what, darlin'?"

"What happened to Pa." She set the sack in the nearest chair and produced the journals and Lucky's letters. "Lucky told me about some letters Pa wrote him. He said I could read them, so I took them back to our ranch and read both the letters and Pa's journal entries from around the same dates." One hot tear streaked down her cheek. "I finally know what happened to him."

Mrs. Dempsey approached, three steaming mugs of coffee in hand. "Sit, child. Tell us what you've found."

Despite the invitation, Maisie stood. "Those men that Lucky and I saw have been around this area for a lot longer than we thought. Pa wrote about them in his journal *six* years ago."

Mr. Dempsey sipped his coffee. "What'd he say about 'em?"

"Just after Lucky went to prison, they showed up. Pa figured out they were connected to the old Freeman gang. He actually believed they were the real leaders but smart enough to stay out of the day-to-day workings of the gang so they wouldn't get caught. Pa started following them. That's why he'd disappear for days. And those things that disappeared from our house?"

"Yeah?" Mr. Dempsey nodded.

"Here." She flipped to a page she'd marked in one of the journals and read of Simeon's blanket reappearing with the bloody message.

From her place at the far end of the table, Mrs. Dempsey covered her mouth.

"He also wrote about Charlotte's doll and later, my diary." A shiver gripped her as she reached into the gunnysack. "Since I was already at the ranch, I went searching." She withdrew the blanket, the doll, and her diary and laid them on the corner of the table.

Mr. Dempsey's face hardened as he smoothed out the blood-soiled blanket then picked up the doll that still sported the noose about its neck.

"Look what they wrote in my diary." Maisie flipped through the pages until she found the jarring message in a strange scrawl.

Mr. Dempsey took it and cleared his throat. "'Found this stashed, secret-like, under your pretty little girl's pillow. Don't think we can't get to you, Blanton. We can. Stop following us, or we will.'"

"I remember the day it went missing." She looked at each in turn as they gaped at her. "I put the diary under my pillow. They were in our house, up in the loft. They pawed through my things." Her skin crawled with the thought of it.

He closed the diary. "You're sure your pa was writing about the same men?"

"His descriptions were spot on. I can show you." She snatched up the journal, but Mr. Dempsey stilled her hands.

"I believe you."

Maisie nodded, mind ricocheting with too many thoughts. "He was so determined to catch them. Each time they left another one of our things for him to find, it made him even more resolute. Until—" Her throat knotted as she reached into the bag and withdrew an old, weathered piece of wood. She handed it to Mr. Dempsey. "Ma's accident. They cut the rungs of the ladder." Pa had given up then, not wanting harm to come to his children like it had to Ma. But his grief and frustration had driven him to drunkenness and an early grave.

After a moment's study of the ladder rung, Mr. Dempsey rose so quickly, the coffee cups rattled. "That right there should be enough to get 'em both strung up. But we gotta find 'em first."

"That's why I need your help. I know where they are, and your hired hand Joe Coppen is working with them."

Please, God, keep Maisie safe. Bring her back to town, and don't let the likes of Percy and Kane Freeman have her.

Lucky paced the length of his small cell, turned, and paced back as the silent prayers boiled through him.

And iffen You would, please, let the sheriff get his sorry hide out of this office to look for her. Better yet, let me out to look for her.

"Would you quit that pacing?" Warburn glared. "I'm trying to get work done."

"Can't. Been sitting still too long." Knowing the woman he loved was out there, possibly in danger, had him wound so tight he could pace a hole in the floor.

Lord, please—

The office door swung open.

"Sheriff?" Mr. Dempsey stepped through the door and headed toward Warburn's desk. "We got us a problem."

On his heels, Maisie also entered, a heavy-laden bag in hand. Her gaze angled his way, and she smiled.

Relief washed through him as he hurried to the bars.

Dark circles rimmed her green eyes, and her clothes and hair were a bit rumpled, but she looked well enough.

"You all right?" His voice came out in a husky rasp.

She nodded. "You?"

"Well as can be expected. Where you been?"

"Out at our old ranch. I went there to read your letters, and I ended up spending the night."

Iffen she were his gal, that wouldn't happen. Not without someone knowing where she was. "Have you been by to see your ma? She's powerful worried. Come to think of it, I been powerful worried as well."

Maisie's cheeks flushed. "Thomas and Charlotte met us along the way. I sent them to let Ma know I'm well." She lowered her chin and looked at him almost shyly. "And thank you for thinking of both me and Charlotte, even in your own time of need."

His heart pounded as every ounce of longing stirred in him. *I think of you every moment of every day, Maisie.*

"Darlin'," Mr. Dempsey called, "come show the sheriff what you found."

She turned as she unknotted the mouth of the bag. "I know just where you'll find the rustled cattle, Sheriff, and I think what I've got to show you will go a long way toward proving Lucky had nothing to do with it."

"Oh, and just how do you reckon to prove that?"

She pulled books, as well as a blanket and a child's doll, from the bag. "Bear with me, and I'll make it all clear."

Chapter 10

An hour before the end of Maisie's shift, Simeon opened the café door and peeked inside. The boy searched the room and, upon finding her, straightened a little.

"They're back." As he closed the door again, he seemed to notice the owner seated behind the counter. The boy's face paled, and he shot the man a sheepish look before slamming the door and darting past the big window out of sight.

Her cheeks flamed when everyone turned her way. Why hadn't Simeon listened? She'd told him to signal her through the window when the posse returned.

As if nothing had happened, she pasted on a smile and turned to the gentleman at the table. "Can I get you anything else?"

Across the room, the owner cleared his throat, and when she turned, he beckoned her nearer.

Her shoulders knotted as she hurried to face her boss.

"What was that about?" He hooked a thumb at the door.

"Nothing important, sir. I'm sorry. I'll remind my brother not to disturb me while I'm working."

"Wouldn't have to do with the posse that rode out to your family's ranch this morning, would it?"

Maisie took one look at his grim expression and hung her head. She'd tried so hard to keep her focus, to care for the customers' needs and not appear distracted. "It was a personal matter, sir. Like I said, I'll talk to Sim. It won't happen again."

"Because iffen that was about arresting the men that caused your ma's accident. . ." He hesitated. "I might could be talked into letting you go a little early today."

She raked her gaze back to his face, eyes suddenly stinging with tears she dared not shed. Now, how had he. . . ? The posse had been so hastily gathered, she thought few knew of it.

Maisie swallowed down the tears. "I wouldn't want to impose, sir. I already missed my shift yesterday."

"You're not. You put in a good day's work. Now go on."

Stunned, she stared for an instant then fumbled with her apron strings. "Thank you kindly, sir."

He quirked a smile as he took the apron from her. "I might be harsh, but I ain't heartless." He jerked his chin toward the door. "Now git."

Before he could change his mind, Maisie shuffled out the door and hurried toward the sheriff's office a few streets away. Reaching the final turn, she rounded the corner and stopped short. A crowd of people and horses had gathered on the street. Most were posse members, judging by the extra guns the men carried. But a core group of towns-folk had also gathered, more than likely looking for the latest gossip. Maisie scanned the faces as she waded through the sea of bodies.

"Maisie!" Robert Dempsey angled her way, grinning as he sidled up next to her. "We got 'em, darlin'."

She stopped to look at him. "Both of them?"

"The Freeman brothers and Joe Coppen, too."

The tension that had knotted her muscles since morning loosened just a bit. "What about Lucky?"

Mr. Dempsey's grin deepened as he motioned toward the open office door. "See for yourself."

She scrambled through the crowd to peek inside. Unable to see anything more than the shapes of three men in the dark interior, she stepped just inside the door to let her eyes adjust to the dim light.

"Maisie Blanton!"

She jerked toward Warburn's familiar voice. "Yes, sir?"

"You and I got some business to attend to."

Business? She squinted at the room as everything gradually took on more form and detail. Able to see well enough, she shuffled toward the lawman but stopped when the hazy form near the corner of Warburn's desk turned her way.

Lucky.

Her pulse quickened. She flashed a quick glance toward the cell he'd so recently occupied. It held three new residents. Percy Freeman sat on one of the two cots, eyes closed and face unnaturally pale. He held his left arm above the elbow as blood oozed between his fingers. Joe Coppen huddled sullenly on the floor, elbows resting on his knees. Kane Freeman stood near the front corner of the cell and stared brazenly her way.

Subduing the shiver that his attention brought, Maisie crossed the distance to where Lucky and the sheriff stood. "Does the fact that Lucky's standing on this side of the bars mean that he's a free man, Sheriff?"

"That's what it means." Warburn glowered at Lucky. "But I'll be watching, Tolliver. You trip up, and I'll know."

"I just wanna go home and do my job, sir. Ain't planning to trip up none."

It was probably too much to hope that Sheriff Warburn could forgive Lucky after he'd been shot by the cowhand years ago. But at least he was free. She grinned Lucky's way, though he'd turned toward the cell.

When Lucky turned back again, he moved nearer, blocking Kane Freeman's glare. "Don't care for the way he's looking at you."

Warmth spilled through her at his whispered words. "Neither do I." Maisie met the sheriff's eyes. "So what business do we have?"

"Let's see. Where are. . ." Warburn shuffled through the clutter littering his desk, and a scrap of paper drifted to the floor near her feet.

She scooped it up, finding the brief warning Lucky had written her in the café: *"Be careful. Bad men."*

Maisie studied the familiar words, noting the little flourishes on the letter *M* and each *B*. Just like on the notes from the flow—

"Oh. . ." She gasped. The casual wordings weren't Thomas's. Her jaw slack and her belly fluttering, she turned. "It was *you*."

His brow furrowed. "What?"

Before she could answer, the doctor swept in, bag in hand. "You sent for me, Warburn?"

The sheriff stopped hunting through the papers and blew out a breath. "Pardon me a minute." He headed toward the doctor. "In the cell. Looks to be a flesh wound, but it ain't quit bleeding yet. Figured you should take a look at it." He shut the office door, the room darkening as he did.

"Dobbs. . ." At Warburn's call, the occasional deputy turned to him. "Get that fella out here so's Doc can see to his wound."

Lucky turned toward the cell and shifted slightly, blocking her view. She stepped to her right, but after a quick glance over his shoulder, he moved in front of her again. Confused, she squinted at his broad shoulders and stepped left, though this time, he darted a hand behind him and caught her waist.

"Stay there." Once more, he shifted in front of her.

Maisie barely had time to consider the command before the metallic grate of the key in the lock sent a shiver down her spine. As directed, she held her position behind Lucky, though she peeked past his shoulder.

"Let's go." Dobbs jerked the cell door open and beckoned to Percy Freeman, who made no move to comply.

Kane glanced at Warburn. "Don't reckon he feels like moving. Maybe you best send the doc in here instead."

"Freeman," Sheriff Warburn called. "You want that hole plugged, you'll get off that bunk and walk out here."

The only recognition Percy seemed to give was to open his eyes an instant then close them again.

Dobbs cleared his throat. "You ain't hurt that bad. Git up."

When he still made no move, both Doc and the deputy stepped into the cell to pull Percy to his feet.

Percy jerked awake suddenly and lunged, knocking Dobbs backward. All three prisoners rushed to the cell door.

As the room erupted, Lucky spun and shoved her toward the door. "Go, Maisie. Get out!"

He gave her another shove. But when gunfire roared in the small office and the sheriff stumbled back against the door, he jerked her to him and sank to the floor. "Stay down!"

Maisie's heart hammered as she huddled against him. Her forehead buried against his chest, they both glanced sideways. A dark stain spread across Sheriff Warburn's sleeve as he fumbled to draw his own gun. One peek around Lucky's shoulder showed Kane Freeman taking aim at the lawman again with Dobbs' pistol.

"When I get that door open, you run." Lucky whispered the command then lunged toward Warburn.

Light flooded the office as the door swung open, though fear rooted Maisie in place.

* * *

As Lucky hit the floor with Warburn, fire flared through his back. Despite it, he jerked the lawman's gun from its holster and rolled to face the cell. With his focus on Kane Freeman, he leveled the pistol, fanned the hammer back with his other hand, and squeezed the trigger.

The outlaw jolted, dropped to a knee.

Lucky fumbled to cock the hammer again then took aim as Percy tried to grab the pistol from his brother. A second time he squeezed the trigger, and the gun bucked in his hand. As it did, his fingers grew weak. The Colt clattered to the floor, and his vision clouded as several men barged into the room.

"Tolliver?" Warburn's voice in his ear tethered him to consciousness. "Tolliver!"

He blinked at the hazy forms, trying to make sense of them. Men. . .but which were rustlers, and which were posse members?

He pried his eyes open wide, trying to clear his sight. He had to stop them. Stop Kane from getting to Maisie. Had she gotten out? Pawing at the pistol, he managed only to knock it farther from reach.

Warburn called to him again. "Lay still now. You're hit."

He lifted his head to look toward the door, though it was if he stared through a dark mist. "Maisie?"

"Dempsey's got her. She's safe."

He lowered his head, and darkness pulled him under.

Chapter 11

Lucky pried heavy eyelids open, blinked a few times, and glanced at his surroundings. Nothing looked familiar, from the small, nondescript room to the narrow bed where he rested.

"You're awake."

He turned toward the angelic voice and found Maisie Blanton seated beside him. Lucky attempted to smile, though a deep ache radiated through him, and he closed his eyes to ward off the pain.

"Lucky?" Her warm hand settled against his shoulder. "How are you feeling?"

Steeling himself, he inhaled carefully and blinked his eyes open once more. Another glance around revealed an open door behind her, leading to what looked like a hallway.

"Where am I?" It took effort to form the question.

"In my home." She put a glass to his lips, and he sipped some cool water. "My brother was kind enough to lend you his bed until you're able to return to Mr. Dempsey's ranch."

He squinted at her. Able to. . . "What's wrong with me?"

The smile trickled from her lips. "You were shot. In the back. Doc says you were fortunate. The bullet hit your shoulder blade, turned, and raked across your ribs. It didn't hit anything vital."

He clenched his teeth as he grew more aware of the pain. "Feels plenty vital to me."

Maisie laughed. "Of course, it does. I only meant that the bullet didn't hit your heart or a lung."

"Right." A moment of contemplation brought the hazy images of the scene in Warburn's office to mind. The lawman had brought in the Freeman brothers and Joe Coppen, but they'd tried to escape. "Kane Freeman got the deputy's gun?"

She nodded. "Yes. You were trying to get me out of the office, and the sheriff was shot. He fell against the door. You were injured while helping him."

"Maisie!"

A door in the hall opened, and Maisie scrambled to her feet as Simeon Blanton darted inside and slammed the door.

"Simeon." She met her brother just beyond the doorway. "Quiet. Remember?"

The boy hung his head sheepishly. "Sorry."

She ruffled his hair.

"I got what ya asked for." He held out a big bunch of wildflowers. "You reckon he'll like—" Simeon glanced into the bedroom and hurriedly tucked the big bouquet behind his back. "Howdy, Lucky. Didn't know you were awake."

He lifted a hand in a slight wave, though confusion pulled at his thoughts. Why the sudden secrecy?

Maisie whispered in her brother's ear, and Simeon disappeared into another room.

Maisie retook her seat. "I'm sorry. I asked him to gather some flowers for a gentleman I've grown rather partial to."

Lucky's chest constricted. A gentleman? That dallying cad, Eddings.

"He's really quite special. Does things to help me and my family, brings me gifts. Watches over us. He even paid our bill in the mercantile."

But *he'd* paid the Blanton's bill, not Thomas Eddings. How would the man have known, and why would he take credit for. . .

Simeon reappeared, toting the pretty vases Lucky'd bought her, each one overflowing with Texas bluebells. "Is this right, Maisie?"

Lucky's gut clenched. She wasn't gonna give away *his* vases to Eddings, was she?

"Perfect, Sim. Thank you." She rose, "Now where shall we put your flowers, Mr. Tolliver?"

Lucky furrowed his brow. "They're for me?"

"Well, you *are* the one who's been leaving the flowers, right?" Her cheeks turned a pretty shade of pink. "And the book of poetry? And the bill—"

"Dempsey told you." He'd begged his boss not to breathe a word.

Simeon set his vase atop the tall chest. "Nah, Mr. Dempsey didn't say nothing, Lucky. You talked in your sleep."

She sat again, depositing her vase on the bedside table. "That, and I finally recognized your handwriting when I saw the warning note in Warburn's office again."

He clamped his eyes shut. "Didn't want you to know."

"Why on earth not, Luke Tolliver?"

Her stern tone drew his gaze. "I came to respect your parents when I was in your pa's jail. I grew to love your family through the things he wrote about you. And the minute I laid eyes on you, I knew I wanted to make you my wife. But you deserve a man that can offer you more than a sullied name and reputation."

"Is that so?"

"Yeah."

She lifted her chin. "There's some things you should know. For one, you're something of a hero after you stopped the Freeman brothers."

His sardonic chuckle sent pain rippling through him. After catching his breath, he shook his head. "Reckon Warburn loves that."

"Warburn said it first, and he hasn't been shy about repeating it."

He stared. "You're joshing."

"She's not." Simeon sidled up to his sister. "The whole town's talking about what you did."

"Word's started getting around about what happened with Pa, too. Folks who've paid us no mind for more than a year have showed up with food and offers to help. Things might be changing for us all, Lucky." She brushed away a tear.

For certain, her family deserved to be treated better than the Blackwater residents had in the last few years. But him—a hero, and because of Warburn's say-so? He never figured such a day would come.

"And you do have something to offer. Your care, your concern, your friendship and love. Those are the things that matter, and you've willingly given them when few others did. You shouldn't have to hide them."

"Those things don't put a roof over your head or feed your family. I ain't nothing but a hired hand, Maisie."

"You let me worry about that part."

He shook his head. "Iffen we was to marry, I wouldn't want you working. But I can't take care of you and your kin on what I make." How many times had he thought it through and come up short every time?

"You wouldn't have to. Sheriff Warburn helped me file to collect the reward money on the Freemans. There's five thousand dollars coming for their captures. That's more than enough to pay what we owe on our ranch and get a small herd to stock it again. We could build from there."

The picture she presented took shape in his mind, and he wobbled a grin at her. "Sounds real nice, but—"

"But what?"

"Somethings a little backwards here. Ain't it the man's place to ask his woman iffen she'll marry him?"

Maisie's cheeks flamed crimson. "It should be, but if I wait on you, I fear you'll get so tongue-tied, you'll never ask."

Oh, he'd ask, and right soon.

Epilogue

One month later.

"Y ou make a lovely bride, darlin'. Your pa woulda been proud."

Maisie's belly fluttered at Robert Dempsey's whispered words. If only Pa could have been here. She clung a little tighter to her friend's arm.

Lord, is he able to see this? Would he be proud?

She could only hope.

When the music began, both she and Mr. Dempsey stepped through the doorway into the church. For an instant, Maisie's feet stalled as she took in the sight of each pew overflowing until people were forced to stand at the back. Had they really all come to celebrate her marriage to Lucky? Much had changed in a short time.

She turned her focus toward the simple altar where her groom stood, dark eyes sparkling and a wide grin on his face. At Mr. Dempsey's slight nudge, she pried her feet loose and walked to the front of the church.

The music ended, and the pastor cleared his throat. "Who gives this woman to be married to this man?"

Mr. Dempsey winked discreetly at her before he looked the pastor's way. "At her ma and pa's request, I do."

Just that quickly, he placed her hand in Lucky's work-roughened palm and took his seat. As she faced her groom, she drank in the sight of him in his dark suit and string tie.

Roguishly handsome, and finally hers.

She tried to focus on the words the reverend spoke, but her mind wandered over every detail of his features. Somehow, she managed to repeat her vows, though the words blurred together until—

"You may now kiss your bride."

Lucky stepped nearer, cupping her face with one hand. "Been wanting to do this for a long time." The whispered words were so low only she would hear.

"Then quit yapping and do it, Luke Tolliver."

He circled her waist with his free arm, and her hands settled against his chest. His lips brushed hers tenderly, though he pulled back after an instant. At his tiny smile, her heart fluttered until she was sure it would come clean out of her chest. She rose on her tiptoes and met his lips again. This time, they lingered, Maisie drinking in his warmth and nearness.

Finally, they broke the kiss, and she settled her forehead against his, her eyes half closed. He caressed her cheek. When the pastor cleared his throat softly behind them, Maisie turned a flame-cheeked gaze toward their guests.

"I now present to you Mr. and Mrs. Luke Tolliver."

Arm in arm, Lucky walked her down the aisle to the back of the church. Outside, he whisked her around the corner and into a small office. He closed the door softly, settled his back against it, and pulled her into his arms.

For a long moment, she stared at her husband. His brown eyes sparkled as he gently stroked her cheek, a grin sprouting across his lips.

"You're looking rather pleased with yourself," she whispered.

"Just thinking how the prettiest gal in Blackwater is wearing my last name."

She laid her head against his chest. Maisie Tolliver.

After a moment, he stirred. "I bought you something."

"You did?" She looked up at him.

He waved to a chair where a small paper-wrapped package sat, a festive blue ribbon adorning the outside. "Open it."

Maisie picked up the small parcel and, handing it to Lucky, glanced at the note he'd written on the crisp brown paper: *"To my beautiful bride, Maisie."*

She ran her finger over the flourishes of his letters then tugged the ends of the ribbon. The paper loosened, and she peeled it away to reveal a leather-bound diary.

"Oh, Lucky." Maisie turned it over, studying the rich brown cover before prying the clasp open to study the blank pages. Tears welling, she looked up at her husband. "This has to be the most thoughtful gift anyone's ever given me. Thank you."

He laid the diary aside and pulled her close, wrapping her in his arms once again. "I did good, then?"

"Better than." She nuzzled against him. "I feel bad though. I didn't get you anything."

"I don't need nothing. Just you. Although. . ." He pulled back and looked at her. "There's one favor you could do me that'd feel like a gift."

"What?"

A shy look, reminiscent of the man who could barely speak two words to her, crossed his face. "I, uh. . ." He shook his head. "I've grown partial to you calling me by my given name."

"You don't want me to call you Lucky anymore?"

He hesitated. "Your pa once wrote that the real Luke Tolliver was buried somewhere inside me, but I've had a hard time finding him. Thing is, you always did see past that lost kid, Lucky, and straight to the heart of the man, Luke. Just feels like a fitting change, given we're starting a new life and all."

Maisie grinned. "A fitting change, indeed, Luke Tolliver."

Jennifer Uhlarik discovered the western genre as a preteen, when she swiped the only "horse" book she found on her older brother's bookshelf. A new love was born. Across the next ten years, she devoured Louis L'Amour westerns and fell in love with the genre. In college at the University of Tampa, she began penning her own story of the Old West. Armed with a BA in writing, she has won five writing competitions and was a finalist in two others. In addition to writing, she has held jobs as a private business owner, a schoolteacher, a marketing director, and her favorite—a full-time homemaker. Jennifer is active in American Christian Fiction Writers and is a lifetime member of the Florida Writers Association. She lives near Tampa, Florida, with her husband, teenage son, and four fur children.

Beside Still Waters

by Becca Whitham

Dedication

For the real Sarah Maffey
Thanks for letting me use your name and beautiful face for this heroine.
All other resemblances are coincidental.
Mostly.

Acknowledgments

I generally don't include acknowledgments in a novella, but this story would not have happened without some very special people. I wrote this story in six days after four months of nonstop deadlines. My creativity was drained. Darcie Gudger helped breathe life into flat characters; Kim Woodhouse "fluffed" my terse prose; and Karen Ball edited out the dry stuff, fixing it by writing many of the best parts. I must also thank my long-suffering husband, Nathan. He cleaned house, went grocery shopping, and made dinner over and over and over again. A few friends came to the rescue with dinners and gifts: notably Michelle Samples, Rachel Harrison, and Julie McCammon, all of them fellow chaplain spouses stationed at Fort Wainwright, Alaska. And I was blessed by countless prayer warriors. I owe them all a huge debt of gratitude. I also want to thank Becky Germany at Barbour Publishing for letting me add a little twist to my secret admirer.

Prologue

Boston, Massachusetts
May 1901

"Y ou'll be the most beautiful bride Boston has ever seen, Miss Maffey."

Sarah twisted to see the back of her wedding dress in the full-length mirror. Although the saleswoman, Mrs. Robertson, was prone to flattery, she wasn't entirely wrong...about the dress at least. It was a masterful creation of creamy satin, lace applique, and decorative pleating worthy of the exorbitant price tag.

"Here." Mrs. Robertson held out a wide-brimmed hat trimmed in matching lace and sporting an enormous tulle rose on the side. "Put this on for the complete picture."

Sarah fit the hat over her brown hair, a smile spreading across her face. "It's quite lovely."

"Yes. Such a shame Miss Hensley isn't here to see it."

Sarah frowned. It was rather odd of Trudy to miss the last dress fitting when, as maid of honor, she'd been to all the previous appointments. "I'll have my driver take me by her house on the way home so I can show her."

"So you don't need any further alterations, miss?" Mrs. Robertson held out a hand and helped Sarah descend from the fitting room dais.

"No. This is perfect." Sarah removed the hat and returned it. "Please have everything boxed up and carried out to the car."

"I'm so glad you're satisfied. I'll send Eliza in to help you remove the dress."

Sarah pressed her hands against her waist. "I almost hate to take it off. I feel quite pretty in it."

Mrs. Robertson's kind smile warmed Sarah. "You're beautiful in it, Miss Maffey, because you're a beautiful person. I know you don't want to hear me say it again, but thank you for your kindness to my Jenny. She's still talking about the delicious lemon tarts you made special for her."

Sarah ducked her head, embarrassment heating her cheeks. "It was nothing."

The dressmaker placed the hat on a nearby chair then stepped forward to take both of Sarah's hands. "No, Miss Maffey, it was a gift of your time, talent, and mostly your attention. Not many great ladies bother to notice those less fortunate. My Jenny may never walk, but her spirit soared when you came to visit. My entire family will never forget it."

Such a small thing to engender so much gratitude. . .and vexation. Eugene had lectured her for five minutes about coddling the lower class, while Trudy—where was she?—stood beside him, nodding her approval. They grumbled like Sarah had served hundred-dollar bills instead of pastries.

She shook off the memory. "It was my pleasure. I love lemon tarts myself, so it was a joy to make them and share with friends."

Mrs. Robertson squeezed Sarah's hands then whirled around and grabbed the bridal hat on her way out of the fitting room. "Eliza, come help Miss Maffey, please."

Thirty minutes later, dress box tucked under her arm, Sarah knocked on the door of the Hensleys' red-bricked brownstone. No one answered, but she heard voices overhead and leaned back enough to see that Trudy's bedroom window was open. Was the slug-abed just now waking up? It was eleven o'clock in the morning. Sarah opened the door, sneaking in like she'd done a hundred times before, to creep up the stairs and surprise her friend.

She was about to turn the doorknob when she heard a man's voice inside Trudy's room. A voice that sounded like—could it be?—Eugene! Sarah snatched her hand off the brass knob, her breathing shallow and rapid. Her fiancé and best friend alone together. . .in a bedroom!

A shudder rippled down her spine. Her lungs filled with shock, leaving too little room for air. Images of them laughing, standing side by side, and sharing whispers filled her mind. She'd thought it wonderful that the two people she loved most got along so well. Had she been a fool? Had they been lovers all along?

Sarah pressed a fist against her lips to keep from crying out and leaned closer to the door, inexorably drawn to discover the worst.

Eugene's voice came through the wood, muffled but distinguishable. ". . .got it in her head to move from Boston. Some nonsense about fresh air."

Nonsense? Was he talking about her idea to put their names into the Oklahoma Land Lottery? He'd called it a brilliant idea. Agreed it would be good for them to make their own way instead of relying so heavily on their parents. Said he couldn't wait to build their little castle on the plains.

Why would he lie to her?

"What did you say?" Sarah pictured her best friend—her *former* best friend—with both hands pressed against her ample chest, blue eyes wide. Was Trudy's blond hair pinned up. . .or falling about her shoulders?

"Exactly what you said I should—whatever it took to keep her happy."

"That's good, Gene. Flattery is your best friend right now."

Sarah's stomach hardened beneath her corset. Trudy wasn't some innocent taken in by a handsome face. She was orchestrating this betrayal.

"Where does Sarah want you to go?" Even through the wood, the calculating tone in Trudy's voice was clear.

"Does it matter?" Eugene sounded more like a nine-year-old brat than a twenty-five-year-old banker. "My tailor is here. My club is here. *You* are here."

Tailor first, club second, then his—what?—mistress? If Sarah wasn't so heartbroken, she'd find his priority order comical.

"What are you going to do?"

Sarah bent nearer, her ear touching the white-painted wood.

"Same thing I've been doing these past six months. I'll pander to her vanity until we're officially married and her inheritance is under my control. Then you and I can finally be free of her."

Everything inside Sarah stopped—her heart, her lungs, the blood pumping in her veins—then roared back to life, pulsing pain and outrage through her body.

"Oh, Gene. You're so smart." There was a rustling that, in Sarah's imagination, sounded like bedcovers, but could be stiff petticoats under a skirt. "I'm so lucky to be your mistress."

The scandalous confirmation snapped the dreadful curiosity rooting Sarah's feet to the floor. She reeled around to flee, not caring that the dress box under her arm smacked against the wall, alerting the traitors to her presence.

A moment later, Trudy's bedroom door slammed open.

Proof was worse than imagination. Eugene was shirtless, his dark chest hairs tangled across his pasty skin like the underside of a beginner's embroidery project. Trudy, her hair mussed, clutched a bedsheet beneath bare shoulders.

In a haze of bitterness and grief, Sarah ran down the steps and out the door, ignoring calls for her to stop, be reasonable, and not make a fuss.

A fuss!

They wanted to downgrade this. . .this *treachery* to a *fuss*?

Sarah thrust the wedding dress box into Jenson's hands and picked up her skirts to scramble into the Stanley Steamer. "Take me home. Hurry!"

"Yes, miss." He handed her back the box then climbed into the seat beside her. He reached below his seat to press gauges and levers, bringing the steam engine to life, and pulled into traffic.

Sarah clutched the box against her chest like a shield, tears streaming down her cheeks. Humiliation squeezed her heart with merciless fingers. She choked on the sobs juddering inside her chest.

Trudy and Eugene. For as long as she lived, Sarah would picture them *déshabillé*. A bitter laugh ripped open her tight throat. Mother once said five years of French lessons would come in handy someday. Yes, quite handy. . .to refer to something base and vile and crushing.

Sarah swiped at the tears heating her cheeks, transferring the evidence of her misery to her butter-colored kid gloves. Wet splotches stained the pink satin bow tied around her dress box. She ducked her chin, reviling herself for displaying her mortification the entire six blocks between the Hensleys' brownstone in Louisburg Square and the Maffey mansion on Cambridge Street.

The moment Jenson stopped next to the sandstone portico and set the brake, Sarah jumped from the automobile and rushed inside. She threw the box on the parquet floor in her haste to find her father.

"Daddy? Where are you?" She ran toward his study.

"I'm in here, princess."

The endearment threatened to break her tenuous hold on the tears.

The mahogany doors to his study were wide open. As she rounded into the tobacco-scented room, she saw her father set the phone handset into its cradle. She tripped on the edge of the Persian rug, catching herself by bracing both hands against his massive desk. "Who—who was that?"

Daddy smoothed his salt-and-pepper goatee. "Eugene."

She wouldn't cry. Not again. Not at the mere mention of the reprobate's name. "What did he want?"

"To warn me that you might be a tad upset when you got home. It appears he spoke truth." The clipped diction expressed his displeasure. His blue eyes scanned her from head to waist, indicating it was with her.

She latched on to what Eugene had said. "A *tad* upset? I find my fiancé half-naked in my best friend's bedroom, and he thinks I'll only be a tad upset?"

"Be reasonable, Sarah."

Her knees buckled and she grabbed onto the desk again before she fell down. "What are you saying? That it's reasonable for the man I'm about to marry to be unfaithful?"

Daddy huffed. "When did you become so dramatic? Of course it was wrong for Eugene to choose your friend as his paramour and not to exercise discretion, but honestly, princess. A man needs an outlet."

The room rippled. She couldn't breathe. If she didn't sit, she'd fall down. She waved a hand behind her back until she felt an armrest and sank into the leather chair. "He. . . she. . .they're after my inheritance."

Daddy rested his interlocked hands on the desktop. "You're Sarah Maffey. Every man in Boston is after your inheritance."

Rage swirled in her chest. At Eugene and Trudy. At her father. At every man in Boston. "Then I'll move to Oklahoma."

"Don't be ridiculous."

His huff drove the knife further into her chest. Why wasn't he exasperated with Eugene? Why her? She was his daughter!

Her spine stiffened. "I'm not being ridiculous. I've been researching all about homesteading." In preparation for moving there with Eugene, but that hardly mattered now. "Did you know there's a company in New York that will sell you a house as a kit? Everything is pre-cut. All you have to do is assemble it."

"And then what will you do? Entertain Indians and soldiers?" His mockery fueled her anger and resolve. "If you decide not to marry Eugene—although I don't see that you'll do better—I will support you. But I'll never release your inheritance if you run off half-demented to Oklahoma."

Weightlessness took over every limb—as though she had landed so hard, she'd bounced and now hung suspended in midair. Over the haze of hurt. Above the confusion. "I have the ten thousand dollars Mother left me. I'm sure that would go a long way in Oklahoma. There's to be a land lottery in August. If I win, I can claim a full forty acres. If I don't win, I'm sure someone will be willing to sell me their plot. I hear that's quite a common practice."

The more she thought about it, the better she liked the idea. Forty acres without a single Boston man in sight? Perfect!

Her breathing settled into an even rhythm. "I'm not a complete stranger to homesteading." Mother's parents had claimed land in Montana Territory, striking gold and turning into millionaires almost overnight. They'd returned to Boston for Grandfather's health, but Grandmother still told stories of their homesteading days. "Three months is plenty of time for Grandmother Novak to teach me how to stake a claim."

"A little money and a smidgeon of research are poor substitutes for common sense." Father reached his hand across his desk. "Stop bluffing, princess. A woman alone would never succeed at homesteading."

Ignoring his proffered hand, Sarah rose from the chair and willed her legs to hold. Was she bluffing? No. . .no, she wasn't. She would do it!

"We'll see about that."

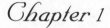

Chapter 1

Fort Sill, Oklahoma
Land Lottery Claim Office
August 2, 1901

John Tyler studied the map hanging on the canvas wall of the land claim tent. Good acreage near East Cache Creek was still available since most of the land lottery winners had chosen lots in what would be the new city of Lawton, Oklahoma. Two more numbers before his.

Water was the key, both for his own needs and the needs of those downstream. He'd suffered enough abuse at the hands of his upstream neighbors in Texas, and he was *never* going to let it happen again. Not to him, and not to anyone else if he could prevent it.

"Twenty-four!"

John turned away from the map. An older man in faded overalls limped toward the land agent's table, his hand clenched around rolled paper. Greedy eyes followed him. The tent was full of every class and color of men and a smattering of women. How many of them were ticket holders, and how many were hoping to steal their way into a claim? Although every lottery ticket listed the name, age, and occupation of its owner, most folks—like the limping man—held their ticket and birth certificate or proof of citizenship together. Stealing both was as easy as stealing one.

John's ticket was inside the toe of his right sock, and his birth certificate was folded inside the left one. They'd stink, but they were safe.

He rested his right hand on the Colt .45 strapped to his hip. In his days as a Texas Ranger, he'd seen avarice maim and kill far more than he cared to count. Anyone who wanted to steal a lottery ticket would have to go through him first.

"C'mon, darlin'. I'd make ya a good husband."

"Don't listen to him. I'm the man you want. See here? Muscles."

John diverted his attention. A whole passel of men—one of them flexing a stringy bicep—surrounded an enormous hat decorated with all kinds of frilly nonsense. Presumably there was a woman under it, but why would anyone wear her Sunday-go-to-meeting clothes inside a tent filled with grimy, sweating bodies on a day hot enough to fry chicken?

"Get away from me," the feminine voice squeaked.

After checking to see that Twenty-four was safely seated at the land agent's table, John edged closer to the pack of jackals surrounding the woman.

"Don't be huffy, lady. I just wants to take good care of you." The man was sixty if he was a day.

"You don't know how to take care of nothin'." The skinny guy who'd been flexing his bicep rolled down his red shirtsleeve and leaned nearer the hat. "I know how to make a woman purr with—"

"Hey!" John grabbed the guy's skeletal arm before he could spout whatever foul thing he'd been about to say. "That's enough out of you."

"Git your hand offa me!" The skinny man jerked free, hitting a man behind him in the chin. That man stumbled back, knocking another string bean of a man sideways.

Oops.

Fists and swearing cut through the air, rippling outward in circles of mayhem. John elbowed his way toward the hat while keeping one hand on his Colt.

"Let me go, you cretin!" Hat Woman screeched. "No! That's *mine*! Give it *back*!"

Pushing through the last bodies between him and the hat, John grabbed hold of a loutish forty-something man who was fighting off delicate hands trying to pry his pudgy fingers off a lottery ticket.

"I said, give it *back*!"

A flying fist knocked the hat sideways.

Dark hair, blue eyes, pretty features. The woman was in her early twenties at the most. John took in her features while wrestling with the varmint who'd stolen her ticket. The ham-fisted man fell, taking John and Hat Woman with him. Odd that a man was stealing a woman's ticket, but perhaps he had a wife or daughter nearby to pass off as the ticket holder.

A gunshot split the air.

Surprise loosened the meaty fingers, giving John an instant to snatch away the lottery ticket.

"That's enough!" An authoritative shout filled the shocked silence. "Everyone who doesn't have a claim ticket between twenty-four and thirty, out."

Groans and cursing.

"I mean it. Out, or the next bullet is going into someone's foot. Won't kill ya, but it'll hurt like the dickens."

Whoever this guy was, John liked him.

Hat Woman struggled to pull herself up, but that didn't keep her from pointing her finger at John and shouting. "That man stole my lottery ticket!"

"What? No!" John pointed at the real thief. "It was this man."

For such a large fellow, the lout moved with remarkable speed. He shot to his feet and bowled through people on his way out the tent flap door while John—who had jumped up to go after him—struggled to pull free of Hat Woman without injuring her. He bent down to pry her fingers from his ankle, but the look in her eyes immobilized him.

Not the accusation or alarm on their gray-blue surface, but the anguish one level deeper. She'd lost someone dear to her—either by death or betrayal—and the grief was fresh.

John knew grief. It had been his constant companion for six years. At first, it was handcuffed to him in a dark cell where it taunted and tortured him. When thin light penetrated the prison walls he'd built with his own hands, grief was still there and still his enemy, but one he'd learned to anticipate. Over the years, he'd made peace with his nemesis, learning to embrace it every spring when bluebonnets filled the meadow or when riding past Miller's Soda Shop. Sometimes he and grief shared a gentle memory of times past, sometimes they persevered through gut-twisting regret for a memory never made.

Yes, he knew grief.

And the woman standing before him still considered it her enemy.

———————————◇◎◎◇———————————

Sarah snatched her lottery ticket from the thief's slack fingers. He didn't flinch. Or resist. Or even seem to notice. He stared down at her, a tenderness in his green eyes that irritated and mesmerized her. Was it fair to label him a thief? He didn't look like one. And he wasn't oafish like the man she'd wrestled with. This man looked. . .intrepid. And sturdy. And not at all like Eugene. But still.

He'd had her ticket.

Maybe he wasn't a thief, but he wasn't a gentleman either. The least he could do was offer to help her up.

"Everything okay here, ma'am?"

Sarah yanked her attention away from the—whatever he was—to address the craggy soldier holding a pistol in his hand. "I believe no permanent damage was done."

Except to her hat, poor thing. Mrs. Robertson insisted Sarah keep it as a you're-better-off-not-wedding-him present. It was too fancy for the plain, sturdy clothing she'd ordered from the dressmaker in lieu of a wedding trousseau, but Sarah wanted to wear it today for good luck. . .or to bolster her spirits. She'd been prepared for crude surroundings. She hadn't been quite as prepared for the crude men.

"Allow me to help you up."

She retrieved her crushed hat, looping the still-tied bow around her arm, and lifted her arms toward the soldier. . .who was walking away. Strong hands fit themselves under her armpits and hoisted her to her feet. As soon as she got her balance, she whirled around. It was *him* again. Her anti-Eugene. Tall, blond, tanned, and what Tru—

What *some* people might call swoonworthy.

"Ma'am." He pinched the brim of his dusty gray cowboy hat.

"Twenty-five!"

Sarah flinched at the land agent's shout for the next claimant.

"Are you all right?" He asked like he wanted a real answer instead of one that assured him she'd not bother him with her troubles.

Very anti-Eugene.

Embarrassed, and not entirely sure why, Sarah mumbled, "I'm fine."

Instead of dismissing her with a shrug as Eugene would have done, Anti-Eugene tilted his head to the side as though studying her. "Please allow me to apologize. I wasn't trying to steal your claim ticket."

Three years of finishing school prompted an automated, "Thank you, sir." But she still didn't believe him. After all, he *was* the one holding the ticket.

"My name is John Tyler, by the way." He took off his hat and dipped his chin in one movement. "Originally from Fort Worth, Texas."

If she were home, she'd curtsy or flutter a fan when introduced to a handsome stranger. Now, she stuck her hand out. "Sarah Maffey." No longer from Boston.

He stared at her hand for a moment, like he wasn't sure if he should shake it or raise it to his lips. He did neither. Returning his hat to his head, he gripped the brim and nodded. "Nice to meet you. Good luck with your pick."

Sarah dropped her hand. How rude! She, out of good breeding, had offered an olive branch to acknowledge he might—*might*—be telling the truth about not stealing her ticket. And he? He *snubbed* her.

"Twenty-six!"

Mr. Tyler cut a glance at the land agent. "That's me."

What did he want? Applause?

He dipped his chin and headed for the table.

Using her ruined hat as a fan, Sarah sauntered over to the map on the wall. She was next to pick, and she needed to be calm. Rational. Not riled up over some man who may or may not have tried to steal her—

Wait. Why would he be after her land when he had a claim ticket of his own—one ahead of hers? Maybe he'd been telling the truth after all.

Doubtful. So far, all the men she'd met in Oklahoma were as greedy as the ones she'd left behind in Boston.

Sarah brushed dirt from her gray skirt as she studied the map. No one had claimed either of the plots she wanted. Although she had plenty of money to build a house and purchase supplies, one of the requirements for proving up a homestead was improving at least ten acres of land over a five-year period. That meant plowing and planting, which meant water. Both of her choices had plenty of creek frontage. Even if Mr. Tyler chose one of them, she'd take the other.

Both Grandmother Novak and the accounts she'd read about homesteading advised good relations with neighbors. Did she want John Tyler as a neighbor? Would she have a choice?

The map might not have been updated since before the limping man selected his land. What would she do if both plots were gone? There were a few places west of town with small creeks, but they were much farther away from Lawton. She might want to be forty acres away from Boston men, but it didn't mean she wanted to live like a hermit.

Her eyes were drawn back to where East Cache Creek ran near the city boundary. Even if both her choices were gone, there were some plots where the creek ran through a corner. It wasn't ideal, but there were over a hundred claims yet to be settled. Not all of them would have ideal creek frontage, so it must be possible to prove up even without water running through the middle of a claim.

"Twenty-seven!"

Sarah's heart lurched. She touched a hand to her chest and started toward the land agent's table.

Mr. Tyler rose. Whatever claim he'd taken, the smile denting his cheeks with a pair of dimples said he was pleased. "Miss Maffey."

She returned his smile out of basic good breeding. And in case they ended up being neighbors, heaven forbid.

"Are you twenty-seven, miss?"

Recalled to her purpose—which was choosing land, not admiring how a cowboy sauntered out of a tent—Sarah hurried to the table.

"Claim ticket and birth certificate, please." The touch of humor in the land agent's voice might have helped settle Sarah's nerves, but her eyes were fixed on the L-shaped outline on the map before her.

"He can't do that." She looked to the land agent. "Can he?"

The land agent nodded. "Rules say claims can be in several configurations. This one's legal."

Sarah's face burned. John Tyler had shaped his claim to encompass all but a sliver of East Cache Creek.

There would be no neighborly relationship with the man. He might not have stolen her claim ticket. . .

But he'd most certainly stolen her water.

Chapter 2

Sarah stood upwind of the man she'd hired to load and unload her supplies. Crates and barrels filled with everything her research deemed either critical or worthwhile came off the back of the mounded wooden cart. Once they were on the ground, out came the bigger items: tent, cookstove, and the tick mattress—something that, when she first read about it, almost broke her resolve to leave Boston for Oklahoma. However, further research revealed that the bedding was *not* stuffed with insects but straw. She could live with that for the two or three weeks it would take for the house kit to be delivered and built. Then she'd send for a real bed and a feather mattress.

"You sure you don't want help settin' up this here tent?" The round man who went by the name Otis lifted his perspiration-drenched shirt to wipe dribbles from his red face.

If she had to spend one more minute surrounded by the smell of the unwashed, she'd lose the greasy lunch rolling around in her belly. Despite the fresh air surrounding the delivery cart, Sarah had held a lilac-scented handkerchief over her nose the entire ride from the train depot to her land. She wasn't sure which smelled worse: Otis or the hind end of his horse. "No, thank you. I can handle the rest of this myself."

Otis gave her a *suit yourself* shrug.

Sarah dug the agreed-upon payment from her reticule, adding a small tip to be neighborly. "Again, thank you. When the supplies for my house arrive, I will be sure to let you know."

Unless she could find a worker who occasionally bathed.

Otis inspected the coins. "This is too much."

"I added that to thank you for your excellent service."

He squinted one eye, drawing his top lip into a crooked line. Had he never heard of a tip, or did his vocabulary not include the word "excellent"? He picked out a couple of coins and offered them back to her with an open palm. "Don't hold with takin' more than what's fair."

The saying, "Honor among thieves," came to mind—which only reminded her of John Tyler and all the things she wished she'd said to him this morning.

Sarah retrieved the coins. "Once again, thank you."

"Ma'am." He doffed his fraying straw hat and climbed into his cart. With two clicks of his tongue, the draft horse started forward.

Sarah waved good-bye, even though he didn't turn around to see the gesture. Outside of John Tyler—her nearest neighbor and the man she most hoped to avoid—Otis and his horse were the only people she knew in all of Oklahoma.

Not that the horse was a person, but Otis talked to him like he was. In this vast expanse of land, with no one to witness your comings and goings, it actually made sense that an animal could become a friend.

She marched toward her pile of belongings, rolling back the cuffs of her cotton blouse. The white fabric was already tinted rusty brown from the drive. "Next time, plain brown fabric."

Normally, she didn't talk to herself aloud, but the silence was unnerving. She'd lived her entire life surrounded by the sounds of city life. And people. Lots of people having lots of conversations. Solitude was going to be a challenge—one she could alleviate by creating her own conversations. That was her theory, anyhow.

"All right, then, enough dawdling. It's time to get to work. Tent first."

That's what the book on homesteading said was most important, because "protecting yourself and supplies from rain is paramount."

Sarah shook her head. Rain was the least of her problems. There wasn't a single cloud in the endless blue sky to offer a patch of shade. Only her wide-brimmed hat offered relief, the poor thing. It had been so pretty before it got trampled. "You, Mr. John Tyler, are a thief and a destroyer of hats."

Yes, talking aloud helped.

But grumbling never made work easier, so Sarah straightened her shoulders and marched toward the large square of canvas. It took two seconds to realize that, with all the bending and lifting she was going to be doing, her corset needed to be loosened. Maybe removed.

The mere thought of unbuttoning her blouse without the protection of four walls and shaded windows made her heart beat faster. She checked on Otis's progress. Not far enough. And the only thing between her and his back were her household goods.

After a deep breath to fortify her nerves, Sarah ducked behind the largest crate. Her fingers shook as she unbuttoned from the neck down. She kept checking to make sure she wasn't putting on a burlesque show, so it took longer than necessary to wriggle out of the corset and button back up again. Since she was already being daring, she left the top four buttons of her blouse open to allow the faint breeze to cool her skin.

She stood up and brushed grass from her skirt. "All right, Sarah Allison Maffey, where are you going to pitch your tent?"

It took five minutes of wandering along the edge of the creek to find a spot that met most of the suggested criterion. But how was she to haul the tent that far? All the parts were bundled inside the canvas fabric and tied with thick cording. She'd never be able to lift it. She tried dragging it. After four attempts, she'd managed a mere eight inches. Wiping her sweaty hands on her skirt, she gave it one more try, tugging and yanking with all her might. Her hands slipped, and she landed on her backside in the red dirt.

"Ow!"

If everything about homesteading was going to be this difficult, she might as well go back—

"No. You are not giving up this quickly. Besides, what are you going to do in Boston? Watch Eugene and Trudy get married? Listen to Daddy gloat about how he told you running off to Oklahoma was ridiculous?"

She rolled onto her side and pushed herself to her feet.

"Besides, you've already paid for your house kit and sent word where to have it delivered. In two or three weeks, all this will be behind you. It's only a tent. You are smarter than a piece of fabric."

She crossed her arms over her chest and glared at the offending canvas square.

If she couldn't drag the entire tent to her chosen site, she'd take it there a piece at a time. After finding the pocketknife in the bottom of the largest crate, Sarah sliced the cord around her tent kit and spread out the canvas. An instruction sheet was tucked inside.

Item number one: Lay out all pieces on the ground to be sure you have everything at hand.

Sarah planted her hands on her hips. "You might have told me that before I tried to drag the entire kit in one try."

Five sweaty minutes later, the wooden posts, ropes, and stakes lay on the ground near her chosen site. Dragging the canvas when it was just one layer proved almost as difficult as when it had been wrapped around the rest of the parts, but she managed.

After reading through the rest of the instructions, Sarah trekked back for a shovel and hammer, lecturing the tentmaker the entire way. "You promised this was easy to assemble. Well, let me tell you something, it hasn't been so far. And if I have any more trouble I will be writing you a sharply worded letter about false advertising."

An hour later, Sarah's complaints against the tentmaker were as long as a Tolstoy novel.

❖

John squinted against the afternoon glare. Off in the distance was the strangest sight he'd ever seen. It looked like prairie dogs popping up and down under a bedsheet. He slapped the reins, telling the borrowed team of horses to step up their pace. His supplies bumped around in the wagon bed, but he'd packed carefully. A little jostling wouldn't hurt them.

Detouring off the path that would take him to his new homestead, he rode closer to the bedsheet. About the time he realized the white fabric was too large for any bed, he heard a high-pitched voice. Her words weren't yet distinguishable, but her situation was clear.

He shouldn't laugh. He shouldn't, but. . .whoops of laughter bounced inside his chest. Someone—and he had a very good idea who—was trapped under a tent tarp. By the time he was close enough to hear Miss Maffey's monologue, his sides ached with mirth. He pulled the horses to a standstill and set the brake. She didn't stop her tirade, but he wasn't surprised. Not only was she buried under thick canvas, she was yelling loud enough to be heard all the way back in Lawton.

"How do you expect me to hold up two poles while stretching the canvas over the top? Who even thinks such a thing is possible? Have you ever tried to follow your instructions? Because, if you had, you would never have advertised yourself as easy to assemble!"

"Miss Maffey?"

"By the time I'm through with you, there won't be a soul in the entire United States of America who will ever purchase—"

"Miss Maffey!"

A scream split the air. Tirade and movement ceased.

He approached the edge of the cone-shaped canvas. "Do you need some help?"

Silence.

"Miss Maffey?"

"Yes."

He leaned over, pressing his palms against his thighs, his mirth reignited. Several shallow breaths and a deep inhale later, he recovered his ability to speak. "Is that, 'Yes, I need help,' or 'Yes, this is Sarah Maffey'?"

Another pause. Longer this time. Then, "Yes."

He lifted the edge of the canvas above his head. "Come on out."

The woman who emerged was a far cry from the one in the land claim office earlier. Where Hat Woman had been buttoned up and proper, this woman had dark hair in her face, dirt on her chin, stains on her blouse, and sweat glistening in the hollow of her neck.

He liked this one better. "I take it you're having trouble putting up a five-person tent all by yourself."

She smoothed hair away from her face. "The advertisement said it was easy to assemble."

"So I gathered." He battled against more laughter. "Would you like some help?"

The way she pinched her lips tight told him what she wanted to say, but he chose to pay attention to her nod instead.

"It will take me a few minutes to see what"—*kind of a mess*—"you've got here. I have a canteen on the seat of my wagon if you'd like some water."

Her chin jerked up. "Thank you, but, no. I wouldn't want to steal water from you."

What in the world? He was offering her his help and a drink of water. How did she get from that to stealing? "Are you still mad about this morning and the claim ticket?"

She eyed him like he'd offered her a plate of steaming horse manure.

"If you will take a moment and think back, you'll see that I was helping you get your ticket back, not taking it from you."

Her nostrils flared. "Are you saying I'm being ridiculous, Mr. Tyler?"

The woman jumped to conclusions—and wrong ones at that—faster than jackrabbits zipped across these plains. He ought to drive off and leave her to her own devices—

Her sniff stopped him. And seeing her touch her ring finger to the corner of her eye.

Someone had called her ridiculous. Someone she trusted. Someone who should have known her better.

"Miss Maffey, I would never call you ridiculous. I think you're trying very hard to do something that requires a great deal of courage, intelligence, and stamina."

She looked away, the tendons in her neck visible behind her open collar.

"I also think this has been a trying day. First that pack of jackals surrounding you at the claims office, then the near theft of your claim ticket, and now a tent that won't assemble as advertised. Since my track record is fifty–fifty in helping you, I will understand if you decide you're better off putting this tent up by yourself."

Her eyes returned to him first, her head following at a slower pace. "What do you mean your track record is fifty–fifty? I remember your attempt to steal"—she held up a hand to stop his protest—"what *appeared to me* as an attempt to steal my claim ticket."

"But you remember the—I hesitate to call them men, so let's just refer to them as males—surrounding you just before the scuffle that broke out."

She nodded.

"I'm afraid my attempt to defend you from a rather foulmouthed one went a little awry."

Understanding dawned in her slate-blue eyes. "That was you?"

He scratched the whiskers under his chin. "Yeah. I grabbed his arm, he hit someone's chin, and a fight broke out that allowed that. . ."

A smile tugged at the corners of her lips. "Odorous male?"

". . .to steal your ticket." Had she said odorous or onerous? He bent his head toward his armpit and sniffed. Nope, couldn't prove it wasn't him if she was going by smell.

She held her hands in front of her skirt, fingers interlocked and thumbs tapping together. "All I remember is it being snatched out of my hand. When the tussling stopped, it was in yours."

"I'd just grabbed it out of his fingers."

She continued to tap her thumbs. "Why didn't you shake my hand?"

"What?"

"My hand. I offered to shake your hand and you refused. Why?"

He showed her his palms. "Because my hands were filthy and you were wearing nice gloves. I didn't want to get them dirty."

"Oh." She looked between him and the tent canvas lying on the ground.

Him.

Canvas.

Him.

Canvas.

Deep breath. "All right, Mr. Tyler. I accept your help with the tent. If we are successful, *then* I will consider your track record to be fifty–fifty."

It took him a moment to figure out his other black mark. "I promise I will never even *think* of you as being ridiculous."

Her laugh was brittle. "You might not want to make that promise until we put up this tent."

Chapter 3

Y ou miserable beast!" Sarah chased after the runaway horse. *Vigorous*, the horse salesman said.

Vigorous, her eye! Ornery, mean-spirited, and uncontrollable was more like it.

And she'd thought nothing could be more difficult than that miserable tent.

She slowed her chase to a fast walk. Proving up her land required that she cultivate ten full acres over the next five years. Two acres a year *had* seemed reasonable. Easy, even.

Until she met her equine nemesis. If she didn't know better, she'd think he was trying to sabotage her efforts.

At her first attempt to improve the land, Shakespeare—a beautiful name for a beast that didn't smell sweet at all—raced off, taking the plow along for a ride. Sarah's land looked like a toddler's first scribbles on paper. After three hours, Shakespeare tired of playing hide-and-seek and returned home.

Her second attempt, the horse bolted as soon as Sarah tried to slip the bridle over his head.

Today, the dumb animal bolted the moment she opened his stall door.

Was coming to Oklahoma a mistake?

It couldn't be.

She'd come with a plan.

Choose good land. Yes, except for John Tyler stealing almost all the water.

Pay someone to build a house and barn. Yes. She'd ordered lumber for the barn and the house kit back in May, paying extra for delivery as close to the date of the land lottery as possible. The barn was already up, and the precut kit for her house would be delivered soon.

Cultivate two acres a year. No, not yet.

If only it didn't involve a horse.

Horseless carriages had been around for ages. Why couldn't someone invent a horseless plow? And why couldn't she have a horse like all the ones in those cowboy novels—the steadfast companion that saved the hero from death, that instinctively knew what was needed, that *returned* when they were supposed to? She raised her hand above her brow to shield the sun from her eyes. Shakespeare headed straight through the creek, ignoring her demands that he come back.

Through the trees lining the streambed, she saw John Tyler emerge from his dugout. She'd not been inside it—she'd never even stepped on his land—but she'd read about dugouts. They were nothing more than dirt caves. They might cut the heat, but she'd take her tent *and* the heat if it meant she didn't have spiders dropping on her head at night.

John whistled, and the traitorous horse raced straight to the man. Stopped right in front of him and ate something out of his hand. Out of his *hand*! Sarah picked up her skirts and ran, exposing her ankles in a most hurly-burly way, but she didn't care. "You leave my horse alone, John Tyler!"

He cupped a hand around his ear and shouted something she couldn't hear.

She trudged through the shallow creek that cut across the northwest corner of her land. "I said, leave my horse alone!"

"What?"

She started to run again, careful not to step in one of the prairie dog holes between her and her wicked, insufferable horse. By the time she got close enough to yell again, she was out of breath. She slowed to a fast march, dropping her skirts back into place. "I said, give me back my horse."

"It's not like I'm trying to steal him."

Maybe not, but Shakespeare was *her* horse and he needed to listen to *her*, not eat out of John Tyler's hand.

Shakespeare stood there munching away, a contented expression in his big brown eyes.

Sarah slowed down as she got closer. She needed to take charge. Show Shakespeare who was boss. Not be afraid of him. But one kick from his powerful leg would send her halfway into the next county.

"Would you like me to—"

"No!" Whatever he'd been about to offer, she wanted no part of it. Yes, the tent required two people, but plowing only took one. That's what all the books said. "I can do this myself."

She could.

She must.

But, gracious, that horse was big.

The closer she got, the more skittish Shakespeare became. A malevolent light entered his eye as if to say, *Just try to get the better of me, you puny woman.*

She never should have bought a male horse.

Shakespeare tossed his head and backed up a step.

John Tyler tightened his fingers around the leather strips, pulling Shakespeare's head down. "Easy, boy. Nothing to worry about."

"Give me the reins." Gracious. What call did she have to be rude to the man? All he did was catch her horse. Why couldn't she be nice? Her hand trembled as she reached out and took a deep, calming breath. "Thank you for catching my horse." There. That was nice.

"You're welcome." He handed her the reins. "Keep a firm hold, and don't be afraid of him."

"Easier said than done." As she turned to haul the stubborn beast back to her side of the creek, she saw dozens of beautiful, straight rows of tilled earth that filled her with awe and envy. "How do you do that?"

"Do what?"

Sarah tugged on Shakespeare's reins and headed home. "Nothing."

John let her go without further comment. Whatever possessed a woman who didn't know her way around horses to select a plot of land that required proving up? Why hadn't she selected a town lot?

Sarah Maffey was a mystery wrapped in porcupine quills. Trying to figure her out was like trying to solve a crime, and the Texas Ranger in him was intrigued.

The key to unlocking the enigmatic Sarah Maffey was kindness. But, though he'd helped her with her enormous tent and at her barn raising—*and* remained calm when she accused him of stealing her ticket and now her horse—she remained leery of him. What more could he do to earn her trust?

Maybe he'd offer to teach her how to plow. Poor woman would never get her wheat in at this rate. And the horse wasn't helping. Stubborn Beast, meet Stubborn Hat Woman. He shook his head and laughed.

Maybe he could. . .

No. For the time being, he needed to focus on getting his own land plowed. Homesteading would offer plenty more opportunities for him to return kindness for her mistrust. And, one of these days, he'd hit on a good solution to the problem of Miss Sarah Maffey.

John ducked back into his dugout. His beans and coffee were lukewarm now, but he swallowed them down. He'd survived on the plain fare for weeks on end before; he could do it again. Except, those times he'd not been downwind of heavenly smells. Sarah Maffey might not know her way around a horse, but she sure knew how to cook. Saliva pooled along the sides of his tongue just thinking about the pie she'd made to thank the men who helped put up her barn.

He shoveled the last bite of beans into his mouth and shuddered. Imagining the sweet apple pie made the unsalted beans taste like mud. Some meat would go a long way toward making meals tastier, but hunting had to wait until the wheat was in.

Mr. Harrison said the winter wheat seed would arrive today, and he'd agreed to let John pay off his order by building shelving and display cabinets once a wood-framed building replaced the grocer's tent. It was a good trade, and one that preserved the dwindling reserves in his cash box.

After washing up and setting another pot of beans to soak, John hitched Homer to his new wagon and headed to town. What had been nothing more than open land a few weeks ago was now a combination of tents, wood buildings, and a few half-walls of brick. Soldiers from nearby Fort Sill, men in aprons, cowboys and ranchers in Stetsons, and even a few women all went about their business. Most wore smiles and discussed the excitement of starting a new town from the ground up; a few troublemaking types groused about not winning a land claim and how the system had been rigged.

Some people could find a conspiracy in a kettle of water.

His attention snagged on a black-suited dandy escorting a blond in a tight-fitted dress and enormous hat. His lawman instincts shouted, "Out of place," but as he had no authority in Lawton, and they were doing nothing but strolling down the street, he continued toward the grocer's tent. He tied Homer to a hitching rail and went inside, stooping to fit under the flap. "Good afternoon, Mr. Harrison."

"Afternoon, Mr. Tyler. You here for your wheat?"

"And a couple other things, if you have them."

Mr. Harrison's eyes brightened. "Just got a shipment in from Dallas. If you don't see what you need in the opened crates"—he swirled his head in a circle to indicate the length and breadth of his tent—"I might have it in an unopened one out back."

"Great. I'll let you know."

Another man ducked inside the tent. Mr. Harrison wandered closer to him to give the same speech, but the new man turned out to be a pastor asking if the grocer would distribute flyers announcing services on Sunday.

John worked his way around the store. Rows of open crates lined all four sides of the tent walls from floor to ceiling, and another row of back-to-back crates ran through the center. If only he had the money for canned peaches and tins of meat. With a sigh, John passed them by for coffee, axle grease, and stationery. He took them to the makeshift table, setting them down before hoisting a large bag of beans and the bag of wheat with his name pinned on it from under the sagging wood to add to his purchases.

Mr. Harrison hurried over and began ringing up the items. "Did you find everything you wanted?"

"Pretty much." John pointed to the stationery. "I was hoping to find a fountain pen."

Mr. Harrison held up a finger, dashed out the back side of his tent, and returned a minute later with a small wooden box. He broke the paper seal and slid the top lid aside to reveal at least a dozen. "How many?"

"One, thanks."

"Anything else I can get for you?"

John cast a longing look at a tin of salt. He could afford it. His finances weren't that tight. But. . . "No, thanks."

"You heading back out to your spread?" Mr. Harrison looked up from the cash register.

John nodded.

"Would you mind taking Miss Maffey's wheat out to her? It would save me a delivery."

"Sure."

Mr. Harrison pointed below the table. "Hers should be somewhere down there with her name on it."

John found the bag easily, added it to his supplies, then loaded up his cart and headed for Miss Maffey's spread. While he was there, he could offer to plow an acre for her.

A new thought took root. Maybe he wouldn't offer. He could just *do*. And maybe, just maybe, over time, she'd unbristle herself when they spoke. Who knew? One day, they might have a civil conversation.

In a decade, they might even be *real* neighbors.

Sarah was in the barn, lecturing Shakespeare on proper equine etiquette, when she heard John Tyler's voice shouting her name. She cupped her hands around her mouth. "I'm in the barn."

A moment later, he poked his head through the doors. "Mr. Harrison asked me to deliver your wheat seed. I have it in my cart. Do you want it in here or inside your tent?"

Did it matter? Either way it was going to sit unused until she figured out how to bribe Shakespeare into obedience. But, if she didn't answer, John Tyler would stand there with his eyebrows raised, waiting. "Here is fine."

Instead of retreating to get the seed, he stepped fully inside the barn. "What are you doing?"

Sarah lifted her chin. "Having a little discussion with Shakespeare."

"A discussion?" He lifted his eyes to the heavens and shook his head. "That's it. You go get the bag of wheat while I harness up this beast and teach him some manners."

"Now wait just one minute. This is *my* horse."

John Tyler came close enough to touch. "And a worthless one until he learns his job. You've got a few more weeks before your wheat needs to be in. At this rate, it'll be next summer before you even get started. Now, I'm hitching up this horse and teaching him how to plow. You can either come along behind me and sow your wheat or not. Up to you."

Sarah swallowed. Goodness, the man could be imposing. And maybe a little impressive. Not that she'd ever admit it out loud. She swooshed her skirt to the side and marched out of the barn with as much dignity as she could muster, given how she'd just capitulated to the stronger will.

But he was right. The wheat did need to go in, and she hadn't the foggiest notion how to make Shakespeare plow. Grandmother Novak warned a time would come to swallow pride for the sake of getting a job done. Why did help have to come from John Tyler, though? Twice.

Sarah leaned over the edge of his cart to hoist the heavy bag of wheat onto her shoulder. The horse swung his head to look at her before returning to munching grass. "I'll pay you a hundred dollars to run off."

The horse didn't react.

"Two hundred?"

Still nothing.

Sarah checked to see if John Tyler was anywhere near before stepping closer to the annoyingly well-behaved horse. "I will give you five *thousand* dollars if you will run off and leave your owner stranded." It would be worth it to see the look on her neighbor's face.

"You about ready?"

Sarah gasped and swung around, grabbing for the bag of wheat before it fell off her shoulder.

John Tyler pulled a fully harnessed Shakespeare from the barn. The horse gave her another of his speaking looks: *See, the problem isn't me.*

Sarah gritted her teeth. "I'm ready."

"Take the reins while I go get the plow." John held the leather straps toward her.

She dropped the bag of wheat on the ground. "And what am I supposed to do if Shakespeare bolts again?"

"Hang on." John grinned, dimples appearing in both cheeks. Why did the man have to be so attractive?

"Very funny." Sarah took the reins. Shakespeare didn't even flinch.

Stupid horse.

Not that she wanted him to run away. . .yet. After the heavy iron wedge was secured and John Tyler was plowing would suit her fine.

But, of course, Shakespeare acted like a perfect gentleman the whole time John plowed and she walked behind dropping seed into row after perfect row. She was so incensed, she overlooked the odd feel of paper inside her wheat sack until it poked her in the palm.

"Ow."

John Tyler glanced over his shoulder. "You okay back there?"

"Fine." Sarah waited for him to turn his attention to plowing again before pulling the paper from her sack. It was an envelope addressed to her. She opened it and unfolded the page to see the signature: *"From your Secret Admirer."*

"Which one of you two fillies is ready ta get yourselves hitched?"

Sarah bit down a wholly unacceptable reply to Elias Zediker's proposal. Unacceptable inside a church, at any rate, even if it was just a tent with makeshift pews and walls too thin to keep out the smell of manure.

Her new friend, Mattie Beal, whose land lottery ticket had been chosen second, rose from the pew, patted the man on the shoulder, and smiled. "Go on, you old coot." As he passed by, she added, "I expect something more eloquent next Sunday."

Zediker paused. "Ela-what?"

"Like this." Young Abe Ventner put one hand over his heart. "Miss Beal, I simply can't take another refusal. I have eyes only for you. Please say you'll be mine for always."

"Hmmm. A little too flowery. Try again." Mattie tugged Sarah to her feet.

Sarah eyed the man. Young. Attractive. And proposing marriage to a complete stranger because he wanted land.

Mr. Ventner kept his hand over his heart, but his Adam's apple bobbed and the sparkle left his eyes. "Uh. . .Miss Maffey, would you. . .um. . . Oh, never mind."

A chorus of jeers greeted his hasty retreat, but none of the other eleven men bothered to take their chances with Sarah. They all scooted into the center aisle to join the long line of people waiting to greet Pastor McCammon on their way out of the tent.

Sarah sat back down to give the men time to move down the line before she entered the aisle. She'd traded Boston men who wanted her money for Lawton men who wanted her land. Both were abhorrent, but at least the Boston men were genteel about it.

"Since Mr. Ventner didn't actually propose, I'd say that's two for me and one for you." Mattie's voice lilted with humor. "I'm up to two-hundred forty-two. What's your count?"

"Ninety-seven." Sarah drew her gloves on and picked up her Bible. "I don't see how you find any of it funny."

"Because it *is*."

Maybe she was right. "I'm sorry. My sense of humor seems to have deserted me of late."

"Homesteading isn't much fun, so I'm not surprised." Mattie retrieved her own Bible from the pew and cast a glance at Mr. Charles Payne, the lumberyard owner. "I wish he would join my circle of beaus."

Sarah put a hand on Mattie's forearm to keep her from stepping into the center aisle. "May I ask you something?"

"Sure."

Leaning close to her friend's ear, Sarah whispered, "Have you received any of these?" She opened her reticule and pulled out the letter she'd found in her wheat bag.

Mattie gave her an odd look and opened the letter.

While she read, Sarah looked around the crowded tent. Who had penned the secret admirer note? Her first thought was John Tyler. After all, he'd brought her the wheat. But since her name was on a piece of paper pinned to the burlap sack, anyone who'd been in town that morning could have slipped it inside.

"This is"—Mattie turned her lips down—"worrying. And, no, I've not received one like it."

Sarah pressed a palm to her aching chest. Whoever this secret admirer was, he was targeting only her.

Chapter 4

John urged Homer into a faster trot the moment he saw Sarah's familiar figure in the distance. After he showed her how to handle Shakespeare, why wouldn't she ride the horse to church? The walk to town was way too long on such a hot day. Amazing she hadn't already collapsed in a field somewhere.

Idiot! Why didn't you offer her a ride to church?

Well, to be fair, he hadn't known she was the churchgoing type. But even as the unkind thought hit, he pushed it away. Of course she was a churchgoing woman.

He shook his head. Apparently her barbs bothered him more than he cared to admit. No sense excusing his lack of manners by thinking less of the woman just because of a tongue-lashing or two.

Or three.

"Miss Maffey!"

She twisted her neck then turned her body toward him. "Good afternoon, Mr. Tyler."

He reined Homer to a halt beside her. "Would you like a ride home?" He scooted left on the small bench to make room.

As she'd done with his offer to help with the tent, she looked back and forth between him and the road several times before extending her hand so he could help her into the wagon. "Thank you."

They were making progress. Instead of being rude first, then muttering a grudging thank-you, they'd skipped straight to the thank-you—a *sincere* one at that.

Unwilling to ruin the peace between them by saying the wrong thing, John searched for a topic of conversation that wouldn't get her riled up. Which meant they rode in silence for several minutes. "Did you enjoy the service this morning?" That should be safe enough.

"Not entirely."

Guess not.

"I should clarify. I enjoyed the service itself. I disliked what came before and after."

John turned his head to look at her. "Care to tell me about it?"

She didn't face him, but he read her discomfort in the way she nibbled at her bottom lip and fiddled with the strings of her reticule. "If I ask you something, will you answer me honestly?"

What a question! As though he'd be dishonest! John turned his attention to the road again. "I will."

She opened her reticule and pulled out a letter. "Did you write this?"

The paper looked identical to the kind he'd bought at Mr. Harrison's general store. "Not to my knowledge. What does it say?"

"It's a. . .secret admirer note."

The fear in her voice caught him in the stomach. "Why is it causing you such distress?"

She pulled away from him, like he'd raised his fist instead of asked a simple question.

"Please, Miss Maffey. I used to be a Texas Ranger. I can tell when someone is in trouble, and that"—he pointed his elbow at the letter—"is causing you trouble."

Silence settled between them again, but not an uncomfortable one. The sound of Homer's steady steps filled the air, an occasional bird chirping in answer.

"I was engaged to a man before I left Boston."

John tensed.

"I discovered that he and my. . ." she cleared her throat, ". . .the woman I *thought* was my best friend were plotting together."

Since she seemed disinclined to explain, and he had no clue what she was talking about, he prompted, "Plotting to what?"

"To steal my inheritance after Eugene and I were married. In fact"—she sniffed twice—"I think my former friend instigated the plot."

So. That was the reason for the grief in her eyes the day they'd met. He'd known it was something bad the same way he'd known who was responsible for killing his wife and daughter long before evidence confirmed it was the Malangers. "What ties their plotting and that letter together?"

"It looks and sounds like a woman wrote it, although it's not Trudy's handwriting." She straightened her spine, her upper arm coming into contact with his.

He jerked away. Not because the contact had been unpleasant, but because it had been decidedly the opposite. Only one woman's touch had ever jolted through him that way before. He nodded in an attempt to clear his thoughts. "In that case, I think you'd better read it to me."

She did, a slight tremor in her voice.

"Dearest Sarah,
You are the light of my life. Your face runs through my dreams, and I can think of little else.
> *I watch you from afar and ache with loneliness.*
> *When you run your fingers through your hair, I wish it were my own hand rather than yours.*
> *I will make you mine. No matter what it takes.*
> *I will see you again soon.*

Your Secret Admirer"

She folded the letter and stuffed in back into her reticule, her fingers trembling the way they had when she reached for Shakespeare's reins a few days ago.

"You said your fiancé and best friend were plotting together?" The out-of-place man and woman he'd seen on the street when he went to Mr. Harrison's general store came to mind. "Dark-haired fellow, blond lady?"

She gasped. "How did you know?"

"Because I saw a couple like that in Lawton the day I picked up your wheat."

"That was the day I found the letter inside my bag."

He pulled Homer to a stop. She needed to see his face—to read his eyes—when he spoke. "Miss Maffey, for your protection, you and I will work together from now on until we figure out who sent that letter."

<hr />

Sarah clenched her teeth. Four emotions begged to be spoken simultaneously—outrage at his high-handedness, relief for a reason she'd figure out later, skepticism that a silly letter posed a threat, and pique that he would think her stupid enough to fall for Eugene and Trudy's tricks. . .again. But the one that came out of her lips was incredulity. "What makes you think I'd trust a man like you to protect me?"

He jerked back like she'd slapped him. "What do you mean 'a man like me'?"

Sarah gulped. She had a right to be leery of him, so why did she feel the need to apologize? "A man who is only out for himself." Like every other man in Boston and Lawton and probably the whole, wide world.

Muscles in his jaw moved up and down. His chest rose and fell in short bursts. Then in one swift movement, he spun away and jumped to the ground.

"You can't deny it, can you?" Sarah scrambled down, steadying herself against the side of the wagon when her skirt caught on the brake release. After regaining her balance, she marched after him. "You can pretend to be nice by helping me with my tent or plowing a field or"—she swung a hand toward his wagon—"giving me a ride, but you revealed your true nature the first day I met you, and I'll not be taken in by you—nor any man, for that matter."

He whirled around. "Are we back to that stupid claim ticket again? How many times do I have to tell you? I wasn't trying to steal it."

"Oh. . .you've said it plenty. But I'm on to your tricks. I was taken in once; I won't let it happen again."

"*What* tricks?"

"Making me think you want to help me, getting me to trust you, all so you can steal my land by getting me to fall in love with you. Did you know who I was? Did you use your Texas Ranger network of spies to find out I was Sarah Maffey of Boston? How do I know you didn't set up that whole fight and get a buddy to steal my ticket so you could play the hero and give it back? How do I know you didn't do the same thing with this letter? That you aren't making up seeing Trudy and Eugene in town? Am I supposed to just trust you about that? Well, I don't. *You* were the one who brought me that bag of wheat. I didn't ask you to; I didn't ask you to do *anything*, but here you are!"

He didn't move. Didn't speak. Didn't respond in any way.

Why wasn't he yelling at her? Calling her ridiculous? Fighting back? She wanted him to do something. Say something. Anything but stand like a statue in the middle of a field silently driving her crazy.

Was that his plan? To make her feel foolish? To make her question every word and action until he convinced her he wasn't who she knew him to be? Sarah took a deep breath, willing herself to calm down. "You can try to confuse me all you want, but I knew you were a selfish, greedy, callous man the moment I saw how you configured your land to steal every possible drop of water."

That got him to move!

He marched so close she inhaled the tang of lye soap. "Water? This is about *water*?"

Sarah lifted her chin. "That's right. And I dare you to justify yourself."

"You dare me?" The calm in his voice couldn't mask the fire in his eyes. "You? Who have made so many assumptions and accusations, I can't even begin to answer half of them." His eyes narrowed. "All right, you want me to justify myself, here it is. Before I came to Oklahoma, I lived in Texas with my wife and daughter."

Reverence and misery colored the last three words.

"We lived downstream from a family named Malanger. You think you've suffered from others' greed? You don't begin to understand the meaning of the word. They dammed up the creek to flood their fields with more water than they needed for the sole purpose of starving us out. They wanted our land, wanted to build themselves an empire in the middle of Texas."

Sarah's pulse pounded in her ears as a sickening feeling spread in her stomach.

"My work as a Ranger often took me away from home for long periods of time. I had to leave my wife and child *alone* to manage our crops and tend our animals. Six years ago, I came home from a five-month chase to find. . ." His voice broke. Tears welled in his eyes and spilled down his cheeks.

Oh, no. . .no. . .

"They were dead." He mouthed the words, only the consonants filled with enough air to make sound. "Dehydrated and starved because Malanger salted our well on top of stealing our water. And I wasn't home to stop it."

She reached a hand forward an inch but pulled it back. Shame crushed the last of her anger. "I'm sorry. I'm so sorry."

"So, you're right. When I chose my land, I configured it to capture every last drop of water. But it was so you and everyone else downstream of me would never, *ever* suffer what my family did."

Chapter 5

Sarah climbed out of the wagon by herself. Same way she climbed into it by herself after John's startling revelation. He hadn't spoken—hadn't even looked at her—the whole way home.

Not that she blamed him.

She'd called him selfish and greedy and callous. How could a simple apology even begin to cover such a terrible misjudgment? She had no words when he finished his story, or on the drive home, or now as she watched him drive away.

She'd gone too far. Been ridiculous. Completely, totally, and utterly ridiculous in her assumptions, her accusations, and her animosity.

What happened to the girl Mrs. Robertson called a beautiful soul? Had Eugene and Trudy's betrayal robbed her of the ability to view others with compassion?

She walked toward the field she and John plowed on Thursday. She couldn't beg forgiveness of the man—not yet—but she fell to her knees, in that place that would forever remind her to be careful what seeds she sowed into her life, and begged forgiveness of God.

How could she have been so. . .wrong?

Her lips trembled, but even as her spirit cried out to God, her heart cried out a defense.

God, you know I only acted the way I did because I was hurt!

Truth struck hard. Of course, she'd been hurt. Everyone got hurt at some point in life. But she'd let that pain fester, poisoning her perspective and her trust—not just in people but in God.

"Forgive me!"

Hot tears coursed down her face as the truth flooded her mind. She'd found enemies because she created them. She'd looked for reasons to be offended. Returned kindness with suspicion. Let bitterness determine her actions and words.

What was it Pastor McCammon said this morning? Trust must be earned. Until then he hoped the congregation would give him the benefit of the doubt.

Sarah hadn't given anyone the benefit of the doubt for a long time.

She fell to her face in the field. "Please, Father, please. . .remove the bitterness rooted in my soul. . . ."

She didn't know how long she lay there, watering the earth with her tears, but slowly the recriminations for how she'd treated others—her neighbor in particular—faded. And in its place. . .

Peace.

Forgiveness.

God had heard. And He'd answered.

Sarah sat up, wiped the wetness from her cheeks, and breathed deep the sweet air of God's grace until she felt ready to do. . .something. "All right, Sarah Allison Maffey. What now?" Breaking the silence seemed like the first step, so she kept talking as she rose and walked back to her tent. "If you were John Tyler, what would you consider a peace offering?"

Plowing was out. So was cleaning—his floor was dirt anyway. But baking? Now there was an idea! He'd served himself a second slice of her apple pie the day he came to help raise the barn.

"Apple pie it is."

A quick trip to the creek later, she dropped dried apple slices into water to let them soak while she worked on the crust. Hymns sprang from her lips, an effective shield against the doldrums seeking to seep their way back in. "This is going to be the best pie you've ever tasted, John Tyler. It might not make up for everything, but if it doesn't put a smile on your face and make you the teensiest bit happy to be my neighbor, then. . ."

Her hands paused in the dough. What *would* she do?

She didn't know, so she added a little extra sugar to the filling.

Fifteen minutes later, she set the pie to baking then went down to the barn to check on Shakespeare.

"I've decided to be nice to you, too, though you've done nothing to deserve it. Here." She held out a few slices of dried apples, scrunching up her facial muscles, equal parts repulsed and amused at how his nose tickled her palm. "We're going to be friends one day, mark my words. Or, if not friends exactly, at least we won't be enemies."

Shakespeare was more interested in finding more apple slices than in making friends, so she left the barn before he devoured her apron.

The pie would take another forty to fifty minutes to bake, but with all this new energy pouring through her, she couldn't just sit there and wait.

"What to do? What to do?" She surveyed her land and the tent, pride filling her heart at how much she—and John—had accomplished in two and a half weeks. And because she'd survived. Her father thought she'd come running home the moment she laid eyes on Oklahoma. She'd proved him wrong. In a few more days, her house kit would be delivered. Mr. Harrison had managed to squeeze that information in before the crowd of men surrounded her and Mattie to propose after the service ended. Once she had a real house and a real bedroom, a real bed and feather mattress wouldn't be far behind.

"Hallelujah!" She sang Handel's *Messiah*.

In the meantime, she should turn the tick mattress. Grandmother Novak said that turning mattresses regularly was important.

The scent of baking apples greeted her as Sarah approached the tent. Sometimes thin walls that allowed smells to penetrate them weren't so bad after all. Smiling, she stepped inside and turned her attention to the bed.

Her heart stuttered.

Lying on the pillow was another letter.

John smelled apple pie before he heard Sarah call his name. If the order had been reversed, he would have rolled over on his bed and pretended sleep, snoring loudly if she needed extra convincing to go away and leave him alone.

He'd spent two hours calming his spirit, and the last thing he wanted was another encounter with his irascible neighbor.

Except, if his nose was correct, she'd brought food. Pie, to be exact, and his stomach didn't care what he wanted. *It* wanted that pie.

He opened the door and his hello died in his throat. Not because of the pie, but because of the alarm on her face—and the cream-colored letter resting on top of the pie.

"Come in."

She stepped inside, and John rushed to clear his table of dirt and bugs that had fallen from the dugout ceiling since the last time he cleaned it.

"I baked a pie."

He stopped cleaning to look at her. Why was she stating the obvious?

"It's apple." She held it out with stiff arms, thick oven mitts protecting her hands.

"I see that. Why don't you set it down here?" He indicated the table.

She nodded but didn't move. "I'm so sorry, John. I didn't know what else to do to make it up to you, so I baked a pie because you seemed to like the last one I made, and then, while it was baking, I was thinking of other things to do so I decided to turn my mattress, and that's when I found"—she took a breath—"this."

Sakes alive! From nothing to jackrabbit speed in an instant. "That pie smells delicious. Why don't you set it down?"

She nodded again, this time placing the pie on the table. "I haven't opened it. The letter, not the pie." She closed her eyes and exhaled. "I'm sorry. I'm babbling away and making no sense at all, it's just. . .it was on my bed. Inside my tent. Whoever wrote it has been inside my home, maybe even. . ."

Touched my things is what he imagined she couldn't say. He'd seen the same reaction in robbery victims. The loss of property didn't violate as much as knowing someone was in your home looking at pictures, rifling through treasures, touching clothing worn close to the skin.

John led her to the stool, pulling it out from under the table so she could sit. "Would you like me to read the letter to you?"

She tugged off the oven mitts and placed them beside the pie. "Just read it to yourself and tell me what I need to know."

"All right, but while I do that, would you mind slicing me a piece of that pie?" His stomach had been patient long enough.

While she rummaged around for a knife and plate, John pulled a crate to the table, sat down, and read:

Dearest Sarah,

I have found you, my darling. You are mine and I am yours.

So I linger and take in your scent, your world, your air.

It won't be long now, my dear.

Good night, good night. Parting is such sweet sorrow, That I shall say good night till it be morrow.

Your Secret Admirer

John again noted the similarity in color and weight to what he'd purchased at the general store. Next time he was in town, he'd check with Mr. Harrison to see who else had purchased stationery. Perhaps a dark-haired man and blond woman?

Sarah set a steaming slice of heaven in front of him. "So. . .what do I need to know?"

John folded the letter. "I think you need to tell me the whole story about this Eugene character."

By the time she recounted how she'd discovered her fiancé and best friend together, he was on his second slice of pie. She sure was a talkative thing when she got a full head of steam behind her. He kind of liked it. Made a nice change to the unending silence of the plains.

"And when I got home and told my father what happened, he said I should marry Eugene anyway because he doubted I could do better."

John's fingers squeezed on his tin fork. How could a father *ever* say that to his daughter?

"So I told him I'd move to Oklahoma instead of marry that no-good, two-timing. . . actually, I don't think I *said* that to Daddy, but it's what I was thinking."

"I can see why."

Sarah's jaw went slack. Was he teasing her? Or serious? She stared at him, trying to discern what it meant when he made a flat, unembellished statement then forked pie in his mouth and chewed. He glanced at her for an instant, a look of expectancy telling her to keep talking. "Sorry. Where was I?"

"No-good, two-timing. . .rather move to Oklahoma?" He cut himself a third piece of pie.

"Right." Sarah stood up to fetch another fork and plate. "I hope you don't mind if I have some, too."

"Why would I mind?"

She'd expected him to say something like, "Help yourself," or "Go right ahead." His surprising response highlighted how little she actually knew him.

"Trust must be earned. Until then, I hope you'll give me the benefit of the doubt." Were the pastor's words ringing in her head as a warning? Or as an encouragement to give John Tyler the benefit of the doubt?

All right. She'd tell him a little. But she wasn't going to trust him with her entire history. "After I told my father I'd move to Oklahoma rather than marry Eugene, I did some more research on homesteading, took advice from my grandmother, then purchased supplies and came down here. If my name hadn't been drawn, I would have purchased land outright with the money my mother left me."

He slanted a look at her. "Wait a minute. Are you telling me you have enough cash on hand to purchase land?"

"Yes." And a whole lot more. . .even though she left half of her ten thousand dollars back in Boston in case things didn't work out here.

His lips rounded. Pie fell from his fork. He caught it with his hand and popped it in his mouth. "Please tell me you didn't stuff cash under the mattress in your tent."

"Most of it is in the bank." She scooped pie onto her fork. "I only kept three hundred in cash."

John covered his mouth, coughing several times before he swallowed. "Sorry. Didn't mean to do that." He cleared his throat. "You're saying that somewhere in your tent is three *hundred* dollars in cash."

She swallowed her morsel of pie. Was that a lot of money? If so, it explained why Mr. Harrison's mouth had fallen open when she gave him a thousand to open a line of credit at his store, and why Mr. Atwood at the bank shortened his prediction of how long it would take to accept wired funds after she said she'd be transferring two thousand.

Should she tell John what she'd done? Or was it irrelevant? He already knew Eugene and Trudy were in town—well, *might* be in town. Seeing a dark-haired man and blond woman together didn't prove anything.

"Did you tell anyone you had that much cash?" John reached behind him to grab the coffeepot off his potbellied stove.

She set her fork down. "Why do you ask?"

He half-stood to take a couple of ceramic mugs from the shelf embedded in the dirt wall above the table. He poured her a cup of coffee and one for himself. "Based off the number of marriage proposals I overheard at the land office and at church this morning, you already know men want your land. You've paid men to build a barn and are set to pay them again when your house materials are delivered. Plus you purchased a horse and other supplies. It wouldn't be a stretch for someone to think you have a lot of money."

He had *no* idea. Sarah sipped the coffee then forked another piece of pie into her mouth so the sweet could cut the bitterness. "Are you saying this secret admirer of mine is looking for cash?"

John sipped his coffee without cringing. Did he *like* it lukewarm and so acidic it bit your tongue? "It's possible."

First Eugene with his smiles and flattery, now some nameless letter writer. Would she never be free of men who were after her money? "What do you think I should do?"

He tapped a finger on the letter. "Until we catch whoever wrote this, I think we need to trade houses."

It was her turn to choke. "You want me to sleep"—she looked around the tiny dugout—"*here?*"

His immediate recoil said she'd offended him. Again. "Do you have a better plan?"

She placed her hand on his arm to get him to look at her. "I'm sorry, John. I didn't mean to sound disparaging. I was just surprised." Movement out of the corner of her eye made her glance away. A fat-bellied, black spider descended from the ceiling. Straight toward the table.

Smack! John smashed the offensive intruder. With his bare hand.

She shivered. "In my world, the very idea that a woman would. . ." She tilted her head toward his mattress.

His skin blanched and then got red. "I wasn't suggesting—"

"I know. But even if you aren't here, even if you were in another state, it's still improper for me to. . .sleep in your bed."

"Would you rather be kidnapped from yours?"

She jerked straight. "Do you think it's that serious?"

He wiped his hands on his jeans and huffed. "Do you think I'd suggest trading places otherwise?"

The question hung between them while Sarah looked around the dugout again. Could she do it? Trade places with him? Sleep in what amounted to a dirt cave?

She reined in her escalating emotions. Now was the time to be practical, not dramatic. She'd read about homesteaders who lived in dugouts—which was why she'd chosen an overlarge tent and a house kit. But she wasn't going to live here, just stay for a few days until they could catch the letter writer.

So. . .for a few days, what would she need to survive? First, her oil lamp. There were no windows in this place. At night, with the door closed, it would be pitch black. She could handle almost dark, but full dark was another matter. The dugout's small size didn't bother her so much as the low roof, but at least his bed area had wood slats above it so no spiders would fall into her face. She *hoped*. As for the impropriety. . .was it any worse than when she changed out of her corset in the open air?

She was already leaning toward saying yes when she recalled where she'd found the letter.

"All right. We'll trade."

Chapter 6

After two nights in John's dugout, Sarah decided she preferred a quick death by letter-writing assassin. Anything was better than the bugs.

They fell on the meager table, on the paltry stove, into her undercooked food, and into her tangled hair.

She hadn't slept well or eaten much for thirty-some hours, and she wanted to go back to civilization—actually visualized apologizing to Eugene for making a fuss. If not for her house kit delivery scheduled for today, she'd buy a ticket for Boston on the next train.

To make matters worse, John forbade her from leaving his property. She'd agreed at the time because he'd couched it in terms of her safety and setting a trap for the secret letter writer, *and* because she thought it would be a nice break from the unending work of homesteading.

But she'd developed a routine over the past few weeks that started with biscuits and coffee at sunrise and didn't end until she and Shakespeare plowed one crooked gouge at least three feet long, after which she rewarded him with oats and a good brushing, and God rewarded her with a sunset.

The sunrises and sunsets were the same at John's place, but everything else was all wrong—especially the coffee. She leaned into the dugout to toss the dregs of her current cup on the floor, still amazed and disgusted that this was how John hardened the dirt.

His house, his rules.

With a sigh, Sarah walked to the water pump five feet away to rinse the cup. She'd researched pumps and wells, but she'd always assumed they needed to be placed near a water source. John's dugout was quite a distance from the creek and located in a small hill. If he got water in a spot like this, maybe she should ask him if she could do something similar so she could place her house in a location less susceptible to flooding.

Oklahoma weather didn't believe in half measures. When it was sunny, the whole sky was blue. When it rained, the drops came fast and hard, swelling the creek to twice its size in no time as water soaked the ground and ran into the streambed. After the first rainstorm, Sarah understood why John's land configuration protected everyone downstream of him. East Cache Creek angled through the middle of the long end of his L shape, into the northwest corner of her square, then back into the short end of his *L*. If John lived up to his promise not to block the flow, and if she didn't block up her section, ground water from miles around would collect and run downstream.

She stilled, the picture of his face when he spoke about how his wife and daughter died haunting her. She gave a slow nod.

Yes, he'd keep his promise.

Hot on the heels of that thought came another: How would it feel to be loved as he'd loved his wife?

Daddy seemed to get over Mother's death within a few months. Of course, there were plenty of women willing to—

"Oh! Gracious!" Sarah bent over, pressing a hand against her ribs. But the pain piercing her wasn't physical.

Women flocked around Daddy even *before* Mother died. Had he been unfaithful to her in the same way Eugene was unfaithful to Sarah? Was *that* why Daddy was upset with *her* that day in his office? Had he told her to calm down and be reasonable because—

Because he was guilty of the same sin?

She flailed her right arm until it hit the pump, and then ran her fingers over its shape to find the handle. Pumping furiously, she splashed water onto her face and neck to cool her heated skin.

In her whole life, was there even *one* man worthy of trust?

John Tyler's face filled her mind's eye. She wanted to believe in him, wanted him to live up to the strong, trustworthy image he projected, if only because she couldn't stand the idea that every man was disloyal. If they were, she was doomed to live alone forever—an idea that had lost much of its appeal in the last few weeks.

She was Sarah Maffey of Boston, heiress. Always had been and always would be, even if she moved halfway across the country to get away from the effect her money had on men. Before discovering Eugene's treachery, she'd never minded that her money was part of her appeal—she just didn't want it to be the *only* thing a man wanted from her.

She splashed more water on her neck, not caring that she was soaking her blouse, too. The day was already hot, her skin hotter, and there wasn't a soul around to see her dishevelment.

She looked around. There had to be *some*thing she could do to occupy her increasingly troubled mind. She grabbed the tin pail and filled it with water. The dugout needed a thorough cleaning, and she was in the mood to scrub until everything inside was shiny. And, by golly, if any spiders or centipedes or bugs of any kind dared to bother her, she'd kill them with *her* bare hands!

Thirty minutes and four pails of dirty water later, Sarah was finishing up when she stood too quickly and knocked her head against the shelf above the table. Coffee cups, tin plates, and a wooden box rained down. *Why* did the dugout have to be so small? A person couldn't even— Sarah caught her breath on a gasp.

Stationery the same color and size as her secret admirer's letters spilled across the muddy floor. Suddenly, the gouge to her head was nothing compared to the stab to her heart.

John had tricked her!

The theft of her ticket, the unnerving love notes, the offer to trade homesteads to "protect" her...it was all staged to make her trust him. And she'd almost—*almost*—fallen for it.

Half of her wanted to sit down and cry, the other half was furious. Was he after her for himself, or was he being paid to trick her? Were Eugene and Trudy behind this betrayal as well? They must be! How else would John know to say he saw a dark-haired man and blond woman in town?

She was such a fool. "Such a fool," she repeated, because saying it once—and only inside her head—didn't seem to be enough to cover how ridiculous she felt.

It was time to go back to Boston. If she was going to be pursued for her money, she might as well do it surrounded by comfort and the few people who loved her.

Before she went, however, she was giving Mr. John Tyler a piece of her mind. And maybe a piece of her fist while she was at it!

She swiped the stationery from the floor and stomped out of the dugout.

Twenty paces later, she heard someone shouting her name and the thundering of horse hooves an instant before she saw John flying across the prairie on Shakespeare.

Shock rooted her feet to the ground.

The anguish on John's face was the same as when he'd told her about his wife and daughter. His expression cleared to immeasurable relief the moment he saw her. He'd been worried about her? That look was for *her*! And he'd tamed the world's most ornery horse to come to her rescue.

She crumpled the offending stationery in her hand. Her rage fled, taking her doubts with it.

John's betrayal was a lie. The undeniable truth was in the way he leaped off a racing horse, ran to her, and crushed her to his chest while whispering, "Thank God, you're all right. I was so worried."

He smelled of sweat and horse and desperation—and she loved him for it.

Sarah paused outside her tent to take a breath. This was going to be bad.

"You don't have to go inside. I can clean it up later." John squeezed her hand.

She shook her head. "I want to see."

He pulled back the tent flap so she could step inside.

Even though he'd warned her, seeing two settings of Mother's china laid out on the table—as though she were waiting for Sarah to join her for tea—jolted her with horror. On the floor surrounding the peaceful tableau were shards of what used to be the other six place settings.

An icy finger traced her spine.

"I'm so sorry," John repeated for the tenth time since finding her outside his dugout. "I don't know how he got past me."

She did. Faithful to what she finally realized was his true character, John had been serving her by plowing another acre of her land and sowing wheat. All her letter-writing vandal had to do was keep out of sight whenever John faced west.

She crept closer. Propped against one of the tea cups was another letter. She looked at John. "Did you read it?"

"No. The moment I saw this, I jumped on Shakespeare's back and headed straight to you."

For as long as she lived, Sarah would remember watching him race toward her, being held close and sighed over, being *cherished*—even if only for an instant. It gave her courage to reach for the letter.

These violent delights have violent ends.

No "Dearest Sarah" or signature. What did that mean? She turned around and handed the letter to John.

His mouth twisted with a wry grin. "You really need to change the name of your horse."

She chuckled, partly because it was funny and partly because there was nothing else to do. "Poor Shakespeare. First he gets saddled with a woman who doesn't know how to handle him, and now some lunatic is quoting his namesake."

John crumpled the letter and walked toward her cookstove. "I don't know about you, but I've had enough of this guy." He tossed the paper into the fire.

"Me, too." What she wouldn't give for solid walls— "Oh!" She spun around, tilting precariously before John reached out to catch her. Gracious, she could get used to being in those strong arms. "My house kit is arriving today. It might not help us catch anyone, but it sure would make me feel safer if I could lock a door at night."

A warm smile spread across his face, denting his cheeks with those dimples she adored. "Then let me escort you into town."

A new sensation surrounded her. Her temperature skyrocketed—and it had nothing at all to do with the weather.

For the first ten minutes as they rode toward Lawton, John was too busy with his own thoughts to notice that Sarah hadn't said a word. He slid his eyes her way to see her hands cradled together in her lap, thumbs tapping.

She needed something else to think about. Something other than her mother's china and that disturbing letter. And he needed a few answers to figure out who was writing the blasted things.

"A few days ago, you said something about being Sarah Maffey of Boston, only it sounded like there was more to it than Boston just being your home. What did you mean by that?"

She squeezed her hands together. Seconds passed. A deep sigh. "I'm something of. . .an heiress."

His hands slackened on the reins for an instant. He recovered his grip and then looked her way.

Her cheeks were pink under her sensible bonnet. "It's why Eugene wanted to marry me. My father said every man in Boston was after my money, so I came to Oklahoma."

A wry chuckle. "Where they're all after my land."

"How much do you stand to inherit?" The question was crass, but he needed to know.

She nibbled her bottom lip and shot him a glance filled with. . .guilt?

John returned his attention to Homer, giving her a little space to think. "I understand why you're hesitating. . .at least I think I do. After what Eugene did, what your father said, and the number of complete strangers who've proposed to you since you won a land claim, you think your worth is tied up in things instead of your character. I don't believe that. I've seen how hard you've worked and, now knowing a little of your history, how much you've sacrificed to succeed against long odds. I'm only asking the size of your inheritance so I know how desperate this Eugene fellow might be."

She turned on the seat to stare at him, probably summing up how much she could trust him with the truth. "Before I answer, may I offer you my sincerest apology for how I've treated you these past few weeks?"

John was too startled to speak, so he nodded.

"I used to be such a nice person." She cut him another guilty look. "I don't know how you've put up with me, nor what makes you say there's worth in my character since I've done little except accuse you of outrageous things. My only defense is that I was acting out of deep hurt. I've asked God to forgive me, and I would be forever grateful if you could find it in your heart to forgive me, too."

He understood deep hurt and how it turned a person inside out. It had taken years to forgive Malanger, not because the man deserved it but because John's own bitterness had turned him into a man he hated being. "I forgive you, and I hope that we can now be both neighbors and friends."

Her smile stirred a fire in his gut that made him wish for something more—much more—than mere friendship.

"I like the idea of us being friends." Sarah gripped her hands together. "And friends tell each other the whole truth. So, to answer your question, aside from the ten thousand dollars my mother gave me, seven hundred thousand dollars will come to me upon my marriage or my thirtieth birthday, whichever comes first. And I will receive more when my father passes into glory—unless, of course, Daddy follows through on his threat to disinherit me. Then I will just receive the seven hundred thousand."

Land sakes alive! He was sitting in a wagon with a bona-fide heiress—who lived in a tent! He didn't know which fact stupefied him most.

"I can see the gears turning inside your head." She turned toward him an inch more. Her knee touched his. "What are you thinking?"

So many things that he couldn't get his brain to hold one long enough to form a sentence. And the heat burning through his knee and setting his heart to racing was no help at all! How could a man focus?

He took a deep breath and returned his attention to Homer, snapping the reins against his rump to get him moving again.

"Start with the letters." Sarah's thumbs started tapping again. "I need to know your thoughts about them."

"Until this last one, the writer used fairly common language for love letters. It could be your Eugene or some other beau from back home, because I imagine the disappearance of an heiress would make headlines."

"My father put out a statement that I had taken ill and wouldn't be attending society functions until I'd recovered." Another wry chuckle. "It's his way of saying he thinks I've lost my sanity and will be running home soon."

That father of hers needed a good pounding. "You've been gone almost three weeks now. Someone has to be asking questions."

"Perhaps, but the lack of newspaper reporters flooding the streets of Lawton indicates I'm still incognito here." The sparkle in her tone said she was quite pleased. "Still, I may have let the cat out of the bag when I gave Mr. Harrison a thousand dollars to open a line of credit at the general store and wired another two thousand into Mr. Atwood's bank."

He pulled up on the reins and swiveled his neck to stare at her. "You did *what*? And you're just now telling me about it?"

She rounded her shoulders, making herself smaller. "You already knew about Eugene, and it seemed like the three hundred I had in cash was distressing to you, so. . ."

He didn't know whether to laugh or cry. "If either Harrison or Atwood talked, every man in town will consider you wealthy beyond their dreams—and that's before they know how much you're *really* worth. A single woman in possession of land is enough of a temptation for some men to propose marriage—"

"As is demonstrated every time I go to town or to church."

"But a woman of means? That garners even more attention. So combine your land with your apparent wealth, and you're far and away the richest person in Lawton. Maybe in all of Oklahoma."

She chewed on her bottom lip for a moment then turned those wide, worried eyes to him. "So what you're saying is, my secret admirer could be anyone."

Chapter 7

When they pulled onto First Street, Sarah suspected word had gotten out about her thousand-dollar line of credit at Mr. Harrison's. Men crowded around his store smoking, leaning on the hitching rail, and chatting. They snapped to attention when they saw her and John.

John gave a nod. "Looks like Mr. Harrison already assembled your building crew. That'll save time."

Sarah relaxed...until John sucked in a breath.

His voice was tight and low. "Keep facing straight ahead, but look left with your eyes. The couple I told you about is coming toward us."

She did as he instructed and squinted to see better—the couple was still a good distance away—but the racing of her heart caused her vision to blur. She closed her eyes and took a long, deep breath. What if it was them? What would she do?

Well, one thing was certain: getting riled wouldn't help. She needed to stay calm. And maybe just a little bit angry. She and John would take this one step at a time. She felt his sturdy hand on her elbow.

Together.

Fortified by his comforting presence, Sarah opened her eyes. The seconds crept by. She waited until the couple came close enough to see under the brims of their fancy hats before exhaling. "It's not them. Which makes me feel both better and worse."

John squeezed her elbow. "Don't worry. I promise we'll find whoever is writing those letters."

Tears threatened. There was such safety in his promise. And comfort. And a whole host of other things she probably shouldn't feel for someone she'd known for such a short amount of time and decided to trust only a few hours ago. But she did feel them. Deeply. "Thank you, John."

He pulled Homer to a stop and turned to look at her. "You're welcome, Sarah."

Maybe she was reading more into it than he intended, but the sincerity in his voice and the tenderness in his green eyes seemed to say, *I'm glad we're friends now.*

Was he glad? She hoped so!

He swiveled on the seat and jumped to the ground. When he helped her out of the wagon, his hands lingered on her waist for a moment longer than necessary.

Or was it just her desire to slow time whenever he was near that made it seem so?

"Miss Maffey!"

Startled out of her wishful thoughts, Sarah turned her attention to Mr. Harrison.

"I was beginning to think you'd forgotten about your delivery today."

"Mr. Tyler and I ran into a small problem this morning, that's all." Sarah looked past the grocer to see if any of the men clustered behind him reacted to her statement. No one looked away or flinched. It wasn't proof positive none of them were her secret admirer, but her pulse slowed to a more normal pace. "I see you assembled the building crew."

Mr. Harrison nodded. "They've been here for an hour waiting for you."

"An hour they'll be paid for." Sarah straightened and gave a brief nod. Firm, without a smile. These men needed to know she was in charge. And no amount of fear-laden-Shakespearean-mumbo-jumbo letters would get her to give up her land.

Tension left the men's faces, some of them going so far as to crack a smile. One elbowed his neighbor and whispered, "Told ya."

As they loaded bundles of cut boards, posts, and boarded-up rectangles that she presumed were windows, Mr. Harrison drew her attention to a second, rather large pile waiting in the gap between his tent and the wooden half-walls of the store he was building. "I wasn't expecting your load to be this large."

Large? The house was only two stories, and a quarter of the total square footage of her home in Boston.

"I took the liberty of asking Otis if he'd be willing to hire out a wagon for a second load."

Sarah looked around for the rotund man. "Did he agree?"

"Not sure. I sent Don Lesta to—oh. I think that's them now."

Sarah turned to see Otis and another man she recognized as part of her barn building crew. "Do you think his wagon will hold the remaining supplies?"

"I'm not sure."

Half an hour later, the two wagons were loaded with everything the horses could safely haul.

John wiped his forehead with the back of his hand. "We'll have to send someone back for the rest after we offload one of the wagons."

"Do we have room for a bag of dried apples?" Sarah eyed the mounded wagons. "I'd like to bake a few pies, but I can wait until—"

"Yes!" It was a collective shout from John and several of the men close enough to hear her.

Mr. Harrison scurried into his tent and reappeared with a large burlap bag a moment later. He gave her a broad grin. "I'll put it on your tab."

Back at Sarah's property, as the rest of the men unloaded the house supplies, John grabbed the bag of apples and followed Sarah inside her tent, grateful for a moment alone. "Sarah." She turned around to look at him. He'd never seen her look so relaxed. "I know it's a relief that the couple in town didn't turn out to be Eugene and Trudy, but I still need you to be careful. If you go anywhere besides here or the barn, let me know." He dropped the apples near her cookstove. "Actually, even if you go to the barn, let me know."

Her smile was soft. "Thank you, John."

He frowned. "For what?"

Instead of answering, she smiled wider. "I'll be sure to stay where you can see me or let you know where I'm going."

Hoo, boy. He was in big trouble. He'd known it as soon as he saw the smashed china and his heart stayed inside his throat until he saw she was safe. Add the apology and that incredible smile, and he was a goner. Even with her prickles and accusations, she'd worked her way under his skin. But there was work to be done, so he went back outside to help with the offloading.

Despite Sarah's promise to stay vigilant, John suspected she'd let her guard down once she verified that the couple he'd pointed out weren't her former friend and fiancé. He kept a wary eye on the men, counting heads every few minutes to be sure none of them wandered off for longer than it took to find a bush and take care of business.

"Hey, John!" Don Lesta waved a handful of papers above his head.

For a split second, John thought they might be another letter—until he saw a picture. "That the house plans?"

Lesta nodded. "You gonna ride back for the last load, or you want me to do it?"

John took the house plans and eyed the man. "What's your background, Mr. Lesta?"

"Name's Don, and I used to own me a carpentry shop. It burned down." He swiped a finger under his nose and sniffed. "Didn't have the wherewithal to start over."

"Since you have carpentry skills, I'd prefer you stay here. We'll find someone else to pick up the last load." John stuffed the papers in his back pocket and headed toward his wagon to help with the unloading.

For half an hour, he and the other five men Sarah had hired offloaded supplies, carted them to the building site, and organized them into piles.

Sarah came out a few times to offer biscuits and coffee, check on progress, and let John know she was making a quick trip to the barn. Five minutes later, she waved at him on her way back into the tent.

John actually enjoyed how *domestic* this all felt. Sarah baking pies in her tent, him working hard on her house—no, her *home*. He shook his head. It had taken long enough, but she was finally accepting his help.

But he wanted more. Much, *much* more. Sparring with Sarah these past few weeks had shaken loose the comfortable friendship he'd made with grief, reminding him of the things he'd liked best about himself when Ada and little Josie were alive. He'd been a protector and provider, someone whose labor benefited more than just himself, and he missed it.

God had offered him a second chance at love, something he never dreamed possible. No wonder it caught him by surprise. He should have known though. From the moment he met Sarah and saw the hurt in her eyes, she'd been his. That's why her distrust and accusations had hurt so much.

He shook his head. Sarah's safety was at stake and here he was having romantic notions. Those could wait.

But hopefully not too long.

Don Lesta came up to John. "You sure I can't be more help goin' for that last load?"

Why was the man so insistent? John smelled trouble, even if he was somewhat side-tracked by the scent of apple pie drifting on the air. "I think we should send Otis. He's looking a little tuckered out."

Lesta shrugged. "Suit yourself."

John watched him wander away, then turned and scanned the men. "Otis!"

The rotund man pulled up his shirt to wipe sweat from his red face. "Yeah?"

"You ready to go get the last load?"

"Figured that'd be my job." He lumbered closer. "Give me a minute to catch my breath, and I'll be off."

John took a few steps toward the building site before swinging around. He'd better check with Sarah and see if she needed anything else while Otis was in town.

"John!" Don hollered out. "We need your help lifting!"

Asking Sarah would have to wait.

A few minutes later, wagon wheels rolled and a harness jangled. John looked up. Otis was already on his way. Oh, well. He'd ask Sarah later about what she needed, and it would give them a good excuse to ride to town together again. Meanwhile, he had a load to lift.

Forty minutes and a gallon of sweat later, John caught the scent of something burning. He felt his heart skip a beat and he raced for the tent.

"Sarah?" He ducked through the flap. Smoke poured from the oven. "Sarah?" Her oven mitts rested beside the cookstove. "Where are you?" He pulled the black-crusted pie from the oven and set it on the flat top then stuck his head outside. "Hey! Anyone seen Sarah?"

The men started yelling her name, their voices coming from several directions.

John sprinted for the barn.

Shakespeare poked his head over the stall door, but Sarah?

She was nowhere to be found.

Chapter 8

Sarah roused.

What. . .what was happening? She struggled to focus.

Why did her middle hurt so? She blinked then realized she was bent over a beefy shoulder like a sack of grain. The stink of sweat and horse assailed her.

Where was she? The last thing she remembered was the same smells mixed with chloroform as she struggled against a cloth held over her nose and mouth.

Otis.

He'd come into the tent while she was baking to say he was heading to town and to ask if she needed anything. She'd turned her back on him to check whether her pie was bubbling. . .

And someone pressed the cloth over her face.

How long had she been unconscious? Where were they? What did Otis want with her?

Her hands were tied behind her back, a cloth was between her teeth, and she was wrapped in a scratchy blanket. She squirmed against her captor's hold on her legs.

"Now, now, love. Don't make things difficult for the man."

Eugene! That was his wretched voice purring with self-satisfaction. "After all, he gets paid to haul things for a living. It doesn't much matter to him what, as long as he gets paid. Isn't that right, Mr. Otis?"

"That's right." Otis shifted his stance, lowering Sarah to the ground.

The blanket around her fell. Eugene and Trudy stood there, side by side.

"Hello, my dear friend." Trudy placed a hand over her bosom, a malicious grin contorting her beauty. "You can't know how wonderful it is to see you. . .like this."

Eugene brayed. Like a mule. His long face and overlarge teeth added to the comparison. How could Sarah ever have thought him handsome?

Someone, presumably Otis, tugged at the cloth wrapped around Sarah's mouth.

"No, no. Leave that in place, Mr. Otis." Eugene pulled a bag of coins from his pocket. "Here's your fee. I can handle my fiancée from here."

The tugging stopped. Otis stepped into Sarah's peripheral vision. He reached for the bag, opened it, and poured coins into his palm, pushing them around with his finger while he counted under his breath. He picked out two dollars and gave them back. "This here's too much. We agreed on twenty."

Twenty dollars? That was the fee for abducting a person? If her gag wasn't in place, Sarah would offer him a hundred times that to haul Eugene and Trudy somewhere—*any*where—as long as it was sweltering hot and crawling with bugs!

Otis stepped back, and the swishing of canvas announced he'd left the tent.

Sarah battled against the fuzziness still clouding her brain to look Eugene straight in the eye. She'd beaten a tent, tamed a horse, and bested spiders. Eugene Fromm was *nothing* compared to all that.

His smug grin wavered. "Come now. We've delayed our nuptials for too long already." He stepped to her right side, while Trudy stepped to the left.

Sarah managed to look around. They were inside the church tent, and a man stood behind the wooden pulpit. It wasn't Pastor McCammon or anyone she recognized. In fact, if she was any judge of people, the man was a drunkard, which, unfortunately, didn't mean he couldn't be a preacher. Sarah saw two women sitting in the front pew, facing forward.

Witnesses?

"That's right, *dear* Sarah." Trudy looped her arm through Sarah's. "I've waited a long time to be your maid of honor. But, more than that, I've waited long enough to see the great Sarah Maffey brought to her knees."

Despite her resolve not to show fear or weakness, Sarah couldn't keep back the tears.

Trudy's blue eyes glittered. "You've always lorded your wealth over me, over everyone, with your charity and hand-me-downs. Well, how does it feel to know that, this time, you're getting *my* hand-me-downs? That Eugene was mine first, and that, as his mistress, *I* will be spending every penny of your wealth?"

Sarah yanked her arms free and ran for the door. If Trudy wanted Eugene, she was welcome to him. Sarah no longer cared two beans or a pickle for the man. Not when men like John Tyler lived and breathed.

John! Where was he now? Did he even know she was missing?

Cruel fingers closed on Sarah's arm, gouging her skin. Trudy pulled her close. "You aren't getting away again. Not if you value your new friend's life."

What? What friend? Had they done something to John? Sarah stumbled and fell to the tent floor.

Trudy yanked Sarah to her feet and pulled her down the aisle to where Eugene stood, mouth gaping. "Grab hold of her, and don't let go this time."

Were it not for the threat hanging over her, Sarah would have laughed at the shock on Eugene's face. Clearly, this side of Trudy was new to him. Nonetheless, he obeyed, and the two tugged Sarah toward the man waiting behind the wooden pulpit. Now that Sarah had a better look at him, he seemed familiar, but why? Where had she seen him before?

One of the women in the front pew was Mattie Beal, her face stained with tears. Next to her was an unfamiliar woman holding a gun.

Trudy leaned close and whispered, "Just think what it would be like to live with the death of an innocent woman on your conscience. You will say nothing except your vows, or I swear on all I hold dear, I will shoot your friend myself."

Had they held a gun to her head, Sarah would have let them pull the trigger rather than be forced to marry Eugene. Defeat knocked the stiffness from her posture. She wouldn't risk Mattie's life.

"Good girl." Trudy's viselike grip relaxed. She reached around the back of Sarah's head and untied the gag. "Now, let's get you married."

Sarah cast a longing look toward the back of the tent. . .and saw one of the corners jiggle.

Someone was loosening a stake.

Was it John? *Please, God, let it be John!*

Sarah jerked her head back to Trudy. "Fine, but I want to know why." And to stall in case it *was* John and he needed time to do whatever a Texas Ranger did. "Why the letters? Why smash my mother's china? What was it all for?"

Eugene twisted, dropping Sarah's elbow from his grip. "I thought I told you we weren't going to do those things."

Trudy jutted her chin. "And I told you I wanted to make her suffer for running away and making us follow her to this wretched place." She glared at Eugene. "I let you have your way by agreeing we wouldn't kill her after you controlled her fortune, so you owed me that much. Now, grab her arm and help me get her to the altar."

After a long pause, he complied.

Sarah sucked in a breath at his painful grip on her bicep. What had she ever seen in this weak-willed man? Were he not marching her toward a drunken preacher to gain control of her money, she might feel sorry for him. Then again, he'd made his bed, so he could jolly well sleep in it!

"Dearly beloved, we are gathered here. . ." The preacher gave her a wary look, and Sarah's breath caught. It was the lout! The man she wrestled with to reclaim her land lottery ticket. Once he performed this mockery of a marriage, would he be rewarded with the deed to her land? Was the woman holding the gun on Mattie his wife? "Eugene Eustace Fromm, do you take this woman to be your lawfully wedded wi—"

"Wait!" Sarah held up a hand. Trudy had turned at a slight sound from the back of the tent.

Trudy spun back to glare at her. "What are you doing?"

Sarah lifted her chin. "If I'm going to be married, I at least deserve to wear a hat."

"Well, you're not getting mine." Trudy placed a hand atop the wide-brimmed concoction.

"I would have thought you'd jump at the chance to give me another of your hand-me-downs." Sarah raised her voice to cover whatever noise John needed to make.

"Just give her the hat, Tru." Eugene mopped his forehead with a white handkerchief. "Let's get this over and get away from this beastly place."

With another glare at Sarah, Trudy unpinned her hat and handed it over. "I'll be burning it tomorrow."

"And then you can buy yourself a new one with my money, so I don't see why you're pouting." Sarah held out her hand, eyebrows arched.

Trudy smirked. "I suppose you're right."

Oh, what she wouldn't give to poke her former friend with the long hat pin! Sarah snatched the frilly hat, fit it atop her hair, and returned her attention to the dubious minister. "You may continue."

"I don't think so."

The simple comment caused Eugene to gasp, Trudy to swear, and the minister to snap to attention.

Sarah spun around. John stood there—behind Mattie—every inch the Texas Ranger with guns in both hands. The other woman was staring at her now-empty hands, a look of bewilderment on her face.

"Are you all right, darlin'?" Though John spoke to Sarah, he kept his gaze on Trudy. Even more proof of his excellent instincts.

A crazy fluttering filled Sarah's stomach. He'd called her *darlin'*. In a church, so he had to be serious. Should she be bold? Call him an endearment in return? In front of God and witnesses? "I'm just fine, sweetheart."

"Does that mean you're getting hitched, Miss Maffey?"

Sarah spun around again. While she'd been focused on John, two more men had snuck inside the tent and now held guns trained on Eugene, the preacher, and Trudy. There would be no escape for the villains.

"Mr. Ventner." Sarah smiled at the young man who'd proposed so awkwardly a few days ago. "I suppose this means I'm unavailable to receive another offer from either you or"—she shot a look at the second man—"Mr. Zediker over there."

Abe Ventner tipped his head and leaned toward Mattie. "Miss Beal? Any chance my brave rescue will get you to marry me?"

Mattie managed a shaky laugh. "Not right now, but you and Mr. Zediker just went to the top of my list."

The news made both men whoop, but neither Mr. Ventner nor Mr. Zediker allowed their guns to waver. They rounded up the four villains and escorted them out of the tent. John started to help, but Abe Ventner whispered something in John's ear to make him stay behind.

Mattie rushed to Sarah, pulling her into a bone-crushing hug. "I was so worried about you."

Sarah pulled away. "You were the one with the gun to your ribs."

"I don't think that woman would have—"

"Mattie!" A man's voice came from the back of the tent. Sarah turned to see Mr. Charles Payne run into the tent. "Are you all right? Otis told me you were—"

"Otis?" Sarah's amazement doubled when the burly cart owner followed Mr. Payne inside the tent. "I would have thought you were long gone with your twenty dollars."

John shook his head. "Now, Sarah girl, don't go accusing a man before you've heard all the facts."

The reminder of how she'd done just that so often of late snapped her lips closed.

"Otis here was sworn to not say a word, isn't that right?" John patted Otis on the back. "However, it didn't keep him from driving so slowly a man riding a fast horse couldn't catch up to him at the edge of town and follow him to where he was taking you."

Shocked, Sarah walked closer to Otis.

"I took the job 'cause they said they was your friends and just tryin' to get you home to your pappy. Said you was touched in the head." Otis shrugged. "After you said you didn't want no help with that there tent a' yours. . ." Another shrug filled in his assessment of her mental capacity.

"Then why let John catch up with you?"

"Some a' the things they said about you made me suspicious. And they never said I couldn't say nothin' 'bout Miss Beal," Otis added. "Didn't know about that 'til I got you inside here. I'm right sorry, Miss Maffey.

A laugh bubbled through her chest and burst into full-throated bloom. She pulled the man into a quick hug, his distinctive odor no longer offensive. "Mr. Otis, since you don't much care what you haul in your cart, I will pay you two hundred dollars to take those four to the nearest jail."

Otis's mouth dropped open. "That's too much."

She squeezed his beefy biceps. "You saved me from a fate worse than death. Allow me to put the proper price on my gratitude."

Either out of shock or because he didn't want to give Sarah a chance to change her mind, Otis flopped his straw hat in place and ran out of the tent. Mr. Payne and Mattie, their arms wrapped around each other's waists, followed.

Leaving Sarah and John alone.

"That was kind of you." John tilted his head toward the tent flap. "Otis will be able to purchase land with that much money."

Sarah didn't know what to say. . .or where to look. She wanted to talk about the endearment, what it meant, or even *if* it meant anything. She needed to know what the green fire in John's eyes meant, too. Only a proper lady didn't ever bring up such an intimate subject.

Oh, who was she kidding? She stopped being a proper lady when she left Boston. She didn't want to ask because she was a coward.

"You called me 'sweetheart.'" John proved his bravery yet again.

She mustered every shred of courage. "You called me 'darlin'' first."

"Because that—I don't wish to disparage the term by calling her a woman, so let's just call her a female, shall we?"

Sarah chuckled at the reminder of his similar description of the men who'd surrounded her that first day in the land office tent. It strangled into a choke inside her tight throat.

"Because that female was talking about how she wanted you to have her leftovers." John shrugged a shoulder. "I wanted her to think you'd already replaced that no-account, miserable excuse for a man with someone better."

Disappointment stabbed her throbbing heart. She'd hoped it meant something else, something wonderful and too good for what she deserved. She wanted to run, get as far away from John Tyler as possible and how he was unknowingly crushing her heart. Only she'd done that once before. And, unlike with Trudy and Eugene, this time Sarah wasn't an innocent bystander in her pain. This time, she'd brought it on herself with her callous treatment of John.

She touched her ring finger to the corner of her eye before a tear fell. "That's what friends are for, right?"

"Friends?" John stepped so close she smelled the combination of earth and soap and strength she loved. "I didn't do it because I want to be your *friend*."

Sarah couldn't stop the tears. "Of course not. I ruined any hope of that when I accused you of—"

John's lips covered hers in a crushing kiss that stole the last breath from her lungs. She wrapped her arms around his neck, pulling him closer in case he let go. In case this was a dream. And in case her legs gave out. His kiss cleansed her, transported her, and made her weep with joy. Against everything she deserved, John Tyler loved her and was proving it with action instead of words.

Eugene had kissed her. Once. The day they got engaged. True to everything else, John Tyler's kiss was very anti-Eugene.

Very!

Becca Whitham (WIT-um) is a multi-published author who has always loved reading and writing stories. After raising two children, she and her husband faced the empty-nest years by following their dreams: he joined the army as a chaplain, and she began her journey toward publication. Becca loves to tell stories marrying real historical events with modern-day applications to inspire readers to live Christ-reflecting lives. She's traveled to almost every state in the United States for speaking and singing engagements and has lived in Washington, Oregon, Colorado, Oklahoma, and Alaska. She can be reached through her website at www.beccawhitham.com.

The Princess of Polecat Creek

by Kathleen Y'Barbo

Dedication

For Jack Jack

*I will lift up mine eyes unto the hills, from whence cometh my help.
My help cometh from the LORD, which made heaven and earth. He will not
suffer thy foot to be moved: he that keepeth thee will not slumber.*
PSALM 121:1–3

Chapter 1

East Texas
May 15, 1886

The Bible said to look to the hills because that's where our help comes from. Try as she might, Pearl Barrett could spy neither help nor any other sign of rescue among the forested hills of this part of East Texas.

Sliding her father a sideways glance, she reminded herself that in that same psalm, God promised that her foot would not be moved. To her mind, that meant she would stay right where she'd been born and raised until that stubborn Deke Wyatt finally came to his senses and asked her to marry him.

And yet here she sat in a fine railcar with all her worldly goods packed in trunks in the luggage car and a ticket marked Denver, Colorado. Worse, one of those trunks held her wedding dress.

Her best friend, Frances, or Frank, as she preferred to be called, had encouraged her not to lose hope. In Frank's last letter, she'd offered her own example of the benefit of waiting for the Lord to bring the man she loved to his senses. That might work for Frank, but Pearl was losing hope.

After all, she'd been quietly waiting for Deke Wyatt most of her life.

Offering up yet another prayer, she clung to the hope that the Lord was listening even as the train whistle blew and the conductor called a departure warning. Papa might think marrying her off to that Simpson fellow in Denver would be good for all of them, but the way Pearl saw it, the only improvement would be to her father's bank account.

"Sit still, Pearline," Mama said as she nudged her. "A lady does not fidget."

"A lady also does not marry one man when another holds her heart," she said under her breath, echoing the very words she'd written to Frank this morning.

"What's this?" Her father folded his copy of the *New York Times* and swiveled to face her. "Would you kindly repeat that?"

"Go back to your paper, dear. Our daughter is overcome with the excitement of this trip and the anticipation of her wedding. She's saying things that are quite ridiculous."

Mama gave Pearl a warning look with her eyes before offering Papa a smile. The elbow that had nudged her became a solid object wedged tightly against Pearl's ribs.

Despite this, Pearl repeated her statement. Frank would be proud that she'd finally stood up to Papa. Now to survive his response.

Kind eyes narrowed until Papa wore his most impatient look. "Don't be foolish, Pearl. Your life in Denver will be far better than—"

"But I don't want that life," she interrupted. "Just because you and Mr. Wyatt had a falling out, that doesn't mean I can't marry Deke someday like both families planned.

I'm sure he'd say that himself if he were here."

Her father instantly looked apoplectic. Rather than back down, Pearl stood her ground. Figuratively, of course.

"That boy hasn't given you or his father's ranch a second thought in years," he sputtered. "The minute Zebediah let that boy go off to Harvard like his mama's people, I knew he'd never be back. He's only come back to Polecat Creek Ranch to settle his father's affairs."

"May Zebediah rest in peace," Mama murmured beside her.

"Mark my words," he continued after giving Mama a nasty look. "He'll be off and gone before the ink has dried on the last document. That boy is as stubborn and as shortsighted as his father was."

Pearl shook her head and once again looked to the hills. Hills where the Wyatts' ranch was nestled. Then her father's words hit their target.

Deke was home. "Oh, Papa. You must let me out of this train. If Deke has come back, then he's come back for me. I'm certain of it."

"That is quite enough," Mama said.

"Indeed," her father echoed.

"But he promised," she insisted. "The last time I saw him he said. . ."

Pearl clamped her lips shut. What transpired between her and Deke Wyatt was not for her parents to know. Every moment of that last conversation, held beneath the stars at Polecat Creek Ranch, was committed to memory.

Everything from the way he teasingly called her Princess to the streak of a shooting star that lit the sky between them. She could recollect it all with complete accuracy.

Deke had smiled in that slow, lazy way he had, and he'd said something about making a wish. She'd been much younger then, just a girl of not quite thirteen whose main connection to the older boy was a shared love of horses and a family history that had been tangled up for years, but she'd known exactly what to wish.

I wish Deke would kiss me and then ask Papa if we can marry.

A bold wish for certain, especially since Deke was on his way to Harvard while she was barely out of the nursery. Of course, she hadn't meant right then. She could certainly wait until she was a more acceptable seventeen or eighteen, although the waiting would be absolutely awful.

"What did you wish?" Deke had asked.

So Pearl told him, not knowing how he would respond. To her surprise, he merely nodded. "Perhaps someday, Princess," he said. "For now you'll have to wait."

With her twenty-second birthday looming, she was still waiting. And the waiting was still awful. She'd just written her dear friend Frank about that very thing. The girls had become fast friends in their first year at Wells College, bound as they were by romances held in secret and love that was as yet unrequited.

Now that they were young women no longer bound by the schoolroom, it appeared Frank would be getting her wish. Pearl sighed. Perhaps someday she would as well.

"What did the Wyatt boy promise?" Papa demanded in that tone he usually reserved for his employees at the paper mill.

"Nothing of consequence," she told him as she pushed her reverie away. "I was a child, after all."

It wasn't true exactly; she hoped the answer would serve to soothe Papa's irritation. His expression quickly told her it had not.

"You were old enough," he snapped. "All those hours of horseback riding that your mother allowed while she visited over at the Wyatt ranch? Surely our trust in him was not misplaced."

Mama's expression told Pearl she wasn't pleased at being named in this manner. Her mother held her tongue. Pearl, however, could not.

Pearl squared her shoulders and straightened her backbone then looked her father in the eyes. "Those hours were spent exactly as you were told. Deke is an expert horseman. I love to ride, as you well know, and he was most informative in teaching me to be adept on horseback." She paused. "Now, Papa, I understand it is your wish that I marry your Denver associate, but I must know something first."

Her father's brows rose. "And what would that be?"

"Did Deke ever ask you for my hand? I know you've had some silly disagreement with his family, but when something is meant to be, those sorts of disputes mean nothing."

A deep scarlet flooded her father's cheeks above his whiskers. Rather than respond, he appeared to sputter. Pearl sat back and averted her eyes.

She'd truly done it now.

"Look at me," he demanded. When Pearl complied, he continued: "What transpired between me and Zeb Wyatt is none of your business, nor is it for you to determine the character of the disagreement between him and me. As to the eldest Wyatt boy, no, he never made a request of your hand. Nor will he."

Papa paused and took a deep breath then let it out slowly. "Now, you will answer honestly and immediately. Has the Wyatt fellow made any improper advances or contacted you in any way in these past few years? To the point, did he make any promises or compromise you?"

"He did not," she managed, her voice barely above a whisper as tears blurred the edges of her vision.

"And he will not." Papa's fingers fisted on his knees. "Just so I understand completely, did he pay you any visits while you were away at school?"

Again she had to admit the truth, though it stung. The main reasons she insisted on attending Mama's alma mater, Wells College in upstate New York, were its distance from Papa and its closer proximity to Deke Wyatt.

"He did not," Pearl said, though she would never tell Papa it was despite the fact she'd certainly invited him to do so in a letter sent to Deke at his grandfather's law firm.

Papa seemed to search her face as if looking for signs of deception. Finally, he nodded. "Then this discussion is at an end. The name of Wyatt will never be said in my presence again."

Her father gave her one more look and then picked up his paper. Mama, however, dug her elbow into the tender spot between two of Pearl's ribs and leaned in close.

"But why?" Pearl asked as tears shimmered.

Papa lowered the paper just enough so that his eyes were now on her. "Because it is none of your concern. Nod if you understand, and then do not speak again until you are spoken to."

Pearl nodded as she dabbed at her eyes with her handkerchief. She understood, all right.

However, believing she would actually be required to put on that dress and wed herself to a stranger nearly old enough to be her father was another thing entirely. And all because of some silly misunderstanding between Papa and Mr. Wyatt, Sr.

Mama pulled her elbow away as the train lurched forward. Pearl inhaled sharply and gave those hills one last long look as they disappeared from sight. If the Lord was going to do something, He needed to be quick about it.

And then, just like that, the train's whistle blew as the brakes squealed. Papa's brows rose. "Now that's strange," he said to Mama. "We've only just left the station. Why in the world would the train be slowing down?"

Pearl hid her smile as her parents moved toward the window and she headed the opposite direction. While her father exclaimed something about train robbers and Mama swooned, Pearl inched toward the exit. As the train lurched to a stop, she fled to the corridor. A few more steps and she found the door that led to freedom.

Gathering her skirts, Pearl climbed down the narrow metal steps. The distance to the ground was still a bit more than she liked, but she jumped anyway. Landing in a puddle of skirts, she scrambled to her feet, while on the other side of the train whoops and shouts echoed.

Only then did she realize the gravity of the situation. The Lord might have orchestrated her escape, but it appeared she had stepped right into the midst of a train robbery.

Without considering what a lady would do, she picked up her skirts and ran for those same hills where she'd expected her help to come from. With each step, the noise of the commotion on the other side of the train quieted just a bit.

Once she put the train and all its noise behind her, she found that the hills had indeed sheltered help. For right there tethered to a tree was a decent-looking horse and wagon that would make a perfect means of escape.

She knew just where she'd go. Just on the other side of the ridge was Polecat Creek Ranch. Wasn't it just like God not only to stop that train but also to drop her right at the edge of Wyatt land?

Pearl smiled as she worked at the knot. Last she heard, Deke had gone off to Washington, DC, to work at his grandfather's law firm.

Rumors swirled that he had been assigned to something important, some secret division of the government that aided the president himself. Papa called the statement rubbish, but Mama and her friends certainly passed along every juicy tidbit of the story with smiles and knowing nods.

Whatever he did in Washington notwithstanding, Pearl shouldn't be surprised that Deke came back when old Mr. Wyatt passed on last month. With things standing poorly between the Barretts and the Wyatts, Pearl hadn't been allowed to attend the service for the elderly rancher. However, she'd hoped and prayed that Deke had.

And that eventually he'd find a way to call on her.

She paused in her efforts to glance around and make certain no one had followed. As she went back to work on the knot, Pearl allowed her thoughts to return to Deke. It was madness that he'd come for her, of course, for Deke likely had some other woman's attention now. And yet, the Bible said the Lord would give us the desires of our hearts if we just continue to seek Him in prayer. So why not keep praying for the one thing she desired most?

Or rather, the one person.

The knot refused to budge, so Pearl went around to the back of the wagon in search of something sharp that might cut twine. A rustling sound in the brush caused her to turn and look.

Satisfied she was still alone, Pearl returned to her search. She spied what looked to be the handle of a saw sticking out of a box filled with tools and scrambled up into the bed of the wagon.

Pearl pulled the saw out of the box and declared it fit to cut the rope. The horse whinnied and stamped at the dusty ground as Pearl climbed down and retraced her steps.

"Hush now," she said as she set the saw down beside her and ran her hand across the nervous horse's muzzle. "I know you don't know who I am, but I'm just trying to cut that rope so you and I can pay a visit to the Wyatts over at the Polecat Creek Ranch."

"Step away from the horse, ma'am," a deep voice said from behind her.

The horse reared. Pearl stumbled backward. Bracing herself to land on the ground, instead she landed against a wall that turned out to be a man wearing a bandanna covering his face.

"I mean no harm," Pearl protested. "I was being held against my will on that train back there. The Lord provided a way for me to escape, and now I'm just trying to get to Polecat Creek Ranch. Will you help me, please?"

Four other men scrambled toward her through the brush and then stopped short. Dressed as if they were going into town rather than intent on robbing a train, all five of the train robbers were of average height and build.

Dark strands of hair could be seen beneath their hats, and four of the five had eyes the color of strong-brewed coffee. The fifth man's eyes were blue as the Texas sky.

Something in those eyes seemed slightly familiar. "Please, just help me escape and I won't tell anyone I've seen you," Pearl said.

"But you haven't seen us," the man nearest to her said as he adjusted his bandanna. The other four nodded. One added a soft, "That's right."

She surveyed the group and took note of a gun on each man's hip. The robber nearest her wore two.

"You are correct. I haven't seen you. In fact, I don't know you at all," she said as she tried to recollect where she had heard these voices.

Pearl dusted off her skirt and then turned her attention to Blue Eyes. "I would like to offer a deal. If you'll just see me as far as the Wyatt place, I'll trouble you no more, and I certainly won't let on as to how I came to arrive there."

"The Wyatt place?" Blue Eyes said as the others looked at one another.

"What business you got with the Wyatts?" the man nearest her snapped, his voice sounding strangely British and his palms now resting on his guns.

Pearl straightened her backbone and determined she would not be frightened. "Business meant to be kept private."

As she spoke, Pearl took a tentative step backward. The robbers circled closer, likely fearing she might bolt and run. If she thought she could get away, she might have made the attempt.

The better plan was to recruit these savages to assist her escape, but that looked doubtful as well. So she decided on a third option: bluffing.

"All right," she said as she moved toward the wagon. "I can see you're contemplating what to do. While you're thinking about it, I'm going to give you one last chance to help." She patted the side of the wagon and looked right into those blue eyes. "You there. Untie this horse so we can get going." Then she turned to the man nearest her. "I'll need assistance getting into the wagon. Would you mind?"

"Not at all," he said as he reached over to lift her into the back of the wagon. "The rest of you climb up and let's get out of here before someone finds us."

Pearl landed hard on her backside but bit back a response. It wouldn't do to upset the men, who were finally appearing to do her bidding.

Blue Eyes climbed up behind her and reached for the reins while one of the robbers made short work of untying the horse. The other three settled themselves in with two on either side of her and one blocking her exit at the back of the wagon.

The rope that had held the horse swung over Pearl's head and landed in her lap. "Tie her up," Blue Eyes demanded. "And do something to cover her eyes."

"There ain't nothing back here but a feed sack," one of the men said.

"Then put her in it," Blue Eyes said as the wagon jerked into motion, allowing Pearl a moment's chance to try and scramble away.

Despite her best efforts, it only took a few minutes before the ruffians had her hog-tied inside a smelly feed sack with a length of cloth in her mouth to muffle her screams. Pearl took some satisfaction in the fact that she'd managed to kick at least one of them hard enough to make him howl and her fingernails had drawn blood on another's arm.

"Hush up and we won't have to hurt you," one of the robbers told her.

"Aw, you know we can't hurt her, Eli," said the man holding her in place.

Eli. Blue Eyes. Five men of similar build and hair color.

Pearl stilled, a smile rising despite the rag in her mouth. The Lord had indeed sent help, and they had come from the hills. The hills of Polecat Creek Ranch where five of Deke Wyatt's brothers still lived.

And one of them, Eli, had the same blue eyes as his older brother Deke.

She rode in silence now, her mind attempting to work out why the five Wyatt boys might be trying to rob a train. She'd find out eventually, Pearl decided. For now, it was enough that she'd be seeing Deke soon, for he surely was still in town. If he'd gone already, Papa would have made sure to mention that fact.

Now to decide exactly how to make the most of this opportunity.

Chapter 2

Deke Wyatt knew something was wrong when all five of his brothers were waiting for him on the front porch when he rode in from town. Not a one of them ought to be sitting there at this time of day when there was work enough to keep them busy elsewhere.

"Eli," he called to the eldest of the group as he pulled back on the reins. "What's going on here? You boys get up off your rears and get to work."

"We got a situation, Deke," Eli said as he rose and walked toward the hitching post. "There's something you ought to know before you go inside."

He glanced past Eli to where his brothers still sat. Zeke had appropriated Pop's rocker, and Ben was sitting on an upturned wooden keg. The other two, twins Matthew and Mark, were leaning against the house with their legs stretched out in front of them.

No one had moved a muscle, nor were they smiling.

"What kind of situation is that?" Deke asked as he stepped down and tied up the reins.

"We got a woman in there," he said.

Deke straightened and glared at Eli. "You know how I feel about that sort of thing. We're God-fearing people. Get her out of there right now, and then I'll have the name of whichever one of you idiots thought this was a good idea."

"Keep your voice down," Eli said. "And settle yourself, brother. It's not like that. She's a good girl, and we only just brought her here a little while ago. We didn't know what else to do with her after she, well. . .we just didn't know what else to do."

He shook his head. "I don't follow."

"No, I don't suppose you do." He paused to look back at the other four then gestured to the twins. "I guess it all started when those two started jabbering about what it might take to stop a train. I stayed out of it until Matthew there declared he could stop a train with a stick. Well, I got to tell you, when he said that and told us he'd back it up with action 'cause he'd heard it was so from a farmhand over in Craddock who'd done it once before, I just had to find out if he was telling a tall tale or not."

Deke held up his hands. "Stop blabbering and get back to the reason you've got a girl in the house."

Zeke joined Eli. "She's not just in the house. We put her in Mama's parlor, right and proper."

"We ain't heathens," Mark added from his place on the porch.

"Aren't heathens," Matthew corrected.

"I think that gal in there might disagree," Ben said. "She did take particular offense to being tied up in that feed bag. I'm just glad we were smart enough not to talk in front of her so she don't know who's got her."

"Doesn't know," Matthew said as he dodged a blow from his twin.

Words he'd never say in front of a woman or a preacher rose in his throat, but Deke squelched them. "Where is she?" Deke managed as he calmed his temper just enough not to take a swing at the nearest brother.

"Like Zeke said, she's in Mama's parlor," Eli said to Deke's retreating back. "But the real question might be: *Who* is she?"

Deke stalled and grabbed for the porch post. Before he could respond, Eli jumped in front of him and opened the door.

"Trust me on this," Eli said, his voice a low whisper. "You won't believe it until you see. But a word of warning." He paused. "Don't get too close. Even with that blindfold, she's got pretty good aim."

Ben nodded as he rubbed his shin. Deke shook his head and pushed past Eli to step inside. One of the geniuses had closed all the curtains and moved the furniture up against the walls. He took two steps forward and slammed into Mama's breakfront.

"What the. . ." he said under his breath as pain radiated up from his knee and right elbow. With a shove, he moved the furniture back against the wall.

As Deke's eyes adjusted to the dim light, he turned on his brother. "Which of you idiots thought rearranging the furniture was a good way to pass time until I got back from town?"

"Ben thought a little preparation was in order in case someone tried to bust down the door and save her. Me, I couldn't see the logic in it, but it kept the others busy while we waited so I went along with it to keep the peace."

"That is the most ridiculous thing I've heard yet," he said as he made his way around three chairs that ought to have been in the dining room and a washstand that was missing its bowl and pitcher. "The same idiots who thought of this are going to put everything back where it goes. If someone comes for the woman, we'll greet them civilly. I'm sure you've all considered what you'll say to this person's family, haven't you?"

"Quiet now," Eli reminded him. "You don't want her to hear you coming. I wasn't joking about her aim. That girl is lethal. And, yes, we have thought of what we'd say, but there wasn't any kind of agreement. We just figured you'd handle it, what with you being all educated and a lawyer and such. Grandpa probably taught you just what to do when there's trouble, didn't he?"

The reference to the man who had made it possible for him to leave this place and seek his purpose in a bigger world than Polecat Creek Ranch was too much. Deke moved in close and grabbed Eli's throat.

"I'm not going to tighten my grip any more, but my fingers just might twitch if I don't get a straight answer. Nod if you understand."

He nodded. "I'd be obliged if that didn't happen, Deke. You're a might stronger than you know, what with you being all citified and everything."

"And you talk too much. Just tell me who's in our mother's parlor and I'll let you go.

No embellishing or offering opinion. Just a name. Understand?"

"Yeah, I do. See, I was going to tell you, but the others, they were against it. Said you'd be mad, but me, I thought you'd be mad anyway, what with Matthew and Mark and their harebrained bet to see whether a train would stop if—"

Deke tightened his grip only slightly, but it was enough to halt his brother's jabbering. "Just. A. Name."

"Princess."

Deke let go. "You threw a princess into a feed sack and brought her here? That doesn't make a bit of sense." Realization dawned. "Oh, I get it. This is all a big joke."

"I wish it was," Eli said. "See, we was all minding our own business and there she was trying to steal our wagon."

"A princess was trying to steal your wagon." Deke shook his head. "Just come clean and admit you're pulling my leg and I might not hurt any of you."

Eli took a step backward and collided with the same breakfront that had stopped Deke's progress. "Truly, I would love to tell you that, Deke, but it ain't so. She's in there right and proper."

"A princess," he said as he curled his fingers into fists.

"Well, of a sort," Eli said. "It's that Barrett girl you used to call Princess. Name of Pearl. Remember her? 'Cause she sure grew up pretty."

"Pearl Barrett tried to steal the wagon so you put her in a feed sack and brought her here?"

"That's the short version, yeah. But don't forget it was them twins that caused it, what with they stopping the train like they did."

"You're sticking with that answer?" Deke ground out through clenched jaws.

Eli stood a little taller, but fear now showed in his eyes. "I got to because it's the truth."

"This is not funny," he managed.

"No, Deke, it ain't."

Deke's temper sent him out the door and back into the yard. It was either leave or hit his brother square between the eyes.

His boot heels rang out on the stone path he and the other Wyatt boys had put down when they were just kids. He hadn't wanted to come back here after conducting the remainder of his business in town, but obligation sent him back on the trail home.

Thanks to these clowns and their ridiculous behavior, his obligation was over. They could pull their pranks on someone else because he wouldn't be darkening this doorstep for a long while. Maybe ever, if he could manage it.

Indeed, he could go back to Washington, DC, and the life he preferred with a clear conscience and the happy knowledge that his brothers were doing just fine without him.

Grandpa was right. He was meant for more than Polecat Creek Ranch.

Anger propelled him the rest of the way across the yard and onto his horse. He was about to ride away when a woman carrying a feed sack appeared on the porch.

"Not so fast, Deke Wyatt. I believe you and I have some unfinished business."

All the anger escaped along with his voice. All Deke could do was stare until finally he managed one word. "Princess?"

Deke hadn't seen Pearl Barrett since she was a gangly girl who liked to follow him around with stars in her eyes, but he'd know her anywhere. Despite whatever mistreatment his idiot brothers had dealt her, Pearl looked like she'd just stepped out of one of his mother's ladies' magazines.

Thanks to her upbringing, she'd always been fashionable. Her mama and daddy had raised her to find a man who would bring money where it was sorely needed. This much he'd learned from Mama, who'd had a letter from a mutual friend of the Barretts warning her that Pearl's family was looking to marry her off.

At the time, Deke had only given the news a passing thought. Now as he stood in close proximity to God's handiwork in crafting a gorgeous woman out of an awkward and bookish child, he tried to recall whether that search for a groom had concluded or was still ongoing.

"Princess?" He said it again, though he had no idea why, beyond the fact it used to make her smile. And the pretty lady on the porch was in dire need of a smile.

Not that he cared now, he reminded himself. She was probably in on the joke.

"Don't you 'Princess' me, Deke Wyatt. Get off that horse and get back here right now. You and your brothers have some explaining to do, and I'll not have a one of you running for help."

"I tried to tell you," Eli said as the rest of the Wyatt clan gathered behind him.

Oh, yes, Deke decided. She was definitely in on the joke.

Pearl paused to allow a sweeping and disdainful glance across the entire Wyatt clan. "Inside with the lot of you," she continued. "Your mother would be horrified to find that you've treated her home so poorly, so you'll be putting everything back where it goes, and I want all windows raised and the rooms aired out."

When no one moved, she clapped her hands. "This instant, if you please."

Though not a one of his brothers looked like they were pleased, they did exactly what she said, leaving him sitting on his horse in the midst of a dilemma. He could easily set off toward town and leave this whole mess to the ones who created it.

It didn't take a Harvard-educated lawyer to figure that out. And yet here he sat powerless to do anything but stare at the woman who wielded command over the men of Polecat Creek Ranch with an ease he hadn't seen since his mama fled to her family in Boston a decade ago.

The object of his thoughts returned her attention to him. "Are you daft?" she demanded.

The challenge in her voice was unmistakable.

"Or do you plan to ride away without looking back again? Again," she continued.

Deke had long ago learned to stop trying to guess what a woman was thinking, although the lawyer in him occasionally made the attempt. He dared a look and found her staring, hands on her hips and a light breeze lifting the ends of her hair. Her chin jutted up just so, as if daring him to answer.

"Good afternoon, Miss Barrett," he said in that tone he reserved for the most reluctant of witnesses. "I see my brothers have been up to no good. Or is their story of abducting you in a feed sack just another of their elaborate jokes? They're quite good at joking but not so good at anticipating the results."

"Nor apparently are you," she snapped. "Else you would have already removed yourself from that horse and would be standing right here on the porch."

She gave that order as if she expected him to carry it out. Oh, she had grown into a lively one. The girl he knew would never be so bold as to instruct him where and when to place his person.

"Well, now," he said slowly as he sorted through several responses. "I believe I'll sit right here until I figure whether you're in on this joke or not."

Well, that did it. He only thought her feathers were ruffled before. Now she looked positively livid as she threw down that feed sack.

"Joke? Do I look like I am amused?" Her hands crossed over that tiny waist of hers, and her toe went to tapping. Oh, but she was a beauty when she was angry.

Who was he kidding? Pearl Barrett was a beauty. Period.

And, no, she did not look amused.

Once again he thought of the marriage hunt that had so worried his mother. Whoever ended up with this spitfire was to be pitied.

She tilted her head slightly and a ray of afternoon sunshine slanted across her face. Perhaps *pitied* wasn't exactly the right word, for no matter what sort of orders her groom would be receiving, he would still be putting his boots under the same bed where that woman slept.

Deke shook off the thought and aimed his gaze at the blue sky overhead. Patience had never been one of the virtues the Lord bestowed on him, but it didn't hurt to ask for an extra dose of it right now.

So he asked. And he waited, but only long enough to hear his name being called yet again. And not in a particularly fond manner.

He shifted his attention in time to see Eli once again walk behind Pearl, this time carrying the washstand. He paused as if watching the interaction between them.

Half of his family tree might have originated on the best side of Boston, but the other half's roots were dug deep in Texas soil, Polecat Creek Ranch soil to be exact. That little woman might think she could order him around, but she was sadly mistaken if she thought he'd sit on this horse and ignore her shrewish behavior.

"If you're telling the truth about not playing any part in this situation—"

"Other than being the person stuffed into the feed sack, you mean? That, I will claim a part in, though I did not go willingly."

"That's the truth," Eli called. "She bit Ben on the hand, though she didn't draw blood."

She turned and said something to Eli that Deke couldn't hear. A moment later, Eli disappeared. Pearl returned her attention to him. "You were saying?"

"I was saying that if you're telling the truth, then we've got a situation that needs dealing with."

"Oh, I am, and you know it. And, yes, we do."

Deke took in a deep breath and let it out slowly. "All right, then. Given those facts, which I suppose I can agree with you on, there's something else you need to know before we commence dealing with the situation."

Her eyes narrowed. "And what is that?"

"I'll go where I want when I want, Miss Barrett. I am a grown man, and you are neither my wife nor my mother. This is my home, and you will not be ordering me around while your shoes are standing on Wyatt property. Do you understand?"

Her brows rose, and the prettiest pink color flooded her cheeks. For a second, Deke allowed himself the thought that perhaps he'd gotten away with his statement. That just maybe he'd silenced Pearl Barrett's rant.

"I understand you have been called to the porch where a serious discussion regarding our current situation needs to take place. However, you are still sitting on your horse. Apparently you've chosen to respond like a child when given instructions rather than as a grown man would."

That did it. He threw the reins aside and climbed off the horse, his decision made. Stalking toward the porch and the frustrating female, he spied his brother had returned and was once again watching.

"Move along," Deke demanded, causing Eli to at least move to a place where he couldn't be seen from the porch.

Deke stopped just a hair closer to Pearl than he ought to have. He could smell her lavender perfume and could just about count the few freckles that dared to dance across her pretty nose.

With one last wave of supreme irritation, he pushed away any thought of her feminine attributes. Or at least tried to.

"All right, Miss Barrett. I am on the porch. Now what?"

Chapter 3

Now what, indeed. Pearl hadn't thought that far ahead.

Yet here he stood, the man she'd been hopelessly in love with as long as she could remember. He was taller than she expected, and broader at the shoulder. In her dreams he was much more slender, likely owing to her faulty memory of their last meeting.

Sadly, she'd fallen in love with a boy but found a man had taken his place. This was not how things were supposed to happen.

She allowed her gaze to travel up the front of his shirt to meet his stare. Now she had done it. There was no mistaking Deke Wyatt was angry.

Furious even.

And rightfully so. She'd behaved horribly. Even as she said those awful things to her future husband, she'd known she sounded like an awful shrew.

Pearl shifted positions and moved slightly away from Deke. Surely the Lord didn't provide a way for her to escape that train only to have her end up here on a porch with a man who obviously did not know he was supposed to save her. She gathered up her wits and thought hard on how to fix this.

Or tried.

But he was standing so close. So very close.

So she looked to the hills. Where was her help?

"Miss Barrett," he snapped as he reached down to pick up the feed sack.

She straightened her backbone and looked him in the eyes. Beautiful blue eyes she'd long ago committed to memory. And she knew in that moment that she couldn't possibly let Deke Wyatt know that he was indeed saving her, though exactly how he would do that remained uncertain.

So she decided to ask.

"Mr. Wyatt," she responded in a similar tone. "This morning I was a passenger on a train, and now I am here. My father and mother have surely begun to worry. As the elder brother, what is your plan to remedy this situation?"

Of all the reactions she anticipated, a smile was not among them. Deke shouted for his brothers, and they piled out on the porch far too quickly to have come from anywhere but nearby.

"Eli, you hitch up the wagon, and the rest of you climb in the back. We're taking Miss Barrett back."

Pearl allowed Deke to lead her to the wagon, but with every step she searched her mind for a reason to stay at Polecat Creek Ranch a little longer. "Wait," she said when an idea occurred to her. "I can't be seen in the company of all of you looking like this."

Deke's gaze swept the length of her, and then their eyes met. "I fail to see a problem."

"Look at my dress. It's wrinkled and smells like the inside of that feed sack. And my hair? What the trip here didn't ruin, the ridiculous blindfold they put on me did. I simply cannot be seen like this, not after having been gone for hours."

"I think she's right," Eli said. "What with her being a young lady and all."

"I don't want to hear another word from you," Deke told him. "Or the rest of you."

He lifted Pearl up onto the wagon's seat and then walked around to the back of the wagon. "All right," he said to his brothers. "Just so I'm clear, the twins started a ruckus about being able to stop a train with a stick, and you all went down to the tracks to see if they could do what they claimed."

"Wasn't me who claimed that," the younger twin said. "See, I heard it, and—"

"Hush," Deke said. "Then you came back to the wagon and found Miss Barrett."

"She was stealing the wagon," Ben said. "So we figured we couldn't let her do that."

"I wasn't stealing it," Pearl said. "I just needed a way to escape from the train. And besides, I never got the rope untied."

"I'm pretty good with knots, aren't I?" Eli asked.

"You are," Pearl said. "Do you think you could teach me how to—"

"Stop talking," Deke said. "Am I wrong in saying that you tossed Miss Barrett in a feed sack and hauled her home with you?" The brothers nodded in agreement. "All right. Miss Barrett, is there anything you would like to add?"

Rather than say what she was thinking—that this truly was not how she envisioned her escape to turn out—she settled for a shake of her head. Then he turned his attention to her.

"I will have a truthful answer, Miss Barrett. Have you been harmed by any of these idiots?"

She glanced back at the wagon full of Wyatts and then back at Deke. "Other than the indignity of being stuffed into a feed sack and held hostage in a parlor, I have not been harmed."

"We do apologize for that feed sack," Eli said. "We panicked just a little, what with the folks from the train thinking we were trying to rob them and all."

"Apology accepted," Pearl said with a smile. "And though this isn't the current topic, please allow me to offer my condolences for the passing of your father."

His expression softened. "Thank you."

"I wished to attend the services, but. . ." She let the words fall between them, unwilling to offer a reminder of the feud that separated the two families.

"Back to the topic at hand. You said you were trying to escape the train. Why would you want to do that?"

She gave the question a moment's thought and decided against revealing too much of the reason she'd been on that train. "I was not consulted regarding the travel plans."

Silence fell between them. That response had certainly made her sound like a petulant child. Perhaps she should have given him a more detailed answer, but she just couldn't discuss her father's wedding plans with a man she had spent years wishing to wed.

"Then I know what I need to do." Deke climbed up beside her and took up the reins. They rode in silence until he passed the turn for the Barrett home.

"Hey, Deke," Eli said. "Where you going?"

"Town," was his curt answer.

"Not sure why you'd do that," Eli said as the other Wyatt brothers in the back of the wagon nodded their agreement.

"Deke," she said gently to the man whose shoulder touched hers. "If you drive this wagon through town, there's no telling who will see us." She touched his sleeve. "My reputation will be ruined."

Deke spared her a sideways look. "I will not let that happen."

"Thank you," she said.

So he would help her after all. Pearl's smile lasted all the way to town but disappeared when the wagon pulled up on a side street near the sheriff's office. "Stay right here," Deke told her as he climbed down and indicated for his brothers to follow him.

"Why, Deke?" Eli asked as his brothers nodded and asked similar questions. "I thought we were seeing to Miss Pearl."

"We are," Deke said as he opened the door and gestured for them to all step inside. "But first you fools need to have a conversation with the sheriff about that incident with the train."

The door slammed shut, leaving her alone on the wagon. At least Deke had thought not to park out front where anyone walking down the main street would see her. Pearl smiled. He was taking care of her, even in this small thing.

She held on to that thought as she heard a familiar voice. "I don't care what the sheriff says," Pearl's father shouted. "I will see justice."

"Justice will be done, dear," her mother said in that soothing voice she often took with him. "Just listen to what he says. That is all I ask."

Scooting to the edge of the seat, Pearl gently climbed down. She tiptoed over to peer around the corner just in time to see her mother's skirt disappearing into the sheriff's office.

Pearl leaned back against the brick wall and calmed her pulse. Whatever was happening inside that office, it couldn't be good. Not with Papa so riled up.

Of course, he was worried about her. Yes, that was it. He hadn't seen her since she left the train during its unscheduled stop. As soon as Deke explained what happened, Papa would be...

Pearl sighed. He would be furious. At her, of course. Especially after their disagreement regarding Deke on the train.

She glanced over at the unattended wagon and briefly considered making good on the attempt that had failed earlier in the day. But where would she go? Certainly not home and most certainly not to Polecat Creek Ranch without Deke.

So she climbed back up in the wagon. And she waited.

And waited.

Finally, the sheriff came ambling around the corner. "Miss Barrett," he called, "I'd be much obliged if you'd come inside with me."

She followed the sheriff then stalled at the door. Mama and Papa rose, and though her father remained in place, her mother rushed to embrace her. Deke and his brothers were nowhere in sight.

"We were so worried when you disappeared," Mama said against her ear. "So very worried."

"I'm sorry," she managed. "I didn't think of how you might feel when I—"

"Wife," her father said, "do gather your wits. We've got more important things to discuss than your worries regarding our delinquent daughter. Come back over here and try to remember you are a Barrett."

"Yes, of course." Mama let her go with one last long look and then returned to Papa's side.

"All right," the sheriff said as he leaned against the corner of his desk. "We've got a situation here, and I'm the one who's going to decide how it all turns out." He turned his attention to Pearl. "I've spoken to your father, and he says you were with him on the train and then disappeared when it was stopped by the Wyatt boys. Would you agree to that version of the story?"

"Yes," she said. "I agree."

"All right, then. I'll move on to the next part of the situation, namely, how we resolve all the laws that have been broken." He glanced over at Papa. "Your father and I are in disagreement. See, I don't believe you had any part in stopping that train, but he believes otherwise, owing to a conversation the two of you had right before it stopped on the tracks. So I will need the truth out of you."

"The truth?" she echoed as she tried not to shrink away under her father's angry gaze. "The truth is that I prayed for something to stop that train. That much I admit to. However, I had no idea how God was going to answer that prayer."

"And you'll swear an oath to that effect?" the sheriff asked.

"Yes," she said slowly, "I will."

"Good enough for me," the sheriff said. "What say you, Barrett?"

Her father's expression remained unchanged, though he offered a curt nod. "Yes, I do suppose I can agree that while she most certainly did not want to accompany her mother and me to Denver, she is not so impetuous that she would plan a train robbery to achieve this."

"Or a false kidnapping," the sheriff added.

At the word *kidnapping*, Mama let out a soft wail and dabbed her eyes. Papa patted her shoulder but otherwise barely blinked.

"I would never arrange a kidnapping," she assured Mama. "You have my word that when I boarded the train to Denver, my only plan was to pray that the Lord would intervene." She offered a weak smile. "And He did."

"And yet your reputation now has been ruined." Mama sank to her knees and dissolved into a fit of tears.

Papa lifted her to her feet and then helped her to the nearest chair. "See what you've done to your mother," he said to Pearl. "And though I have much to say on what you've done to my credibility with my esteemed business partner, we shall reserve that discussion for a less public venue."

"Credibility or bank credit, Papa?" Pearl snapped as her temper rose. "For I would assume your credit would rise with my arrival in Denver. He was paying you substantially, wasn't he?"

"You ungrateful child," her father said. "I only arranged a situation that would be the best for you."

"And for you," Pearl said. "I am very glad my heavenly Father arranged a better one."

Now she'd done it. The Barrett family secrets were never to be aired in public, and here she'd said things in front of the sheriff that hadn't needed to be spoken. "I'm sorry, Papa," she said, her voice contrite. "I should not have spoken so harshly."

Her father frowned and turned away. Mama grasped his hand, tears shimmering in her eyes.

"Let's get back to the goings-on of this morning. Is that what you're saying happened?" the sheriff said as he stood. "You said a prayer and the Wyatt boys showed up to rob the train?"

"I don't believe the Wyatts robbed the train. Stopped the train would be the accurate description," she said. "But, yes, the rest of your statement is accurate."

The sheriff crossed his arms over his chest and seemed to be considering her statement. Finally, he rose.

"All right, Barrett," he said to Papa. "I've heard enough. For all that those Wyatt boys have been prone to stupid decisions, especially the twins, I've never had any occasion to call them criminals. You've known them all as long as I have. Can you offer any evidence to the contrary?"

Papa looked as if he wished he could. Finally, he shook his head. "I cannot."

"Given the fact nothing was taken from the train, I cannot charge these boys with train robbery," he said. "Stupidity, yes, but not train robbery."

"But, Sheriff," Papa protested. "We agreed there would be compensation for my daughter's reputation. She was forcibly removed from a train and hauled away. It won't be long before the whole town knows this."

Pearl's heart sank. Where was Deke?

"Just hold on, Mr. Barrett. I'm coming to that part," the sheriff said as he turned to Pearl. "Way I see it, those boys kidnapped you and brought you back to Polecat Creek Ranch where you were kept against your will for a length of time with no female chaperone in attendance. Can you deny any of this?"

"I cannot," she said. "But nothing untoward happened. Once they removed me from the feed sack, that is, they were perfect gentlemen."

At the mention of a feed sack, Mama resumed wailing. This time Papa left her to her noise as he crossed the room to come face-to-face with the sheriff.

"If you've got a plan to repair this situation, I will hear it now. My wife is beyond distraught, and my daughter and her reputation have suffered greatly at the hands of the Wyatt brothers. What justice do you offer for this?"

"Miss Barrett," the sheriff said, seeming to ignore Papa, "I want you to understand that I have taken both your father's wishes and my need to keep the peace into consideration as I make my decision on what's going to happen here."

He glanced back at her father. "Because I'm the law here, I've got final say in the situation. However, I'd be much obliged if you'd agree now not to go against whatever I decide."

"I'm not sure I can do that, Sheriff," he said. "I'm a man of commerce, and as such, I do not agree to a deal until after I have heard it."

"Then this'll be a new experience, Barrett, because if you disagree with what I'm going to propose, then the alternative is that your daughter was acting with these Wyatt boys and not a victim. Do you want the whole lot of them, Miss Barrett included, to be charged with something? I guarantee that'll get around town fast."

Papa lifted his chin in defiance. It was a look Pearl knew well. Mama said she copied it when the need arose, but Pearl didn't think so.

"I thought you said you didn't have anything to charge those boys with."

"Changed my mind," the lawman said. "I think criminal mischief'll do to start. I'm sure the railroad company'll have some complaint about the delay, so I'll be factoring that in. Probably a fraud charge for falsifying a kidnapping. And I'm mightily aggrieved I had to investigate a false claim, so I'll tack something on for that, too. Might just come up with a few other charges once I set my mind to it."

"All right," her father said. "I'll agree to whatever you decide, with one qualification. I want my daughter's reputation unscathed. Do you understand?"

"Quite well," he said. "You know I've got a girl of my own, and while she's not of marriageable age yet, she will be someday. A reputation's a thing that must be protected until such time as a woman is wed."

"Well, at least we agree on that," Papa said. "So what's this plan of yours?"

The sheriff grinned. "Miss Barrett, you're going to get hitched."

Mama's crying and Papa's protests drowned out most of the sheriff's explanation, but Pearl managed to understand that there would be a jailhouse wedding with her as bride. She struggled to figure out just to whom she might be wed.

Surely the sheriff hadn't found some way to contact Mr. Simpson in Denver. That would be just awful.

The sheriff nodded toward the back hallway. "Now if you'll just pick out a Wyatt boy, I'll go fetch him out of the jail and let him know today's his lucky day."

"Oh, no, not a Wyatt," Mama said. "John, don't let her marry a Wyatt."

"Mama?" Pearl pressed past the sheriff to kneel beside her mother. "You know I've loved Deke Wyatt since I was a girl. I've prayed for this day, and now here it is."

Her mother looked her in the eyes and swiped a tear. "Your wedding was supposed to be a grand affair with all of society in attendance. Look where you are. It's just not right."

Pearl wiped away her mother's tears with the back of her hand and then mustered a smile. "It may not be what you wanted for me, but it is what I want." She turned to look at the sheriff as the odd thought occurred: what a surprising letter to Frank this would be!

"I'll marry Deke if he'll have me," she told the sheriff, suppressing a smile for the benefit of her mother.

"Oh, he'll have you," the sheriff said. "Just let me go fetch him. Might take a minute or two to explain things, but he'll have you."

"I won't have her," Deke said loud enough to be heard by the conniving woman and her family. "I don't care if you have to lock me away for the rest of my life, I will not be trapped into marrying anyone, especially not the Barrett girl."

"That's fine, then," the sheriff told him. "Looks like you and your brothers'll do a little time here in the jailhouse. Then the railroad company'll come and get you and take you up to where they're based. I forget. Is it Philadelphia? Boston, maybe? In any account, you'll likely stand charges there of delay of commerce and fraud, just to get started."

"Fraud?" Deke shook his head. "That's a serious charge, and you have no proof of it."

"Don't need proof, son. There's a whole bunch of people on that train who saw the Wyatt boys out there this morning. Now, while you all probably won't do more than five to ten years on the federal charges, that's enough time away to cause your law practice to suffer and the Polecat Creek Ranch to go to ruin." He shrugged. "But if that's how you feel."

Eli tapped the sheriff on the shoulder. "I'll marry up with her. She's right pretty."

"I'll marry her," Ben said. "She's feisty. I like a feisty woman."

The rest of the boys offered their opinions on why they should be the one to take the Barrett woman as a bride. Finally, the sheriff held up his hands to silence them.

"I'm sorry, boys, but the deal is Deke marries her or you'll be making yourself at home here until it's time to head off to the federal prison." He turned to Deke. "It's a shame about those young brothers of yours. They won't last long in the penitentiary. Anyway, what'll it be, son?"

"This is ludicrous," Deke said. "There are no statutes to back up the charges you're making, and no evidence to warrant a federal trial." Before the sheriff could lecture him on evidence and such, Deke shook his head. "However, I'd like to make a deal of my own. Let me go to jail and let these idiots go free. I may not be able to argue my way out of local charges, but I'd be happy to take my chances with a federal prosecutor."

"Nope. We've got a young lady out there whose reputation could be seriously damaged if word gets out she was kidnapped by five men and held against her will without a female companion to chaperone. Now, if the word gets out that she eloped, well, that's a whole other thing, now, ain't it?"

"Eloped?" Deke thought through several scenarios and then came to the only possible conclusion. The sheriff was right.

"You sure she only wants me?" Deke said. "As you noticed, any one of my brothers would be glad to marry up with her."

"I'm sure." He paused. "So I'll just let you be for a few minutes so you can make your decision. Just so we're clear, it's either marry Miss Barrett or the whole lot of you goes behind bars for a long time."

Deke felt a hand on his shoulder and turned to see Eli standing there. "I won't tell you what to do. The boys and me'll stand behind you no matter what you decide. However, I do not see anything wrong with marrying up with that Miss Barrett. She just might be what the good Lord thinks you need."

He let out a long breath and then nodded. There really was no other choice. Either he married Pearl Barrett or he risked ruining his brothers' lives and losing the ranch that his father worked so hard to build.

"All right, Sheriff," he called. "I will marry her, but I want the official record to reflect that I am marrying her under duress."

"Oh, shoot, son. There ain't going to be no official record of this. The only thing the busybodies in this town are going to know is that a young man who had been away from our fair city for a while pined away for his childhood sweetheart to the extent that he had his brothers stop a train to fetch her for him to wed. Now ain't that romantic?"

"It sure is, Sheriff," Eli said. "Can I be his best man? I mean, what with me being part of the elopement and all. I'd even be happy to claim I organized the elopement, if that will help."

As the other brothers began to argue over which of them would stand beside Deke as he was led to the slaughter, he leaned against the iron bars and wondered how he would explain this to his mother. And worse, to his grandfather.

The explanation that he was trading one prison for another was not far from the mark. The only difference was, in the prison to which he was going, he was the only man there.

And he would be shackled to Pearl Barrett for the rest of his life.

Chapter 4

That was possibly the fastest wedding I've ever attended. I can't wait to write Frank about it. Frank's my college friend. Frank is just a nickname, but, well, anyway, we've daydreamed about our wedding days, but never did I imagine mine would be like that."

Pearl slid a sideways glance at her new husband in hopes that he might respond with a nod or a smile. Or even a grunt.

Instead, he continued to stare straight ahead, his fingers gripping the reins so tight that his knuckles had long ago turned white.

"You know it's the funniest thing," she said. "I was just remembering how when I was just a girl you told me that someday you'd come back and marry me. And look at this. You did."

Silence.

"You called me Princess back then, and I always loved that. Of course, I was just a girl." She paused. "But then even a grown woman likes to think she's special. Not that I expect you to think that of me now. But maybe someday, when we've been married awhile."

No reaction.

Pearl sighed and looked away to watch the familiar landscape roll past. This was not what she envisioned when she and Frank daydreamed about their wedding days. She certainly hoped Frank would fare better. Considering Frank's situation, there was a good chance her fairy-tale wedding would actually happen.

She stewed on that fact just long enough to realize that no matter how it had come to be, she was indeed married to Deke Wyatt. If a big beautiful wedding with all the trimmings was her goal, then she shouldn't have been so upset about the arrangements Papa made with Mr. Simpson. That certainly would have been quite the social event.

Oh, but the marriage that followed any wedding was much more important. She hadn't been able to imagine a life with Mr. Simpson, but Deke? Yes, indeed, they would have a fine life together.

Just as soon as he stopped being so grumpy about marrying her.

She decided right then to be a good wife and cheer him up. "I will need to know all your favorite meals so I can learn to cook them."

Silence.

"And I must know whether you like your coffee black or with something more like sugar or milk."

Nothing.

All right. She would try another topic. "Your brothers certainly looked surprised when you told them they had to walk back to the ranch tomorrow after they stay the night in jail. I don't think they expected that."

"Nor did I expect a few things that happened today," he muttered.

Success. He spoke!

"Nor did I," she said. "I was sitting in the railcar heading for Denver and. . ." Pearl let the words hang between them, unwilling to talk about her near miss with marriage to another man. "Well, anyway, I had one plan this morning, and the Lord changed that right quick, didn't He?"

Deke snorted and shifted positions but never spared her a glance. "You think the Lord did this?"

Her heart lurched. Surely Deke still believed in God and the power of prayer. "I know He did. I asked Him to." She hesitated. "You do still believe in God, don't you?"

"Yes, I do, which is why all of this makes no sense." Deke pulled back on the reins to slow the wagon and then looked her direction. "You mean to tell me you set off this morning to marry me? That certainly explains the way I was railroaded into this."

In any other situation, Deke's pun, however unintentional, might have been funny. At this moment, it was not.

"*You* were railroaded into this? Did you not notice that *I* was also given no choice?"

His expression remained stony. "What I noticed was that you didn't seem too unhappy to be taking my name when the sheriff fetched the preacher. I also noticed it was me you picked out of the lot of us. Any one of my brothers would have been proud to marry up with you and call you his wife."

"But not you," she said, her feelings a jumble of anger and hurt.

Rather than respond, Deke slapped at the reins and set the wagon in motion again. His lack of answer was all the answer Pearl needed.

"Look," he finally said, "I have no desire to hurt you, but I am a busy man. My Washington practice is just getting started and I have no time for a wife. I really had no time to come back here and handle my father's affairs, but my grandfather insisted, so he sent someone from his firm to cover my work until I return."

"I see."

"No," Deke said, "I don't think you do. I'm losing more of what I worked so hard for with every day that I am not there to see to the firm. This marriage is just one more complication."

"So I am a complication," she said, anger rising slightly over the pain she felt at Deke's attitude. "Then I shall prove you wrong."

Deke's laugh held no humor. "Go ahead and try, Princess, but I do not hold out much hope for success. I was forced to marry you, but I am not forced to bring you with me when I leave."

He turned the wagon down the road leading to the Polecat Creek Ranch. Off in the distance she could see the home and lands she had married into.

"Wherever you go, I will go, too, like it says in the Bible."

"That verse wasn't meant to refer to a husband and a wife," he said.

"All right," she said. "What about this one: 'And unto the married I command, yet not I, but the Lord, let not the wife depart from her husband.'"

When he ignored her, Pearl tried again. "'Therefore shall a man leave his father and his mother, and shall cleave unto his wife: and they shall be one flesh.' Or this one: 'Husbands, love your wives, even as Christ also loved the church.'"

"All right," he said as he held his hand up to silence her. "I get the idea. In my absence you've become a Bible scholar."

"Hardly," she said as she smoothed her skirts. "But I did attend university. You might recall I sent an invitation for you to visit Wells College on one of their open houses?"

"I do not," Deke said. "To what address did you send this invitation?"

"To your grandfather's law office," she said. "I assumed it would reach you."

"It did not," he said as he urged the horses on. "Tell me about this education of yours."

She smiled. "The usual classics, of course. And the Bible."

"As I guessed."

Pearl nodded. "Along with mathematics and sciences. I especially enjoyed my courses in astronomy and languages."

For a moment, Deke looked surprised. Then his expression returned to something akin to neutral. "That is impressive," he finally said, almost grudgingly.

"Father wasn't pleased that I had chosen to study so far away, but since Mama was an alumnus, she was quite supportive."

"Well, of course." His steely tone had returned.

"What does that mean, Deke?"

He shrugged. "Probably not a discussion best held on our wedding day, my dear."

Had he not used such a sarcastic tone when he called her that endearment, Pearl might have been slightly encouraged. Instead, she sank lower on the bench.

"Considering the situation, I don't see how any discussion will make the day any worse."

"Point taken," he said as he nodded toward the ranch house. "But we no longer have to carry on any sort of conversation, because we've arrived. Welcome home, Mrs. Wyatt."

The piles of legal documents on the corner of his father's desk kept Deke busy for more than an hour after their return to Polecat Creek Ranch. With his grandfather's political aspirations, it was more important than ever for the firm to make a good impression should they manage an introduction to the new president once he took office.

He was halfway through the text of a Supreme Court decision on *Hollister v. Benedict & Burnham Manufacturing Company* when he felt someone watching him.

Pearl stepped inside the door and then made her way toward him. Deke couldn't help but notice she walked with a confident shyness that was both appealing and intriguing.

"What are you reading?" she asked as she settled onto the chair on the other side of the desk.

"A Supreme Court decision regarding a bill in equity to enjoin the alleged infringement of letters patent," he said as he leaned back in his father's chair to await her purpose in interrupting him.

"Was it reversed or affirmed?" At his surprised look, she smiled. "What? I know a thing or two about the law."

"So you do," he said. "It was reversed."

She nodded. "And do you agree with the reversal?"

"I haven't read the case thoroughly, so I am withholding judgment." He paused. "I have a lot of work to catch up on and a short time to get it done. My grandfather has an important meeting in a few weeks, and I've been charged with accomplishing a few critical things beforehand on his behalf. Is there something you wanted?"

"Actually, I was hoping I might divert your attention and have you accompany me on a short ride. I would go alone, but I don't have my riding boots with me and I hesitate to go far alone and without being properly attired for riding."

"Yes, I can see the problem with that." He glanced down at the paperwork and back at Pearl. "I shouldn't."

"Probably not." She cast her gaze downward and then slowly lifted her attention to him once more. "I'm sure I can manage, then."

"You could wait for one of my brothers."

"I could," she said, "but you made sure they wouldn't be home until tomorrow."

"Yes, I did." He let out a long breath. The two of them would be alone the rest of the evening.

And tonight.

What was he thinking?

"All right, then," Deke said as he rose and stretched out his back. "I don't suppose it would hurt to leave this work briefly, but we will take the buggy."

"But you know how I love to ride the ranch horses," she protested.

"When you've assembled the proper clothes to ride, then you'll ride. Until then, it's either the buggy or I go back to my work."

A slow smile began, and as it blossomed Pearl looked even more beautiful. He almost forgot how irritated he was that she'd chosen him of all the Wyatt brothers. Worse, he was actually happy for the interruption from his work.

The feeling terrified him.

Rising abruptly, he made his way around the desk and out into the hall. "I'll harness the horse."

A short while later, they were seated in the buggy and headed toward the ridge. "I look to the hills," Pearl said. "It is where my help comes from."

Deke nodded. "You like the Bible references, don't you?"

"Don't you?" she countered.

"Sure, I do," he said, "although I haven't found as much need to use them in conversation as you have."

"Then perhaps you're talking to the wrong people." She shrugged. "Or just having the wrong conversations. Do head toward the hills, please."

"It's a good long distance, Pearl. We'll be lucky to get there and back before dark."

His companion grinned. "I'm willing to try if you are."

"You always were a daredevil," he commented as he flicked the reins and urged the buggy forward. Pearl's laughter trailed behind them and curled up in his heart. He remembered that laugh, but that had been so long ago.

After a few minutes, Pearl nudged him. "Let me take the reins, please."

Though he argued with her, his opposition was halfhearted at best. He knew Pearl could handle a buggy. He was the one who'd taught her.

"Just don't get us killed," he said as he handed the reins over to her.

It had been years since Pearl felt the wind blowing in her face and the feel of a buggy racing across the open prairie. For too long she'd been so occupied being prim and proper to gain her parents' approval, so busy learning her lessons at college and at the hands of her deportment tutor, that she had forgotten how to have fun.

And this was fun.

She let out a whoop that stunned her new husband. "What?" she demanded.

"Oh, nothing," he said with a grin. "I just didn't expect you to. . ." He shook his head. "Well, you just seem like you've grown up to be a lady who doesn't. . ."

"Doesn't whoop?" She laughed and urged the buggy around a tight curve between two rocks with an expertise that had never left her. "That would be a sad lady."

"I see," he said, his fingers gripping the edge of the seat so tightly that his knuckles were white. "May I suggest you slow down a little, or you will be a sad lady when you turn the buggy over and land us down there in Polecat Creek. I've been baptized once in that creek, and I am not of a mind to do that again today."

"Don't be silly," she said as she cleared the curve and set the horses moving faster once again. "It's just a little hill and we're almost to the top."

"And it's just a big creek and we're pretty close to landing in it."

Once they reached the thick trees at the top of the hill, Pearl slowed the buggy down to a more reasonable pace. "See," she said. "We've arrived and all in one piece with no creek water anywhere on us."

Deke pulled out his handkerchief to dab at his forehead. "Just a little perspiration from worrying whether I would live to see another day."

She nudged his arm with her elbow and then handed the reins back to him. "It's beautiful up here. I'd forgotten how much I like the view."

Before Deke could help her, Pearl climbed out of the buggy and walked toward the precipice that looked down over the valley on the other side of Polecat Creek Ranch. The sun was already trailing deep orange colors toward the horizon, but Pearl felt no need to hurry back to the ranch house.

Not when the rest of the evening would likely pale in comparison to this moment.

She glanced back at Deke, who appeared to be watching her closely. Or would it?

Surely her husband wouldn't want to, well. . . Heat rose in her cheeks as Pearl contemplated the fact she was, indeed, well and truly married to Deke.

She was officially Mrs. Deke Wyatt, with all the responsibilities that went along with that new name. Though she'd had a cursory education in what to expect on her wedding night, she and Frank hadn't discussed that part of their wedding plans in much detail.

It was all too embarrassing.

She sighed. She did so want little Dekes and Pearls running around. And truly the fuss Deke was making about their forced marriage would end soon enough and he would assume his full role as husband.

Thus, she needed to be prepared.

"Something wrong?" Deke called. "You look like you've seen a ghost."

The only way to learn anything was to practice. She'd proven adept at horsemanship because she'd ridden horses.

She marched toward the buggy. Without offering a word of warning, she kissed her husband on the lips. Though she had no idea what she was doing, she felt she pulled off the maneuver quite well.

Until she ended the kiss and saw the look on Deke's face.

"What?" she said.

Deke seemed incapable of response. Slowly he released his grip on the reins and scooted to the other side of the bench then climbed down.

With the entirety of the buggy's seat between them, Pearl let out a long breath and closed her eyes. Searching her mind for what she knew of kissing, she replayed the event in her head. Perhaps she'd done something wrong.

Something to cause Deke to dislike her even more.

"Pearl," Deke said, causing her to open her eyes, "I'm going to help you into the buggy now."

She nodded as he made his way around the back of the buggy, still trying to figure out where her kiss went wrong. "So was it my technique or perhaps the length of the kiss that was at issue?" she asked him.

Deke placed his hands at her waist and lifted her into the buggy without comment. A moment later, he took his seat and reached for the reins.

"Just as it was when you were teaching me to ride a horse, I need to know what I am doing wrong before I can learn to do it right."

She watched for a response and thought perhaps Deke might speak. Instead, he turned the buggy around and headed down the hill.

It didn't take long for the hills to fall behind them. With nothing but flat prairie between the buggy and the ranch house, Deke allowed the horses to find a brisk pace.

"Now who is the daredevil?" Pearl demanded when the buggy hit a rock and she almost tumbled out.

He halted the buggy and turned toward her. "Are you hurt?"

"I'm fine," she managed. "But I, too, have been baptized in that creek. Unlike you, I think it might be great fun to go swimming there again, though perhaps not in the only dress I have with me."

"I'm sorry. I should have been concentrating on the trail and my mind was elsewhere."

"On *Hollister v. Benedict & Burnham Manufacturing Company?*" she asked with a grin.

"No."

"Then perhaps you were thinking about our kiss?"

"Perhaps," he said tersely.

"About that." Pearl touched his sleeve. "I apologize for my lack of wifely knowledge, but I will improve." She paused. "With the proper instruction."

She thought she heard Deke groan as he resumed their travel toward the ranch, this time at a slower pace. He stared straight ahead as if his neck no longer turned. Once again, his knuckles were white.

When Deke stopped in front of the ranch house, Pearl shook her head. "Go on to the barn and I will help you with the horse like I used to."

Deke seemed to consider this a moment then nodded, and off they went. After taking care of the horse together, they walked back up to the ranch house. Just as Pearl stepped onto the porch she turned to look up at the stars.

"I forget how pretty the stars are out here," she said. "With all the gas lamps Papa insists on burning at our home, I can hardly see them."

Standing on the step below her, Deke turned to look up into the sky. She followed his gaze in time to see a star fall.

"Oh, Deke," she said, her breath catching. "Did you see that?"

He turned back around and nodded but said nothing.

"It's just like the night so long ago when you told me you'd come back to marry me." She paused. "And now you have."

Rather than respond, he walked past and took his pride and those awful growing feelings of caring for Pearl Barrett with him. He couldn't speak about either.

No, he wouldn't.

Chapter 5

Deke almost felt bad ignoring his new wife on their wedding night. She'd been petulant since their conversation under the stars, not that he blamed her. He hadn't wanted to marry her, and he wasn't a man given to false pretense.

Then there was that kiss. He groaned once again at the thought of her lips pressing against his. Of the way her amateurish attempt had put a fire in his blood despite her lack of practice.

And worse, of the fact all he could think of was taking her up on her request to teach her the wifely skills in which she felt she was lacking. Deke's greatest fear, however, was that Pearl wasn't lacking at all in that department.

Concentrate, he admonished himself.

Grandfather's last letter indicated he had a good shot at a meeting with the newly elected president. He'd demanded Deke put in extra hours of work on the firm's cases in order to show the president just what an impressive job they could do.

Unfortunately, he'd been too busy to do anything else. And now he was too distracted to give the papers in front of him more than a cursory glance.

He gave up on *Hollister v. Benedict & Burnham Manufacturing Company* and set it aside in favor of the next assignment on the long list he needed to address.

"I'll have my dinner in here tonight," he called to her as he returned his attention to the mountain of legal papers he'd brought with him from Washington, DC. He'd been so involved working out all the details of his father's estate that he'd only just cracked open the valise that contained them.

After a while, Deke's stomach growled, and he realized Pearl had not yet brought his dinner. He called her name and waited then called her again.

When she did not respond, he went looking for her. The kitchen was dark, as were all the public rooms. He thought about calling her name and then decided against it when he spied a light coming from beneath a door at the end of the hall.

How had she known, of all the rooms in the ranch house, which one was his?

Deke halted in front of the door, which was open slightly. Pearl was curled up in a chair in the corner, a pen and paper in hand and a quilt wrapped around her. Her hair was undone and tumbled around her shoulders in the lamplight as she scribbled on the paper.

His heart jumped to his throat as he took in the sight of this beautiful woman. His wife.

John Barrett's daughter.

The thought was enough to sober him. Deke turned around and walked away, grabbing a blanket and pillow from the room next to his. In a few days he would leave her quietly and go back to his life in Washington, DC. The only fair thing to do was spend tonight and every night until he left out in the bunkhouse.

But as he tried to get comfortable on the straw mattress, all he could think of was how he realized he had missed Pearl Barrett. True, he'd teased her and called her Princess, but he had also enjoyed matching wits with her and teaching her to ride and rope.

Deke smiled. She'd been better at roping than he had. He wondered if she'd kept that practice up and then quickly discarded the idea. An educated and cultured woman like Pearl Barrett hadn't the inclination to rope cattle when she could sip tea in a parlor instead.

Though he awoke the next morning hungry, sore, and picking straw out of his hair, at least he'd done the right thing. Pearl was his wife in name only, and that's how it would remain.

Having gone to bed without supper, he was starved this morning. By the time he got the stove lit and the eggs cooked, Pearl wandered in. "It appears I have married a man who can cook."

Though she was beautiful in the lamplight, Pearl Barrett was stunning in the morning sunshine. She padded across the kitchen in her bare feet with that same quilt from last night draped around her shoulders. Her hair was a tangled mess, and yet his fingers itched to reach out and touch the glossy curls.

"I never learned to cook," she said as she reached for the plate of eggs and scraped a third of them onto a smaller plate. "I look forward to learning from you. Will you teach me?"

Her pleading look almost melted the heart he'd decided would remain cold. Deke turned away to grab two forks and then handed her one. "I'm sure that won't be necessary."

She shrugged and the quilt fell away from her left shoulder. Her skin was pale, a luminous ivory that made him take a step back for want of running his hand over it.

While he stabbed his fork into the eggs and attempted a bite, Pearl took her plate and wandered out, oblivious to the state she'd left him in. When Deke heard the front door open and then slam shut, he followed her in spite of all good sense.

She'd found the rocker and settled herself onto it. Deke walked past her to sit on the steps. They ate in silence until Deke pushed his empty plate away and swiveled to face her.

"Legally this is your home now," he told her. "So you're welcome to stay once I've gone."

"Thank you," she said.

Thank you? That was all? Had she come to her senses after a night under his roof? Deke could only hope.

"All right, then," he said instead of questioning her any further. Better not to ask what had caused her to stop arguing about accompanying him north.

Something caught his attention on the horizon, and he rose to get a better look. "Seems like the boys have hitched a ride with someone," he told her. "Best get some decent clothes on."

"My decent clothes are in trunks down at the train station," she said. "Remember you told my father you'd have them sent."

He had said that, then in his anger and hurry to leave town, he'd elected not to fetch them. "Do your best with what you have, then," he told her. "I don't know but there might be something left over from when my mother lived here. Her trunks are in the room next to the one where you slept last night."

"Yes, that's where I found this nightgown. It's lovely, don't you think?"

"I try not to think when it comes to nightgowns," he said, though the quip sounded much less witty out loud than when he'd just thought it.

She rose slowly and set her plate on the porch rail. He couldn't help but notice that she'd barely touched her food.

"Don't like my cooking?" he asked.

Pearl shook her head. "It's not that. I'm sure the eggs were delicious, but I just don't have much of an appetite this morning."

He couldn't speak to that fact, but he could urge her to hurry. "Whatever wagon's bringing those idiots is moving fast. I'd suggest you do the same, or you're going to get caught in your nightclothes."

She collected her plate then walked toward him; he assumed to gather up his plate. Though surely this woman wasn't a practiced flirt, she certainly had his attention as her elbow brushed his arm. Once again the quilt fell just enough to bare her shoulder.

As she reached for the plate, she seemed to think better of it and looked up at him instead. Using the corner of the quilt, she reached up on tiptoe to swipe at the corner of his mouth.

Then, with one hand gripping his biceps, she smiled as she let go of the quilt. "Thank you for cooking breakfast. I slept quite well in your bed."

She turned to grab his plate before disappearing inside with the quilt trailing behind her like a regal queen. Or a princess.

The princess of Polecat Creek came to mind, but Deke was powerless to do anything but nod, even though Pearl was long gone before he managed it.

Shaking off whatever it was that had him acting like a fool, Deke turned to face the brothers who would be arriving back on his doorstep any minute. Their doorstep, he corrected, because he would be gone soon.

As the wagon neared, he spied a familiar figure seated beside Eli. "Grandfather?" he called as he stepped out to greet the wagon. "What are you doing here?"

"I had business in New Orleans and thought to take the train out here to join up with you for the trip back to Washington, DC. My railcar is waiting at the siding in town, and I've been told a train will be coming through in a few hours. The car will leave with that train, and you will leave with me." He paused. "Unless you've got something keeping you here."

"What? No, the estate has been settled, and I was planning to leave in a few days. I suppose a few hours works just fine."

He watched his grandfather climb down from the wagon and marveled at how a man of his age whose livelihood kept him indoors never seemed to age. True, his hair had grayed, but he was still fit and strong, and his senses were just as finely tuned as when Deke was a child.

Several of his brothers piled out of the back while the rest of them waited their turn. Eli nodded a greeting and then headed off in the empty wagon toward the barn. Meanwhile, the rest of his brothers let their grandfather take the lead as they all headed toward the house.

Rather than shake hands, as was their custom in the law office, Grandfather enveloped Deke in a hug as the other Wyatts hurried past them in silence. "It's good to see you, boy. The firm misses you, and so do I."

"And I have missed the firm." Deke paused to smile. "And you."

Deke opened the door to invite his grandfather into the ranch house, and a thought occurred. For a man whose five grandsons spent the night in jail and the sixth one spent the night—theoretically—with his new bride, he was acting awfully calm.

"Grandfather," he said slowly once the older man had settled himself on a settee near the front windows. "Did you and the boys happen to have any sort of discussion on the way out here?"

"Oh, about their great train adventure and their night in jail? Yes, of course, we did," he said as he rested his palms on his knees. "Didn't bother me much. I figure to leave boys to their youthful folly, don't you think?"

"Youthful folly?" Deke shrugged. "Yes, well, I see your point. My guess is they won't be stopping trains again anytime soon."

"Yes, that's true," Grandfather said. "And I reinforced that fact with a promise that should they determine another train needed stopping, they should be more afraid of me than any small-town sheriff." He paused. "Now, as for you, Eli said you had some news for me."

Eli appeared at the window behind their grandfather, his grin easily seen even from this distance.

"So they didn't tell you what that news was?" Deke asked, ignoring his brother.

"Well, the twins tried, but the rest of them decided it was better if I heard from you. Or at least that was the consensus." He shrugged. "So shall we talk here or in your father's study where we might be afforded a bit more privacy?"

Given the fact three other faces had joined Eli's at the window, Deke's choice was simple. "The study," he said as he ushered his grandfather down the hall to the room that had become his office in his father's absence.

Without asking, Grandfather settled into the chair behind the desk as if he owned the place. "All right, Deke. What have you done?"

"Well," he said as he contemplated just how to break the news. "I saved the boys from the penitentiary, for one thing. And possibly myself as well, or so the sheriff said. But then you probably heard that part already."

"As we've already discussed, I have heard their versions but want to hear yours as well."

He took a deep breath and let it out slowly. What was it about his mother's father that made him feel like a child again every time he was forced to carry on a difficult conversation with him?

"You see," he began, "the railroad company was likely to press charges, and there seemed only one simple solution to it all, I mean, given the fact that. . ."

Deke's words stalled. "Oh, this is ridiculous. I am a grown man. I don't have to justify the decisions I make."

"No, generally you do not. However, I wonder if what you are about to tell me might be the exception to this?"

"It might," he admitted, "but what's done is done. I got married yesterday." He paused. "To Pearl Barrett."

"Barrett!" It came out like an explosion as Grandfather slammed his fist on the desktop and sent a stack of paperwork flying. "What on earth possessed you to marry the daughter of that man? You and I both know how your mother will react."

"How will she react, sir?" a feminine voice asked.

Deke whirled around and found Pearl standing in the doorway. She'd somehow managed to don a gown of pale pink sprigged with tiny roses, and she'd tamed her hair into a braid that she'd coiled at her neck. Once again, he found himself speechless.

"Well, hello, Miss Barrett," Grandfather said tersely.

"Mrs. Wyatt," she corrected, albeit with more gentleness than his grandfather deserved. "It's good to see you again, sir. I believe I was just a child the last time you visited the ranch."

Grandfather's eyes traveled the length of Pearl and then settled on her face. "Indeed, that must have been some time ago, for you definitely are no longer a child. That being said, you are a woman and this conversation is for men only."

Pearl's expression told him she did not take kindly to the remark. Heading off an argument he had no patience to hear, Deke stepped between Pearl and his grandfather to escort his wife out into the hallway.

"Go," he said quietly as he blocked the doorway.

When she opened her mouth to protest, Deke shook his head. "Yesterday you quoted several Bible verses to me regarding marriage. I've just got one for you right now."

She looked up at him, eyes narrowed. "What would that be?"

" 'Wives, submit yourselves unto your own husbands, as unto the Lord. For the husband is the head of the wife,' " he quoted from the book of Ephesians. "Now go, please."

Without waiting for Pearl's response, Deke stepped back into the study and closed the door. When he turned around, his grandfather was watching him with an expression he couldn't quite identify.

"At least you know how to handle her," Grandfather said. "Your father never could manage that feat with your mother." At Deke's stunned look, he continued. "He let my daughter go off and leave him here by himself. He ought to have come after her, but he didn't, and we both know why."

"He told me that they agreed he wasn't cut out for city life and she never adjusted to life on the ranch." Deke paused. "But I recognize things must have been difficult after John Barrett's dirty business dealings came to light."

"*Difficult* is a kind word for the situation Barrett put them both in. Had your mother not been in possession of a sizable bank account of her own, this ranch would have gone to the taxman years ago."

"And I am very glad it has not," Deke said. "Keeping the ranch in the family is precisely why I accepted the sheriff's offer. I doubt my mother would bail it out a second time."

"Yes, doubtful indeed. But your father should never have left you boys in this situation, although I must admit Eli and the others have done an excellent job of making the business profitable again."

"How do you know that?"

"As head of this family, I still see the banking reports, Deke. Still, I cannot stress enough that making the wrong match, as I have always maintained your mother did, never ends well."

Grandfather continued to complain about Father while Deke crossed the room to take a seat across from the desk. Though he was relieved at the temporary change of topic, Deke knew it wouldn't take long for Grandfather to get back to discussing the current situation.

"Enough of that. The child should not have to listen to a recitation of the sins of his parents, yes?" He swung his gaze back to Deke. "I believe you were explaining your reasoning behind this disastrous situation we now face."

"We, sir?" Deke asked. "Because although I mean no disrespect, I fail to see how my marriage affects you beyond having to listen to my mother complain about it."

"Oh, that's rich. You're the one I've groomed to take over my firm. I cannot have you ruin what I have worked so hard for by marrying the wrong person. We are this close to getting a meeting with the new president. Do you think he will want to consider me for a cabinet appointment given the reputation of your new wife's family?"

Deke shifted positions. "I don't disagree that there was very little thought put into this marriage beyond saving my brothers, the ranch, and my position at your firm, but it's done now. What comes next is to assess how to deal with the situation. As to the president, I'm sure he has more important things to do than listen to gossip and worry about one man's poor business decisions."

"Facts, not gossip, Deke," he said. "And, yes, I believe the president is kept informed on all the details of those he is considering for office. The man who made those poor business decisions, as you call them, not only bankrupted your father, but he also may be covering up serious financial misconduct of a criminal nature."

This much Deke had already considered. More than one of the documents on the desk involved Barrett transactions and items related to Barrett Industries. Little did he know when he set out to clear his father's name in the business world that he would end up married to the prime culprit's daughter.

"So, I'll tell you how we deal with it," Grandfather continued. "We get this atrocious joke of a marriage annulled immediately." He paused. "You and she didn't...that is, there was no..."

"I slept in the bunkhouse last night, if that's what you're asking."

"Then it's settled. I'll draw up the papers, and we'll have this handled on our way out of town."

"With all due respect, Grandfather, I'm a grown man, and I will handle this in the way that I intend."

"And what might that be?" he demanded.

"I had planned to leave in a few days, but I'm happy to accompany you in the railcar today. Until I decide how to proceed—and I have not ruled out an annulment, but I must be sure my family and the ranch are safe—Pearl will stay here at the ranch. Should she disagree with this arrangement, then her alternative is the one you've suggested."

Grandfather looked skeptical. "I assume you and she have not discussed this."

"We have not. This is my decision, not hers."

"And when she sees you gathering your things to leave and decides to join you?"

"She won't. I will arrange for Eli to take her for a ride. She always loved to ride the ranch horses. Once she's gone, we can take the wagon."

His grandfather rose and walked around the desk to clasp his hand on Deke's shoulder. "You make me proud."

For once, the statement did not make him happy.

Chapter 6

Pearl stepped away from the study door, her temper rising. More than anything else, she was hurt that Deke would plan to deceive her in such a way.

Keeping her silence though she wanted to scream, Pearl hurried outside and headed toward the barn, where she hoped she would find Eli. He was there as she expected, grooming a beautiful roan mare.

"Something wrong, Miss Barrett?" He shook his head. "I mean Mrs. Wyatt, I guess."

"Just call me Pearl like you used to," she said. "I know you love your brother, but I need a big favor, and what I'm going to ask might make him mad at you."

"Then I don't think I ought to do it," he said.

"Well," she said slowly, "what if it was the right thing to do?"

He dropped the brush and turned to face her. "Pearl, you're going to have to explain yourself, because I'm lost."

So she told him what Deke intended and her own plan, a plan that had been concocted on her trip over from the house. When she was done, Pearl added a silent prayer that Eli would become her ally in saving her very brief marriage.

Deke's younger brother nodded. "You're right that a husband and wife ought not be apart, especially when they're just freshly hitched." He gave the matter another moment's consideration. "You're also right that Deke won't be happy about it, but I'll do it."

"Remember, we will need to play our parts well once we are in town. The object is to get me on that train no matter what. If Deke sees us, you'll need to be prepared."

"Don't you worry, Pearl. You're going to get on that train, no matter what. Now go get ready to leave, and I'll do my part here with the horses."

"Thank you," she said as she touched his sleeve. "You're a good man, Eli. I hope God brings you a good woman someday."

He grinned. "I'll let you pray that one for me. I'm too busy taking care of the ranch to worry about wooing a woman."

"I will do that." She reached into her pocket as a thought occurred. "Oh, do you mind posting these letters to my dear friend after you've left me off at the train station?"

"Course." He accepted the stack of correspondence then lifted a dark brow before returning his attention to her. "These are addressed to someone named Frank. You sure you want to send them, what with you being a married woman and all?"

Pearl laughed. "Of course, I do. Frank has been my closest friend since college. I wrote Deke several letters during my college years that mention our escapades. He is fully aware that we correspond."

Eli looked doubtful but shoved the letters into his pocket anyway. "If you say so."

"If it makes you feel any better, the last letter is a brief scribble letting Frank know my husband and I are returning to Washington and would love to arrange a visit. I managed it on the way out the door, but I think the message will be clear."

The rest of the details, including the story of the great escape she was about to make against her husband's will, would be the subject of the next letter. Or perhaps that was a tale better told in person.

"Off with you, then," Eli said as he disappeared into the tack room.

Pearl offered a smile as she left to return to the ranch house to prepare. As she neared the house, she recognized a familiar buggy parked in front. The trunks she had taken with her on the journey that should have ended in Denver were stacked on the porch.

"Papa!" Pearl called as she stepped inside.

Unfortunately, her voice was covered by the sounds of shouting down the hall. She moved swiftly toward the noise, halting in front of the closed door of the study.

"You always wanted my land, and now you'll have it, I suppose," her father said. "Wasn't it enough that you caused all that trouble between Zeb Wyatt and me?"

"Me cause the trouble?" Deke's grandfather said. "You were the one who made the choices you did in your business dealings. I merely pointed out to my daughter that her husband put blind faith in a man who neither earned it nor deserved it."

"I will have an apology for that lie," Papa said. "Perhaps now is the time to tell your grandson just who got rich off the investments you encouraged that Zeb and I make."

There was a moment of silence, and then Deke said, "Grandfather?"

"He's talking nonsense," the older man said.

"Nonsense is your only defense?" Deke countered.

"My defense is that I would never do anything to harm your mother or her sons, no matter what man sired them."

"See there?" her father said. "Am I the only one who noticed he did not directly answer your question? Of course, he would do what's best for Emma and her boys. And what was best was for him to use me and my company to take everything your father had in the bank plus just about all I had. Did you ever wonder where that money came from that got your father's ranch out of hock?"

There was a pause. Pearl pressed her ear to the door in order not to miss the answer to that very important question.

"Grandfather?" Deke said again. "Defend yourself against this man and his charges."

"I will not," Deke's grandfather said. "Either you believe me or John Barrett, a man who has proven to be a poor businessman and apparently a poor father as he has allowed such things to happen to his daughter as have recently transpired. And perhaps, if you consider how it all turned out, he just may have orchestrated the whole thing. Rather convenient he regains access to the Wyatt monies through his daughter, don't you think?"

"I could make the same charge," Papa said. "Rather convenient that the Wyatts get the rest of my holdings through my daughter."

Once again the room fell into silence. Pearl reached for the doorknob but stalled just shy of opening the door and going in.

"Both of you have made serious accusations of the other," Deke said. "How am I supposed to know who is telling the truth and who is lying?"

"You know because I am family, Deke Wyatt. You are my namesake, my blood and my kin. How could I do such things against you?"

"That's just it, Grandfather. Mr. Barrett hasn't said you've done things against me. He's claiming you've used deception to do things against him that benefits us. I would feel much better about this situation if you would refute the charges in a concrete manner."

The older man laughed and Pearl took a step backward. What kind of man laughed in the face of this sort of charge?

"Think, Deke. You are party to all my confidential files at the firm. Have I once done anything that seemed improper or was illegal? You know as well as I do that I run a tight ship and release any employee who does not do the same. You were warned when you came aboard that the same rules applied to you." He paused. "If you can reconcile the person you know I am to the man Barrett claims me to be, then so be it. But if you cannot, then you must determine that Barrett is lying."

Someone started clapping. Pearl returned her ear to the door so as not to miss a word.

"I know you to be an honest man in your business dealings, Grandfather," Deke said. "What you don't know is that I have been looking into the last deal that my father and John Barrett did together."

"And you have not found any improprieties yet, have you?" Papa said.

"Not yet," Deke admitted, "but my investigation is ongoing."

Pearl's heart sank. So her husband had been trying to prove her father had done something improper in his business dealings that had harmed the Wyatt family? Her eyes narrowed as she tried to reason this through.

Why would Papa hurt his dear friend? Or rather, his former dear friend. Papa and Mama never would discuss what led to the falling out between the families, but as she thought on the timing, the break between the families had come at the same time rumors flew about the financial stability of the Polecat Creek Ranch.

Had Papa arranged the trouble, or were he and Mr. Wyatt caught in a trap set by Deke's grandfather? It was all too much to consider.

"So you are unwilling to admit your grandfather stole not only your father's profits but mine, Deke?"

"Yes, sir, I am at this time, although I will be the first one to say so should I learn that this accusation is true."

"You're a Wyatt, boy, so, of course, you will stick with what the family tells you to do," her father said. "You're just like him, only he just took my financial stability. I can earn that back, and I will. But you?" Papa paused. "You stole my daughter, too."

"Your daughter was thrust on me, Mr. Barrett. I did not want to marry her, and I am not certain how long I will remain—"

"Deacon Wyatt, cease your talking," his grandfather shouted.

There was a long pause, and then Papa said, "So the schemes continue. I should not be surprised. I will see my daughter now. She has a choice to make."

Pearl shoved open the door and stepped inside. She found Deke's grandfather seated behind Mr. Wyatt's desk and Deke standing near the window that faced the creek. Papa was nearest the door, though he made no move toward her.

"Of course, she'd be skulking about in the hallway," the older man said. "You taught her well, Barrett."

Pearl was about to object when her father stepped between them. "You've a choice to make, Pearl." He glanced over his shoulder at Deke's grandfather and then looked back at her. "This man and his kin have waged war against our family for some time now. He cloaks it as honest business and makes me out to look like the man who is of ill reputation, but he's very clever in how he goes about this. Your husband there will never find a trail of deceit because his grandfather has covered that trail so well. But they are vile as snakes, the whole lot of them."

"Mr. Barrett," Deke said. "You will not insult me and my family in my own home. I'll have an apology or you will leave and never come back."

"You'll never have the former, and I will be happy to do the latter. The only question is whether my daughter goes with me." He turned his back on Pearl to face Deke. "She has a much better offer than yours, son. Didn't she tell you that? She was already affianced to a gentleman of much greater means and influence than you when her trip was so rudely interrupted by those ruffians you call brothers."

Deke looked past her father to set his attention squarely on her. "No, she did not tell me she has promised to wed another."

"I did not make that promise," Pearl said. "My father did. As for me, I prefer—"

"Dear," Deke's grandfather interrupted, "no one here cares to hear what you prefer. It is far too late for that now." He cleared his throat and turned toward Papa. "We are men of business and commerce, and as such, we seek the best answer to whatever trouble besets us. Wouldn't you agree, Barrett?"

"I would, in general."

"Fair enough." The older man smiled in the direction of his grandson. "Then perhaps the men could hold a more rational discussion about how to reach a reasonable conclusion to this whole fiasco."

"If you're going to discuss an annulment, I won't have it." Pearl's voice was far too high and full of emotion to sound reasonable, but it was the best protest she could manage under the circumstances.

Her eyes found Deke, his image swirling through the tears. "I won't have it," she repeated, making sure her husband saw her as she said the words.

"Go" was the only word Deke spared for her.

"Go?" she managed.

Deke crossed the room to take her arm. "Leave this discussion to the men, Pearl. We can make a rational decision that will be best for all of us."

"That will be best for you," she said as she swiped at her eyes so she could better see him.

"No," he said when he'd led her around the corner and out of sight of Papa and his grandfather. "I do consider you in this. If I didn't care what happened to you, would I be married to you?"

She reached up and touched his cheek and then lifted up on tiptoe to attempt another kiss. Deke turned his head just before she reached his lips, causing her to kiss his cheek.

"So that's how we are leaving it?" she said.

He looked back down at her. "I must make my decision with a rational mind."

"No," she said softly. "You must make your decision knowing what you will miss if you cast me off and send me to that man in Denver."

Deke released her to take two steps back toward the study. Then he stopped short and turned around. Before she could blink, he had returned to her side to sweep her into his arms to carry her into the parlor.

He set her on her feet long enough to shut the door and then closed the distance between them again. "Give me one reason why I should remain married to you when all good sense and the facts tell me I should go through with an annulment."

Pearl placed her palm against his cheek. "Because you know as well as I do that we were meant to be wed. Didn't you think of me while you were away all those years?"

The question was as unfair as the current situation. Of course, he'd thought of her. She'd been the girl who'd shadowed him as a child, but she had somehow grown to be a beautiful woman over the years. Now that she was back in his life, he knew for certain he would miss her when she was gone again.

But she didn't have to go. He could remain married to her.

The question was should he?

Grandfather's story was arguably the stronger of the two, and his mother, who was an excellent judge of character, had never liked John Barrett. Or so she claimed.

Being a man of facts had helped him in his law career. However, being a man of action caused him to reach for his wife and hold her close. He did need to know what he would be missing should he end this marriage through annulment.

Looking down at his bride, Deke felt his heart thud against his chest. The trusting way Pearl looked up at him, though her eyes were misting with tears and her feelings were likely trampled, undid him.

"Pearl," he said in a gruff whisper, "your attempts at kissing were appreciated, but you have obviously not had the proper attention to your studies in that area."

"Then teach me, husband," she responded softly as her eyes slid shut.

So he did.

They were still kissing when a knock at the door ended the moment. "What?" Deke growled as he held Pearl close to him.

"I will have my daughter now," John Barrett said from the other side of the door. "She and I must have a conversation, and you will not prevent it."

Deke looked down at Pearl, her lips now slightly swollen from their most pleasant encounter. "You should speak to him."

"I know," she said, though she lifted up to kiss him once more. "And I shall."

"He will want you to leave with him," Deke said as he traced the line of her jaw.

"What do you want me to do? It appears I have a choice."

He wanted to tell her to stay with him. The words were right there. However, he was a man of facts, and right now the facts did not point to a clear conclusion.

"I want you to do what you think is best," he said as he released her to walk over and open the door.

Facing John Barrett caused him the odd urge to want to punch him. Not because of the things he said about the Wyatts and Grandfather, but because he was the man who could take Pearl away.

His feelings were too little and too late, at least in his estimation. He should have realized what he had when Pearl first declared her feelings. Instead, he was reduced to standing aside and allowing Pearl to choose.

He listened as her father effectively argued the point that the Barretts had been treated poorly and deceived by the Wyatt family. Had he chosen lawyering, John Barrett might have made a fine one.

"I will have you choose," Barrett finally told her. "Me or the Wyatts."

"Would you give us a moment, Deke?" Pearl asked.

He nodded. "I am leaving with my grandfather in fifteen minutes. If you're going with us, have Eli put your trunks in the wagon. If they're not in the wagon, I'll know you've left with your father."

"Oh, Deke," she whispered against his ear. "All you have to do is ask me to stay and I will."

He wanted to ask her to stay, but logic clearly dictated he allow her to make this decision on her own. Then there was the slight possibility that foul play on her father's part had led to this.

Deke clamped his lips shut and left the room, all the while praying Pearl would choose him over her father.

Papa hadn't understood, but then she figured he wouldn't. He would come to understand someday, just as she knew that somehow Deke would come to love her as she loved him. Their kisses conveyed promise enough that this would happen.

Perhaps it already had.

She gathered up the few things she'd had with her and tucked them into the reticule along with writing paper and pens. The next letter to Frank would likely be a long one, but she could write that on the train.

Deke and his grandfather were nowhere to be seen, but fifteen minutes had not yet passed so she had no concern of their whereabouts. Stepping out onto the porch, she found Eli waiting for her.

Oh, their plan. She'd almost forgotten.

"Look, things have changed. I don't need for you to do what we planned. If you'll just take my trunks out of the buggy and put them in the wagon, we will call it all off."

"Oh, no," he said. "I can't do that. We made a deal and I swore a promise."

Pearl shook her head. "You don't understand. See, Deke and I mended our differences. We're leaving together."

"Yes, that's true. Now get on in so we can surprise your husband."

"No, that's not what—"

Her words were squelched when Eli picked her up and deposited her in the buggy. "Remember, I promised I'd get you there no matter how it happened."

"Eli, please listen. I'm going in the wagon with Deke. It's fine."

He regarded her from his place on the seat beside her. "You made me swear a promise, Pearl, and I am keeping it. Now I am going to need you to get in that feed sack like we planned."

"No, truly, I—"

The air went out of her as Eli snatched her across the seat and placed a bandanna over her mouth. "I'm so sorry, Pearl. I'm just doing what you told me to. Remember that, won't you?"

He settled her gently into the feed sack and placed her on the floor of the buggy then drove along the back trail leading to town, all the while apologizing that he'd had to do as she asked despite her protests. Once she realized that she would end up on the train whether she fought this and somehow got out of the feed sack or whether she went along with the plan and ended up surprising Deke, Pearl relaxed. Indeed her husband would be surprised.

If only she could see well enough to write another letter to Frank. But then Frank had no patience for Deke's stubbornness. Urging Pearl to make another choice, to pick a man who was worthy of her, had become a common theme.

Pearl knew Deke was that man. She prayed now that he would prove this to her.

Chapter 7

Pearl's trunks were not in the wagon. His heart still hurt when he recalled the empty wagon and the absence of both Pearl's trunks and her father's buggy.

She'd gone. The princess who'd stolen his heart beneath a falling star had been pushed so far away by his stubbornness that she'd given up on him.

Deke made himself as comfortable as he could manage in the salon of his grandfather's railcar as the porter busied himself preparing the table for dinner. They left the station more than an hour ago, and guilt had chased him the whole time.

Perhaps if he'd been more insistent to keep her close rather than allow her to be alone with her father, she would not have returned home with him.

And she might have chosen him rather than that fellow in Denver as it appeared she had. Then there was the kiss that still seared his lips. He'd been kissed before, but never like that.

To distract himself, Deke went to the pile of work demanding his attention. Grandfather walked through the salon, but Deke did not look up. In the absence of conversation, the old man returned to his chamber.

Several times, however, the porter returned and seemed to give him strange looks. Finally, Deke said, "Is there something wrong?"

"No, I don't suppose," he said, "although I do wonder if you've checked your sleeping chamber since arriving on the train to. . ." The porter seemed to be at a loss for words, though a deep crimson rose in his cheeks. "Well, I just wondered about your luggage, sir."

"My luggage?" Deke shrugged. "I'm sure everything is fine. No need to check."

He edged a step closer. "You're certain about that?"

"I am," he said to the pesky porter.

"Yes, all right. Very well, Mr. Wyatt," he said before hurrying away, his brows raised.

Deke pulled the folder of documents on the Barretts that he'd yet to go through and began reading and making notes. Though he had no idea how long he'd been staring at the pages, Deke did realize the porter had somehow managed to light the lamps without him taking notice.

He lined the pages up under the lamplight as a growing dread surfaced. Here in front of him was undisputable proof that the deposits made by Wyatt and Barrett companies totaled exactly the amounts Grandfather had written into the firm ledger.

Deke dug further and found transactions that made no sense. Ledger entries that spoke of deceit at a level that stunned Deke.

"So you've found them, I see."

Deke whirled around to see his grandfather standing there.

"I did it for you," he said. "For your mother, too, of course, but more for you. You're my heir apparent, Deke. I had to secure your future."

"My future is fine," he said. "Though yours is in doubt."

"What will you do?" Grandfather asked as he scrubbed his face with his hands.

"I don't know." He paused. "But I know what you will do. Make this right. Go through every transaction and account for it. Pay back every cent to John Barrett and admit to him and my mother and brothers what you've done."

Grandfather closed the distance between them to place his hand on Deke's shoulder. "I was wrong to do this. My intentions were good, but I took the wrong path in carrying them out. However, I was right in saying you are the heir apparent. You're a wise man, Deke Wyatt."

"I wish I could agree," he said as he patted his grandfather's hand and then rose. "I am guilty of a terrible choice, and I wish I had a way of repairing it."

"The Barrett girl?" Grandfather said.

Deke nodded. "I think I'll go to bed now," he said. "I just don't feel up to dinner."

Grandfather nodded. "Thank you," he said as he embraced Deke. "I am proud of you."

Deke walked down the hall to his bedchamber, one of two in the railcar, and found the gas lamps had not been lit. Fumbling for the lamp, he heard a woman's giggle.

Before he could react, a distinctly female voice said, "Hush, husband, or your grandfather will know your wife is here."

Deke grinned. "Princess?" he said as he fumbled around in the darkness for his wife but found feed sack burlap instead.

"I do like the sound of that," Pearl said softly.

"When your trunks weren't in the wagon, I thought you'd left me."

"There's actually a funny story connected to that, but first, would you mind turning on the gas lamp? I'm in need of assistance."

"Of course."

After a moment, he managed to light the lamp, plunging the room into brilliant light. As his eyes adjusted to the brightness, he spied a feed sack on the bed where he expected to find his wife.

"Princess?"

"Yes, Deke," she said. "I'm in the feed sack again, though I don't think it's the same one. This one is nice and clean."

Deke made short work of releasing his wife from her burlap prison then held her tight. "Who did this?"

"Eli," she said with a giggle. "See, when I thought you were leaving without me, I went to Eli with a plan to save our marriage. He agreed to help. Please don't be mad at him, because he did this for you."

"He stuffed my wife in a feed sack and delivered her to the railcar instead of allowing her to just ride in the wagon with me?" Deke swept the feed sack onto the floor and sat on the edge of the bed. "I assume this is the funny story you planned to tell me."

"It is. See, the plan was to get me on this train no matter what I told him once we'd set everything in motion, even if I told him later that I had changed my mind. My thinking was that I knew I needed to be with you and, should someone talk me out of it, I wanted a backup. Does that make sense?"

"Not a bit," Deke admitted.

"Well, in any case, Eli played his part too well. When I met him at the preplanned spot to let him know I was going with you after all and all was well, he did as I asked him to and ignored me."

Deke shook his head. "You told him you were going to the train so he threw you in the feed sack and took you to the train." He paused. "I assume that's how you got here."

"It is," she said. "Eli was determined to follow the plan exactly."

He shrugged. "I admit it's an odd plan, but I cannot complain, because it brought you here to me."

"Yes, it did," Pearl said as she wrapped her arms around him.

"Never leave me again. I'm an idiot and slow to admit things, but I love you. More than anything, I love you." He paused. "Although I have to warn you that once we get to Washington, DC, we may end up turning around and coming right back to Polecat Creek Ranch."

"I don't mind," she said. "Wherever you go, I will go."

"Then I declare you the princess of Polecat Creek," he said as he pulled her closer and traced the line of her jaw with his kisses. "I had hoped to promise you all of Washington, DC, at your feet and possibly the chance to be married to a man who had dealings with the president himself, but I would rather have you than all of that. I know that now."

He swooped in to kiss her, but to his surprise, she pulled away. "You never told me you wanted to work with the president."

"No," he said slowly, "I don't suppose I did. It's just been a dream of mine to use what I have learned as a lawyer to make a difference. I study cases like the one I told you about yesterday in order to learn as much as I can about patents and laws related to new ideas and inventions. I don't believe we're doing enough as a country to keep those who invent things protected from those who wish to steal those inventions." Deke chuckled under his breath. "Listen to me. The wife I thought was gone is right here in my chamber and I am talking business." He lifted her hand to kiss her fingers. "Will you forgive me? I promise not to say another word about work or politics or anything else you don't want to hear about."

"Of course," she said, "but only if you will make just one promise."

"Anything."

She smiled. "Just take me to a wedding next week. I cannot give you the details right now because I am sworn to secrecy. However, I promise it will be one place where politics may be acceptable to be discussed. As long as you aren't opposed to the new president's views."

He thought a moment. "Will I know the couple?"

Again she giggled. "I feel certain you will know the groom, which is why I am sworn to secrecy. I can tell you the bride is my dear friend Frank."

"I am earning forgiveness by escorting you to a highly secret wedding between a mystery groom who is known to me and a woman named Frank who is known to you?" Deke shook his head. "Woman, you are as perplexing a female as ever drew a breath, but I wouldn't have it any other way."

Epilogue

June 2, 1886
The Executive Mansion
Washington, DC

Deke walked through the door of the White House's Blue Room two steps behind his wife. In the time since they arrived in Washington, DC, he had come to realize how incomplete his life had been before she stepped back into it.

His gaze scanned the room, catching sight of an impressive group of a half dozen or so men whose reputations in world politics preceded them. Though these men effectively ruled most of the free world, their women stole this show. Between their lively conversation and their even livelier dresses and hats, the political wives were an impressive lot on their own.

But the most beautiful of all was the woman who woke up beside him this morning.

Pearl turned to bid him follow, and he did as she asked. "I do so wish I could have introduced you to Frank before the wedding, but there's just been no time."

Just as Deke was about to sit down beside his wife, one of the White House staff tapped him on the shoulder. "Mr. Wyatt, I have a message for you with best wishes on your recent marriage to Mrs. Wyatt."

Deke accepted the folded note and returned to take his seat. Turning the note over, he broke the wax that displayed the seal of the president of the United States, and then showed the note to Pearl.

"How nice," she said as if receiving a personal note from the president of the United States with congratulations on your marriage was the most natural thing in the world.

Unfolding the note, he read these words:

Mr. Wyatt,
I have been remiss in offering a proper congratulations to you for marrying our dear friend Pearl. Please accept my deepest apologies for this grievous error. May I make it up to you by sending for you Tuesday next at nine in the morning? I have heard from reliable sources that you show great promise in the field of laws regarding patents. I have a great need for a man like you to advise me in this important matter.

The signature read simply "Grover Cleveland, President of the United States."

When he could manage to assemble a coherent thought, Deke turned to his wife and thrust the note in her direction.

"That's very nice of him," she said after she'd read it.

" 'That's very nice of him'? That's all you can say? Do you realize this is—"

"The president," she supplied. "Well, of course, I do, but you're simply going to have to put that note away. The music is starting and, oh, look, there's Frank."

Deke turned in the direction where his wife had nodded and spied a lovely young woman in an ivory-colored bridal gown. The bride winked at Pearl as she walked past them.

"Isn't she lovely?" Pearl asked.

"Not as lovely as you," he said as he turned back around to where the bride had stopped beside her groom.

He reached for his wife's hand and drew her close enough to whisper. "You didn't tell me she was marrying. . ."

"Grover?" Pearl shrugged. "I told you I was sworn to secrecy. However, Grover is keen to get to know you. He is such a dear."

"You refer to a United States president as a dear and you knew before anyone else he was marrying your friend." Deke shook his head. "Will the rest of our life together be filled with surprises like this?"

Pearl grinned. "As princess of Polecat Creek, I declare it shall be so."

Even though the wedding of the century was happening nearby, while all others were watching the president marry his bride, Deke gave his wife a proper kiss to celebrate.

Author's Note

While I try to stay as true to history as possible, I did break a few time line rules in this novel. Frances Folsom, known as Frank to her friends, did attend Wells College, did have a long and secret courtship with Grover Cleveland, and did marry him on June 2, 1886.

In the story, the marriage was a surprise to everyone but very close friends of the bride and groom, including my fictional lead character Pearl Barrett. In reality, the group of less than thirty close friends and political allies who attended the ceremony did have five days' notice in the form of a written letter from the groom himself. The wedding was held at seven o'clock in the evening in the Blue Room of the Executive Mansion, and the Marine Band, directed by John Philip Sousa, provided the music.

President Cleveland was forty-nine years old when he wed twenty-one-year-old Frances Folsom. Cleveland was her late father's law partner and the executor of his estate. He was known to say that he had to wait for his bride to grow up before he could marry her.

Bestselling author **Kathleen Y'Barbo** is a *Romantic Times* Inspirational Book of the Year winner as well as a multiple RITA and Carol Award nominee of more than eighty novels with more than two million copies of her books in print in the United States and abroad. A tenth-generation Texan and certified paralegal, Kathleen resides in central Texas with her very own hero in combat boots.

To find out more about Kathleen or connect with her through social media, check out her website at www.kathleenybarbo.com.

Love from Afar

by Penny Zeller

Dedication

To my oldest daughter. I am beyond blessed to be your mom.

Wait on the LORD: be of good courage,
and he shall strengthen thine heart: wait, I say, on the LORD.
PSALM 27:14

Chapter 1

Another wedding dress completed.

Another happy ending.

Just never her own.

Pushing reality aside, Meredith Waller bustled up the front steps of the Goff residence. She draped the wedding dress over her arm and tapped on the door, eager for the recipient to see her latest sewing creation.

"What a pleasure to see you. Do come in, Meredith." Mrs. Goff, a round and jolly sort, beckoned Meredith to enter the humble home she had visited so many times throughout the years.

But this time was different. This time, Meredith would be assisting her best friend, Roxie Goff, in starting a new chapter of her life. A life that involved matrimonial vows.

A life that seemed more distant and unreachable for Meredith as the years passed by.

Meredith promptly quelled the feelings of jealousy not only of Roxie but of all the other young brides who had come before Roxie, as well. These women were Meredith's friends. How could she even think of entertaining such covetous thoughts?

"Meredith, you have my dress!" Roxie, a younger version of her mother, rushed toward Meredith, her arms outstretched in anticipation. She offered to take the quilt-covered gown.

"I hope you like it."

"How could I not? You are only the best wedding dress seamstress west of the Mississippi."

Meredith laughed at her friend's proclamation. "I don't know if my legendary wedding dress skills are known from that great a distance."

"Of course, they are. I heard some women talking at the mercantile the other day about what exquisite dresses you sew. And I'm number nine, correct?"

Meredith took a deep breath. Nine dresses she had sewn for her friends and members of the Ellis Creek community. Nine dresses she had sewn for happy brides-to-be who had found the love of their dreams.

Would she herself ever know the joy of wearing such a dress?

With great care, Roxie removed the quilt from around the wedding dress. "It's breathtaking," she gasped.

"I'm thrilled you like it."

"Like it? I love it! May I try it?"

"Of course."

Meredith waited in the parlor while Roxie tried on her dress. Then, presenting herself for Mrs. Goff and Meredith, Roxie entered the parlor and twirled around as though a princess.

"Meredith, you really do fine work. Such a gift you have with the needle and thread," declared Mrs. Goff.

"Thank you, Mrs. Goff. It was my pleasure. After all, Roxie has been my best friend all these many years."

"And you have been such a dear friend to me as well." Roxie paused for a moment as if the realization Meredith had already contemplated finally settled in her heart, too. The thought that soon, after Roxie married Perry, things would change between them, and Roxie's time would be spent as that of a rancher's wife and, within a year, likely a mother.

Meredith pushed from her mind the speculation. She refused to let dismal thoughts ruin this special moment together with her best friend.

Roxie left the room and changed back into her everyday dress, all the while chatting about the wedding dress Meredith had sewn.

"Would you like some lemonade on the porch?" Roxie asked.

Meredith smiled. "That sounds delightful." How many times had she and Roxie shared lemonade on the Goff's porch? Too many to count.

Within moments, Roxie reappeared with two glasses of lemonade and took a seat beside Meredith. "Before you know it, you'll be stitching a wedding dress of your own, Meredith."

"That's decidedly unlikely." The words left her mouth before she could pay them any mind.

"God has someone planned for you, Meredith. I just know it."

"If you'll recall, I was the one everyone thought would marry first out of all of our friends, and by the age of eighteen, no less. Mind you, that definitely was not in God's plan."

"Who would guess that Idella would fall in love with Richard practically the day she met him during his visit to Ellis Creek?"

Meredith laughed. Idella and Richard had already been married nearly three years. They brought new proof to the old adage that love might just happen at first sight. "True. They do have a wonderful story to tell their daughter when she grows older."

"You do know that we will still be the best of friends, even after I marry Perry, right?"

"I know things will change, Roxie."

"They will change. Perry will be my main priority, after the good Lord, of course. But we will still pay each other visits, chat about the goings-on of this town, and sit and drink lemonade on the porch. We haven't been friends for all these years to suddenly stop."

Meredith smiled at her dear friend. "You're right, Roxie. We shall remain grand friends, no matter what."

"True. And don't you let the fact that God hasn't sent the man He aims for you to marry bother you. His timing is different than our timing. Isn't that what the reverend always says?"

"Yes, and I know that the Lord knows and sees everything, but sometimes I wonder if He may have forgotten that in a few short months I'll be twenty-one years old. A spinster by any standard, especially in Ellis Creek."

"Fiddlesticks! The Montana Territory may be behind the times a bit. But in less than twenty years, we'll be entering a new century. Spinsterhood will be considered much later. Maybe even into a woman's mid-twenties."

"Well, whether or not that's true," said Meredith, taking a sip of her lemonade, "how can a girl find a man to marry when there are no options? And not just no options, but *absolutely* no options."

"Perhaps there are options we aren't seeing. Options right there before us."

"Please, Roxie, do give an example."

"Well, let's see. There's Mr. Griggs."

Meredith shivered at her friend's suggestion. "Mr. Griggs might be a worthwhile choice were it not for his lack of teeth and failure to bathe."

"I do suppose that Mr. Griggs is, shall we say, rather disheveled."

"Disheveled, indeed."

"Mr. Norman from the post office would make a fine choice."

Meredith giggled at that suggestion. "If it wasn't that he is at least ninety years old."

"Marvin Pratt?"

Meredith held out her forefinger and thumb with only a small space between the two. "Only one inconsequential problem with Marvin Pratt: he will likely insist we live at his parents' home since he doesn't understand the verse in the Bible that states 'therefore shall a man leave his father and his mother, and shall cleave unto his wife.'"

"Give poor Marvin time. He's only thirty."

"Any other suggestions, Roxie?"

"What about that new banker in town, Leopold Arkwright? He's quite sought after by some of the young women in Ellis Creek."

Meredith wrinkled her nose. The arrogant man had tried to court several of the young women in town, to no avail. "I dare say that Mr. Arkwright is quite one to put on airs. Also, wouldn't he be perturbed to know we weren't addressing him by his full name, Leopold Lawrence Arkwright III?"

"He would indeed. But don't you find him the least bit dapper?" Roxie winked teasingly at her friend.

"Not in the least."

"He is one of the wealthiest men in Ellis Creek."

Meredith shrugged. "Riches are not all there is. Give me a poor man with a strong faith in the Lord and a kind and gracious nature over a wealthy one possessing Mr. Arkwright's personality any day."

"All right. I'll not press on about the notorious Leopold Lawrence Arkwright III. Hmmm." Roxie put her finger to her lips. "Gabe Kleeman?"

"Gabe Kleeman?"

"Yes, Lula's older brother?"

Meredith thought for a moment. Lula was the best friend of Meredith's younger sister, Tillie. Did Lula have a brother?

"Remember, Meredith, when we were in school? He was a head shorter than the rest of the boys—and the girls. A strong wind could blow him away, if I correctly recall."

"I think I remember him. Didn't he go to Minnesota to help his relatives?"

"Missouri, I believe."

"I recall he would retrieve Tillie from our home and from school on occasion. But it's been several years." Meredith pondered for a moment. "Oh, yes, I do vaguely recall him. Such a sickly fellow. It seemed he missed a lot of school."

"Yes, a nice boy, not like the others in school always pulling on our braids or teasing us." Roxie thoughtfully tapped her chin. "I do believe I heard from Mother, who heard from Mrs. Smith, who heard from Mrs. Plunkett, that Gabe has returned to Ellis Creek."

"I don't think there's anyone for me in Ellis Creek, Roxie. I may have to travel to the distant corners of the Montana Territory and beyond."

"Don't give up yet, Meredith. God has a plan."

Meredith offered a weak smile. She hoped God's plan didn't include spinsterhood.

Chapter 2

Gabe Kleeman stood in the field and, turning, gazed in every direction. The Madison Range in the distance, the plentiful ranch land, and the numerous trees gave testimony to how blessed he was to have acquired such a fine piece of land. He couldn't have done it, of course, without Pa's help. Adjacent to his parents' property, the spread had come up for sale when the Potter family had moved to Iowa. Pa had suggested Gabe take out a loan on the property and start his own ranch.

From the beginning, that had been Gabe's dream—to own his own ranch.

Now, after three years, he was back in Ellis Creek. Not that he had minded traveling to Missouri to assist his aunt and uncle after his uncle's accident. The years spent there drew Gabe and his extended family closer, giving Gabe the opportunity to help ensure that his aunt and uncle didn't lose the farm they had worked so hard to keep.

God had answered the prayers of Gabe's entire family throughout the past couple of years. Gabe was stronger and healthier than he had ever been, and the days of his rough start in life as an ailing youngster would forever be in the past.

Gabe's return to Ellis Creek sealed the fact that he belonged here. Always had. His family, the land, the cattle, the beautiful summers, and the crisp winters would always beckon him to the place he had lived since a young lad. He had missed much since his time away and was glad to be back.

Three days later, Gabe sat in church, awaiting the sermon. He hoped the reverend would preach another convicting sermon as he had done last week when he spoke of allowing God to take all your worries. The reverend had reiterated that the Lord cared for the smallest of sparrows. Gabe would need to remember that as he started this new chapter in his life, operating his own ranch.

The Waller family sat in the fourth pew from the front. A fine location for the family in Gabe's humble estimate, as it afforded him ample time to take in the fine beauty of one Miss Meredith Waller. Not that Gabe wasn't listening to the goings-on at the church service and particularly the sermon, for indeed he was. But there was just something about the woman who had captured his attention all those years ago during their early school days. She hadn't known he existed then, and she certainly didn't know now.

Meredith might never know if Gabe didn't figure out how to use the mouth God gave him to actually speak to her.

Old Mrs. Plunkett began playing a hymn on the piano, and Gabe focused on his hymnal. When the song concluded, everyone took their seats to listen to the announcements. Out of the corner of his eye, Gabe had a perfect view of Meredith. Her long brown hair cascaded down her back in what Lula would call ringlets. She had expressive, pale blue eyes that he remembered from school when she appeared to be looking his way once. More like looking past him while in a daydream, but Gabe still recalled her sparkling eyes.

Meredith looked back over her shoulder, and Gabe redirected his attention to the front of the church. It wouldn't do to have Meredith discover he was staring at her. Did she realize he had returned from Missouri? Had she even known he had left?

When Meredith faced forward again, Gabe's eyes wandered once again to gaze upon her beauty. What would she say if she ever knew he fancied her? Would she laugh? He had attempted once several years ago to speak to Meredith by asking her to a barn dance. When Gabe had finally forced the words from his mouth, he'd been horrified with embarrassment when he realized he had asked her to a *yarn bance*.

If only Gabe hadn't been born shy, maybe he would have a chance with the prettiest girl in Ellis Creek.

He could talk to just about everyone else in town, but when it came to Meredith, his tongue got tied into hopeless knots. Better not to say anything at all than embarrass himself again, as he had with the "yarn bance" incident.

A nudge to his rib cage drew his attention from Meredith to his younger sister sitting to his right. A sly look in her eyes told him he'd been caught. "What is it, Lula?" he whispered.

"I saw you."

"What?"

"I saw you staring at Meredith Waller. You are supposed to be listening to the announcements."

Gabe felt the warmth travel up his neck. He shook his head. Why was it that his parents decided to have another child when Gabe was ten? Couldn't he have remained an only child? Not that he didn't love Lula with all his being, but a pesky sort she was, especially at times like these.

"I could listen if you weren't talking."

Lula narrowed her eyes at him. "I know you fancy Meredith Waller."

"She seems nice enough."

"Maybe I should tell Tillie."

"You wouldn't dare."

Lula merely shrugged, her long brown braids bobbing as she did. She stuck her chin out and focused her attention on the reverend, acting as though she had been listening intently to the announcements all along.

In all his shyness, and there was plenty of it, Gabe would die an early death if Lula ever breathed a word of her suspicions. He would have to purchase more of those jawbreakers she had grown so fond of and bribe her with one each week to keep her conjectures to herself.

Chapter 3

Tillie Waller couldn't wait until recess to speak with her best friend, Lula Kleeman. If lunch recess didn't arrive soon, she might be forced to sneak over to Lula's desk during arithmetic and let her know all about the grand plan she had concocted in her head while doing her chores last night.

But that would never do. Miss Apgar would tan her hide for sure if Tillie dared speak out of turn in class.

So instead, Tillie sat, attempting to do her best at listening to reasons why she had to learn double-digit multiplication, although Miss Apgar's reasons clearly lacked merit. Tillie prided herself on being more of a word-girl than a number-girl.

She removed her spectacles and rubbed her tired eyes. Arithmetic had a way of boring her. If she lasted the next hour without drifting into a deep sleep, it would be nothing short of miraculous. Tillie quietly drummed her fingers on the desk and every so often glanced Lula's way, hoping to catch her eye.

Finally after what seemed like a multitude of hours, Miss Apgar announced that lunch recess had arrived. "Now pupils, as always, please, eat your lunch first then play."

Tillie and the rest of the students chorused, "Yes, ma'am." For as smart as Miss Apgar was, she certainly never provided a variety of words to her standard "eat first then play" speech.

All of the students clamored for their tin pails on the shelf in the back of the classroom with youngest going first and elders toward the back. Tillie tapped her toe on the floor, attempting her best to be patient. Finally, her turn came, and she grabbed her tin pail and bolted out the door.

"Lula!"

"Tillie!"

The two embraced as if they hadn't seen each other just yesterday. Such was the case with best friends, Tillie supposed.

"I have the grandest plan in all the West."

Lula stared at Tillie with wide eyes. "Really?"

"Yes, I must tell you or I fear I shall be unable to endure the rest of the day."

"Let's go sit under the tree, and you can tell me all about it."

Tillie followed Lula to the large tree at the edge of the schoolyard. "What is it?" Lula inquired.

"You know how you and I were discussing that your brother is so lonely since returning from Missouri and that my sister is so distraught over everyone else having a beau?"

Lula removed a sandwich from her tin pail. "Yes?"

"Well, while I was doing chores last night, I had the most splendid plan."

"Do tell!"

"Why don't we arrange for your brother and my sister to fall in love?" Finally, Tillie had set free the words of her heart. Surely Lula would see the importance of the plan, just as Tillie had when the idea had popped into her head.

"Do people arrange for people to fall in love?" Lula asked.

"Well, sure."

"All right. So what is your plan?"

Tillie placed her apple back in her tin pail. Who could eat at a time like this? "I'm glad you asked, Lula. You see, we could write love letters."

"Love letters? Wherever did you ever get that idea?"

"I overheard Mama telling Papa that during the war, Grandmother and Grandfather wrote letters back and forth to stay in touch. Mama said that Grandmother was a fright, wondering if Grandfather would return from fighting for the North unscathed."

"You and your big words, Tillie."

"That's why I do well in writing but not in arithmetic. Anyhow, we write love letters, and soon Meredith and Gabe fall in love, get married, and we'll be sisters forever."

Lula absentmindedly placed a finger to her lips, seemingly pondering the thought. Tillie had known her best friend since they were little. She just knew Lula would see the importance of such an endeavor.

"We're only eleven. How could we possibly help two people fall in love?" Lula asked.

"It's been done before. Besides, we'll both be twelve soon."

"How do we deliver the letters to them?"

Tillie scrunched her nose. "I hadn't thought of that yet. I only thought about composing the letters." She refused to allow this complication to hinder her plans. "There has to be a way. Say, what about mailing the letters?"

"That would get mighty pricey. Have you seen the price of a stamp lately?"

"True. Perhaps we could ask someone to deliver the letters for us."

"And risk that person telling either Gabe or Meredith that we are behind this scheme?"

"Lula, you are always so pragmatic." Couldn't Lula be a dreamer like herself, just once?

"Not pragmatic, just realistic. We mustn't allow anyone to find out it is us writing the letters. Our plan would never work then."

"There has to be a way." Tillie decided just this once to eat her dessert before her sandwich. Taking a bite of her cookie, she closed her eyes in quick prayer. Surely the Lord saw the importance of the situation, didn't He?

"Are you sure Gabe and Meredith want to fall in love?"

"They do. They just don't know it yet." Tillie spoke with her mouth full of cookie, glad that Mama wasn't around to witness her appalling breach of manners.

"I've never heard Gabe say he wants to fall in love."

"Do boys even talk about such things?"

Lula shook her head. "Not that I know of. You have a brother. Does he ever swoon over any girls in town?"

"Charles is a scatterbrain. All he thinks about is hunting and catching fish. His days are boring, to say the least. But he's only fifteen. In time, he'll realize the importance of falling in love. Meredith is different." Tillie leaned in toward Lula and reduced her voice to a whisper. "Don't tell anyone, but I heard her sniffling a bit when she was finishing Roxie's wedding dress."

"Perhaps there was dust in the air. Maybe she wasn't sad at all."

"Oh, she was distraught, all right. She kept pulling the dress toward herself, and I could see the wistful gaze in her eyes."

Lula shot a suspicious glance Tillie's way.

All right, so maybe there was dust in the air, and maybe Meredith's wistful gaze was because she would not be spending as much time with Roxie as they had in the past once Roxie married Perry. Tillie had overheard Mama and Meredith speaking about how things change once a woman marries and her husband takes top priority in her life. But Tillie wouldn't admit all of that to Lula.

"Gabe is content running his new ranch. I don't think he cares about—wait a minute. I did happen to see him staring at Meredith at church Sunday."

"Really?"

"Are you thinking what I'm thinking, Tillie?"

"And are you thinking what I'm thinking, Lula?"

Both girls nodded. "We must arrange for them to fall in love," Tillie proclaimed.

"A most excellent plan, indeed! When do we start?"

"Tomorrow. Tonight, we will each come up with a plan on how to deliver the letters and how best to keep this a secret."

"And," added Lula, "what to write in those letters."

Tillie pointed her thumb at herself. "You leave that to me."

***

The following day at lunch recess, the plans were in place to arrange a falling-in-love between Meredith Waller and Gabe Kleeman.

"We mail the first letter to Meredith," Lula announced.

"Do we have two cents for the stamp?"

"I have a penny saved. If we can come up with another penny, this plan could very well work."

"I have a penny."

Lula grinned. "Perfect! But I haven't an idea about the rest of the letters. We need to write several back and forth."

They had come this far. They couldn't let this minor obstacle block their path. "I know!" Tillie announced. "We can hide the letters in that sliver of a space behind the big knot on that huge oak tree at the edge of town, just past the Jones' place. It would be a perfect hiding place. We can tell Meredith in her first letter that each letter thereafter will be at the tree. She can place her return letters to Gabe there, as well. It's an excellent hiding place if no squirrels haul off the letter, and no one in town will know since the tree is off of the main road."

"Yes, but you forgot something."

"What's that?" Tillie panicked. What of her well-planned idea?

"You forgot that Gabe is a boy. Do boys even like writing letters?"

"Some must. Our McGuffey Readers were written by William Holmes McGuffey, who was a man. Or look at Noah Webster. His dictionary is one of my favorite books of all time."

"True. But. . .Gabe is neither Mr. McGuffey nor Mr. Webster, and I'm not sure Gabe will be all right with the idea. He might be embarrassed. He's a reticent fellow, after all."

"That is true." Tillie bit her lip and pondered their latest hindrance. "I have a splendid idea! Why don't we write the letters for Gabe? At least until he warms to the idea. Then he can begin writing his own."

"When do we tell him?"

"After ten letters at least."

"When do we start?"

"We'll write our first letter right now. It won't do for me to pen it, as Meredith will recognize my penmanship, so you'll have to accomplish that task. This will meet with imminent success. I can feel it in my bones, as Grandmama Waller would say." The contents of the letter began to crowd her mind.

"This is quite thrilling. Can you imagine if our plan works? I declare, the way Gabe stared at Meredith in church could put us one step closer to being sisters forever."

This truly was more exciting than just about anything Tillie had experienced as of late. She removed a piece of writing paper that she had pilfered from Meredith's stationery pile, and together, she and Lula wrote the first of several letters.

After all, if they couldn't discover a new world like Christopher Columbus or sew the American flag like Betsy Ross, they could certainly make a difference for all humanity in their own small way.

Chapter 4

Not since Meredith had corresponded with Grandmama had she received any mail. When Mr. Norman waved her down on the boardwalk, she thought he must be mistaken. "Miss Waller, I have a letter for you!"

Perhaps the letter was for Mama. Meredith turned and started toward the elderly postmaster.

"This here came for you just today." Mr. Norman held the envelope in his wrinkled hand.

Arching an eyebrow, Meredith took the letter. "Thank you, Mr. Norman. It isn't often that I receive mail."

"I always feel like I'm giving folks a Christmas present. Unless, of course, the letter is bad news." Mr. Norman grinned, his aged face showing his years. "Am I to assume you have received good news, Miss Waller?"

Meredith turned the letter over in her hands. She didn't recognize the penmanship. "I do hope it is good news, Mr. Norman. I'm not expecting anything to the contrary."

"Well, I'll leave you be then to open your letter. Tell your folks I said hello."

"I will, Mr. Norman. Thank you."

Mr. Norman waved and ambled back to the post office.

Meredith claimed a bench outside the mercantile to open her letter. The stationery looked rather familiar, like her own cream-colored writing paper. The two-cent stamp had been placed rather haphazardly and crooked in the corner.

Who could be sending her a letter?

She carefully opened the seal and unfolded the ivory sheet of paper. Her eyes traveled across the words, not once, not twice, but three times:

Dear Miss Waller,
It has taken me considerable courage to write to you. I believe you are not only lovely but also kind and charitable.

Yours Truly,
Your Secret Admirer
P.S. If you would like to write back and forth, please check the sliver of a space behind the big knot on that huge oak tree at the edge of town, just past the Jones' place. I will place another letter there for you in the coming week.

Meredith shook her head. Was the letter written in jest? She looked around at all the people walking up and down the street, down the boardwalk, and into the stores. Who in Ellis Creek would send her such a letter? And did she want to write back and forth? How could she if she didn't even know who had sent the letter?

On the other hand, she allowed herself, just for a moment, to believe that someone really did find her lovely, kind, and charitable. A handsome prince of sorts, only in the modern times of 1884. As quickly as the thought entered her mind, she dismissed it. For who in Ellis Creek was a handsome prince? And who in Ellis Creek would call her lovely, kind, and charitable, and wish to write to her? Perhaps the writer of the letter hailed from another town in the Montana Territory or beyond. If so, how had he known to write to her? How did he even know her?

Questions filled her mind in rapid order as she folded the letter and returned it to its envelope. One thing was certain: she aimed to discover the author.

<hr />

Meredith removed the pan of biscuits from the oven. Mama had invited the Kleeman family over for supper, thinking it a good idea and adding that it was the perfect way for them to welcome Gabe Kleeman back to Ellis Creek after his time in Missouri. Meredith hadn't seen Gabe in at least three years, possibly longer. In her mind, he was the very same boy Roxie spoke of in their conversation a few days ago. Puny in stature, sickly, and shy. The poor man. Had he improved in health? Meredith recalled someone, Mama maybe, mentioning that Gabe Kleeman hadn't been healthy as a child due to a long illness.

Mama, Meredith, and Tillie set the table while Papa and Charles finished the out-side chores. Before long, the Kleemans arrived at the front door. Mama and Mrs. Kleeman eagerly greeted each other as if they hadn't just seen each other in church a few days ago. Tillie and Lula squealed in exuberance and immediately began whispering and giggling. Mr. Kleeman shook Papa's hand, and talk of the prices of cattle began.

Meredith was about to shut the door when a large foot blocked the door, causing her to jump back in surprise. "I'm so sorry! I didn't see you there." Her face was just inches from that of a young man in the doorway. One of those salesman touting fake remedies that had been rumored to be arriving in Ellis Creek, perhaps?

"May I help you?" Meredith asked.

The man fiddled with the button on his shirt cuff. "Uh, I'm Gabe Kleeman."

"Gabe Kleeman?"

"My family. . .was. . .invited over for supper."

A flush found its way up Meredith's neck. *How embarrassing! Could I just disappear now and avoid this whole humiliating course of circumstances?* "I'm so sorry, Mr. Kleeman. Do come in."

While opening the door, Meredith stumbled back, nearly losing her footing. Gabe Kleeman stepped through the door as she eyed him with suspicion. Where was the puny, sickly, small-statured boy she recalled from school?

Mama rushed toward the young Mr. Kleeman. "It's so nice to have you back in Ellis Creek, Gabe. We can't wait to hear about your time in Missouri."

"Thank you, Mrs. Waller, for the supper invitation." Gabe Kleeman took a seat at the table next to Charles.

"I heard you've been back about a week," Pa said.

"Yes, sir."

Meredith assisted Mama with the remaining food then took her seat next to Tillie and across from Gabe Kleeman. The humiliation of nearly shutting the man's foot in the door still flooded her mind. What must he think of her? Thankfully, no one else in either family seemed to have noticed.

Pa said the blessing, thanking the Lord for the meal. Commotion then ensued as food was passed and plates heaped. "How was Missouri, Gabe?" Mama asked.

"I was thankful for the opportunity to be able to help my aunt and uncle." Gabe moved some green beans on his plate with his fork, maintaining eye contact with Mama. "Reckon I am glad to be back though."

"We are so glad to have him back," said Mrs. Kleeman. "Gabe has purchased some land just west of ours and is going to have his own ranch."

"That's wonderful!" Mama buttered a piece of biscuit. "We are so proud of you, Gabe."

Meredith watched Gabe nod, seemingly nervous, at Mama's outburst of excitement. But then, Mama was nearly always excited about something. Pa said that was one of the things he loved about her the most—her cheerful fuss over everything from big things to seemingly mundane things. Gabe shifted in his seat and pushed more green beans to the side of his plate. The poor guy radiated nervousness under all the scrutiny.

"I see Tillie often, but, Meredith, how are you doing, dear?" Mrs. Kleeman asked.

"I am well, thank you."

Mama beamed, her smile lighting up her entire face. "Meredith sewed another wedding dress, this time for Roxie Goff. She is getting quite well known for her elegant creations."

"That is just delightful, dear. Perhaps someday you will sew one for yourself," Mrs. Kleeman said.

While there was no unkindness in her words, Meredith wanted to shrink beneath the table all the same. Why did everyone make such a fuss about her spinsterhood? "Yes, maybe so," she squeaked. Or maybe not.

The letter she'd received in the mail entered her mind, and she brushed the thought aside. That one lonely letter could hardly be considered an auspicious foretelling of her marital future.

The conversation turned to Tillie and Lula and their schooling. Meredith took a deep breath and sent a prayer of thanks to the good Lord for His provision in allowing the supper-table discussion to turn from her. Meredith needn't be reminded of the imminent arrival of spinsterhood and the immense distress it caused her.

She took a bite of meat loaf and caught Gabe Kleeman's gaze as it connected with hers. An unexpected shiver traveled through her. Mr. Kleeman hurriedly looked away, his nicely shaped ears turning red.

Nicely shaped ears? Where had that silly notion come from? Sure, the young Mr.

Kleeman did have nice ears, a nice face, too. But why was she noticing? And how had a man changed so much in the past three years? Puny did not enter the description of this now over six-foot-tall man with strong arms.

Meredith had never been considered shy. Quite the opposite, actually. She was a lot like Mama in her outgoing nature, although more realistic. Sitting here at the table with the changed Gabe Kleeman, however, did something to her insides she couldn't quite explain.

Gabe found sleep difficult that night. He tossed and turned, thinking of Meredith Waller and her pretty face across from him at the dinner table. He beheld in his mind the way a few strands of loose hair, the color of freshly upturned topsoil, hung around her shoulders. Her blue eyes had glinted every time she spoke, and Gabe had tried not to stare.

She had almost shut his foot in the door, not that Gabe minded. For a chance to court her, he would allow Meredith to shut his foot—both of his feet—in the door once a day if she desired. If only there was some way to make his intentions known. If only there was some way to know if she'd ever feel the same for him as he felt for her.

He deemed admiring Meredith Waller from a distance much safer.

Sure, Gabe was shy toward a few people, but he did quite well articulating his thoughts to those he had known for a good portion of his life. With Meredith, however, the words barely rose past his throat. She likely thought him a bumbling fool. Ma would remind him that muttering wasn't gentlemanly, and Gabe would chastise himself once again for his apprehensive disposition.

God had richly blessed Gabe with a loving family, a good-sized spread of a ranch, and, after so many years, the healing of his body. Gabe would never take good health for granted, not after having lived as an unhealthy boy without the ability to walk far without tiring, only to become a robust man with energy to spare.

Lord, I reckon this is a bit out of the ordinary, but could You please help me find words to speak to Meredith? And if it's Your will, Lord, might I ask that she be favorable toward me?

Chapter 5

The second letter arrived a week later. Meredith had checked the hole in the tree every day, not that she'd admit to anyone her curious obsession with an old tree on the way to town. Or why she made numerous trips to town when she had more important matters to tend to.

She scrutinized the obscure writing that she recognized from the prior letter. Her heart thumped loudly as she unfolded the letter:

> *Dear Miss Waller,*
> *The rose is red, the violet's blue,*
> *The honey's sweet, and so are you.*
>
>   *Yours Truly,*
>   *Your Secret Admirer*

Meredith blushed at the words. Yes, she knew they weren't original, but to have been copied by this mysterious secret admirer's hand and placed in the tree thrilled her.

Reaching into her reticule, Meredith retrieved her own envelope. Opening the flap, she read it one last time before depositing it in the secret place in the tree:

> *Dear Secret Admirer,*
> *Thank you for your kind letters. Can you give me a hint as to your identity? Are you from Ellis Creek? Elsewhere in the Montana Territory? Do I know you? How do you know me?*
>
>   *Yours Truly,*
>   *Meredith Waller*

Perhaps she had asked too many questions. What would etiquette books say of her superfluous curiosity?

At the notion of the etiquette books addressing the topic of conversing by letter with a secret admirer, Meredith laughed. Perhaps she should pen her own etiquette book and discuss such an unorthodox topic.

Weighing her options, Meredith finally persuaded herself to place the letter in the tree. If the questions in her letter were answered, the list of names Meredith had compiled for possibilities could be considerably narrowed.

Not that her mental list proved lengthy. No, it contained just four possibilities:

Leopold Arkwright, Mr. Griggs, Marvin Pratt, and an unnamed, unknown man from outside Ellis Creek. Not good choices. Well, except for the man from outside Ellis Creek; he could have potential.

Meredith sighed. Maybe she didn't want to know the identity of her mysterious suitor, after all.

Meredith slowed the wagon in front of the home of Widow Jones. A humble home, the one-story whitewashed house provided just enough room for the widow and her two young grandchildren.

Clutching her basket of sewing in one hand and two loaves of bread in the other, Meredith prayed she would bless the widow who had lost her beloved husband of fifty years and her son and daughter-in-law all in a year's time.

"Widow Jones?" Meredith called while tapping on the door.

"Meredith, what a delight to see you." With fingers gnarled from painful arthritis, Widow Jones opened the door and beckoned Meredith to enter.

"I brought your mending and two loaves of Mama's bread, fresh out of the oven."

Widow Jones smiled, bringing more prominence to the fine wrinkles that lined her soft face. "You are a dear, Meredith. Do come in."

Meredith followed Widow Jones into the home, placing the loaves of bread on the table. She reached a hand toward the widow's shawl-covered arm. "How are you doing today?"

"I am blessed. I don't know what I'd do without the body of Christ," Widow Jones continued. "You have all been so gracious to me in my time of need. How do people go through rough times without Jesus and the ones He calls to help us?"

Meredith and the widow chatted for some time until a knock at the door interrupted their conversation. "I wonder who could be paying me a visit. Would you mind seeing for me, Meredith? Getting out of this chair is a mite difficult anymore."

Meredith opened the front door to see none other than Gabe Kleeman. For a moment, her heart left her at the sight of the man before her. "Mr. Kleeman, what brings you here on this fine day? Do come in."

Gabe Kleeman had a nervous way about him and avoided her gaze. He appeared as though he wanted to say something but couldn't quite find the words. Instead, he nodded at Meredith and followed her into the widow's home.

"Gabe, is that you?" Widow Jones called.

"Yes, Widow Jones, it is."

Meredith observed that the handsome man had found his voice. He walked toward the widow, a crate in his arms. Arms with sleeves rolled up to his elbows and showing fibrous, sinewy muscles in his forearms.

Not that Meredith noticed.

Because Gabe Kleeman certainly didn't notice her at all. Not one bit.

"Ma wanted me to deliver a jar of jam and some spuds. I thought I'd also mend that fence while I'm here."

"You are such a dear, Gabe. That would be delightful. Before you mend the fence, why don't you join Meredith and me for some of your ma's jam on her mama's delicious bread?"

"Reckon that sounds fine, Widow Jones." Gabe sauntered toward the table, where he set the crate. "Nice day outside. Perhaps I could assist you outside on the porch for some sunshine."

Feeling a bit left out of the conversation, Meredith set about slicing three pieces of bread. Then, standing near Mr. Kleeman, she waited for the right moment to inquire if she might unload the jar of jam from the crate he still hovered over.

"That would be resplendent, Gabe. Perhaps we could carry this chair to the porch." Widow Jones patted the arms of the rocking chair.

"No need for that, ma'am. I brought a chair for you in the back of my wagon."

Widow Jones's eyes grew wide. "You brought a chair for me to borrow? An outside chair?"

"Better than that. I made you a chair you can keep. That way, you can watch over your grandsons while they do their chores or play outside."

"My, but isn't he a fine young man, Meredith?" Widow Jones beamed. "A handsome one at that."

Meredith didn't have to have Mama's handheld mirror to know her face was covered with a bright red blush.

The tips of Gabe Kleeman's ears grew red, and he glanced at her out of the corner of his eye. The poor man must be just as embarrassed.

Meredith cleared her throat in the most ladylike way possible. "Mr. Kleeman, might I have the jar of jam? I'll prepare each of us a slice of bread." There. She had changed the subject. Now she would will her face, likely the color of the strawberry preserves in Gabe Kleeman's crate, to return to a normal pallor.

Mr. Kleeman nodded and reached into the crate for a jar of jam. He turned and, without meeting her eye, handed it to her.

Only something happened and the jar didn't make its graceful transition from Mr. Kleeman's hand to Meredith's. Instead, it began a quick descent to the floor.

With agile and nimble fingers, Gabe Kleeman caught and rescued the jam before it splattered all over Widow Jones's floor.

Meredith released the breath she was holding as Mr. Kleeman returned to his normal height. "Here, uh, Miss Waller," he muttered, handing her the jar.

When his fingers lightly brushed hers, Meredith almost dropped the jar of preserves all over again. "Thank you."

Gabe Kleeman's eyes darted from Meredith's face to some unknown spot on the wall behind her. Did he blame her for the awkward transition of the jam jar? Meredith hastily found an empty space on the table and continued her preparations. She inhaled the delectable scent of the strawberry preserves and attempted her best to forget that Mr. Kleeman stood nearby.

"Meredith, don't you and Gabe know each other from your school days?" Widow Jones asked.

Meredith almost jumped plumb out of her skin at the widow's voice. "Begging your pardon, Widow Jones?"

"Are not you and Gabe acquaintances from school?"

Meredith attempted to reconcile the puny and feeble boy she remembered from school with the strong and healthy man not far from her side. "Yes, ma'am, we are."

"And don't you two know each other from church, Gabe?" Widow Jones questioned.

"Yes, Widow, we do."

"Then why is it that you are both so formal? 'Mr. Kleeman' this, 'Miss Waller' that. Ellis Creek is a small town. Now, I understand calling older folks by their surnames and with all the politeness your mamas taught you, but you two are young folks and have known each other nearly all of your lives. Why not just forgo the Waller and Kleeman notions and make good use of your given names?"

"Yes, ma'am," Meredith and Gabe chorused.

Meredith mused that calling Mr. Kleeman "Gabe" would be so much easier if he knew she existed. Liking him from afar was a challenge.

Would he ever notice her?

She might just have to give up on that quest if shutting his foot in the door and clumsily dropping jam hadn't worked.

Gabe started his work on the fence, all the while knowing that the beautiful woman of his affections stood nearby on the porch as Widow Jones sat in her new chair. If only he had made a good impression on her. Instead, his fumble fingers had almost dropped the jar of preserves. What must Meredith think of him?

He could hear her sunny laughter as Meredith and the widow conversed. With a squint of his eyes from the sun, Gabe caught a glimpse of her slender form. Meredith was taller than most women, but he wagered—no he knew—that the top of Meredith's head reached his chin. If she tilted her pretty little head back just right, he could plant a kiss atop those lips without even having to bend much.

Whoa, Gabe Kleeman! Back up the horse! What kind of thoughts were those? That he could kiss her without even bending much? Gabe shook his head. He had no business thinking such thoughts, especially about a woman who didn't and wouldn't likely ever know of his affections.

But then, he couldn't just tell her of his fondness for her. Not when his tongue either didn't work or was tied up in knots at the very sight of her. It happened each time Gabe was in her presence. His knees shook beneath his trousers, he had a strong desire to run in the opposite direction, and words that formed in his throat never made it to his mouth.

He wished beyond wishes the good Lord hadn't made him so shy. Gabe could have done with just a minute bit of the boldness God gave other men.

Standing so close to her in the widow's house had almost been his undoing. When the jar of jam nearly fell and then his fingers brushed hers—was this what it felt like to be in love?

Fiddlesticks! What was a man doing thinking of such things anyway? He would be laughed all the way to a water-filled trough where he'd be dunked for sure in a quest to empty his head of such foolish notions.

Gabe glimpsed a moment into his far-off future. He would be ninety years old and still eyeing Meredith from a distance. His voice would crackle with age—not that many words would leave his lips when in Meredith's presence. Meredith would have white hair like the Widow Jones and wrinkles aplenty, yet he'd still find her easy on the eyes. And while Gabe would have likely lost all his teeth and his eyesight would be starting to deteriorate, things would still be the same in one way: his admiration for Meredith would remain.

In the middle of mending the fence, a thought occurred to Gabe. Should he retrieve a chair for Meredith from the house? Surely she would enjoy sitting with Widow Jones on the porch. And if Meredith continued to stay on the porch in a comfortable chair, Gabe could admire her all the more. From a safe distance, of course.

Gabe rolled his eyes. When had he become a lovelorn fool? He had never been able to speak to Meredith at school on the rare days when he'd attended. He'd missed so many days from illness, having to partake in studies in his bed or, when feeling better, at the kitchen table. When he attended school, Gabe took to staring at Meredith when she was facing the opposite direction. She never knew, not once, that he had admired her from the back of the schoolroom. She also never knew that he was the one who'd brought her a fresh apple from the neighbor's apple tree and placed it at her desk at school. She'd thought for sure it was that obnoxious Dean Floshour.

Years later, Gabe's feelings for Meredith endured. He sighed and sauntered toward the house. Even if he couldn't find the words to speak to her, he could be a gentleman. His ma had raised him right.

"Gabe, dear. This chair is right comfortable. Thank you for making it for me. Isn't Gabe a fine carpenter, Meredith?"

"Indeed, he is, Widow Jones." Of course, Meredith would be polite and agree with the widow, even if Gabe had built a shabby and ill-constructed chair.

"I was wondering if—" Gabe took a deep breath, and instead of addressing his question to Meredith, he took the safer route and addressed Widow Jones. "I was wondering, Widow, if I might retrieve a chair for Miss Wal—Meredith from the house so she might sit with you, rather than stand."

"Sounds right fine, Gabe. Although I must insist you ask her if she would desire a chair."

Gabe was afraid of that. Perhaps he should retreat back to the field. The fence wouldn't mend itself. He glanced back at the field. It wasn't that far, and since Meredith likely thought him a fool, it would hardly strike her as odd if he retreated without directly asking her.

"Go ahead, Gabe. Ask her," Widow Jones prodded. The kindly old woman sure didn't help matters much.

"Uh, Meredith?"

"Yes?"

If only he could have continued without her gazing up at him with those sparkly blue eyes. Suddenly, he lost all nerve.

If he'd ever had any to begin with.

Silence filled the air. Gabe looked away. He focused his attention on the mountains, the ground, the corral, and then the barn. Finally, he had a solution to his dilemma. Sauntering past Meredith and Widow Jones, he entered the home, retrieved the chair, and set it next to the widow's chair.

Meredith threw him an odd glance. "Thank you, Gabe," she said, taking a seat on the house chair.

Gabe touched the brim of his hat, hurrying back to mending the fence. He shook his head. Whatever would Meredith think of him now?

Meredith took a seat on the house chair and watched as Gabe returned to the field. Had she done something to offend him? He certainly seemed peculiar and hesitant around her. He rarely looked her in the eye, and he spoke less often than that. Maybe his illness had rendered him unable to speak many words.

Then why did he have no problem speaking to others? Meredith shrugged. The man perplexed her.

"That Gabe must not be feeling well. He is usually chattier than that," Widow Jones said, interrupting Meredith's thoughts. "It's so nice having him back in Ellis Creek. What with him helping his aunt and uncle in Missouri for those years, I know his family here missed him something awful. Can you believe how much healthier he looks?"

Meredith turned her face to avoid allowing Widow Jones a chance to see her flushed expression. Gabe looked healthy, all right. Downright handsome with those brawny shoulders.

Widow Jones continued. "I recall how burdensome it was for him always feeling poorly as a young'un. Here about four or five years ago, he started to feel much better. Do you remember that?"

"I'm sorry, I don't, Widow Jones." Where had she been, for goodness' sake, that she could not remember seeing much of Gabe? Meredith recalled him in school, but then as they got older, she hadn't seen as much of him, even though their parents and their sisters were friends.

"Then he goes to Missouri and breathes in that fresh Midwestern air and the Lord heals him, what appears to be completely. Can't anyone say the Lord doesn't perform miracles anymore. Look what our gracious Father did for Gabe." Widow Jones held out her gnarled fingers. "I'm praying for a miracle with this arthritis."

The topic of conversation needs to be changed from the discussion of Gabe. "Widow Jones, you know I aim to be of assistance to you with the sewing or baking or whatever else you need, as is my mama."

"Yes, and I thank you kindly for that. Now back to Gabe."

So much for changing the subject, thought Meredith.

"Such a fine man. Do you know if he's entered into a courtship with anyone in Ellis

Creek?" Widow Jones scrutinized Meredith, seemingly prying for details.

Meredith swallowed hard and prayed that Widow Jones missed the rosy tint that dotted her face. "I can't say as I know for sure, ma'am."

"Perhaps you ought to ponder such a thought yourself. You'd make a right fine couple. And what's there not to like about that young man out there mending my fence? A godly, kind soul if there ever was one."

"That he is, Widow Jones."

Meredith chastised herself for hoping that the eyesight of Widow Jones wasn't what it had once been. Otherwise, the elderly woman would see the embarrassment Meredith found impossible to disguise.

Chapter 6

Meredith hadn't received a letter from her secret admirer in over three days. Disappointed, she decided to walk to church ahead of the rest of her family to check the tree for a letter and, of course, get some fresh air. Thankfully, Tillie hadn't suggested Meredith needed a little sister to join her on that walk.

When Meredith reached the tree, she eyed the surrounding area, reassuring herself there were no onlookers. For what would one think about Meredith Waller reaching into an old tree to claim personal letters? That latest piece of gossip would ripple through Ellis Creek in less than five minutes.

Sure enough, an envelope with the same writing had been placed in the tree. Taking several steps away from the tree, Meredith promptly opened it:

> *Dear Miss Waller,*
> *Thank you for writing me and for your questions. I am somewhat from Ellis Creek. Yes, you know me. Yes, I know you. I hope you are having a splendid week. Are you going to the church potluck?*
>
> > *Yours Truly,*
> > *Your Secret Admirer*

When had the author delivered this most recent letter? Would he be attending the potluck today after church? For that matter, did he attend church?

He mentioned that they knew each other. Meredith's brow furrowed. He had answered all of her questions, although the answer about his residence bordered on obscurity. *Somewhat from Ellis Creek?*

Such revelations could only mean one of two things. Either her secret admirer was indeed Mr. Pratt, Leopold Arkwright, or Marvin Griggs, although none of these choices held even the least bit of appeal. Or Meredith's admirer could be someone she hadn't yet considered.

Meredith chose the latter scenario.

Reaching into her reticule, she placed another letter in the tree. She had to have hope. Otherwise, this constant writing back and forth was futile.

The church potluck followed the service, and Meredith watched as her parents joined with friends. Tillie, Lula, and Charles bounded toward their classmates, and the group

Mama had termed "the young folks" met on the east side of the church. Meredith headed toward the group, many of whom she had known since childhood.

Soon-to-be-married Roxie and Perry joined other young couples, including Idella and Richard and Enid and Hugh. Meredith felt a bit out of place with all the other couples either already married or courting but took comfort when she saw Gabe. *Thank You, Lord, that I am not the only one without someone.* Her eyes connected with Gabe's for a brief moment before he looked away. Could that have been a slight twinge of a smile on his lips?

Greetings took place around the circle of friends, and conversation began. *Perhaps this won't be so bad, after all*, Meredith thought, engaging herself in talk with her female friends about the newest fabric patterns at the mercantile.

They stood in line for their food then regrouped, sitting on the grass. Meredith thought perhaps her heart might thump right out of her chest when Gabe took a seat next to her on her left.

What if she dribbled lemonade down her chin or plopped a piece of pie right in her lap with the object of her affection sitting so close? A surreptitious glimpse at Gabe's strong profile told her he might be just as nervous as she.

Roxie sat to her immediate right. "What a perfect day for a potluck," her best friend exclaimed in between bites of her sandwich. "Oh, look. There's Widow Jones."

The group waved at the widow and her young grandsons, as they headed toward friends. "Were you able to convince Widow Jones to allow you to assist her with her mending, Meredith?" Enid asked. "Ma says the widow can be a bit stubborn at times."

"I was. Her arthritis is so painful sometimes. I told her I was happy to retrieve her mending once a week, or more often if need be." Meredith saw Hugh shoot a mischievous glance toward Gabe.

"I hear that you and Meredith were out helping the widow on the same day last week," Hugh said, a smirk lining his dark features. Hugh had always had a wit about him. Meredith just wished this time it hadn't been directed toward her and Gabe and the irony of their visit to Widow Jones on the same day. Thank goodness Hugh hadn't been there to observe the falling jam jar episode.

"Yes. I mended a fence for her," said Gabe.

"So you and Meredith were able to assist the widow on the same day. That's good." Hugh nudged Enid, and they gave each other a knowing glance.

Meredith knew her cheeks had to be the color of the red flowers on her calico skirt and from her peripheral view, she saw Gabe shift to a different sitting position.

The conversation soon changed to another topic, and Meredith attempted to relax. Suddenly, a strong gust of wind blew, causing Meredith's handkerchief to float from her lap.

She leaned forward to retrieve it.

Gabe did the same.

Their heads connected with a clunk, and Meredith winced.

"I'm. . .sorry, Meredith." Gabe whispered.

When Meredith opened her eyes, Gabe's face was directly in front of hers. Their eyes connected. His, so handsomely hazel. And then with that lock of brown hair falling over his forehead. . . Meredith knew her heart stopped for certain. The awkwardness of the situation hampered her breathing, and she stared into his eyes, and he into hers. For a moment, she forgot all about the threatening headache from the collision with Gabe's noggin.

Several chuckles and giggles interrupted Meredith's whimsical thoughts, and she and Gabe hastily pulled away from each other. Meredith placed a hand on the sore spot of her head.

Silence ensued. All of their friends waiting to see what happened next in this awkward, yet romantic situation, perhaps? Meredith inwardly cringed. She'd never hear the end of it from Roxie, Enid, and Idella.

"Sorry," Gabe said.

"Begging your pardon," squeaked Meredith, their words colliding in chorus.

"Here." He handed her the handkerchief that had caused all the troubles in the first place. She attempted to reclaim the handkerchief, only to miss it and have it drift to the ground in front of her. Careful not to have a repeat of their heads colliding, Gabe cautiously picked up the handkerchief and again handed it to her.

"Goodness, but I fear I have butterfingers today." Meredith found it odd that her voice sounded like someone else's entirely in her ears, all high-pitched and shrill. Since when was she so antsy?

When the dapper Gabe Kleeman was sitting within a foot of her, that's when.

Gabe offered a slow, handsome smile, and his face and ears turned a bright red. He said nothing, returning his attention to his food.

Meredith dared to look around at their friends. Roxie and Perry winked at each other; Enid and Hugh smirked; Idella appeared perplexed; and Richard was too busy eating his midday meal to notice. This event would certainly be fodder for the gossip mill.

Finally, Roxie, bless her heart, brought up the subject of the weather.

Chapter 7

Over the past few years, the Waller and Kleeman families had spent a lot of time together. But that was when Gabe was in Missouri. With Gabe's return, visiting each other's families had become a trifle awkward.

As they walked toward Gabe's home the following Saturday evening, Meredith noticed that Mama and Mrs. Kleeman began chatting about the happenings around town and how Charles was assisting Widow Jones this evening. Behind them, Pa and Mr. Kleeman chatted about grain prices. In the back, Tillie and Lula giggled about schoolgirl notions. Soon Gabe fell into step with Meredith.

The silence between Meredith and Gabe was awkward, but not as awkward as Lula and Tillie's giggles and whispers. Meredith could only imagine what they must be saying, and she was sure it involved her and Gabe, especially since news of the potluck incident had reached its way to Tillie's ears.

"Sure has been nice weather," Meredith commented, just to take her mind off of the discomfort she felt.

Gabe avoided her gaze and continued down the road. "Uh, yes, it has been."

"I wouldn't trade the summers in Ellis Creek for anything. Not that I've lived anywhere else, mind you, to know about the summer season in other places." Yes, she was rambling. Meredith closed her mouth and worked her lip between her teeth. Why must she always sound like a blabbering ninny? It didn't help that Gabe proved not to be the most proactive conversationalist.

What must he think of her? Meredith tried not to stare at his strong and handsome profile. Why had she not noticed what a dapper man he was before this year? Clearly, she had been spending far too much time sewing dresses and far too little time noticing the man she'd known since they were children in school.

"How were the summers in Missouri?" There she went again. Her mouth opened before she could tell it to remain closed.

"Uh. . .reckon they were fine. Humid."

Gabe kept his focus forward. Why was the man so difficult to talk to? Did he think her a simpleton?

"Are you glad to be back in the Montana Territory?"

More giggles and snorts from the obnoxious factory greeted Meredith's question to Gabe, and she noticed that if Lula and Tillie were any closer, they would be stepping on her heels. She whirled around and narrowed her eyes at her sister.

"Yes."

"That's good."

"That's good," Tillie mimicked Meredith in an exaggerated voice.

It was then that Meredith noticed that the girls had been copying everything she and Gabe had said, with Tillie mimicking her and Lula mimicking Gabe. Meredith had every mind to let that little sister of hers know that if she didn't stop posthaste, Tillie would be doing all of Meredith's chores on top of her own until Tillie was at least fifty-six.

She again turned and glared at the girls.

Gabe caught her glare, and a deep blush covered Meredith's face. Oh, dear. Now he must think of her as harsh. Meredith faced forward once again. It was just far too difficult to carry on a conversation with Gabe, the man of few words, especially with two annoying pestilences mocking every bit of the nearly one-sided conversation.

They reached Gabe's ranch, and fortunately, Gabe joined his father in showing Meredith's pa the barn, the corrals, and finally, the humble home.

"Impressive for a man so young, wouldn't you agree, dear?" Mama asked.

Meredith didn't need to see Gabe's ranch to be impressed. She was already captivated by his love for the Lord, his kind and thoughtful ways, and, of course, his dapper appearance.

Yesterday, Roxie had asked Meredith if she fancied Gabe. Meredith admitted it, to which Roxie had exclaimed, "Wouldn't it just be wonderful if the two of you began to court?"

"He doesn't know I exist," Meredith had answered.

"Oh, he knows you exist, all right."

"How can you be so sure?"

"Trust me. He sees you, Meredith."

Meredith hadn't told Roxie about the secret letters she'd been receiving, although she had been tempted to share the news. It was one of those rare things she decided to keep even from her best friend.

If only the man who was delivering the letters could be someone like Gabe instead of the likely prospects of Leopold Arkwright, Marvin Pratt, or Mr. Griggs.

Thinking back on her conversation with Roxie, Meredith wished she could see the big picture the Lord saw, instead of the small tintype she managed. Then she would know for sure if Gabe fancied her, or at the very least, knew she existed.

Gabe tossed a pile of hay to the horses in the corral. If he showed wisdom in how he spent his earnings, he should be able to add a few more cattle to his herd by next year. If he continued to grow his herd, he should be able to provide a nice home for the woman he would someday marry.

Marriage?

Meredith Waller had messed with Gabe's mind. He had never contemplated marriage until he'd returned from Missouri and seen Meredith sitting in church.

The woman he'd never truly forgotten.

What must she think of him? After the potluck and him thudding his head into hers while she reached for the handkerchief, she must think of him as a buffoon. A woman as lovely as her could have a choice of any man to court. Why would she choose someone like him? Someone who was clumsy and wordless?

Although, Gabe had to admit, his speaking when around her had improved, thanks to the countless prayers he'd sent heavenward. While they were walking to his home with the families last week, he had actually said more than one word at a time. Twice. He had actually articulated words, rather than grunts, in her presence. God was steadily helping him improve. Hopefully, those small improvements would be enough to win her heart.

Gabe perused the area around his ranch. With the exception of the animals, he was alone. Perhaps this would be as good a time as any to practice his speaking skills. He beckoned his horse, Dottie. She ambled toward him, and he fed her an apple. "Now, Dottie, I need your help. You see, there's this girl named Meredith. I've fancied her for many years." Gabe paused and scanned from right to left, just to be sure no one had arrived at his ranch.

Seeing no one, he continued. "Dottie, I'm going to pretend you are Meredith so I can work on my speaking skills. For some reason, I'm tongue-tied beyond belief when I'm in her presence. Are you ready?"

As if she understood, Dottie nodded her head and neighed.

"Hello, Meredith. You look beautiful today. You have the prettiest blue eyes I've ever seen." Gabe grinned and tried his best to imagine Meredith stood before him, rather than his horse. "Reckon it is still two months away, but I would be much obliged if you would attend the—" He paused. He really had to practice this part so he wouldn't make the same mistake he'd made years ago when he'd called the barn dance a *yarn bance*.

"I was wondering if you'd accompany me to the harvest barn dance at the Randels'."

Dottie seemed distracted, as she nodded her head to and fro.

"Is that a yes?"

Giggles and snorts interrupted Gabe's conversation. He turned to see Lula snickering behind him. He felt his face flush as he gritted his teeth. When had she arrived, and how much had she heard? "Lula, what are you doing here?"

"Watching you carry on a conversation with a horse." She started giggling again.

"Don't you talk to your pets at home? I reckon you've spoken to your puppy many times."

"True, but I never pretended he was Meredith!"

"Lula, you will not tell anyone about what you just saw."

"I won't?" With that, Lula took off down the road, her long braids flying behind her.

Gabe ran after her. He recalled a time, not too far in the past, when he couldn't run to save his life. His weak legs could barely walk on some days. But not today. God had healed him, and he would catch that impudent sister of his if it was the last thing he did.

With his long stride, it didn't take long to catch up to her. "Lula, please stop."

Lula whirled around to face him, her face flushed from laughing so hard at his expense. "Will you, please, not tell anyone about what you saw and heard here today?"

She seemed to ponder his question. "So you admit that you were pretending that Dottie was Meredith and that you were telling her how beautiful she is with her pretty blue eyes?"

Gabe sighed. "All right. I admit I was practicing my speech for Meredith on Dottie."

"That's what I thought. So you do like Meredith then?"

"Maybe."

"For a bag of jawbreakers, I might be persuaded not to utter a word about this to anyone." Lula paused then whispered, "Except Tillie."

"For a bag of jawbreakers, you'll not utter a word to anyone, not even Tillie."

Lula's shoulders slumped. "But she's my best friend."

"Not even Tillie, Lula."

"All right. I'll do my best."

"Were you stopping by for a visit?"

"Ma wanted me to invite you to supper." Lula's eyes darted to and fro, as if she were hiding something. Of all the sisters God could have given him, the good Lord had to give Gabe a mischievous one.

"Lula, you're acting mighty peculiar."

Lula shifted her shoes in the soft dirt. "I just might have an idea, that's all."

"An idea?"

"An idea to help you be able to speak to Meredith without being such a shy fellow."

So Lula had noticed. Just grand. "What's your idea?"

"Not so fast. First, you must agree to two things."

"Two things?"

"Yes. First, you must agree that I may call an important meeting with Tillie to discuss this matter before I share with you my magnificent idea."

Gabe exhaled. This was not boding well for him. "And second?"

"Second thing is that you, under no circumstances, can be angry with me for my idea or any ideas in the past."

"This sounds suspicious, Lula. Reckon I can't agree to your terms."

Lula folded her arms across her chest. "Then I'm afraid I can't tell you my idea, and you will really want to hear it."

"All right, all right," Gabe said, after offering prayers for patience. "I reluctantly agree to your terms."

"Then give me an hour, and I'll be back to present my idea to you before supper." With that, Lula bounded off, braids flying behind her, as she headed toward their parents' home.

True to her word, Lula returned about an hour later. Gabe had agonized about her idea. It would either be an impressive one, or it would be the worst idea he'd ever heard. He banked on the latter.

"I spoke with Tillie. She regrets she is unable to attend this meeting due to the fact that she may have exaggerated about having her chores completed. Sometimes children make bad decisions of that sort."

Gabe narrowed his eyes at Lula. Hadn't she pulled that same antic with their parents a time or two?

"So Tillie and I did something. Now remember, Gabe, you promised not be angry about anything I am about to tell you."

"Go on, Lula."

"You see, some time ago, Tillie and I decided we wanted to become sisters forever. The only way to do that was for us to convince you and Meredith to get married."

"What?"

"Wait. It gets much better. We had this grandiose plan to write letters to Meredith from you."

"Write letters to Meredith from me?"

"Is there an echo on this ranch?"

Gabe shook his head. "Lula, please, tell me you did not write letters to Meredith from me." If Meredith didn't already think him a buffoon, she certainly would after some crazy letters supposedly from him.

"We did. But here's the good news. We've only written. . ." Lula counted on her fingers. "We've only written her five of them."

"Five?"

"Yes. And more good news. We signed them from a 'secret admirer.' According to a good source, Meredith does not suspect it is you writing the letters."

A good source? That could only mean Tillie.

Whom did she suspect? It could be good. . .or bad that Meredith did not suspect him. Did she wish it was a certain fellow? Someone like Leopold Arkwright? Gabe had seen many an unmarried woman swooning over him a time or two. "I can't believe you and Tillie did that."

"Some call us geniuses. I prefer the term *creative*."

More like impish. "How can this help me?"

"Well, she has written back. Her letters are rather dull and full of questions, but if you started really writing the letters"—Lula paused for effect—"if you really were the one writing the letters, you could win her heart without uttering a word."

Gabe mulled over Lula's words. This might not be so bad after all. Surely on paper, he could say things he would never have the nerve to say in person. "Reckon I could give it a try. How are you delivering the letters?"

"In the sliver in the knot of the old oak tree near the Jones' place."

"Do you have the letters she's written?"

"For a bag of jawbreakers for Tillie, she says I can give them to you."

Gabe would be poor for certain if he continued to spend his hard-earned money on jawbreakers. "This is bribery, Lula."

Lula shrugged. "I think Meredith would delight in receiving letters from you. You could ask her questions and find out more about her. Then when you fall in love you'll know what her favorite color is and all those good things to know about the woman you court."

The crazy idea could work. Perhaps through the letters, Gabe could gather the courage to make his intentions toward a particular young lady known.

If his letters to Meredith were deemed as favorable.

And if he could write better than he could speak.

Chapter 8

The letters arrived with more regularity, but that wasn't the only thing Meredith noticed had changed. The handwriting was different. Her curiosity piqued. Had this suddenly become a prank? Were there two authors?

She would have to ponder this latest development.

Meredith shut the door to the room she shared with Tillie. She certainly did not want her younger sister to know about the letters. Tillie would undoubtedly share that tidbit of juicy gossip with Lula, who would manage to find a way to share it with others until the entire town of Ellis Creek was privy to the letters. Or they would find a way to publish it in the *Ellis Creek Journal*, which was always on the lookout for intriguing stories. Meredith cringed at that thought.

She plopped on the bed and noticed an open bag of jawbreakers on the chest of drawers she and Tillie shared. It certainly seemed as though Tillie ate far more jawbreakers than usual as of late.

Brushing the strange observation aside, Meredith opened her stash of letters and dumped them on the quilt to peruse. There had been five letters in the same handwriting and now two more recent letters in different handwriting, so seven letters total. She didn't recognize the penmanship of either batch of letters, but the second batch appeared more deliberate, interesting, and thorough.

She reached for a piece of stationery and penned a letter. Since her admirer hadn't been clear on his residence in one of his past letters, she decided to again address the issue. Knowing if he resided here would certainly assist her in determining his identity:

Dear Secret Admirer,
Are you a man of religion? For what are you most grateful? Do you reside in Ellis Creek?
Yours Truly,
Meredith Waller

The response arrived in two days.

Dear Miss Waller,
Yes, I reside in Ellis Creek. Yes, I am a man of religion and a devoted follower of Christ. I am most grateful for the many blessings He has given me, including family and good health. For what are you most grateful?
Yours Truly,
Your Secret Admirer

Meredith read and reread the most recent letter. While thankful that he loved the Lord and had gratitude, she was determined more than ever to solve the mystery.

Stopping at the mercantile the following day, Meredith spied Marvin Pratt. Could he be the one who was writing to her?

She hoped not.

Although he would be better than the other possible admirers.

Meredith stood next to the shelf containing the sugar and flour and attempted to spy on Mr. Pratt while remaining discreet.

Marvin Pratt held a list in his hand and handed it to Mrs. Burris, the proprietor. "I'll be needin' these items for my ma."

"Very well, Marvin. Give me just a moment."

Mrs. Burris, who with her severe hair and glasses reminded Meredith more of a schoolmarm than a co-owner of the lone mercantile in Ellis Creek, bustled about, locating items for Mr. Pratt. When she finished, she placed the list on the counter and began calculating the total due.

"That'll be three dollars and eighty-seven cents," she told her customer.

Mr. Pratt dug his hands into his trouser pockets. "Can you put that on my pa's account?"

"Certainly."

"Thank you." Mr. Pratt grabbed the crate with some effort and seemed to rest it on his protruding stomach for ease of carrying. "Well, hello there, Miss Waller. Pleasure seeing you here today."

"Hello, Mr. Pratt."

"What brings you out on this fine day?"

"Oh, just some errands. And you?"

"Retrieving some items for Ma. She's making my favorite supper tonight: meat loaf with mixed vegetables. Couldn't survive one day without her fine cookin'." Mr. Pratt paused. "Reckon I enjoyed the church sermon a whole lot this past Sunday. Am thankful that my back isn't giving me grief like it does on occasion."

Meredith swallowed hard. Hadn't her secret admirer mentioned he was a man of God and thankful for good health?

Not that Marvin Pratt wasn't a nice man. On the contrary, he had always been polite. But at age thirty, he hadn't yet found a way to live on his own without the care of his parents. "Have a fine day, Mr. Pratt."

"You as well, Miss Waller." With an amiable bob of his round head, Marvin Pratt exited the mercantile.

That's when Meredith saw it. Mr. Pratt's item list. Could it be the key to solving the letter mystery?

She hoped the list was in Mr. Pratt's penmanship, rather than his mother's.

"Mrs. Burris, may I see that list?"

Mrs. Burris gave Meredith a befuddled look. "Mr. Pratt's list of items?"

"Yes, ma'am."

With a perplexed facial expression, Mrs. Burris handed Meredith the list. It was a man's penmanship, Meredith was sure about that. But it didn't match the handwriting of either batch of letters she had received.

She let out an enormous sigh. "Thank you, Mrs. Burris." Eyeballing her own list, she added, "I see that I need some baking powder."

Mrs. Burris's eyes rolled behind large wire-rimmed spectacles. "Oh, that's why you needed to see Mr. Pratt's list. So you could discern what item you had forgotten. I thought as much."

Meredith didn't want to lie, so she instead smiled. She offered a prayer of gratitude that Marvin Pratt was one more person to mark off her list of possible suspects.

Gabe found that he enjoyed receiving and writing the letters. But most of all, receiving them. Meredith had elegant penmanship, and each letter held her soft scent of lavender. Who'd have thought he, Gabe Kleeman, man of few words, would become the author of letters? And who would have thought that Lula and Tillie would have actually thought up a worthwhile idea?

Of course, the letters that the two best friends had written made Gabe cringe. Especially the poem. He would never write anything like that. Ever. Gabe did not consider himself a poet in any sense of the word, and he had never been syrupy or lovey-dovey.

Through the letters, he found that he and Meredith had much in common. Not that he had ever doubted that. Having known her since school, he knew they shared many similar interests.

Gabe read her most recent letter:

Dear Secret Admirer,
What traits do you most admire in others? What things in life vex you most?
Yours Truly,
Meredith Waller

The answers to those questions weren't difficult, although Gabe was glad he was writing the answers, rather than speaking them. Tillie had offered him stationery, and in his best penmanship, he wrote:

Dear Miss Waller,
The traits I most admire in others are kindness and helping those in need. What trait do you admire most in others? The things that vex me most are liars and those riding through town too quickly and nearly running someone over. What most vexes you?
What is your favorite color?
Yours Truly,
Your Secret Admirer

Gabe placed the letter in his trouser pocket. Later today, he would ride into town and deliver it. While it had become costly to keep Lula and Tillie in jaw-breakers, it had been worth it. Gabe had all of the letters they had collected from

Meredith. He also had their promised silence.

What would become of this odd situation? Would Meredith ever find out it was him who had written the letters—well, the most recent letters? If she did find out, would she be thrilled or disappointed? Perhaps she'd rather it be someone like the wealthy Leopold Arkwright.

· ❖ ·

Two days later, Gabe found a letter from Meredith in the tree. The objective was to avoid being there when Meredith was, lest she discover his secret. So far, he'd been lucky in that aspect. Climbing on his horse, he rode a short stretch before opening the letter:

> *Dear Secret Admirer,*
> *Thank you for your letter. I am glad you appreciate helping those less fortunate. I, too, agree that liars and those riding too quickly through town are vexing. For me, I would add that sewing a crooked seam and having to resew it is irritating as well. Another thing that perturbs me is ungentlemanly behavior. As for traits I admire most in others, those would include honesty, thoughtfulness, and loyalty.*
> *My favorite color is purple.*
>
>

Yours Truly,
Meredith Waller

Gabe caught the scent of Meredith's perfume on the letter and inhaled. He had been giving the letters much thought lately. Perhaps it was time to reveal who he was to her. But then again, maybe not. What if Meredith abhorred the thought of him being her secret admirer? While she was pleasant whenever they met in person, Gabe figured she likely had several other suitors vying for her hand in courtship.

One of them was likely that brash Leopold Arkwright. Would Gabe have a chance against someone as wealthy and dapper as Leopold?

If Meredith discovered that it was Gabe who sent the letters, would she be thrilled? Or would she kindly reject him? Forget about *when* he told her. *How* would he tell her? While the Lord had given him assistance in the shyness department, Gabe still struggled with stringing words together in her presence.

Gabe nudged Dottie into a gallop as he passed by the Randels' farm. That's when an idea came to him.

Later that evening, he penned yet another letter to Meredith:

> *Dear Miss Waller,*
> *Are you attending the barn dance at the Randels' next week? I plan to attend and would like very much the honor of dancing with you. I will be wearing a red bandanna on my left arm.*
>
>

Yours Truly,
Your Secret Admirer

Chapter 9

More letters had arrived in recent days, and Meredith again contemplated the conundrum of why the most recent letters contained different handwriting than the earlier ones. If she were a Pinkerton detective, she would have already solved this mystery.

As she shoved open the door to the Ellis Creek National Bank, an idea came to her. Perhaps she could cross another likely letter-writer off her list by asking for a sample of Leopold Arkwright's penmanship.

"Well, Miss Waller. To what do I owe the pleasure?" Leopold Arkwright adjusted the glasses on his pointed nose and offered her a wide grin.

A grin that rendered many eligible women in Ellis Creek flustered and giddy. But not Meredith. Mr. Arkwright's "charms" had no effect on her.

Meredith retrieved her coin purse and placed four coins on the counter. "I'd like to make a deposit, please, Mr. Arkwright."

"Certainly." Mr. Arkwright leaned toward her through the banker's window and offered a coquettish wink. "How are you this fine day, Miss Waller?"

Meredith took in the site of Leopold Arkwright's mutton chop whiskers, which framed his narrow aristocratic face; his thick glasses; and his even thicker eyebrows; and she offered a silent prayer heavenward: *Lord, please, can my secret admirer not be Leopold Arkwright?*

Not that the man wasn't amicable, because he was. But Mr. Arkwright had an excessive sense of self, and his intentions were a bit forward. "I'm fine, Mr. Arkwright. And you?"

"Doing quite well. I certainly appreciate you choosing to do your banking at Ellis Creek National Bank."

Meredith didn't mention that the Ellis Creek National Bank was the only bank in town.

She pushed aside her thoughts of banking and deliberated about the real reason she had visited the bank: to discover if Mr. Arkwright was her secret admirer. Had he written any or all of the letters to her? She pushed aside the dismal thought.

"Mr. Arkwright?"

"Yes, Miss Waller?"

"Could I kindly ask a favor of you?"

"Most certainly. A buggy ride? A picnic? Accompaniment to the Randels' barn dance next week?"

At the latter, Meredith widened her eyes, and her heart raced. Hadn't one of the most recent letters mentioned the Randel barn dance?

"No, no, thank you, Mr. Arkwright. Rather, could you please write *dearest bandanna dance* on a slip of paper?"

"Dearest bandanna dance? Why, Miss Waller, you are not only winsome, but you also have a marvelous sense of humor." Leopold Arkwright threw his head back with a chortle, causing his neatly combed hair to flutter to the other side of his head.

Without hesitation, the banker retrieved a slip of paper from his desk and wrote the words Meredith had requested. She held her breath. He then pushed it through the teller window toward her. "Now then, is that what you requested?"

Meredith glanced at the writing, but she couldn't ascertain if it was the same writing as the writing in the letters she had received. Did all men write in a similar fashion? "Could you also add the words. . ." Meredith made a show of pretending to think up more silly words. "Could you also write the words *secret*, *forward*, and *barn*?"

"At your service, dear lady."

Meredith did her best not to roll her eyes at the banker's exaggerated words and posture. He wrote the words on the same piece of paper then again slipped it under the teller window. "Thank you, Mr. Arkwright."

"My pleasure. Now, tell me, Miss Waller, shall I convene with your father and request his permission to accompany you to the annual barn dance at the Randels'?" His thick, dark bushy eyebrows knitted together to form one long, substantial eyebrow.

Such a presumptuous man! "My apologies, but I will have to decline. Perhaps another time."

"Not to worry. As they say, it is to man's benefit to be patient, as long as he is waiting on such a handsome woman as yourself. Although, I must say, I have been secretly admiring your loveliness."

Meredith swallowed hard. Had he just said *secretly admiring*? Did that mean secretly admiring by letter? She suddenly felt faint.

"If you'll excuse me." She grasped her coin purse and the slip of paper with his writing sample on it. Then with what was left of her dignity, she hurried out of the bank.

Never, ever had she wanted anything so badly as to not be the object of Mr. Arkwright's affections or his letters. While some women in Ellis Creek would be honored to capture the man's fancy, Meredith was decidedly not one of them.

Later that afternoon, Meredith sat under the large cottonwood tree at her parents' home. The letters she had received lay sprawled before her, open. Beside the letters, she had placed Leopold Arkwright's penmanship sample.

Counting on her fingers, she listed the things she knew to be fact. She knew that her secret admirer resided in Ellis Creek. At church last Sunday, she had glanced around several times to see if she could spot any other young unmarried men she'd not known of before.

Her eyes had lingered on a certain Gabe Kleeman. Unfortunate that he couldn't be the author.

Meredith knew that the first letters were written in different script than the latter letters. Could it mean two different admirers? If so, that led to a larger conundrum.

Reaching for her pencil, Meredith jotted down the names of her possible admirers with notes beside each name:

Marvin Pratt: Handwriting does not match; however, discussed topics that could be related to topics mentioned in previous letters.
Mr. Norman: Never really a suspect. Old enough to be my great-grandfather.
Mr. Griggs: Lack of teeth, failure to bathe, never has expressed interest.
Leopold Arkwright: Handwriting may or may not match (difficult to ascertain); could be a possibility; asked about dance in person.
Gabe Kleeman: Wishful thinking. Does not know I exist.

Meredith bit the inside of her lip. Was there anyone she was missing? If not, then all clues pointed to Leopold Arkwright. If that was the case, she would cease writing to him immediately, and she certainly would not look for him at the barn dance.

Tillie took a sip of her lemonade. She loved attending the barn dances with Lula. Once in a while, someone asked Tillie to dance, but mostly it was that vexatious boy named Willard, who sat in front of her in school. His flaming, bright red hair gave Tillie a warning anytime he was about to approach her. "Have you seen Willard?" she asked Lula.

"Not yet. I'm sure he'll be here to ask his favorite girl for a dance." Lula winked and giggled.

"Meredith says that boys don't always stay peculiar as they get older. If Willard wasn't so downright idiosyncratic, I might take a liking to him. Do you think there's any hope for Willard?"

"No. Boys are all odd, if you ask me. Say, what do you think Meredith thought of the latest letters? Do you think she realizes the writing is different?"

Tillie shrugged and popped a jawbreaker in her mouth. "If she has any suspicions, she hasn't mentioned them to me. I'm just glad Gabe knows about the whole situation now. Makes things a lot easier with him writing the letters."

"Meredith does look a bit sheepish over there by the punch bowl. Do you suppose she's waiting to see who walks in with a red bandanna?"

"Won't she be surprised! I don't think she has any clue it's Gabe. I know that Mr. Arkwright down at the bank fancies her. Say, there he is right now." Tillie pointed toward the entrance.

"We for sure cannot have Meredith marrying Mr. Arkwright. How will we ever be sisters forever if that happens?"

Tillie looked at her friend's concerned face. "No, we mustn't allow Mr. Arkwright to set his sights on Meredith. It's a right good thing that Gabe is smitten with her, too." Tillie watched as Mr. Arkwright approached her sister. "A right good thing, indeed."

Chapter 10

Meredith attempted not to appear nervous, but she knew she wasn't successful. The man who'd written her the letters would be arriving any moment, if he wasn't here already.

She eyed the many people in attendance. Her parents were already dancing, as were Mr. and Mrs. Kleeman. Roxie and Perry were sipping lemonade on the sidelines, and Tillie and Lula stood in a nearby corner whispering and sharing giggles. Where was Gabe Kleeman? Had he decided not to come with the rest of his family? Meredith felt a twinge of disappointment in her heart. Would Gabe ever know of her secret admiration for him? Would he ever feel the same for her? The man rarely spoke and seemed to not notice her presence. Had someone else captured his fancy?

"Care to dance?" Marvin Pratt sidled up alongside her with a hopeful grin on his pudgy face.

"I'll have to pass at the moment, Mr. Pratt, although I appreciate your inquiry."

Marvin hung his head and pooched out his bottom lip. "All right, Miss Waller. But iffen you wanna dance, I'll be happy to oblige."

Meredith acknowledged his response politely, grateful there was no bandanna on Mr. Pratt's beefy arm. Ma would have her hide and then some if she wasn't anything but polite. But she didn't want to dance with Mr. Pratt. No, she wanted to wait and see who the man was who'd been writing her the letters—the man who had promised to attend the barn dance with a red bandanna around his arm.

She squinted toward the entrance just as Leopold Arkwright sauntered in, his arrogance emanating across the room.

Meredith gasped. His red-and-black flannel shirt caught her attention. She squinted in an attempt to reassure herself that a red bandanna had not blended in with the pattern. His gaze connected with hers, and he strutted toward her. Was there still time to hide?

"Fancy seeing you here, Miss Waller." Leopold Arkwright coyly grinned at her, exposing a mouth full of far too many perfectly straight teeth.

"Hello, Mr. Arkwright."

"From your comment at the bank the other day, I took it to mean you weren't going to be in attendance."

Meredith swallowed. To lie would never do. But how could she explain to the man that she hadn't wanted to attend with him in a proper and kind way? Coming to the conclusion that there was no honest way, Meredith attempted a polite smile and avoided the question.

"Would you like for me to continue writing letters to you?"

Meredith's palms grew clammy, and she tried to wipe them on her dress in as lady-like a fashion as possible. More letters? Had *he* been the one? "What letters?"

"Why, such as the letters you had me write in the bank the other day."

He thinks those were letters? Relief flooded over her. "Oh, those letters. No, thank you, Mr. Arkwright. Now, if you'll excuse me, I must—"

"Dance with me?"

Meredith didn't try to hide her shock at the man's cheeky behavior. "Not at the moment, Mr. Arkwright. Now, if you'll please excuse me."

Hurrying past Leopold Arkwright, Meredith continued along the outskirts of the dance floor. She turned to take a second glance just to be sure Leopold wasn't following her. That's when something most embarrassing happened.

She ran right into Gabe Kleeman.

Gabe's arms reached for Meredith as she teetered toward him. When he righted her, Meredith's gaze connected with his. Gabe swallowed hard. Hadn't he often dreamed of holding Meredith in his arms?

Perhaps so, but not due to this awkward circumstance. "Hello. . .uh. . .Meredith," he said, hearing in his own ears that his voice sounded like the croak of an ill frog. He shoved the insecure thoughts aside. She smelled of roses, and he inhaled again.

His heart leaped a bit in his chest just at the mere sight of her.

"Hello, Gabe."

Gabe realized he was still holding her in his arms, but to Meredith's credit, she didn't seem like she was trying her best to escape his gentle hold. He released her, took a step back, and willed his mouth to speak rational and intelligible words. "Um. . .are you all right?" Not quite as intelligent-sounding as he'd hoped, but it would have to do.

Meredith nodded and pressed her hands against the wrinkles of her blue dress. My, but wasn't she a sight to behold! Realizing he was staring, Gabe averted his gaze toward the folks on the makeshift dance floor then back again to Meredith. That's when he realized Meredith staring at the red bandanna on his arm.

What would she think now that she knew he was her secret admirer? Well, not her secret admirer exactly, as he'd just only recently begun to take over the task of writing letters to her. But still, would she be happy to discover his feelings toward her? Or disappointed? A wave of insecurity washed over him.

Meredith's gaze returned to his face, her expression unreadable. Should he ask her if she would like to dance? Prefer some lemonade? Escape his presence? The loud music sounded in Gabe's ears. "Uh. . ."

"Yes?"

Gabe took a deep breath. *Lord, please, can You make my mouth work with coherent words?* "Uh. . .hello, Meredith." *It was a start, if not redundant.*

"Hello, Gabe."

What a fool he was! They'd already made introductions. "Meredith?"

"Yes?"

Was that expectation he saw in her eyes? He hoped so. She hadn't fled yet. That comforted him.

"Would you...would you care to step outside for a minute of fresh air?"

"Certainly."

Just speaking those fourteen words drained him of energy. But how else could he explain about the letters with all the commotion that surrounded them?

Gabe followed Meredith outside. Several other folks had the same inclination, as many couples and children were enjoying the fresh air. Gabe offered a prayer. He would need a miracle if he was going to be able to utter more than a few words.

Meredith's heart seemed as though it might beat plumb out of her chest. Was Gabe sporting a handkerchief around his arm in case he needed to use it, or was he *the one*?

Her mind brimmed full with the memorized contents of all the letters she had received. If the handkerchief was on Gabe's arm because he was the one who had written them, it could only mean one thing.

He liked her as much as she liked him.

Would it be proper to ask him if he'd sent the letters? Just to be sure? Or should she wait for him to say the first word? What if he never said anything?

Meredith stopped by the fence post and watched a colt with boundless energy kick up its heels.

"I...uh...it's a nice night." Gabe had stopped beside her near the fence and wiped his hands on his pants. He looked quite dapper this evening with his blue chambray shirt that further enhanced his broad shoulders. He smelled of pine, like the forests near Ellis Creek.

"It is a nice night."

They stood in silence for what felt like an hour. The tips of Gabe's ears had begun to turn red, a trait that Meredith found endearing. She looked out over the sun that was starting to set. "Are you...are you the one who sent me the letters?" What would Mama say of her forwardness?

He took so long to answer that Meredith regretted asking the question. Perhaps Mama and Pa would announce it was time to return home and save her from this embarrassment. If Gabe said no, then what would he think of her? Yet why did he sport the red handkerchief on his left arm? She leaned over just to be sure it was still there.

"Oh, there you are, Meredith!" Tillie skipped toward her. "I was looking for you. Hello, Gabe."

That girl had the worst timing ever. "Did you need something, Tillie?"

"No. I was just wondering where you went. That impertinent Mr. Arkwright is looking for you."

Meredith grimaced. Would the man never realize she wasn't the least bit interested in him? "I'll thank you kindly not to tell Mr. Arkwright where I am." Meredith tossed a threatening big-sister glare Tillie's way.

Tillie made a motion to appear she was buttoning up her lips. "Not a chance. I'd never do something cheeky like that. Mr. Arkwright is a cad if I ever knew one. But Gabe here, well, he's the opposite of a cad. A gentleman, to be precise."

"Thanks, Tillie." Good. Gabe had found his voice again. Now, if Tillie would leave them to their discussion, Meredith might find the answer to her important question before nightfall.

"I better return to the dance. That ridiculous boy Willard, with the pumpkin hair, persists in asking me for a dance."

Meredith laughed at her sister's exaggerated words. "Give him one dance, Tillie, and then rest assured he'll likely cease pestering you."

"That would be seemly, but highly improbable." Tillie rolled her eyes. "I'll leave you to your conversation."

"Thank you, Tillie." Meredith marveled at how intelligent her sister always sounded with her large vocabulary. The girl's dream of someday teaching school seemed attainable. With a swish of her skirts, Tillie turned on her heel and returned to the barn.

Would it be too brazen for Meredith to ask Gabe her question again? She chewed on her bottom lip. If she did ask again, might she receive an answer this time? If she didn't ask again and he hadn't heard her the first time, she might never know.

She must know.

Therefore, she must ask.

"Gabe, are you the one who wrote the letters to me?"

"Somewhat."

"Begging your pardon?"

Gabe cleared his throat. "I am somewhat responsible for the letters."

"Somewhat?" This conversation was going nowhere. Did he have a partner in writing the letters? Had he, or had he not, written the letters?

Gabe turned to face her. His eyes were so hazel. His handsome face so serious. Could it be that she'd made some mistake? She hoped not. "Begging your pardon, Gabe, but I received a letter stating that the author would be wearing a red handkerchief on his arm at the dance. Have I mistaken the red one on your arm?" She hated the way her voice sounded so desperate. More than anything else at this moment, she truly wanted her secret admirer to be Gabe. What a wonder it would be if he had admired her from afar, just as she had admired him.

"I wrote the last five letters."

"Only the last five?" Then who had written the prior letters? *Please, not Leopold Arkwright!* "May I inquire as to who wrote the previous letters?"

The corners of Gabe's mouth turned up in a large smile. He seemed to be able to converse easier now than in the past. "Our dear sisters."

"Tillie and Lula?"

"Two and the same."

Meredith put her hand to her chest. Her sister, along with Gabe's sister, had dreamed up this scheme?

"But then. . .how? Why?"

Gabe chuckled, a flush creeping across his handsome cheeks. He shrugged but said nothing, so Meredith continued. "I suppose I don't rightly understand. Why would our sisters do something so unconventional? That would explain, however, why some of the letters were written in a different penmanship. I'm assuming that's because they wrote some of them and you wrote some of them." Meredith paused to take a breath as she processed the information. "I'm surely thankful that your decision to wear a red handkerchief on your arm is because you are the one who sent the letters. Well, not all of the letters, mind you, but some of the letters. And I'm ecstatic that that Leopold Arkwright didn't write any of those letters. After all, he mentioned writing letters, and I do declare, the thought of him being the one was enough to make a girl faint dead away from dread." She took a deep breath. "Oh, dear me. I'm rambling."

Meredith's oval face had taken on a rosy tint, one to match his own, to be sure. If she wanted to ramble, that was quite all right with him. He wouldn't utter another word. Gabe would just watch Meredith's face light up with excitement as she spoke.

It was as if the words he wanted to say were mushed down in his throat and unable to make their way the short distance out his mouth. He tried to pretend she was someone else while explaining about Tillie and Lula, and it had worked for a second. But one look at her face and he was reminded all over again that this was Meredith.

Meredith Waller.

The girl he had secretly admired and had looked upon with great fondness since their school days. While the words seemed to flow with more ease than ever before, there was no way the words would ever come easily in her presence. So just how was a tongue-tied oaf like himself supposed to ask her the important questions, like the question of courtship? Or how could he tell her how pretty she was or that he wished he'd written all the letters, not just the last few? With his luck, he'd probably drool all over the place from his tongue being tied in more knots than an unworkable rope. What then? Would she still be thankful that it was he, and not Leopold Arkwright behind the letters?

She was gazing at him expectantly, awaiting a response. He prayed then mustered up some courage that must have come all the way from his curled toes in his boots. "Meredith." Her name caught in his throat.

"Yes?" Meredith's eyes were bright with anticipation.

"I..."

Her head bobbed slowly as she waited for him to speak.

"I...I'm glad it's me, too."

"You're glad it's you?"

Lord, could You please help me be long-winded just this once? I know You're in the business of miracles, and I reckon I could sure use one right about now!

Gabe took a deep breath. "Meredith, I reckon I'm glad I'm your secret admirer and not Arkwright. I'm glad you're glad it's me and that I wore a handkerchief on my arm. I'm honored to be here with you tonight. I wanted to write all those letters, but I'm much obliged for our sisters starting off this whole thing." There. He'd said it.

And the Lord had performed a miracle.

An even brighter smile lit her face. "I can't wait to hear all about how Tillie and Lula ever came up with such a plan."

"Would you care to dance?"

"I'd love to dance."

Gabe led her back into the barn, relieved, for dancing was easier than conversation. He took her left hand in his and placed his right hand gently on her back. Every ounce of embarrassment had been worth it for this moment.

Reckon you're turnin' soft, Kleeman, he chastised himself.

Gabe drove Meredith home in his wagon that evening. She didn't want the night to end. Over and over, Meredith had thanked the good Lord above that it hadn't been Mr. Arkwright or Marvin Pratt or Mr. Griggs who had been writing the letters.

She never would have guessed that Gabe fancied her.

The only sound during the ride home was the *clop-clopping* of the horses' hooves on the dirt road and the song of crickets in the night air. Meredith found the silence to be agreeable. It gave her time to rehash the night spent dancing with Gabe. Not once, not twice, but at least six dances. A time or two, she had noticed Leopold Arkwright starting to meander toward them, presumably to ask her for a dance. Gabe must have noticed, too, for he quickly swept her aside.

Moments later, Gabe assisted Meredith from the wagon. "I had a nice time."

"Thank you, Gabe. I did, too."

They stood facing each other. Meredith looked up into his eyes. His strong arms had been around her tonight, both when she'd run into him and then when they had danced. What would it be like to be kissed by Gabe Kleeman?

Meredith hastily chastised herself. A night spent in Gabe's company at a barn dance did not equal courtship. Although she did hope he would ask to see her again.

Chapter 11

Widow Jones put her hand on Meredith's arm. "Thank you again for all the mending you've done for me."

Meredith smiled at the dear woman. "You are more than welcome, Widow Jones."

As they stood conversing, a wagon approached. The driver glimpsed their way then took a second glance. He promptly turned the wagon around and headed toward Widow Jones's home. Meredith's heart stopped in her chest when she realized it was Gabe. She hadn't slept much last night thinking about their time at the dance and Gabe's admission to writing the letters. Maybe someday Meredith would even thank Tillie for her role in bringing them together.

And now, here the man of her affections was once again.

Gabe removed his hat. "Hello, Widow Jones." He turned toward Meredith. "I'd be much obliged if I could speak to you for a moment."

"Certainly. Is everything all right, Gabe?"

His face flushed before he answered a hearty yes.

Widow Jones stood nearby, a smirk on her precious wrinkled face.

While waiting for him to continue, Meredith looked into Gabe's eyes. Such handsome eyes on such a handsome face. Not only that, but he was kind, generous, and a man of God. What was there not to like? How could she have not noticed him before he left for Missouri?

"Could you. . .would you. . ." Gabe paused and threw a glance at the widow as if begging her to step aside. Was he hoping for a moment of privacy without their chaperone? What was he about to ask?

Meredith held her breath.

Gabe again darted his eyes toward Widow Jones in some type of unspoken message.

Instead of taking the hint, Widow Jones merely grinned, did the opposite, and took a step closer. To be privy to the interesting goings-on, perhaps?

"Meredith. . ."

"Yes?"

Gabe took a deep breath. "Would you do me the honor of courting me?"

"Yes, Gabe. I will court you."

Gabe nodded, returned his hat to his head, and strolled toward his wagon. With a wave, he beckoned his horses and rode off down the road.

Leaving Meredith to wonder if what had just happened was truly a reality.

Widow Jones held her hand to her heart. "Such a darling man. It befuddles me that he took so long to ask you. I could see it in his eyes the day you were both over here helping me that he fancied you. Ah, to be young and in love."

Meredith didn't have a response for Widow Jones, but she was thrilled about what had transpired. Courtship with Gabe? She couldn't wait to tell Roxie.

"He does seem to suffer from a lack of words where you are concerned, dear," the widow continued. "Not to worry, however. My beloved Harold had a shyness about him, as well, until the day we married. Then he had words-a-plenty, and some mighty sweet words at that. Just takes some men a bit of time to find their words. Not one person who knew Harold would say he wasn't long-winded."

All this time, Meredith had figured Gabe wasn't interested in her. But now, with their time spent at the barn dance and his subsequent request for courtship, Meredith realized how wrong she'd been. Gabe had only been shy and reserved.

Thank You, Lord. Thank You that You care about every detail in our lives. Even about courtship.

Gabe's stomach knotted, as he rode his horse toward the Waller home. He had prayed since yesterday that he would summon the fortitude to do what he was about to do. If he survived this meeting, Gabe could survive anything.

Perspiration beaded his brow. What if Mr. Waller didn't find Gabe fit to court his daughter? What if Mr. Waller had someone else in mind for his eldest child? What if—

Quit it, Gabe. You've given the situation to the Lord. It's only fitting you let Him handle it. Besides, if you can string together enough words to ask Meredith about courting in front of Widow Jones, you can assuredly ask her father.

But then, once Meredith gave you her answer, you just rode off as hasty as a varmint escaping a predator. What must she think of that? Gabe shook his head. He still needed assistance where shyness was concerned. A lot of assistance.

After scolding himself, Gabe experienced a renewed sense of courage. He traipsed toward the Waller home, noting that Tillie sat outside on the tree swing. "Hello, Tillie."

Tillie removed herself from the round circular chunk of log that constituted a swing. "Hello, Gabe. Say, I am about out of jawbreakers."

"Reckon you've had enough jawbreakers in the last few weeks to render you toothless."

"If you'd like me to keep your surreptitious messages to Meredith incognito, might I suggest another bag of jawbreakers?"

Gabe chuckled. "Nice try, Tillie. You forget that I have a sister who has already attempted enough bribery in jawbreakers to last until she's forty-five. Anyhow, Meredith knows about the 'surreptitious messages,' as you call them."

"She does?" Tillie's eyes grew large beneath her spectacles. "Who divulged the confidential information? The last I knew, she feared it was Leopold Arkwright delivering the letters."

"Meredith feared it was Arkwright?"

"She did. Or even that Mr. Pratt. Now, he's an interesting sort."

Gabe blew out a breath of relief. He needn't have worried that Meredith had wished the letters to have been written by Arkwright. Pratt had never been a concern. "So, do you think she's grateful it was me?"

"For a bag of jawbreakers—"

"No more jawbreakers, Tillie. Can you tell me where your pa is?"

"Reckon he's in the barn. What are you going to discuss with him?"

Gabe shook his head. The only downside of someday asking for Meredith's hand in marriage was that he would inherit another younger pesky sister.

Meredith was worth the sacrifice.

Moments later, Gabe found Mr. Waller in the barn. "What can I do for you, Gabe?"

"Hello, sir. May I have a moment of your time?"

Mr. Waller set aside his work. "What's on your mind?"

Gabe walked to the barn door and peeked outside. Sure enough, Tillie held her ear to the wall. He closed the door and returned to Mr. Waller. "I spied an eavesdropper."

Mr. Waller let out a rumbling chuckle. "That Tillie. God has some plans for her life for sure. But she's a bit on the meddlesome side."

Gabe couldn't agree more. But he hadn't come here to discuss Tillie's meddlesome ways. He removed his hat and reached his forearm up to wipe the perspiration on his forehead. "Mr. Waller, I've come to ask you an important question."

"Go on."

"I reckon I'd be much obliged if I could court your daughter." The words were out, and there was no retracting them. *Lord, please, let him say yes!*

Mr. Waller narrowed his eyes but said nothing in response. Gabe considered sneaking out of the barn, climbing on his horse, and returning home. Instead, he pleaded his case, drawing upon his rehearsed speech. "Sir, I have a right fine ranch that I'm continuing to expand. I will provide for Meredith and love her and care for her always."

"Just one question for you, son."

"Yes, sir?"

"What took you so long to ask?"

"Beg your pardon, Mr. Waller?"

"The missus and I suspected that you've fancied Meredith for some time now."

Had everyone known of Gabe's intentions toward Meredith? "Yes, sir. Since we were in school together."

Mr. Waller raised his eyebrows. "We hadn't figured that long. Anyhow, you have my blessing to court my daughter. I couldn't ask for a finer man to make that request."

"You mean it, sir?"

"Yes, I do."

They shook hands until Gabe was certain he'd shake the hand right off the shorter, older man standing before him.

While **Penny Zeller** has had a love for writing since childhood, she began her adult writing career penning articles for national and regional publications.

Today, Penny is a multi-published, award-winning author of inspirational books. She is a homeschool mom of two and actively devotes her time to coaching homeschool P.E. and teaching a variety of classes at her local homeschool co-op. Her passion is to assist and nurture women and children into a closer relationship with Christ.

When Penny is not dreaming up new characters, she enjoys spending time with her husband and children while camping, hiking, canoeing, reading, running, gardening, and playing volleyball.

more would he love the woman of his affections from afar.

Her dainty hands unfolded the note—hands he'd have the privilege of holding far into the future as they took long walks along his ranch. Their ranch.

Last week, Gabe had penned the words *Will you marry me?* on some special lilac-colored stationery he had purchased from the mercantile. Finally working up the nerve to deliver his letter, he held his breath for Meredith's response.

Her eyes scanned the paper then gazed up at his. "Yes, Gabe. I will marry you."

In a romantic sweep, he had her in his arms. In an even quicker movement, his lips found hers, sealing the promise of their hearts.

For two months, Meredith and Gabe had spent time together. Today, Gabe had promised a picnic near the river, not far from Ellis Creek.

Meredith finished packing the picnic basket and then tucked in a checkered table-cloth she'd sewn last week.

"Are you departing with Gabe again?" Tillie asked, perching herself on the table.

"Yes. Today we're going on a picnic."

"That sounds romantic," Tillie swooned. "And to think, it all began with Lula and me and our brilliant idea."

"Thank you, Tillie."

"You're welcome. I received quite a few jawbreakers for our good deed." Tillie pushed her spectacles up on her nose. "Do you think someday Willard won't be such a nuisance? Maybe he'll be handsome and dashing like Gabe."

"That could very well happen, Tillie."

Tillie smirked and pointed out the window. "Here comes your beau now. I'll leave you to your swooning," she tittered, fleeing the room.

Less than an hour later, Gabe assisted Meredith from the wagon. She put her arm through the crook of his elbow as they walked toward the creek. Would God see fit to join them in matrimony someday?

Over the past couple of weeks, Gabe had improved in his efforts to overcome shyness. Meredith giggled to herself. Perhaps what Widow Jones had said was true about men becoming more long-winded as time passed.

They looked into each other's eyes for a few moments until Gabe leaned toward her. "Meredith?"

"Yes?"

"May I steal a kiss?"

She'd thought he'd never ask. "Yes, you may."

He held her face gently in his large hands and leaned toward her. He smelled of pine trees and soap. She closed her eyes as his face neared hers. His mouth sought hers, the soft touch of his lips growing more passionate as the seconds passed. So this was what kissing Gabe would be like.

No disappointment there.

When the kiss ended, Gabe stroked her cheek with his fingers. He seemed to be searching for words. "Meredith?"

"Yes?"

"Reckon I'm in love with you."

She reckoned—no she knew—that she was in love with him, too. Meredith marveled that the Lord had brought the right person to her in His timing.

Gabe suggested Meredith retrieve one final letter from the oak tree. He stood a short distance from her and watched as she reached her hand into the sliver for his letter. No